MI

I'm an ex-media technician turned rock-music-loving author of hot, sexy romance and chick lit with a kick! My love of books began the second I could read, and some of my happiest memories are of me curled up in bed as a child devouring every Malory Towers and Famous Five book I could get my hands on. As the years progressed I read everything from horror to Harry Potter, Jackie Collins to Jilly Cooper, but I always knew that I wanted to write romance. I love the idea of escapism – of creating a world in which readers can lose themselves, and characters they'll want to spend time with. And thanks to inspiration from the aforementioned Ms. Collins, I always knew that I wanted to write romance of the more racy variety, and to be able to do that every day is a dream come true for me.

After a spell living on the beautiful Canarian island of Tenerife, I'm now back in the UK and settled in County Durham with my wonderful husband and my gorgeous West Highland Terrier, Archie. A proud Geordie girl, I adore the north east of England, but I also love the odd glass of wine, Keanu Reeves, a decent TV drama, Peter Kay… and darts!

You can follow me on Twitter @michellebetham, find me on Facebook www.facebook.com/AuthorMichelleBetham or chat to me on my blog http://michellebethamwriter.blogspot.co.uk/.

This book is dedicated to all those people who've believed in me, supported me, and encouraged me when I've needed that push. You all know who you are, and I can't thank you enough.I got there – eventually!

To my amazing publisher HarperImpulse for making my dream come true.

And to all the footballers out there – you gave me a lot of inspiration... but this one's for the WAGs!

Chapter One

'Jesus! I'm home,' Ryan sighed, pulling open the blinds of his hotel room to reveal a miserable, grey drizzle falling steadily from a gunmetal-grey August sky, the familiar sight of the Tyne Bridge looming large in the distance, reminding Ryan that he was, indeed, back home.

Downing a mouthful of coffee as he watched the morning rush-hour traffic cross that famous North East landmark, he felt a tinge of unfamiliar apprehension as he thought about what was to come. When people realised all the rumours were true they'd be expecting something akin to the return of the Prodigal Son, a homecoming hero; was he really going to be able to live up to all those expectations? Yeah. Of course he fucking was! What a ridiculous question.

Smiling to himself, he finished his coffee and turned away from the window, pulling off the white Egyptian cotton towel that was tied around his waist. He had one hell of a body – hard, toned and tanned thanks to a recent trip to Marbella followed by a pre-season tour of California. And hadn't *that* been a blast? Who knew those American girls would be so into their 'soccer' – as they called it over there. Or their soccer players? He probably had David Beckham to thank for that one.

He smiled again, checking out his naked reflection in the

full-length mirror. Yeah. He was going to live off those American memories for a while, that was for sure. Not just because of the women, but because that had been the last time he'd played for a club he'd been a part of for over four years. But, in the world of football, you went where the money was, and right now the money was here, back in his native North-East England.

Pulling on battered jeans, black t-shirt and expensive trainers, Ryan ran a hand through his short, dark hair as he sat down on the edge of the huge king-size bed, watching the traffic steadily crossing the Tyne Bridge in what seemed like a constant, never-ending stream. He had a long day ahead of him – interviews, photo calls, not to mention moving into the house his new club had sorted out for him. Another roller-coaster of a ride was about to begin, and just because he was back up north, away from the bright lights of London and all the temptations that had been thrown his way, none of which he'd declined, it didn't mean that this chapter of his life was going to be any less crazy. Why would it be? Ryan Fisher had it all – money, talent, any woman he wanted. He had the lot. And he had no intention of letting go of any of it any time soon.

'Ten-thirty, at Newcastle Red Star's ground. Did you get that, Amber?'

Amber Sullivan looked at her boss. Shit! Had he just asked her something? Her mind had been temporarily distracted by the constant arrival of texts being sent to her phone regarding the ongoing rumours of Ryan Fisher making a return to the North East; only, *she* knew they weren't rumours anymore.

'Sorry, Kevin. I was…'

'Distracted, yeah. I got that. Just get your head together in time for this interview, okay? We've got an exclusive here. He isn't speaking one-on-one to any other local news programme, so…'

'Are we talking about Ryan Fisher here?' Amber asked, swinging her chair round and crossing her long legs as her producer sat down on the edge of her desk, clasping his hands together on his lap.

'Who else has just signed a record-breaking transfer deal with one of the biggest clubs in the region? Come on, Amber. I need you focused here. I'm sending *you* to interview him.'

'Why me?' Amber began rooting around in her desk drawer, looking for the Dictaphone she remembered throwing in there the other day after a particularly second-rate interview with a Durham cricketer who'd quite obviously been in no mood to talk sport but had been quite happy to make a move on her in the most clumsy and irritating of ways. 'I thought you were sending Harry to Tynebridge?'

'I was. Until we got word that Ryan Fisher was willing to speak to us one-on-one before the main press conference, so your plans for the day have changed, kiddo. You're the only one I can trust to do this interview properly.' Kevin Russell pushed a hand through his light-brown, slightly ruffled hair and stood up before shoving both hands in the pockets of his well-cut black trousers. 'Ten-thirty, Tynebridge Stadium. There's a pass waiting for you at reception. Come and see me when you get back.'

Amber threw her head back and closed her eyes. She actually loved this time of year, when the new football season was just beginning, the summer transfer window was drawing to a close and rumours and speculation were rife. There was a certain kind of energy filling the Sports Department as everyone tried to second-guess just who might be signing who, or which player was about to leave English football behind for the chance to experience, say, the excitement of La Liga over in Spain, or the opportunity to make more money than they could ever dream of over in Asia.

She'd been working on Newcastle-based regional news programme News North East for over ten years now, starting out as a junior reporter before climbing to the dizzy ranks of the show's first ever female Sports Editor five years ago at the age of thirty-two. She loved her job. She was also extremely good at it.

Amber Sullivan had grown up surrounded by sport, so it was

only natural that her work revolved around it. Her father, Freddie Sullivan, was an ex-professional footballer – and an ex-Newcastle Red Star player – who now managed a local lower-league club, so being around sportsmen, and footballers in particular, was nothing new to her. Although, as she'd got older it had become less of an enjoyable experience, because Amber had grown up to be nothing short of beautiful. Which brought with it its own set of problems. With long, naturally dark hair that hung in loose waves around her shoulders, pale blue eyes and olive-toned skin she'd inherited from her late Spanish mother it was as if, one day, she'd suddenly turned from that tomboy who loved a kick-about with the lads into a stunning young woman, which in turn meant that a lot of the sportsmen she knew suddenly stopped seeing her as 'one of them', and began seeing her as more of a conquest. Especially the footballers. Even though they knew her father, respected him, looked up to him, they didn't seem to have the same respect for his daughter.

Because of that, Amber had always made a conscious effort to stay away from relationships with sportsmen of any kind, but she steered clear of relationships with footballers more than any other sportsmen in particular. She wasn't perfect, though, and she'd strayed from that self-imposed rule only briefly a few years back when she'd embarked on a short relationship with a player called Ronnie White, a man who had gone on to become one of her closest friends. But Ronnie had been different to the others, an exception. So she had no intention of going there again, no desire to become emotionally involved with men who could quite easily hurt her with their selfish behaviour and egos that seemed to need boosting on an hourly basis. It just wasn't on her agenda, despite these men being the people she hung out with both professionally, and personally, on a frequent basis. Amber Sullivan had no desire to be a WAG. The whole lifestyle some of those women signed up for was nothing short of abhorrent to her because, deep down inside, she was still that tomboy who'd accompanied her father to

10

nearly all of his matches, learning all about the so-called 'beautiful game' from the very best. Her interest was in the sport – not the men who played it. Unless it was on a purely professional level, of course.

No, she was quite happy being single. Feisty and fiercely independent, Amber had no room in her life for a man. Except her dad. He was the only man who mattered to her right now, especially since the loss of her mother just two years ago. As an only child, that had pushed her and her father even closer together, so, in between making sure he was okay, and her job at News North East, she had no time for anything resembling a serious relationship. She had no time for relationships, full stop. They would only get in the way.

She sat up and looked over towards Kevin's glass-fronted office. He was standing at the window tapping his watch and shrugging. Amber couldn't help but smile. He was going to give himself another angina attack if he didn't learn to relax a bit more. She'd never been late for an interview, never missed an appointment. Amber Sullivan let nothing get in the way of her work, and Kevin Russell knew that. Yet still he stressed out.

She stood up, grabbed her bag and mouthed 'I'm going' at her producer, who smiled his thanks and turned away from the window to answer his constantly ringing phone. Amber had a feeling today was going to be one of those days when her feet didn't touch the ground, but those were the kind of days she loved – when she was part of something big and exciting. And, right now, as far as the world of North-East football was concerned, there was nothing bigger or more exciting than the arrival of Ryan Fisher.

It was something he should be used to by now, being shoved from room to room, passed on to every person who wanted a piece of him, but it still didn't sit well with Ryan. Even after all his years in the top-flight of professional football this was the bit he hated the most – the interviews, press conferences, photo calls. But it was all part of the package, and it was a package he'd wanted ever since he'd been old enough to kick a ball.

Ryan Fisher was twenty-six years old, just over 6ft tall with beautiful, deep – almost navy – blue eyes, short, slightly unruly dark hair and a beard that gave him a somewhat rough-and-ready look that only made him all the more attractive, as did the multitude of tattoos he'd collected over the years that graced his extremely toned and incredibly sexy arms. In fact, the only word to describe Ryan Fisher was handsome. Very, very handsome. And it was this – combined with the hard, toned body – that had made him the pin-up player of the football world, which meant he didn't just get the women, he also got the sponsorship deals, the modelling contracts, the invites to every celebrity party going. But Ryan also had a natural talent for the game that hadn't been seen in a long time.

Growing up on a large, sprawling council estate just outside of Newcastle-upon-Tyne, he'd only ever wanted to be a professional footballer. As a child he'd spent all of his spare time kicking his beloved football against walls or organising five-a-side games with his mates on the playing field at the back of his house. Saturdays had been his favourite day of the week, when he'd sit with his dad, eagerly watching the football results roll in, then spend the rest of the evening waiting for *Match of the Day* to start so he could watch the professionals at work, hoping that, one day, he could be one of them, playing out there on some of the most famous pitches in the world in front of thousands of loyal supporters. When his father could afford it, they'd even go into town to see Newcastle Red Star play, giving Ryan a taste of what it felt like to be part of the excitement football could create. Days like that had only made him want it more.

It was all he could think about. He'd thrown himself into every school team at the earliest age he could, rising from a star of the under-13s into a promising under-16 prospect, which is where he was first spotted by a scout from a London club on the lookout for local talent. He'd been fourteen at the time, and he'd never forgotten the excitement he'd felt when that scout had approached his father on the touchline one rainy Thursday afternoon as his team took on another local school in the Under-16's county tournament. That one meeting had been the beginning of what was turning out to be one hell of a career for Ryan.

He'd been whisked down to London for a trial at a First Division club, with their coach eager to sign him to their Youth Team almost immediately, and whilst his mother had been reluctant to let her son move down south – away from his family, his school, his friends – at such a young age, his father had seen the wisdom in not letting this chance pass Ryan by. It was an opportunity that might not have come along again.

And so the journey began. His days had been split between the training field and the classroom as he'd combined those first steps of his dream career with studying for his GCSEs and, thanks to a tutor whom Ryan had never forgotten, he'd come away with passes that could have guaranteed him a place at college to study A Levels. If that's what he'd really wanted. But that had never been Ryan's plan. Despite the fact he'd been – and still was – an intelligent young man, he'd only ever wanted to play football, and those that mattered could see that natural talent he possessed. They'd known it was an ambition he could easily fulfil.

By the age of sixteen he'd been playing first-team football, still unable to believe that he was actually living his dream. But that dream had only grown bigger when, at seventeen, a big-name club had shown more than a little interest in him. And suddenly, before Ryan's feet had had a chance to hit the ground, he'd been surrounded by agents and managers and PR people as word began to spread of this new, young talent that was setting the football world alight. There was talk of big money and sponsorship deals, figures that – at the time – Ryan couldn't even begin to comprehend, so it was just as well there'd been people around who could deal with it all for him. It had been a confusing but exciting time.

But all Ryan cared about was playing football. For a while, anyway. Because, once the money had started rolling in and he'd become more savvy with the way the system worked, he'd begun to realise that the amount you could earn depended very much on what you had the balls to ask for.

By the age of nineteen Ryan Fisher had become one of the most recognised faces in English football. And one of the highest paid. He had a sharp business mind, able to steer agents and managers in whichever direction he wanted them to go as easily as he could direct a ball into the back of the net. Contract negotiations were never a sticking point because Ryan wasn't just business-smart, he also had a knack for turning on the charm, both on and off the pitch.

As a young, top-earning player he had no shortage of women throwing themselves at him. And that was one perk he was more than willing to capitalise on. By the time he was twenty-one he'd become one of *the* biggest players in the English Premier League, with a life that was way beyond even *his* wildest dreams. Clubs were falling over themselves to sign him, men wanted to *be* him, and women wanted to be *with* him. He had everything he could ever have wished for, and he was doing the job he loved because, despite everything else that was going on around him, Ryan's first love was the game itself. But, if that game brought with it all the trappings of luxury and fame that he was experiencing, then that was a bonus he was happy to take.

He'd been lucky enough to not only play for some of the biggest and best clubs in England, he was also a regular member of the international squad, having represented his country on numerous occasions – the pinnacle of any serious footballer's career as far as Ryan was concerned. And it never hurt the old bank balance, either.

But now, after almost twelve years away from his native North East, he was finally coming home in a record-breaking, multi-million-pound transfer deal that was seeing him sign for one of the region's biggest and most famous clubs – the club he'd supported as a boy. It was a deal he hadn't been able to ignore. For a number of reasons. The time was right for Ryan to leave London behind. The time was right for him to finally come home.

'If you'd like to follow me, Mr. Fisher,' a pretty, young blonde girl smiled at him as she ushered him through the main lobby area of the huge and impressive stadium his new club had just had built. Ryan followed her, his hands buried deep in his pockets, his eyes fixed firmly on her backside – which looked nothing short of perfect in a tight black pencil skirt – as she took him through a set of double doors, past the Players' Lounge, before stopping outside the Press Lounge opposite.

Ryan couldn't help but smile back at her, noting the way she blushed slightly before quickly turning away to open the door for him. Even though he was more than capable of opening it himself.

He looked around, peering inside the still-quiet and empty Press Lounge that, in less than an hour, would be full of journalists, reporters and photographers all waiting to hear what he had to say. All waiting to find out just why he'd finally chosen to come home and play for the club he'd supported all his life.

Somehow or other he'd managed to shake off both Max – his agent – and the club official who was to sit in with him when he did this pre-press-conference interview with a local news programme. How he'd managed that he had no idea because they'd been stuck to him like limpets ever since he'd got out of the car not two minutes ago – a car he'd been bundled out of in a rather unceremonious fashion in some ridiculous attempt to keep news of his signing a secret until the very last minute. Which was a waste of time. It was probably old news by now, thanks to the recent Twitter rumours and media speculation that had been rife for the past couple of days.

Taking one more quick glance around, he followed the pretty PR assistant into the room, not missing the slightly panic-stricken look that took over her face when she realised he was alone.

'Oh, I'm... I'm sorry, Mr. Fisher. We need to wait for the club official, and your agent. They should be here, too. I don't know where they've… If you'll just excuse me…'

Ryan put his arm across the doorway, blocking her exit, smiling that smile that had turned a thousand women's heads over the years. 'So we're alone? Does that bother you?'

'I… I could get into trouble, Mr. Fisher…'

'Quit with the Mr. Fisher crap, will you? It's Ryan. And you are…?'

She looked at him with eyes that were still full of panic – but there was a tiny hint of excitement there, too; he could see it. A tell-tale sign that she was torn between this chance to be alone with a good-looking, extremely famous footballer, and the need to carry out her job with the utmost professionalism. 'Erm… my name's… I'm Ellen.'

Ryan grinned, his arm still resting against the doorpost, still blocking her exit. 'Ellen… well, what are you doing after all this bullshit has finished then, Ellen?'

'I don't know what *she's* doing but *you're* moving house then getting your head down for an early night. You've got training tomorrow morning.'

Ryan groaned as Max Mandell appeared in the doorway, pushing Ryan's arm out of the way to allow the cameraman from News North East through.

Max Mandell was one of the most respected and revered football agents in the business, with some of the biggest names in the game on his books. Renowned for always getting his clients the best deals possible, he was a straight-to-the-point, hard-nosed businessman who took no crap, which meant he had few friends, but one hell of a client list. Max Mandell was one of those men who didn't care much about anyone else – unless they could earn him big money. 'And for Christ's sake, Ryan, behave yourself, will you? For five frigging minutes. Let's show this club the professional player they've just signed over millions for, not some jumped-up playboy that might just make them regret shelling out all that cash.' He looked at Ellen as she backed up against the wall, studying her clipboard with probably more interest than was necessary. 'Is this going to get started soon, sweetheart? Only, we've got a shitload of stuff to be getting on with today.'

Ellen looked at him before quickly checking with the News North East cameraman, who gave her the nod that he was almost ready to go. 'As soon as Ms. Sullivan arrives…'

Ryan looked up. '*Ms.* Sullivan?'

'Jesus Christ,' Max sighed, throwing his head back. He knew of Amber Sullivan. He knew her father, Freddie, because he'd been one hell of a player in his day. And Max knew that Freddie Sullivan's daughter was one very beautiful young woman. But he also knew that she was good at her job. In fact, from what he'd heard, she could be as hard-nosed as him at times. She had a bit of a reputation for it, apparently. He'd often wondered why she'd never moved out of the North East to try for a job on national TV – she was just as good as any of the females who were gracing the world of sports broadcasting right now, and she'd always struck him as extremely ambitious, the few times he'd met her. Not to mention the fact her father was an ex-professional footballer. Surely she had the necessary contacts that could make all that happen for her? Maybe he should have a word with her, see where her thoughts for the future lay. He was sure he could broker some kind of deal to get her into the big wide world of football broadcasting. Max Mandell was never one to say no to a potential client, even if she wasn't the kind of client he usually went for. 'Just do the fucking interview and no shit, Ryan. Do you hear me?'

'Alright, Max. Jesus… I'm not a frigging five-year-old.'

Max looked at Ryan, arching an eyebrow. Ryan Fisher was probably one of the most talented players in football right now but, like most other lads of his age, earning too much and becoming so famous so quickly had side effects that weren't always pleasant. There were some, of course, who resisted the urge to have their heads turned, but there were others, just like Ryan, who chose to live that stereotypical footballer lifestyle to the hilt. And that wasn't always an attractive trait. Still, he wasn't there to keep an eye on their personalities. As long as they stayed fit and did their job, keeping the money rolling into both their pockets, *and his*, he didn't really give a shit what they got up to. Not unless it started to affect *him*.

Ryan stood at the back of the room, his hands in his pockets, his head down, scuffing his trainers against the skirting board in an action that told everyone in the room he wasn't happy. It wasn't even lunchtime and already he was pissed off. There were days when he felt as if his life wasn't his own, and this was fast turning into one of them. Sitting down on a comfortable black leather bucket chair, which quite obviously didn't belong in that room on a permanent basis, he folded his arms in an almost defensive manner as the somewhat flustered club official finally caught up with them. He smiled at both Ryan and Max before taking his seat, checking a large red book he'd had tucked under his arm, all ready to make sure that only questions the club had authorised were asked. Max had decided to take his usual, rather more intimidating stance of leaning against the wall, also with folded arms, to keep an eye on things. Ryan was just bored. He hated interviews, and he couldn't even remember agreeing to this one, but then, how many times had he found himself 'agreeing' to things just to humour some sponsor or to earn a few thousand extra pounds for a public appearance?

'Ah, Ms. Sullivan. You're here.'

Ryan looked up as he heard Ellen – maybe he could still corner her somewhere along the line and grab that date – welcome the reporter whose heavily vetted questions he was about to spend the next ten minutes answering. And, as his eyes met hers, all thoughts of that date with the beautiful but nervous Ellen flew right out of the window.

Amber diverted her eyes away from Ryan Fisher's gaze to check with Alec, her cameraman, that he was ready to record this interview before looking down at her list of questions. About half a dozen of them had been edited by the over-exacting club official, with many not being deemed suitable to ask at all, although Amber had no idea why. It was hardly as if she was asking for his bank account details. But she'd done this enough times and knew enough about this game and the way it worked to know that even the smallest thing could be considered far too personal to ask. So, it was just a case of gritting her teeth and getting on with it. As usual.

'Hey, good to meet you,' Ryan grinned, standing up and holding out his hand, not waiting for anyone else to introduce him. Not that he needed any introductions. Even if you weren't overly familiar with the world of football, most people knew who Ryan Fisher was. He'd been on the cover of enough glossy gossip magazines or the front pages of the tabloid newspapers, for a variety of reasons. But reasons that usually involved some would-be model, actress or even the odd reality TV star.

Amber looked at him. Was that smile intended to impress her? Sweep her off her feet? Or have her falling at his? He was going to have a long wait, then. 'Are we all ready to go?' Amber asked, directing her question at the club official, knowing only too well how tight a schedule these events were run on.

Ryan was even more pissed off now. Was she blanking him? Jesus! She might look hot, but she was one cold bitch. Mind you, that was actually a bit of a turn-on. Ryan had never been one to shirk a challenge, although, to be honest, he'd never really been challenged all that often. In fact, he'd be hard-pressed to think of a time when a woman had blanked him like this.

'Okay. Mr. Fisher...'

'My name's Ryan, sweetheart. Can we lose the "Mr. Fisher" crap? I'm a footballer, not some fucking businessman in a board meeting.'

Amber's eyes bored into his. Who the hell did he think he was talking to? She was all too aware of this man's reputation – both

19

on and off the pitch – but she was more than ready for him. Fixing him with her best smile, she crossed her legs and sat back in her chair, glancing over at her cameraman again. He gave her the nod – he was ready to go, so she might as well get this show on the road. 'Okay then… Ryan. Shall we get started?'

Ryan smiled, too, although he was finding it hard to make that smile reach his eyes. She was one hard-faced cow. It was just a pity she was so attractive because, despite the fact she was quite obviously not in the least bit impressed by who he was, he still found himself drawn to her. Not that he had any intention of acting on it. Why put himself in a situation that would only succeed in denting his delicate ego when there were women out there who would quite happily massage it – and other parts of him – with just the click of his fingers? He'd get this over and done with then go see if he could find Ellen. She was a dead cert, whereas this one wasn't even going to get off the starting blocks.

'Fire away,' Ryan sighed, sitting back and clasping his hands over his stomach.

Amber looked down at her notebook, mainly because she had no real desire to look at this man in front of her, although, as a professional, she knew she'd have to, sooner or later. Even if she couldn't really care less what he had to say. He may well be on his way to becoming a footballing legend, and even *she* had to admit that she'd been more than impressed with his performances on the pitch. But as a person, she could, quite frankly, take him or leave him. And preferably the latter. He was doing nothing to eliminate the sometimes misguided stereotype of the modern-day professional footballer with his arrogant behaviour, but it wasn't like he was the first sportsman she'd come across who acted like this. She knew how to deal with them.

'So… how does it feel to be back home, then – Ryan?'

Ryan waited until she lifted her head, his eyes immediately locking onto hers in a stare he wasn't in any hurry to break. 'How does it feel to be back home?' A smile spread slowly across his handsome face as he continued to stare at Amber. 'It feels fucking fantastic!'

'He's an arrogant prick,' Amber said, watching from the dugout as her father's team played an evening match. The miserable weather from earlier in the day had given way to a beautiful, clear August night – conditions that were perfect for both playing the game, and watching it. The reason why, Amber suspected, the club's modest, lower-league ground was almost full to capacity which, in terms of her father's club, was a few thousand, compared to the fifty-four thousand that his old club, Newcastle Red Star, could now command in their new, purpose-built stadium.

Freddie Sullivan looked at his headstrong daughter. 'You've let him get to you, kiddo. That's not like you.'

Amber sat up straight and looked at her dad. 'Huh? I have *not* let him get to me…'

'I'm just saying, pet. Look, come on. Everyone knows what Ryan Fisher's like. He's one hell of a player, both on *and* off the pitch. You should know that by now.'

'He's reinforcing every stereotype there is, Dad. And it isn't like he's stupid, either. He's probably one of the most intelligent players I've ever met.'

'And he knows how to work reporters like you, kiddo.'

Amber looked at her dad again. 'Like *me*? What? Women, you mean?'

Freddie laughed, sitting back and stretching out his legs – legs that had once been insured for quite a bit of cash back in the 1970s and 80s. 'I didn't say that, Amber. *You* did.'

Amber stuck her hands in her pockets and sat back too, directing her eyes at the action on the pitch. The interview with Ryan had gone okay, considering. He'd answered most of the questions she'd put to him in a professional and articulate way, which had really frustrated her. More than she'd thought it would. He was an incredibly intelligent young man, yet he chose to act, at times, as

21

though he was nothing more than an empty-headed poster-boy, full of crap and arrogance. She'd almost hoped, as she'd made her way to Tynebridge that morning, that all the rumours she'd heard about him from those who'd met him weren't true, but it seemed they were. More's the pity.

'It was a good interview, though, don't you think?' Freddie commented, quickly jumping up from the bench to yell an instruction at one of his floundering defenders.

Amber waited for him to sit back down, still staring at the action on the pitch. 'The edited version looked fine, yeah. But he's still an arrogant prick. And that came across in all the bits you didn't see on TV tonight.'

Freddie looked at his daughter again. 'You've been in this business a long time, Amber. And I've never seen you react to any player like this before, and let's face it, you've interviewed some of the biggest idiots this game has ever had the pleasure of spawning. Why's Ryan Fisher got you so rattled?'

'He hasn't got me rattled, Dad. It's just… it's been a long day, and I'm tired.'

'Then maybe you shouldn't have come to the match tonight. You should have gone straight home, had a bath, watched some TV.'

'I *wanted* to come to the match. I didn't *want* to go home and sit on my own watching soap operas and drinking wine… Actually, I quite like the drinking wine bit.'

'Join us in the bar after the match, then. I'll buy you a pint.'

Amber laughed, finally starting to feel relaxed for the first time since the interview with Ryan Fisher. 'Yeah. You always did know how to make a girl feel special, Dad.'

Freddie Sullivan leaned over and ruffled his daughter's hair, pulling her in for a quick hug before jumping back up to yell yet more instructions at that same wayward defender, using language that turned the air bluer than the late-August evening sky.

Amber smiled, leaning back in her seat for the final few seconds of the first half, a little part of her suddenly warming to the idea of soap operas and a bottle of anything cold and white. She wouldn't miss anything here. Freddie's team was wiping the floor with the opposition, and anyway, he'd fill her in on everything when she popped round to see him tomorrow. No, despite feelings to the contrary just a few seconds earlier, now she really fancied just sinking into a hot, bubble-filled bath with the radio on low and a glass of ice-cold wine by her side. Because, no matter how much she tried to deny it, Ryan Fisher *had* got to her. For a reason she couldn't yet work out.

Ryan rolled over onto his back and stared at the ceiling, his breathing heavy and shallow. She may well have been shy and quiet at the club earlier, but Ellen certainly knew how to shake off those inhibitions once she'd set foot in the bedroom. Talk about wild! To look at her you wouldn't think she'd know how to do half the things Ryan had asked her to do, but she'd done them all, willingly. It was over now, though. The sex was done, and he really wasn't in the mood for conversation and cuddles, which is what so many of them wanted these days. They seemed to think that just because you took them home, gave them champagne, told them how beautiful they were and then let them do anything they wanted to you that it constituted a pre-cursor to a full-blown relationship. It didn't. And it probably never would. Ryan had no doubt he'd settle down one day, but that day was still far away in the future. He had a lot of living to do, and he had no immediate intention of doing it with the same girl. Not yet, anyway.

'You're really not as bad as everyone says you are,' Ellen smiled, turning onto her side and resting up on one elbow.

Ryan looked at her. She really was pretty. Very pretty. Would it hurt to keep her on the scene for another couple of days? After all, he was still settling in here, wasn't he? He could do with a bit of company until he found his feet.

'And what does everyone say about me?' Ryan smirked, feeling just a touch uncomfortable as she snuggled in against him. He usually didn't encourage this from any of the women he slept with in case it led to those mixed signals he was so wary of. But he didn't really have the heart to push her away. Especially as he was still considering keeping her around for a little while longer.

'They say you're an arrogant, self-centred, selfish bastard,' Ellen went on, her arms circling his waist, her head now on his chest. Ryan resisted the urge to put his arm around her shoulders. The signals were already mixed enough, and he figured the only way he was possibly going to be able to end this when *he* wanted to was by being as distant as he could. He'd done it before, it wasn't exactly hard. 'But an arrogant, self-centred, selfish bastard with talent.'

Ryan couldn't help but smile a wry smile, putting both hands behind his head as he stared at the ceiling again. 'You've heard that a lot, then?'

Ellen shrugged. 'Quite a few times today.'

Ryan laughed. Yeah, that'd be right. He was all too aware of what people thought about him, but what did their opinions matter, anyway? He did the business on the pitch, didn't he? And that was all they really cared about. In the long run. As long as you didn't push them too far, clubs would usually turn a blind eye to anything you got up to off the pitch, within reason, of course. But it didn't stop them voicing their opinions to anyone who'd listen.

'Oh, I'm sorry…' Ellen said, letting go of him and sitting up, covering her pretty, pert breasts with the thin bed sheet. 'I haven't offended you, have I?'

Ryan sat up, too. He was fast reaching the point where he wanted her to leave. Being alone seemed like such a great idea right now. He'd had his fun; he didn't need the company anymore. 'Sweetheart, you couldn't offend me if you tried. Listen, if I took notice of everything everybody said about me I doubt I'd have got very far in this game. And anyway, maybe they're right. Maybe I *am* an arrogant, self-centred, selfish bastard.'

Ellen looked at him for a second, frowning slightly, until she realised he was speaking with his tongue very firmly in his cheek.

'Look, Ellen, this has been fun, but… I've got training in the morning, y'know? New club and everything. I don't want to turn up late on my first morning, or even worse, worn out. You know how it is.'

'Oh… Oh, yes, of course. I'm… I'm sorry. I should go.' She leaned over the side of the bed and quickly retrieved her discarded underwear, hurriedly slipping it back on as though she didn't want him to see her naked anymore. Which was pointless. He'd seen it all, and so much more, so trying to hide it now was a waste of time. 'I've got things to do, too.'

She looked at him with an expression that seemed as though she was dying for him to ask just what those things were exactly, to show some kind of interest in her life, but why would he? He'd known her all of five minutes and, in all honesty, he'd probably wake up tomorrow morning unable to even remember her name. Maybe he should write it down somewhere, get her to leave him her number, because he *did* want to see her again. But only because he hadn't had enough time to check out what else was on offer yet.

'Listen, sweetheart, scribble down your number, okay? Leave it there on the bedside table.' Ryan indicated to a scrap of paper lying beside the empty condom packet before sliding out of bed and walking naked to the en-suite. Why the hell should *he* be shy? If you had it, flaunt it. And Ryan Fisher certainly had it. In spades. 'You can see yourself out, can't you?' In Ryan's eyes the fun was over, and in his world *he* called the shots.

Chapter Two

'Have you done something to your hair?' Kevin asked, cocking his head as he stood at the side of Amber's desk.

'I've dyed it,' she replied, without looking away from her computer screen.

'I thought it looked different. It suits you.'

This time Amber looked at her producer, frowning slightly. 'Are you alright?'

'Of course I'm alright. Why the hell wouldn't I be alright?'

'Since when have you cared about the state of anyone's hair? Come to think of it, I've had God knows how many changes of hair colour, and styles, since I've worked here and you've never noticed any of them. What's the matter with you?'

Kevin shrugged, throwing a press pass down on her desk. 'It's pretty hard to miss *that* hair colour to be honest.'

Amber ran a hand through her newly-coloured, dark red hair, smiling at her producer. For some reason she'd felt like a change – of what, she hadn't been entirely sure, but dyeing her hair had seemed like the easiest option. And she liked it. A lot. So much, in fact, that she was considering keeping it that colour. 'You said it suits me,' she smiled, chewing on the end of her pen, a habit she'd never been able to break in all of her years working on News North East.

'It does. It matches your frigging temper. You're off-site again today, kiddo.'

Amber groaned, throwing her head back, her pen still stuck in her mouth. 'I've got so much stuff to catch up on, Kevin. I could have done with a day at my desk.'

'Tough. You're off to Red Star's training ground. We're covering Ryan Fisher's first day with his new club. Oh, and let's not forget the double whammy Red Star have just thrown up by signing Jim Allen as their new manager. That's being made official today. You could maybe try grabbing a word with him, too, while you're at it. If he's there, that is.'

Amber sat up straight, taking the pen out of her mouth. 'That's definite, then?'

'*What's* definite?' Kevin asked, looking through a pile of newspapers he was holding.

'Jim Allen, coming back to Red Star as manager.' She'd heard the rumours concerning ex-Newcastle Red Star player Jim Allen joining the club as their new manager, but she hadn't thought anything would come of it. He'd been in charge of a huge and extremely successful London club for some time now, and as far as she'd been aware they were trying to hold onto him with some eye-watering new contract negotiations, so determined were they to keep him where he was. So she hadn't thought coming back to the North East was an option for him, despite Red Star desperately wanting a successful, big name manager to help them with their league-winning efforts this season. And who better than a man who'd been one of their most popular players back in the day?

Jim Allen was also a good friend of her dad's. He'd joined Newcastle Red Star just as her father was ending his professional playing days, but Freddie Sullivan had taken Jim under his wing, become his mentor almost. They'd stayed close ever since. So she'd have thought Freddie would've said something to her about this if he'd known what was going on. She wasn't sure how often they talked these days, but it really would have been nice, if he did know something, to have let her know. For a number of reasons. None of which he would actually have been aware of.

Kevin looked at her through slightly narrowed eyes. 'Remind me, what job do you do again? Jesus Christ, Amber, come on. Isn't Jim Allen a family friend or something? Surely you of all people should be keeping up with all of this. He signed the contract this morning. They're holding a press conference at Tynebridge later today, so it's possible he won't be at the training ground when you're there, but if he is… Anyway, I'm sending Phil to the press conference, if you don't mind. I'd rather you concentrated on Ryan Fisher, for now.'

Amber stuck the end of her pen back in her mouth, looking briefly out of the window. 'That's fine with me.' Another meeting with the charming Mr. Fisher. She couldn't wait. 'Anything in particular we're looking for here?'

'Not really,' Kevin said, flicking through a copy of one the local newspapers. 'I suspect the place'll be swarming with press and TV, so we'll just be one of many trying to get a glimpse of the returning hero in action.'

'He's hardly a hero,' Amber muttered, throwing her phone and press pass into her bag. She suddenly had a headache forming right behind her eyes.

Kevin arched an eyebrow. 'Well, whatever he is – and I've heard him called plenty – keep an eye on him, and just try and get a word with him after training, okay? See how his first session's gone, find out how he's feeling about making his debut for the club on Saturday, what he thinks of Jim Allen as a manager; you know the kind of thing. You don't need *me* to tell you.'

'Gonna be difficult to get a one-to-one if everyone else is going to be there. And didn't we cover most of that in yesterday's interview?'

'You know how this works, Amber; you've done it enough times. And *you* shouldn't have any trouble getting his attention, anyway. Not with that hair colour.'

Amber contemplated wearing a hat, because she wasn't all that keen on attracting the attention of Ryan Fisher. She hadn't liked him on sight yesterday, and she didn't think she was going to feel any different today. But this was her job, so she was just going to have to suck it up and get on with it.

'Okay,' she sighed, throwing Kevin a look that told him she wasn't happy but she'd do it anyway. 'I'm on my way.'

'You're such a trooper, Amber,' Kevin said with his usual dose of dry wit. 'I've already sent Alec over to the ground to do camera and sound, so, when you're ready you might like to get over there and join him.' He made a point of looking at his watch before walking back towards his office. 'Any time in the next five minutes would be ideal,' he shouted over his shoulder. 'Come and…'

'… see you when I get back, I know.' She sighed again, shutting down her computer.

'Whoa! What's happened to your hair?'

'Ronnie!' Amber squealed, jumping out of her chair and throwing herself into her best friend's arms.

She'd known Ronnie White for almost ten years now. An ex-professional, North-East-born footballer – and a pretty famous one at that – he was now a popular TV football pundit and commentator after his career had been ended due to injury five years ago, at the age of thirty. He now split his time between his home in Northumberland, and London, but Amber never saw enough of him. He was the only footballer who'd caused her to break her *no relationships of any kind with any footballers* rule, and she loved him. Like a brother. Despite that very brief and very physical relationship during his time as a top-flight player. But that was all over now. She was just glad their friendship had survived the post-sex period. 'What are you doing here?'

'I thought I'd come and surprise you,' Ronnie grinned, swinging her round before putting her back down, holding her out at arm's length. 'I'm back up north to cover Ryan Fisher's first game with Newcastle Red Star at the weekend.'

'I didn't know that match was being televised,' Amber said, ridiculously excited to see him. It'd been a while, and she hadn't realised how much she'd missed him, until now.

'You know how they change these things. With the arrival of both Jim Allen *and* Fisher at Red Star, suddenly this game looks like the more exciting option. And it gives *me* the perfect excuse to come home for a few days. You did *know* about Jim Allen signing as Red Star's new manager, didn't you?'

'Yeah. Of course I knew,' Amber said, pushing a hand through her newly-dyed hair before giving Ronnie another big hug.

'Put him down, Amber, and get your arse out of here and over to Red Star's training ground,' Kevin said, reappearing beside her desk again. 'Hello, Ronnie.'

'Kevin… Look, I'm at a bit of a loose end right now, so why don't I go with Amber this morning? I'm dying to get a look at Fisher in action.'

'I don't need your help, Ronnie,' Amber said, leaning back against her desk and folding her arms, that headache showing no signs of dissipating.

'Hey, Miss Defensive. That's not the reason I want to go with you, alright?'

'Yeah, but having him around might help you get closer to Fisher,' Kevin pointed out.

'What? Because *he's* famous, too?' Amber asked.

'Err, yeah,' Kevin replied, looking at Amber as though she'd just made a really stupid comment. 'He might feel more inclined to come over and speak to somebody he used to share a dressing room with.'

'To be fair, Kevin,' Ronnie started, '… me and Ryan Fisher only played for the same club for about three months. And we were never what you'd call the best of friends. He was just a kid… Anyway, I don't want to go with Amber to help her get an interview. She's more than capable of doing that all by herself.'

'Thank you,' Amber smiled, sticking her tongue out at Kevin, who responded by giving her a rather rude finger gesture.

'I want to go with her because she's my best mate, and I haven't seen her for far too long. I just want to spend some time with her.'

'Aaah, isn't he lovely?' Amber said, still smiling, squeezing Ronnie's arm and poking her tongue out at Kevin again.

'Do that too many times and your face'll stay that way,' Kevin smirked. 'And then you won't stand a chance of luring *any* players over for an interview, never mind the really famous ones.'

'I'm sure I could do you for some kind of sexual harassment with that comment, Mr. Russell,' Amber said in a mock-shocked tone.

'Just get your arse out of here, now. Go on. And take him with you,' Kevin smiled, indicating Ronnie. 'Fancy a drink later, Ron? Usual place? Around eight-thirty?'

'Sure. Make mine a pint. See you there.'

Amber glanced over at her best friend. He looked tanned and handsome with his messed-up, dark brown hair and hazel eyes; he also looked happier than she'd seen him in a long while. That long-overdue holiday to Majorca must have done him the world of good, and he'd needed it. The recent divorce from his wife, Karen – who'd left him for a big-name goalkeeper after seven years of marriage – had knocked him for six and Amber still wished she could have been there for him more than she had been.

'Everything okay with you?' she asked, linking her arm through his as they made their way to the underground car park.

'If you mean am I getting over Karen, then yes. Slowly. I've stopped blaming myself, anyway.'

Amber squeezed his arm, stopping briefly to plant a quick kiss on his cheek. 'It never *was* your fault, Ronnie.'

He shrugged, sliding his arm round her waist and giving it a quick squeeze. 'Maybe I just wasn't there for her enough.'

'That's not an excuse to go shagging about though, is it? She knew what she was getting into when she married a footballer. I mean, that's half the reason I steer well clear of relationships with you lot.'

They stepped into the lift and Ronnie leaned back against the wall, his hands in his pockets, a slight smile on his face. 'That's the reason, huh? You don't like to be alone too much, is that it?'

Amber smiled back. 'On the contrary. I *love* being alone.'

'Bollocks! Come on, Amber. You've been on your own for far too long now. Isn't it about time you found yourself a nice young man to share your life with?'

She looked at him out the corner of her eye as the lift finally reached the underground car park. 'Who are you? My father? And, for your information, I don't want a "nice young man" to share my life with.'

'Whatever you say,' Ronnie sighed, following her out into the strip-lit car park. 'I just hope it wasn't me who put you off relationships with footballers.'

Amber said nothing for a few seconds, continuing to walk with her head down before she fixed a smile on her face and turned to look at him. 'You flatter yourself, Mr. White.'

They finally reached Amber's car, Ronnie resting his arms on the roof of her pale blue Fiat 500 as he smiled at her. 'So, what do you think of Ryan Fisher?'

'Not much,' Amber replied, climbing into the driver's side, relieved he'd changed the subject.

'He didn't win you over with the famous Fisher charm, then?' Ronnie slid into the passenger seat, immediately fiddling with the radio to try and find the sports station he occasionally did some work for.

'No. He didn't.' Amber backed out of the parking space and drove slowly out into the late-August sunshine, sliding her sunglasses down over her eyes the second they hit daylight. 'Has he always been such a cocky bastard?'

'He's always been extremely confident, if that's what you mean.'

'No. That's not what I mean. There's a difference between cocky and confident, and he was most definitely cocky. Almost as if he just expected me to fall at his over-insured feet. And the second it was evident that I wasn't going to do that, his mood changed.'

'Well, one thing I *do* know about Ryan Fisher is that he's never had a problem getting the women. So, what happened? Did you knock him back?' Ronnie grinned.

Amber briefly looked at him, smiling slightly. 'No, I didn't knock him back because he never *asked* me anything.'

'Ryan Fisher doesn't *need* to ask, Amber. He just gets. Whatever he wants, usually. That's the way this game plays out these days, with players at his level.'

'Did *you* always get what *you* wanted when you were playing?'

'I already had what I wanted, didn't I? I had Karen. I didn't need to look anywhere else. I didn't want to.'

Ronnie turned to look out of the window and Amber threw her head back for a second as they pulled up at traffic lights. 'Ronnie, I'm sorry,' she sighed.

'It's okay, really,' he smiled. 'I guess I'm still just a bit over-sensitive about everything, that's all. Which is why I'm glad to be back here in the North East for a while. I get to come home, hang out with you, and forget about all that crap.'

Amber returned his smile, leaning over to quickly kiss his cheek again before the lights turned to green and she sped off out of the city centre towards Red Star's training ground on the outskirts of town. 'Having a good time sounds like a plan to me. It's been ages since I've had a decent night out.'

'That's because you work too hard and never let yourself go,' Ronnie said. 'It's not a crime to enjoy yourself, y'know.'

'Yeah, thanks, I know that, Ronnie. But there aren't all that many people around to have a good time *with*.'

'Rubbish! You just hate letting your guard down. You hate letting people see beneath that ball-breaking exterior.'

Amber couldn't help laughing. 'Ball-breaking exterior?'

'Yes,' Ronnie laughed. 'You've got a bit of a reputation, kiddo.'

'Have I now,' Amber remarked. 'Well, we might have to do something about that, then.'

'Is that a promise?' Ronnie grinned as they pulled into the visitor's car park at Red Star's training ground.

'Tell you what,' Amber smiled, getting out of the car and slamming the door shut. 'Tell Kevin you've got other plans for tonight and I'll show you that I can let myself go just as much as the next person. Alright?'

'You're on,' Ronnie said. 'So, Amber Sullivan, party girl, is coming out to play?'

Amber just smiled, sliding her sunglasses up onto her head as she turned away and started walking towards the entrance to the training ground. 'I never said that. Come on. I've got work to do before I can even start thinking about having any kind of fun.'

But, all of a sudden, fun seemed like a really great idea. Especially if she was sharing that fun with Ronnie. Yeah. Maybe a night out *was* something she needed. After all, what harm could it do?

Ryan was having a good day. So far nothing was telling him that this move back to his native North East was one he was going to regret, but even if it was, he couldn't go back. Anyway, wasn't playing for the club you'd supported all your life a really big deal for a professional footballer? That hadn't been the first thing on Ryan's mind when he'd asked Max to find him a northern club, but he was secretly over-the-moon that Newcastle Red Star had wanted him so much they'd agreed to all the terms Max had put forward. His wages had increased significantly, they'd provided him with a fabulous, if not slightly-out-of-the-way, house to live in, and everyone was treating him like a returning hero. Everyone except that reporter from News North East. The one with the hard-faced attitude and the sexy-as-hell body. What a conundrum *that* posed. Despite the fact he'd been seriously unimpressed at her reaction towards him – being cold-shouldered wasn't something he was used to – he hadn't been able to get her out of his head. More's the pity. He'd never had to chase after a woman in his life and he wasn't about to start now. It was pointless even trying with her, anyway. Pointless going after something that was only going to kick you in the balls, metaphorically speaking, of course. Why bother with all that shit when he had Ellen ready and waiting for him to just click his fingers whenever he wanted her? Not to mention all the potential conquests that would doubtless be lining up to meet the newest addition to North-East football when he hit the town later. Some of his team-mates were taking him into the city centre for a bit of a 'welcome to the club' night out, and even though it was a Wednesday, and probably not the kind of night that was going to throw up the biggest choice in women, Ryan was absolutely certain there wouldn't be a shortage. It was almost as if these girls could sniff out a footballer at fifty paces, and before you knew it you were surrounded by a barrage of them all trying to 'get to know you'. Ryan couldn't fucking wait!

'Okay you lot, back on the pitch, come on!'

Ryan pulled himself up off the ground, glugging back one last mouthful of water. He had no intention of ignoring Colin Bailey. The man was a legendary football coach who, along with Jim Allen, the charismatic, American-born ex-player-turned-manager, had joined the club in the hope that they could bring Newcastle Red Star the success that had eluded them for far too long. Bailey had a reputation as a stern but fair coach, and it was a reputation that had gained him the respect of any player who'd trained under him. But he could also put the fear of God into you if he thought you were slacking in any way. Ryan, however, intended to start as he meant to go on – getting on the good side of his new coach.

'Over here, Fisher!' Colin yelled in his tough Glaswegian accent. An accent that only solidified his no-nonsense attitude. 'A quick kick-about to end the session, okay? But let's not treat this like a piss around in the park, alright? I'm watching the lot of you. Especially you, Fisher. We need to know exactly what to do with you on Saturday.'

Ryan ran back out onto the pitch, ready to give not just the coach but also the gathering crowd of press and TV that had been allowed access into today's training session something to really look at. Ryan Fisher was one of the greatest strikers out there right now, and he was in the process of showing them just what it was this club had paid millions for.

Fifteen minutes later and all he had to do was talk to a couple of journalists, give a handful of quick interviews to camera, and he was done for the day. But Ryan didn't intend to waste the afternoon playing golf or spending money on some ridiculously overpriced shirt to wear tonight; he had enough of those already. No, he intended to give Ellen a ring, see if she could get away for an hour or so. He was going to spend the afternoon getting some practice in for his night on the town. Ellen was the warm-up act, but Ryan was definitely on the lookout for a different main performance.

'You ready, then?' Max asked, sauntering over to Ryan, his mobile phone attached firmly to his ear.

Ryan rubbed a towel along the back of his neck, looking over towards the throng of assorted journalists and reporters who were across the other side of the pitch talking to some of his teammates. 'Yeah. I'm ready.'

'Great. Hang on a second; I'll just take this call. Don't wander off, okay?'

Ryan sometimes wondered if Max actually knew how old he was, because, at times, he still treat him like the nineteen-year-old kid he'd been when Max had first started representing him. Or maybe he just knew him too well.

Looking over once again at the crowd of reporters, Ryan squinted slightly as a familiar figure stepped back from the crowd. Was that Ronnie White? What was *he* doing here? Hang on; was he with that reporter from yesterday? What was her name again...? Amber. That was it! Amber Sullivan. Daughter of Freddie Sullivan, apparently. So Max had told him. Pity she hadn't inherited any of her father's charm. Shit! She looked even sexier with that new hair colour. Red suited her. Ryan guessed it matched her temperament, which probably meant she was shit-hot in the bedroom – Jesus; he had to quit thinking like that. It wasn't easy, though. This was one tough girl with attitude that Ryan was suddenly pretty desperate to get closer to. Even if it meant enduring a few more kicks in the teeth. Maybe that's what she got off on.

'What're *you* smirking at?' Max asked, sliding his mobile phone back into his jacket pocket.

'Nothing.'

Max followed Ryan's gaze. 'Right,' he sighed. 'Best leave well alone there, kiddo. She'll eat you for breakfast.'

'Yeah,' Ryan grinned. 'That's what I'm hoping for.'

'For fuck's sake…' Max sighed again, rolling his eyes. 'Come on. Focus for at least five minutes, then you're out of here. Although, Christ knows I'd feel more comfortable if you were being chaperoned twenty-four hours a day.'

'If they looked like that…' Ryan smirked, indicating Amber as she laughed at something Ronnie White said to her, '… they can chaperone me all they like.'

'I thought it was hate at first sight with you two,' Max said, guiding Ryan towards another local sports reporter who wanted a quick word.

'Hey, I never said I *hated* her. I hated being *ignored* by her. That's different.'

'You hate being ignored, full stop. Now, turn on the charm and do what you're here to do. The sooner we get this out of the way, the sooner we can all go home.'

Amber smiled and waved at a fellow sports reporter she knew from a local radio station as he made his way out of the training ground. He'd had his five minutes with Ryan Fisher, whereas Amber had yet to approach him. It just wasn't something she was particularly keen to do, even though it was the reason she was there. She'd spoken to a couple of the other players to see how *they* felt about their new team-mate, but so far she hadn't set foot

37

near the man himself.

'I think I know why you don't want to go near him,' Ronnie said, leaning nonchalantly against a wall, his hands shoved deep in the pockets of his more-than-likely stupidly expensive designer jeans. He was a footballer, after all.

'Do enlighten me with your theory, then,' Amber sighed, watching from across the other side of the pitch as Ryan Fisher charmed the pants off another female reporter. It was quite a sight to see. He almost had it down to an art form.

'You fancy the arse off him.'

Amber swung round and fixed Ronnie with a stare that would kill, given half a chance. 'Sorry? Did you just accuse me of fancying the arse off Ryan Fisher?'

Ronnie shrugged. 'It's obvious.'

'Oh, is it? Care to fill me in on how you came to that conclusion?'

'How many footballers have you been around, Amber?'

She said nothing for a second, aware that she still had to talk to Ryan at some point before he disappeared off to do whatever it was footballers did for the rest of their days once training was finished, otherwise Kevin would doubtless have something to say.

'Loads,' Amber replied, checking her watch before looking over at Alec.

'Okay. So, how many of them have you deliberately avoided talking to? For any reason.'

She looked at Ronnie again, narrowing her eyes. 'None. And what the hell are you talking about?'

'You fancy him. Come on, Amber. You said yourself you avoid relationships with footballers, but you've never actually avoided *talking* to any of them, especially not in a professional capacity. But look at you! Even *you* know you're actually looking for an excuse not to go over to him. Am I right? Or am I right?'

Amber gave Ronnie one last glare through still-narrowed eyes, turned on her heels, and strode purposefully over to where Ryan Fisher was busy talking to his agent.

'Have you got a couple of minutes to say a few words to News North East about your first training session with Red Star?' Amber asked, her stomach – for some completely unexplainable reason – turning somersaults. Mind you, that was probably due to the fact she hadn't had any breakfast that morning. Yeah, that had to be it. She couldn't think of any other reason.

Ryan turned to look at her, a smile – or was it more of a leer? – spreading slowly across his undoubtedly handsome face. 'For you, sweetheart, I've got all the time in the world.'

Amber groaned inwardly. What the hell was Ronnie thinking? Her? Fancy Ryan Fisher? He needed to give her a little more credit as to the kind of men she went for, because this man here, with a wage packet that was probably as over-inflated as his ego, was so far away from the kind of men she wanted to spend time with.

'Two minutes, Ryan,' Max said before leaving them to it.

Yeah, Ryan thought. Two very *long* minutes, if *he* had anything to do with it. 'Loving the new hair colour,' he smirked, taking another swig from his water bottle, his eyes not leaving Amber's. 'Makes you look even sexier than yesterday.'

Was this guy for real? 'Anyway,' Amber began, shaking all other thoughts out of her head, '…the training session…' She looked around for Alec, whom she'd assumed was right behind her. He *had* been a second ago. Where the hell had he gone now? She wanted this interview done and dusted as soon as possible, but she couldn't do a thing without her cameraman. 'I'm sorry. My camera guy seems to have disappeared…'

'I'm in no rush,' Ryan said, leaning back against the wall, draining the last of the water from his bottle. 'So, Amber… can I call you Amber?'

She just looked at him before turning round to see if she could spot Alec anywhere.

'How do you know Ronnie White?' Ryan asked, running a hand through his dark hair, fixing her with another look as she turned back round to face him. 'I'm assuming you *do* know him, because

39

the two of you look pretty friendly to me.'

Amber toyed with the idea of telling him to piss off, but then thought better of it. 'We're friends. I met him when he was still a player, about ten years ago, not that that's any of your business. My dad introduced us at a charity dinner we were all attending at the Civic Centre.'

'What's the relationship there, then? You seeing each other? I've heard he's recently divorced…'

'What the hell has any of that got to do with *you*?' Amber interrupted, quite unable to believe that someone could ask such personal questions of somebody they didn't even know. 'I've told you, we're friends.'

'I'm just interested,' Ryan shrugged, still refusing to divert his eyes away from hers.

Amber shuffled from foot-to-foot, becoming slightly agitated at Alec's absence now. She just wanted to get this over and done with and get back to the safety of her desk back in the News North East offices.

'Good friends, are you?' Ryan asked, arching an eyebrow, which did nothing to lessen the agitation Amber was feeling. She was beginning to dislike him more and more with each passing second. Ronnie couldn't have been more way off the mark – how on earth did he even *think* that she could possibly go for someone like Ryan Fisher? If he was the only man left on earth, she'd rather stay single for the rest of her life. 'Best friends with benefits, huh?' Ryan winked.

Amber swore she could actually feel her blood begin to boil, and she was about to furnish him with some sort of reply to let him know just how inappropriate that comment had been when Alec finally showed up.

'Sorry, Amber. Got talking to Jason from North News Tonight. Lost track of time. Are we ready to go here?'

Amber kept her eyes very much on Ryan as she spoke, suddenly feeling the need for that night out with Ronnie more than ever now. 'Oh, we're ready to go, Alec. We couldn't be more ready.'

And, as far as Ryan was concerned, she couldn't have spoken a truer word.

Chapter Three

The bar was unusually crowded for a Wednesday night, but for Ryan that just meant more choice. He'd had a more than pleasant afternoon sampling the delights of the lovely Ellen; so pleasant, in fact, that he'd been almost sorry to leave the sanctuary of his bedroom behind. She certainly knew how to keep his attention, but Ryan didn't care too much for playing with the same friend for too long. He liked variety, and plenty of it.

'Hey, you okay, mate?' Gary Blandford, the club's Sunderland-born star defender asked, sliding onto the stool next to Ryan. Gary had a bit of a reputation himself, never one to shirk the lifestyle or benefits that came with his job, despite being engaged to a very pretty local model called Debbie who, with her glamorous image and local-celebrity lifestyle, had earned herself the nickname of Queen of the Red Star WAGs. They had a lot in common, did Gary and Ryan. Which is why they'd become friendly with each other very quickly.

Ryan looked at Gary as he handed him another pint. 'Have you had many dealings with Amber Sullivan?'

Gary grinned, taking a mouthful of ice-cold lager. 'Yeah. 'Course I have. I mean, I've come across her a few times. She's interviewed a lot of us local players over the years. She certainly makes a welcome change from all those run-of-the-mill blokes-in-suits I used to get at me old clubs. Why do you ask?'

Ryan shrugged. 'No reason.'

'You do know she's Freddie Sullivan's daughter, don't you?'

'Yeah, I know. I'm assuming she takes after her mother in the looks department.'

Gary laughed. 'Yeah. She's pretty easy on the eye, isn't she?'

'I've certainly never been interviewed by anyone with legs like hers before, that's for sure.' Ryan smirked, also downing a mouthful of lager.

'She's got a reputation for being a bit of a cold bitch, though,' Gary went on, grinning at a couple of girls in short skirts and extremely high heels as they sauntered past. 'Won't touch footballers with a bargepole, apparently. Although, she did have a fling with Ronnie White. Just before he met his ex-wife.'

Ryan looked at his teammate. 'Really? They used to be a couple?'

Gary nodded. 'It was never something the whole world knew about. You know Ronnie, he's a pretty private person. It didn't last all that long, apparently. But they've stayed friends ever since.'

Ryan took another drink. 'Do you think there's anything going on between them now? I mean, Ronnie – he's recently divorced, isn't he? Was that because of her, do you think? Because of Amber?'

'Nah, mate. His wife left him for Frankie Greenham, Kennway Town's goalie. Had nothing to do with the lovely Amber Sullivan. Like I said before, Ronnie White was the one and only exception to her "no footballers" rule. *I* should know. I've tried.'

'What? *You've* asked her out?' There was more than a hint of surprise in Ryan's voice.

'Half the squad's asked her out, mate. She's said no to all of us. Doesn't want to know.'

Ryan said nothing, just took another slow swig of lager.

'Anyway, do you want another one? We're gonna hang round here for a bit longer before we hit the club.'

'Nah, I'm alright for the minute,' Ryan smiled.

'Fancy a game of pool?' Gary asked, sliding off the stool and grabbing his pint.

'I'll be over in a bit. Just got to nip to the loo.'

'Okay. Well, we're just over there. See you later.'

Ryan watched Gary walk over to the rest of the lads before turning round on his stool and taking a look around the crowded bar. Sometimes, being a professional footballer at the highest level was akin to being like the proverbial kid in a candy shop. All around him was temptation, and all he had to do was give the nod and whatever he wanted would just appear. Would he ever get bored of that feeling? Would the day ever come when he just didn't want to do this anymore? When all he wanted to do was settle down and get on with his life? Maybe. But it wasn't happening any time soon, that was for sure.

Turning back to face the bar, he held up his empty glass and indicated to the barman that he was ready for another. One more then he'd join the rest of the lads. This night was only just beginning, and he had a gut feeling it was going to be a good one.

'You do know that practically every male head in this bar has turned to look in your direction at least once, don't you?' Ronnie smiled, returning to the table with a bottle of champagne and two glasses. 'Because *you* have scrubbed up pretty nicely, Ms. Sullivan.'

'Champagne?' Amber asked, ignoring Ronnie's comment. 'Are we celebrating something?'

'Yeah. You finally leaving the house for a few hours and actually enjoying yourself.'

'Cheeky bastard.' But she couldn't help smiling. 'And you don't scrub up too badly yourself, Mr. White.'

Ronnie White may not have been as obviously handsome as the Ryan Fishers of this world, but he had a quirky quality about him that made him just as attractive, in a different kind of way. Probably more so, because Ronnie wasn't just some pretty shell that drew women's attention towards him purely because of his looks. He was also one of football's nice guys. He always had been; that was just the kind of person he was, and it still seemed unbelievable to Amber that Karen hadn't been able to see what a gem of a man she'd had in him. As far as *she'd* been concerned, the grass was greener elsewhere, but in Amber's eyes she thought Karen had made a huge mistake. Ronnie was a wonderful man, but if Karen hadn't been able to see that then she really didn't deserve him. Amber just hoped that, next time, he'd find someone who really loved him and appreciated him. Because he deserved that.

'You alright?' Ronnie asked, breaking into Amber's thoughts.

'Yeah. Yeah, I'm fine. I was just thinking, that's all.'

'Well, quit thinking and start enjoying yourself. Here. Get this down your neck.' He leaned forward, handing her a glass of champagne.

'You're such a charmer, Ronnie,' Amber smiled, taking a sip of the cold, bubbly liquid. 'And isn't this a bit excessive? Champagne, on a Wednesday night?'

'I'm an ex-professional footballer, Amber. There's no such thing as excessive.'

Amber smiled again, because he'd said that with his tongue very firmly in his cheek. Ronnie had never really lived the extravagant footballer's lifestyle, which was partly the reason why she liked him so much. But was that also partly the reason why Karen had left him? Had she wanted that lifestyle more than she'd wanted Ronnie? It was something that had crossed Amber's mind on more than one occasion since Ronnie's marriage break-up. But it was something she still couldn't get her head around. Ronnie was genuine. He never did things because he felt he had to, or because he just could. Karen really had no idea what she'd thrown away.

'Do you fancy going clubbing?' Ronnie asked, taking a sip of his own champagne, his eyes fixed on Amber as she shuffled about in her seat, the short black dress she was wearing riding up her legs slightly to reveal probably a little more tanned thigh than she'd intended.

'Clubbing? Are you joking? The last time I went clubbing flares were still in fashion. And you're hardly John Travolta yourself.'

'You're supposed to be having fun.'

'I *am* having fun, thank you. This is me, having fun.'

Ronnie leaned forward again, clasping his hands together between his open knees, fixing Amber with a look that defied her to turn away. 'Do you *ever* relax? I mean, I've known you for almost ten years now and in all that time I've only seen you really let yourself go once, maybe twice – my wedding, and that Christmas party we went to when we were a couple, when I was playing for United. The club Christmas party, remember?'

'How could I forget? You should never have let me have that Long Island Iced Tea. It was lethal.'

Ronnie smiled, and Amber loved the way his eyes crinkled up at the edges. 'You had such a good night, Amber. You were the life and soul of that party, so I know you *can* let your hair down, when you want to.'

'When I'm drunk, you mean,' Amber half-smiled as she took another small sip of champagne.

'Well, maybe you should get drunk more often,' Ronnie sighed, sitting back in his seat. 'Everything doesn't have to be so serious *all* the time, y'know.'

Amber put her glass down and crossed her legs, quickly pulling the hem of her dress down over her thigh. 'I just want to be taken seriously, Ronnie. I want to be a success, I want to be good at what I do…'

'You *are* good at what you do. But sometimes you need to shake off this cold exterior you give off.'

Amber looked at him. 'Is it really that bad? Do I really come across as cold?'

'Not all the time, no. But you always come across as incredibly professional.'

'And what's wrong with that?'

Ronnie leaned forward again, smiling as he looked at her. 'Nothing. There's nothing wrong with that. But I know you, Amber.

46

And I know you're anything *but* cold. I just think you put up too many barriers. It's almost like you're afraid to let anyone in.'

Amber said nothing, just took another sip of champagne.

'Don't you get lonely?' Ronnie asked. She was such a beautiful woman, he found it difficult to understand how she was still alone after all this time. Since their brief relationship all those years ago he didn't think she'd been seriously involved with anyone. She'd certainly never spoken to him about any relationships she'd been in or any men she'd met. Yet, she spent her life around men. So surely she couldn't have been alone for all that time?

'I haven't got time to be lonely, Ronnie. I'm a busy girl.'

He sat back again, pushing both hands through his hair, his brown eyes still looking straight at her. 'Hmm... well, you know what they say – all work and no play makes Amber one very boring young lady.'

She stuck her tongue out at him before taking another sip of champagne. She could get a taste for this, she thought, as the cool bubbles slid effortlessly down her throat. She could feel it going to her head already, but it was a nice feeling. Maybe Ronnie was right. Maybe it wouldn't hurt to enjoy herself for once.

'Refill?' Ronnie asked, knowing for sure he'd hit a nerve now. She listened to him, so he hoped that she'd taken what he'd said the right way. He didn't want to criticise her, he just wanted her to know that he cared about her, and all he wanted was for her to be happy. To make the most of her life. To have some fun.

'Yeah. Why not?' Amber smiled, holding out her empty glass for him to fill up. 'I might as well start the night as I mean to go on.'

'Is that a promise?' Ronnie grinned, filling up his own empty glass.

'Yeah. It's a promise,' she laughed. She just hoped it wouldn't be one she'd end up regretting in the morning.

Ryan pushed his way through the crowd, for once glad that it was so busy hardly anyone recognised him. If he saw someone he wanted to get to know better he'd make himself known. Why attract all and sundry when he didn't really have the energy to fight off the ones he couldn't be bothered with? Ryan Fisher was picky when it came to women, despite what the papers might say to the contrary.

'Shit! Jesus, will you look where you're going?'

Ryan stopped and turned around, coming face-to-face with the last person he'd expected to see in a busy Newcastle bar on a Wednesday night. He just hadn't had her down as the type of person to have fun on a weeknight. He didn't have her down as the type of person to have fun, full stop. He suspected she'd been one of those kids who'd always handed their homework in on time, too.

'Well, hello there, Ms. Sullivan. We meet again.' He flashed her the famous Ryan Fisher smile, to no effect. Christ, she was a hard one to crack. But he was almost turned on at the prospect of the challenge.

'Sorry would have been nice,' Amber muttered, rubbing her shoulder. 'You nearly took my arm off there.'

'Okay… Sorry.' He was still smiling, and Amber didn't know whether that was making her angrier, or whether it was actually diffusing a situation that didn't really need to become heated. At least four other people had bumped into her harder than he had just then, yet she hadn't called any of those out for doing so.

'Apology accepted,' she said, repositioning the strap of her dress back on her shoulder. Very nice shoulders, too, Ryan thought.

'You here on your own?' Ryan asked, shoving his hands in the pockets of his black jeans.

Amber narrowed her eyes as she looked at him. Was there no end to this man's rudeness? Although, he did have really beautiful eyes. A deep blue colour that Amber had never seen before. Jesus, that champagne really must have gone to her head.

Ryan reached out to quickly grab her arm as she briefly lost her balance. 'Whoa there, gorgeous. You been knocking them back like there's no tomorrow, then?'

Amber ignored him, trying desperately to sober up, pulling her arm free from his grip. 'If you'll excuse me...'

'Are you here with Ronnie White?' Ryan asked, not caring that he was getting personal again and that it was something she quite obviously didn't like. Tough. He wanted to know what was going on there. Gary had said there was nothing between the ex-footballer and this incredibly pretty sports reporter, but what did *he* know? He'd rather hear it from her. Although the chance that she was going to impart any information to him on that score was probably less than zero.

Amber looked at him, right into those deep-blue eyes, and she had to steady herself again by grabbing onto the table behind her as her heart gave another surprise somersault. She really had to start eating more before she drank alcohol. She just wasn't used to these kinds of nights out anymore.

'What's it got to do...?'

'With me? Nothing. It's got nothing to do with me. Not really. But, hey, I just want to know. And you get nowt if you don't ask, do you?'

Amber couldn't help smiling. His cocky attitude was something she truly hadn't come across in such close proximity before, despite all her time around footballers just as famous as he was. But his Geordie accent *was* just a little bit sexy. She couldn't deny that. She'd always loved the Geordie accent. And all that time away from the North East certainly hadn't softened his.

'You're smiling,' Ryan pointed out. Was he making progress here? Was he actually beginning to melt the ice-queen's frosty exterior?

'Am I?' Amber asked, knowing that she was, and not really caring. She was having a great time tonight, even if she *had* somehow found herself in the middle of some sort of conversation with Ryan Fisher, arrogant bastard and self-styled northern playboy. And now she couldn't even remember the question he'd asked her not two minutes ago. 'Sorry, did you just ask me something?'

'Are you here with Ronnie White? I mean, I know you said you're just friends, but, someone told me you two used to go out, once-upon-a-time.'

'Did they now,' Amber said. It wasn't a question.

'You never told me that.'

'Because it's got nothing to do with you.'

'So, did you? Go out with Ronnie White, I mean. Only, I hear you've got a bit of a strict "no footballers" rule going on.'

'You've been hearing a lot tonight, haven't you?'

'Makes a change to hear stuff about other people, rather than me.'

'Must be such a pain in the arse, not being the centre of attention.'

Ryan shrugged. 'It's good to get a night off.'

She couldn't help smiling again, despite herself.

'Anyway, you haven't answered my question. You and Ronnie White…'

Amber looked over towards the corner table where Ronnie was talking into his mobile phone, laughing at whatever was being said down the line. 'This really has got absolutely nothing to do with you, and I don't even know why I'm telling you, but yes, we used to go out. For all of five minutes, really.'

'Nothing mind-blowingly serious, then?'

She looked at him. 'No. Nothing serious.'

Neither of them said anything for a few seconds, and then Ryan took his chance, gently grabbing her arm and steering her out into the quieter corridor that housed the toilets and an entrance that led to the bar's outdoor terrace area.

'What are you doing?' Amber asked, taking a few seconds to register just what it was that was happening. That'd teach her to down champagne too quickly. She'd only had two glasses, but it was enough to make her reflexes slower and her judgement that little bit clouded.

'Look, when I first met you yesterday I really didn't like you.

I mean, you're this great-looking woman, but your attitude was crap...'

'Ex*cuse* me? *My* attitude was crap? And which charm school did *you* graduate from? I've got to get back to Ronnie...'

'No, hang on, Amber...' He reached out to grab her arm again, swinging her back round to face him.

'What? What do you want from me?'

He looked at her, not exactly sure how to answer that. He wanted to sleep with her, yeah. Of course he did. But, despite the fact he was Ryan Fisher – and if he wanted to sleep with someone then it usually happened – this was a whole different ball game. She wasn't going to just fall at his feet like the girls he usually went for. He was going to have to work hard to get this one anywhere near his bed, and hard work outside of the football pitch wasn't something Ryan was keen on. Would she be worth the effort? 'I just want to get to know you,' he said, his eyes not leaving hers.

'Oh. Really.' Again, it wasn't a question.

'Yeah. Really.'

'You do know I'm a good few years older than you, don't you?'

Ryan shrugged. 'So? What's *that* got to do with anything?'

Amber narrowed her eyes as she continued to stare at him. 'So, you're telling me you're bored with all the young and pretty football groupies all vying for your attention. You thought you'd try your hand with an older woman instead. Is that it? You're tired of the wannabe WAGs, huh?'

'I'm not tired of anything, Amber. I'm not bored of anything and I'm not even thinking too hard about any of this. I just like what I see and I want to find out more. Where's the harm in that?'

Amber just looked at him for a few more seconds before turning on her red high heels and walking away.

'Amber! Jesus, come on... Shit!' Ryan leaned back against the wall and ran a hand through his short, dark hair, closing his eyes for a moment. Under normal circumstances he'd give this up as a bad job and move onto the next one, but two things were different here: one – he'd never had to give anything up as a 'bad job' before because nobody had ever walked away from him like she'd just done. And two – he didn't *want* to move onto the next one. He wanted Amber Sullivan.

'Where've you been?' Ronnie asked, looking up as Amber threw herself down on the sofa opposite him.

'Fending off Ryan Fisher,' Amber replied, taking her compact out of her make-up bag and checking her face. No, her make-up looked fine – mascara still in the right place, lipstick unsmudged.

'Huh?' Ronnie laughed.

Amber snapped her compact shut and looked straight at Ronnie. 'Do you fancy some really hot sex with no strings attached?'

Ronnie looked around, almost as if he was positive she was talking to someone else and he was trying to see who that person was.

'Well?' Amber asked, standing up and sliding her bag up onto her shoulder.

'Erm, I…'

'Do you want sex or not, Ronnie? It's a perfectly simple question. I'm not asking you to marry me or even take me out to dinner, and I know neither of us wants a relationship out of this so, hot sex, no strings. Are you up for it?'

Ronnie stood up, too, holding out his hand. 'Why the hell not? You only live once.'

Ryan had had enough. He wasn't really in the mood to hang around any longer, and with training in the morning, and him still with a point to prove at his new club, maybe going back home and getting some rest was the best option. And even though he could easily have gone back out there and picked any woman he wanted to take his mind off Amber Sullivan, he just didn't feel like it anymore. And that worried him. Was he losing his touch? When had Ryan Fisher *not* been in the mood for sex? Especially when it was so readily available to him.

Keeping his head down as he pushed his way out of the bar, he took his phone out of his pocket and began texting Gary. He lied, of course. He told him he'd met a girl and was taking her home for fun of the more private kind, when really he was waiting for a taxi to take him back to the huge, empty house the club had stuck him in until he found a place of his own. But Gary and the lads didn't need to know that. They'd only rib him rotten if they thought he'd joined the ranks of footballers Amber Sullivan had given the brush-off to. He shouldn't have even bothered trying but all of a sudden Ryan had the ridiculously uncharacteristic urge to take up the challenge Amber had unwittingly offered up.

Never before had Ryan Fisher had to do the chasing, but it looked like, this time, if he wanted something to happen, then he was going to have to start running.

Amber kicked the door shut behind her, hardly having time to take a breath before Ronnie pushed her back against the wall, kissing her hard and deep, his tongue running over the roof of her mouth as their hands pulled at each other's clothes. Amber had every idea why she suddenly needed to have sex like this – something she hadn't felt the need to do in a long time – and she also knew that she was using the fact she was having wild and spontaneous sex to forget about that very reason. But who cared? Right now it was time to enjoy what was happening and think about the consequences in the morning. Not that there'd *be* any consequences. They both knew the score. They were both free agents. They were both in this for a quick release, and nothing else.

Sliding her dress down to the floor, Amber stepped out of it and kicked it away, pulling Ronnie back against her, his mouth covering her neck in soft kisses as his fingers gently ran over her breasts, sending tiny shivers right through her. She'd forgotten how talented this man was at making her feel good. Their brief relationship had been an intense and physical one at the time, in fact, if Amber remembered rightly, they'd spent a hell of a lot of time in bed, which is probably why it had never really gotten off the ground in any other way. That, and the fact that Amber had already made the decision never to get involved with footballers. For a very good reason. What had happened with Ronnie had been a blip, a lapse of concentration on her part, because once that need for almost constant sex had gone, that was when they'd realised they worked better as best friends. Ronnie had gone on to meet and marry Karen, and Amber had thrown herself into her work. In reality, it would have been hard to have had a relationship anyway because, at the time, Ronnie had been playing for a Manchester club and Amber had been based in Newcastle. So best friends it had stayed, and Amber was glad of that because she needed him around as her friend. Which, in a way, made it quite a strange feeling, having him touch her like this after so long, but at the same time, it felt safe and familiar. And that's what she needed right now. Something safe and familiar.

She gasped out loud as his fingers slid down from her breasts, trailing over her stomach, down to a place he hadn't been in a long time, but Amber was quite happy to welcome him back, moaning quietly as he touched her gently, his own groans matching hers as the intensity built.

She could feel her heart racing, so fast it was almost making her dizzy. She hadn't had sex with anyone for so long and it felt good to be able to let go, to have that sweet release, and it felt even better to be sharing it with a man she trusted, rather than some random person she'd picked up just for the hell of it. How Ryan Fisher could possibly get any kind of satisfaction from doing that, she had no idea. Jesus, why was she even *thinking* about Ryan Fisher? But she knew why. She knew exactly why, and she really didn't *want* to think about him, so she pushed him very firmly to the back of her mind, concentrating totally on what was happening here, with Ronnie.

She hadn't realised how much she'd missed sex until now, and in a way Amber wondered if that had anything to do with the fact she'd been so uptight lately. Right now, though, she felt anything *but* uptight as Ronnie lifted her up, and she quickly wrapped her legs around his waist as he pushed into her with a force she welcomed, backing her right up against the wall. She wanted it hard and rough, she didn't want gentle or careful. She wanted to feel every move he made, every push he gave as he thrust deeper into her, and even though it was over far quicker than Amber would have liked, it had given her a taste for something she hadn't realised she'd missed quite so much.

But it also made her realise something else. Something that didn't make her feel comfortable or safe, and it certainly wasn't something she wanted to dwell on. But it was real, and she had a feeling that it wasn't going to go away, no matter how many times she slept with Ronnie or tried to forget it wasn't happening. It wasn't going to go away. She'd let Ryan Fisher get to her. And Amber had no idea how she was going to deal with that.

Chapter Four

The sun was shining and the sky was blue, but Ryan wasn't in the mood to be cheerful. He'd gone to bed alone, even though that hadn't been his intention when the evening had started. He'd wanted to party with his teammates, see what his hometown had to offer up in the way of women, and then bring one or two back to play with. That's how last night had started out, and yet here he was, waking up by himself, feeling like crap. And he hadn't even drank that much.

Walking out into the vast back garden of his temporary home, Ryan knew he had to get out of there. He was stuck in middle-class suburbia, surrounded by doctors and bankers and wealthy accountants with their two cars and their privately-educated children and it felt stifling. This wasn't where he belonged. Oh, he was grateful to the club for giving him a place to stay, but he needed to move on, needed to find his own place, and fast. He'd give Max a call; get him to line up some riverside apartments for him to look at closer to the city. That was much more his kind of thing. Whereas this wasn't. This screamed weekend dinner parties and Sunday mornings mowing the lawn or washing the car, and whilst that may be fine for some people, a life like that terrified Ryan.

Sitting down under the shade of a canopy that covered the patio, he threw his head back and closed his eyes, the image of

Amber Sullivan in that figure-hugging black dress and those killer red heels filling his brain. It was an image that had been there all night, he couldn't shake it. He'd gone to sleep thinking about her and woken up with the same thought still running through his head, accompanied by a hard-on he'd had to deal with all on his own. He wanted to know what she felt like. He wanted to know if she felt as uptight and rigid as she seemed to come across. He couldn't help smiling as he thought how that could actually be a plus point, where sex was concerned. The more uptight the better. Shit! Ryan wasn't used to having one woman on his mind. On the rare occasions when he'd actually had a girlfriend, none of the relationships had ever lasted all that long because he just couldn't concentrate on one woman at a time. And why should he? He had this incredible opportunity to play a field bigger than Wembley and he was sure as hell going to make the most of that opportunity. What man in his position would turn it down? Well, quite a few, actually. Ryan knew a lot of players who'd settled down with the 'right' woman, got married, had kids, given up the partying to concentrate on a more conventional life. But that just wasn't for him. Not yet. At least, not *just* yet. But then, was that only because he hadn't yet managed to meet his own 'Miss Right'?

Come on! What the hell was he thinking? Settling down, getting married, having kids, they were things that were still way off in the future. So what if he couldn't stop thinking about one woman in particular? What was so wrong with that? Amber Sullivan was different, that was all. He never usually went for the older woman, but she gave no man any other choice but to take notice of her. And she'd looked as hot as hell last night. It was almost like she was two different women – the professional, uptight sports reporter who gave off attitude and a look that could break your balls, and the red-haired vamp who oozed sex appeal the like of which Ryan hadn't seen in a long time. It was one hell of a turn-on, and he knew that if he didn't get to sleep with that woman soon it was going to kill him. He wanted to go where others had failed. Many before him had tried, but he wanted to be the one to succeed. So far, the only footballer she'd ever slept with, to his knowledge, had been Ronnie White, but Ryan was going to change that. He'd make it his mission.

Amber Sullivan may be oblivious to him right now, but he'd find a way to thaw that ice-cold exterior. She'd give in, he knew she would. She'd give in. And she'd give in soon. Ryan Fisher was up for the challenge, but he didn't play the long game. He was going straight for the goal, and there was no doubt in his mind that he was going to score.

'Shit, Ronnie, I'm sorry,' Amber sighed, opening her eyes and rolling onto her back. 'I'm not sure last night should have happened.'

'Oh, I don't know about that,' Ronnie smiled, lying on his side, resting up on his elbow as he looked at her. 'You promised me you'd show me you could let yourself go, but even *I* have to admit I wasn't expecting *that* to be quite the way you meant.'

Amber turned to look at him, giving him a small half-smile back. 'No. Can't say I was expecting that, either.'

'So, what made you suddenly decide you wanted some of the old Ronnie White magic, then? You been missing it, huh?'

She couldn't help laughing, because she knew he wasn't being serious. 'Yeah, sure. It's all I've been able to think about for the past heaven knows how many years.'

'Yep. I've still got it,' Ronnie sighed, sitting up and stretching out, quickly winking at Amber before he slid out of bed.

Amber watched as he walked into the en-suite, naked and handsome and still as fit as he had been when he'd been playing professionally. But they'd never get back together as a couple. They'd never go there again. *She* knew that, and Ronnie knew that. Last night had been a bit of fun. She'd needed it to take her mind off something that had been niggling away at her all day yesterday, and it was back to niggle away at her again today. With a vengeance. She'd known it wouldn't go away, she'd known last

58

night had been nothing but a temporary measure, even though she'd hoped she'd wake up thinking that, whatever had been going round in her head yesterday, it had been nothing but a silly error of judgement. A stupid lapse of rational thinking. She had self-enforced rules she wanted to play by, and it was up to her to make sure she didn't stray from those. What had happened with Ronnie had been an exception, of course. The one and only exception.

Slipping out of bed, she wrapped her robe around herself and walked over to the window. She loved the view she had from the back of her modest, semi-detached house on the outskirts of Newcastle-upon-Tyne. It was a view that could almost lead you to believe that you were anywhere but a few miles from the city centre. With green fields stretching as far as the eye could see, it felt more like the countryside than a suburban village, and that's what Amber loved about it. It was peaceful, yet just a few minutes' drive from work and less than half an hour from the coast. She'd bought the house not long after she'd started working at News North East and over the years she'd slowly made it her own, so much so that she couldn't see a time when she'd ever want to leave. She had a life she loved, a career she'd worked hard for, and a home she adored. What else could she possibly need?

Walking downstairs and into her cosy kitchen, she filled the kettle and sat down on the brown suede sofa next to the French doors that led out onto a small patio area. She liked to call the sofa 'lived in', whereas some people would probably call it tatty, but she'd had it for years and it was probably the most comfortable piece of furniture she owned, so she had no intention of getting rid of it just yet. It was where she spent most mornings, sitting on that sofa, watching the sun come up with a huge mug of tea, thinking about the day ahead and what it might bring – just like she was doing now, although the tea hadn't yet arrived. The sound of the kettle boiling told her it wasn't far away, though. And exactly what *was* today going to bring? Amber pulled her knees up and hugged them to her chest, resting her chin on them, looking out over her simple yet pretty garden as the sun began to sweep across it.

She wondered what Ryan Fisher was doing right now. Was he waking up with yet another young and beautiful stranger in his bed, ready to pack her off out into the cold light of day, marking her down as nothing but another conquest he'd managed to notch up? Another disappointed young woman whose dreams of becoming that glamorous footballer's wife would now have to rest with someone else? Because it seemed apparent that Ryan Fisher didn't do commitment. And why would he? He was a twenty-six-year-old professional footballer with the world at his feet.

Amber threw her head back and sighed heavily, closing her eyes as she listened to Ronnie padding about upstairs. Sometimes she wondered if her life would have been simpler if she and Ronnie had just got it together, stayed a couple. Who's to say what might have happened? But it would never have worked. She had absolutely no desire to be a footballer's wife. Not even Ronnie's. She couldn't do it. It just wasn't her.

The sound of the kettle switching off brought her back to reality and she opened her eyes, jumping up off the sofa to fill the teapot, sliding two slices of bread into the toaster, even though she was anything but hungry. Her head was spinning with thoughts she couldn't seem to shake off, feelings she wasn't used to experiencing, and it frustrated her because it was almost as if she couldn't control them, which she couldn't. Not really. If she could control them then she could stop them from infiltrating her usually rational and sensible brain, and that just wasn't happening today. But, the scariest thing of all, and it was something that Amber still couldn't quite get her head around, was that she couldn't stop thinking about Ryan Fisher.

'I like it,' Ryan smiled, spinning 360 degrees on his expensive trainers as he took in the vast space that surrounded him. 'I like it a lot.'

'It's the first one you've seen,' Max said, leaning back against the breakfast bar and folding his arms, watching as Ryan spun around again, looking like a kid in a toy store who'd just been given free rein to play with anything he wanted. Mind you, as far as Max was concerned, professional footballers like Ryan were no different, in reality. On the kind of money some of them earned they really could have anything they wanted and bugger the price. Which is what was happening here, with Ryan. He wanted a place of his own, money was no object, therefore he could live anywhere he wanted without so much as a thought as to what it might be costing. Max doubted very much whether Ryan – along with most of the other footballers he had on his books – actually had any real idea of how much things cost, anyway. Whatever they wanted – be it a new car, a holiday or, in Ryan's case, a new home – they could have it just by asking someone to find it for them.

'So why waste time trailing round other places when I've already found the one I want?' Ryan pointed out, nudging Max out of his daydream about a quiet, footballer-free retirement in Monaco.

'This is the one you want, then, is it?' Max asked, already pulling his phone out of his jacket pocket, ready to call the estate agent who was waiting downstairs in the lobby.

'Yeah... Why not?' Ryan grinned, looking out at the view of the river, the famous Tyne Bridge just a stone's throw away. He could even see Red Star's Tynebridge Stadium in the distance. This place was perfect. There was a residents' gym and swimming pool downstairs, private car parking, a concierge service, and the best thing of all – it was close to the city centre bars, clubs and restaurants he still had yet to explore. Yes, this was much more Ryan Fisher, not that vast detached house way out in the country. This was what Ryan called a home. 'How soon can I move in?'

'Give me a chance, kiddo. I've got to talk to the agent yet... Oh, yeah, this is Max Mandell, Ryan Fisher's agent... Yeah, he wants the apartment...'

Ryan left Max to make the deal and walked out onto the balcony, shielding his eyes from the late-summer sun as he looked out across the city. It was good to be home, in a funny kind of way. But he still couldn't help wondering if he ever would have returned back here if this move hadn't been borne out of some kind of necessity. Because, in reality, the decision to return to the North East wasn't one he'd made because he'd been missing his roots. Far from it. He'd *had* to leave London. He'd had to. He couldn't stay there any more, even though his club had done everything in their power to try and keep him. But circumstances and events had seen to it that Ryan had been left with no choice but to return back up north and leave the bright lights and the London lifestyle behind him. Because it was exactly that which had led to him needing to leave in the first place.

'Next Monday,' Max said, slipping his phone back into his pocket.

'Huh?' Ryan asked, turning round and leaning back against the balcony railings as Max joined him outside.

'You can move in next Monday. The agent's on his way up with papers for you to sign, and I'll organise the finances, okay? Get everything transferred for you.'

'Yeah. Yeah, thanks, Max.' Ryan suddenly felt a little bit dizzy. It was all real now, wasn't it? The moving back home, the brand new club, a fresh start. If it could *be* a fresh start, that is. Because Ryan had no idea how this was going to pan out. Not really. Nobody did. But it was a risk he'd had to take.

'You okay?' Max asked, the look on Ryan's face not escaping him. He'd been with the kid for far too long not to notice these things. Max had a kind of unwritten rule to stay away from close personal relationships with his clients, but Ryan was different. He actually cared about this one. Maybe it was the northern solidarity thing – Max was a Lancashire lad through and through – or maybe it was just that, sometimes, he could see beneath that cocky exterior Ryan liked to hide behind.

Ryan nodded, looking at Max. 'This *is* all going to be alright, isn't it, Max?'

Max shoved his hands in his pockets, looking down at the ground as he spoke. 'We did the right thing, Ryan. Coming here.' He looked up at his young client. 'We did the right thing. You needed a new start.'

Ryan turned back around, staring down at the murky river below him. 'It was *my* fault, though. Wasn't it? I should have…'

'It happened, Ryan. You weren't the first and you certainly won't be the last, but it's over now, okay? It's over, it's sorted. The rest is up to you.'

Ryan smiled at his agent, a man who'd become more like a second dad to him. He knew for a fact that, without Max, his career would be all but over, so he had no intention of messing things up a second time.

'Thanks, Max. I owe you.'

Max just gave him a look that spoke volumes and walked back inside the apartment, leaving Ryan in no doubt that Max was right. He *had* done the right thing in coming here. Now all he had to do was make sure he didn't regret it.

'No Ronnie today?' Kevin asked, perching himself on the edge of Amber's desk.

She looked up at him, leaning back in her chair. 'We're not joined at the hip, y'know. And he's not here for a holiday. He's got work to do. Especially with the transfer window closing tomorrow night, and then Red Star's televised match on Saturday.'

'I'm just making conversation,' Kevin said, checking his phone as a text message pinged its arrival. 'Anyway, I want *you* there on Saturday, too. At Tynebridge. It's big news, what with Ryan Fisher's debut and Jim Allen's first match in charge, so I'm sending you to cover it.'

'Yeah, okay. Fine,' Amber replied, turning back to her laptop.

'I know it's okay. It's your job,' Kevin said, sliding down from her desk. 'I wasn't giving you a choice. You're the Sports Editor, not to mention my best reporter, so obviously you're going to cover the game. We're looking for a big piece to put out on Monday's show.' He started to walk back towards his office before turning back around and looking at Amber, his hands in his pockets. 'And anyway, you seem to have a way with Ryan Fisher that I can't imagine any of the others would have.'

Amber swung round in her chair, fixing her producer with a look. 'And what's that supposed to mean?'

'He fancies the arse off you, Amber. That's what that's supposed to mean. He's been talking a lot about you, apparently. And because of that he's quite happy to talk to you.'

'Not sexist in the least, huh, Kevin?'

'I couldn't give a fuck, Amber. Just get used to hanging around him, okay?'

'Yeah, thanks for that,' Amber muttered, turning back around to face her laptop, her train of thought now completely lost. She didn't know whether that comment from Kevin had angered or flattered her. The idea that somebody more than ten years younger than her fancied the arse off her, as Kevin had so eloquently put it, of course it was going to be a bit of an ego-boost. But Ryan Fisher was a footballer, and Amber didn't *do* footballers. Especially those so much younger than she was, which accounted for a fair chunk of them. So why was *he* still on her mind? It was ridiculous. It was just an ego-trip, nothing else. He'd shown some interest in her last night, flirted with her, even, and she couldn't help but be flattered by that. After all, she was within spitting distance of turning forty, so who *wouldn't* be flattered by the attentions of a younger man? Especially one as good-looking as Ryan Fisher.

Aware that she could quite possibly have some kind of unchar-acteristically ridiculous expression on her face, Amber grabbed a pile of papers that needed to be taken down to the main reception and took the opportunity to escape the confines of the Sports Desk for a while.

'Hey, Amber.' Tracy, News North East's receptionist, smiled at her as she arrived at her desk in the main lobby of the building.

'You taking a break? Do you want a coffee?'

'The answer to both those questions is yes, thank you, Tracy. And these are for you.'

'Oh, thanks. I was just about to send someone up to get those.'

'Saved you a trip, then,' Amber smiled, leaning against the reception desk as Tracy disappeared into a back room to get her coffee. 'Anything or anyone interesting pass through those doors today?'

'Not really,' Tracy replied, reappearing with a steaming mug of coffee for Amber. 'Ooh, except Ryan Fisher, that is.'

'Ryan Fisher?' Amber frowned, taking the coffee Tracy held out and blowing on it to cool it down. 'What's *he* doing here?'

Tracy shrugged, sitting herself back down behind the huge oval reception desk. 'He didn't say. Just gave me that gorgeous smile of his and said he was popping up to the Sports Desk. I'm surprised you didn't pass him on your way down. He only arrived a few seconds before you came down here.'

Amber said nothing, just blew on her coffee again, more as a distraction than anything else. 'No. I didn't see him.' For some reason she just couldn't explain – or maybe she could, but she was too scared to admit it – she began to feel a touch unsettled. Her mind wandered back to yesterday; what Ronnie had said to her at the training ground, seeing Ryan in the bar last night. Ever since Ryan Fisher had arrived on the scene she'd felt slightly preoccupied, and it would be a lie if she tried to tell herself that she had no idea why. She had *every* idea why. She just didn't want to admit it. Or tell Ronnie he was right. Well, sort of right, anyway.

'Are you okay?' Tracy asked, breaking into Amber's thoughts.

Amber looked up, immediately shaking herself back to reality. 'Yeah, sorry. I'm fine. I've just remembered, there's something I need to do, that's all. I'd better get back up to the Sports Desk. Thanks for the coffee.'

'Don't mention it,' Tracy smiled, but Amber was already at the lift, half running half walking as she tried to get back to her desk before – before, what? Before Ryan Fisher left? Was she *really* thinking that way? When had she turned from sensible, grown-up sports reporter to simpering fan-girl? But she really needed to see him, if only to get something straight in her own mind. Which was why she picked up the pace once the lift reached the Sports Desk on the third floor, although she was doing her best to look calm and not bothered in the slightest that one of the country's most famous and fanciable footballers was in the building. Why should she care, anyway?

Walking purposefully towards her desk in the corner of the room, Amber couldn't stop her heart from beating hard against her ribs as she noticed somebody sitting in her chair, leaning back with his feet up on her desk. Feet that were covered by trainers that he'd doubtless not paid a penny for but had been given gratis purely because the publicity he could generate just from wearing them was priceless.

'Someone to see you, Amber,' Kevin said as he walked past, flinging his jacket over his shoulder. 'And be nice, okay? He's come here especially to see you. I think he's taken a bit of a shine to you, kiddo, so you might want to try a bit of flirting, y'know, see if you can get something out of him that nobody else is getting.'

'Can we please stop going down the overtly sexist route, Kevin? It's so offensive it's making me feel quite queasy. And what do you mean, he's taken a bit of a shine to me? You make me sound like a second-hand car.'

'I couldn't give a flying fuck *what* I'm making you sound like, Amber. All I'm saying is, if you get close to Ryan Fisher then *we* – as the North East's leading local news programme – could have access to breaking news on the football front before anyone else. Do you see what I mean?'

'Have you always been this prehistoric in your views on women reporters and I've just had blinkers on for the past heaven knows how many years?' Amber couldn't help throwing a glance over towards the corner of the room, where Ryan was still sitting in her chair, his feet still on her desk as he concentrated on his mobile phone. She was almost shocked at her own reaction; the way her heart missed that stupid and clichéd beat, her stomach flipping over, and that was just from looking at the back of his head. She had a real fear of her knees giving way the second he turned around. Was this *really* happening to her? Thirty-seven-years-old and acting like a teenager. Two days ago she would have thought this behaviour hilarious, and something she would never have indulged in. But then, two days ago, Ryan Fisher hadn't been on the scene. 'What's he want to see me for, anyway?' Amber asked, trying not to sound bothered.

Kevin shrugged, looking at his watch. 'No idea.' He looked straight at her, smiling a wide smile and throwing her a wink. 'Just be nice to him. Alright?'

Amber sighed as she tried not to smile back at her pain-in-the-arse producer. 'Like I'd be anything else.'

'You're a true professional, Amber. Right, I'm off to meet Ronnie for a drink, seeing as you hijacked him last night.'

'Jealous?' Amber smirked, now itching to get away and see what Ryan wanted.

Kevin just pulled a face and walked off in the direction of the lift.

Amber waited a few seconds, just so she could compose herself, really. Something else she wasn't used to doing – composing herself. Amber Sullivan was usually ready for anything. But not this.

Taking a deep breath, she quickly ran a hand through her long, dark red hair and strode over to her desk by the window, kicking the seat of her swivel chair so it spun round to face her, knocking his feet off her desk in the process.

'What are you doing here?' she asked, that hard exterior making a comeback, belying everything she was really feeling inside. Because, inside, she was feeling all mushy and mixed-up like some star-struck wannabe WAG, but she didn't want *him* to see that. She wanted him to be on the receiving end of the full-on, couldn't-care-less attitude.

Ryan grinned at her. Yeah, he was right. Last night she might have been that sexy sports reporter that wet dreams were made of, but today she was right back to her uptight self. 'Where'd you get off to last night, then?' he asked, still leaning back in her chair like he owned the place. And he could probably afford to.

'Not altogether sure that's any of your business,' Amber replied, his arrogant attitude still one she couldn't quite get her head around. But, oh God, he looked so hot sitting there with that sexy, messed-up hair, his tattooed arms hard and toned in a white t-shirt that showed off his tanned skin to perfection. Shit! Her heart was going ten-to-the-dozen here, what the hell was wrong with her? She fancied him; *that's* what was wrong with her. Ronnie was right – the bastard! She wished he wasn't, and she'd spent the past day or so trying to deny it and pretend he was so far from the truth it was laughable, but she'd only been kidding herself. There was something about Ryan Fisher that was gradually knocking down all her well-built defences, and there was nothing she could do about it. But he really didn't need to know that. Despite everything she'd told herself, she was finding his arrogance and bare-faced cheek one hell of a turn-on. 'I'll ask you again – what are you doing here?' But she still had to keep up the cold-bitch act. For now.

'I came to see *you*,' Ryan said, fixing her with a stare that may just have ever-so-slightly dented her steely exterior. 'You busy tonight?'

Amber sat down on the edge of her desk, looking briefly out of the window at the view of the city centre, the traffic down below streaming past the building, letting her know that rush-hour was almost upon them. 'I've got work to do,' Amber lied. She had absolutely nothing to do; she was finished for the day but, once again, he didn't need to know that.

He sat forward, clasping his hands between his open knees, his eyes still boring into hers. 'Can we cut the crap, Amber?'

She stared back at him, those deep-blue eyes of his making her feel quite dizzy. 'I… What do you mean?'

'You *know* what I mean. Don't you?'

She swallowed hard, a tingling in her thighs that she should not be feeling at 4:15 in the afternoon sending warning signals to her brain that she really shouldn't be thinking about doing what she was doubtless going to end up doing, but what the hell. Ronnie was right on another score – maybe she *did* need to let her hair down more often. So, yeah, she knew what he meant. And even though it went against everything she'd ever stood for, broke every self-enforced rule she'd ever set herself, she wanted to see what was going to happen next. If she let it. Because she could still stop it, if she wanted to. But she *didn't* want to. That was the problem.

Ryan smiled, a smile that sent a shiver right through Amber's body, that tingle in her thighs only increasing with every second his eyes were on hers. 'I'm giving you the chance to welcome me back to the North East in a way nobody else could ever do.'

'You're giving me the *chance*?' Amber asked, half laughing at his never-ending arrogance. 'You'll be telling me it's a one-time-only offer next.'

Ryan sat back, shrugging, and Amber laughed again, throwing her head back, yet knowing full well that she was going to grab this chance with both hands in an act of total recklessness that was so beyond anything she'd ever done before – well, maybe not in a long time, anyway.

'There are two reasons why I shouldn't go anywhere near you,' she said, sliding down from the desk, leaning over to write something down on a post-it note. As she wrote, she deliberately stuck out her bum, arching her back downwards, completely aware that she was flirting outrageously now, but not because Kevin had told her to. It was because she wanted to. Probably just to see if she still could.

Standing up straight, she smiled at Ryan, quite flattered by the flustered look he sported, even though it was obvious he was trying to look cool. Okay. So she *could* still do it. 'Reason number one – you're a lot younger than me, and two – you're a footballer.' She handed him the piece of paper, his fingers quickly brushing against hers as he took it from her, an action which sent a wave of something almost electric shooting right through her. 'Anytime after seven-thirty. Now get out of my chair. I've got work to do.'

Chapter Five

Ryan felt like he'd just scored the winning goal in a cup final. Sticking the yellow post-it note to the dashboard of his black Jaguar XK coupé, he entered the postcode into his satnav, waiting a few seconds until it finally plotted the route to what he hoped was going to be a very successful night. He knew he should really be taking it easy; he should be leaving the fun until after Saturday's match, *that* would be the sensible thing to do. But Amber Sullivan was something else. She was also the kind of woman that was almost guaranteed to change her mind if you left her hanging on for too long, so he wasn't going to play games. She wasn't one of those ten-a-penny pretty girls; she was different, a distraction he hadn't banked on, but one he couldn't ignore.

Switching the radio to a rock station, he turned up the volume and headed out onto the motorway, barely able to keep the smile off his face. Was he going to be the one that made this ice-cold sports reporter break her own rules? That in itself was enough to turn him on, but the thought of what lay beneath the surface of a woman who was quite fascinating, to say the least, made everything just that little bit more exciting. And the one thing Ryan Fisher couldn't live without was excitement. It was something that had got him into a lot of trouble in the past, and maybe he should be listening to the warning shots that were ringing out now, telling him to back off and lay low, play it cool, settle down. But he couldn't do it. He just couldn't do it. That would be like rolling over and admitting defeat, and anyway, who's to say that what had happened in London would happen here? He knew the pitfalls now. He'd promised Max he'd left all that behind, and he had. But that didn't mean to say he had to stop having fun altogether. Jesus, he was only human.

Shaking those thoughts from his head, he knocked the radio's volume up another notch and began tapping his fingers on the steering wheel as The Killers' *Somebody Told Me* blasted out. Max had assured him that moving back home had been the right thing to do, and Ryan believed him. It was time for a fresh start, a new beginning, but none of that meant he had to start living like a monk. He just had to be careful, that was all. He was still hot property in the football world, and nobody could take that away from him. Nobody.

Amber wondered if she'd done the right thing. Or had she just made the biggest mistake of her life, inviting Ryan Fisher into her home? Had she just taken the first step towards losing her so-carefully-kept-intact dignity just because she'd developed some silly little crush on a handsome footballer? Had she really allowed her head to be turned by Ryan Fisher and his hardworking charm offensive? After all, how many good-looking footballers had she been around in all her years as a sports reporter? Loads of them. And yet, she'd never allowed herself to feel this way about any of them, despite a fair few of them trying to gain her attention, without much success. And surely, after what had happened all those years ago, she should know better.

She shook thoughts of the past out of her head and let her hand hover over the phone as she contemplated ringing Ronnie. Maybe he could talk her out of what she was about to do. Jesus! She was a grown woman, for heaven's sake! She didn't need somebody else to tell her whether what she was doing was right or wrong.

Pulling her hand away from the phone, she went over to the cupboard and pulled out a large wineglass, filling it with the last of the bottle of Rioja that was sitting next to the microwave and taking a long drink. It went to her head almost immediately, which was what she'd hoped it would do. Just a small dose of Dutch courage.

Checking the large clock on her kitchen wall, she watched the second hand tick round, as if it was in slow motion. She needed some music or something, anything to take away the silence and her mind off what she'd done. Not that she'd done anything *yet*. She could just be asking him round for a drink, couldn't she? A harmless drink, that was all. *Oh, bollocks, Amber,* she thought as she walked into the living room. She could try and convince herself otherwise, but it would be a complete waste of time. Ryan Fisher was coming here for one reason and one reason only, but it was still up to her how far she let things go. She had to remember that.

Scrolling down the playlists on her iPod, she settled on a classic Janet Jackson album before walking over to the living room window, peering through the wooden blinds and watching the street outside as everything and everybody carried on with their usual daily routine. And then she saw it – the flash Jaguar sports coupé that certainly didn't belong to anyone on her street, that was for sure. So it could only belong to one other person, couldn't it?

She felt her stomach give a large and nausea-inducing flip as she watched him pull up outside her house, climb out of the car and run a hand through his dark hair before walking up the driveway to her front door with the kind of swagger only a man so young, famous and full of attitude could get away with.

Amber quickly backed away from the window and leaned back against the wall, the sound of the doorbell causing her heart to beat so fast she thought it might burst out of her chest at any second. Oh, Jesus, this was ridiculous! What the hell was she thinking? She was eleven years older than him, this young and volatile footballer with a reputation for excess but a talent that meant he was popular for all the right reasons, as well as all the wrong ones. She shouldn't be going anywhere near him; it was crazy and stupid, and probably a touch unprofessional, too.

She closed her eyes as the doorbell rang out again. She'd let him in, and she'd tell him. Decision made. This wasn't going to happen. She'd let him in, he could stay for a drink, but then he had to go because this wasn't going to happen. No matter what Ronnie had said or thought, and even if he was right, even if she *did* fancy him, it didn't matter. It wasn't going to happen. It couldn't. Not after everything she'd been through in the past – she'd be really stupid to go there again, wouldn't she?

Opening her eyes, she took a deep breath and walked out into the hall, exhaling quietly one last time before slowly opening the door.

'About time,' Ryan smiled. 'You gonna let me in, then?'

Amber just looked at him for a few seconds, aware only of how incredible he looked in a simple yet undoubtedly obscenely expensive outfit of jeans, white t-shirt and black boots; and with that sexy dark hair and those deep-blue eyes shining out of that handsome face of his, he looked hot. There was no two ways about it. He looked hot, and Amber felt a warm flush spread right through her as she stood aside to let him in, her head spinning again as her heart began overruling her head. Something she hadn't wanted to happen.

'Go… go through to the living room,' she managed to say, acutely aware that her voice may have sounded slightly strange there. More high-pitched than it normally did.

'Champagne,' Ryan grinned, handing her a bottle of something Amber recognised as certainly not the cheap stuff. A bit predictable, maybe, but at least he'd brought something. It proved he had manners, anyhow, even if he probably wasn't going to be around long enough to actually drink much of it. 'Predictable, I know, but I didn't want to turn up empty-handed.'

Amber looked at him, and suddenly the pair of them just burst out laughing. 'Oh, I'm sorry,' Amber said. 'But, yeah. Footballers and flash bottles of champagne are a touch on the stereotypical side, I suppose.'

Ryan shrugged, sticking his hands in his pockets, and for the briefest of seconds Amber was certain she saw a slight flash of vulnerability cross his face. But that only made him seem all the more attractive, unfortunately.

'You look great, by the way,' Ryan said quietly, his dark blue eyes locking onto hers. 'I forgot to tell you that, when you opened the door.'

Amber felt an uncharacteristic blush heat her cheeks and she looked down at her feet for a second or two, feeling like a shy teenager on a first date instead of the strong, independent woman she was. Or *thought* she was. It was all a bit confusing, but before she could even begin to get her head around just what was supposed to be happening here, she felt him prise the bottle of champagne out of her hand, place it on the table beside them and gently touch her face with his fingertips. She looked up at him as she asked probably the most obvious question ever. 'What are you doing?'

He pulled away slightly, taking a small step back, and she couldn't stop the stab of disappointment from happening. 'Amber, I…'

'You couldn't stand me a couple of days ago,' she said, aware of the tension building and the fight she was now going to have, to stop the excitement rising up in her.

'You couldn't stand me, either,' he replied, a small smile playing at the corners of his mouth and Amber couldn't help but smile back. This wasn't going quite to plan, although, that all depended on which plan she was talking about – the original plan, or the change of plan. And she wasn't entirely sure herself.

'No. I couldn't,' she said. 'I thought you were the most arrogant, self-centred, egotistical prick I'd ever set eyes on.'

He moved a little closer, his hands back in his pockets but his eyes locked onto hers. 'And I thought *you* were a cold, uptight bitch.'

'Oh, really?'

75

'Yeah. Really.'

He moved closer still, and Amber felt her resolve fading fast, but she was ceasing to care. That glass of red wine she'd had just minutes ago was starting to have an effect, and it felt good. *She* felt good. So she really didn't care anymore. He was hot, she felt like having some fun, what was the problem? Well, there was probably a list longer than a ten-mile tailback on the central motorway as far as problems were concerned, but she'd deal with those in the morning. Right now, she wasn't going to think about them.

'So, I'm cold, am I?'

'A regular fucking ice-queen. But you're no match for this arrogant prick, sweetheart.'

Amber couldn't tear her eyes away from his. She couldn't remember the last time she'd felt this excited about anything. Sure, she'd had sex with Ronnie only last night, but that was different. That had been nothing but an act carried out only to, temporarily at least, stop her thinking about this man standing here in front of her. No other reason. Compared to what she was feeling now that had been almost mechanical in comparison. A paint-by-numbers act of sexual release. This was something else.

'Oh, I think this ice-queen can take on the arrogant prick any time.'

'You think so?'

'I know so.'

She felt herself burning up, the heat from his body making her head spin. He was so close now she could feel the electricity practically fizzing between them. One glass of wine couldn't be having *that* much effect, surely, could it?

And then, before she had a chance to draw another breath, his hand was in the small of her back, pushing her against him, his mouth covering hers in a hard, fast kiss that took her completely by surprise for some reason. Considering it had obviously been building up to that for the past few seconds. But it didn't take long for her to lose what few inhibitions she had left, falling against him as the kiss got deeper and harder, the taste of him overwhelming her with feelings she'd kept repressed for so long that even sleeping with Ronnie last night hadn't managed to quell them.

It was like the release she'd been waiting for ever since she'd set eyes on him just a couple of days ago. The sexual tension that had been building ever since that initial interview was now being allowed to come to the forefront, cut itself loose, and as Ryan pushed her down onto the sofa, his fingers pushing her dress up over her thighs, hurriedly pulling down her underwear and discarding it like unwanted rubbish, she felt unusually liberated. Maybe she *had* been uptight for too long. Nobody could accuse her of that now, though, could they?

Stretching her arms up above her, she closed her eyes as he slid her dress up over her head, removing her bra in one swift movement, his mouth immediately lowering down to cover one of her breasts. It was a strangely warm and comforting feeling, and Amber arched her back, her arms still up above her head, almost pushing herself at him, but hey, she was in this too deep now, wasn't she? It was a bit late to hit the reverse button. But, oh, it felt so good, so fucking good as his fingers stroked her naked skin, running over her thighs, up to her breasts, every touch sending a million tiny tingles coursing through her entire body.

And that feeling ended only briefly whilst he discarded his own clothes, and Amber watched as that young, toned, incredibly fit body became visible in front of her, in all its naked glory. No wonder the women fell at his feet. He wasn't even her usual type – she never had gone for the six-pack and bicep brigade before – but there was something about this man that was making her confused and excited all at the same time. She couldn't just ignore that, could she? She was only human after all.

Ryan was trying desperately not to let the hard-on he'd found difficult to hold off from exploding way sooner than he wanted it to, but it was killing him. It was almost painful, so desperate was the need to get inside her. But he didn't want to come across as some stereotypical fuck-'em-and-run footballer, which he'd been more than guilty of in the past. So why was this any different? Trying to answer that question was enough to keep that ultimate release at bay for just a little while longer as he continued to thaw the ice-queen. And it hadn't taken long. He wouldn't call her a pushover – not to her face, anyway – but she hadn't exactly put up much of a fight. And he wasn't complaining. Just because she'd been a slightly easier conquest than he'd first anticipated didn't make this any less enjoyable. So far he was having the ride of his life, enjoying taking his time to explore a body the like of which he hadn't seen in a long time. He was used to fake tans, false tits, and more make-up than was absolutely necessary, but Amber Sullivan was in a different league. She was curvy in the true sense of the word, with wide hips, a perfect, small waist and the most amazing breasts he'd ever set eyes on. And they were all her own. Her thighs were hard and toned, and she had a body you could actually get hold of, rather than the skin-and-bone bodies of girls who thought that being thin was the be-all and end-all of looking good. It wasn't. He'd never really liked that look of being able to see a girl's ribs whilst two ridiculous-sized false 'footballs' were stuck to her chest, making her look entirely out-of-proportion. Amber Sullivan was a real woman. Amber Sullivan was sexy and beautiful – and real.

He ran his fingers gently over her stomach, down to her inner thighs, watching as she slowly opened her legs wider, giving him a perfect view of heaven. Shit! He was sure he was breaking out in a sweat – Ryan Fisher, stressing out over sex with a woman. But no ordinary woman. Not this one.

He knelt up, sliding his arms around her waist, gently pulling her up so she was sitting astride him, her legs automatically wrapping themselves around him as he gave in to what he'd been wanting to do ever since he'd got there – he was about to show her that Ryan Fisher could be just as talented off the pitch as he was on it.

Amber held onto him tightly as she finally felt him enter her, pushing herself down onto him as he pushed in deeper. It was a feeling she couldn't even begin to describe, that warm and beautiful tingle she was so familiar with now intensified tenfold as their bodies became one, moving in almost perfect rhythm together. She'd never meant to take it this far, yet from the second she'd seen him sitting there in the Press Lounge in the Tynebridge Stadium the day of their first meeting, she'd always known something was going to happen between them. She just hadn't been sure what. But this was fine, this was okay. This was better than okay.

She held onto him tighter as the rhythm they'd created became faster, harder, building up to a crescendo of a climax that surprised even Ryan, her body shuddering in his arms as he finally felt his own release sweep through every inch of him. Jesus, that felt good! He couldn't speak, so hard was his breathing, but as he looked at her, into those pale blue eyes of hers, he had realised that, although he'd finally been the one to conquer this ice-queen, the one to make her break her own 'no footballers' rule, he didn't care about that anymore. All thoughts of running back to the lads tomorrow morning at training to give them every tiny detail of how he'd turned her from cold and uptight into hot and horny, all those thoughts had disappeared. He had no intention of doing that now, even though he'd had every intention of doing it before.

'You can't stay the night,' Amber said, suddenly feeling as though she'd just sobered up from one hell of a heavy night out.

It took Ryan a few seconds to get his head together before he realised she was already pulling her clothes back on, running her fingers through that sexy, dark red hair of hers. He'd never been one for those post-sex cuddles that women always seemed to like, yet he couldn't help but feel disappointed that she was up and off him in what had to be record-quick time. That was usually *his* trick.

'Yeah. Yeah, okay,' Ryan said, slightly confused by what was happening now.

'So?'

He looked at her as he hurriedly pulled on his own clothes,

still unable to shake that disappointed feeling. 'So, what? You… you want me to go *now*?'

She nodded, standing by the fireplace, her arms folded, her eyes unable to meet his.

'Jesus…'

'Please, Ryan.'

He stood up and walked over to her, reaching out to gently touch her cheek, and even though he'd half expected her to flinch away from him, she didn't. She stayed right where she was, but she still couldn't look at him.

'You're something else, Amber. Do you know that?' Ryan said, stepping away from her and making his way to the door.

She finally looked at him as he walked out of the living room, closing her eyes as she heard the front door close behind him. But even then, she knew it was too late. Amber Sullivan had let her guard down. Worst case scenario.

Chapter Six

Ryan could feel the atmosphere from the stadium outside before he even reached the tunnel; the noise and the music and the excited cheers from the thousands of fans who'd turned up to see how the returning local hero was going to fit into this beloved club of theirs. He could hear it all the second they'd stepped out of the dressing room, the decibel level rising with each step of the short walk to the tunnel. He had a lot to prove, and he knew the pitfalls that would be waiting for him if he managed to stuff up his debut appearance.

He could feel his heart racing, his stomach turning in a mixture of excited and nervous somersaults, the noise of the crowd reaching a crescendo as both teams finally approached the tunnel, standing still for a few seconds side-by-side, hands behind their backs as they took in the sheer wall of sound that seemed to reverberate around the stadium outside.

Ryan smiled as a couple of his new teammates patted him on the shoulder and wished him good luck, whilst a player on the opposing team whom he'd never got along with threw him an altogether different expression that conveyed the hope that he'd break a leg or smash a shin bone. Ryan ignored him. Nothing like that was going to get to him today. Today he was focused, totally on his game, ready to prove that he was going to deliver everything he'd promised.

He closed his eyes and said a silent prayer, opening them quickly as more music blared out from the stadium tannoy system signalling the players' cue to run out and get this match underway. And as Ryan jogged out of the tunnel, out onto a perfect pitch, the roar of the crowd was almost deafening. But it was exactly that which gave him the will to play this game to the best of his ability. It was that feeling only a stadium-full of football fans could give a player like him – a feeling of absolute determination not to let them down. He'd do it for them, and show them he was worth every single penny of those multi-million pounds this club had forked out for him. Ryan Fisher was home.

'There's no doubt about it, the guy can play football,' Ronnie said, leaning against the small corner bar in the Players' Lounge as the post-match crowd started to drift in. Everybody from journalists and sports reporters to pundits, players' wives, friends and girlfriends would congregate in the Players' Lounge to dissect the match, catch up with people they hadn't seen in a while or, in the case of some of those aforementioned wives and girlfriends, bitch about somebody's ill-advised choice of shoes, hairdo, or personalised number plate on their brand new, salmon-pink Range Rover.

'Are you expecting somebody?' Ronnie asked, taking a much-looked-forward-to sip of cold beer. He'd just spent the best part of two hours stuck in a commentary box and he was parched. The cups of tea he'd been given during the game just weren't going to cut it anymore.

'Hmm? Sorry?' Amber said, turning to face him. 'Did you say something?'

'You keep looking at that door as if you're expecting somebody to come through it.'

'No I don't.' Amber frowned, her voice a touch more defensive than she'd wanted it to be.

'Yeah. You do,' Ronnie went on, taking another sip of beer. 'So, when did you sleep with him, then?'

Amber almost choked on her lager. 'Jesus Christ, Ronnie! How the hell do you know I've slept with Ryan Fisher?'

'I didn't,' Ronnie said, leaning back against the bar again. 'But you've just admitted it now.'

'Shit! I hate you, do you know that?' She took a long drink of lager. 'Thursday night, if you must know.'

'And you haven't spoken to him since?'

'Only when I grabbed a few words with him seconds after the match for News North East. Professional capacity only. In front of the camera wasn't really the right time to discuss our sex life.'

'So, you've got one, then?'

'Got what?' Amber asked, still somewhat distracted.

'A sex life. Me on Wednesday night, Ryan Fisher on Thursday…'

'You're making me sound like some kind of slapper. It wasn't like that.'

'Well,' Ronnie sighed. 'I don't want to say I told you so, kiddo…'

'Then don't. Because it was *me* who sent *him* packing, if you must know.'

Ronnie looked at her, frowning slightly. 'Huh?'

'He came to see me at work, I invited him round to my place, he looked hot – he looked *really* hot, actually – we had sex, then I told him to go. Simple as that.'

'Why?' Ronnie asked, wanting to ask so many questions but thinking better of it. She didn't look as though she was in the mood for the Spanish Inquisition.

Amber looked over towards the door again, not caring that she was making it obvious now. 'I got scared. I let my guard down, and I let it down in front of Ryan fucking Fisher, of all people.' She took another drink of lager and slammed her glass down on the bar, putting her head in her hands. 'Jesus, Ronnie. What have I done? I slept with one of the most notoriously arrogant, self-centred footballers there's ever been, he's probably told God knows how many people, and now my "no footballers" rule is tarnished forever.'

'Wasn't it tarnished the second you slept with *me*?'

'You don't count, Ronnie.'

'Gee, thanks, Amber,' Ronnie replied, a touch sarcastically.

'You know what I mean,' Amber sighed, suddenly feeling very tired. If the truth be told, she hadn't really wanted to come to the match today, but she'd had to work, and she was nothing if not professional. Any personal feelings towards Ryan Fisher that she may be experiencing right now had to be pushed aside. She was just having a bit of trouble managing that.

'Look, Amber, sweetheart. This ridiculous "no footballers" rule that you gave yourself was pointless anyway.'

'Was it?' Amber asked, looking up at him sharply. 'How's that, then?'

'Because you're around them all the time. The law of averages says you're probably going to end up becoming involved with one at some point in your life.'

'Well, thank you, Gypsy Rose Ronnie.'

Ronnie pulled a face and Amber poked her tongue out at him, her head turning to check out the door once more in a reaction that was almost reflex-driven by some kind of sixth sense, because just as she turned her head, he walked in. Tall, tanned, handsome and hot. Ryan Fisher. And practically every female in the room stopped what they were doing to stare at him. He had that kind of aura about him. But his eyes had locked straight onto hers, staring at her, a slight smile playing at the corners of his mouth. A mouth that had been covering her breasts and sending her to heaven only a couple of nights ago. And just the thought of that made her shiver, made her want to turn away and try and forget what she was feeling, but she couldn't. She couldn't do it.

'I'd better go grab a few words with him,' Amber swallowed, keeping her eyes on Ryan in case he disappeared into a crowd that was quite obviously very pleased to see him. Despite it being called the Players' Lounge, it wasn't all that often that any players actually came in there, so when they did they always attracted attention. And Ryan Fisher was hot property today. Hotter than usual, if that was actually possible. 'On a professional level, of course.'

'Of course,' Ronnie said, arching an eyebrow before turning his attention to a fellow pundit who'd just arrived in the lounge.

Amber quickly weaved her way through the growing crowd of people now amassing in the small but comfortable Players' Lounge, over towards Ryan, who was talking to his new boss. Her heart raced as she tried to adopt her professional stance and forget all about Thursday evening, after all, *he* probably had. There was no doubt that he'd be moving onto the next conquest at some point tonight when he did the usual footballer's thing of celebrating a home win with a stupidly expensive night out. And the women, of course, would be queuing up. Shit! Why did that actually bother her?

As she approached Ryan, she accidentally caught the eye of Red Star's new manager, Jim Allen. He'd come over to the UK from Washington DC over twenty years ago, a young and extremely talented soccer player who'd been lucky enough to play for some of the biggest clubs in the world in his time – including Newcastle Red Star, where he'd spent the final few years of his professional playing career. But he hadn't just played in England; he'd also spent time in Spain and Germany, not to mention numerous international appearances for his country. He loved the game, and he'd been a great player in his day, but now he was making a name for himself as a pretty successful manager. And to say the Red Star fans had been over the moon when he'd been appointed as the new man in charge of their club was an understatement. Not only had they acquired Ryan Fisher, one of the greatest players around right now, they'd also managed to steal Jim Allen away from one of the biggest, most successful London clubs.

Jim Allen had come into management fairly young – at the age of thirty-five – but he'd already confirmed he was a force to be reckoned with over his thirteen or so years as a manager.

Football was in his blood. He'd been a great player, and now he was proving to be an accomplished and well-respected manager; a natural people person, a savvy businessman. And it also didn't hurt that Red Star had recently been bought out by a large, New York-based consortium who were more than happy to have a fellow American at the helm.

Amber had known Jim a long time, due to the close relationship he had with her father, but he almost always made her feel slightly uncomfortable every time she was around him. And she didn't really want to be around him right now.

She looked away quickly as he smiled at her, staring down at her feet, her hands in her pockets. 'Could I have a quick word with Ryan, please? For News North East?'

'He's all yours, honey,' Jim Allen winked, giving her his best smile, and Amber looked away again, this time pretending to root around in her bag for some imaginary object. 'How's your old man, by the way? I hear he's doing okay over there at Bracken Town.'

'He's fine,' Amber replied, still rooting around in her bag, aware that Ryan's eyes were on her. She could almost feel them boring into the back of her neck.

'Well, tell him to give me a call, okay? It's been a while since we've had a proper catch-up.' His eyes met hers again. 'Yeah… It's been a long time.' He turned his attention back to Ryan, leaving him with a friendly slap on the shoulder. 'Proud of you today, kiddo. Be nice to Amber, okay? She's a good friend of mine.' He looked at her again. 'A very good friend.'

Amber watched Jim leave, almost breathing an inner sigh of relief, before slowly turning round to face Ryan.

'Not *one* word since Thursday?' he asked, his comment, not to mention his tone of voice, taking her completely by surprise. She had no idea it would even have bothered him. She'd given him what he'd wanted, hadn't she?

'You've been holed up in a hotel since Friday afternoon, Ryan. There was no way *to* get in touch with you.'

Jim Allen was a great believer in making sure his players had as few distractions as possible before a match. The day before any game – be it home or away – he'd take his team to a hotel, away from everything, away from all outside distractions, and make sure they were focused on nothing but football. No contact of any kind with wives, girlfriends or any family members was allowed – unless it was an emergency, of course. He wanted everyone to think only about the forthcoming match, and nothing else.

'That's crap, Amber. We didn't leave for the fucking hotel until after 3 o'clock…'

Amber quickly switched to professional mode, looking him straight in the eye. 'Any more thoughts on this evening's match?'

'For fuck's sake, Amber, we've already done this… I loved every second of it, the crowd were amazing, the boss is a legend, and I was proud to get a hat-trick on my debut for the club. There. Anything else you need to know? Not one frigging word, Amber.'

'Hang on, can we rewind a bit here because I'm a touch confused. You *are* Ryan Fisher, aren't you? The one who, quite frankly, will sleep with anything that shows him the slightest bit of interest and then prays they never want to see him again once the sex is over? That *is* you, isn't it?'

'*You* were different, Amber,' Ryan hissed, trying to keep his voice down, but he was more than agitated that she didn't seem to care about what had happened between them. Because *he* did. Oh, he didn't *want* to. Jesus, of course he didn't *want* to feel that way, but he did. 'I didn't want to leave; you *do* know that, don't you?'

Amber said nothing at first, just looked at him, searching his handsome face because there was something different about him today that she hadn't really noticed before. Sincerity? Was that it?

'I needed you to go, Ryan,' she whispered. Her stomach felt as though it was tied up in knots, the confusion she'd been feeling since Thursday threatening to overwhelm her again. For so many reasons.

'Why, Amber? Why did you need me to go? Because you actually enjoyed yourself and were afraid to let anyone know that?'

'Come on, Ryan. I'd just slept with you – with *you,* so how do you ex*pect* me to react?'

'What the hell's *that* supposed to mean?'

She looked away for a second, looking over at Ronnie who was deep in conversation with a couple of reporters she recognised. 'I didn't want to be another conquest, Ryan.'

'You weren't. You *aren't.*'

She looked at him. 'Why should I believe you? I mean, you have such a reputation, a reputation that…'

'That means I couldn't possibly find someone that makes me feel different?'

Amber stared at him. She just stared at him, because she couldn't actually think of anything to say.

'Okay, I have a reputation, I'll hold my hands up to that,' Ryan began, staring down at his trainers for a second. 'And, as you've just pointed out, I've obviously got a lot of work ahead of me if I ever want to leave that reputation behind.'

'Why would you *want* to leave it behind?' Amber asked, narrowing her eyes as she continued to stare at him. 'I mean, this is what you do, isn't it? This is you. This is the way you live your life.'

'Have you ever thought that I might actually want to give a proper relationship a go?'

Amber couldn't help laughing. 'Ha! Come on, Ryan. You've tried that before and it just doesn't work. You don't really want that…'

'Hey, do you want to quit telling me what it is I want?' He ran a hand through his hair, those incredible dark blue eyes of his full of confusion, which only served to make him look twice as handsome, Amber noticed. If that was possible. 'Look, come out to dinner with me. Tonight.'

'Why?'

'Because I like you, Amber. I like being with you, I like the vibes you give off, and I even like the fact you're a pain in the arse who refuses to give footballers a chance. And I can't lie – the sex was amazing. Jesus, sweetheart, you have one killer body.'

Amber felt herself blush. What was she? Sixteen?

'Look me in the eye and tell me you don't want to see me again. Come on. Look me in the eye and tell me that was it, and if you can do that, well…' He shrugged, '… end of story.'

She looked him right in the eye, but she couldn't say it, could she? Because she wouldn't mean it. 'Okay,' she sighed, rolling her eyes as though accepting a dinner date with Ryan Fisher was the world's biggest chore, when really she felt elated that he'd told her all those things. Maybe he *did* deserve that chance she'd denied him on Thursday. 'Dinner it is. Where?'

'Franco's. Do you know it? It's in town…'

'Yeah, I know it,' Amber said, trying not to let the smile she was dying to let loose escape onto her face just yet. She didn't want him to know she was actually looking forward to seeing him later. 'I'll meet you there. Eight-thirty?'

Ryan wasn't used to women making the decisions quite as forcefully as she did, but on her it was a turn-on. He couldn't help wondering if she brought that dominating streak into the bedroom, but maybe if he played his cards right tonight he'd find out.

'Eight-thirty it is,' he grinned, sticking his hands in his pockets. 'Looking forward to it.'

Amber just gave him a small smile back then turned and walked away. Ryan had absolutely no idea why this woman had got to him, but she had. Maybe it was because she was just so different to all the other girls he was used to. Maybe it was because she didn't fall at his feet with the click of a finger. He didn't know, but whatever it was he wanted to find out more.

'Great match, lad. You did me proud out there.'

Ryan swung round at the sound of the strong Geordie accent behind him, leaning back against the wall, sighing heavily. 'Dad.'

'I thought you would've been to see us, Ryan. Your mam's been looking forward to having her boy back home after all these years.'

'I've been busy.'

'Too busy to spare a few minutes to come and see your mam and dad?'

Ryan looked at his father. 'I don't need the nagging, Dad. Mam treats me like I'm still a kid sometimes.'

'With good reason, son. Because sometimes you act like it.'

Ryan continued to stare at his dad. 'Those days are over now. Okay?'

'I hope you're right, Ryan. Still, at least you're back home now. Back where you belong.'

Ryan looked at his dad through slightly narrowed eyes, but said nothing.

'Your mam's worried sick about you, lad.'

Ryan threw his head back and sighed again. 'Jesus...' He looked straight at his father, running a hand through his dark hair. 'I'm fine, alright? Everything is just fine.'

'Is it? After everything...'

'It's fine, Dad.' Ryan's voice left his father in no doubt that his son didn't want to take this conversation any further. But that was easier said than done.

'Your mam always told me that letting you settle in London was a bad idea. She blames me for everything...'

'Christ, Dad, come on. None of it was *your* fault. It was nobody's fault but mine. *I* got myself into all that shit.'

'And I hope you're well out of it now, son. It's good that you've come back home.'

'Where you can keep an eye on me? Is that it?'

'If that's what it takes, Ryan. Yes. I hear you've just bought a brand new flat down on the Quayside.'

Ryan looked at his dad, his hands jammed firmly in his pockets, not enjoying this unwelcome interrogation. 'I need somewhere to live.'

'The club had given you a perfectly good house to stay in. For as long as you needed it.'

'I want my own place, okay?'

'Is the city centre the most sensible choice of location, son? It's a bit close to…'

'That house, it wasn't me,' Ryan interrupted. 'I wasn't comfortable there.'

His father fixed him with a stare that demanded the truth. 'Are you…?'

'Am I, what?' Ryan asked, his stare just as determined.

'You know what I'm asking, Ryan.'

'I'm getting there, Dad. That's all you need to know.'

'Aye, well, as long as you are, lad. As long as you are.'

'Do I look alright?' Amber asked Ronnie as he pulled up at the corner of the street where Franco's restaurant was situated.

'You look fine,' Ronnie replied as he fiddled with his in-car MP3 player.

Amber looked at him. 'Fine. I look *fine*?'

Ronnie stared at her. 'Yeah. You look fine.'

Amber said nothing, just raised her eyebrows and gave him a wide-eyed look. Ronnie shrugged, genuinely confused. 'What? What do you *want* me to say? Who the hell *am* I? Gok frigging Wan? You look great, okay? Is that better?'

Amber still said nothing, just pulled down the visor and checked her face in the small, side-lit mirror, running her tongue over her teeth just in case any pale pink lip gloss had found its way on there.

'Do you know what you're doing?' Ronnie asked, finally finding a playlist he was happy with.

Amber looked at him. 'Of course I know what I'm doing. I'm having dinner with Ryan Fisher.'

'You know what I mean. I want to make sure you know just what it is you might be getting into. Although, if you want my opinion…'

'Which I don't.'

Ronnie ignored her. 'If you want my opinion, I don't think you should be getting into it at all.'

'I'm not getting "into" anything, Ronnie.'

'Well, with the greatest of respect, Amber, you already *are* into something when you sleep with somebody.'

'So, what does that make *our* relationship then? Huh? Do you want to explain that one?'

Ronnie looked out of the window for a second. She kind of had him there.

'No, didn't think so. Because you can't, can you? Look, Ronnie, like I said before, I'm not getting "into" anything. I'm just having dinner. That's all. Ryan and I both know where we stand, and just because we appear to be doing things a little back to front, it doesn't actually have to mean anything's going on.'

'Y'know, you might think you're all hard-faced and nobody can tell you anything, but you're still my best friend and I care about you, okay? And, let's face it, where men are concerned you're not exactly experienced, are you?'

'Yeah, thanks for that, Ronnie.'

'Amber, sweetheart… you said that all of this doesn't have to mean that anything's going on, but…'

'But what?' Amber asked, looking right into Ronnie's eyes.

'But… do you *want* something to happen? Even just a little bit?'

She sat back in the passenger seat of his black BMW, the dark leather interior cool against her skin. 'Look, Ronnie, I know I've always said I really didn't want to get involved with footballers, mainly because I assumed you were all like Ryan Fisher. But *you* proved me wrong, and I think Ryan might actually prove me wrong, too. I don't know. Maybe I'm just getting softer, but I'm willing to see how tonight goes. People *can* change, y'know.'

Ronnie raised a concerned eyebrow. 'You think so, huh? You think someone like Ryan Fisher is just going to change overnight? Don't go rushing into anything, Amber. Please.'

'It's a bit late for that, isn't it?' Amber smiled, grabbing her handbag and opening the car door. 'I mean, like you said before, we've already slept together, haven't we?'

Ronnie gave a resigned sigh, smiling back at her as she leaned in through the open passenger window, blowing him a kiss. 'Have a good time, kiddo.'

'I'll try,' she winked at him before waving him off, standing still for a few seconds, just to compose herself. Again. She seemed to be composing herself a lot where Ryan Fisher was concerned.

The restaurant was busy when she finally walked in, but then it *was* Saturday night in the centre of town. She'd never actually been inside Franco's before, mainly because it was the haunt of local celebrities and footballers and therefore the price range was a little out of her league, but she'd always wondered what it would be like to eat there. She was also one of life's truly nosy people, and to be able to get a glimpse at the clientele that frequented this famous local restaurant was something she was particularly looking forward to.

Sliding her clutch bag under her arm, she scanned the room as she waited at the front desk for the maitre d', but she couldn't see Ryan anywhere. What if he'd had a better offer from someone younger, thinner and blonde? She could do without *that* kind of kick in the teeth.

'You look amazing.'

She swung round at the sound of that now-familiar voice, trying to keep the smile off her face as she saw him standing there behind her. Dressed in a dark suit and white shirt, no tie, and that sexy, messed-up hair that he really was carrying off so well, it was all Amber could do to stop a sharp intake of breath from escaping. As usual, Ryan Fisher looked hot. Handsome, sexy, young and dangerous. Cocky, arrogant, selfish and smug. All things that described this man in front of her, but Amber was willing to give him that chance he seemed so set on having. But if he blew it, then she was walking away. No second chances, no lame explanations. She was breaking the biggest rule she'd ever set herself and if he gave her cause to regret that then this was going no further.

93

'I was at the bar,' he went on, his hands in his pockets, a smile on his handsome face. She couldn't help noticing how sexy that beard of his really was. He suited it. It made her think of a young George Best in his heyday, and then she couldn't help hoping that he didn't resemble him in other ways, too. Because she'd heard the stories, listened to the rumours. 'Do you want a drink before we get settled at our table?'

'Please,' Amber smiled, positive she was breaking out in some kind of hot flush. She was only eleven years older than him but she felt like some kind of Mrs. Robinson figure. She felt as if all eyes were on her, which they probably weren't. But they could quite possibly all be on Ryan. 'And make it a large one.'

Ryan laughed a deep, almost rough-edged laugh that made Amber's skin break out in a zillion goose bumps. Was there anything this man did that *wasn't* sexy? 'That kind of day, huh?'

She looked at him as they walked over to the dimly-lit but cosy bar area, the low lighting making him look younger than his twenty-six years. She could only hope it was as kind to her. 'Not really. I'm just nervous. There, I've said it. I'll have a white wine, please.'

'Okay. Coming up,' he said, smiling slightly as he turned to order their drinks. 'So,' he went on, turning back to face her, '… want to know something? I'm nervous, too.'

'Really?' Amber asked, unable to hide the slightly cynical tone in her voice. She did, however, hope that he meant it and he wasn't just saying it to make her feel better. Although even *that* would be a really kind thing for him to do. Hang on, had she just described Ryan Fisher as 'kind'?

'Yeah, really,' Ryan replied, handing her a large glass of white wine. 'Even arrogant, self-centred bastards can get nervous sometimes.'

She took a sip of wine, keeping her eyes on his on all the time. 'I still find that incredibly hard to believe. Come on, Ryan, you can't blame me. There's hardly a week goes by when you're not in some gossip magazine or showbiz section of some newspaper or other with something that falls into the category of Z-List celebrity hanging off your arm. There *was* a time when footballers only used to feature on the *back* pages of newspapers.'

'You're not in the least bit cynical, then?' he asked, although it was purely a rhetorical question. Boy, it was going to be a long haul to get this one on side. She was going to be hard work, but something was telling Ryan she'd be worth it. He hadn't realised how exciting a bit of a challenge would be until he'd met Amber Sullivan. And maybe she was just what he needed right now – someone to take his mind off everything else.

'Cynical? Me?' Amber smiled, taking another sip of wine. 'As if.'

Ryan smiled, too, holding out his hand. 'Shall we sit down?'

Amber nodded, slipping her hand into his, her stomach turning a tiny somersault as his fingers curled around hers. It had been a long time since she'd experienced those somersaults, those little stomach flips that told you something exciting might be about to happen. But, as Amber was the eternal pessimist, she never let herself get carried away with such feelings. And she had to remember who she was dealing with here.

'So, the lure of the post-home-win-celebrations with some of the lads wasn't grabbing you, huh?' Amber asked, resting her chin in her hand as she looked at him across the candle-lit table.

Ryan shrugged, giving her that famous smile of his again. 'I fancied a change.'

'Oh, so *that's* what I am, then? A *change*. I see…'

'I didn't mean it like that…'

'I know you didn't,' Amber smiled. 'I just wanted to see how genuine you are.'

'Are you gonna constantly test me like this?'

Amber shrugged. 'Probably. It takes a lot for me to trust some-body, Ryan. I've been around sportsmen too long, believe me. I know what a lot of you are like.'

He leaned forward, keeping his eyes on hers, not willing to break the stare. 'Do you, though? Do you really? You said yourself you've kept away from relationships with footballers in particular, so, if that's the case, then you only know what you see on the surface – what you read about, what you hear them talking about, and believe *me*, Amber, there are a few of them out there who like to furnish the truth quite a bit. So, you see, you only *think* you know what we're like. You don't actually *know* anything.'

'Don't I?'

He shook his head. 'No. You don't.'

'How do you know that, huh? You don't really know anything about me, so how do you know that?'

'Because, bar your relationship with Ronnie White, you've never let yourself get close enough. At least, that's what you're leading me to assume. So, what you think you know only scratches the surface in reality, doesn't it?'

'You really *are* arrogance personified, aren't you?'

'Look, Amber, all I'm saying is that if you, maybe, stopped being so cynical, tore down those barriers you seem to have built around yourself and just let someone in, you might actually find something there that could change your mind. If you're willing to give them a chance.'

She *wanted* to give him a chance. She'd told Ronnie as much, and there was no doubt that she was attracted to him. But she'd spent so long backing away from relationships and concentrating on her career that she didn't really know what to do next. Or how to handle it all. How the hell *did* you handle a relationship with somebody like Ryan Fisher? And is that what they were talking about here – a relationship? Is that what was happening? Is that what she *wanted*? What *he* wanted?

'I can pull 'em down, if you like,' Ryan said, giving her that grin of his.

She couldn't help smiling back. 'Pull *what* down, exactly?'

He sat back, adopting a more-than-casual stance. Cocky, even. But that was just the way he was. The way he chose to showcase himself. And she figured she was just going to have to learn to deal with it if she really wanted to get closer to him.

'Those barriers of yours,' he smirked, causing Amber to laugh out loud, against her better judgement. 'There you go. You're not such an ice-queen after all, are you?'

'Jesus, is that how I really come across?' Amber asked, smiling her thanks at the wine waiter as he topped up her half-empty glass.

'Sometimes. But, hey, you just need warming up a bit.'

'Reel it in, will you, Ryan. I get it, okay?'

He looked at her through slightly narrowed eyes. It was all a front as far as he was concerned, this ice-queen image. She was using it as some kind of shield to hide behind, and he should know. 'I just want to get to know you, Amber. Is that such a bad thing?'

She shook her head, finally allowing herself to feel comfortable with him, although the drink could be helping on that score. But a little bit of help never hurt, did it?

'No. It's not a bad thing at all.'

'Okay. Then, let's start again, shall we? My name's Ryan, and I'm pleased to meet you.'

She couldn't help smiling at him as she felt herself relax. 'Pleased to meet you, too, Ryan. I'm Amber.'

'Well hello, Amber.' He leaned forward, clasping his hands together on the table in front of him. 'I think you and I are gonna get along just fine, don't you?'

She leaned forward, too, copying his stance, looking into those deep, almost navy, blue eyes of his. And she had absolutely no reason to argue with that.

Chapter Seven

'You're my secret weapon,' Ryan whispered, his lips close to her ear as he pushed her over onto her back, parting her legs with his knee. 'My very own lucky charm.'

Amber laughed out loud, throwing her head back as she wrapped her legs around him, the prospect of a few more minutes in bed so much more appealing than another day at the Sports Desk over at News North East. But she was going to have to make a move some time soon, whether she liked it or not. 'Hmm…' she groaned, stretching languidly as his mouth covered one of her breasts, his tongue flicking across her naked skin, his rough beard tickling her slightly, which only heightened the shivers that were shooting right through her. 'I think you might be right. I'm certainly feeling lucky right now.'

He looked at her, those deep-blue eyes of his showing no signs of the little sleep they'd had the night before, whereas Amber was almost dreading looking in the mirror when she finally managed to summon up the enthusiasm to get out of bed.

'Since I met you, Ms. Sullivan, I've scored in every single match I've played in, won "Man of the Match" three times, and am currently being lauded as a saint here on Tyneside. They are loving me, baby. *Loving* me. And *you've* done that.' He quickly kissed her unsuspecting mouth, an action which Amber was growing to love more and more as each day around Ryan Fisher unfolded. He had the sexiest mouth, and one that could deliver everything from the lightest of touches to the deepest, most erotic kiss she'd ever experienced.

She smiled up at him as he pulled away slightly, that familiar, almost boyish smirk on his handsome face. 'Oh, come on, Ryan. I'm not sure I can take *all* the credit for your winning streak.'

'Well, I can't deny my incredible talent doesn't have *something* to do with it.'

Amber grabbed a pillow and hit him with it, squealing loudly as he grappled the pillow from her hands, pulling her up into his arms.

'Hey, you don't want to be injuring this sporting legend now, do you?' he smirked, his arms falling around her waist as she sat astride him.

'If I really wanted to injure you, you egotistical pig, I could think of far more interesting ways of doing it.'

'Oh yeah?' he asked, arching an eyebrow.

'Yeah,' she smiled, closing her eyes and groaning quietly as his mouth once again covered one of her breasts, his tongue sending a million tiny electric shocks coursing through her all at once. 'Jesus, Ryan, come on. I'm going to be late for work.'

He pushed her back onto the bed again, his hands holding onto her wrists as he pulled her arms up above her head, pinning her down, pushing his way inside her before she had any more chances to protest.

'Ryan!' Amber moaned, half of her angry at him for giving her no choice here, and the other half excited that the early morning sex wasn't quite over yet. She was sure she could smooth things over with Kevin if she *did* happen to be a little late into the office. 'You're such a bastard!'

'But an incredibly sexy one, huh?' he grinned, holding tightly onto her wrists as he pushed in deeper, feeling her respond with a thrust of her hips and another long moan.

'Yeah, alright, I give in. I really am sleeping with God's gift to the football pitch, aren't I?'

He gave a low, deep laugh and Amber couldn't help but laugh, too. She'd tried so hard to fight this relationship with Ryan over the past few weeks, but it was a fight she'd lost in spectacular fashion. He'd reeled her in, and now she was hooked. And making no attempt to wriggle free. He was a breath of fresh air in her usually routine life. He was everything she needed, everything she'd wanted but had been too afraid to go out and get. He was a necessity, and he was becoming a fixture she didn't really want to let go of just yet.

'You are such an arrogant prick,' Amber groaned, closing her eyes and falling back against the pillows as those final few post-sex shivers tingled their way up her body, leaving her slightly breathless but totally satisfied, and more than ready to go and face whatever it was that Kevin had in store for her today.

'Yeah,' Ryan sighed, rolling off her and sliding out of bed. As much as he loved being with Amber, he still wasn't big on the post-sex cuddles. But it seemed she wasn't all that bothered about them, either. She was fast turning into his perfect woman with that red-hot hair and a figure that was real, in the true sense of the word. Not one thing about Amber Sullivan was false, and she was just one of the many factors that contributed to the fact he was having the time of his life right now. His football was flaw-less, he was having the best sex he'd had in years, and all he had to do was make sure he kept those demons in check. And he was trying. He was. He was trying really hard. 'But don't tell me you don't find that one hell of a turn-on.'

Amber laughed again, throwing her head back as he ripped the covers away from her naked body before retreating into the en-suite, leaving her to stretch out on his ridiculously huge bed, taking in the view of the River Tyne from the floor-to-ceiling windows that lined one entire wall of Ryan's bedroom.

Smiling to herself, she sat up and hugged her knees to her chest, still staring out at the early morning rush-hour traffic streaming across the Tyne Bridge as the sun began to rise. The dark skies were slowly turning lighter and she knew she'd have to make a move soon. As much as she'd love to hang around in Ryan Fisher's bed all day, she had work to do. More's the pity.

She was just fastening her watch onto her wrist when he walked up behind her, sliding his arms around her waist, his bearded chin resting on her shoulder. 'You running away from me?'

'I've got a proper job to go to,' Amber half-smiled, turning her head slightly to kiss him quickly. 'Unlike you, you part-timer.'

'Ooh, fighting talk,' Ryan laughed, squeezing her waist, making her giggle like some star-struck teenager. 'Maybe you need to spend more time watching me train, huh? See exactly just what it is I do all day.'

She turned round, slipping her arms around his neck as he pulled her against him. 'I *know* what you do all day, Ryan. I was brought up around footballers, remember? Although my dad swears blind you all get away with murder these days. He says in his day you wouldn't have had it so easy.'

'Oh, I see where you get that fighting talk from now, kiddo. Inherited from daddy, huh?'

She just smiled, kissing him slowly, loving the feel of his half-naked body against her clothed one. She would be the envy of so many women if they knew just how close she'd become to this famous footballer, but for now their relationship was pretty much a secret. Not deliberately so, but they weren't going out of their way to advertise the fact, either.

'Don't work too hard, okay?' she winked, reluctantly pulling away from him and grabbing her bag from the chair by the door.

'Am I gonna see you later?' he asked, a question he wasn't really used to asking. Usually *he* called the shots in whatever relationships he was involved in, but this was so different to anything he'd ever been involved in before. And he suddenly felt a little vulnerable. Another unusual feeling in Ryan Fisher's world.

'Yeah. If you want to,' Amber replied, stopping briefly by the door.

'I want to,' he smirked, pulling the towel he was wearing from around his waist, giving Amber one last look at something else Ryan Fisher was famous for.

'Then later it is,' she winked, closing the bedroom door behind her.

Ryan couldn't help laughing, running a hand over the back of his neck as he looked down at the floor. She was good for him, Ms. Amber Sullivan. There was no doubt about that. Over the past few weeks he'd managed to break down some of those barriers she'd built up around herself and got to know the woman behind that ice-queen façade. Because that's all it was. A façade. She was hiding from something, protecting herself from something and he didn't know what, he wasn't even sure he cared. He just knew that she was somebody he wanted to spend time with.

Pulling on his jeans and a t-shirt, he bent down to pick up his kitbag, accidentally knocking a jacket off the back of the chair in the process. He turned round quickly as something fell out of the pocket, clattering to the floor, rolling underneath the sideboard. He crouched down, stretching his arm out to pick up the object that had rolled under there, sliding it out across the dark-wood floor. Standing up, he leaned back against the sideboard, turning the rogue casino chip over and over in his fingers. It must've slipped into his pocket somehow the other night. Opening a drawer and quickly throwing it inside, he slammed the drawer shut and leaned back against the wall, closing his eyes for a second. He hadn't wanted to go, he really hadn't. And he shouldn't have gone. Max would go spare if he found out, but he was still the new guy at the club and he didn't want to isolate himself by turning down nights out with the other lads. He wanted to fit in, and as much as Ryan didn't want to think about it, he knew, deep down inside, that it was his desperate need to fit in that had caused all the shit in the past. But as far as Ryan was concerned, it wasn't

102

a step backwards. He'd been in control, he hadn't done anything stupid. It wasn't going to be like it had been before, so there was no need to panic, no need for anyone's concern. This time he was completely in control. This time it would be different.

'How's it all going, then?' Ronnie asked, folding his arms as he perched on the edge of Amber's desk.

She looked at him briefly before continuing to tap away on her keyboard. 'How's *what* all going?'

'You and Ryan Fisher.'

She swung her chair round to face him, crossing her legs and clasping her hands together in her lap. 'Keep it down, will you? It isn't public knowledge yet.'

'Oh, I see. It's a *secret* relationship then, is it?'

'It's not like that, Ronnie. We just don't see the point in broadcasting it, that's all.'

Ronnie sniffed. 'That's unusual, for Ryan. Usually he's first in the queue to be papped when he's got a new piece of arm candy to show off.'

Amber couldn't help laughing. 'Arm candy? Hardly, Ronnie.'

'You're not the usual type Ryan Fisher goes for, I have to say.'

Amber looked at her best friend. 'Do you want to carry on? Give yourself a few more minutes and you might just get a touch more insulting.'

'You know what I mean, Amber.'

'I'm not sure I do, actually. Look, I really think he's changed, Ronnie.'

'Jesus, come on, Amber. What do you think you are? Some kind of miracle cure? You're better than that. The likes of Ryan Fisher don't change, it isn't in him.'

'Well, maybe people like *you* should try and give him a chance. Stop being so judgemental.'

Ronnie narrowed his eyes, looking at her as though he couldn't quite believe what he was hearing. 'Okay. You're scaring me now.

What's caused this sudden turn-around in your opinion of one of football's most arrogant pricks? A couple of dinner-dates and suddenly you think he's a saint?'

'Maybe I've just learnt not to judge a book by its cover.'

'Yeah, but it's not just the cover, though, is it, Amber? It's backed up by everything that's inside, too.'

Amber swung back around on her chair and started shutting down her laptop. She was tired and she needed to get home quickly tonight, shower, change, and then get herself over to the Tynebridge Stadium where she was covering a charity dinner for News North East that Newcastle Red Star were throwing. And it may be a night of working that lay ahead, but she still had to look good.

'Look, Ronnie, it's just a bit of fun, alright? And, if you remember, it was *you* who told me I should be having more of that.'

'Yeah, but I don't remember telling you to have it with Ryan Fisher.'

Amber smiled at Ronnie as she closed the lid of her laptop and stood up, slipping her coat on and grabbing her bag up off the floor. 'You jealous?'

'As if,' Ronnie smirked, following her as she walked towards the lift that took them down to the underground car park. 'You're in a bit of a hurry, aren't you?'

'That's because I'm in a rush. I've got to get home, shower, find something glamorous to wear and get my arse down to Tynebridge for seven-thirty. Kevin's got me covering this charity dinner the club are throwing tonight.'

'Oh, right. I'm off there, too. Quite a few ex-Red Star players are going to be there, so I gather. Your dad's going, isn't he?'

'Yeah, he is,' Amber replied, stepping into the lift, closely followed by Ronnie. 'I wondered why *you* were back up north again.'

'Well, somebody's got to keep an eye on you, obviously,' Ronnie winked, sticking his hands in his pockets as he leaned back against the wall. 'So what's your dad think about you getting involved

104

with Ryan Fisher?'

'He doesn't know, yet,' Amber said, standing by the lift doors as they opened slowly, stepping out into the underground car park, her heels click-clacking across the concrete floor as she walked quickly towards her car.

'Christ, what have you and Fisher been doing all this time? Non-stop sex and no dates anywhere public?'

'Pretty much, yeah,' Amber smirked, flinging her bag into the passenger seat of her little Fiat 500.

'Are you *kidding* me? Jesus, I go away for a couple of weeks and you turn into some sex-crazed cougar.'

'Cheeky sod!' she laughed, playfully punching his arm. 'Look, we just didn't see the point in advertising the fact we're together, okay? Especially when we don't really know what's happening yet.'

'So, it's nothing serious, then?'

Amber leaned back against her car, folding her arms. 'No, Ronnie. It's definitely nothing serious.'

He stood beside her, copying her stance. 'Good.'

Amber looked at him. 'Why do you say that?'

'Because this is Ryan Fisher we're talking about here. Remember? And I care about you. I don't want to see you get hurt.'

'He won't hurt me.'

'Won't he?'

She fixed Ronnie with a determined stare. 'No. He won't.'

Ronnie looked out across the cold and unfeeling car park, his arms still folded across his chest. 'What about tonight?'

'What about it?' Amber asked, looking at her watch. She really was going to have to make a move in a minute or she'd never be ready in time.

'Are you and Ryan going to spend the entire night avoiding each other so as not to let the cat out of the bag, so to speak?'

Amber shrugged, stepping away from the car and opening the driver-side door. 'I guess we'll just have to play that one by ear, won't we?'

'Whoa! Freddie Sullivan's little girl really *has* grown-up, hasn't she?'

Amber swung round, finding herself face-to-face with Newcastle Red Star's new boss, Jim Allen. She'd successfully managed to avoid him for a few weeks now, but it looked like that had been nothing but a minor stay of execution. Although, if she thought she could get away with it, she'd turn and run straight to the Cooper Suite – where the dinner was being held – and forget this had ever happened.

The way his eyes looked her slowly up and down in the knee-length black sheath dress and matching stiletto-heeled ankle boots she was wearing made her feel more than a little uncomfortable, but, short of turning her back on him and walking in a completely different direction to where she needed to be, she had no choice but to speak to him. Even though it was the last thing she really wanted to do.

'I'm thirty-seven, Jim. I grew up a long time ago. I had to. And you more than anyone should know that.'

There. It was done. She'd seen him, she'd spoken to him, that was enough. But as she turned to go he gently grabbed her arm, swinging her round to face him. 'You look beautiful, Amber.'

Amber could feel her cheeks flush, her heart picking up the pace as far as beats were concerned. This wasn't how she'd wanted the night to start. She had work to do, she didn't need this.

'I'm working, Jim.'

He reached out and touched her face, the palm of his hand resting lightly on her warm cheek as his green eyes looked right into hers. 'It really is so good to see you…'

'I don't need this…' She tried to walk away from him but he somehow managed to grab her hand, giving her no other option but to stop and face him again.

'I've signed a four-year contract, honey, and considering your line of work, it's gonna be pretty damn hard for you to avoid me forever.'

She stared into his eyes, wishing this wasn't happening but

knowing it had only been a matter of time. The second she'd heard Newcastle Red Star had appointed him as their new manager she'd known this day would come. She'd known she was going to have to face him again, after years of trying to forget he even existed. 'And this… this relationship we have… We need to do something about that, don't we?'

'We don't *have* a "relationship", Jim.'

He smiled at her, that full-on, all-American smile that had made him one of the most lusted-after football managers by bored housewives and female football fans alike. To describe him as a good-looking son-of-a-bitch wouldn't be too far from the truth, but Amber had messed with Jim Allen one time too many. And been hurt badly in the process. 'Now, y'see, I don't agree with you there, Amber. I think we have what people might call a "special" relationship, don't you? Jesus, sweetheart, you are taking my breath away in that dress. I guess my baby girl really did grow up into a beautiful young woman.'

Amber felt her stomach turn, a sick feeling taking over. 'I'm not your "baby girl", Jim. Not anymore. And you don't get to do this to me again, okay? You don't…'

A door opening at the far end of the corridor made them jump apart, and Amber took that as her cue to walk away from him, her heart still thumping so hard inside her chest it hurt. She felt breathless, the need to compose herself before she entered the Cooper Suite a necessity now. So, taking a few long, deep breaths as she approached the huge double doors that led into the suite, she shook out her dark red hair, closed her eyes for a second just to make sure she was focused, and then made her way into the room.

It was crowded, and she craned her neck to see if she could find Ronnie, or her dad, or even Ryan, but she couldn't see any of them. Not yet, anyway. So, moving away from the doors, she made her way to the bar, ordering herself a small glass of red wine. She was working, so it was minimum alcohol tonight. Unfortunately. Because that encounter with Jim Allen had shaken her slightly.

107

Now that he was back up north she could feel that panic she'd tried to suppress for all those years well up inside her again; panic that people would find out just what had gone on, that her father would one day discover the truth. And she really didn't want that to happen. He didn't need to know, nobody did. It was enough that *she* had to live with the constant memories every time she saw him; she didn't want her father to have to cope with that, too. Jim was a friend, a good friend of her dad's. He had been for a long, long time. Although, if Freddie Sullivan knew exactly what had happened between Jim Allen and his daughter, he may not think he was such a good friend after all.

'You look as though you need that.'

Amber swung round, a smile instantly lighting up her face when she saw him standing there, handsome and sexy in a dark grey suit and white shirt. The memories of the lunchtime sex they'd had at his flat just a few hours ago – the last time she'd seen him – made her stomach flip over and dance those ridiculous somersaults it seemed to dance every time he was around now, but that was good. She could cope with Jim Allen tonight knowing Ryan was around. Knowing she could go back to his place after all this was over and forget what had just happened.

'Yeah. It's a pity I'm here to work, though.'

'Not *all* night, surely?' Ryan asked, leaning back against the bar, his hands in his pockets.

'Well, I think I'm allowed to have a little bit of fun,' Amber smiled, sipping her wine. 'Look, I know you don't want anyone to know about us...'

'I never said that, Amber. Did I?' Ryan looked her straight in the eye and she felt a little shiver run right up her spine.

'No. No, you didn't.'

He looked out over the room as it began to slowly fill up with local celebrities, sportsmen, Red Star players past and present. He didn't really want to be there, if he was honest. This kind of gig wasn't his thing, but it came with the territory. And anyway, now that Amber was here things could only get better. 'I kind of assumed it was *you* who didn't want to tell the world you were with *me*.'

Amber looked at him. 'Ryan, I… I don't… What's actually going on with us?'

'Apart from great sex?'

'Be serious, will you? My night hasn't exactly got off to the best of starts so I don't need…'

'Do you want to talk about it?'

She looked away for a second, catching the eye of Jim Allen as he walked into the room, her heart leaping about like it was on some kind of trampoline as he held her gaze, causing her to look away first. 'No. I don't want to talk about it.'

'Amber…'

She took another, longer sip of wine, shaking out her hair as though that would rid her of all the negative energy seeing Jim Allen had created. 'I want to be with you, Ryan. Okay? I don't know what we have here, exactly, or even where it's going. All I know is that I like being with you. I like being around you.'

'I like being around you, too, Amber.'

She looked at him, slightly taken aback because she'd half expected him to run a mile. She wasn't exactly telling him that she wanted to get married and have his babies, but considering the type of person Ryan Fisher was, what she'd just told him almost constituted a serious relationship. But that was the last thing either of them wanted. At the minute. 'You do?'

He smiled, a smile which wiped all thoughts of Jim Allen clean away. For now. 'Yeah. Jesus, Amber, I've never met anyone like you before, so don't think for a minute I'm giving you up that easily. And besides, we're having fun, aren't we?'

'Yeah. We are.' She really wanted another drink but she'd just seen Kevin walk in, so she had a feeling best behaviour was going to be called for from now on. She really wished she didn't have to work tonight. The last thing she felt like doing was mingling with a roomful of local celebrities, grabbing a word here and a short interview there. She just wasn't in the mood. But that was what she was here to do. Whether she liked it or not.

The touch of Ryan's hand on her hip made her turn her attention back to him as he gently swung her round to face him. 'Wanna give them something to talk about?' he grinned, and Amber couldn't help but grin back. Why did he make her feel sixteen again? And was that ultimately a good thing? She'd done a lot of things at sixteen she hadn't been proud of, and it wasn't a place she particularly wanted to revisit. Even though circumstances could mean she had no choice.

'I really don't know what I'm getting myself into with you, Ryan Fisher. But do you know what? I'm tired of being sensible, boring Amber. I'm tired of being serious all the time. I *need* some fun, before I forget how to have it.'

'Sounds like a plan to me,' Ryan smiled, pulling her against him, kissing her slowly. And maybe it wasn't the wisest of places in which to make their relationship public, but it was done now. They couldn't exactly press rewind.

'Okay, handsome. As much as I'd like to stay here with you, I've got work to do.' She looked over towards Kevin, who was staring back at her with raised eyebrows and an expression that asked '*Is there something you want to tell me?*'

'You coming back to mine later?' Ryan asked, reluctantly letting her go. She looked incredible tonight in that tight black dress and those killer heels. Although he had no doubt that he'd rather see that dress down around her ankles. She could keep the heels on, though. Jesus, that image was giving him a hard-on he was going to have put back in the box until later.

'Yeah,' Amber smiled, shaking her hair out again, quickly running her fingers through it. 'You bet I am.'

Leaving him standing by the bar, she walked over to Kevin, who was still looking at her with raised eyebrows and a surprised expression.

'If the wind changes you'll stay like that,' Amber pointed out, taking a glass of something sparkling from the tray of a passing waiter. Sod it. One more drink wouldn't hurt.

'How long has *that* been going on?' he asked, jerking his head in the direction of Ryan.

She took a sip of what tasted like champagne. 'Long enough.'

'Shit! Amber!'

'What? What difference does it make to *you*? You said it wouldn't hurt if I got closer to Ryan Fisher.'

'I didn't say shag him for news stories, did I?'

'Oh, you think I'm with him purely to get you scoops from the sporting world?'

'No, of course not…'

'I'm joking, Kevin. Look, it's just a bit of fun, alright? It won't affect my work, I'll be professional at all times – when I need to be – and if there *is* any juicy news from the world of football that I think we should know about, I'll make sure Ryan tells us first, alright?'

Kevin looked at her, his eyebrows thankfully returning to their normal position. 'You're a dark horse, Amber Sullivan. I always thought you and footballers…'

'Yes, well, you know what thought did.' She took another sip of champagne and scanned the room, noticing her dad deep in conversation with Jim Allen. Her stomach momentarily lurched again as his eyes briefly met hers, a million memories flooding her head that she quickly pushed aside. She turned her attention back to Kevin. 'Right. I'd better start mingling then, hadn't I? Is Alec here with the camera yet?'

'He's just setting up,' Kevin replied. 'I'll give you a shout when he's ready. Go on. Go talk to your dad for five minutes.'

Amber watched Kevin walk away, reluctant to go over to her dad while Jim was still around.

'So, it's all official then?' Ronnie asked, sidling up beside her, a pint in one hand, the other stuffed deep in the pocket of his black suit trousers.

'Why is everybody suddenly making me feel like I'm twelve years old? I'm thirty-frigging-seven, and Ryan isn't my first boyfriend.'

'Touchy,' Ronnie smirked, taking a sip of lager.

Amber nudged him, unable to stop herself from smiling. 'Fuck off, Ronnie.'

'Nice. Does your new boyfriend know what comes out of that mouth?'

'He's more concerned with what goes in it,' she winked, walking away from him, finally plucking up the courage to go over to her dad.

'Oh, that's ladylike, Amber. That's very ladylike,' Ronnie shouted after her. Amber just gave him a dismissive wave over her shoulder as she walked away, trying not to let the sick feeling in her stomach take over as she approached her dad, who was still talking to Jim Allen.

'Amber,' Freddie Sullivan said, giving his daughter an almost stern look. Was he *really* going to start lecturing her on boyfriends? At *her* age? *Really*? 'Jim tells me you two have already caught up with each other?'

She looked over at the handsome American. He might be forty-eight years old now but he hadn't lost any of those good looks that had made him the pin-up player of his day. If anything, he'd only got better looking. 'Yeah. We have. Briefly.'

'And I've told her she's looking beautiful tonight,' Jim smiled, a smile loaded with more meaning than Amber cared to think about. 'Your new boyfriend really is one very lucky man.'

Amber swallowed hard, trying desperately to keep the smile on her face, although she wasn't altogether sure it had travelled to her eyes.

'Don't you go wearing him out now,' Jim winked. 'We've got a big match this weekend. I'd hate our star player to be – tired.' He turned away from her and smiled at her father. 'I'll catch you later, Freddie. Good to see you again, after all this time.'

'You too, Jim.'

Amber watched him walk away, swallowing hard again before she looked at her dad, sighing the second she saw his expression. 'Jesus, Dad, come on. Don't start, alright?'

'I'm not going to lie and say I'm happy about this, Amber.'

'I don't need your approval.'

'Maybe not, but he's eleven years younger than you…'

'And what's *that* got to do with anything?'

'Ryan Fisher is trouble, kiddo. And you know that as well as I do. He's trouble, and that concerns me when I suddenly find out that my daughter is involved with him.'

'Y'know, contrary to belief, I'm all grown-up now. I think I can handle Ryan Fisher.'

'I hope so. I really hope so. Because I don't want to have to be the one to pick up the pieces when he fucks up.'

'Dad…'

'You might not be my little girl anymore, Amber, but that doesn't stop me from worrying about you. So just be careful, okay?'

Amber sighed again, looking up at the ceiling for a few seconds as she heard Kevin's voice calling her over, grateful for the well-timed distraction. 'I've got work to do, Dad. I'll catch you later.'

'Are you fucking kidding me?'

Amber swung round as she heard that American accent behind her. She'd thought nobody had noticed her sneak off for a sly cigarette, donated by a News North East colleague – the kind of night she'd had so far had caused her to revive her old smoking habit – but she'd been wrong. Some people had quite obviously been watching her more closely than others.

'I'm busy, Jim.'

He grabbed her arm again, almost dragging her round the corner to a quiet area behind the stadium, pushing her back against the wall. 'Ryan fucking *Fisher*?'

She stared into his eyes. Maybe facing him head-on was the only option she had left now. Avoiding him obviously wasn't working.

113

'And that's got *how* much to do with you, exactly?'

'I'm his fucking manager, honey. So what he's doing and who he's doing it with is very much my business.'

She couldn't help laughing. Was he serious? 'Bullshit, Jim!' She pushed him away and he staggered back slightly, quickly composing himself, straightening his jacket collar, his eyes meeting hers once again. But she was standing her ground. 'Fucking bullshit!'

He laughed, too, a deep, almost sinister laugh, moving closer to her again, reaching out to stroke her cheek with his fingertips. 'Your dad's none-too-pleased about your new – boyfriend, I gather.'

She made no attempt to remove his hand. She made no attempt to move at all, her eyes still staring into his. Eyes she hadn't stared into for almost two decades now. For good reason.

'But then, I'm sure daddy wouldn't be too pleased if he knew what me and his little girl had got up to. His baby. You were so young, Amber…'

'I was too young, Jim.'

'I never once heard you say no, honey. Not once.'

'I'd just turned sixteen,' Amber whispered, her stomach turning over and over as he moved ever closer, his thumb now running over her slightly open mouth, and Amber wished with all her heart that she wasn't feeling the things she was feeling right now.

'And you were beautiful. You were so beautiful. And you're even more beautiful now…'

'Why did you come back here, Jim? You promised me, you said you would never come back here once your playing days were over.'

'Promises are made to be broken, Amber. And you can't expect me to turn down the opportunity of a lifetime now, can you? Expecting me to turn down this job just because *you* don't want me around anymore, that's pretty selfish, don't you think?'

She closed her eyes as his fingers continued to stroke her skin, moving down over her neck, her shoulders, trailing slowly along her collarbone. 'Please, don't do this to me, Jim. Don't do this. I can't go there again. What you did to me…'

'I was in love with you, Amber. I was in love with you for so long…'

She shook her head, trying desperately not to cry now. She'd tried so hard for so many years to forget her teenage affair with this handsome American who'd swept her off her feet and made her feel like a princess. She'd tried to forget the first time he'd made love to her, just days after her sixteenth birthday. He'd been this twenty-seven-year-old, incredibly charming, drop-dead gorgeous footballer who'd made her feel like the most special person in the world. But he'd also been the man who'd told her they had to keep their relationship a secret because nobody would understand, and she'd never questioned that because, back then, she would have done anything for him. Anything.

For almost two years her life had been a whirlwind of daydreams and fantasies as she'd studied for her A Levels and he continued to be a footballing god, becoming one of Red Star's most successful players ever. They'd snatched secret meetings together at a city centre apartment at any opportunity, making love and talking about the future, but it was a future she soon found out he'd had no intention of spending with her.

The day his relationship with a local model hit the headlines was the day Amber had left the North East to go and study for her degree in Manchester. She'd needed to get away. She'd needed that distance in order to cope, because coping wasn't something she'd dealt with all that successfully at the time. How could she possibly have stayed in the North East with Jim a major player at Red Star, flaunting his beautiful new girlfriend all over the place? This stunning new couple that everybody was talking about. He'd used her as nothing but a plaything, something with which to amuse himself until he'd found the girl he'd really wanted. And it had shattered Amber. Because she'd been convinced, absolutely convinced, that he'd meant every word he'd said to her. How stupid had she been?

After finishing university she'd moved back to the North East, finally believing she was over Jim Allen. Had it hurt to see him again? Had it hurt to go home and find him there, at her parents' house? Smiling at her as though he hadn't been the one to take her precious virginity, lie to her, and then walk away the second he'd got bored? Yeah. It had hurt like hell. So why, then, did she just erase all those bad memories and replace them only with the beautiful ones she remembered? The ones where he'd hold her in his arms and touch her in a way she could only ever have dreamt about before? Why did she forget the lies and the secrets and the hurt he'd put her through? Why did she do that? Because Jim Allen had got under her skin, embedded himself there like some kind of permanent tattoo that she couldn't remove, no matter how much she wanted to. And to get home and find out that his relationship had ended, that his girlfriend had left him for a musician she'd met on a modelling shoot, that was the news Amber had wanted to hear for so long. The news that Jim Allen was free again. Everything else – the past, the lies, all the hurt and the pain, none of that had mattered. All that mattered was that he was back in her life. It hadn't bothered her that he'd still been determined to keep everything a secret, to hide their relationship away like something seedy and sordid. She wasn't that naive sixteen-year-old who'd had her head turned by a handsome face and empty promises, she wasn't that person anymore, so why hadn't she questioned the secrecy second time around? Why hadn't she done that? Because she'd been blinded by an obsession that had taken her over, that's why. And once again she'd believed everything he'd told her. She'd believed that, this time, there was a future for them, that they *did* have something worth fighting for. And it had been worth it just to have him back where she'd always wanted him – back in her life, back in her bed, back making love to her in a way that made her feel like the most beautiful woman in the world. Jim Allen was addictive. Jim Allen was dangerous. Jim Allen had the ability to hurt her all over again, so when it came out that he was involved with a famous soap actress, it shouldn't have come as a surprise to

Amber. She should have known it was going to happen all along. But when he tossed her aside a second time it was still as much of a shock as it had been first time around. Yet still she couldn't tell a soul. She couldn't tell anyone why her heart was breaking all over again, why she refused invitations from friends to go out and have fun in the pubs and clubs of Newcastle, like any normal young girl in their twenties. She couldn't tell them that she didn't want to meet some random boy in a bar. She didn't want that. She didn't want some meaningless relationship – yet, in reality, wasn't that exactly what she'd had with Jim?

That was when she'd thrown herself into her work, deciding to carve out a career in sports reporting rather than having fun and finding love. She'd already found love, and look where that had got her. She couldn't go through that again. It was then that Amber had made her decision never to become involved with footballers ever again. Despite what she'd told Ronnie, despite what she'd told anyone else, that decision had never really been about the Ryan Fishers of this world. She could handle them – the arrogant, cocksure bastards who thought everything revolved around them. They were just little boys who earned far too much money and lived their lives in some kind of fantasy bubble. They weren't a problem; she could deal with them. No, everything was Jim Allen's fault. Everything. *He* was the reason she was a cold-hearted ice-queen. *He* was the reason she'd never had a decent relationship with any man for all these years. *He* was the reason she was shaken up and confused. *He* was the reason.

He'd seen out his professional playing days at Newcastle Red Star, and following his retirement he'd finally left the North East with his soap-star girlfriend to move down south and start his managerial career, giving Amber the distance she'd needed all over again. And he'd promised her, he'd told her that was it. If she didn't want him to come back up north then he wouldn't. He'd leave her in peace, let her move on with her life and, despite everything, that's what she'd done. She'd moved on. But now he was back. Back in the North East, back in her life. Back to break her heart all over again?

'You were never in love with me, Jim. Never.'

He shook his head, his eyes following the movement of his fingers as they traced the curve of her breasts, and Amber was unable to stop a small gasp of pleasure from escaping, even though she'd tried to do so by biting down on her lip.

'You have no idea, Amber…' He gave that low laugh again, his eyes back on hers. 'You used to bite down on your lip when we made love, do you remember?' His arm snaked around her waist, his hand sliding down to rest in the small of her back, his mouth moving closer to hers as he spoke. 'I can still see it now. Your eyes would always be open because you liked to look at me, didn't you? You liked to look at me when I pushed inside you. But you'd always bite down on that bottom lip of yours. Always.'

'Please don't do this,' Amber whispered, afraid of what she might do now, afraid of what might happen because she hadn't even thought about the consequences Jim Allen's arrival back on Tyneside might have. She'd known she was going to have to face him again, but she hadn't even thought about what could – what *would* – happen when she did. Thirty-seven years old and, even though she'd tried so hard to believe that she wasn't, she was still as naive as that sixteen-year-old girl who'd believed every promise this man had broken. 'Please.'

'I didn't just come back for this job, Amber.'

'No.' She shook her head again, silent tears now streaming down her cheeks, and as he leaned forward and brushed his lips over those tears, gently kissing them away, she felt her heart break into a million tiny pieces. 'Don't say that. Please, don't say that.'

'I'm a free agent, Amber. No ties, nothing holding me back. And I don't believe for one second that this ridiculous relationship you have with Ryan Fisher is anything but a front…'

'You don't know anything,' Amber said quietly, quickly brushing away fresh tears with the back of her hand. 'Ryan… he's not what everybody thinks he is. He's changed.'

'Are you really still that naive, Amber? Ryan Fisher doesn't care about you, he never will. You're the older woman, the novelty he hasn't yet had a chance to try out. Believe me, honey, when he's finished with you he'll just toss you aside and move onto the next new toy.'

'Like you did, you mean?'

Jim looked at her, right into her pale blue eyes that were still shining with tears yet, at the same time, were steely and cold. 'I came back for *you*, Amber.'

'No, you didn't, Jim. Jesus, will you stop playing me again? This isn't fair, *you're* not being fair…'

'I saw you with him, and it hurt. Okay? He's a boy, Amber. A boy. And he'll never love you, not like I can. Never.'

'Who says I *want* love? After what *you* did to me why would I want to leave myself open to that kind of hurt again? Huh? Why would I want to do that? I'm having fun, Jim. For all those years I threw myself into my work as a way of forgetting *you* and what you did to me; I became obsessed with my career, with being the best at what I did, and in turn that made me into this cold, almost bitter person who trusted no one and let nobody past the barriers I had to put up. Because of what *you* did. So now I'm having fun, okay? I'm not in this to find love, or to find that perfect man, because he doesn't exist. I'm just having fun.'

He pulled her against him, his hand still resting firmly in the small of her back, his mouth almost touching hers as he spoke, the smell of his aftershave overwhelming because it was the same aftershave he'd worn when they'd been together. Both times. He smelt the same, he felt the same; he sounded the same. But everything was so different.

'I didn't come back here purely for this job,' he whispered. 'Believe that.'

'I don't have to believe anything where you're concerned, Jim.'

He smiled, a smile that sent Amber's heart racing so fast she

119

could almost feel the blood rushing through her veins, making her feel dizzy and slightly disorientated. 'My baby girl,' he whispered, gently stroking her hair. 'My beautiful baby girl.'

Amber had lost all control now. He was too close, he was far too close and she couldn't stop him, couldn't stop it from happening. Before she'd even had a chance to realise what was going on, his mouth was touching hers in a kiss that sent her heart racing even faster, a kiss so beautiful, so full of memories that it made her cry all over again, hot, fresh tears soaking his skin as well as hers. But she couldn't pull away; she didn't want to. Not at first, anyway. His mouth was soft against hers, moving slowly as he kissed her long and deep, his hand resting on her damp cheek as she held him close – this man who'd hurt her so badly. This man who'd walked back into her life as though nothing had happened.

But then reality kicked in. All the memories of the pain and the tears, the nights she'd lain in bed crying her heart out, falling to pieces because she'd loved him so much, the humiliation enough to make sure she'd never, ever told a soul about what had happened between them. All that hurt came flooding back like a tidal wave, crashing over her with a force so overwhelming it was as if someone had just turned on a light and all of a sudden she could see exactly what was going on.

Pulling away from him, she pushed him backwards, with a much harder force this time, wiping her mouth with the back of her hand as she looked him right in the eye. 'You don't get to do this to me a third time, Jim. You don't get to do that.'

And with that she walked away from him, back inside, back to the life she'd been trying to get on with before he'd walked back into it.

'Everything okay?' Ryan asked as she joined him at the bar.

She looked at him. 'Have you been here all night?'

'Who are you? My mother?'

'Fuck you, Ryan. I'm not in the mood.' She started to walk away from him, tired and desperate to forget this night had ever happened. But he wasn't letting her get away that easily.

'Hey, come on.' He gently took her hand, swinging her back round to face him. 'What's up with you, huh? You've been tense all night. Is there something you want to tell me?'

'Like what?' she asked, her skin prickling as Jim Allen walked back into the Cooper Suite, looking every inch the charismatic character he'd become. Amber found it hard to believe he didn't have some glamorous model or stunning pop star by his side. Past history showed that was the type he went for. The type he'd brushed her aside for.

Ryan narrowed his eyes as he caught the look she gave his manager. 'Has something happened between you and the boss?'

Amber swung round to look at him, hoping to God that her expression gave nothing away. Ryan finding out about her teenage affair with his new manager would just put a lid on this crappy night. 'No. No, of course not. Why – why would you ask that?'

'He's a family friend, isn't he?'

Amber quickly ordered herself a large brandy, immediately taking a long sip, not looking at Ryan when she spoke. 'Yeah. So?'

Ryan shrugged. 'Nothing. But… the way you looked at him just then… it was a bit weird, that's all. Maybe there's a bit of history there, I don't know…'

'For fuck's sake, Ryan, I'm just tired, alright? I've got people on my back because of who you are and what we're doing, and technically I've been working since 7.30 this morning, so I'm just tired. Okay? Nothing else.'

Ryan held up his hands in surrender, smiling at her in the vain hope that it might calm her down. Having said that, though, she did look more than a little bit sexy when she was in a mood. And that could be beneficial when they got back to his apartment. Sometimes angry sex could be the biggest kick ever. 'Okay, okay. I get it. Do you think sex'll help sort you out?'

She looked at him, and she couldn't help laughing, the effect of the brandy and his cocky sense of humour going a long way towards helping her relax. And forget. 'Shit, Ryan. You have no idea how much I need you right now.'

'*Right* now?' he asked, arching an eyebrow.

She finished the last of her brandy and slipped her arms around his waist, kissing him quickly. 'Well, as much as that might get you more headline space, and I know how much you adore the publicity, no. Not *right* now. But, if you're willing to finish that drink as quickly as is humanly possible…'

He put his half-finished pint down on the bar and pulled her closer, tilting her chin up and kissing her back, a kiss so different to Jim's, but a kiss she could quite easily get used to. 'I'm done.'

She smiled, gently stroking the rough beard that covered his strong jawline with her fingertips. 'And those are two words I don't want to hear from you again for a good few hours, you got that?'

He smiled, too, his hand sliding down onto her backside as he kissed her again, the feel of her breasts pushing against him enough to make him realise they were finished here. It was time to go home. 'I got it.'

'Good,' she whispered, playing with the collar of his jacket. 'Then let's get out of here.'

Chapter Eight

'I can't believe you kept that a secret from us!' Tracy mock-scolded before Amber had even had a chance to get through the revolving door of the News North East entrance. 'You and Ryan Fisher! How did you manage to keep *that* one quiet? I'd have been shouting it from the rooftops if it was me.'

'I didn't keep anything a secret, Tracy,' Amber said, loosening the coat she had wrapped tight around her. Autumn had well and truly hit the North East now and it was freezing outside. 'I just didn't choose to make it public knowledge, because we're not exactly Brad and Angelina.'

'Posh and Becks then?' Tracy smiled.

Amber couldn't help but smile back. 'Not even close,' she laughed.

'Well, *you* might not think you're news, but it seems the press have other ideas,' Tracy said, holding up a copy of a well-known tabloid newspaper. Emblazoned across the front page was a picture of Amber and Ryan, hand-in-hand, leaving an Indian restaurant in Newcastle. Amber sighed, rolling her eyes. She really wasn't dealing with the sudden publicity her relationship with Ryan had caused. She never had been one to revel in any kind of limelight; she hated being the centre of attention in any situation, and the fact she hadn't even realised that people would be interested in her relationship with this young, famous footballer just proved that she really was still painfully naive. 'You're the newest WAG on the block now,' Tracy grinned as Amber took the paper from her. The picture of her clinging onto Ryan's hand, leaning into him as they walked, made her cringe slightly. She had her head down, thankfully, but he was looking straight into the camera, a slight smile on his face. He loved all that shit, but it was very much a downside for Amber.

'Looks like we won't even be able to nip out for a curry in peace now, then,' she sighed, handing the newspaper back to Tracy.

'So, come on,' Tracy said, unable to hide the eagerness in her voice. 'What's he like?'

Amber looked at the pretty receptionist through slightly narrowed eyes. 'He's a bloke, Tracy. That's all he is. He just happens to be a bloke who's very good at football.'

'How can you *say* that?' Tracy gasped, placing a hand over her chest, her eyes wide with shock. 'Ryan Fisher is probably *the* most *gorgeous* footballer out there right now.' She returned to a somewhat more composed position behind her desk. 'Mind you, a few of my friends think that Jim Allen is a bit of alright, too. For an older man. *I* certainly wouldn't say no. Who knew football could be so sexy, huh?'

Just the mention of Jim's name made Amber's skin prickle and she stepped away from the desk, picking up her bag.

'Personally, either of them would do me,' Tracy went on, sorting through a pile of mail on her desk. 'Your dad used to play alongside Jim Allen at Newcastle Red Star, didn't he?'

'Briefly, yes. Look, Tracy, if you'll excuse me I've got quite a bit to get through this morning if I want to make it to the match this afternoon.'

'Feel free to pop down for a coffee later,' Tracy smiled, looking up as Amber made her way towards the lift. 'Y'know, if there's any more gossip you want to share.'

Amber gave Tracy a small smile back before disappearing into the lift. With the doors safely closed, she leaned back against the wall, closed her eyes and breathed out slowly. She really wished she'd been more prepared for the publicity being involved with Ryan Fisher was creating. She could kick herself for being so stupid. Had she really thought that people would just shrug their shoulders and let them get on with things? Talk about burying your head in the sand! But, and this was the biggest surprise, she was really growing to like Ryan. Despite his reputation. Despite the age gap. Despite the fact she still couldn't trust him 100%. But then, could *he* really trust *her*? Now that Jim Allen was back in her life, could she really trust her*self*?

Since the night of the charity dinner at the Tynebridge Stadium, Amber had tried her hardest to avoid bumping into Jim again, and thanks to a run of away matches she'd succeeded. Of course, the double-edged sword there was that Ryan had been away from home, too, and she'd found herself missing him. More than she'd thought she would. Oh, she wasn't talking love's young dream or anything like that. She wasn't pining for him or sitting there night after night scribbling his name down on pieces of paper and imagining what it would be like to be Mrs. Ryan Fisher. Far from it. They weren't joined at the hip or desperate to be around each other twenty-four hours a day. All it had been so far was a lovely few weeks of fun, which suited Amber just fine. And she was sure it suited Ryan just fine, too. But it *did* feel good knowing someone was there if she needed them. It felt good being able to let go and enjoy herself. It felt good to have that physical relationship again, and nobody could deny that Ryan Fisher wasn't a man most women would kill to get into their bed. That in itself brought a slightly smug smile to Amber's face as she stepped out of the lift and made her way to her desk.

'I won't ask what you're smiling about because you'll probably tell me,' Kevin said, throwing a pile of post onto Amber's desk as she sat down, swinging her chair round to face her laptop. 'I take it you're going to the match this afternoon?'

'Oh, you're not gonna make me work, are you?' Amber groaned. She really wanted to go to Tynebridge that afternoon and just watch a game of football without knowing she had work to do, too.

'Chill out, will you? You're free to go whenever you want. I didn't even need you in this morning, if you must know.'

'Yeah, well, I wanted to get this report done before Monday. And I've got an interview at the cricket ground to sort out for next week that I'd rather get out of the way now. That's the only reason I'm here.'

Kevin sat down on the edge of her desk, folding his arms.

Amber looked at him, frowning slightly. 'Do you want something, Kevin?'

'Is everything alright?'

Amber sat back, crossing her legs, resting one elbow on the desk beside her, tapping the nails of her other hand on the arm of her chair. 'What's the matter? Come on, you've got that "*I'm about to give you a bit of a talking to*" look on your face.'

'Are you coping okay with all this publicity you and Ryan Fisher are getting at the minute?'

Amber glanced briefly out of the window, watching the steady stream of Saturday morning traffic flowing past the News North East offices. 'I don't like it, but, yeah…' She turned her attention back to Kevin. 'Why? Have *you* got a problem with it?'

Kevin shook his head, almost *too* defensively, Amber thought. 'No. No, I don't have a problem with it. Why would I have a problem with it?'

'I don't know,' Amber said, chewing on the end of her biro as she stared at Kevin. 'Why *would* you?'

Kevin looked down at the floor for a few seconds before meeting Amber's eyes again, coughing quickly. 'I know I made a joke out of things in the beginning, telling you to get closer to Ryan because it might benefit us, but…'

Amber couldn't help smiling. She and Kevin Russell had known each other a long time – ever since she'd joined News North East as a young trainee – and despite their often clashing personalities, she cared a lot about him. And she knew he cared about her, too. He just had trouble expressing his real feelings.

'Kevin, I'm fine. Okay? I know what I'm doing, I know the kind of person Ryan is, and I'm well aware of his reputation. So I don't need another "dad" on my back. Alright?'

He looked at her, a sideways smile starting to appear at the corners of his mouth. 'You sure?'

'I'm sure,' Amber replied, still smiling as she swung her chair back round to face her now fired-up laptop. 'Now, go on, get off my desk. I've got work to do.'

Opening up her emails, Amber scanned the list to see which, if any, required urgent attention, but the sound of her phone ringing distracted her almost immediately. She picked up and pressed *answer* without checking the caller's number, and the second she heard his voice she knew that had been a mistake. 'Hello, Amber.'

'Who gave you my number?' Amber asked, her voice almost a whisper.

'Come on, honey. Your dad gave it to me. We're old friends, baby, remember? He just wants us all to stay in touch this time.'

'You aren't being fair, Jim,' Amber carried on through gritted teeth, leaning forward, desperate to make sure nobody overheard this conversation.

'I just want to get to know you again, Amber. What's so wrong with that? It's been so long... too long... Look, I'm back now and there isn't really anything you can do about that, so why don't we start again, huh? Start over.'

'Because I can't do that, Jim. I *can't* start over, I *can't* begin again. I can't do that. So just let me deal with this in my own way, alright? And that means leaving me alone.'

She ended the call and threw her phone down onto the desk, dropping her head into her hands. Jim Allen wasn't going to go away, she wasn't stupid. He was back, and it was something she was just going to have to deal with. She just didn't know how to, yet. She just didn't know how.

Ryan watched as his laptop screen sprang to life, his heart racing. He was alone in the hotel room, but that could change at any time. Jim Allen had a strict ban on computer use on the day of a match – he even confiscated everyone's mobile phones for the last few hours leading up to kick-off. They were too much of a distraction as far as he was concerned. Nobody should be thinking about anything other than the match ahead. But Ryan had sneaked his laptop in, burying it under a pile of clothes at the bottom of his holdall. He was big enough to be able to decide what was considered a distraction, and right now, sitting there with nothing to do and nowhere to go until they were called for a team lunch at midday, the silence was a bigger distraction than the internet could ever be.

He looked at the computer screen, his fingers flying over the keyboard as he logged into his account, but for some reason he just couldn't bring himself to do what he'd intended to do, so he quickly logged off and threw himself down on the bed, staring up at the ceiling. He wished Amber was with him. She'd be able to take his mind off things, even though pre-match sex was usually way off-limits. It wasn't something that was encouraged because it could have a habit of draining vital energy needed to kick the arses of whomever you happened to be playing later. Shit! Ryan wasn't handling this well at all today. He was usually so focused, so totally fixed on nothing but the football, so why was he suddenly distracted? It all felt too familiar, too much of a sense of déjà vu and that only served to make Ryan nervous. He'd thought he was dealing with this. He'd thought he could do it.

A knock at the door made him almost jump out of his skin and he sat bolt upright, shoving his laptop underneath a pillow as Gary popped his head round the door. 'Hey, you alright? You look like you've just seen a ghost?'

'I was… I was asleep. I woke up with a bit of a start, that's all.'

'Sorry, mate. But it's lunchtime. The boss wants us all downstairs in five. Okay?'

Ryan smiled, standing up and running a hand through his dark hair. 'Yeah. Okay.'

It was time to get his focus back. He had a match to play, and everything else had to be put to the back of his mind – for now, at least.

'Hey, you,' Amber smiled, kissing Ronnie on both cheeks as she joined him at the bar in the Players' Lounge at Tynebridge for a pre-match drink. 'It's so good to see you.'

'And you, kiddo,' Ronnie smiled back, giving her a big hug. 'It makes a change for us both to be able to enjoy a match without either of us being here in a professional capacity.'

Amber leaned over the bar, ordering them both bottles of lager. If neither of them were working, then there was no reason why they shouldn't kick back and enjoy the afternoon. 'You're not here to babysit me, are you?' Amber asked, looking at Ronnie with a slightly suspicious expression as she slid up onto a barstool.

'Jesus, you're a bit paranoid, aren't you?' Ronnie laughed, leaning back against the bar and folding his arms. 'Why? Do you *need* babysitting?'

Amber stuck her tongue out at him, taking a swig of lager straight from the bottle.

'Everything still going okay with you and Roy of the Rovers?'

'Yes, thank you,' Amber smiled, scanning the room to see if there was anyone else in there she recognised. 'Everything is just fine.'

'Any sign of it getting serious?'

'Jesus, no!' Amber said, almost choking on her lager. 'Far from it! But it's good to be having some fun, y'know? Without the burden of commitment.'

'Yeah. I can see that,' Ronnie smiled, reaching out to squeeze her hand. 'Maybe we're all wrong about him, huh? Because he certainly seems to be making *you* the happiest I've seen you in a long time.'

'Well, I can't deny I like being with him. He's proving to be a very reliable stress-buster.'

'What have you got to be stressed about?' Ronnie asked, frowning slightly.

Amber took another swig of lager, looking away for a second, which was a mistake. Because Jim Allen chose that exact moment to walk into the Players' Lounge, his hands in the pockets of his dark suit, that smile lighting up his handsome face as he stopped to talk to people. It wasn't a usual occurrence to see the manager of the home team in the Players' Lounge so soon before kick-off, and just the sight of him made Amber suddenly feel quite anxious.

'Nothing,' Amber replied, turning back to face Ronnie. 'I've got nothing to be stressed about.' She slid down from her stool, straightening her top before kissing Ronnie quickly on the cheek. 'I've just got to nip to the loo. I'll see you up in the executive box in a bit, okay?'

'Yeah. Okay.'

She almost ran out of the Lounge, hoping that Jim hadn't noticed her, her heart beating like a jackhammer because she really couldn't face talking to him. Not now. Not today.

'Amber! Amber, wait…'

She stopped walking and leaned back against the wall, closing her eyes and sighing heavily. 'What do you want, Jim?'

'Come to my office. Please. I just want to talk to you.'

She looked at her watch, tapping the face as her eyes met his. 'You *are* aware of the time, aren't you?'

'Colin's got everything under control. Please, Amber. Five minutes, that's all.'

'What do we need to talk about, Jim? You're back, and I've just got to deal with that. We don't need to *talk* about anything.'

He reached out and gently ran his thumb over her cheek, and as he did so his eyes never wavered from hers, his stare almost mesmerising, bringing with it a hundred and one memories that Amber had tried so hard to keep hidden. 'I think we do.'

She threw her head back, sighing again, pushing a hand through her dark red hair. 'Five minutes. That's all.'

Amber could feel her anxiety levels rising as they walked the short distance downstairs to Jim's office. She shouldn't be doing this. She really shouldn't be doing this. The manager's office was directly opposite the home team's dressing room, the tiniest of spaces separating the two rooms, and it was just too close for comfort in Amber's eyes. She should have been strong enough to say no to him. She should have been strong enough to turn around and walk away, but she'd never been strong enough to say no to Jim Allen. And that was what scared her the most. From a distance she could cope, but when he was this close to her she didn't know if it was going to be that easy.

Closing the door behind them, Jim took off his jacket and flung it over the back of the chair behind his desk, sticking his hands in his pockets again. He walked round to the front of his desk, leaning back against it, looking straight at Amber. 'You seem nervous.'

'Of course I'm nervous. I'm alone in a room with you, and I'm not entirely sure how I let that happen.'

'I'm not going to hurt you.'

'Not in the physical sense of the word, no,' Amber said quietly, still all too aware that Ryan was just metres away in the dressing room opposite. She could hear the players' voices; she could hear the noise, the hum of all that pre-match chatter, and it didn't make her feel comfortable.

'Amber, please. I really want you to…'

'Trust you? Is that what you were going to say?'

He pushed a hand through his dark, grey-flecked hair, looking down at the ground. 'I don't think you're ever going to trust me again, are you?'

'Too damn right I'm not.' She backed away towards the door, almost as if placing herself there meant she could make her escape that much faster. 'Twice, Jim. I trusted you twice, and both times you threw it back in my face.' She looked right at him. 'So how

131

can you ever expect me to trust you again?'

He looked down at the floor. 'I can't.'

'No. You can't.'

He walked over to her and Amber made no attempt to move, even though a huge part of her was screaming *back off, get out of there*! She was doing everything she'd promised herself she'd never do again. She was letting Jim back in, letting him wield that power over her that only he could inflict. And all of a sudden she was that sixteen-year-old girl again, looking up into the eyes of a man who should have known better. A man who was about to take over her entire life, just as he had done all those years ago.

'If I could walk away, Amber, I would. Believe me.'

'That's bullshit, Jim. Of course you can walk away.'

'Can *you*?' He reached out and touched her face, stroking her cheek with his fingertips, so lightly it made Amber catch her breath, his green eyes staring deep into her soul, or that's what it felt like. 'Why do you think I've never managed to hold down a real, solid relationship for all these years, Amber? I'm forty-eight years old and I've never been married, never even been engaged, never let anyone get that close to me, so why *is* that, huh?'

'Because nobody can trust you, Jim. You take people's feelings, scrunch them up into a tiny ball and then you throw them aside as though they never mattered to you in the first place.'

'Is that what you really think?'

'You've never given me any cause to think otherwise.'

She could feel her heart pounding as his fingers slid down over her neck, her shoulder, running lightly over her arm until his hand slipped into hers. He was holding her hand, and it felt just like it had done all those years ago – it felt magical, almost. They'd shared this big secret, the two of them, and it was a secret that seemed destined to continue. Despite everything Amber had promised herself.

'I would have done anything for you, Jim,' she whispered, staring up into his eyes. 'Anything. But the one thing I didn't do is the one thing I *should* have done – I should have told people what happened between us because, if I had, then *this* wouldn't be happening now. You wouldn't have had the chance to come near me again, my dad would've seen to that.'

'So why didn't you?' Jim asked, watching as Amber slipped her hand out of his, walking away from him.

'I was scared.' She swung back round to face him. 'I slept with you when I was just sixteen, Jim. I'd been sixteen years old for just a few days when I let that happen, because I wanted you *so* much, and to know that you wanted me, too – you have no idea how that made me feel. But if my dad ever found out… How do you think he'd react, huh? Even after all this time, do you really think he'd just shrug it off because it happened all those years ago? If it was *your* daughter…?'

Jim ran a hand through his hair, walking over to her as she leaned back against his desk. 'He'd hate me. Of course he would. But nobody needs to know what happened back then. Nobody got hurt…'

'Nobody got *hurt*?' Amber gasped. '*I* got hurt, Jim. *Me*. You hurt *me*.'

'I know, baby,' he whispered, stroking her cheek with the back of his hand. 'I know. And I'm sorry, I'm so, so sorry. But all that matters is what's happening now. You and me. We could be so good together.'

Amber shook her head, but her heart was screaming for him to touch her again, to kiss her mouth the way he'd always used to, to hold her in his arms and make love to her, because she knew it would feel as if he'd never been away. She knew that. And that's what frightened her the most, but it was something she'd wanted more than anything – from the very second she'd laid eyes on him again.

'We can't be together, Jim.' But what she was saying and what she was feeling were two completely different things, and it was taking more effort to stay strong than Amber could have ever

133

imagined. 'We can't. And this… this isn't fair, this is so unfair…'

His mouth was on hers before she'd had a chance to draw breath, his tongue touching hers, his arm circling her waist, pulling her against him. And that kiss, just the feel of his mouth moving against hers, it was as if it had wiped every ounce of that hard-fought-for strength clean away, leaving Amber as that sixteen-year-old girl once more – powerless to do anything because she loved him. So much. She always had done. Was that the *real* reason why she'd never really wanted another serious relationship? Because, in the back of her mind, she'd always been waiting for him to come back to her?

Lost in the moment now, too far down that road to turn back and forget this was happening, Amber closed her eyes and threw her head back as his mouth brushed the base of her neck, his fingers sliding up under her top, cool against her naked skin, but all that did was send a shiver running through her that heightened everything she was already feeling. She was under his spell once more.

Pulling her top up over her head, she leaned right back, closing her eyes again as she remembered the very first time he'd touched her this way; how she'd felt just a little bit scared, but with an excitement inside that had been almost unbearable. She'd been worried it would hurt, worried the pain would detract from what she'd so wanted to be a fairy tale experience, and whilst it hadn't been quite that, he'd made love to her so carefully, so gently that she'd cried, because she'd had such a crush on Jim Allen. Such a huge, heartbreaking crush, and to feel him actually making love to her had been the biggest dream come true.

She bit down on her lip as his fingers gently stroked her breasts, his quiet groans turning her on to the point where she didn't think she could take anymore. She didn't even care that his office had no lock, that anyone could walk in at any second, it didn't matter. She didn't care. She'd waited so long to feel this way again, waited so long to have him touch her naked skin, waited so long to feel him this close, but the pain it was actually causing now that he was here was indescribable. Because this shouldn't be happening.

'Jesus, Amber, baby. You grew up good…' Jim groaned, lifting her up onto his desk. She kicked off her shoes, allowing him to slide her jeans down over her thighs, throwing them aside before doing the same with her underwear until she was naked and exposed, but it felt almost exhilarating. Freeing himself with a speed that was almost record-breaking, he pushed her legs apart, taking just a second to look at her, just a second before he'd taken his place back where Amber had let very few men go since.

She closed her eyes again, leaning back and wrapping her legs around him as she felt him push inside her, and it was a feeling she'd never forgotten. A feeling she'd missed like the most addictive drug there ever was, and not even Ryan Fisher could give her the fix she really needed. Even the most beautiful man in football couldn't compare to this man here with her now.

'Don't think about him,' Jim whispered, his mouth resting on hers. 'Don't do that. Don't. You're with *me*, baby. You're with me now.'

'Jim…'

'Sshh, it's okay. It's okay.'

She should be feeling guilty, but then, why should she? Her and Ryan, they may be a couple, but as far as a committed relationship went they were so far away from that. It wasn't something Amber thought either of them were ready for, and the fact she was here, with Jim, went a long way to proving that point even further. For all she knew Ryan had been with other women when she wasn't around – they'd never laid down ground rules or issued conditions. It wasn't that kind of relationship, so she couldn't let guilt get in the way.

Sliding her hand round the back of his neck, she pulled Jim closer, desperate to feel his mouth on hers again, his lips soft and welcoming as they kissed her slow and deep. Kisses that sent her head spinning and her stomach cartwheeling; kisses that spelt trouble, but what was she supposed to do? She could feel him inside her, deep inside her, and every memory, every beautiful, painful memory of the past came crashing over her like a tidal wave of emotion that was hard to control. But he was holding her so tight, saying all the right things, making her feel everything she'd ever wanted to feel, and as she felt the white-hot climax begin its climb, nothing else seemed to matter. Not Ryan, not the fact that she was getting into something she really shouldn't be going anywhere near; none of it mattered. All that mattered was that Jim was with her; he was back. But for how long?

That question flashed briefly through her mind as she felt his body jerk inside her, his muffled cries signalling the end of the ride for him and Amber kept her eyes closed as she felt that hot rush filling her up, spreading through her like a blanket of beautiful pins and needles, each tingle reaching every last, tiny part of her. It was the most incredible feeling. Even more incredible because he'd never forgotten – he'd never forgotten that, sometimes, he needed to help her reach that endgame, too, and as he slowly withdrew he gently touched her with his fingers, their eyes locked together as his hand moved slowly back and forth until Amber reached that same white-hot climax, burying her face in his shoulder as she shuddered in his arms, her skin tingling once again. It was as if every time he touched her it sent a wave of something she couldn't explain sweeping over her; that's how it had been then, and it was exactly how it was now.

'That's why we need to be together,' Jim whispered, lifting her down from the desk and pulling her against him. 'It feels right, Amber. You and me.'

She looked at him, right into those almost-mesmerising eyes of his, suddenly feeling extremely vulnerable. 'I promised myself I would never let you go there again,' she said, pulling away from him and retrieving her discarded clothes, quickly pulling them back on. 'I promised myself…'

Jim gently grabbed her wrist, giving her no choice but to look at him. '*That* was meant to happen, Amber.'

She shook her head, reality hitting her like a speeding truck. It was as if someone had just flicked that switch again and suddenly she could see everything so much clearer. 'No. It wasn't. It happened because I was weak.'

'It happened because you *wanted* it to. Don't you believe in fate, honey?'

'I don't know what I believe anymore,' Amber whispered, clarity slowly taking over. Okay, so she'd let that happen, but it was out of her system now. She'd given him what he wanted, and yeah, maybe she *had* wanted it, too, but that had to be the end. She wasn't prepared to put herself through the pain and the hurt that Jim Allen could bring to her door. She couldn't do that, not again. She couldn't. Maybe she was always going to love him – he'd been such a huge part of her life from such a young age, she couldn't just brush that aside – but being with him was another matter.

'I love you, Amber. I've always loved you…'

'Yeah. So you keep saying.' Amber ran her hands through her hair, all the strength she'd temporarily lost flooding back as those protective barriers crept back up around her.

'You're just gonna *leave*?' Jim asked, his face a mask of genuine confusion. 'You're walking out on me? After what we've just done?'

Amber turned round to face him as she stopped by the door, her fingers already gripping the handle, a determination she'd never felt before taking over. 'It's not a nice feeling, is it, Jim?'

'Where the hell have *you* been?' Ronnie asked as Amber finally took her seat in the executive box Freddie Sullivan commandeered every season at Tynebridge. His own club had a match that afternoon, though, so he wasn't around, of which Amber was glad. Facing her father after what had just happened wouldn't have been something she was keen to do.

'Nowhere,' Amber replied, staring straight ahead. The match had just started and she scanned the pitch, looking for Ryan's number 9 shirt.

'Nowhere,' Ronnie repeated.

Amber looked at him. 'Yeah. Nowhere.'

'You sure about that?'

She turned to look at him, frowning. 'Is there something wrong, Ronnie?'

'You and Jim Allen. What's the story?'

She quickly looked away, but Ronnie wasn't giving up.

'No, come on, Amber. You're gonna talk to me.'

'About what?' Amber asked, standing up and walking over to the window of the large executive box. She didn't really like watching games from behind glass. She much preferred to be out there, amongst the crowd, watching football the way it *should* be watched.

'About you and Jim Allen. When you ran out of the Players' Lounge before, you seemed a bit – I dunno – upset.'

'I wasn't upset,' Amber said, shoving her hands in her pockets as she contemplated walking out onto the private balcony attached to the box. At least that way she might feel a bit of the atmosphere outside, because the one inside was starting to get a bit claustrophobic.

'Flustered, then.'

'I wasn't…'

'I followed you outside, Amber. I wanted to make sure you were okay. But he got to you first.'

Amber turned away again, desperate to catch a glimpse of Ryan, anything to make her absolutely sure that she'd done the right thing in walking away from Jim. Before *he* walked away from *her*. Again.

'He's an old family friend, Ronnie. You know that. He just wanted to catch up with me, that's all.'

Ronnie's eyes narrowed as he looked at her, even though she was still staring out of the window, quite obviously avoiding his gaze. Didn't she realise how guilty that made her seem? Of what, Ronnie had yet to find out.

'So close to kick-off? You're telling me he wanted a catch-up chat at twenty-five-past-two on a match day? I'm not buying that,

138

Amber. I saw him. He was touching you, he was looking into your eyes and he was touching your cheek, and believe me, sweetheart, the *way* he was looking at you, that wasn't the way *I'd* ever greet a family friend. You didn't find that weird then, huh?'

Amber stared at him. 'Not here, okay?' She walked out of the box, closely followed by Ronnie, not stopping until they were outside the stadium. She needed the fresh air because she suddenly felt quite sick. 'This really isn't the time or the place, Ronnie.'

'Is there something going on between you two?'

Amber looked down at the ground, scuffing the heel of her shoe against the wall behind her. She didn't really have much choice left but to tell him. He kind of had her backed into a corner and she couldn't think of anything off the top of her head that would placate him, apart from the truth. 'We had – Christ, I don't even know how to put this – we had a, relationship, I suppose. If you could call it that…'

'When? Recently?'

She shook her head, still looking down at the ground, aware of the stadium inside erupting. It sounded like Red Star had scored an early goal. 'It was a long time ago. When he was a player, here, at Newcastle Red Star.'

Ronnie frowned again. 'Before you and me met, I take it?'

'Way before. It was a long time ago, Ronnie.' She shrugged. 'Y'know, these things happen, we move on.'

Ronnie leaned back against the wall beside her, shoving his hands in his pockets as they both stared straight ahead. 'I'm not getting this, Amber. Why did you never tell me?'

Amber shrugged again. 'It's not something I like talking about.'

'And is there a reason for that?'

'I was in love with him, Ronnie. I've been in love with him since I was fifteen years old…'

Ronnie looked at her. 'Fifteen? Jesus, Amber, how long has this been going on?'

'Twenty-two years,' Amber whispered, still staring straight

139

ahead. 'It's been going on for almost twenty-two years.'

'Hang on…' Ronnie moved so he was standing right in front of her, giving her no choice but to look at him. 'Are you telling me that you and Jim Allen… You were *fifteen* years old?'

'My dad had wanted him at Red Star for so long,' Amber said, trying to avoid Ronnie's eyes, but failing. 'He pushed for the club to sign him, but you probably know that.'

Ronnie nodded. 'Yeah. Yeah, I remember all the stories about him moving to Red Star. But…'

'They hit it off straightaway, y'know? Him and my dad. Jim looked up to Freddie. He'd always admired him as a player, apparently, and even though my dad was at the end of his playing career, they still became really close. That's why he was round our house so often. My dad had wanted him to settle in to North-East life quickly so he could concentrate on his football…'

'Amber…'

'The second my dad brought him through our front door, that was it. I can still remember the day. I was sitting on the sofa, watching something on TV; I don't know what, exactly… I was making a list of people I wanted to invite to my sixteenth birthday party – my dad had arranged for me to have it at the club, the old ground, as it was then. Tynebridge didn't exist back in those days…'

'Amber, I know all of that…'

'I remember looking up when my dad walked into the living room; Jim was close behind him, and… my heart just stopped, Ronnie. It literally stopped. I know it did…'

'But surely that was just some silly teenage crush? You were just a kid.'

'I was old enough.'

Her eyes met his and Ronnie stared at her, frowning again. 'Old enough for *what*, Amber?'

She looked back down at the ground, twisting the ring she wore on her right hand round and round her finger. 'He came to the party. A few of the Red Star players did. I mean, it was my dad's club at the time, wasn't it? Of course a few of them would be there. I think that was half the reason I had so many guests, when word got round the whole school who was going to be there…' She trailed off for a second, still staring down at the ground. 'Jim he… he paid me so much attention. I felt like the luckiest girl in the world, having this gorgeous footballer smiling at me and talking to me and… He wanted me, too, Ronnie. I could see it, I could *feel* it…'

'Jesus Christ, Amber.' Ronnie ran a hand through his hair, turning away for a second. 'You were just a kid. Please tell me nothing happened.'

'Not that night it didn't.' Amber's voice was quiet, her attention distracted slightly as the crowd inside the stadium erupted again, signalling another Red Star goal. Was Ryan out there playing the game of his life, thinking she was watching him, when she'd missed it all because of her ridiculous attempts at trying to get Jim Allen out of her system? 'I went to his apartment a week or so later…'

'You went to his apartment? Amber, you were sixteen years old!'

'It wasn't fucking illegal, Ronnie!' She hadn't meant to raise her voice but he was starting to aggravate her now. Or maybe she was just frustrated with herself, for being so weak.

'You *slept* with him?'

'What the hell did you *think* I went to his apartment for? A post-match report? My head was turned, okay?'

Ronnie stared at her, grabbing her hand so she couldn't get away, couldn't avoid telling him exactly what was going on. 'And?'

Amber felt her shoulders sag. She hadn't *wanted* to tell anyone about this, but it didn't look as though she had much choice now. 'We met in secret after that. Regularly. I just wanted to be with him, that was all. I fell in love, and I just wanted to be with him. And for almost two years…' She swallowed hard, looking away for a second. 'But then he found someone else, didn't he…? He found someone else, and he just walked away from me as though I'd never even existed.'

141

Ronnie loosened his grip on her hand slightly, the pain in her eyes more than evident now. 'Is that when you moved to Manchester? To do your degree?'

She nodded. 'But then I went back home, didn't I? Once I'd graduated I went back home to find that Jim's relationship was over, and I let him back into my life, Ronnie. Just like that. I let it happen all over again, and that's the way it was for another couple of years – back to the secrecy and the lies because nobody could know about us. He didn't want that, and neither did I. And it was good, y'know? Good having him back in my life, because I'd never stopped loving him. Never stopped wanting him. Everything he did… stupid little things like… like the way he said my name with that accent of his… it used to make my stomach flip over and over and… I loved him, Ronnie. I loved him. And things were so good, things were great, until… until he hurt me a second time. Until he just walked away and left me as though I'd never mattered to him at all.'

'It sounds as though you didn't.'

Amber looked up sharply, slightly angry at Ronnie's response. What did *he* know? 'I mattered to him, Ronnie. I know I did.'

Ronnie said nothing. He thought better of it. She was quite obviously not in the mood to listen to his opinions on the matter. 'But you didn't run away a second time, did you?'

She shook her head, still twisting the ring round and round her finger. 'I didn't need to. His playing days were over by that point. He had no real reason to stay in the North East.' Amber kicked the heel of her shoe against the wall in a reflex, almost nervous, action. 'He promised me he would never come back up here, Ronnie. He promised me that. He'd hurt me so badly – so, so badly and he knew that, and he promised me with all of his heart that he wouldn't come back up here. Because as long as he was around, I was going to want him. And that wasn't fair, because if I couldn't have him…'

'But you can now.'

She looked back up at Ronnie. 'Yeah. I can.'

Ronnie leaned back against the wall beside her, running a hand through his hair. 'What happened just now, Amber?'

She continued to kick the wall behind her, staring down at the ground. 'We had sex. In his office.'

'Jesus… with Ryan next door? Amber…'

'But that's it. That's it. He's out of my system now, and somehow I found the strength to walk away from him, okay? I turned and walked away from him. Just like he did with me.' She looked up at her best friend, her voice quiet, although its calmness defied everything she was actually feeling. 'It's been so hard, Ronnie. I really thought I was over it, over *him*. I mean, it's not like I haven't set eyes on him for all this time, is it? I've seen him on TV, I've always known he was there, existing… but I always thought I was handling it well. I'd feel a slight pang of – something, I don't know what, but whatever it was I always managed to push it away and get on with my life, but… but seeing him in the flesh… that's so different…'

Ronnie turned his head to look at her. 'I'm assuming Freddie knows nothing about any of this.'

Amber nodded. 'And I don't ever want him to know, Ronnie. So please, don't tell him. Okay?'

'Come on, Amber. What do you take me for?'

'And that goes for Jim, too. I don't want him to know I've told you anything about what happened between us.'

Ronnie turned his head away from her, staring straight ahead again. 'And to think I was worried about you and Ryan.'

'I can handle Ryan. I can handle the likes of him better than anyone really gives me credit for.' She looked at her best friend, well aware that this news had shocked him slightly. Maybe she wasn't as bad at keeping a secret as she'd first thought she was. 'It wasn't that I didn't ever want a serious relationship, Ronnie. But, when Jim hurt me the way he did it… it made me put up that wall, shut myself off from any other offers. I didn't want to put myself in a position where someone could hurt me like that again.'

'Is that why you really ended it with me?'

She shrugged. 'I don't know. Maybe subconsciously that was the reason, I really don't know. Maybe I got scared and ended it before anything could happen that could leave me open to the kind of hurt Jim put me through. All I know is that he messed me up. He instilled something in me that made me unable to trust people. Which is why, I guess, I prefer spending time on my own rather than in the company of other people.' She smiled weakly at Ronnie, who reached out to take her hand again, squeezing it gently. 'Except you, of course. I *love* spending time with you because, for some reason, you're the only person I can really trust.'

'What did he do to you?' Ronnie whispered, reaching out to push the dark red hair from her eyes.

'He didn't *make* me fall in love with him, Ronnie. That was my own fault.'

'And now he's back?'

She looked at him. 'I've got to be strong this time. I can't let him do it to me again, not a third time. That would just be embarrassing.'

Ronnie couldn't help but laugh as she smiled at him. But even though she was making a joke of it, he knew it was far from trivial. 'So where does Ryan fit into all this, then?'

Amber started stroking Ronnie's fingers as they clung onto hers. 'I genuinely love being with him, Ronnie. But I really did go into that relationship with my eyes wide open. Despite what you all think, and what you probably *definitely* think now, I know the kind of person he is. I'm aware of his reputation, and I'm by no means looking for a future with him. I just want some fun. And maybe it's about time I got back on that horse, huh? Maybe it's time I really did try to forget Jim Allen once and for all and move on with my life.'

'Do you think you can do that?' Ronnie asked, squeezing her hand again.

'I've got no choice. I can't let him get to me, I mean, I'm not that sixteen-year-old girl with a crush anymore, am I? I've grown up.'

'It's not going to be easy though, is it? I mean, you have a working relationship with this club, too. You're gonna have to face him for all sorts of reasons.'

'Yeah, I'm well aware of that, Ronnie. But what else can I do? Quit my job because I just might have to interview Jim Allen at some point in the future?'

'You could move away. You heard what Max Mandell said to you a few weeks ago. There's work for you down in London…'

'I don't *want* to move to London, Ronnie. I want to stay here, and I'm sorry if that makes me sound like some kind of small-town girl, but I like it here. I like my life. I like my job. And I like Ryan Fisher, okay?'

'And, are you sure you're not just using him, Amber? As a way of deflecting your feelings for Jim Allen?'

'Jesus, hark at Mr. Psychologist over there. No. Alright? I'm not "using" him. But we're not exactly exclusive, either. He can do what he likes, and I'm sure he feels the same way about me.'

'Do you think he'd be happy if he thought you were sleeping with his boss?'

She let go of his hand, heading back inside the main entrance, ignoring his question. 'And anyway, what happened today was a one off. It won't happen again.' She looked straight at Ronnie, that determination she'd felt when she'd walked away from Jim making a welcome return. 'It won't happen again.'

Chapter Nine

'A few of us are going down the casino later, if you're up for it.'

Ryan tucked the phone between his shoulder and chin as he filled the kettle, listening as Gary laid out his and a few of the other Red Star players' plans for the night. A few drinks in a bar on the Quayside, a few hours in the casino, then maybe a club followed by, who knew? That last instalment all depended on who happened to be around at the time. 'I don't know, Gaz,' Ryan said, flicking the switch down on the kettle. 'I'm kind of tired, y'know?'

Gary laughed down the line. 'Come on! Ryan Fisher turning down a night of drinking, gambling and women?'

That was *exactly* what Ryan should be turning down. 'Hey, I'm with Amber now, remember?'

'And she's got you by the balls then, has she?'

'No…'

'Then get your arse out with the rest of us tonight. Come on, mate. Just because you've been one of the few to conquer the ice-queen it doesn't mean to say you have to stop enjoying yourself, does it? You're not fucking married. Jesus, I'm frigging engaged and I've got more freedom than you have.'

Ryan sighed inwardly. Part of him knew what Gary was saying – he was young, he was living the dream, and he really wasn't ready for cosy nights in in front of the TV. Not *every* night, anyway. But part of him also knew that he was on dangerous ground. He'd been here before. And he should know what he needed to do to stop from going there again.

'We'll be in Goodyear's Bar, eight-thirty,' Gary said. 'We'll see you there.'

Ryan quickly ended the call, looking up sharply as Amber entered the room, all sleepy-eyed and sexy in one of his t-shirts, and very little else, from what he could see. He filled two mugs with boiling water as Amber walked up behind him, circling his waist and kissing his naked, tattooed shoulder.

'Who was that on the phone?' she asked, playing with the waistband of his jeans.

'Oh… nobody, babe. Just Gary asking if I wanted to join him and the lads for a drink later tonight.'

'And? Are you going?'

Ryan shrugged. 'Have you got a better offer?'

'Oh, baby, I'm sorry. I'm working late tonight so you might as well do your own thing. All I'm gonna be fit for when I get home is sleep.'

Ryan couldn't help wishing that she'd given him a different answer, given him the option to back out of tonight. If she'd made him that better offer then he would've had an excuse not to turn up, because he wasn't sure his willpower was strong enough to do that all on his own. 'You didn't need to get out of bed,' he smiled, turning round and stroking strands of dark red hair from her eyes. 'I was just making us a cup of tea. I was gonna bring it in to you.'

'If I'd hung around in bed waiting for you to come back it was only gonna end up in sex,' Amber whispered, kissing him lazily. 'And I can't be late for work again.'

'Sex, huh?'

'Yeah. You know, that thing we did last night, and again at half-past-five this morning.'

Ryan smiled again, letting his hands wander up underneath the t-shirt she was wearing, realising that she really wasn't wearing

147

anything else. At all. He groaned as his fingers gently stroked her hips, pulling her even closer against him as his mouth covered hers in a long, slow kiss. 'We don't have to go back to bed for sex, y'know.'

Amber threw her head back, the feel of his lips on her neck and his hard-on digging into her thigh telling her she was going to have to drive like Lewis Hamilton to get to work on time now. Because it looked like breakfast was going to be a purely physical one today. Not that she was complaining. 'I know,' she moaned, leaning back against the counter as he pushed her t-shirt up over her hips, sliding his hand between her legs, parting them to allow him in. 'Jesus, Ryan, you are such a bad fucking influence on me. I used to be such a good girl.'

He laughed that deep, sexy laugh of his as he buried his face in her hair. 'Good girls are no fun,' he whispered, running his fingers up and down her spine, settling in the small of her back, keeping her pressed against him as he pushed inside her, backing her up against the counter. 'Bad girls are so much better.'

She couldn't help laughing, but he was right. She'd been too good for far too long, but he was slowly making her realise that life could be fun. He was good for her. They were good together. She was having a blast, and that's what she needed right now.

She closed her eyes and clung onto him as he pushed in deeper, rocking her whole body with every thrust until she finally felt that beautiful release, felt her body shake in his arms as they both reached a quick but more than satisfying climax. She could think of worse ways to start the day.

'Well, baby, this bad girl had better go put some clothes on and get to work,' she smiled, pulling her t-shirt down over her thighs and standing up on tiptoe to kiss him quickly, running her hands over his naked chest as she backed away from him. 'So you're gonna have to amuse yourself until it's time to go training.'

He leaned back against the counter and folded his arms, watching her almost sashay her way back towards the bedroom.

She sure was one sexy older woman, and someone Ryan was happy to spend more and more time with. She made him feel things he'd never felt before; she made him realise that maybe he really was changing. Was Ryan Fisher finally growing up? But, if he really *was* growing up, then why was he even contemplating going out tonight? Pushing a hand through his hair, he threw his head back and sighed heavily before running into the bedroom after Amber. 'Amber, hang on.'

She swung round to face him. 'What's up?' she asked, dragging her hair back into a high ponytail.

He came over to her, pulling her into his arms. 'Let's do something really crazy.'

'Like what?' she laughed, running her hands up and down his heavily tattooed arms.

'Move in with me.'

Amber looked at him for a few seconds, too stunned to say anything. 'Sorry?'

'Look, I know this isn't something you – or anyone, really – expected to hear from me, but… You've changed me, Amber.'

She frowned as she continued to stare at him, trying to work out if he was being serious. 'And… is that a *good* thing?'

'I dunno. It *feels* like a good thing.' Did it?

Amber laughed again, turning her head slightly to stare past him outside at the view of the River Tyne, the early morning November sun bouncing off the water. 'Ryan, baby, I don't know how much coffee you've been drinking, but you can't come out with something like that just as I'm about to rush out the door and expect me to give you some kind of definitive answer.'

'I'm being serious, Amber. Since meeting… since meeting you, everything feels different. It's like I can suddenly see what really makes me happy.' Was that true?

'And you're happy to put your playboy past behind you and move in with *me*? A female sports reporter eleven years your senior?'

'Will you stop banging on about age? You've got a body women ten years younger than you would kill for.'

'Oh, I should move in with you purely for that comment alone,' she laughed, running her fingers over his chest, the muscles hard and taut beneath her fingers.

'Then do it. Come on, Amber. Live dangerously.'

She smiled, kissing him slowly, her fingers now playing with the waistband of his jeans. 'Yeah, but not *that* dangerously.' She gave him one more kiss, grabbed her bag from the chair by the door and walked out of the bedroom, blowing him a kiss and winking at him over her shoulder.

He looked down at the ground, running a hand over the back of his neck before looking back up at her retreating figure. 'I'm serious, Amber!' he shouted after her. But the front door closing out in the hall told him the subject was over as far as she was concerned.

All of a sudden he needed a release, something to take his mind off all the unwelcome temptations that had suddenly appeared. So much for moving back up north to get away from everything. That had worked, hadn't it? He'd been stupid to think running away was going to solve anything.

Sliding his phone out of the back pocket of his jeans, he scrolled through his contact list until he came to a number he'd been given by a 'friend' back in London. Just in case he ever needed anything once he was back up north, they'd said. A number he should have deleted, but he hadn't. And right now he was glad he'd left it where it was. He pressed *call* before he had a chance to change his mind. They answered after just three rings.

'Hey, Ryan. Callum told me I might be hearing from you. What can I do for you?'

Ryan closed his eyes and took a deep breath. 'The usual. Did Callum tell you what that is?'

The voice at the other end of the line laughed. 'Hey, man. No problem. Welcome home. Personal collection? Or do you want

150

somebody to come round?'

'No!' A million second thoughts suddenly raced through his head. But what was the problem? He knew what he was doing. He could handle it. It was just a release, that was all. A brief escape from everything. Something to calm him down, chill him out. He could control it now, couldn't he? 'I'll come to you. Give me an address.'

Ryan quickly scribbled down the address he was given and ended the call, his heart beating hard against his ribs. He'd forgotten how weird, but also how exciting, the rush could be. Scrolling down his contact list again, he found another number. Something else that could give him that brief escape. And anyway, once training was finished he had a whole afternoon to kill, didn't he? He might as well make good use of it.

Amber sat on a bench overlooking the River Tyne, the cold autumn air penetrating the material of her coat and she pulled the collar up to shield the back of her neck from the cool breeze that seemed to be growing stronger as the afternoon wore on.

She didn't have to work late that night. Not really. She'd had quite an easy day, if the truth be told. But, for some reason, she'd felt the need to lie to Ryan – why? Because she was scared of what she was starting to feel for him? Or was she scared of the fact that she just didn't want to spend as much time with him as she'd first thought? Because of someone else.

Cupping her hands around the steaming carton of coffee she'd just bought, she continued to stare out at life going on all around her, the bustling atmosphere of the Quayside somehow pulling her back to reality, giving her some kind of clarity. She couldn't let Jim Allen back into her life. She couldn't. It would be stupid, it would be wrong. Why would she put herself through all of that again? When he'd only hurt her, just like he'd hurt her before. He wasn't going to change. Not now. But Ryan, he just might. If she gave him a chance.

She took a sip of hot coffee, sitting back against the wooden bench, the low November sun hitting her face. Shielding her eyes, she watched the steady stream of people walking across the Gateshead Millennium Bridge – a stunning pedestrian and cyclist tilt bridge that linked Gateshead's Quay's arts quarter on the south bank and Newcastle's Quayside on the north. She loved this place. She never really wanted to leave the North East, it was her home. But the reappearance of Jim Allen had tarnished everything slightly. He was a distraction she had to forget about, before it took over again. And she could do that. It would be hard, but she could do it. She had to. She had no choice.

Taking another sip of coffee, she thought about what Ryan had asked her that morning. He was trying really hard to prove to her that he wasn't that playboy the tabloids would have you think he was, she knew that, and that was sweet. But who was he kidding? He couldn't switch all of that off just like that. He was a twenty-six-year-old professional footballer with the world at his feet, so no matter how much he told her he'd changed, she wasn't going to hold her breath. She'd just enjoy what they had and take each day as it came. What else could she do? At least Ryan provided a decent distraction from Jim. And any distraction was better than none at all.

She put her coffee to one side and pulled her phone out of her bag, looking at it for a few seconds. Should she call Ryan? Tell him she wasn't working late? Tell him she had that better offer for him after all? One he wouldn't be able to refuse? Her finger hovered over his number for a few seconds as she looked up at the river again, the sun bouncing off the water, making her squint slightly. No. He'd probably made plans now, anyway, and she didn't want to be one of those girlfriends who made him feel guilty about going out with his friends just because she was now at a loose end. She wanted him to spend time with her because he *wanted* to, not because he felt he had to. No, she'd leave it. She'd see him tomorrow. They could do something together then, if he had nothing else planned. She'd go and see her dad tonight; spend an evening catching up on things.

Stuffing her phone back in her bag, she picked up her coffee and stood up, walking slowly along the Quayside, one hand shoved deep in the pocket of her coat. Now she'd given herself that silent talking to she felt better about everything. So maybe now it was time to finally begin the rest of her life, without Jim Allen constantly being at the forefront of her mind. Maybe now it was finally time to start living.

Ryan closed the door and leaned back against it, closing his eyes as a surge of uncharacteristic guilt swept over him. Maybe he should have been stronger, but when you had a whole afternoon stretching out in front of you with nobody to spend it with and nowhere to go, what else was he supposed to do? Training had finished not long after lunch, and after a quick pint in the pub with Gary and a few of the other lads, he'd had nothing else to do but amuse himself. And he'd managed that, although if Amber found out just how he liked to amuse himself, he wasn't sure she'd stick around long enough to hear his explanation. Not that he had one, anyway.

Walking over to the mirror, he stared at his reflection, quickly wiping the faint dusting of white powder from underneath his nose. He looked tired, too. Mind you, who wouldn't after the afternoon *he'd* had?

Running a hand through his ruffled dark hair, he smiled. Jesus, he was one good-looking son-of-a-bitch! It wouldn't take much to get him back up to full strength – all he needed was a cool shower, some clean clothes and a splash of something expensive and he'd be ready to hit the town. He may not have been all that keen on the idea this morning, but now he couldn't wait to get out there and see what the night had to offer. And if it brought anything even close to the afternoon he'd just had, Ryan Fisher was going to be one very happy man. One very happy man indeed.

'Hey, kiddo,' Freddie Sullivan smiled, closing the front door behind her. 'You look very relaxed, I have to say.'

Amber gave her dad a half-smile, looking at him out the corner of her eye. 'Are you saying I look stressed-out most of the time?'

Freddie laughed, taking the bottle of wine she held out for him from her. 'No, Amber. I'm not saying that at all. Can I not pay my little girl a compliment now and again?'

'Yeah. Of course you can,' Amber smiled. 'And yeah, I *am* feeling quite relaxed as it happens. It's been a good day. Something smells great by the way. What are we having for dinner?'

'Roast beef and my homemade Yorkshire puddings. Do you remember how your mam used to love my homemade Yorkshire puddings? Oh, and I hope you don't mind, sweetheart, but we've got a guest.'

'A guest?' Amber frowned as she followed her dad into the living room, her heart stalling in her chest as she saw just who that guest was.

'I invited Jim over. I haven't had a chance to catch up with him properly since he got back to the North East, and he's on his own up here, so I thought it'd be nice to have him over for dinner. Let him spend some time with old friends.'

Amber's eyes met Jim's, her stomach turning a million somer-saults as she swallowed hard.

'You don't mind, do you, Amber?' Jim asked, standing up and smiling that smile, a smile that sent Amber's heart into overdrive as she remembered the last time she'd seen him. The way he'd touched her, kissed her – the way it had felt so right when he'd made love to her, like that was where he was supposed to be. Where he belonged. Then she shook all those thoughts from her head and stared at Jim, defying him to do or say anything stupid. This wasn't the place.

'No. No, of course I don't mind.' She looked at her father who, thankfully, seemed to have absolutely no idea of the atmosphere between herself and one of his oldest friends. He had no idea at all, and she needed to make sure it stayed that way. 'Can I… can I have a drink, Dad?'

'Of course you can, sweetheart? What do you fancy?'

'Gin and tonic, please. A large one.'

Freddie looked at her through slightly narrowed eyes. 'I thought you said it'd been a good day?'

'It has.' Amber tried to sound bright and cheerful, when she now felt anything but. 'I'm just in the mood to unwind and relax.'

'Okay. Well, one large G&T coming up. I'll be back in a tick.'

Amber waited until he'd disappeared into the kitchen before she turned her attention back to Jim. 'Did you know I'd be here when he invited you?'

'He's a good friend, Amber. And I'm really looking forward to talking over old times…'

'Did you know I'd be here?' she repeated slowly, looking right into his eyes. His beautiful, mesmerising green eyes. Shit! She needed this tonight, didn't she? She'd spent all day turning everything over in her mind and finally coming to a conclusion she was happy with, comfortable with, and now *he* was here and it was like he'd just undone every decision she'd worked so hard to achieve.

'Your dad did mention that you'd be coming over, yes.'

'Then you should have said no. You should have told him you had other plans.'

'You can't avoid me forever, Amber.'

'So you keep saying, but this is deliberate, Jim. You, being here, this is deliberate.'

He walked over to her, gently tilting her chin up so she had no other option but to look into his eyes. 'You do crazy, stupid things when you're in love.'

Swiping his hand away in one swift movement, she walked away from him, over to the bay window that overlooked the long gravel driveway and the street outside, keeping her back to him as she focused on the huge weeping willow tree that stood in the centre of her father's large, lawned front garden. 'I should go,' Amber

155

whispered, folding her arms. Suddenly she just wanted to be with Ryan. She didn't want to be here, with a man who only had the ability to confuse and distract her. She wanted to be with Ryan.

'Okay, so you leave, all of a sudden, just like that, and you don't think your dad's gonna find that odd?'

She swung round to face him, looking up as he stood right in front of her, all handsome and rugged and everything she'd ever wanted. For most of her life she'd only ever wanted this man. But she couldn't have him. For her own sanity she had to keep away, otherwise her entire life was just going to be one long cycle of loving him and losing him and she couldn't live like that. Not anymore.

'He'll want to know why, won't he?'

'I'll tell him I don't feel well. It wouldn't be so far from the truth.'

'I don't want you to go.'

She stared up at him, the smell of that familiar aftershave and the warmth of his body so close to hers making her feel weak and she hated herself for it. She'd never been weak, unless Jim Allen happened to be around. And then she suddenly turned into a completely different person, and one she wasn't altogether sure she liked.

'Don't make tonight hard for me, Jim. Please.'

He smiled again, leaning forward slightly, close enough for his lips to ever-so-gently brush over hers, but he said nothing. He just backed away, smiling at her as he picked up his drink from the coffee table and took a sip, his eyes never leaving hers.

Amber turned her head away, looking back out of the window as a large blackbird swooped down to land on the roof of her dad's silver Audi. It was strange the things you focused on when you didn't want to face something else.

'Here you go, sweetheart.'

Freddie Sullivan's voice shook Amber back to reality and she turned to look at him, smiling as he handed her a tumbler of gin and tonic, a small slice of lemon bobbing about around the top of the glass. Yeah, it really was strange the things you focused on, the distractions you created.

'You okay?' Freddie asked, frowning slightly, but Amber quickly fixed a smile on her face, leaning forward to kiss her father on the cheek.

'Of course I'm okay. I had a long walk along the Quayside this afternoon and I think all that fresh air has just made me a bit tired, that's all. I'm not used to it.'

'Well, sit yourself down and relax, young lady. I'll leave you and Jim to catch up while I go and finish dinner, if that's alright with you two? I'm sure you've got more than enough to talk about.'

Amber looked over at Jim as he took another sip of his drink, his eyes meeting hers over the rim of his glass. As far as Amber was concerned they had very little left to talk about. But Freddie Sullivan didn't need to know that.

Ryan pushed the pile of chips onto black, sitting back in his chair as the croupier swung the roulette wheel round with a measured flick of her wrist. Folding his arms, he leaned back, aware of the crowd around him, the rest of the Red Star lads cheering him on, the group of women they'd somehow become attached to hanging onto his arms and shoulders, leaning over him as they screamed in overexcited tones at the spinning wheel. In all his years in top-flight football Ryan was only too aware that professional players at his level seemed to attract women like the Pied Piper had attracted rats. Not the best analogy, maybe, but it was true. They'd not been inside the casino two minutes when they'd suddenly become surrounded, and not just by any old women, either. These girls were beautiful, glamorous and on the prowl for a famous face.

He leaned forward again as the roulette wheel started to slow down, that tiny white ball flicking in and out of the red and black compartments, causing everyone around the table to draw breath then exhale loudly as the ball flew out of one colour and into another, setting nerves on edge and the excitement rising. It finally settled in red and Ryan sat back again, running his hands through his hair and closing his eyes for a second, letting the groans of some of the people around him wash over him. He might have been successful in attracting the women tonight, but as far as luck was concerned, it had run out by the time he'd reached the roulette wheel.

'How much is that you've lost tonight, then?' Gary asked, patting Ryan on the shoulder as they left the table and made their way to the bar.

'Too fucking much,' Ryan sighed, shoving his hands in his pockets as a pretty, young blonde girl slipped her arm through his, snuggling in against him as they walked. He looked at her, then at Gary.

'What the eye don't see…' Gary shrugged.

Ryan looked at the girl again. He didn't even know her name. He couldn't even remember whether she'd told him what it was in the first place, because this night was slowly becoming a blur. Too many Jagerbombs in too short a time had dulled his senses somewhat.

'A few of us are going to The Goldman after this,' Gary said, leaning over the bar and waving a fifty pound note in front of the barman to gain his attention.

The Goldman was probably one of the most exclusive city centre hotels the region had to offer. It was a popular haunt for footballers and celebrities, for all sorts of reasons, but the Jagerbombs hadn't dulled Ryan's senses enough for him not to know just why Gary and the lads were heading over there later. You only had to check out the group of women that had latched onto them to see what the rest of the night had in store.

'You gonna join us?' Gary asked, shoving a drink into Ryan's hand. He wasn't even sure what it was, but he'd drink it anyway. It was that kind of night. 'Or are you running off home to the missus?'

Ryan bristled slightly at the way Gary referred to his relationship with Amber. He knew he was probably just jealous in some small way because Ryan had managed to go where Gary had tried and failed. But there was also a part of him that sensed his teammates thought he was just a touch under the thumb. Which he wasn't. Best not to tell them he'd asked her to move in with him, though. Mind you, it wasn't as if that was going to happen anyway, was it? Amber's reaction to his idea hadn't exactly sent her running off to pack her bags, so why shouldn't he enjoy himself tonight? He'd wanted to take their relationship to the next level, she didn't. Her loss.

'Count me in,' Ryan smirked, leaning his elbows on the bar. 'It sounds like too good an invitation to turn down.'

'Good man,' Gary grinned, slapping Ryan on the back. 'You won't regret it. And, like I said before, what Amber doesn't see won't hurt her, will it?'

Ryan looked at the pretty, blonde girl who was still by his side, now sipping delicately on a flute of something sparkling, her gloss-covered lips pouting sexily against the rim of the glass, her heavily made-up eyes looking right at him. She was silently promising him a night he'd never forget, but Ryan had seen it all before. It wouldn't be a night he'd never forget – it'd be a night he'd forget quite easily, because he'd had so many of them they almost all blended into one. The same actions, just different women. But who was he to turn it down when it was quite obviously being handed to him on a plate? So he smiled at her, watching the way her false eyelashes fluttered manically in an attempt to prolong the flirting, and tried to push all thoughts of Amber Sullivan to the back of his mind.

'So, how are you and Ryan getting on, then?' Freddie asked, pouring Amber a brandy to finish off the lovely meal he'd cooked. A meal Amber had more than enjoyed because, as far as cooking was concerned, it wasn't her strong point. But her dad had picked up a lot of tips from her mother during their marriage, which was more than could be said for Amber.

She picked up her brandy glass and took a quick sip, letting the warm liquid slide down her throat, aware that Jim's eyes were on her, waiting for her answer. 'We're getting on fine, thanks.'

She put her glass back down on the table, her fingers almost involuntarily fiddling with the stem. It was a nervous reaction, obviously.

'She's not proving to be too much of a distraction for your star player then, is she?' Freddie laughed, looking over at Jim.

'No,' Jim replied, leaning back in his chair. 'The club's still managing to keep his full and undivided attention.' His eyes were still on Amber, and she didn't miss the loaded content of that reply. 'For now.'

'Good,' Freddie said, beginning to clear away the debris from dinner, stacking a pile of plates together to take back into the kitchen. 'That's the way it should be. Full concentration on the pitch, then he can do what he likes when he gets back home.' He winked at Amber, and she smiled weakly back before looking down at her fingers which were still fiddling with the stem of her glass. 'Amber knows the score, though, don't you, pet?'

'Hmm? Sorry?' Amber asked, quickly looking back up at her dad.

'You know the score, as far as not distracting Ryan is concerned.'

'Yeah. Yeah, of course I do.' She looked over at Jim, who was still staring at her, a slight smile on his far-too-handsome face. 'Anyway, it's not like we're joined at the hip or anything.'

'She might even be a good influence on him,' Freddie went on, picking up the pile of plates and cutlery. 'Might be able to get him to curb that playboy image of his.'

'Jesus, Dad…' Amber sighed, pushing her chair back and going over to the sofa. 'He isn't twelve, and I'm not his bloody mother. I'm sure Ryan's quite capable of doing all the growing up he needs to do all by himself. He doesn't need *my* help.'

Freddie Sullivan looked at his daughter as she threw herself down on the sofa, taking a long sip of her brandy. 'Right. I'll just clear the table, then we'll have a bit of a nightcap, okay?'

Amber looked at her dad, smiling at him. She didn't want him asking any questions as to why she was slightly on edge tonight. She wasn't in the mood to make up some excuse. 'Dad… thanks for tonight. That roast beef was fabulous.'

He smiled back, throwing her another wink. 'You're welcome, kiddo. Keep Jim entertained for a few minutes, will you? While I load the dishwasher. I won't be long.'

Amber watched as he pulled the living room door shut behind him, her stomach flipping over as she heard Jim push his chair back and come over to her, sitting down beside her.

'It's been good, seeing you here. It's like old times, isn't it? All of us here, at your dad's place.'

Amber looked at him, a million emotions clashing inside her head, giving her a headache that now pounded away behind her eyes. 'This isn't like old times, Jim. Old times never *were* like this, were they?'

'They were *exactly* like this, Amber. Me and you, exchanging looks, making each other silent promises when we thought no one was looking…'

Amber shook her head. 'You think that's what's been happening here? Huh? Really? You couldn't be further from the truth.' She put her almost-empty brandy glass down on the side table, tucking her legs up underneath her, looking straight at him as she spoke. 'Ryan asked me to move in with him today.'

Jim's expression changed in an instant, his eyes darkening, his smile disappearing. 'He asked you to move in with him?'

Amber nodded, suddenly realising that she only had one option left open to her if she was to move forward. An opportunity she had to grab with both hands if she had any chance of leaving the past behind. As much as she could, anyway. And this was a start. 'Yeah. And I'm about to say yes.'

Chapter Ten

Amber closed the door of her beautiful little semi-detached home behind her, taking one last look at the pink front door she'd loved so much. She'd never thought she'd leave this place; this house had been her sanctuary, but in a couple of hours someone else would be living here. It wasn't hers to come home to anymore.

'You okay?' Ryan asked, slipping his arm around her shoulders and pulling her close, quickly kissing the top of her head.

'Yeah,' Amber nodded, hugging his waist. 'It's only bricks and mortar, as my dad is so fond of saying. And anyway, I'm only renting it out, aren't I? It's not like I've lost it forever.'

Ryan swung her round into his arms, sliding his hand into the small of her back as he pushed her against him. 'No second thoughts, then?'

She smiled, running her fingers lightly over his bearded chin. 'No. No second thoughts.' Maybe that was a little white lie, but, on the whole, she didn't really regret the decision to move in with Ryan. Although she'd put her foot down about moving into his Quayside apartment. She'd never been a fan of open-plan loft living, so the past couple of weeks had been taken up with house-hunting as she and Ryan had looked for the perfect home. Although that probably made things sound a touch more permanent than they actually were. She still couldn't say that she truly loved him, but she did know that she wanted to be with him. She *needed* to be with him.

They'd finally found a lovely four-bedroom detached house to rent on the outskirts of the city, not that far from her old home. The area was perfect, the house had a good feel about it and it was private enough for Ryan not to be bothered too much. They'd moved in together just over a week ago, and although it was taking some getting used to – neither of them had ever shared a home with a partner before – it was going okay. Things were okay. But it was all going to take time, wasn't it? It was just going to take time.

Ryan smiled at her, kissing her slowly. 'I guess we've both just got to get used to a different routine, huh?'

She rested her forehead against his, her fingers stroking the back of his neck. 'Do you think you can manage that, then, Mr. Football Star?'

He shrugged, grinning at her. 'I'll give it a go.'

She couldn't help laughing, playfully punching his arm. 'Yeah, well, come on.' She let go of him and headed off down the drive towards Ryan's car that was parked on the road outside. 'We'd better make a move. You're due at Tynebridge soon. We don't want you late for this afternoon's match, do we? Especially as you were so kindly given permission to leave the hotel and help me this morning.'

Ryan shoved his hands in his pockets as he followed her to the car. 'Yeah. Strange that, though, isn't it?'

Amber swung round to look at him, sensing something in his voice that didn't sound right. 'Is something wrong, Ryan?'

He shrugged, pressing his key fob to open the doors of his black Jaguar. 'If Jim Allen's so keen to keep us away from distractions before kick-off, then why let one of his players out to help his girlfriend, of all people, on a Saturday morning? It doesn't add up, Amber. Unless the rumours are true.'

Amber frowned. 'Rumours?'

'Some of the lads have heard a few things, that's all,' Ryan said, looking down the quiet, typically suburban street that Amber had called home for so long now.

'And what exactly have they heard?' Amber asked, stopping him before he got into the car.

Ryan sighed, leaning back against the driver's door, folding his arms. 'Just something the boss said.'

'What, Ryan?' Just the mention of Jim Allen made Amber feel uneasy. She didn't know what Ryan was going to tell her, but already she didn't like the sound of it.

He threw his head back, sighing again, closing his eyes for a second or two before looking at Amber. 'There are rumours flying around that the boss is going to drop me this afternoon.'

Amber felt her blood run cold. 'Drop you?'

'Yeah, as in, not play me.'

'I know what it means, Ryan. You're not injured, are you?'

He shook his head, staring straight ahead.

'Then why is he dropping you?' Amber had a good idea why. She just didn't want to believe it was true.

'I don't know, Amber. Alright? And I don't even know if he *is* going to drop me, it's just things the lads have heard, that's all. Can we go now?'

She nodded, standing aside to let him get into the car, taking one last look at her old home before she finally left it behind to carry on with life in her new one. Things really were changing for Amber Sullivan. And she had a feeling not all of those changes were going to run smoothly.

'Shit!' Ryan shouted, throwing his football boots onto the dressing room floor. 'What the fuck…?'

'I want to try a different formation, Ryan…'

'That's bollocks, boss. And you fucking know it,' Ryan hissed, squaring up to Jim Allen.

'You might want to curb that attitude, kiddo,' Jim said, his tone cool and calm. 'Or you could be looking at a longer hiatus than just one game.'

'Fuck!' Ryan yelled, turning away, pressing his hands against the tiled wall, his head down as he tried to get it together. 'I just don't fucking understand...'

'This is the way this game works, Ryan,' Jim went on, leaning back against the table in the centre of the dressing room, his hands in the pockets of his black suit trousers. Jim Allen wasn't one of those tracksuit-wearing managers, he never had been. He always liked to wear the suit; he liked to look smart, exude a certain air of authority. 'You know that. It's nothing personal.'

Ryan closed his eyes, breathing in deep. Something was going on here, something wasn't right and he didn't know what it was exactly, but he'd find out. A club didn't pay all that money for a striker they desperately needed only to drop him before the season was even halfway through. He'd suck it up for now, because he didn't want to do anything that could see him slapped with a ban or a hefty fine he could well do without. But this wasn't the end of it. Far from it.

Ryan turned round and sat down, clasping his hands together between his open knees. 'Okay. Have it your way. Drop me. I'm not the one who's got to answer to the board, am I?'

Jim just smiled, folding his arms. 'They'll understand that I have to do what I think is right...'

'But *is* it the right decision, boss?' Gary chipped in, pulling his red and white strip down over his head. 'I mean, we're woefully lacking up front, which is why the club bought Ryan in the first place...'

Jim threw Gary a look that stopped him in his tracks. 'Keep going, son, and you'll find yourself on that subs bench next to your friend. I'm giving Henderson a chance up front with Yates. I want to see what he's got. This should be an easy game for us. We're not playing one of the big boys so we don't need to go out all-guns-blazing, do we? I can use this opportunity to take a look at a couple of our younger players.' He turned to Ryan again. 'After all, a team can't rely on one person alone, can it?'

Ryan knew Jim wasn't telling him everything. He wasn't stupid. He just didn't get it. Newcastle Red Star had paid a ridiculous amount of money for him because they'd needed him, apparently. Yet all of a sudden Jim Allen thought it was time to drop him in favour of a young and as-yet untried striker who wasn't even done coming through the Red Star Training Academy.

'Colin's got a few things he wants to run through with you all due to this change,' Jim said, shoving his hands back in his pockets as he made to leave the dressing room, looking over at his Head Coach. 'I'll be in my office if you need me, Colin.'

Ryan threw his head back and closed his eyes, sighing heavily. Something wasn't right. But, for once in his life, it was something he couldn't control. And that's what frustrated him the most.

'Did *you* know about this?' Ronnie asked Amber as she joined him in the Players' Lounge for a pre-match drink.

'About what?' Amber asked, throwing herself down onto one of the comfortable red suede sofas that were dotted about the room.

'About Jim Allen putting Ryan on the bench this afternoon.'

Amber looked at Ronnie, pushing a hand through her hair. 'He's done it, then.' It wasn't a question. More a statement of recognition.

Ronnie narrowed his eyes as he looked back at her. 'You *did* know about it?'

Amber sighed. 'Ryan told me he'd overheard rumours that Jim might drop him this afternoon. I just can't believe he's actually done it.'

'Why, though? *Why's* he dropped him?'

'How the hell should *I* know? I'm not the bloody manager, am I? I don't know what goes on in his head. He might have a perfectly good reason for doing this.'

'And you believe that, do you?'

Amber looked at Ronnie for a few seconds, saying nothing. 'No. I don't,' she said, standing up. 'I won't be long.'

'Where are you going? You've only just got here… Amber…?'

But Amber wasn't stopping to chat any longer. She might not be the manager of this club, but even she could see that there was absolutely no reason why Ryan should be dropped from the first team. He wasn't injured, he wasn't serving any match bans; so there was no reason that Amber could see for Jim to have done this. No professional reason, anyway.

'What the hell is going on?' Amber asked, closing the door of Jim's office behind her, not bothering to knock before she barged in, showing no concern that he might have someone in there with him, not even caring that the home dressing room was just opposite and that her raised voice could more than likely be heard if it was quiet in there. It was almost like she had some kind of tunnel vision going on.

'Well, this is a lovely surprise, I have to say,' Jim smiled, getting up from behind his desk and walking over to her.

'Cut the crap, Jim. You've dropped Ryan.'

'Ah. You've seen the team sheet, then.'

'What are you playing at?'

He looked at her with a slightly confused expression. 'Playing at? I'm running a football team, Amber. And you more than anyone should know that that sometimes involves making decisions that aren't always popular.'

'Jesus… That's bullshit, Jim. And you know it. No way should Ryan be dropped from the first team, it's a ridiculous decision…'

'Oh, I see. You think you can do my job better than me, is that it?'

'You're playing games, Jim. And you're doing that in a very dangerous way.'

He laughed, a low, deep laugh as his eyes bored into hers. 'A game? Amber, you're paranoid, sweetheart. Ryan understands why I've had to do this…'

'Ryan will be biting his tongue because he doesn't want to do something that might get him banned, but he won't be happy about it. He *won't* understand why you did this, because he doesn't know the real reason, does he?'

Jim walked back to his desk, leaning against it and folding his arms. 'I've explained it all to him, Amber. Ryan and the rest of the lads know exactly why I'm doing this today. Ryan is an excellent player; he's a great asset to the squad I'm building here at Red Star, but a team can't run on one man alone, can it?'

It was Amber's turn to laugh out loud, pushing a hand through her hair. 'Jesus, you actually sound as though you believe all that shit you're spinning.' She looked at him, right at him, fixing him with a stare that told him she wasn't taking his crap anymore. 'You dropped Ryan to get back at me, didn't you?'

'You flatter yourself, honey.'

'It's all just a touch too coincidental, Jim. Ryan and I move in together, then all of a sudden he starts hearing rumours that you might be dropping him from the first team this afternoon, and what happens next? Come Saturday *he's* on the subs bench, and *you* think you've won.'

'That's quite a serious accusation you're making there, young lady. Are you accusing me of acting in an unprofessional manner?'

'You know the truth, Jim. I should let everyone know what you're doing…'

'But you won't do that, will you? Because if you do, then that means everyone will know exactly what went on between the two of us. And I'm sure you don't want that, do you, Amber?'

'Jesus!' Amber turned away, pushing both hands through her hair. 'Why are you doing this, Jim?' She swung back round to face him. 'Why? I thought you cared about me. I thought…'

'I do. I've always cared about you, Amber. Always.' He walked over to her, gently touching her cheek with the palm of his hand, his eyes looking down into hers. 'I love you.'

'Don't say that. Saying that isn't fair and it hurts, don't you understand? Everything you're doing hurts. If you really loved me, why won't you just let me get on with my life? Why can't you just do that?'

'Because he isn't right for you, Amber. Ryan Fisher isn't right for you. What kind of life is he going to give you?'

Amber stepped away from him, walking back towards the door, her arms folded defensively against her. This was a match Ryan should be playing, not one he'd been deliberately excluded from, and it was all her fault. If she wasn't with him, Jim almost certainly wouldn't be acting this way. He was a manager who had a reputation for being the ultimate professional, but today he was being anything but. And there wasn't a thing she could do about it.

'He won't treat you any better than I did, don't you get that?' Jim said, walking towards her, reaching out and resting his hand lightly on her hip, which Amber quickly removed with a swift slap.

'The difference, though, Jim, is that I know exactly what I'm getting into with Ryan. We're having fun; he's good to be around. He's changed me, and he's changed me for the better. He's made me lose some of that bitterness, that cold exterior. He makes me laugh, he's taught me how to have fun again; but, most importantly, he's made me no promises. And I don't want him to. You said it yourself, Jim. Promises are there to be broken, so I don't ever want to have to deal with promises again. From anyone.'

'So why move in with him if you've got no intention of this relationship going anywhere?'

'I didn't say I had no intention of it going anywhere, did I? I didn't say that. Nobody knows what's going to happen in the future, and I've given up second-guessing anything. I'm taking it one day at a time, and we'll just see where it goes. No promises.'

'You're making a mistake, Amber. Letting Ryan Fisher into your life, it's a mistake.'

She looked up at him, into eyes she hated looking into because they made her feel weak, made her feel as though everything she'd just said had been nothing but a smokescreen to hide behind because she was too scared to admit the truth. 'No, Jim. The only mistake I ever made was letting you touch me again.' She backed away from him, edging closer to the door. She needed to get out of there now, before she did something she was going to regret. 'Please don't take this out on Ryan. Okay?' Amber looked straight at Jim, an almost pleading expression on her face. 'He's got nothing to do with any of this, and he doesn't deserve it, so please, keep him out of it.'

'Are you okay?' Amber asked, leaning back against the bar in a crowded post-match Players' Lounge as Ryan joined her. He had his head down, his hands buried deep in the pockets of his jeans. She could almost describe him as lost, and that wasn't something you could say about Ryan Fisher all that often.

'What do *you* think?' Ryan said, looking straight at her, his voice agitated. 'Not even fucking substituted, Amber. We go one goal down and the fucker doesn't even stick me on as a substitute, I mean, what the fuck is *that* all about?'

Amber turned away from him, taking a long sip of her lager, catching Ronnie's eye from across the other side of the room. He knew as well as she did that Jim Allen was playing a dangerous game here; a game that nobody else was aware of, a game that could ultimately cost him his job if he continued to act recklessly by leaving out players that should obviously be first-team choices. The fans had already made their feelings known both at half-time and again at the end of the match, with boos and jeers all aimed at Jim. His decisions had been wholly unpopular with most people today, and all Amber could hope for was that now he'd made his point, he'd go back to doing his job in the professional manner he was known for. Before he lost all that hard-earned respect he'd built up over the years.

'Red Star managed to pull two goals back, though,' Amber pointed out, immediately wishing she'd kept her mouth shut, because the look Ryan gave her made her stomach turn over, and not in a good way.

'That's not the fucking point, Amber. Jesus…'

She turned away again, leaving him to it and walking over to

Ronnie.

'Is he alright?' Ronnie asked, giving Amber's shoulder a quick squeeze.

'Not really, no. He's pissed off, and who can blame him?'

'He doesn't need to take it out on you, though, does he?'

'If it helps him get it out of his system then I'd prefer it if he used *me* as a sounding board rather than do something stupid that could see him slapped with a three-match ban.'

'It's not your fault, though, is it?'

Amber looked at Ronnie. 'Well, yeah, it is, really. He just doesn't know that.'

'Still no excuse,' Ronnie said, looking over at Ryan who was standing alone at the bar, staring into his pint. 'He should know you don't hit out at the ones you love.'

'He doesn't *love* me, Ronnie,' Amber frowned.

Ronnie just shrugged. 'You know what I mean. You're together, he should realise you're there to support him. There's no need for him to take any of this out on you.'

'Yeah, okay.' Amber was a little taken aback at Ronnie's outburst. He very rarely got agitated about anything much – in his day he'd been one of the most placid and calm players around, which was why he'd been chosen to not only captain his club, but also the international squad on numerous occasions. Even in the midst of all the crap Karen had put him through, Amber had never seen Ronnie get too worked up. He'd always told her it was a waste of energy. 'Have you seen my dad?' she went on, quickly changing the subject.

Ronnie shook his head, then jerked it towards the door just as Freddie Sullivan walked in. His team weren't playing until Monday evening, so he'd finally made it to a Red Star match. Amber loved it when her dad turned up to watch games with her. It reminded her of the old days, when she was just a kid, sitting there in the stands, watching him play and wishing she could do the same. It was where she'd fallen in love with this so-called beautiful game.

It was where she'd fallen in love with Jim Allen.

She shook all thoughts of Jim out of her head as her dad approached, kissing him quickly on the cheek. 'Where've you been?' she asked, turning her head slightly to see if Ryan was still at the bar. He was.

'Talking to Jim,' Freddie replied. 'He's just been hauled in front of the chairman who wants some answers regarding his team choices today.' He looked at his daughter; his tough but beautiful daughter. 'Do *you* have any idea why Jim would do this? I mean, dropping Ryan like that. No one can get their head around it.'

'Why is everyone asking *me*?' Amber sighed. She just wanted to go home now. She wanted to go home and snuggle up on the sofa with some reality TV and a huge bar of chocolate. And maybe a large glass of wine. Yeah, that sounded like a perfect idea. It had been a long and tiring day – beginning with the emotional job of saying goodbye to her little house in Gateshead, and ending with this fiasco. She'd had enough. And she was positive Ryan had, too.

'Well, I'd have thought it was quite obvious why people are asking *you*, Amber,' Freddie said, leaning back against the bright-red painted wall. The whole room was decorated in the colours of Newcastle Red Star – red walls, matching carpet, and dark red sofas and chairs all scattered with red and white cushions – which made for a warm and cosy atmosphere, even when the room was empty. Although the atmosphere Amber was experiencing that afternoon was anything *but* cosy. 'As Ryan's girlfriend… Did *he* have any idea he might be dropped?'

Amber looked at Ronnie who smiled at her, giving her arm a little squeeze. She really didn't want to get into this right now. And certainly not with her father. 'Look, I'm sure Jim had his reasons. I'm going to find Ryan and get out of here, okay? I think we could both do with a quiet night in.'

She kissed both of them quickly on the cheeks and walked back over to the bar, where Ryan was still nursing his pint, although he looked a little less angry than he had done when she'd left him not ten minutes ago. He smiled at her, a smile that gave Amber no choice but to smile back. 'Hey, babe, I'm sorry. I'm sorry for going off on one there – for taking it out on you. I shouldn't have done that.'

'It's okay,' Amber smiled, taking his hand and squeezing it tight.

'No. No, it's *not* okay. None of this was your fault. It's Jim Allen I *should* be having a go at.'

Amber could still see the frustration in his eyes and she leaned forward, kissing him slowly, falling against him as he slid an arm around her waist, kissing her back. He tasted of shower gel and soap, his body still warm from the shower he'd just had and all Amber wanted to do was get him home and make him forget what a bad day it had been. 'Listen, baby, let's put today behind us, okay? Let's go home, order a takeaway and have an early night. What do you say?'

She saw his expression change almost immediately, and she felt her heart sink.

'Amber, babe, I've promised the lads I'll go with them to this new club…'

'Oh. I just… I thought…'

'I know,' Ryan smiled, stroking her red hair out of her eyes. 'I know, and it's a lovely thought, it really is. And if I hadn't prom-ised the lads I'd go out with them I could think of nothing better than a night in with you in that amazing new bed of ours…' He ran his thumb lightly over her cheek as he moved in for another kiss, his open mouth moving gently against hers. 'Wait up for me, okay? Please?'

She looked at him, her stomach sinking even further. 'You're not even coming home to get changed?' She was aware that she'd probably sounded a bit like a nagging wife there, but she was genuinely upset that Saturday night now stretched out ahead of her and she was going to have to spend it alone. She'd really thought he'd be in the mood for nothing other than a quiet night away from all of this. How wrong was *she*?

'We're going for something to eat first. Amber, look, I really am sorry. If I'd known…'

She forced a smile, remembering what she kept telling everyone who questioned her relationship with Ryan – she knew what she was getting into; she knew what he was like. So this shouldn't be a surprise to her. Of course he'd rather forget today by hitting the town. She'd been stupid to think he'd drop that for a night in front of the TV. 'It's alright. I understand. You've got to let off some steam, of course you have.'

He grinned, kissing her quickly. 'So, you'll wait up for me, yeah?'

She folded her arms, nodding as she watched his expression change, his eyes lighting up. Did he really have any idea how dejected she felt right now?

'I'll see you later, then.' He smiled as he started walking backwards away from her. 'You're a star, Amber.'

'You're a mug, more like.'

Amber swung round to see Jim standing beside her, his suit jacket off and his shirtsleeves rolled up. She said nothing. She had nothing left *to* say.

'You really think he wants to be with you, huh? When he can't even be bothered to spend a few hours with you? He'd rather go out with the lads and drink himself into oblivion than be with you. What does that tell you, Amber?'

She looked at him, feeling nothing, just a numbness she couldn't shake. 'You know nothing, Jim. Okay? So just keep out of it.'

He gave a small laugh, a cynical laugh, before looking down at the ground. 'He'll hurt you.' His eyes met hers again, his face serious. 'That's what his type do.'

Amber stared back at him. 'Well, you'd know all about that, Jim. Wouldn't you?'

Chapter Eleven

'What do you want, Max?' Ryan asked, leaning against the door-post, sleepily wiping his eyes.

'You not going to invite me in?'

'I've just got out of bed. Do you know what frigging time it is?'

'Best to catch you early, Ryan. Before you slip under the radar again.'

'What the hell's *that* supposed to mean?' Ryan really didn't need this. He'd already had his sleep interrupted once this morning by Amber getting up at the crack of dawn, and now Max had woken him a second time. He didn't even think it was eight o'clock yet, and considering that he didn't have to be at the training ground until ten, Ryan was pissed off that he'd been forced out of bed.

'It means you've been avoiding my calls, Ryan.' Max pushed past him into the house. 'Is Amber in?'

'No. She's at work,' Ryan sighed, closing the front door, realising he had no choice but to wake up now. Max obviously wasn't going to go away.

'Good. Because I need to talk to you.'

Ryan followed Max into the kitchen, turning the thermostat up as he passed. The North-East winter had kicked in big time now and Ryan was freezing.

'Talk to me about what?' Ryan asked, getting two mugs out of the cupboard.

'You've been out and about a lot lately, haven't you?'

Ryan turned round and leaned back against the counter, folding his arms, fixing his agent with a confused look. 'Huh?'

'New clubs, bars down the Quayside… the casino. The Goldman Hotel.'

Ryan threw his head back and sighed.

'You'd better not be falling back into old habits, Ryan,' Max said, walking over to the French windows at the back of the kitchen that looked out over an impressive walled garden.

'Who are you? My fucking father?'

'No, but I bet he's just as worried about you as I am.'

'Have you spoken to him…?'

'No, of course I haven't. But I'm sure he's concerned, Ryan. As am I.'

'So I've been out a few times with the rest of the lads,' Ryan said, pouring boiling water into the mugs. 'What do you want me to do? Live like a frigging monk?'

'Don't be childish, Ryan.'

He looked at his agent. 'Trust me, okay? I'm not going back there, I promise.'

Max just continued to look at him, his hands in his pockets, an eyebrow arched in surprise. 'You need to keep your head down, Ryan. You need to behave yourself and stop thinking that you can still do whatever you want.'

'What you gonna do, Max? Keep me under fucking house arrest? What the hell *is* all this?'

'You can't afford a repeat performance, Ryan. You got a second chance without anyone actually realising that you'd almost blown the first one. You may not be so lucky again. Picking up the pieces a second time might not be so easy.'

'Jesus Christ…'

'You need to curb the fucking playboy image, okay?' Max said, walking back towards the huge island in the centre of the room.

'You've got a great girl in Amber, so why not try settling down for a change? Because I don't want to hear about you hanging around bars and clubs every chance you get, you got that? And I especially don't want to hear about you frequenting the casino, okay? That's a habit you really cannot afford to go back to. Do you want to start a whole new nightmare, huh? Is that what you want?'

'Of course not,' Ryan sighed, suddenly feeling like a five-year-old who'd been told off for forgetting his homework.

'Then listen to what I'm telling you. We can do this, okay? Without you losing everything. But you need to be sensible. Right, I'm out of here. I've got a meeting with a player from Wearside Spartans in an hour and I need to make a few phone calls first.'

'You not stopping for coffee?' Ryan asked, probably a touch more sarcastically than he'd meant it to come out, but he was pissed off. Big time. Max was treating him like some wayward teenager, who the hell did he think he was?

'No, Ryan,' Max replied, looking him up and down – this cocky kid with the big attitude. Something which had got him into trouble in the past, and could quite easily do so again. 'Remember what I said. Keep your head down and your nose clean and we can do this. I'll see myself out... Oh, and one more thing, Ryan – learn from your mistakes, okay? Don't repeat them.'

Ryan sighed heavily, throwing his head back and staring at the white ceiling. He needed *that* shit first thing in the morning, didn't he?

He took a long sip of hot coffee and reached over for his phone, scrolling down his speed-dial list until he found the numbers he was looking for, pressing the one at the top of the list first. He knew what he *really* needed. And in just a few minutes time he'd have it.

'You're looking very chipper this morning,' Kevin said, perching himself down on the edge of Amber's desk.

'If by that you mean I seem quite cheerful then yes, you'd be right.'

'Good, because you're out on the road today.'

Amber shrugged. 'Fair enough. Where am I going?'

'I want you to get yourself down to Wearside Spartans ground. We've set up an interview with their manager and a few of their summer signings to talk about the fact they're doing really well this season. Ask them what they think of their chances in the forthcoming derby match against Red Star; are they going all-out for that league title, how are the new signings settling in, you know the kind of thing. It'll make a nice piece for the sports bulletin this evening. Alec's packing the van, so just grab your stuff and join him when you're sorted. Okay?'

Amber nodded and smiled at Kevin. 'Okay.' Yeah, she really was in a good mood today, despite the fact Ryan hadn't made things easy for her lately. He was spending more time out with his team-mates than he was at home with her, and although she kept telling herself that she'd known full well what she was getting into when she moved in with him, that excuse was in danger of wearing thin now. But when he *was* at home, that's when Amber knew she'd done the right thing moving in with him. When he wanted to be, he could be the most attentive, the most caring man she'd ever been with. He was smart and funny and handsome – Jesus, he was handsome! There were times when she couldn't keep her hands off him, and those were the times she relished. The times when she felt the happiest she'd felt in a long time. She had this amazing man in her life, and she should be grateful for that. She was having fun, but there were times – those times when Ryan was out and she was home alone – when she wondered whether, at her age, she should be looking for more. She wondered whether her feelings for Ryan were changing, and that scared her, because she'd almost promised herself that wouldn't happen, and if it did then she'd run. She'd get out of there. She couldn't afford to fall into another one-sided relationship with a footballer. She didn't think she could put herself through it. But, right now, she was staying put. Her time with Ryan wasn't over yet. Not by a long shot. The times when she enjoyed herself far outweighed the times when she second-guessed the relationship, and that's all Amber needed for her to be sure she was doing the right thing. For now, at least.

Gathering her things together, she pushed her chair back and slung her bag up onto her shoulder, smiling to herself. Yeah. Things were going okay. It was a whole new adventure for both of them – living together, being together. Being a couple. It was just a whole new adventure, that was all.

Ryan couldn't shake the guilt, and guilt wasn't something he felt all that often. When people described him as selfish, they weren't all that far from the truth, and as far as what he was doing to Amber right now was concerned, he was being incredibly selfish. But she'd never understand. She'd never understand that everything he did he was doing purely because it helped him to forget, and he needed to do that. He needed to forget. She wasn't with him all the time, and he hated sitting around with all those dead hours stretching out in front of him. All that did was make him overthink things. People assumed that being a footballer was all glamour and fun, but there were times when it could be extremely depressing. When training finished – usually around lunchtime – all that lay ahead was a whole afternoon of nothing to do, and that could be soul-destroying at times. So Ryan needed an escape, something to take his mind off it all. Something to make him forget that his life wasn't perfect, no matter how much he tried to pretend it was.

Throwing himself down into a chair by the living room window, he watched as the figure retreating down the drive pulled her coat tighter around her, the cold north-easterly wind blowing her hair over her face. He watched as she opened the door of the cab that had just pulled up, sliding inside. He watched as she pulled the door shut, watched as the cab sped off into the distance, and all the time Ryan knew he was playing a dangerous game. What if that cab driver knew he lived here? All it would take would be for him to mention this afternoon's pick-up and word could spread like wildfire about just what Ryan liked to do on those afternoons when football wasn't there to distract him. But something else was.

He threw his head back and closed his eyes, breathing in deep. He felt anything but calm. Despite what had just happened, it hadn't settled him or made him feel any better about anything. Today it just hadn't had the desired effect. He needed something else, some other kind of rush to give him that shot of excitement he craved. Amber was doing the teatime sports bulletin on News North East so she wasn't going to be home until at least seven-thirty, which meant he still had a good few hours left to kill. And he knew just how he wanted to kill them.

He jumped up out of the chair, suddenly feeling refreshed and invigorated. Just thinking about heading off into town had changed his mood. Running upstairs to the bedroom, he grabbed his jacket, taking out his wallet and checking the cash inside. There was at least three hundred pounds in there, but he might need more. It all depended on how the afternoon went. But if recent luck was anything to go by, yeah, he'd need more. He checked his reflection in the mirror and smiled, running his hands through his dark hair. He had a positive feeling about today. It was going to be a good session, he could sense it. However, it wouldn't hurt to give himself that little extra boost, would it? What harm could it do?

Pulling open the sideboard drawer, he rooted around at the back, finally retrieving the tiny packet he'd hidden from Amber. Taking a credit card out of his wallet, he crouched down beside the small glass table by the door of the en-suite and opened the packet, shaking the white powder onto the surface, cutting it with the card, another momentary flash of guilt sweeping over him that caused him to take a step back and stop what he was doing for a second. If Amber ever found out…

He closed his eyes and tried to put all thoughts of Amber out of his head. He was being careful, and she need never know what he was doing, as long as he kept it discreet and didn't overdo things. Sliding a fifty-pound-note out of his wallet, he rolled it up and leaned back over the table, quickly snorting the white powder, sniffing hard to make sure it reached its destination. He could feel the hit almost immediately. He could feel that warm, calm sensation washing over him, and all of a sudden he felt as though he could take on the world. Any guilt he'd felt a few minutes ago was now a thing of the past. He had nothing to feel guilty for. Ryan Fisher was untouchable. He had the world at his feet, could have anything or anyone he wanted, and right now, he wanted a huge dose of lady luck, and anything else that might come his way would be an added bonus.

Grabbing a towel from the rail in the en-suite, he quickly wiped the glass table down, making sure there was no residue left over, nothing that would make Amber suspicious should she get home before him, before slinging it into the washing basket. All done. And now that he was suitably fired up and raring to go there was nothing stopping Ryan from having another afternoon to remember. Jesus, he loved being a fucking footballer…

'Hello there. We meet again,' Max smiled, approaching Amber as she helped Alec load the equipment back into the van. The interviews had gone well, but now they had to get back to the News North East offices to edit the piece for that evening's programme, so she could do without any distractions. And she really wasn't in the mood for a conversation.

She looked at Max, frowning slightly. 'What can I do for you, Mr…?'

'Max, please. Max Mandell. I'm Ryan's agent.' Max held out his hand, which Amber took, shaking it quickly before letting it go.

'Oh, yeah. I remember you now. So, is there something I can do for you, Max?'

'I just need a quick word, if that's okay?'

'I'm a bit busy, but… Is it something to do with Ryan?'

Max stuck his hands in his pockets and looked at Amber. 'In a way, yeah.'

Amber frowned even more. 'I'm confused.'

'Has Ryan… Have you noticed anything strange in his behaviour lately?'

Amber gave Alec a nod that said she was fine, she'd be along in a minute, before turning back to Max. 'What do you mean, a change? I don't understand. Ryan is a law unto himself at the best of times, so what exactly am I supposed to be looking for here?'

Max kept his hands in his pockets, shuffling his feet slightly as he continued to look at Amber. 'Is he out a lot? And I don't mean anything football-related, I mean, out at night, in the evenings. During the day, even. Without you.'

Amber leaned back against the side of the News North East van, folding her arms. 'Well, yeah. I suppose he is. But it's not like we're joined at the hip, I don't monitor him 24 hours a day, so… why? What's the problem?'

Max arched an eyebrow and Amber felt her skin prickle. Just what was this man trying to say? 'How much has he told you about his past, Amber?'

Amber looked at her watch. 'I thought much of his life had been lived as an open book anyway. Is there anything more to tell?'

Max gave a small laugh, but a laugh that was full of hidden meaning. 'Amber, sweetheart, there's so much about Ryan Fisher that you have no idea about. Believe me.'

She locked eyes with Ryan's agent, not sure whether he was being like this out of spite, or because he felt there were things she needed to know. Either way, she wished he hadn't chosen now to have this conversation. 'Then tell me. What exactly do I need to know?'

'Maybe you should ask him.'

'No, I'm asking *you*. You started this, so I think it's only fair you finish it.'

'He needs pulling into line, Amber. Before it starts happening all over again.'

'Before *what* starts happening all over again? Listen, Mr.

Mandell…'

'Max, please.'

'Max… I'm really busy today, and I don't have time to stand here playing guessing games…'

'Did you know he'd spent time in a rehab clinic?'

Amber took a few seconds to digest what Max had just told her. 'Rehab? I… No, I had no idea. There was… there was no…'

'It was never public knowledge,' Max went on, knowing just what Amber was trying to say. 'Only a handful of people knew and, thankfully, that's the way it still is today.'

'I… I don't understand,' Amber said, slightly stunned. *Should* she be surprised? Given the kind of person Ryan was? 'Was it… was it drugs?'

Max shook his head. 'That wasn't the major problem, no.'

'That wasn't the *major* problem? Max, can you just tell me what's going on here, please?'

'He was young and stupid; he was earning way too much money at far too young an age. He spent too much time in bars and clubs, gambling that money away in casinos every spare minute he had, drinking himself into oblivion. How it didn't affect his football more I'll never know, but he's obviously one hell of a resilient character…'

'What are you trying to say, Max?' Amber asked, suddenly feeling something close to agitation.

'It got too much,' Max went on, looking Amber straight in the eye. 'He lost so much money, and he'd got himself in so deep he didn't know how to get out of the hole he'd dug himself into. He was drinking most days, dabbling in drugs…'

'What kind of drugs?' Amber's voice was quite calm, considering.

'Coke. It got him through the dark days he'd created for himself, or that's what he told the rest of us, anyway. Those of us who knew. I'm just glad it all came to a head before he had the chance to dabble any further, or his career really *would* have been over…' Max looked at Amber again, her face almost passive as she stared back at him. 'I don't know if you remember, Ryan was out with an injury problem a while back. Towards the middle of last season. It kept him out of the game for a good couple of months.'

'I remember,' Amber said quietly, her mind racing now. She really shouldn't be surprised that Max was telling her this. But she was.

'We got him into a clinic in the South West. An isolated, private clinic that helped him tackle the problems he'd got himself into – the gambling, the drinking, the... Look, sweetheart, I'm sorry you have to hear this, but I really thought you should know.'

Amber said nothing. She just continued to stare at Ryan's agent.

'He came out of that clinic a different man. Or, at least, I thought he did. But that's when we made the decision to get him out of London, to try and get him home, where he belonged. His parents were worried about him, *I* was worried about him. He's a fucking amazing player, Amber. A player the likes of which we haven't seen in a long time, but the bloody idiot just couldn't handle everything that came with the status this job afforded him. We had to get him out of there. Out of the way of temptation before...'

'Before it started again,' Amber finished off Max's sentence. 'But it didn't work, did it? Because it's started anyway, hasn't it?'

Max looked briefly down at the ground before meeting Amber's eyes again. 'Yeah. I think it has.'

Amber looked away, squinting into the low winter sun as she stared out at the rows of trees in front of her, the last of their yellow and orange leaves rapidly falling onto the ground below, the sound of traffic speeding by in the distance along the busy motorway. 'And what do you want *me* to do about it?'

'I just needed to see it in your eyes, Amber. And one look at you when I was talking there, you knew, didn't you? You knew that something wasn't right?'

Amber swallowed hard, trying to work out why she felt so upset all of a sudden. This wasn't like her, to feel this way. She'd gone into this relationship knowing Ryan wasn't a saint, knowing they were a long way off declaring undying love. But a little bit of trust would have been nice. If she'd known the truth…

Max sighed, pushing a hand through his mop of dark grey hair. 'Look, I know this isn't really your problem, but… he needs a steadying influence, Amber.'

'Does he sleep with other women?' She wasn't even aware she'd asked that question out loud, but it appeared she had. And she didn't even know why, because she had a feeling she already knew the answer.

'I don't know, Amber.'

'Were women part of the problem before? Before he went into rehab?'

'He's a young, professional footballer, sweetheart. Of course women were part of the problem. He's one of those players who thinks he's something close to God half the time and unfortunately there are women out there who believe him. And what kid of his age is gonna turn them down?'

Amber felt uncharacteristic tears prick the back of her eyes and she had to turn away again. She really was some kind of idiot for getting herself into something that she'd only known would end up this way. Had she learnt nothing from her time with Jim? Why had she ever gone near Ryan in the first place? Because she'd been sucked in by a handsome face and a distraction from Jim, that's why. Why was she even upset? Despite telling Ronnie otherwise, she knew she'd used Ryan just as much as he'd used her, so there was no need for her to be feeling this way. But she couldn't help it.

'He cares about you, Amber.'

'Does he?' She looked at Max again. 'He's obviously not ready for a relationship, though, is he?'

'But it's what he *needs*, and the fact that he asked you to move in with him tells me that somewhere, deep down inside, he knows that. He *knows* that. He's just too bloody stubborn to admit it. Too frightened of everything changing.' Max's face was deadly serious as he spoke. 'I care about that kid. I've looked after him since he was nineteen years old. I've seen him hit the big time and then I've seen what that did to him, but throughout it all he was still one hell of a brilliant footballer. He nearly lost all of that once, Amber, and if you care anything – *anything* – for that lad, then I'm sure you don't want to see that talent go to waste.'

'It's not my problem, though, is it, Max? You said that yourself. I mean, if he doesn't want to help himself – if he's willing to push himself to the brink again and bugger the consequences, how can anyone stop him?'

'All I'm saying, Amber, is if you care even just a little bit about him – and I think you do, I really think you do – if you feel anything for Ryan then, please, realise that he needs you. More than you think he does. Right now, he really, really needs you.'

Ryan closed the door of the hotel room behind him and leaned back against it, watching as the pretty, dark-haired girl with him threw her coat aside and quickly relieved herself of the rest of her clothes before he'd even had a chance to blink. Within seconds she was standing in front of him wearing nothing but black high-heels and a smile that told him she was ready to take him to heaven and back, and all he'd have to do was lie there and enjoy the ride. Jesus, this was one hell of a fucking kick! He'd won big time in the casino, and the adrenalin rush that had given him was still making him feel like he could take on the world. It made him feel like he could do anything, but all he wanted to do right now was lose himself in another round of meaningless sex, no strings attached, no feelings involved.

The image of Amber waking up that morning in bed beside him, looking all sleepy-eyed and beautiful passed briefly through his mind and he closed his eyes for a second, willing that image to go away. All it was doing was confusing him, making him feel things he didn't want to feel. He didn't do complicated, it wasn't him, he couldn't do it. *Yeah, really? So why did you ask her to move in with you, then?* Silencing the argument inside his head,

186

he opened his eyes and smiled at the nameless brunette in front of him. Another girl, another pointless fuck that meant nothing, and they never would.

Ryan Fisher knew what he really wanted; he was just too shit-scared to admit it.

'What do I do, Ronnie?'

'You actually *want* my opinion on this one, then?' Ronnie asked as he grabbed a quick drink with Amber in the pub across the road from the News North East building. She'd just finished her evening sports bulletin, but going straight home hadn't been an option. She needed to talk to someone first, and thankfully Ronnie was up north for a few days, providing that perfect shoulder to lean on.

Amber looked at Ronnie, nervously chewing on her thumbnail. 'No. I'm not sure I do now.'

'Why? Because you already know what I'm going to say?'

She couldn't actually say anything to that, because he was right.

'Okay,' Ronnie sighed, sitting back in his seat. 'So, why ask me to come here in the first place, then? If you already know the answer to your own question?'

'Because I need to talk to somebody, Ronnie. And you're my best friend.'

'Yeah, I am, Amber. And it's because I'm your best friend that I'm telling you to back off from Ryan. Don't get involved, kid.'

Amber stared down into her half-drunk glass of non-alcoholic lager. She was driving, so the alcohol kick she really needed was just going to have to wait, for now. 'How can I not be involved, Ronnie? I'm living with the guy.'

'And I still can't quite work out why you made that crazy decision.'

'Because I…' She knew why she'd really moved in with Ryan. He was a perfect distraction from Jim Allen, and she'd thought – stupidly – that by moving in with him maybe something stronger would develop between them, a relationship that would actually mean something. Not the most adult of reasons, but Amber's head was all over the place right now. All rationality had seemingly gone out of the window. 'Because I wanted to be with him. I still do.'

'Even after everything Max told you this afternoon?'

'Yes. Even after everything Max told me. And don't you breathe a word of that to anyone, Ronnie. Promise me.'

'I promise. Although why I should do Ryan Fisher any favours when he seems quite happy to throw his own career away, I don't know.'

'Ronnie. Please.' Amber looked back down into her drink.

'Aren't you even angry?' Ronnie asked. 'That he kept all that from you?'

'It's not like we're married, is it? We never promised total disclosure of our pasts, never said there'd be no secrets…'

'You're living together! For Christ's sake, Amber, what is *wrong* with you? What's happened to that level-headed, sensible woman I used to know?'

'I'm confused, alright?' She looked up at Ronnie, who just stared back at her with an almost incredulous expression on his face. 'I'm confused. Because I *am* angry at him for keeping all of that from me, but at the same time I know that our relationship isn't exactly without complications… Shit!' She threw herself back into her seat, pushing a hand through her dark red hair. 'Sod it, Ronnie; I'm going home to have it out with him. We can't go on like this. We can't…'

'What's the matter?' Ronnie asked, noticing Amber's sudden change of expression. He followed her gaze, rolling his eyes and sighing heavily again. 'What's *he* doing in here?'

'I don't know,' Amber replied, watching as Jim Allen was stopped by a group of eager Newcastle Red Star supporters on his way to the bar.

'Something to do with you?' Ronnie asked, raising an eyebrow.

Amber looked at him, slightly annoyed at the way he was talking to her. Like she was some wayward teenager who needed bringing into line. 'No, Ronnie, it is *not* something to do with me. I have as much of an idea as to why he's here as you do. He's not someone I'm particularly keen on bumping into. He's a complication I can do without, believe me.'

Ronnie leaned forward, resting his elbows on the table as he stared straight at her. 'You've put Jim Allen to the back of your mind, then, have you? All those years of feeling the way you did about him, they're all forgotten now, are they? Just like that?' Amber said nothing, just stared back, giving as good as she was getting. 'You'll be telling me you've fallen in love with Ryan next.'

'And what if I have?' She'd surprised even herself with that totally unexpected comment, and that was something that didn't escape Ronnie's notice.

'You don't really believe that, do you, Amber?'

She sat forward, too, still staring right into Ronnie's eyes. 'Maybe that's been the whole problem all along. Maybe I've always known that these feelings were going to rise to the surface at some point, but I've just been too scared to admit them.'

'You'd be crazy to let him know you feel that way, Amber. I mean that, kiddo. You let Ryan know how you really feel and he'll have you right where he wants you, because don't think for one minute that he'll ever love you back.'

'How do you know that, Ronnie? How can you say that when you've spent no time with him? No real time. Not like I have.'

'What, you mean, like the five minutes he's spent with you lately in between all the nights out and the afternoon disappearing acts?'

'You can be such a bastard when you want to be.'

'Oh, so caring about you is me being a bastard, is it?'

'You know what I mean.'

'No, I'm not altogether sure I do, actually.'

'I'm going home.'

'Amber… wait, come on…'

'I'm going home, Ronnie. I'm tired, and I need to talk to Ryan. Anyway, you'll be late for your date with Anna if you don't leave now. And I like Anna, she's lovely. You need someone like her.'

Anna was Ronnie's new girlfriend – she was one of the PA's who worked over at Red Star's training ground and they'd met at the charity function at Tynebridge a couple of months ago.

'Amber, sweetheart, believe me, this is only because I care about you. Everything I'm doing, everything I say…'

She looked at Ronnie, forcing a smile as she reached out to take his hand, squeezing it gently. 'I know, Ronnie. And I'm really grateful to you for listening to me go on and on about all of this. I'd go crazy if I didn't have you to talk to. But I need to talk to Ryan now, do you understand? To work out just what the hell happens next.'

'Just, be careful, okay?'

She nodded, letting go of his hand. 'Yeah. Okay. See you later, Ronnie. Oh, and say hello to Anna for me.'

She'd just stepped outside when she felt a hand on her arm and she turned to see who it was that was stopping her from heading home. Even though she already knew. It was obvious.

'I'm really not in the mood, Jim.'

'I just need to talk to you, Amber.'

'Now isn't a great time, believe me.'

'Is something wrong?'

She looked into his eyes – those beautiful green eyes that could tell you one thing whilst lying so easily. 'No. Nothing's wrong. It's just been a long day and I want to go home. So, if you don't mind…'

'It looked like you were having a pretty heated conversation with Ronnie White in there.'

'Jim, what are you doing here? You haven't drunk in this pub since you were a player at Red Star, so why the sudden revisit? Are you on some kind of nostalgia trip?'

'I wanted to see you. Kevin said you'd gone here for a quick drink with Ronnie after the show, so…'

'You thought you'd continue to stalk me?'

'That's not what I'm doing, Amber. But you won't give me

the chance to talk to you, to let you know how I really feel, how much I've changed…'

'You don't change, Jim. None of you do.'

Jim frowned, letting go of Amber's arm. 'Has something happened between you and Ryan?'

Amber quickly changed her expression. The last thing she wanted was Jim knowing anything about the trouble Ryan might be getting himself into. Although, as his manager, didn't he have every right to know just what his star striker might be getting up to? 'Ryan and I are fine. We're just fine.'

'You sure about that? Because you don't look happy, Amber. You really don't look happy.'

'It's none of your business, Jim.'

'Are you hungry?'

She looked at him, a feeling of complete numbness taking over. And, yes, she *was* hungry, as it happened. She hadn't actually eaten anything all day, except for a quickly consumed cereal bar at around eleven-thirty.

'I know a great little restaurant round the corner from here,' Jim smiled. 'All I'm asking is that you listen to me, Amber. That's all.'

Amber felt her shoulders sag, and although it probably wasn't the most sensible decision she'd made that day, she didn't really have the energy to face Ryan just yet. Not really. And anyway, given what she'd just been told today, there was a good chance that he wasn't even home, so what was the point of her going back to that big empty house just to sit there overthinking everything until he decided to roll in? Decision made. Dinner with Jim it was.

Ryan looked at his watch, the sound of the shower in the en-suite bathroom telling him his companion was now otherwise occupied, and for that he was actually grateful. The sex had been great, while it had lasted, but now it was over he had that familiar feeling of just wanting her to go so he could get his head together. Decide what he was going to do next. Go home, or try his luck back at the casino, see if that winning streak he was on was going to last all day.

He reached for the remote control and flicked on the TV, lying back against the pillows as the screen sprang to life, his fingers hovering over the remote control for a few seconds before banging in the channel number for News North East. And maybe it wasn't exactly wise, given what he'd spent the afternoon doing, but for some reason he really wanted to see her. For some confusing reason that he couldn't explain, he needed to see her. Amber. And there she was, large as life on the screen in front of him with that crazy red hair and that sexy smile and that body that could do things to him that nobody else could. Not even Little-Miss-Brunette in the bathroom. She was years younger than Amber yet she didn't even come close to her in any way.

He watched as Amber read out the sports news, introduced her interviews with some Wearside Spartans players, even talked about Newcastle Red Star, and his stomach turned briefly when she mentioned his name.

'*What the fuck are you doing?*' he whispered under his breath, as though asking himself that question would mean he would come up with a suitable answer. He knew exactly why he was doing what he was doing, and he knew the reason why it would never stop. Until he really wanted it to, and he wasn't sure that he did, just yet.

He heard the shower stop and quickly flicked off the TV as Little-Miss-Brunette came sauntering out of the en-suite, naked and damp and everything Ryan needed right now. No, he wasn't ready yet. He wasn't ready for what he really wanted, but who cared about that when he had the perfect diversion right here to take his mind off it all?

'All those years, Amber. All those years and I never stopped thinking about you. Even when I… even when I was…' He looked into her eyes but she quickly looked away, staring down at the table instead. 'It was always you, Amber. And I was just this crazy, stupid guy

192

who should never have done what I did…'

'You got so many things right there, Jim. You should never have touched me in the first place, never encouraged me…'

'You could have pushed me away.'

She looked up sharply. 'I was sixteen years old, Jim. I was a star-struck teenager who'd had her head turned by this handsome footballer, what did you *expect* me to do? *You* were the grown-up. *You* were the one who should have had the willpower to leave me alone. I would've gotten over it; I would've put it down as nothing but some silly teenage crush if you'd just ignored me. If you'd just ignored what you were feeling, too. But you made sure I could never do that.'

'I fell in love with you, Amber.'

'Well, you had a funny way of showing it.'

He looked up at the ceiling for a second, breathing in deeply before exhaling slowly. 'I'm still in love with you now, baby.' His eyes met hers again. 'It's always been you, don't you see that? Okay, maybe the way I went about things wasn't the best…'

Amber couldn't help but let out a tiny snort of derision.

'But I opened those floodgates, Amber. And I've never been able to close them.'

'Then that's something you're just going to have to live with, isn't it?'

He reached out for her hand but she pulled it away. 'I'm not trying to upset you; I'm not trying to interfere with your life, not anymore. It's wrong of me to do that and I'm sorry if my being here is hard for you, but I need you to know that… that you've been such a huge part of my life for so long and I… I can't push that aside. I came back here for you, yes, I'll admit that. But if I can't have you, then I guess I'm just going to have to accept that.'

'Yes. You are.' She clasped her hands together, searching his face so she could see for herself that he was telling the truth. If he was capable of that, because she couldn't be sure. Not after everything that had happened.

'I'm being honest here, Amber.'

'You know that I never really stopped loving you either, don't you? And it is so hard for me to admit that. So hard.'

He looked at her, his eyes never leaving hers.

'But I can't go back there, Jim. I can't. It hurts too much, and as much as I...' She broke off, turning away to focus on the crumpled napkin by the side of her plate.

'As much as you what? As much as you what, Amber?'

'I just... I can't go back, Jim.' She looked at him, and it hurt, of course it did. It hurt because she'd never wanted to have to face him again. She'd put her life back together and all of a sudden everything was in turmoil. But she couldn't really blame Jim for everything. He hadn't forced her into a relationship with Ryan. She'd taken the decision to go there all by herself. Although there was no denying that Jim was probably the reason why she'd thrown herself into it so quickly. 'I'm learning to cope with having you around again because I don't really have a choice, but I'm moving on with my life now. I have to.'

'With Ryan Fisher?'

'With anybody but you.'

It was his turn to look away for a few seconds, and Amber looked down at her hands, realising they were clutching the napkin tightly and she let it go, pushing it aside. She always had been stubborn, even if it didn't always lead her to make the best decisions in life. Was this what she was doing here? Doing something just because she thought she should? And not because she really wanted to.

'Then I... I don't want to lose you as a friend, Amber. If that's... if that's possible.'

She looked back up, her eyes meeting his again. No. She was doing the right thing. 'Promise me there'll be no more taking things out on Ryan.'

Jim's eyes stayed fixed on hers, but he said nothing.

'I mean it, Jim. No dropping him from the first team just because *you* don't like the thought of him being with me.'

He looked down at the table, fiddling with the cutlery, breathing out slowly. 'Okay. That was really unprofessional of me…'

'So you admit you did that purely out of spite, then?'

Jim looked back up, and it was all Amber could do not to reach out and take his hand, hold it tight. It was an urge so overwhelming she had to try really hard to wipe it from her mind. 'I got a bit crazy, Amber. I guess I just needed a bit more time to get my head around the idea of you and him, that's all.'

'And are you used to it now?' she asked, pulling the napkin back in front of her, giving her something to hold onto.

He smiled, his green eyes crinkling up at the edges. Yeah, he was older now. He wasn't the young, fit footballer who'd stolen her heart then broken it into a million tiny pieces, twice over. But he was still one of the most handsome men in the world of football right now. 'I care about you, Amber. I just want you to be happy. So… friends?'

She returned his smile, despite the fact it was the most painful smile she'd ever had to give. 'It won't be easy. But, for the sake of my dad, I think we owe it to him to carry on as normal, don't you?' Whatever 'normal' was. She wasn't entirely sure.

Jim nodded, although it wasn't the answer he'd wanted to hear. He'd wanted her to say she couldn't handle being around him if all they could have was friendship. He'd wanted her to say that she needed him back in her life the way it used to be, but that was never going to happen. And he knew that, deep down inside. But being the eternal optimist could sometimes bring disappointment.

'I've really got to go,' Amber said, checking her watch again. Surely Ryan would be home by now? It was gone ten-thirty, and he had training in the morning.

'You can't stay for one more drink?'

Amber looked at him; her first love, a man she would once – or should that be twice? – have done anything for, no matter what he'd given her in return. Had she finally grown up? Or was she just moving onto another, bigger mistake?

She shook her head, giving him one more smile as she slid her bag up onto her shoulder. 'Thanks, Jim.'

He smiled back at her – that full-on, beautiful smile that had once had the power to floor her completely. And it still could, if she let it. 'I'll see you around, then?'

'Yeah. I'll see you around.'

She almost ran out of the restaurant, not sure whether she was getting away from a situation she couldn't control anymore, or running towards a situation she had yet to grasp any control over at all. All she knew was that she wanted to get home. She wanted to see Ryan, and even then she wasn't entirely sure how she was going to feel when she did.

The short drive home had seemed to take an eternity, even though the roads were quiet and the traffic light. But, finally sliding her key into the lock, she felt nothing but utter relief as she pushed open the front door. Relief that was short-lived as silence and darkness greeted her, letting her know in no uncertain terms that Ryan wasn't home. Disappointment flooded through her, quickly followed by anger and the realisation that she really had been naive to think this could be anything other than what it was – a sham of a relationship that neither of them really wanted.

She'd had enough, and without even taking off her coat, she threw her bag down onto the hall floor and thundered up the stairs at what felt like a hundred miles an hour, running straight into the main bedroom. Sliding a small suitcase out from under their ridiculously huge bed, she flung it open, taking a second to stop and think about what she could throw in there to tide her over until she felt calm enough to come back and pack the rest.

She'd just about filled the case when she heard the front door open and then quickly close. Ryan's voice called out her name from down in the hall, but she didn't answer him. She was busy. Let him find her if he was that desperate to see her.

'Amber! Hey, Amber! Are you upstairs, babe?'

She could hear his voice getting nearer as he climbed the spiral staircase that led to the first floor. And despite her stomach turning with nerves and apprehension, she stuck to her guns, closing the suitcase and zipping it shut, just as Ryan finally found her.

'Going somewhere?' he asked, standing in the doorway looking sexy-as-hell in dark jeans and jacket, his messed-up dark brown hair still giving him that edge that made him all the more attractive, in an ever-so-slightly-dangerous way. But Amber had to ignore that. Giving into that was trouble, and it was quite obvious that this relationship with Ryan was nothing but a repeat performance of everything she'd ever had with Jim. Wasn't it about time she grew out of that crap? She really was better off alone, she had no doubt about that now.

'I'm leaving,' she replied, immediately tearing her eyes away from him as she hauled the case off the bed.

'And going where exactly?' Ryan went on, blocking her exit from the room.

'Are you going to let me past?'

'Not until you start making some sense. What's going on, Amber?'

She felt that earlier anger come surging back with a vengeance – she just wasn't sure whether it was an anger that was directed at Ryan for what he'd done, or directed at herself for being so bloody stupid. Again.

'You lied to me, Ryan.'

He looked genuinely confused, which only angered Amber more.

'Gambling, drinking – a spell in rehab I had no idea about.'

'To be fair, Amber, only about half a dozen people know about that.'

'And are you sleeping with any of *them*? Jesus, Ryan, didn't you think I deserved to know just *some*thing about what happened in your past? Or did you think that by letting me know what you're *really* like it would mean I checked up on you just that little bit more?'

'For fuck's sake, I need *this*, don't I? Five minutes through the fucking door and you're starting on me. What the hell's the matter with you?'

'Where've you been, Ryan?'

He stared at her, letting out a nervous laugh. 'Huh? Sorry, who are you, my fucking mother?'

'Actually, do you know what? I don't care. I've had enough. I really can't go there again…' Amber grabbed her suitcase, dragging it along the floor, but Ryan moved further into the doorway, blocking her exit even more. 'Get out of the way, Ryan.'

'Not until you tell me how I can leave you this morning and everything's okay, but when I get back home you've turned into some kind of weird, crazed psycho. I didn't tell you about the gambling, Amber, because it's in the past, alright? I got into some deep shit, I sorted it out, it's over.'

'It's over,' Amber repeated, looking into those gorgeous, dark blue eyes of his, and wishing she hadn't. 'It's over. Well, that's alright then, isn't it?' That was said with a more-than-slightly-sarcastic tone. 'Okay, so, if it's over you can look me right in the eye and tell me you haven't been to the casino at all since you moved back up north, can you? You can look me in the eye and tell me you haven't snorted any coke, you haven't got blind drunk just because you can. You can look me in the eye and tell me you haven't slept with another woman since you've been with me. You can do that, can you?'

'Yes, I can. Amber…'

'Then you're a fucking liar!' she shouted, pushing past him, but only getting as far as the landing before he pulled the suitcase out of her grasp and swung her back round to face him.

'Listen, Amber, sweetheart, you knew what you were getting into when we got together…'

'Yeah, maybe I did, Ryan. Maybe I did. But I had no idea you were so hell-bent on ruining a bloody good career quite so much as you are right now.'

'Jesus Christ… who've you been talking to? Huh? Because some-one's said something…'

'Max. Max told me. Because he cares about you, you bloody idiot. He doesn't want to see you make the same mistakes twice, but it seems you're either too stupid or too bloody arrogant to listen.'

'I'll fucking kill him…'

'Y'know, rather than channelling that anger into attacking someone who gives a damn about you, maybe you'd be better off using it to try and keep your head above water, before this amazing life you seem to think you have comes crashing down around you.'

'What the…? Why did Max talk to you, Amber? Why did he do that?'

'I've told you, Ryan. Because he cares about you. And he said if I cared about you, too, I'd try and help you nip this shit in the bud before it spirals out of control again. And I thought I could do that, y'know? I really thought I cared enough about you to actually help you…'

Ryan stared at her, an overwhelming feeling of guilt flooding through him. 'Then… then why don't you, Amber? Why *don't* you help me?'

'Because I'm not even sure you want me to.'

Ryan let go of her arm, taking a step back towards the bedroom. He didn't know what to think anymore. He'd asked her to move in with him for a reason, and he knew exactly what that reason was, so why couldn't he just come out and say it? Why couldn't he just admit it to himself? Admit it to her.

'I want you to help me, Amber.'

She sighed heavily, leaning back against the banister and folding her arms, looking up at the ceiling. 'I don't know what to do, Ryan. I don't know if I can deal with this, if I'm the right person…'

Ryan walked towards her, reaching out to gently touch her cheek, stroking it lightly with his thumb. 'I want you to help me, Amber. I *need* you to help me.'

She looked at him, her eyes meeting his. Was he being serious now? Did he really mean *any*thing he said to her? 'You need me, huh?'

'More than you know,' he whispered, his other hand resting on her hip, pulling her closer.

'I should get out of here. If you knew what...' She stopped herself from saying anything else, because the last thing this relationship needed was another complication. Ryan didn't need to know about Jim. And that might smack of double standards – *she* wanted to know all about *his* past but she had no intention of telling him about hers – but that was just the way it needed to be.

'If I knew what, Amber?'

She shook her head, looking down at the ground. 'Nothing. It doesn't matter.'

He tilted her chin up, forcing her to look at him again. 'I got scared, Amber. All of this – me falling back into old habits, the gambling, the... the other women...'

Amber felt her stomach sink like a lead weight the second he'd said that, a sick feeling washing over her. Now she'd actually heard him say it himself, she knew it was true. And even though, in her heart of hearts, she'd suspected it, thinking it was going on and knowing that it definitely was were two completely different things. And the truth hurt. Like a hard and unnecessary kick to the head.

'I got scared, baby,' Ryan went on, stroking her cheek again, his breath warm on her face. 'I've never felt this way before, about anyone, and I got scared. So I... I thought that if I... if I carried on with my old life, went back to the way it used to be I could push those feelings to the back of my mind and pretend they weren't happening.'

'Why did you ask me to move in with you? If that's the way you felt?'

'Because I wanted to be with you, Amber. Believe me, because that is the truth. And when you said no, that kind of pushed me even closer to my old life because I thought you didn't care...'

'Don't blame *me* for this, Ryan.'

'No. No, baby, I'm not. I'm not blaming you. I just felt… Jesus, I don't know, rejected, I suppose.'

'I said yes, didn't I? Eventually.'

He smiled, running his fingers through her dark red hair. 'Yeah. You did. And I'm so sorry for being such a prick, for putting you through this. I just couldn't get my head around the fact that I… that I just wanted to be with one woman, y'know? I couldn't believe it was *me* feeling that way. It didn't feel right. Not at first.'

'I really *should* walk away from this, Ryan.'

He shook his head, pulling her closer, his mouth ever-so-gently brushing over hers in the tiniest of kisses, but it was enough to send a beautiful shiver right up Amber's spine. 'I'm weak, Amber. I'm weak and I'm stupid and I really don't know if I'm strong enough to do this without you. Baby, I need you. I need you, so fucking much.'

She felt tears start to prick the back of her eyes, falling slowly down her cheeks as she stared at him, and suddenly all she saw in front of her was a lost young man. Was he really telling her the truth? Was the reason why he'd taken things too far really just a desperate attempt to block out his true feelings? She had to be so careful here, given what had happened in the past. But her heart was fast beginning to rule her head. 'What are you scared of, Ryan?'

'I'm scared of falling in love,' he whispered, trying desperately to stop tears of his own from escaping. 'But I think it might already have happened.'

Amber shook her head, putting a finger to his lips. 'No. Don't say that, okay?'

'But…'

'Not yet, Ryan. Please. Everyone's emotions are all over the place right now and I don't think either of us is in the right frame of mind to talk about how we really feel. Do you?'

He took her hand, wrapping his fingers around hers, holding onto her tightly. 'Are you… are you still leaving?'

She looked down at their joined hands, closing her eyes for

a second, blinking back more tears. 'I should…' She raised her head slightly to look at him, his eyes almost pleading with her. It was something she hadn't seen in him before, the vulnerable side of Ryan Fisher. Was this who he *really* was? She had no way of knowing that just yet. But maybe she needed to stick around and find out. Maybe it was time to start trusting people again. She couldn't spend her *whole* life being cynical and judgemental. 'I'm not going anywhere.'

She watched him throw his head back and breathe out a huge sigh of relief. Had she done the right thing? Was she taking a huge risk by staying with this man? One chance, she'd said. She would walk away if he hurt her, that's what she'd told him. Yet despite that happening, she was about to give him another chance. A chance she could quite easily live to regret; she was all too aware of that.

'I'll change, Amber. I promise. Maybe this has been the wake-up call I needed, huh?'

She smiled, looking into those incredible deep-blue eyes again, reaching out to touch his face, running her fingertips over his bearded jawline. She may still have feelings for Jim, but she could live with the fact that they were probably always going to be there and she was just going to have to deal with them. What mattered now was that she also had feelings for Ryan, feelings that were growing stronger by the day, and she was scared, too. He didn't have the monopoly on experiencing new feelings. This was more than a touch alien to her, as well as him.

'Let's go to bed,' she whispered, closing her eyes as his mouth lowered down onto hers, kissing her slow and deep, turning her knees to jelly and making her head spin, which she knew was down to him, because she hadn't touched a drop of alcohol all night.

'I really am so sorry, Amber.'

She put a finger to his lips again. 'Stop telling me that, Ryan, and start showing me. Okay? Start showing me.'

Chapter Twelve

Ryan stood in the doorway of the en-suite and looked over at Amber as she slept. For the past few days it had felt as though a weight had been lifted off his shoulders, and despite all the crazy, stupid decisions he'd made since his arrival back in the North East, at least he'd finally made one that was sensible. A little out-of-character, maybe, for him, but he knew it was the right one. Amber brought some stability into his life, and even though he'd tried to fight it at first, he was slowly learning to accept that this was the better choice for him. Yes, there were times when he itched to get back out there and hit the bars and clubs, times when he would have killed to get back to the casino and have just one more go at finding that winning streak, but so far he'd managed to get through those times because he wasn't willing to lose Amber. But his days were sometimes lonely when she wasn't around, and that's when the urges became strongest – when he had nothing to take his mind off things. Did he feel the need for those other 'kicks' he'd revisited over the past few weeks? Hell, yeah! Of course he did! He wasn't a frigging saint, he was only human. But he loved Amber. He loved her. Had he finally faced up to the fact that he was growing up and that settling down might just be a possibility in his life? Well, he was dealing with it. And that was good enough, for now. Amber was right. It was best to take things slowly, one day at a time. There was no rush.

He walked back over to the bed, leaning over to gently brush her dark red hair from her eyes, kissing her slightly open mouth, and that was enough to let him know that it was time to wake her up now. It was time to give her an early alarm call that she might not be expecting. Or she might. After all, they'd spent the best part of the past few days 'getting to know' each other all over again, and he was quite enjoying this brand new start.

Running his hand slowly along the curve of her waist, down over her hip and thigh, snaking round to gently turn her over, he smiled as she smiled, too, keeping her eyes closed.

'That had better be you, Ryan Fisher.'

'Who else would it be?' he asked, leaning over to kiss her neck, sliding his hand round into the small of her back as she arched it, moaning quietly.

'I know what you footballers are like, remember? And I've read the tabloids.'

'You don't want to believe everything you read, Ms. Sullivan.'

She opened her eyes, arching an eyebrow. 'Really?'

'Really,' he grinned, sliding his hand between her legs, causing her to groan out loud as she threw her head back and her arms up above her head.

'Jesus, Ryan, I'm not even awake yet.'

'Yeah, well, I reckoned you might need a bit of help with that.'

She couldn't help but laugh as he buried his head between her breasts. 'Ryan! What are you doing up so early anyway? It's not like you've got to be anywhere before ten-thirty.'

'The boss has got us in at nine this morning. He seems to think we all need some extra work before the big derby match on Sunday.'

Even the tiniest of references to Jim Allen was enough to make Amber's skin prickle, the guilt of a secret she should have told Ryan preying on her mind more than she wanted it to. But what purpose would telling him serve? What if Ryan kicked off and did something stupid? This was his boss they were talking about here, after all. She had no way of knowing how he'd react, and in the long run it altered nothing as far as her relationship with Ryan was concerned. He didn't need to know.

'Should you really be wasting your energy doing this, then?' she smiled, pushing herself up against him as he pushed his way inside her, slowly and carefully, his hands holding tightly onto her hips.

'He can ban sex the day before matches, babe, but he's having no say in when else I can be with you.'

She really wanted to stop thinking about Jim, but it was too late. He was in her head now, and it was Ryan who'd put him there. 'No,' Amber whispered, reaching up to touch his cheek. 'That's purely *our* business.' Closing her eyes, she wrapped her legs around him, holding onto him tight as they made love. Jim Allen was her past, even if he *had* suddenly become an unwelcome part of her present. But she had Ryan now. Her handsome, young footballer. Together they were dealing with their own demons, it was just that Ryan couldn't help *her* the way *she* could help *him*. Nobody could. She had to be strong enough to deal with it all on her own.

Lying back against the pillows, Amber kept her eyes closed as Ryan pushed harder into her, his mouth kissing her breasts, his fingers stroking her skin, and she tried desperately to push more thoughts of Jim to the back of her mind. Tried desperately to recognise that it was Ryan making love to her, not Jim. It was Ryan who was holding her in his arms, it was Ryan who was touching her so intimately, his fingers stroking her, helping her reach that beautiful endgame as they both came to a crashing climax together.

She kept her eyes closed as Ryan withdrew and rolled over onto his back. She wanted a few seconds to let that post-sex shiver run its course, feel it slow down and dissipate before she opened her eyes and let reality back in.

There was no doubt about it, Ryan Fisher made her feel alive again. He made her feel young and beautiful and she loved him for that alone. She hadn't really known how much she'd needed someone like him until he'd unexpectedly walked into her world.

And she could have quite easily let what had happened with Jim taint the rest of her life; she could have allowed that experience to prevent her from moving forward, and she'd almost rejected Ryan completely because she'd thought that was the only way to go. The only way to forget. She'd been wrong. What she needed was a life – and Ryan was giving her that. And she was slowly falling for him in a way that both surprised and excited her, although she was still yet to let him know that. And until she was 100% certain of how she was feeling, that was the way it was going to stay.

'You okay?' Ryan asked, his breathing slowly returning to normal.

Amber nodded, keeping her eyes closed. 'Yeah. I'm fine.' She was better than fine, if truth be told. She was way better than fine.

'You've gone quiet.'

'I'm good, Ryan. Nothing's wrong…' She broke off as she felt something unfamiliar happening – his hand slipping inside hers, pulling her closer. Usually he was up and off the bed within seconds, still reluctant to partake in those post-sex cuddles. But today it appeared he'd changed his mind. And it was an action that almost made Amber want to cry. They might actually be getting somewhere with this relationship after all.

'Are you going to let me tell you I love you now?' he asked, stroking her hair as he looked into her eyes. There was something there that he couldn't quite read, but she was bound to still be wary of him, wasn't she? But she was still here, still with him. And he meant every word he said now. He needed her, and yes, he loved her.

Amber gently stroked his cheek, smiling as she snuggled against him. 'I don't think I have much choice, do you?'

He shook his head, winding his arm around her waist, keeping her close, and liking the way it felt – keeping someone this close just seconds after being inside them. It felt good. Because he was finally with someone he wanted to be close to, for longer than the time it took to score a quick fuck. He felt his heart skip a beat, a feeling so uncharacteristically alien to him that it made him catch his breath. 'Come and watch me at the training ground, Amber.'

She had the day off, but she hadn't planned on spending it anywhere near Red Star's training ground. It was hard enough as it was to avoid Jim Allen at the best of times without deliberately putting herself in a position where he could be unnecessarily close.

'They don't allow random visitors to just turn up and watch, Ryan. You know that.'

'You're not some random visitor, though, are you, Amber? You're a friend of the boss's. And anyway, I heard a rumour your dad's gonna be there this afternoon.'

That was news to Amber. 'Is he? He never said anything to me.'

'Yep,' Ryan sighed, reluctantly letting go of her and hauling himself off the bed. 'He's gonna help Colin with some training techniques, apparently. That's why the boss has got us there for most of the day today.'

'Yeah, 'cause you slack-arses are usually done by lunchtime, aren't you? Unlike those of us with *real* jobs.'

He turned round and threw a cushion at her. She giggled and grabbed it, poking her tongue out at him. He pulled a face, which only set Amber off giggling again. Pulling her knees up to her chest as she watched him walk back into the en-suite, his hard, toned and naked body on show, she didn't think she'd ever get tired of looking at him. Could she see a future here? It was impossible to tell. All she knew was that she could quite possibly be falling in love for the first time in a long time, with the kind of man she'd vowed she would never go near again.

She could only hope that history didn't repeat itself.

'Jesus Christ, Amber, you've got the day off, woman! What the hell are you doing in *here*?' Kevin Russell met her with an incredulous expression as he found her rummaging about in the drawers of her desk. 'Are you some kind of masochistic workaholic? Can you really not just chill out and relax?'

She stood up and looked at her producer, a hand on her hip, her lips slightly pursed. 'This is a bit of a pot-calling-the-kettle-black situation, don't you think? I mean, you're hardly Mr. "kick back and forget about everything" yourself, are you?'

'Yes, well, I haven't got myself a younger man to play with, have I?'

Amber couldn't keep the slight smirk off her face. 'I'm glad to hear it, Kevin. Otherwise I'm sure Mrs. Russell would have something to say about that.'

'Yeah, you're funny. Dating footballers seems to have given you a sense of humour all of a sudden. You should've tried it earlier.'

'I'm not dating *footballers*, Kevin. I'm dating *a* footballer. Just the one. And that's draining enough…'

'Yes, thank you, can I stop you there before we stray into "*too much information*" territory? I'll ask you again, what are you doing here?'

'I was just getting my Dictaphone, if you must know.'

'Why? You got something planned I don't know about? Is the ever-surprising Ryan Fisher about to spill something of interest that might be useful to us?'

'I'm off to Red Star's training ground.'

Kevin raised both eyebrows in an expression of utter surprise. 'Really? Have you been invited? I mean, I know you're sleeping with their star striker, but I wasn't aware that granted you carte blanche to accompany him to work every day.'

'I'm going with my dad.'

'Your dad?'

'Yeah. Y'know, that ex-footballer who used to play for Newcastle Red Star, he was quite famous back in the 1970s…'

'Jesus. When did *you* turn into a comedian? What's your dad doing over there today?'

Amber shrugged. 'He's helping Colin with some training sessions, apparently. Although the first I heard about it was this morning, when Ryan told me. So when Ryan asked me to go and watch him train, well, I've got nothing else planned, so I might as well go and spend my day off eyeing up sexy, young footballers.'

Kevin narrowed his eyes and stared at her.

'Christ, Kevin, come on,' Amber laughed. 'I haven't suddenly turned into some sex-crazed cougar. I'm joking. But I *am* going to watch Ryan.'

'So what's with the Dictaphone then?'

'Well, I'm a reporter by nature, aren't I? I should always be prepared for a story, no matter where I am. Especially with the derby match against Wearside Spartans coming up on Sunday.'

'I've trained you well,' Kevin grinned, giving her a pat on the shoulder before turning on his heel and heading back towards his office. 'Now, get out of here.'

Amber leaned back against her desk, smiling to herself as she looked out of the window at the view of the city stretching out ahead of her. Usually, once she was here at her desk, she'd find any reason to stay, any reason to lose herself in a pile of work, whether it needed doing or not, because she'd never had all that much else to do. Her career had been her priority for so long, but suddenly things were changing. Okay, so she didn't really need the Dictaphone, and she'd only come into the office to make sure there was nothing that needed any urgent attention, but nobody said the habit was going to be an easy one to break. She just knew that, now she was here, she couldn't wait to get away. She couldn't wait to go and see Ryan. She really couldn't wait.

'You've changed, mate,' Gary said, throwing the ball at Ryan, the cold December wind whipping around the exposed pitch, but none of the lads were feeling it. They were way too busy getting stuck into the various training sessions Colin Bailey – Red Star's Head Coach – had set up for them. And he was leaving no stone unturned in preparation for the upcoming derby match on Sunday. They were being worked harder than they'd ever been worked before.

'Changed, how?' Ryan asked, kicking the ball at goal, watching as it hit the back of the net, sending Rob Howard, their first-team goalkeeper, in the complete opposite direction. 'Got ya there, Rob, mate,' Ryan grinned, returning the good-natured but impolite hand gesture that Rob had given him.

'Enough of that, you lot!' Colin shouted over from the sidelines. 'You're supposed to be practising penalties, this isn't a fucking playground. Let's have some concentration, okay?'

'You're no frigging fun anymore,' Gary replied, holding up a hand in apology to their Glaswegian coach. 'I thought I'd found my partner-in-crime when you joined the club, I mean, your reputation went before you, didn't it?'

'People *do* change, Gary.'

'Yeah, but, overnight? Because that's what it seems like, mate. One minute you're on an all-day bender and the next you're spending cosy nights in and giving us the brush off. For a woman?'

'Amber isn't the reason I've decided not to spend my nights living the footballer-cliché of hanging around bars picking up random women.'

'Yeah? Really? Because that's what it seems like to us, Ryan.' Gary took a shot at goal, his penalty saved by Rob, who just threw him a smug smile. 'Y'know, I'm not saying I wouldn't give a week's wages to go where you go with the lovely Amber, but, come on, mate. We all thought she'd just be a quick shag so you could say you'd been the one to crack the ice-queen, we didn't think you'd be halfway to marriage before Christmas. And talking of the region's sexiest sports reporter…'

Ryan followed Gary's gaze, catching sight of Amber and Freddie Sullivan talking to Colin pitch-side. She was wrapped up against the cold in a waist-length black jacket, skinny jeans and knee-high boots, her dark red hair covered by a beanie hat, and as far as Ryan was concerned she looked as sexy-as-hell. Because *he* knew what she looked like underneath all those layers. He felt his stomach give another one of those uncharacteristic somersaults and he quickly turned away, placing the ball he was holding down on the penalty spot.

'Come on. We're supposed to be training here and I really can't be arsed to face the wrath of Colin today.'

'You don't want to go over and say hello to the newest addition to the world of WAGs?' Gary grinned, indicating Amber at the side of the pitch, who still hadn't looked over in their direction, Ryan had noticed.

'Something tells me she won't be too pleased to hear you call her that,' Ryan muttered, turning his attention back to the task in hand. 'Besides, I'll have plenty of time to talk to her later, won't I?'

'Whatever you say,' Gary shrugged, wincing slightly as Ryan kicked the ball so hard it hammered straight into Rob's chest, almost winding him. 'Jesus, mate, take it easy. What the frig's got into *you*?'

'Your turn,' Ryan said, throwing a ball at Gary and ignoring his comment.

'You talking about penalty kicks there, mate, or are you finally inviting me to have a go on your girlfriend?' Gary smirked, an expression that was quickly wiped off his face as Ryan lunged towards him, grabbing him by his sweatshirt, but Rob immediately threw himself between them, pushing them apart before Ryan had the chance to do anything more than shove his teammate hard in the chest.

'What the fucking hell is going on over here?' Colin Bailey yelled, running onto the pitch. 'Jesus Christ, can I not leave you lot alone for five bloody minutes? Sort it out, whatever it is, and before anyone starts speaking, I don't want to fucking know. Just sort it out, or I'll send the pair of you inside and you can explain to the boss just what the hell you're playing at.'

'That'll be hard, considering he's not even here yet,' Gary said, throwing Ryan a look, one that was quickly returned.

'Less of the smart mouth, Blandford. You're acting like a couple of pre-school kids, so just grow up and get on with things. I'm watching you both.'

Gary directed a mock-salute at Colin's retreating back before walking over to the penalty area, gently nudging the ball back onto its spot with the heel of his boot.

'You need to lighten up again, Ryan.'

'Shut the fuck up and take the penalty, Gary.'

Gary kicked the ball to the left of Rob, and this time it sailed past him, cannoning its way into the back netting of the goal. He turned to look at Ryan, folding his arms as he watched his teammate look briefly over towards Amber. 'You're twenty-six years old, Ryan. You're a professional footballer with one of the biggest clubs in the country, and if that wasn't enough, you're one handsome son-of-a-bitch, too, you bastard! Are you *really* ready to settle down? Huh?'

Ryan looked at his teammate; his best friend here at the club, and he didn't have all that many friends if truth be told. Surely he didn't have to alienate everyone else just to make sure he didn't stray back into everything that was bad for him? What was he? Some fifteen-year-old kid that was easily led? He was an adult. He knew what he had to do now, and he had no intention of returning to anything that could threaten not only his career, but also his relationship with Amber. But that didn't mean to say he had to lock himself away under some kind of house arrest.

Ryan shrugged, leaning back against the goal post.

'You'll be back,' Gary smirked, crouching down to tie his boot-lace before standing back up, looking straight at Ryan. 'I guarantee it.'

'What the hell was *that* all about?' Amber asked as Colin arrived back on the touchline.

'I don't want to know,' he sighed, facing the pitch and folding his arms as he surveyed the Red Star squad at work. 'It doesn't take much to start a kick-off around here, not with this lot. It's like being in charge of a bunch of adolescents at times.'

Amber pulled her collar up, shielding the back of her neck

from the harsh, north-east wind before burying her hands deep in the pockets of her jacket as she looked over at Ryan. He certainly appeared to have the adolescent stance down pat as he leaned against the goalpost, his head down, an expression akin to that of a sulky teenager covering his handsome face. He'd been so cheerful when he'd left for the training ground just a couple of hours ago – what had happened to change all that?

'Jim not here yet, then?'

Her dad's voice broke into her thoughts, and even though she knew this was never going to have been a Jim-free day, she secretly hoped that Colin was going to tell them that he'd changed his mind, that he had things to do over at Tynebridge and he wouldn't be coming to the training ground at all.

'He should be on his way,' Colin replied, and Amber immediately felt her heart sink. 'Should be here any time now.'

'You gonna fill him in on what they've been up to?' Freddie asked, nodding his head in the direction of a now-seemingly reunited Gary Blandford and Ryan Fisher.

'No point,' Colin went on. '*I'm* in charge here, and I can deal with them.' He looked at Freddie, a small smirk playing at the corner of his mouth. 'I like to keep the boss on a need-to-know-basis, if you get my drift.'

Freddie couldn't help but laugh. 'Yeah. I know where you're coming from.'

Amber was slowly beginning to regret turning up at training now. She was freezing cold, Ryan appeared to be acting like an idiot, and her dad and Colin Bailey seemed happy enough to while the time away talking shop and reminiscing over the good-old-days of football. She just wanted to see Ryan and ask him what all that had been about with Gary – although whether he told her the truth or not remained to be seen.

'Speak of the devil…' Colin said.

Amber looked up, frowning slightly, because she really wasn't concentrating on what they were saying at all. 'Huh? Sorry?'

213

'The boss is here,' Colin sighed, pulling his hat down further so it covered his ears.

Amber looked over towards the block of buildings that made up the training ground's offices and indoor facilities, watching as Jim Allen strode over towards them, and she couldn't stop her stomach from flipping over double-time at the sight of him. Dressed in a dark suit and shirt, his eyes shielded from the low winter sun by aviator shades, his mobile phone attached firmly to his ear, he looked every inch the business-savvy football manager that he was. He looked handsome and dangerously sexy, and Amber wished with all her heart that she didn't feel the way she still felt when she looked at him. But she did.

'Everything okay here?' Jim asked, sliding his phone back into his jacket pocket as he approached them.

'Any reason why it shouldn't be?' Colin replied, half-smiling at Jim. 'It's all under control, don't worry.'

Amber wished he wasn't standing so close to her, and she stared straight ahead again, focusing on Ryan as he ran around the pitch, yelling instructions at his teammates. She focused on his strong, toned legs that were now splattered with mud, his heavily tattooed arms, his handsome face as he laughed at something Rob shouted at him. Yeah, *that* little stomach somersault was just for him, she couldn't deny that.

'Everything okay with you and wonder boy over there?' Jim asked, staring straight ahead, too, his eyes still covered by those aviator shades.

'Fine, thanks,' Amber replied. And even though she hadn't really wanted to, she turned to look at him. 'You don't mind me being here, do you? Only, I know how private you like to keep these training sessions sometimes, especially with the derby match coming up.'

'Of course I don't mind you being here,' he smiled, a smile that lit up his entire face, and Amber had to look away briefly again, just to compose herself. 'It's good to see you, Amber. It's always

214

good to see you.'

She pushed her hands deeper into her pockets, unaware for a few seconds that she was clenching her fists, so hard she could feel her fingernails digging into her palms.

'I'm going inside,' she said, turning to walk away, back towards the training ground offices. 'It's freezing out here.'

'You alright?' Freddie asked, frowning slightly as he looked at his daughter.

'I'm fine, Dad.' She looked over at Jim, who held her gaze briefly before looking away again. 'I just need a cup of coffee, that's all.'

'We're off out again tonight,' Gary said, wrapping a towel around himself as he stepped out of the showers, '... seeing as we're all on lockdown at the hotel from Saturday afternoon. Got to have some sort of blow-out before we're confined to barracks. You gonna join us?' He sat down next to Ryan, who was tapping out a text on his mobile phone. 'Something to eat, a few drinks, maybe a club? You up for it?'

Ryan looked at Gary. His immediate reaction was to say yes, he was up for it, he was *more* than up for it. But he couldn't, could he? He'd promised Amber. He'd promised Max. He'd promised his mam and dad. 'I can't, mate.'

'Which is it? "*Can't*" or "*won't*"?' Gary asked, roughly towel-drying his light-brown hair. 'Come on, mate. We know you've got your very own WAG now, and you probably still need a bit of time to wear her in…'

'Jesus, Gary, do you want to try and be a bit more offensive there? I'm beginning to see why she turned you down now.'

'Hey, listen, it looks like I had a lucky escape. If she's the kind of lass that turns you into some kind of stay-at-home bore, then you can keep her. I'll take my Debbie any day. She knows the score.'

'Yeah, thanks for that.'

'A couple of hours, Ryan. That's all we're talking about. A chicken madras down the TyneGate Tandoori, some shots, and a few beers in a couple of bars, maybe a quick visit to the casino, what do you say? There's always some decent talent in there…'

'I'm not *after* any talent, Gary. For Christ's sake…'

'Okay, okay. Hey, listen, if *you're* off-limits then that only means all the more for the rest of us, so don't worry about it. You can occupy yourself at the frigging Blackjack table for all I care, all I know is that I'm on the look-out for a bit of pre-match fun. And I'm sure The Goldman will be quite happy to accommodate us, should we feel the need.'

Ryan sat back, closing his eyes and running a hand through his damp hair.

'What you so scared of, mate?' Gary persisted. 'She hasn't got you on some kind of leash, has she?'

'Fuck off, Gary. Shit!' Ryan sat forward, bowing his head and clasping his hands together between his knees. 'It's not like that, okay? You don't understand…'

'I understand you've suddenly turned into a boring prick.'

'For fuck's sake!' Ryan sighed, sitting back again. 'I'll come, okay? If only to stop you frigging banging on about it.'

'Good man,' Gary grinned, slapping Ryan hard on the shoulder. 'You know you wanted to all along. You've just got to remember how to keep her indoors happy, mate, and you'll have this relationship lark sorted in no time. Take it from one who knows.' He tapped his nose and winked as he got up to retrieve some clean clothes from his locker.

Ryan closed his eyes again. This was all proving to be way harder than he'd ever imagined. Part of him really did just want to stay home with Amber and do all those things normal couples did, whilst another part of him couldn't bear the thought of leaving behind a lifestyle he loved. The fame, the glamour; the women – he'd be lying if he said he could say goodbye to all of that and not regret it. It made him forget all the low times and the bad days that also came with that self-same lifestyle.

'I'm going to see Amber,' Ryan sighed, pulling his t-shirt over his head as he stood up, running his hands through his still-damp dark hair.

'Asking permission, huh?' Gary smirked.

Ryan ignored him. Yes, he knew it was all just dressing room banter, but it was getting to him maybe slightly more than it should do. So it was probably best to get out of there for a while, spend the break they'd been given for lunch with Amber. They weren't supposed to leave the training ground – they still had a couple of hours of training left, with a little bit of help from Amber's dad – but that wasn't a problem. Ryan was sure they could find somewhere quiet, away from prying eyes, to spend a bit of time together. He needed to get her onside, anyway, if he stood any chance of leaving the house that night without some kind of confrontation. Jesus, he felt about fifteen. It wasn't as if he was grounded or anything. He could come and go as he pleased; he didn't need anyone's permission, despite what Gary thought.

'You look as though you've got a lot on your mind.'

Jim Allen's voice caused Ryan to jump. He'd been so deep in thought he hadn't heard him walk up beside him. 'No, I'm… I'm fine. This morning's training was tough going, that's all. I'm a bit tired.'

'Tired? You're young and fit, you shouldn't be tired. I hope this isn't a sign that your love life's beginning to get in the way of your football.'

Ryan looked at his manager through slightly-narrowed eyes. 'No.'

'Well, I hope you're looking after her,' Jim went on, staring straight ahead as they walked together towards the dining room. 'Amber. I hope you're treating her right. She's a very special girl.'

'Know her well, do you?' Ryan asked, suddenly keen to know more about the relationship between his boss and his girlfriend. He knew Jim was a good friend of Amber's dad, he knew he'd been close to the family for a number of years – ever since he'd been a Newcastle Red Star player alongside Freddie Sullivan. But how close was he, really, to Amber?

'I know her well enough to care about how people treat her,' Jim replied, shoving his hands in his pockets as he turned to look at Ryan. 'You're a lucky man to have her in your life. You shouldn't take that for granted.'

What was this? Some kind of lecture? Ryan was slowly getting more pissed off as the day went on. Was everybody out to get him all of a sudden? He was prevented from saying anything else by his phone ringing. It was Max. 'I've got to take this,' Ryan muttered, placing his phone to his ear and walking away from Jim. 'Max. What can I do for you?'

'You behaving yourself?'

'For Christ's sake, what is it with everyone today? I'm at the training ground, Max, what the frig can I get up to here?'

'I wouldn't put anything past you, kiddo. How you fixed for a photo shoot with the club's sponsors next week?'

'Just me? Or is the rest of the team involved, too?'

'Just you. They want you to be part of a new poster campaign – you've got the right look, apparently.'

'What kind of money are we talking about here?'

'I'm in negotiations as we speak, but we're looking at six figures, at least. I just wanted to make sure you were on board. Can I tell them yes? You're not averse to taking your shirt off for a few hundred thousand quid, are you?'

Ryan couldn't help but smile. 'Why not? At least it'll get me out of the house for a few hours.'

'Speaking of which, how are the cosy nights in coming along? I trust you've been a good boy since we last saw each other?'

'I'm not in the mood, Max. I'm having a shit day…'

'And those are the days we need to be aware of, Ryan. Remember that. Don't let them get to you, kiddo. Fight it. You can do it; I've got faith in you.'

Ryan just wished he had as much faith in himself.

'Are things going okay with you and Ronnie, then?' Amber asked, sitting down on the edge of Anna's desk, picking up a hole-punch and examining it for absolutely no reason whatsoever.

'He's just so lovely,' Anna gushed, leaning forward and resting her elbows on the desk as she stared dreamily ahead of her. 'I can't believe he hasn't already been snapped up.'

'Well, the divorce kind of shook him up a bit, I guess,' Amber said, putting the hole-punch back down and smiling at Anna. With her short dark hair and pretty face, she was just what Ronnie needed. She'd given him a new lease of life and Amber couldn't be happier for them. Ronnie deserved someone special in his life, and she hoped that Anna could be that woman. 'But, I have to say, since meeting you I've never seen him smile quite so much.'

'Really?' Anna gasped, looking at Amber with wide, hopeful eyes. 'Oh God, I'm so sorry, Amber. I must sound like some sort of simpering fan-girl, I mean, it's not like I never mix with footballers, is it? It's just that, well, Ronnie's different. And I can't believe he even looked twice at me.'

'Come on, Anna, you're beautiful! And I'll let you into a little secret here – Ronnie said exactly the same thing to me after your first date.'

'He did?' Anna asked, her eyes wide and hopeful again.

'Yeah,' Amber smiled. 'He did.'

Anna sat back in her chair, clasping her hands over her stomach. 'It's hard, though, I have to admit, him being away from the North East so often. I really miss him when he's not here.'

'Yeah,' Amber sighed, sliding down from the desk. 'Me too. But at least he'll be here over the weekend. He's commentating on Red Star's match against Spartans and, if what he told me was true, he's going to be sticking around for a few days afterwards, too.'

Anna's face broke into a huge smile. 'That's good. He did say he was thinking of taking a few days off after the derby game.'

'He wants to spend some time with you, Anna. He really does.'

'Amber… thanks. For introducing us.'

'My pleasure,' Amber smiled, checking her watch. 'I'm just glad you two hit it off. He deserves someone like you. Someone who really cares about him.'

'And how are things with you and Ryan?' Anna asked, leaning forward again, resting her chin in her hand as she looked at Amber.

'We're ticking along,' Amber replied, wondering if that was really the best description of her and Ryan's relationship. Is that all they were doing? Ticking along? She'd thought they'd moved on from that. Yet that's how she'd just described their state of play. Ticking along. 'We're both having to get used to a whole new routine, y'know? But he *is* kind of gorgeous, and he doesn't always act like the egotistical idiot he's sometimes been labelled as.'

Anna smiled at Amber. She really did have a pretty smile. Amber could well understand why Ronnie had fallen for her. 'Everything's alright, then?'

Amber looked at her. She'd become quite close to Anna since her and Ronnie had become an item, and it had been a long time since Amber had had a close girlfriend she could confide in. Did Anna want to be that kind of friend, though? Amber had always been slightly wary of opening up too much to people in case they didn't really want to get that close.

'You can talk to me, Amber. Really. I mean that.'

Amber looked out of the window, out at the muddy pitch down below, the housing estate in the distance that backed onto the training ground, the grey sky that was casting its murky glow across everything, making it all seem slightly more damp and depressing than it probably was. 'I just can't seem to get a handle on him, Anna,' Amber began, turning back round. 'I mean, everything was fine this morning, when he left to come here. And yet, by the time *I* turn up, he's in the middle of a kick-off with Gary Blandford and his mood seems all edgy and agitated.'

'Have you managed to talk to him yet? Since you got here, I mean?'

Amber shook her head, absentmindedly fiddling with the cuff

of her jacket. 'I haven't had a chance. Jesus, Anna...' Amber sat back down on the desk, sighing heavily again. 'I know I grew up with a dad who was a famous footballer, but he never really went in for that extravagant kind of lifestyle some of them want to lead nowadays. Things were different back then. We were comfortable, well off, but both my mum and dad were very grounded. Very – normal, I suppose. If that's the right word. And now I've suddenly been thrust into a relationship with what I used to consider the worst kind of footballer. And I never wanted to be a WAG, y'know? Ever. I can't mix in those circles; I can't be like those women, although I know I shouldn't tar everybody with the same brush. It's just that, some of the wives and girlfriends who get in that Players' Lounge on a match day really freak me out for some reason. I always feel like I should be running out to get myself a pair of five-inch silver-heeled ankle boots and a French manicure before I come to the match.'

'I know how you feel,' Anna sighed. 'I'm not like that, either. That's why I like Ronnie so much, because he never did subscribe to that kind of lifestyle.'

'But Ryan has,' Amber said, staring out of the window again, watching as her dad and Colin Bailey started setting up rows of cones along the pitch ready for the afternoon's training session. 'And I'm still not sure I'm going to be able to cope with that.'

Anna frowned as she looked at Amber, an expression Amber caught as she turned back around, quickly fixing a smile on her face. She couldn't let anyone know the extent of Ryan's problems, or how confused her feelings really were where this man was concerned.

'I'm just being silly,' she said, still smiling. 'It's been that long since I've been in a serious relationship that I'm letting every tiny detail bother me.'

'It's understandable,' Anna smiled back. 'Especially with Ryan being so high-profile.'

Both of them looked up sharply as the door opened and Jim

Allen walked into the room, and Amber didn't miss the look most of the girls gave him as he walked through the large, open-plan office on his way to his own office at the other end of the floor. They were almost swooning!

He stopped by Anna's desk, smiling at the pretty PA, and Amber couldn't help but notice her blush. Jesus, this guy certainly left an impression wherever he went. And that wasn't always a good thing.

'Amber.' Jim turned his smile in her direction. 'I wasn't expecting to see you up here. I thought you'd be downstairs, with Ryan.'

Amber looked at him, those green eyes boring into hers with an intensity she could well do without. Whether he was aware of the fact or not, what he was doing wasn't fair. Just him being there wasn't fair. But there was nothing she could do about that. 'It's not like you to encourage your players to fraternise with their partners in the middle of a training session,' Amber said, keeping her voice steady and her eyes locked on his.

'Five minutes can't hurt. And you're a sensible girl, aren't you?' Jim's eyes continued to bore right into hers. 'You won't distract him, will you? You know the score… Listen, Amber, seeing as you're here, can I have a quick word? Before you go?'

'Erm… yeah. Okay.'

'In my office, if that's alright?'

Amber looked at him, trying to work out what he was playing at. If he was playing at anything. Did he really just want a word, and if so, what about? And when the hell had she become so paranoid about everything? The second Jim Allen had turned up back on Tyneside, that's when. So shouldn't she be running downstairs to grab every precious second she could with Ryan before he disappeared back onto the training pitch? Instead of putting herself in another situation where she could be left alone with Jim.

When they reached his office, he stood aside to let her through first before following her inside, closing the door behind him. Amber immediately walked over to the huge picture window at the back of the room that looked out onto the main training pitch.

Her dad and Colin were now standing on the touchline with their arms folded, chatting away. They'd no doubt be putting the world of football to rights, if Amber knew her dad.

'A little bird tells me your boyfriend is starting to let his feelings get in the way of his football,' Jim began, leaning back against his desk, folding his arms.

Amber turned around, frowning slightly. 'Colin *told* you? I thought he…'

'No, it wasn't Colin. Colin doesn't tell me anything if he doesn't think I need to know about it.'

'Then… Was it my dad?'

'I saw it, Amber. Just because I wasn't outside at the time it doesn't mean to say things escape my attention. I was up here, in this office. And you can see the view for yourself.'

Amber continued to look at him, the frown still etched on her face. 'You don't know what it was all about, though, do you? I mean, none of us could hear what they were saying to each other, even those of us…'

'I don't think we needed to hear anything to know what it was all about. Honey, I'm around these guys a hell of a lot, I hear snippets of conversations all the time.'

'So? What's that got to do with Ryan?'

'A lot of these guys have made a play for you, haven't they?'

Amber's frown showed no signs of going away. 'Yes, I suppose so, but… they were just trying it on, Jim. You know what they're like. A female reporter is still a bit of a novelty in the world of football and some of them start acting like overexcited schoolboys when one appears… Are they saying things to him? To Ryan? Are they winding him up?'

'What do *you* think?' Jim replied, walking over to her.

'Jesus,' Amber sighed, throwing her head back. No wonder Ryan was acting like that. His mood was delicate enough as it was, with everything that was going on, so it was obvious the slightest thing was going to set him off. And he really didn't need that. 'I'd better go see him.'

'Amber, hang on…' Jim said, turning to grab her hand as she walked away towards the door. 'Can I…?'

'Can you, what?' she asked, pulling her hand away, but not before she'd left it there for a couple of seconds longer than she should have done.

'Is he right for you, honey?'

She held his gaze for a moment, reaching out to grab the door handle, giving her no excuse to stay alone with him any longer. 'I don't think that's got anything to do with you.'

'If this relationship starts to affect his game…'

'It won't, alright? I'll make sure of that.'

Before he could say anything else, she walked out of his office, closing the door firmly behind her, striding purposefully through the maze of desks and cubicles, almost running down to the dining room, where she hoped Ryan would be.

'Hey, gorgeous!' His voice stopped her just before she reached the dining room and she swung round to see him standing there, leaning back against the wall, his arms folded, a smile all over his incredibly handsome face. 'I've been looking for you.'

She walked over to him, grabbing his t-shirt and pulling him closer, quickly kissing his mouth. He tasted good – a mixture of energy drink and mint. 'Well, it would appear you've found me. You not eating?'

'I'm not hungry,' he replied, sliding his hand up under her jacket, his fingers gently stroking the small of her back.

'You've got to keep your strength up,' Amber whispered, running her hand lightly over his rough, bearded chin, her eyes focusing on his extremely kissable mouth. A mouth she suddenly wanted to feel touching her in places that nobody but him should be seeing.

'It's not food I want,' Ryan said, moving his mouth closer to hers. She could feel him hard against her thigh, and that just made her want him more. A sudden urge she couldn't back down from now. Because it would help block out all thoughts of Jim Allen?

Did it matter? Whatever the reason, she wanted him. Now.

'I'm sure my dad's going to be working you very hard this afternoon.'

'Then it seems only fair that his daughter helps me with the warm-up exercises, don't you think?'

Amber couldn't help smiling, suddenly feeling like a teenager again, about to do something she shouldn't. And she knew all about *that*, didn't she?

'Come on,' he said, taking her hand. 'I know where it's quiet at the minute.'

They ran like a couple of kids sneaking off somewhere they shouldn't, out of the admin block, back outside into the freezing winter sunshine, and Amber clung onto Ryan's hand, quite happy to let him take her wherever he was heading, which turned out to be the now-quiet and empty dressing room back over in the training centre. Kicking the door shut behind him, Ryan didn't even stop to catch his breath, pushing Amber back up against the wall, kissing her hard, his hands pulling at her jacket. She wriggled out of it quickly, throwing it onto the floor, desperate to keep the momentum going, not to let this moment pass them by, even though she was more than aware that anyone could walk in at any minute. Including her father. For once in her life she was letting the excitement and the danger take over and sod the consequences.

'Come with me,' Ryan breathed, taking her hand again as they walked across the dressing room, over to the showers.

'Ryan...' Amber began, knowing where this was heading but still feeling a fleeting rush of panic.

He grinned, pulling off his t-shirt to reveal that hard, toned body that had made women go weak at the knees – including Amber. There was something about those tattooed arms that just did it for her.

'Oh, Jesus,' she groaned, running her fingers over his chest, her heart racing, her breath almost catching in her throat as she looked at him. Young, beautiful, and all hers. What the hell was she so worried about? Yes, this man was driving her crazy but she'd never had so much fun. When she and Jim had been together – if being together was what you could call it – living dangerously had always given her a kick. There was no reason why she couldn't go there again. She'd been an expert at it back then. And what was happening here was one hell of a turn-on.

She closed her eyes and gave in to it all, the feel of his lips on her neck, his hands stripping her naked, giving her shivers the likes of which she hadn't felt since – well, she hadn't felt like this in a long while, and it was way better stress-relief than anything else she'd ever tried.

'This is crazy,' she groaned as his fingers trailed lightly over her breasts, his mouth almost touching hers.

'You up for this, then?' he smiled, although even he must have been totally aware that it was a purely rhetorical question.

'Somebody could walk in here any second, Ryan.'

'Then they're gonna get themselves one hell of a free show, aren't they?'

She felt her stomach flip over a dozen times, making it feel as though every butterfly there could possibly be was now flying loose inside her. The excitement and anticipation was killing her; a beautiful pain, a sick ache that took over everything was all she felt as she stared into his deep-blue eyes. 'So, what are we waiting for?' she smiled, stroking his cheek with her thumb, pressing her lips against his as he reached back to turn on the shower.

Warm jets of water started cascading down over them, soaking their skin, and they had to hold on to each other even tighter as their bodies became wetter, the steam of the shower turning the room hotter until the atmosphere was heightened to impossible levels. Every ounce of frustration and fear and confusion that Amber seemed to feel on a daily basis with Ryan started to just melt away as he pushed her back against the tiled wall, lifting her up and holding onto her tightly as she wrapped her legs around him, groaning loudly as he pushed inside her, every thrust taking her further and further away from the memories of Jim and a past she may, deep down, still want to revisit, but knew she never could. And why would she want to when she had everything she could possibly need right here?

The water continued to rain down on their naked bodies, their cries drowned out by the heavy flow of the shower as the water thudded down onto the floor, trickling away down the drain. Amber had never felt so free, so alive, not since – oh God, why couldn't she stop comparing what was happening here to what had happened back then? Closing her eyes tight shut, she felt another warm shiver shoot right through her, that white-hot tingle slowly creeping its way up her body as Ryan gave one hard, final thrust, his arms keeping her close, keeping her steady until she reached her own climax just seconds later, helped no end by the warm jets of water hitting parts of her body that gave her a feeling so incredibly beautiful she couldn't help but shout out loud. Shit! She'd just had the best sex ever!

She buried her face in Ryan's damp shoulder as he carefully put her back down, one arm staying firmly around her waist while he turned off the shower.

'Now what do we do?' she said, looking up at him, both of them now soaking wet. Something they were going to have to explain. Somehow.

Ryan shrugged, a slight smirk on his face. 'Tell people we've just fucked in the shower?'

She smiled again, kissing him slowly, enjoying the taste of him, the feel of his still-hard body against her. 'Yeah. That'll go down well. Especially as you've got an afternoon of training ahead. And my dad has a zero tolerance level when it comes to slackers.'

'Oh, I'm a slacker now, am I?' he grinned, sliding his hand round from her hip to her inner thigh, stroking it gently with slow, rhythmic motions.

'Jesus, Ryan, come on,' she groaned, wishing with all her heart that they could go again, but they'd got away with it once, who's to say they'd be so lucky a second time? 'We've really got to get ourselves dried off and get back out there.'

'I'd much rather stay here,' he whispered, his fingers now touching her in the most intimate of places, sending those stomach somersaults of hers back into overdrive.

'Yeah, well, so would I but I'd rather not get you into trouble. Come on.' She reluctantly pulled his hand away, hoping they could maybe resume this game later on tonight, before dragging him back out into the main part of the dressing room. 'We'd better get ready and go show our faces.'

Ryan grabbed a towel from one of the benches, pulling her towards him and turning her around so she faced away from him. He started drying her back with the huge white towel, kissing her neck as he moved lower, slowly covering her body with the thick, warm cotton. He was suddenly making towel-drying the sexiest thing she'd ever experienced as he slowly turned her back around to face him, drying her breasts, moving lower, sliding a hand between her legs until she could take no more. It was too much, he'd gone too far now. She had no choice but to push him down onto the nearest bench, straddling him and lowering herself down onto him until he was back inside her. Back where she needed him to be, for now, for fast and furious sex that had no purpose other than to relieve both of them of the last of their pent-up, sexual frustration.

'Jesus Christ, Amber, I fucking love you, baby. I love you so frigging much,' Ryan gasped as she climbed off him, grabbing the towel off the floor to finish drying her damp body before pulling her clothes back on. Quickly, before anything else could happen.

'You love the sex, you mean,' she said, throwing the towel at him, but she had a half-smile on her face as she spoke. 'Now get dried, come on. We'd better get out of here.'

He opened his eyes and looked at her. He was still naked and beautiful and sexy-as-hell, seemingly in no hurry to cover up. Not that Amber minded. That body was hers. If she could keep him in line long enough to make sure he didn't stray again. 'I love *you*, Amber.'

She walked over to him, taking the towel out of his hands and throwing it aside as she straddled him again, but at least this time she was fully clothed. 'How can one man be so good for me yet still be so bad,' she whispered, resting her forehead against his, wishing with all her heart that she could tell him she loved him, too. Because she might, she just wasn't sure that it was enough to be able to say the words. Yet. 'We've really got to go, baby,' she said quietly, running her fingers lightly over his cheek before climbing off him.

Ryan reluctantly stood up, pulling his clothes back on and running a hand through his damp, dark hair. He felt good – now. Amber was like a drug he needed in order to carry on, and he could have as much of her as he wanted without it doing him any harm. So why did he still feel the need to go out tonight and face losing the closeness today had given them?

'What was all that with you and Gary before?' Amber asked, shoving her wet hair up underneath her hat.

'Hmm? Sorry?' Ryan asked, her voice knocking him back to the here and now.

'This morning. You and Gary. What was it all about?'

He'd forgotten all about that. 'It was something and nothing, babe.'

Amber doubted that very much, but he seemed fine now. So maybe it was best not to push it. She was all too aware of the banter that went on between teammates, and it could quite possibly *be* over nothing. She had to remember that Ryan's moods could be a touch up and down at the minute, so it probably took very little to make him edgy. At least she knew what it took to calm him down, and that was a much more pleasant exercise, as far as she was concerned.

She walked over to him, sliding her arms round his neck as she kissed him quickly. 'Well, if they're trying to wind you up, just ignore them. Okay?'

He smiled, kissing her back as he held her against him, not really in the mood to get back out on the training pitch. 'I'm a big boy now, Amber.'

'Yeah, I know,' she smirked, letting him go and walking towards the door. 'See you later, handsome.'

How much later, however, was entirely up to him.

Chapter Thirteen

'He didn't come home,' Amber said, opening the door to let Ronnie through. He immediately pulled her in for a hug and she held onto him for a few seconds, glad he was there. 'I never asked you to come round here,' she went on, pulling away from him and walking off into the living room. He followed her, his hands in his pockets.

'I know. I know you didn't. But Anna said you were upset, said you two had a long chat last night…'

'You should be with *her*, Ronnie. Not me. She's your priority,' Amber said, folding her arms as she looked out of the window of her and Ryan's home. The one he'd wanted her to share with him, yet it was the one he treated more like a hotel at times.

'Amber, sweetheart…'

'Do you know what?' Amber interrupted, turning round, her arms still folded in a defensive manner, her tone irritated. With good reason. 'I really don't need to do this. I shouldn't *have* to do this…'

'Hang on, slow down, will you? Do what? What are you talking about?'

'He's taking the piss, Ronnie. That's what he's doing. I mean, one minute he's fucking my brains out in the dressing room at the training ground, telling me he loves me, and the next I don't see him for frigging dust! One quick text to say he's having a drink with the lads and that was it. Not one more word. His phone's on voicemail, and that'll be because he knows I want to talk to him…'

'Okay. Look, can we back-pedal a bit here? Because you lost me a good few sentences ago. What is it you don't have to do, Amber?'

She leaned back against the windowsill, looking straight at Ronnie, pushing a hand through her messed-up, unbrushed hair. 'Help him, Ronnie. I don't have to help him.'

'No. You don't,' Ronnie sighed. 'But I've already told you that… Amber…?'

She'd been distracted by a car pulling up outside and she watched as Ryan climbed out of it, watched as he leaned in through the driver's window, saying something to whoever was behind the wheel before turning round and quickly running up the driveway.

'Amber…' Ronnie's voice held more than a touch of warning as he watched her expression change, her body language stiffen as Ryan opened the front door, slamming it shut behind him.

'I can't believe him,' she said, but she didn't move from where she was standing.

'Just… take it easy, kiddo. Maybe he has a perfectly good explanation for staying out all night.'

She looked at Ronnie. 'You actually believe that, do you?'

Ronnie pushed a hand through his hair, looking over at the living room door as Ryan walked through it, throwing him a warning look.

'Ronnie? What… what are you doing here?' Ryan asked. Shit! That's all he needed. Although, maybe having Ronnie around would mean Amber wouldn't kick off quite as much as she would have done if she'd been alone.

'Amber was worried about you.'

'I can speak for myself, thanks, Ronnie.'

Ronnie held his hands up, walking over to her and kissing her on the cheek, squeezing her shoulder. 'I'll leave you to it. You gonna be okay?'

'Yeah,' Amber smiled. 'Thanks, Ronnie.'

'Take it easy, alright?' He looked at Ryan, even though he was still talking to Amber. 'Think of the derby match, kiddo. You can kick his arse after that's over and done with.'

Amber smiled again, waiting until Ronnie had left before she looked at Ryan, the smile fading fast. 'A phone call would have been nice.'

'Amber, I'm…'

'Sorry, yeah, of course you are. After the event.' She looked out of the window, at Gary sitting outside in his silver BMW. 'I take it this is just a flying visit?'

'We've got to get to Tynebridge, Amber. You know how it is. We're off to the hotel this afternoon, y'know, in preparation for the derby match tomorrow…'

'Yeah, I know how it all works, Ryan.'

He looked at her, and he literally felt his heart sink. He was one stupid son-of-a-bitch at times. Why couldn't he just have said no to Gary yesterday? Even though it *had* been one hell of a night – a blast, if Ryan was honest. But, in the cold light of day, after the event, had it really been worth it? 'I'm so sorry, baby. I don't know what else to say.'

Amber just looked at him, taking in his tired eyes and unkempt hair, and she hated the way he still looked so handsome, so hot, even in *that* state. But she said nothing. Just looked at him, her arms still folded against her as a barrier to stop him getting too close. She didn't want him close. He'd get close to her again when *she* felt like it. On her terms. Two could play at that game.

'I… We… we went out for something to eat, and the lads, they… they wanted to go on to a couple of bars and I… I…'

'Couldn't say no.' It wasn't a question. 'Did you go to the casino?'

He said nothing, looking away briefly for a couple of seconds, unable to meet her eyes.

'Jesus, Ryan…'

'I need to be a part of this team, Amber. Believe me, baby…'

She held up her hands as she walked away from the window, past

233

him and out into the hall. 'Save it, Ryan. I knew what I was doing when I got involved with someone like you so I really shouldn't be surprised.' She swung round, fixing him with a stare that told him she wanted the truth from the question she was about to ask him. 'Just tell me one thing, Ryan. One thing – and be honest, okay? Did you sleep with anyone last night? Did you pick up some wannabe WAG in a bar and take her back to The Goldman because, yes, I know exactly where you lot go to indulge in your pathetic pulling games. I'm a fucking reporter, for heaven's sake.'

'No. No, I didn't sleep with anyone. I… I was at The Goldman, I'm not… I'm not gonna lie so, yeah, I was there. And there… there *were* women there, but I didn't sleep with anyone, Amber. I didn't.'

'Did you kiss anyone? Did you touch them? Give them something to remember before they toddled off back to their routine lives?'

He shook his head, his eyes staring into hers all the time.

'You better be telling me the fucking truth, Ryan. Because I will walk away from this in a heartbeat if I find out you've been lying. I swear, I will fucking walk away.'

He made an attempt to reach out for her but she stepped backwards.

'I can cope with you not coming home, okay? Because I've been there and I've done that and I've coped with all of that before…' She quickly stopped herself, because what she was talking about were the things she'd had to put up with when she'd been involved with Jim. Her relationship with Ronnie had been completely different, and most people knew that. What they didn't know was that she'd been through *this* shit before.

'Before?' Ryan asked, frowning as he looked at her, an expression of confusion slowly crossing his face. 'I thought you and Ronnie were…?'

'Me and Ronnie were fine. Everything about that relationship was fine…' She fixed him with a glare that she hoped was as cold as she intended it to be. 'I can cope with most things, Ryan. Believe me. But you touch another woman again while we're together and that's it. I'm gone.'

'Amber…'

'I've already packed your bag for the hotel, it's down by the door,' she said as she turned away, running up the stairs.

'Amber! Jesus… Are you gonna be there on Sunday? Amber? Are you gonna be at the match?'

She stopped and turned around, knowing that if she let him leave the house in the middle of an argument then his mind would be on anything but the game. And she didn't want to get the blame for him putting on a crap performance tomorrow afternoon. Especially in an important derby match.

Sucking up everything she was really feeling, she walked back downstairs, sliding her arms around his neck and letting him pull her close. On her terms wasn't going to work the day before a big game. She loved the sport too much to be petty. She needed him to leave the house thinking everything was fine between them, even if it wasn't completely perfect. Far from it.

'I really am sorry, babe,' Ryan whispered, stroking a stray strand of hair from her eyes, a feeling of utter relief sweeping over him. He really hadn't wanted to leave for the hotel with this on his mind.

'Just stop saying that, Ryan. Please.'

'I don't deserve you.'

'No, you don't,' she said, a small smile creeping onto her face. Jesus, how could she be so angry with him yet still want to fuck him so bad? 'Go on. You'd better get going, Gary's waiting.'

Ryan smiled, too, holding her tight and needing her so bad; it was like an ache that wouldn't go away. 'Sneak into the hotel tonight, Amber. Please.'

'You *are* kidding, aren't you? Ryan, they'd go ballistic!'

'Fuck 'em! I want to fuck *you,* and I know it's against all the rules but, Jesus, Amber, I really need you, baby.'

'You should've thought about that last night, then, shouldn't you?'

235

He lowered his mouth down onto hers, kissing her slow and deep and she couldn't pull away. She wanted to, if only to show him she hadn't forgiven him completely, but she didn't. She couldn't. He tasted too good and felt even better.

'Come on, Amber. Be a bad girl and break some rules with me. You know where we're staying. Come on.'

'The day before the big local derby match against Wearside Spartans? Are you crazy, Ryan?'

'Yeah,' he replied, running his fingers lightly down her neck, his touch sending shivers up and down her spine like some demented, out-of-control elevator. 'Living on the edge is right up there on my list of priorities.'

She couldn't help smiling. 'Jim'd kill you if he found out. And he'd probably drop you from the first team, too.'

'Not for this match he wouldn't. It's way too important.'

'Oh, still as cocky as hell I see.' But Amber knew Ryan was right. He'd be punished, for sure, but he probably wouldn't be left out of Sunday's game. There was pride being played for as much as points in this fixture.

'Please, Amber.'

She looked down at the ground for a second before slowly raising her head to stare into his eyes. 'It's not a good idea, Ryan. Really.'

He threw his head back, sighing heavily. 'Jesus! I need you so fucking bad right now. This is killing me.'

Amber let go of him, leaning back against the banister, gently kicking his holdall towards him. 'Well, like I said before, you should have thought about that last night.'

'So what am I supposed to do then, huh? Because I'm almost sure that being sexually frustrated isn't good for a player's game.'

Amber smiled, almost enjoying the fact he was feeling that way. It served him right. 'Oh, I'm sure an intelligent young man like you can think of some way to relieve yourself.' She leaned back against the wall, sliding her hand underneath her shirt, letting her fingers run lightly over her breasts, her eyes on his all the time.

'Shit, Amber. You're getting a kick out of this, aren't you?'

'Call it your punishment,' she said, pulling her hand away and walking towards the front door. 'Now get out, go on. You don't want to be late.'

He leaned over to pick up his holdall, stopping beside her and sliding an arm around her waist, pulling her in for another kiss, enjoying the taste of her, the feel of her lips against his, before she gently pushed him away.

'And can I give you one piece of advice before you go?' Amber smirked, straightening the collar of his leather jacket, feeling ridiculously turned on considering how angry she'd felt not ten minutes ago. Some self-relief was going to be called for the second he was out the door. 'Try and smarten yourself up a bit before Jim sees you. If he catches you looking like that, he's gonna be asking questions. You look like crap.'

'But sexy crap, huh?' Ryan winked.

'Get out of here.'

He stepped outside but turned back around one more time, his face a little more serious. 'I *will* see you tomorrow, won't I?'

She folded her arms, nodding. 'Yeah. You'll see me tomorrow.'

'I… I love you, Amber.'

'Yeah. I know you do, Ryan. I know you do.'

'What are *you* doing here?'

Amber looked up sharply at the sound of Jim's voice, shutting down her laptop and unplugging it from the power source. 'I could ask *you* the same question,' she replied, sliding her computer into its bag. '*I'm* here because I had a meeting with one of the PR guys about the Christmas Charity Dinner the club is throwing next week, and which News North East is covering. He kindly allowed me to use the Press Lounge to do some work while I was here. What's *your* excuse? Because, unless I've mysteriously time-travelled without realising it, shouldn't you be at the hotel with

237

the squad preparing for tomorrow's derby match?'

'They've gone on ahead, with Colin. I had a bit of work to finish off myself before I head over there.'

'Right, well, I'll leave you to it. I've got shopping to do.'

'Amber…' He reached out and grabbed her arm, causing her to turn around and face him.

'Do you want to let me go?'

'I thought we were friends.'

'We are. Can you let go of me, Jim. Please.'

He reluctantly let her go, putting both his hands in his pockets as he looked down at the ground. 'I'm having real trouble handling all of this, Amber.'

'Handling what?' she asked, sliding her bag up onto her shoulder and checking her watch.

He looked at her, fixing her with those green eyes of his and Amber tried hard to stop her stomach from somersaulting, but that familiar dip happened, causing her to step backwards, away from him. 'You and Ryan Fisher. Jesus, have you got any idea how hard it is for me, knowing you're sleeping with my star striker? Imagining what he does to you, what he…'

'You had your chance, Jim. And you chose to blow it. Twice. Look, I really thought we were past all of this…'

He came closer, his hands still in his pockets but his eyes were fixed firmly on hers. 'I'll never be "past it", as you put it. Ever. And yes, I blew it, but I was stupid…'

'That's not my fault.'

He reached out to touch her cheek, running his fingers lightly over her skin, resting them on her lips before slowly pulling his hand away. 'I can't stop thinking about you, Amber.'

'Again, that's not my fault, Jim.' She wished with all her heart that she could tell him she never thought of him at all now, but she'd be lying. He was all she'd thought about for over twenty years. It wasn't that easy to push those feelings aside. Even with a drop-dead gorgeous young footballer by her side. Someone who loved her, or told her he did, anyway. Whether he really meant that was still yet to be discovered.

Jim's eyes searched her face, sending a million tiny shivers shooting through her body, a warning sign that she should walk away from this, before something really stupid happened. Again.

'I've got to go,' she whispered.

He backed away from her, indicating the still-open door of the empty Press Lounge. 'You gonna be here tomorrow?' he asked, his eyes following her as she walked to the door.

'You *know* I'll be here,' Amber replied.

'Supporting your man, huh?'

She gave him one last look before heading out of the Press Lounge, saying nothing as she walked briskly along the corridor, pushing open the double doors that led back out into the main atrium.

It was only when she was finally outside that she stopped to take a breath, leaning back against the wall, closing her eyes for a second as she rummaged about in her bag for that packet of cigarettes she always kept handy for times such as this.

'*I can't do this,*' she whispered to herself, taking a long drag on the cigarette before stubbing it out on the wall beside her, throwing it onto the floor and grinding it into the concrete with her foot. '*Shit!*' She closed her eyes again, taking a deep breath and exhaling deep. Wasn't she supposed to be this hard-faced bitch with the ice-queen reputation who could handle anything? Except her past, it would seem. When it came to that, she was the weakest, most pathetic person she knew. Someone who seemed hell-bent on making one mistake after another with no real chance of changing anything.

Taking her car keys out of her pocket, she looked at them, turning them over and over in her hand before shoving them back in her bag and walking back inside Tynebridge, striding through the main entrance. Tunnel vision had taken over, and it was wrong and so incredibly stupid what she was about to do, because it would give him the upper hand all over again – unless she shifted the goalposts, laid down ground rules. Played the game the way *she* wanted to play it this time.

'I've left something in the Press Lounge,' she smiled at Patrick, the security guard behind the main desk. He just smiled back and got on with studying something on his computer screen.

Pushing through the double doors that led down to the Players' Lounge, dressing rooms and press areas, Amber walked quickly towards Jim's office. If she stopped for even a second, she knew she could change her mind and actually start acting like an adult about this, but that wasn't what she wanted. Not anymore. She wanted some kind of rush, something to make her feel like she was somebody, after Ryan had quite plainly shown her she could be forgotten quite easily at the drop of a hat. A feeling she should be used to, yet still she kept coming back for more.

Reaching Jim's office, she didn't stop to knock, didn't even think of the fact that someone could be in there with him. She didn't really care. But, thankfully, he was alone, standing by the filing cabinet, his back to the door, which she kicked shut behind her, shrugging off her coat and throwing it down on the floor. He turned around, looking at her with a more-than-surprised expression on his face as she walked straight over to him, taking the papers he was holding out of his hands and tossing them aside. Neither of them said anything as she reached out to gently touch his cheek with the palm of her hand, her eyes never leaving his. There was nothing that needed to be said; both of them knew where this was going because it had been heading that way ever since he'd arrived back in the North East. Ever since she'd let him near her again. That's when the touchpaper had been lit.

Closing her eyes, she slid her hand round the back of his neck, moving closer until her body finally touched his, their mouths meeting in a slow, deep kiss, a kiss that confused and scared her; yet it was a kiss that felt so safe, so familiar that she didn't ever want it to stop.

His arms fell around her, pulling her closer against him, their mouths still moving together in that same beautiful rhythm; a kiss that seemed never-ending. His hands stroked her back, his tongue touching hers as that kiss continued to send Amber's heart racing, her skin breaking out in a million goose bumps as a cacophony of warning signals fired off inside her head, one after the other, all of which she ignored. The deepening kiss was silencing them, her fingers now buried in his grey-flecked hair until, finally, she pulled away, but only slightly.

And still neither of them said anything. Her heart was pounding at what felt like a thousand beats a minute as she reached up under her dress, sliding her underwear down until it fell to the floor, kicking it away, their eyes still locked together. Her mouth had gone dry, but as Jim slid a hand between her legs she knew she was anything but dry down there, and she finally broke the stare, closing her eyes as his fingers began working their magic. But not for long. *She* wanted to take control here.

She pushed him back onto the sofa, freeing him within seconds, smiling at the fact he was already hard, already waiting to take her, just as she wanted him to be, and her head started to spin slightly with the anticipation of what was to come. Crouching down in front of him, she took him in her hand, a strange kind of freedom washing over her as she held him there, touching him; an almost warped, liberated feeling. She held the power, or she believed she did anyway, and right now, that was good enough for her.

Leaning forward, she took him in her mouth, just briefly, so briefly he almost didn't have time to register it was happening at all, but the slight flinch she felt from him told her he had. The groan he gave told her he wanted more, but she was playing by *her* rules today.

She let him go, standing up and straddling him, slowly lowering herself down onto him, taking him in her hand once more as she guided him inside, her whole body relaxing the second he was there. It was like a beautiful, warm injection that she'd only now

241

just realised she needed. His hands were on her hips, pushing her down onto him, allowing him to go deeper, and she threw her head back, unable to stop the moan of sheer pleasure from escaping as she reached down and touched herself, helping her on her way to reaching that beautiful finale. And she knew he was watching her do that, knew he was watching her because he couldn't hold back either, and it was the biggest turn-on. Knowing he was watching her touch herself was enough to bring on those waves of white-hot tingles, cause that incredible, beautiful pain to spread right through her and she couldn't help but shout out his name as everything seemed to come crashing to an end all at once. She felt him explode inside her, both of them accepting the quick climax they'd created, but not quietly. The feeling was too raw, too exquisite, to keep those emotions in check, despite where they were. But, oh God, she didn't want him to leave her body. Not yet. She just wanted to stay there, for a little while longer, living this moment, before the reality of what she'd done hit her head-on.

'I knew you'd come back to me,' he whispered, gently stroking the hair from her eyes, the intensity in his own causing what little breath Amber had left to catch in her throat. What it was she really felt for this man she'd probably never really know. It was like a lifelong obsession she just couldn't shake. But whatever it was, she needed it. Needed *him*. Needed what had happened here. Just as much as she needed Ryan.

'Who said anyone was coming back?' She finally managed to speak, her fingers now stroking the back of his neck as his mouth touched hers again, their breathing still shallow and fast, but all Amber was aware of was that he was still inside her, and this kiss they were sharing was making her heart race and her head spin even faster than it had done before. But, as he slowly withdrew, the action of him leaving her body brought with it a realisation that Amber knew had been there all along. Despite what had happened here.

She climbed off him, hurriedly retrieving her underwear, pulling herself back together as he stood up, too, watching her as she smoothed her dress down, ran her fingers through her hair.

'I'm not sorry that happened, Amber.'

She looked at him, confusion pushing itself forward to become the dominant emotion amongst an already jumbled mixture that were crowding her head. 'Neither am I,' she said quietly, and she wasn't. She'd wanted this; she'd been the one to make it happen. If she'd just let it go, left well alone, would he still have been willing to take that step back and let her get on with her life? 'Jim, I... I can't leave Ryan. I need you to know that because... because he needs me.'

'He doesn't need anyone, Amber. Ryan Fisher is a law unto himself.'

'That's why he needs me.' She walked over to him, gently running her fingertips over his slightly open mouth, watching every move they made, her stomach flipping over and over in those never-ending somersaults she was so used to feeling every time she was near this man. 'He's not as strong as he makes out.'

Jim frowned, taking her hand, his fingers intertwining with hers. 'Are we talking about the same Ryan Fisher here?'

Amber said nothing as a feeling of guilt she didn't enjoy, but should have expected, washed over her. 'All I know is, I can't do it anymore. I can't keep on seeing you, being around you, and not be able to touch you or kiss you, I... I can't do it, Jim. So, you've won, again. Because I can't do without you. I just can't do it...'

'Hey, come on. Come on. Nobody's won anything, Amber. Jesus, honey, we can't help the way we feel.'

'Yes, Jim. We *can*. But it's just too bloody hard to walk away this time, when you're right there, in my life, every day. I can't fight it anymore.'

'Then don't.'

'I care about Ryan... No, I really *do* care about him, despite what... despite what I've just let happen.' Her heart did another little dance as she remembered the feel of him in her hand, her mouth; he tasted so good, felt even better. And she needed him. It was as simple as that. 'I know how he comes across, but he's not half as cocky or as arrogant as he makes himself out to be. Not all the time…'

'He's also not the clean-cut, settling-down type either, Amber. And you know that. Honey, I know he was out all Friday night. I know he didn't come home. I overheard Gary talking when they were outside waiting for the coach. And the state of them… You only had to look at them to see the kind of night they'd had.'

Amber looked down at her hand in Jim's, the way his thumb was absentmindedly stroking her fingers, and it felt nice. It felt safe. *She* felt safe. 'I shouldn't be doing this to him. Especially not with you. How's he going to react if he ever finds out?'

'We make sure he never does. That's all we can do, baby. We just have to make sure he never does.'

She looked up into his green eyes. What was she doing? Did she really know? Because this was dangerous. This was only repeating mistakes she'd vowed never to repeat again, but him turning back up here, taking the job at Red Star, it had changed everything. It had turned her well-ordered, compartmentalised life on its head. He was back, and she couldn't ignore him. She couldn't do it. She just wasn't strong enough. She'd waved the white flag and admitted defeat, in spectacular fashion.

'I've really got to go,' she whispered, although she made no attempt to break free of his grip.

'It's all I've ever wanted, Amber. This. You. It's all I've ever wanted.'

She closed her eyes as his mouth lowered down onto hers again, the taste of him so different to Ryan, so familiar. So calming. She could have stayed there in his arms all afternoon, just holding him again, being close to a man she was never going to forget, mainly because she wouldn't let herself. 'He can't know, Jim. So many things could go wrong if he ever finds out about us. So many things…'

'He won't find out, baby. He won't, I promise. I promise.'

She looked at him. 'Don't promise me anything, Jim. Don't... don't do that.' She pulled away from him as the cold reality of what she was getting herself into finally hit home. Yet still she couldn't walk away. Or wouldn't. That was probably the word she *should* be using. 'I'd better leave.'

'I won't hurt you again, Amber. And that's a promise you can't stop me from making.'

Amber looked at him, reaching out to run her fingertips over his rough chin, leaning in for one last kiss, not sure if she could do without the feel of his mouth on hers now, the touch of his fingers on her skin. 'I'll see you tomorrow,' she said, before walking away. Jim Allen was firmly back in her life now. The game was on. And she'd just signed up for one hell of a dangerous replay.

Chapter Fourteen

The atmosphere surrounding Tynebridge on derby day was something else. Completely different to any other match, this one carried with it feelings of heightened passion, a bellyful of pride; an almost tribal air surrounded the stadium as local fans from opposite sides of the river came together in the first of two local derby games to be played out that season.

The city was heaving with football fans and Sunday shoppers, the traffic busier than usual, roads gridlocked in places as people headed towards Tynebridge in time for the 1.30pm lunchtime kick-off. More police than usual lined the streets that led to Red Star's impressive new stadium on the very edge of the city centre, every single one of them on the lookout for any trouble at an event that had been known to throw up a few altercations between opposing fans in the past as heightened feelings and local pride seemed to blank out the fact this was a game of football, not a war zone.

Amber stood outside the main entrance, leaning back against the wall as she finished her cigarette, watching the crowds of supporters as they filed into the ground through the various entrances that lined the outside of the stadium, the noise tenfold on what it usually was on an ordinary match day. She hadn't slept a wink all night; her head had been too full of colliding feelings of guilt for what she was doing to Ryan, and a selfish need to take what she wanted from a man who owed her so much. And if that wasn't enough, Kevin had rung early that morning to ask her if she wouldn't mind taking over from Harry, the reporter who was supposed to be covering the match for Monday's sports bulletin on News North East. He'd suddenly been taken ill and wasn't up to working. Amber had really wanted to say yes, she *did* mind, because she knew Harry, and she knew he was a huge Wearside Spartans fan and she had every suspicion that his 'illness' was nothing more than the result of a Saturday night out on the drink that meant he'd got so wrecked he was in no fit state to come into work but in a perfectly good enough state to prop himself up against the bar in his local in front of the big-screen TV for an afternoon of football and hair-of-the-dog. Yes, she was quite possibly being over-cynical, but the thought of having to interview Jim after the match, to stand there and talk to him as though he was nothing more than the home team's manager and not the man she'd been infatuated with since the age of sixteen wasn't something she was looking forward to.

'If you can just do the post-match interviews, Amber, and I'll sort out everything else. Is that okay?' Amber turned to see Kevin Russell lean back against the wall beside her, offering her another cigarette from his own just-opened packet. 'And I really must give this up,' he said, sliding a cigarette between his lips and lighting it up. 'I'm getting grief from the wife over me high blood pressure.'

'Well, to be fair, Kevin, she's probably got a point,' Amber half-smiled, continuing to look out at the mass of people still making their way into the stadium's various entrances, the noise level growing ever-louder by the second. 'I mean, those things can't be helping, can they?'

'Don't *you* start,' he mumbled, flicking ash onto the ground. 'And anyway, I thought you'd quit. What drove *you* back to this filthy habit?'

'You don't want to know,' she muttered, checking her watch.

'Go on. Get yourself inside. I've just seen Ronnie pop into the

Players' Lounge. Go say hello and chill out for a bit. You look like you've got the weight of the world on your shoulders.'

Amber looked at him, and she was about to say something when she was distracted by the arrival of the Red Star team coach, turning up for what was being billed as the biggest game of the season so far.

She stayed put, watching as the coach doors opened and Jim Allen stepped off first, exchanging a few words with the waiting press and a large group of fans who'd suddenly crowded round the team coach, before making his way up the flight of steps that led to the stadium's main entrance, handsome and charismatic as always, dressed in his trademark dark suit and aviator shades. Ever the dynamic and popular manager. Her stomach jolted like someone had just pushed her insides hard as his eyes briefly met hers, a smile directed solely at her sending her heart racing. And then he was gone.

With him safely inside, she turned her attention back to the team coach. Colin Bailey was busy ushering the players off, most of them with their heads down, hands in pockets, many of them wearing large headphones connected to their MP3 players to block out the obvious outside distractions. But Ryan had his head up, his face almost impassive as he ran up the steps – until he caught sight of her. Then his expression changed, a smile making his handsome features light up and Amber couldn't stop herself from smiling back, even though the wave of guilt which accompanied that smile made her almost breathless for a second. But no words were exchanged as Colin made sure every player was inside the building within seconds. Standard match practice. They were off the coach and into the dressing room within minutes, no speaking to anyone, no distractions of any kind. Jim had a very strict sense of discipline when it came to match days. He was famous for it.

'Everything alright?' Kevin asked, and Amber almost jumped out of her skin. She'd forgotten he was there.

'Yeah. Yeah, of course it is. Why wouldn't it be?'

'I don't know,' Kevin shrugged. 'You just seem a bit, stressed. More than usual, I mean.'

She couldn't help smiling at him. 'I'm just not sleeping all that well at the minute, that's all.'

'Yes, well, that's what you get for shacking up with a toy boy, so don't go looking at me for any sympathy,' Kevin said, a smile playing at the corner of his mouth. 'Go on. Go see Ronnie. I'll come and find you when I need you.'

She made her way back inside, escaping into the corridor that led to the Players' Lounge before the away team coach arrived.

'Hey, you. I was wondering where you were,' Ronnie grinned, pulling her into his arms for a hug, kissing her gently on both cheeks. 'You've been having a sly smoke, haven't you?' he asked, looking at her with a mock-stern expression on his face.

'Don't start. Is Anna not with you?' Amber looked around the small but incredibly busy Players' Lounge, full of family and friends enjoying a few drinks and a catch-up before the match began.

'She'll be here later,' Ronnie replied, leaning back against the bar. 'She had to go see her mum first.'

'Going okay, is it? You and her?' Amber asked, pushing a hand through her loose, dark red hair.

'It's going better than okay,' Ronnie grinned.

Amber grinned back, nudging his arm. 'That's what I like to hear. I knew you two would be good for each other.'

'Alright, so that's me settled in a decent, honest relationship,' Ronnie went on, and Amber could tell from the tone of his voice what was coming next, and she felt her stomach sink, '… now, what about you?'

'I'm working on it,' Amber replied, going over to a table full of tea and coffee flasks and grabbing herself a mug of something hot and strong.

'Working on it?' Ronnie frowned. 'What's *that* supposed to mean?'

'It means me and Ryan quite obviously still have a lot of talking to do,' Amber sighed, joining Ronnie back at the bar.

'Have you…? Oh, hang on, kiddo. I'd better take this,' he said, putting his phone to his ear and escaping out of the crowded and noisy lounge to take the call.

Amber took a sip of coffee and continued to look around the room, seeing a few faces she recognised, and some she'd seen around now and again. But nobody she particularly wanted to go over and talk to.

'You're Ryan Fisher's new girlfriend, aren't you?'

Amber turned to see who the voice beside her belonged to, recognising her as Debbie Hogan, Gary Blandford's fiancée. All long blonde hair and whiter-than-white teeth, kitted out in the latest designer gear, finished off with a pair of crazy-high stiletto boots she looked every inch the stereotypical WAG. All Amber really knew about her was that she was a glamour model and sometimes 'wrote' a column for one of those celebrity gossip magazines. And she also had a history of affairs with various Z-List celebrities, but then, from what Amber could gather, Gary Blandford was hardly Mr. Monogamous himself.

'Yeah. I suppose I am,' Amber replied, bored already by a conversation she didn't really want to have.

'I've always liked Ryan,' Debbie went on, curling a strand of hair round her finger, making sure everybody could see the ridiculously overstated and far-too-large yellow-diamond engagement ring she was wearing. 'I went out with him once, y'know. For a little while, when he played down south.'

'Really,' Amber said. It wasn't a question.

'I was working on a shoot for a men's magazine at the time, before I met Gary… He's really good-looking, isn't he?' Debbie smiled, finally letting go of her hair. 'Ryan, I mean.'

'Yeah. I suppose he is,' Amber replied, not sure if Debbie could feel the apathy in her voice or not.

'How's it going?' Debbie asked, leaning back against the bar beside Amber. Amber just looked at her. Had she done anything that had encouraged this woman to stay and carry on a conversation that she really had neither the time nor the inclination to continue?

'Erm, well, okay, I suppose,' Amber said, staring down into her coffee, swirling the dark liquid round and round in the mug.

'You should really try and keep him away from Gary, y'know.'

Amber looked up sharply, her eyes meeting the slightly over-made-up, grey-blue ones of the woman beside her.

'What… why? What do you mean?'

'You know as well as I do, Amber, that Gary actually has a worse reputation than Ryan. When it comes to women, anyway.'

Amber frowned, putting her mug down on the bar behind her, turning to face Debbie. 'You *know* what he gets up to?'

'Of course I do,' Debbie smiled, and Amber suddenly felt herself warming to this woman who was so far away from the kind of person she'd usually gravitate towards. 'But I love this lifestyle, Amber. Call me shallow, call me some kind of fame-hungry WAG but that's me. That's who I am. And we've got a good life, me and Gary. Good *lives* – because he kind of lives his and I live mine, and that's fine. As long as I can have that status of being a famous footballer's wife, I don't really care what he gets up to.'

Amber was incredibly confused now. She'd never wanted that kind of life, never been drawn to it any way, shape or form and she found it hard to believe that someone could want to be part of that just so they could have the money, status and the kind of fame that it could, sometimes, give you. Didn't love come into it at all? Or was this whole world just one messed-up concoction of men with a God complex and women who just wanted to spend their days shopping and getting their hair done in the most expensive salons possible? That was such a stereotype, and Amber knew that wasn't the way it really was, but sometimes it was hard to forget that people *did* live outside that kind of world.

'We're no Posh and Becks,' Debbie sighed, resuming the hair-curling again. 'But we love each other, in our own funny kind of way.'

'Does he *know* you know what he gets up to?' Amber asked, knowing full well it was probably a rhetorical question.

Debbie nodded. 'I'm hardly innocence personified myself, chick. Maybe it'll all change when we get married, I don't know.'

'Don't you *want* it to change?' Amber was quite fascinated now. In all her years being involved in the world of football she'd never really stopped to get to know any of the women who shared the lives of these famous, top-flight players. So now that she was one of them – like it or not – maybe it was time to stop and listen. Time to make some friends and enter that inner circle. Although the thought of it still made her shudder slightly.

'I don't know,' Debbie said, looking straight into Amber's eyes. 'I really don't know. We're both so used to living our lives the way we do that getting used to something else might be really strange. Does that make sense?'

'No. Not really,' Amber frowned. 'So if you're so used to Gary's behaviour, why should I keep Ryan away from him?'

'Because Ryan's different,' Debbie said. 'When I was with him, I could see that a lot of what he did was nothing but a façade. Something to hide behind. Ryan is also desperate to be liked, Amber. He came into football so young; he was taken away from what he knew and thrown into this whole new life before he'd even left school and I think that meant he never really had the chance to make any real friends. His whole world was football, with no time to be a kid…'

'Did he tell you this?' Amber interrupted, wondering how this woman knew so much about him for somebody who'd only been with him for such a short time.

Debbie nodded again. 'There were days when all he wanted to do was talk. Just sit and talk and get things off his chest, and that's when I could see the real person behind that big-name footballer with an image that he felt he had to keep up. But he never *really* had to do that, did he? Because he had talent. And that should've

252

been enough. But he wanted to be popular, thought it was all part of that image. So he'd throw himself into anything the rest of his teammates did, and that's when the trouble began, I suppose. When he started to become the person he is now.'

'Do you… do you know anything else about him, Debbie? I mean, do you… how far…?' Amber wanted to know if she knew about the gambling, the drugs, the time Ryan had spent in rehab, but how did you even begin to ask a question like that? Because, if she *didn't* know, then asking that question would certainly mean she would now. Amber couldn't risk that.

'He's just your typical footballer, Amber. But he doesn't need to be. I'd really hoped that when he had that injury – y'know, the one that kept him out of action for months last season – I'd hoped that would have given him time to think about his life. Making the move up here was a good decision, but I'm not sure him becoming best friends with Gary was the best idea.'

Amber sussed from that that Debbie had no real idea of the truth behind Ryan's behaviour; she had no idea of how deep his problems ran, and that's the way it needed to stay. But one thing she *had* done was make sure that Amber tried even harder to keep Ryan away from that lifestyle that had almost destroyed him once. He needed to realise that what had happened on Friday – the bars and the drinking and the staying out all night – that couldn't continue. Not if he wanted his career to stay on track. He was only twenty-six. He still had plenty of playing days ahead of him yet.

'Thanks, Debbie.'

Debbie smiled; a warm smile. A friendly smile. 'You should come out with me and the girls sometime, Amber. We can have just as good a time as the boys can, believe me.'

Amber returned her smile, thinking what a surreal experience this had just been, but a very pleasant one. Surprisingly so.

'Will you?' Debbie asked. 'Come out with us sometime, I mean. With me and the girls.'

'Yeah,' Amber replied, still smiling. 'Yeah. I think I'd like that.'

'Great,' Debbie beamed, pulling Amber in for an unexpected hug.

They'd just exchanged phone numbers when Ronnie reappeared, looking at Amber with a surprised expression. 'Erm, sorry, but was that *you* exchanging phone numbers with Debbie Hogan? Queen of the North East WAGs?'

'So?' Amber asked, probably a touch too defensively.

Ronnie shrugged. 'Nothing. It's just that… *you*? A WAG?'

'I've done it before,' she said, looking at him.

'Well, yeah. I suppose you have. You didn't enjoy it, though.'

She smiled, standing on tiptoe to kiss him quickly on the cheek. 'I enjoyed the other perks. Like being with you.'

'Well, who can blame you there?' Ronnie grinned.

'Shouldn't you *be* somewhere?' she asked, still smiling at him. 'You *are* working on this match, aren't you? Are you commentating?'

'No. I'm up in the studio, in front of the cameras. I'm one of the pundits.'

'Oh, you're on TV this afternoon? And you didn't think to have a shave before you left the house?'

Ronnie felt his rough chin, his expression changing. 'Shit! That's because Anna said she liked me with a bit of stubble.'

'Yeah, well, that's enough information on that score, and I have to agree with her, actually. The rough-and-ready look suits you, but on TV you're only going to look as though you couldn't be arsed to get ready.'

'Your honesty is one of your more attractive traits, Amber, I have to say. Right, well, I'd better get off then. See you later? For a post-match drink?'

'Absolutely.'

Ryan sat with his hands clasped between his open knees, his head down, his brain working overtime as what felt like a million different feelings clashed like warring enemies inside his head, causing a blanket of confusion and a lack of concentration he could well do without.

Sometimes he hated this routine of getting to the ground so early – ninety minutes before kick-off was the norm, and today was no exception. That time was used to warm up in the small gym just off the dressing room; sort out any lingering injury problems with the physio; get their heads together. Something he was finding very hard to do today, of all days.

'Everything alright, Ryan?'

He looked up at the sound of Jim Allen's voice. 'I'm fine.'

'You don't look it.'

'I'm fine,' Ryan repeated.

Jim sat down beside him, copying his stance, staring straight ahead. 'I need you focused, son. This is a big game for us and I really don't intend to lose my winning streak just because *you* can't control your love life.'

Ryan kept his eyes on his clasped hands as he spoke. 'My love life is none of your business.'

'Now, you see, I think it is, Ryan. I think it is, when it starts to affect you as a player.'

This time Ryan looked straight at his manager, their eyes locking in a silent battle that only one of them really knew was going on. 'When it comes to me running out onto that pitch, boss… when it comes to me running out on that pitch there will be no other player out there more focused than me. I can assure you of that.'

Jim said nothing for a few seconds, just continued to stare into the eyes of his extremely talented, but at the same time incredibly mixed-up, striker before standing back up, putting his hands in his pockets as he looked down at Ryan. 'I hope you mean that.'

Or what? Ryan wanted to ask, but Jim had left the dressing room before he'd had a chance to say anything else. Jesus! He could do with a hit right now. Just one quick hit. But that would be suicide, and he knew it. He needed something to take the edge off everything he was feeling, though.

'You coming out with us tonight?' Gary asked, sitting down

next to Ryan, pulling his red and white strip down over his head.

'Jesus, Gary, don't you ever just want a night in with Debbie? Like a normal couple?'

'And you think *she's* spending tonight in front of the TV with the *X Factor* results show and a pot of tea? Huh? Far from it, mate. She's got her own night out lined up, so if she thinks I'm sitting in waiting for her to roll in at all hours she's wrong. And anyway, there's no training tomorrow, is there? No excuse for us not to have a late one tonight.'

Ryan sat back, running a hand through his dark hair. 'I really want to spend some time with Amber, y'know?'

'Has she busted your balls over Friday night yet?'

Ryan looked at him. 'No. Not yet. She was okay when I saw her yesterday morning...'

'Because she didn't want you going into this match thinking she was annoyed with you?'

Ryan frowned. 'She said she was fine about everything. I mean, she had a bit of a go, and I can't blame her for that, but she seemed okay when I left for the hotel.'

'Well, you can believe that if you want to, mate. If you're really stupid. But I'm speaking from experience here, and she meant none of that, I can almost guarantee it. She'll be ready and waiting to kick your arse from here to next weekend, believe me. I've been there. Once this match is over, *that's* when the shit'll hit the fan.'

Ryan sighed heavily, a headache beginning to thump away behind his eyes. 'And replaying the events of Friday night is the best way to deal with that, is it?'

Gary shrugged. 'Look, we've got VIP tickets to that new bar opening up in the city centre. The place'll be full of beautiful women all looking for a famous face to screw senseless. You gonna say no to that?'

Ryan sighed again, but said nothing.

'You need some stress relief, don't you?' Gary asked. 'Something to make all the shit go away? Just for a little while?'

Ryan looked at Gary, still saying nothing.

'No training in the morning, that's practically carte blanche to do what the hell we like, mate. For as long as we like and as late as we like, now who's gonna turn that down? It sure as hell beats going home to an argument with the missus, don't you think?'

Ryan felt his resolve weakening. He needed to see Amber, but was that just for sex? Because he needed some of that, that was for sure. But he could get that anywhere, with anyone. It didn't always matter what it felt like or how long it took, as long as he came and the release was there, he didn't give a shit who he was fucking. As long as he was fucking *some*one. That's the way his past had played out for so many years, and hadn't he had the best time? As long as he kept things under some kind of control then, there was no reason why that past couldn't come out to play again. He could square things with Amber, he was sure of it. She'd understand. Eventually.

'You in?' Gary asked, tightening the laces on his boots.

'Yeah,' Ryan smiled. 'Yeah. I'm in.'

Amber watched the match from a seat in the main stand. She hadn't wanted to see it from the comfort of a hospitality box, she wanted to experience it as the real fans saw it, with all the noise and the language and the jeers aimed at the rival supporters, which were always a touch more personal on a local derby day than any other match. This was how she'd been brought up with the game, and this had always been her favourite way to watch it.

For a small part of the second half she'd joined Ronnie up in the makeshift TV studio in the corner of the ground to watch some of the match, enjoying the banter between the TV presenter, himself an ex-footballer, and the other pundits – a manager of another Premiership team not playing that day, and a Wearside Spartans player who was injured and not able to take part in this particular match.

Amber found it so easy being in the company of men. So much

easier than being around women, but that was just because she'd always been around this sport, these kinds of people. It was where she felt comfortable; it was her territory.

She looked on as Ryan scored two goals towards the end of the match after almost eighty minutes of deadlock in a game that was littered with dodgy tackles and more than a sprinkling of yellow cards. That was the way it always seemed to go on derby days. The referee always seemed to have a slightly tougher-than-usual job as he tried to calm certain players down because the heady atmosphere created by the fans could sometimes filter its way down onto the pitch, meaning that tensions ran higher than usual.

But with one goal in the eighty-fourth minute, and another in the first minute of injury time, Ryan ended the match the hero, deservedly winning the 'Man of the Match' award, and sending Tynebridge wild as the Red Star fans flaunted their victory in the faces of the downhearted Wearside Spartans supporters. Strike one to Red Star. But there was still the visit to Spartans' ground next March that would see this fixture played out again, and who won the next round was anyone's guess. Red Star had certainly looked the stronger side though, and that was something Amber had mentioned in her post-match interview with Jim. The hardest interview she'd ever had to do, despite the fact it had lasted just seconds, as most post-match interviews did. Pretending nothing was going on was an uphill struggle she could never be sure she was managing to hide, and she was only thankful that she wasn't visible on camera. Just Jim. And he was professionalism personified.

After brief interviews with both managers, and a couple of players from both teams – including Ryan – Amber returned to the Players' Lounge. And this time it was alcohol, not coffee, she turned to, a cold glass of lager hitting the spot.

'You look like you need that,' Jim smiled, joining Amber at the bar.

'Shouldn't you be giving your boys a post-match team talk or something?' Amber said, not sure she wanted to be this close to him in a room that was at breaking point with people, including fellow reporters. And she knew the way *their* minds worked.

'They did a great job out there this afternoon. They don't need me to tell them that. I'll leave them to celebrate with Ryan's "Man of the Match" bottle of champagne.'

Amber's heart did a tiny leap at the mention of Ryan's name. 'What are you doing in here, anyway?' she asked. 'We don't normally see managers so soon after the match. You've usually got other, more important things to do.'

'Do you… do you want me to leave or something?' Jim said, turning to face her.

'Well, to be honest, this probably isn't the best place for us to be seen together, is it?'

'We're friends, Amber. Everybody knows I'm close to your family, what's so strange about me sharing a drink with you after a game, huh?'

'Because it isn't that simple, is it? And it never has been.'

'You were so good at keeping things secret back in the day, honey. What's changed now you're all grown-up?'

'I've developed a conscience.'

'Because of Ryan?'

She stared back at him, her heart skipping that beat again, but she had no idea why this time – because of the mention of Ryan's name? Or because Jim was there? So handsome and charming and doing everything he could to take over her life all over again. Because she'd let him.

'Don't make an already difficult situation any harder, Jim. Please.'

'I need to see you tonight.'

'And I need to be with Ryan.'

'Does he need to be with *you*?'

'What's that supposed to mean?'

'Come on, Amber. They're organising a big night out at some new club that's opening in the city centre. You think Ryan's gonna turn that down? After the game *he* had this afternoon? He's the man of the moment, honey. He'll want to make the most of that.'

'You sound as if you've almost encouraged him to get out there.'

'I need to see you, Amber. Alone, away from here, away from the threat of anyone seeing us.'

She finished her drink, pulling her jacket back on as she got ready to leave. She was well aware that she'd opened up these floodgates once again, but she still hadn't quite worked out how to handle it all just yet. 'I'm going home, Jim.'

'Is that it? Amber, come on…'

'*My* terms this time, Jim. My terms. And if you don't like it, then you know what you can do.'

Ryan sank down into the ice bath, the freezing cold water shocking his skin, tightening every muscle with immediate effect as he waited for the numbness to take over. Within five to ten minutes the icy water would've caused his blood vessels to tighten, draining the blood from his legs and as squeamish as it sounded, this ritual was a much-used technique in modern sport. Ice baths were an important part of the recovery process for most sportsmen, not just footballers, helping the muscles, tendons, bones, nerves and all the different tissues used recover from whatever workout they'd been a part of. A quick-fix body MOT, a way of repairing all the necessary parts needed for the next match. And that derby match had been one hell of a workout, with Wearside Spartans players becoming quite brutal and indiscriminate with the tackles by the end of the game. Ryan felt more battered and bruised than usual, and he could do without the aches and pains tonight.

He was planning to go home first, see Amber, gauge her mood, see how the land lay. Although he had every intention of heading out with Gary and the lads, no matter what mood she was in. He'd already made that decision. He cared about Amber, and when he told her he loved her he meant it. But love wasn't a definitive word as far as Ryan was concerned. It had many meanings, on so many levels. You could love someone without wanting to spend every waking minute with them, couldn't you? Besides, she seemed in no hurry to tell him she loved him back. If she'd reciprocated his declaration, maybe that would have made a difference to the way he was feeling, he didn't know. What he *did* know – or what he felt, anyway – was that she was hiding something from him. But then, who was he to call her out on that when he was guilty of hiding things from her, too? Jesus, this was one messed-up relationship, and maybe he should be working on trying to sort it out rather than throwing himself back into the nights of partying and excess. Maybe he should, but he wasn't going to. Not yet.

Immersing himself completely in the freezing water for a second – not because it was necessary, more because he hoped it would clear his head – he finally emerged from the icy-cold and stood up, shaking the remnants of water from his body before stepping out of the bath, grabbing a towel to cover his nakedness.

'Hey, here he is. Man of the frigging Match,' Gary grinned, slapping Ryan on the back before handing him the bottle of champagne given to the recipient of the much-coveted award. Especially on derby days. 'Time to celebrate, mate. You gonna do the honours?'

Ryan looked at the bottle, remembered how it had felt to score those two goals, and returned Gary's grin, shaking the champagne bottle vigorously before popping the cork, cheers ringing out around the dressing room as the amber liquid spurted out of the neck in a cascading arc of bubbles. This was why he loved this game so much – the elation it was possible to feel when you were that player who scored the all-important winning goal, the feeling of camaraderie being part of a team could create. It was possible to feel on top of the world on days like this and no way was Ryan going to let that end by spending the evening at home, not when there was an army of people out there just waiting to congratulate him, spend time with him – tell him how incredible he was. He loved Amber, but he loved this feeling more. This was his life, and she was just going to have to find a way to fit into it.

Sitting on the edge of the bed, Amber held her left leg out in front of her, turning her foot one way then the other, examining the brand-new ankle boots she'd bought on the way home. Black, simple in design, but with a heel higher than anything she'd felt brave enough to wear before, she'd fallen in love with them instantly. Hey, she might still be that tomboy, deep down inside, but she could still scrub up when she wanted to.

She smiled to herself as she stood up and walked over to the huge, full-length mirror at the other side of the room, smoothing down the short, mint-green dress she'd also bought on her spur-of-the-moment shopping trip. The perils of a lunch-time kick-off meant the shops were still open once everything was over. Yeah, she looked okay. Actually, she looked better than okay, she thought, as she pulled her dark red hair up off her face, piling it on top of her head and fixing it with a couple of hair grips. Not bad, considering she'd had the kind of day that would usually have seen her running for the bubble bath and a bottle of wine.

The doorbell ringing caused her to break away from admiring herself and run downstairs, momentarily forgetting that she was doing so in five-inch heels, grabbing onto the banister the second she realised.

'Whoa! Look at those legs!' Ryan whistled, looking her up and down.

'What happened to using your key?' Amber asked, standing aside to let him through.

'It's in the bottom of me bag, babe. Thought it'd be quicker to just ring the bell. And I'm glad I did, when you answer it looking like that.'

He slid an arm round her waist, pushing her back against the hall wall, kicking the front door shut with the heel of his boot as his mouth lowered down onto hers in a long, slow kiss, his hands falling onto her backside within seconds.

'Have you been drinking?'

'Jesus, Amber, you look like my fantasy woman but you sound

like my mother. I've had a fucking amazing day, babe. Two goals, Man of the Match, adulation wherever I go… I'm the returning hero, the local lad who helped Red Star win the first local derby of the season so, yeah, I've had a drink. Of course I've had a drink. In fact, I've only come home to get changed…'

She wriggled free from his grip. 'For Christ's sake, Ryan. After everything I said before…' She started to walk back upstairs, but he quickly followed her.

'Hey, baby, come on. You were there; you saw what the atmosphere was like.' He followed her along the lengthy landing, into their bedroom. 'I'm on a high, Amber.'

She swung round to look at him, her eyes asking him a silent question.

'Jesus, no, Amber. No. Not *that* kind of high, shit! I mean, the kind of high you can only get when you have the kind of game *I* had today.'

'Then maybe you should piss me off more often. It seems to bring out the best in you.'

'Shit! Come on, babe. You know what I mean. I'm hyper, Amber. I can't come down yet, and staying in tonight would just be so fucking frustrating. I've got to get out there, get this out of my system…'

'Have you heard yourself, Ryan? Yesterday morning you were desperate to be with me, yet now you can't wait to get back out of the house to have a waiting brood of over-made-up soccer stalkers throw themselves at you.'

'Hey, cut me some fucking slack here. You're beginning to sound like one long, broken frigging record. What is this? Max is away for a few days so you've taken it upon yourself to be my own personal bodyguard, is that it? Spying on me…'

'I'm not *spying* on you, Ryan. I'm trying to save you from yourself.'

'Well, spare me the sanctimonious crap, okay? I don't need Max issuing the orders and I don't need *you* keeping an eye on me. You got that?'

Amber glared at him, an anger she really hadn't wanted to feel rising up in her, but she wasn't going to give him the benefit of seeing just how angry she felt. Was he really so blinkered, so selfish that he couldn't see history repeating itself? And was she just wasting her time trying to make sure it didn't happen?

'Do you know what, Ryan? Please yourself. Do what the hell you like because I'm really not in the mood to care right now.'

'Amber…'

'Hey, if *you* don't care about the fact you could be throwing your career away, then why the hell should *I*?'

'Jesus Christ, are we not making this more of a frigging drama than it needs to be? Amber…?'

But she'd gone before he had the chance to say anything else, running downstairs to the kitchen, glad – for once – that the house was so big she had room to get away from him. Half of her still wanted to stop him from doing what he was going to do, because she knew that the mood he was in meant he'd probably do things he was going to regret later – or maybe not. She was beginning to doubt what she really knew about him, despite everything Debbie had told her. But, when he was acting like this, she couldn't handle it, couldn't handle *him*.

Noticing her phone lying on the countertop, she grabbed it and began scrolling down the list of numbers until she came to Debbie's. She'd bumped into her in the Players' Lounge after the match and Debbie had asked her if she'd wanted to join her and a few of the other wives and girlfriends for a few drinks in town. At the time Amber had declined, believing that she and Ryan were going to have that cosy night in *she* craved and *he* needed, but now that it was evident that wasn't going to happen, what was the point in moping around on her own all night? She might as well make use of those new boots and get out and enjoy herself. After all, Ronnie had told her she should loosen up a bit. And she felt like loosening up a lot.

A quick exchange of texts with Debbie and Amber's rearranged night was planned. And she was strangely looking forward to it now she'd finally made the decision to go.

'I'm off.'

She looked up at the sound of Ryan's voice. He was standing in the doorway, all handsome and cocky and sexy-as-hell in jeans, boots, a white t-shirt and a dark-brown leather jacket. Bastard! She was still so angry with him, even when he looked that hot.

'I won't wait up.'

'Amber, please. Don't be like this.'

'Don't be like *what*, Ryan? Don't care about what you're doing to yourself? Don't care about the fact you're dangerously close to revisiting a past that you shouldn't be going anywhere near?'

'For fuck's sake, will you just leave it alone? I'm quite capable of looking after myself…'

'Oh, really?'

'Yes. Really. I'm not going back there, Amber. And even if I was, they were some of the best days of my life.'

Amber gave a cynical laugh, folding her arms and throwing her head back, shaking it. 'If that's the way you feel, why did you ask for my help, huh?'

'Because I thought you might actually understand.'

'Oh, I understand plenty, Ryan. I understand plenty.'

They both looked at each other for what seemed like minutes, but it was only a few seconds in reality, before he turned and walked away, the sound of the front door slamming telling her he was gone. And it was anyone's guess when she'd see him again.

He had no idea what he was doing, she was convinced of that now. He had no idea how close he was to throwing it all away if he carried on the way he was going. She'd honestly thought they were making some headway, that he was finally beginning to understand what was really best for him. But it seemed she was wrong.

She was about to head off upstairs to get ready herself when the doorbell rang again. For a second she thought against answering it,

265

thinking it was probably just Ryan back to irritate her even more and she wasn't in the mood for another round. But she hated ignoring it; after all, it could be something important.

It wasn't.

'Going somewhere?' Jim asked, smiling a smile that, much to her annoyance, made her heart skip what felt like a dozen beats.

'What are you doing here? What if Ryan sees you? How are you are going to explain that one, huh?'

'He's out, isn't he? I've just seen him get into a taxi.'

'Are you spying on me?'

'Something like that, yeah. You gonna ask me in?'

'I'm going out myself.'

'Night in with the boyfriend not work out, then?'

'Piss off, Jim.'

'You look amazing.'

'Good. Then I might get some attention when I hit the bars later.'

'Is that what you want? Attention?'

Amber said nothing, just looked at him, not knowing exactly what she was going to do next.

'If you want to talk…'

'I don't want to talk, Jim.'

'Even better. Because I'm not much into talking myself right now.'

'What do you want from me?'

He moved closer, standing right in the doorway so she could neither shut the door in his face nor get out of his way to avoid him. 'I want to be inside you again, Amber.'

'Jesus Christ,' Amber sighed, finally standing aside to let him in. A reflex action brought on by what he'd just said? Probably. She didn't even know if she cared anymore.

'A night out with the girls, then, is it?' Jim asked, looking her up and down which, against her better judgement, only served to turn her on, that familiar tingle between her legs striking up within seconds.

She didn't answer him, just walked on through to the kitchen, finding a bottle of vodka in one of the cupboards and pouring herself a shot.

'Nobody said living with a player like Ryan would be easy, honey.'

She looked up at him before quickly refilling her shot glass. 'You don't know anything, Jim.'

'I know he's pissed you off.'

'And what if he has?'

'You might want to vent your frustration.'

'How, exactly?'

He walked over to her, taking the glass from her hand and placing it down on the counter before slowly sliding a hand up and under her dress, touching her thigh as his mouth moved closer to hers. 'Well, for starters, you could fuck me so hard it hurts. I can take the pain.'

She felt her stomach flip over in a barrage of excited somersaults. Ryan deserved some kind of payback, after the shit he was pulling tonight. And the mood he was in, she'd lay money on him ending the night with some random bimbo in The Goldman, and she didn't even think she'd care if he did. So why shouldn't she take Jim up on his offer? And what a way to start her own night – fucking the league's sexiest, most popular manager.

'You can, huh?' she smiled, backing up against the counter as his fingers slipped under the sides of her panties, slowly pushing them down.

'I can,' he whispered, his mouth now resting on hers, his breath warm on her face, the smell of him overwhelming, taking over everything she was feeling, dissipating that anger that had been building up just enough to make her still want revenge and know that this was the only way she was going to feel any better.

Amber closed her eyes as his hand slid between her legs, making her gasp out loud. His touch was firm yet gentle, his fingers moving back and forth in a slow, rhythmic motion that sent a million white-hot tingles shooting through her, kicking off an ache for him so bad she didn't know how long she could stand it.

'Jim…' she groaned, throwing her head back as his lips started kissing the base of her throat, his other hand in the small of her back, keeping her close. Everything was wrong, what they were doing here, yet it felt so right. She was living that age-old cliché, and for once she didn't care. Ryan had been at his worst tonight, so surely she deserved this? Surely she deserved to have the revenge she badly wanted right now. No matter how childish and petty that revenge might be.

Pulling his hand away, Jim lifted her up onto the counter, pushing her dress up over her thighs, pulling her panties off and throwing them aside. He looked at her, looked down between her open legs, before quickly removing his jacket, tossing it away like a used dishcloth, even though it probably cost more than Amber earned in a month. She wanted him so badly now, so much it physically hurt, and when he finally freed himself, pushing his way inside her before either of them had the chance to change their minds, as far as Amber was concerned it was the most perfect feeling. Within seconds he'd taken her over, and as dangerous and stupid as that may have been, for Amber it felt like coming home. There was no other way she could describe it. Despite everything he'd put her through, despite the pathetic way she'd always run back to him even though he'd never really cared, he was what she needed. He'd been the first person she'd ever given herself to, and she couldn't forget that. She couldn't let that go, no matter how hard she tried. She was stuck in a world in which he was always going to be present, so the only thing she could do was follow her heart. Even if it was going to lead her in every wrong direction going.

Biting down on her lip as he came fast and hard, she held onto him tight as he gently touched her, helping her reach her own climax, his mouth on hers, their kiss as rhythmic as the movement of his fingers, eventually leaving them both breathless. She'd had her revenge on Ryan. And had it made her feel any better? She wasn't entirely sure.

'You feel so good,' Jim whispered, his forehead resting against hers as their breathing finally began to slow down. 'So fucking good.'

'I've really got to go,' she said, her fingers gently stroking the back of his neck. 'I'm going to be late.'

'Call it off, Amber. Ring them up, cancel, and stay here. With me. Stay here.'

She shook her head, letting go of him and sliding down from the counter, pulling herself together as another slice of cold reality hit her. But she didn't regret what she'd just done. Not yet, anyway. 'I'm going to be late,' she repeated. 'You'd better go.'

He bent down to pick up his jacket, quickly slipping it back on over his dark shirt. 'This isn't the end, Amber.'

She turned to look at him, walking over and sliding a hand round the back of his neck, bringing his mouth down to touch hers again, the kiss deepening as his arm held her against him. 'I didn't say it was,' she smiled, letting go of him again, walking slowly backwards, her dark red hair now beginning to fall free of the grips that had been holding it up before, stray strands lying loose over her bare shoulders. 'I'll see you later, Jim.'

He smiled, too, that all-American, drop-dead-gorgeous smile. That charming smile that had gained him a whole army of female football fans. That smile that still made Amber's heart skip a proverbial beat. 'You kill me, Amber. You freaking kill me, baby.'

'Well, just try to stay alive for a little while longer, okay? I haven't finished with you yet.'

He started to make his way out of the kitchen, stopping only when he reached where she was standing, sliding an arm around her waist again, his mouth so very close to hers as he spoke, his voice low and husky. 'And that, Ms. Sullivan, had better be one hell of a promise.'

The music was thumping, so loud it almost felt as though the floor was vibrating, a steady, heavy bass beat reverberating through the club, making it almost impossible to speak without shouting.

Ryan was having a night like he hadn't had in a long time. People were flocking around him like he was the second coming of Christ. Men were shoving drinks at him, telling him how great he'd played that afternoon, how much of a local hero he really was, whilst women couldn't get enough of him, all of them stunning to look at and quite willing to give him anything he wanted. He was seriously considering offers. If Amber couldn't understand how much today meant to him then he might as well spend time with those that did. And surely this was his well-deserved reward after getting Red Star those three winning points that had now sent them to fourth in the league table. He was making his mark at a club he'd supported all his life. Jesus, he was on top of the frigging world tonight!

'You gonna leave a few for us?' Gary winked, joining Ryan at the VIP table they'd commandeered for the night, dumping two more bottles of champagne down in the centre. 'On the house, apparently. You're our lucky charm tonight, mate. No doubt about it.'

'It's not like we can't afford the drink, Gary.'

'That's not the point. If we don't have to pay for it, all the better. And that goes for the women, too.'

Ryan looked at Gary through slightly narrowed eyes.

'Oh, come on, Ryan. Are you telling me you've never used the services of a high-class call-girl? Sometimes needs must, mate.'

Ryan said nothing, just turned to look out onto the dance floor where a pretty and very-young-but-definitely-legal blonde and a brunette with legs up to her armpits were putting on a show especially for him. He could feel himself reacting, too, dangerously close to having to find a quiet corner and relieve the pressure, if truth be told.

'Jesus fucking Christ,' Gary whistled, leaning back and watching the floor-show. 'You are one lucky son-of-a-bitch.'

'You reckon?' Ryan asked, draining his glass of champagne. He was sick of drinking the stuff now, if he was honest. He might start hitting the shorts next. A few vodka shots should set him up nicely.

'Yeah, I reckon. Those two are yours for the taking,' Gary said, indicating the two girls still gyrating against each other on the dance floor, although their eyes were very much on Ryan, ' … not to mention the rest of 'em. You're on fire tonight, mate. On frigging fire!'

Ryan grinned, running a hand through his dark hair, making it even more messed-up and sexy. 'Yeah. I fucking am, aren't I?'

'Looks like The Goldman is gonna get the pleasure of your company tonight, then?' Gary smirked, looking out onto the dance floor again, his expression suddenly changing. 'Oh, shit! Are you frigging kidding me? What the fuck are *they* doing in here?'

Ryan followed Gary's gaze, his stomach flipping an unexpected somersault the second he saw her, looking hotter than he'd ever seen her look before.

'I said to her, I said, "Debbie, babe, you and your WAG brigade can go where the hell you like tonight, just don't fucking turn up here." Frigging brilliant!'

'What? This *bothers* you?' Ryan asked, tearing his eyes away from Amber for a second, although something was telling him not to let her out of his sight.

'Yeah, it frigging bothers me,' Gary replied. 'I mean, me and Debbie, I know our relationship isn't exactly conventional, but doing shit right in front of her, mate – that's off limits.'

Ryan stared at him, and for a brief second he wondered just what the hell he was doing there. Then he looked around him, at the women who wanted him, the men who wanted to *be* him… who the hell *wouldn't* want that? No matter how sick and twisted it could sometimes become.

'Yeah, well, Amber's looking like a wet dream come true, so I'm off over there to see what's happening.'

'What? You're leaving Barbie and her mate to go and see your fucking girlfriend?'

'Yeah,' Ryan grinned. 'Weird, isn't it?'

'You're telling me.'

'I'm sure you can keep those two amused,' Ryan went on, nodding his head in the direction of his dancing fan club. 'I might need them later.'

Gary just laughed, shaking his head as Ryan got up and made his way through the crowd, over towards Amber and the rest of the Red Star WAGs.

'Hey, beautiful. Couldn't keep away, huh?'

Amber turned around, her eyes immediately meeting his. 'Sorry, are you talking to me?'

'Don't play games, babe. You're looking hot tonight, by the way.'

'Play games? Y'know, when it comes to playing games then I can only have picked up tips from the master, Ryan.'

'Whoa! You're still pissed off with me, then?'

'Glad to see the ego hasn't stopped you from being perceptive.'

'Come on, Amber,' Ryan groaned, sliding his arm around her waist, pulling her close. 'You look incredible, babe. And I can't ignore that.'

'What? Even though you're surrounded by heaven knows how many glamorous young things all vying for your attention?'

'It's not the same, though, is it?'

'Isn't it?'

'No. I like the idea of you being there, at home, waiting for me…'

Amber quickly disentangled herself from his grip, backing away from him. 'Yes, well, there we have the problem, Ryan. You want the best of both worlds, don't you? You like the idea of me being there at home, waiting for you, as long as you can have all this shit, too.' She quickly looked around, making sure none of the other girls were within earshot. 'I'm not Debbie, Ryan. *She* might put up with Gary and whatever it is that *he* puts her through, but I can't do that. I've got more self-respect.' She felt a touch uncomfortable saying those words, considering what had just happened with Jim, but it was true. She wasn't going to be the kind of girlfriend who put up with the kind of lifestyle Ryan seemed to be slipping back into. And he needed to know that. 'You've got a lot of thinking to do, Ryan. You've got decisions to make.'

'Amber…' He reached out to take her hand but she pulled it away, shaking her head.

'I care about you, Ryan. So much. But there are some things I just can't do.'

'Amber… hang on… Shit!'

She turned and walked away from him, swerving through the mass of people inside this glitzy new club – which wasn't totally Amber's style, if she was truthful – over to where Debbie was busy organising more drinks for them all.

'What kind of mood is he in?' she asked as Amber approached.

'Close to self-destruction, I reckon,' Amber sighed, gratefully accepting another glass of something cold and sparkling.

'He's had that kind of day,' Debbie said, crossing her legs as Amber sat down beside her. 'They put themselves up on this ridiculous pedestal and then, when they come to places like this and find people who only insist on raising that pedestal even higher, it goes to their heads until they think they're one step away from God. I've seen it all before, chick. He'll come down, eventually. They all do.'

'Maybe,' Amber sighed, watching Ryan as he hit the dance floor, pulling a blonde who couldn't have been older than nineteen against him, moving his body against hers as she stared up into his eyes, silently promising him things he'd probably gratefully accept later on. 'I just don't know if I'm cut out for this, Debbie.'

'Do you love him?'

Amber looked at her new friend. 'I don't know. I really don't know. I mean, I care about him…'

'Then you just have to work out if that's enough. Amber. Believe me, I know Ryan better than you think, and this isn't really the person he wants to be. I honestly believe he wants to change, he just doesn't know how to. And he's scared. And when guys like him get scared, they throw themselves into something they think will keep the status quo intact because that's what's best for them, but it isn't.'

Amber looked back over at Ryan. He was with the darker haired, slightly older girl now, his hands all over her body, which was poured into a dress so tight Amber thought she might need to be sucked out of it.

'He's doing that on purpose,' Debbie said.

Amber looked at her, frowning slightly. 'Sorry?'

'Ryan. He's doing that on purpose, dancing close to those girls, acting the way he is. He wasn't doing it before he'd spoken to you, was he?'

'I… I don't…'

'He wasn't. I was watching him. But he's doing it now. He's trying to get a reaction, Amber. He's trying to make you jealous.'

'He doesn't need to do that,' Amber said, turning her attention back to Ryan.

'Well, he thinks he does. He loves you, Amber. I can see it when I talk to him, I can feel it when he talks about you.'

'So why's he acting like a first-rate idiot?'

Debbie looked at Amber, taking a sip of her champagne cocktail. 'You've been around footballers all your life, chick. So I think you already know the answer to that one.'

Amber sat back, running a hand through her hair. She really wanted to confide in someone about the whole mess she was getting into with Jim, but she knew she could never do that. She couldn't tell anybody, because if it ever got out…

'Let him get today out of his system,' Debbie smiled, leaning forward and placing a hand on Amber's arm. 'Let him act like the hero he thinks he is and then talk to him. Because I think you care enough about him not to throw it all away just yet.'

And, despite everything that was going on with Jim, Amber knew Debbie was right. She just had to work out whether she was up to riding the emotional roller-coaster that stretched out ahead

274

of her, because, all of a sudden, Amber Sullivan's quiet, organised life had disappeared. And she had no idea if it would ever return.

Chapter Fifteen

'Amber, can I have a word?' Kevin asked.

Amber looked up, his voice shaking her out of a daydream she hadn't been enjoying all that much. 'Sorry? Did you... did you say something?'

'A word, Amber. In my office.'

Amber watched him walk away, her stomach sinking. She didn't have a good feeling about this. The tone of his voice told her he wasn't pulling her aside for a friendly chat over a cup of coffee and a doughnut.

Sighing, she pushed her chair back and followed him into his office, closing the door behind her.

'Sit down,' he said, indicating the chair in front of his desk.

Amber said nothing, just sat down and crossed her legs, clasping her hands together on her lap.

'I think you know why I've called you in here, don't you?' Kevin perched himself on the edge of his desk, his eyes meeting Amber's.

She nodded. 'Yeah. Yeah, I think I know.'

'I'm worried about you, Amber. These past few weeks, it's like a different person has turned up for work, and believe me, when you've worked with someone as long as I've worked with you, it can be quite unsettling. So, you gonna tell me what's up?'

'Nothing's up, Kevin,' Amber swallowed, knowing that was a lie.

And one look at Kevin's arched eyebrow told her *he* knew that, too.

'Your work's been suffering, kiddo. You might have noticed I've been sending others out to do jobs I'd much rather you had done, but – and I hate to say this, because I know you, Amber, and I know this isn't like you – I can't trust you to do the job properly right now.'

'Kevin…'

'No, Amber, let me finish,' Kevin interrupted, holding a hand up to stop her from talking. 'Your head is elsewhere, sweetheart. It's obvious. And I can only assume this has got everything to do with Ryan Fisher. Am I right?'

Not entirely, Amber thought. He was only part of the problem. If it was just Ryan she could probably deal with it all, but throwing Jim into the equation just messed things up even more. And that's why her head was all over the place. Oh, Ryan wasn't innocent, far from it. His nights out were becoming more frequent, his time spent with her less and less, but then, she had someone else there to occupy that time, didn't she?

'You're doing it again,' Kevin said, his voice once again jolting Amber from her thoughts. 'Look, Amber. When was the last time you had a holiday? A proper holiday? And by that I mean more than a few days away from this place?'

She frowned slightly, not sure where this was leading. 'I don't know…'

'Exactly. That's my point, sweetheart. You can't remember the last time you had a proper break, can you?'

'No, but…'

'Take some time off.'

'Kevin! No. I don't *want* to take some time off…'

'I'm not asking you, Amber. I'm telling you. It's nearly Christmas…'

'And we're really busy…'

'We'll cope. This place won't fall apart without you.'

'That's not what I meant,' Amber said, with more than a touch of resignation in her voice. How had she let things get this bad? How hadn't she noticed her concentration slipping and her mind wandering off to think about things that didn't really matter? But then, Ryan *did* matter, didn't he? He mattered a lot. And that was the problem. Because, at times, she felt more like a babysitter than a girlfriend, so of course she'd been distracted. Although she would've been less distracted if Jim hadn't been on the scene. And there was another problem. She knew what Ryan was doing to himself, and she was trying to stop him from going down a road he needed to get off, but at the same time she didn't feel Jim needed to know just how unstable Ryan's behaviour could become. In spite of everything, Ryan lived to play football, and if Jim knew what was really going on then there was every possibility he would pull Ryan from the first team, and that was the last thing Ryan needed. But did *she* need all this stress? All the secrets and lies she was having to keep hidden? Now it was starting to affect her work, things suddenly felt a whole lot different. She'd thought she could cope with it all, but it seemed she was wrong. She couldn't really cope at all.

'I know what you meant,' Kevin smiled, his voice quieter. 'I care about you, Amber, I really do, and you know that. You know I wouldn't make you do this if I didn't think it was going to help. But I really do believe that some time off will do you the world of good. Sometimes work isn't everything. And I think the whole problem with you is that you're having a hard time dealing with the fact that *you're* beginning to see that, too.'

She frowned again, looking at him. 'I don't…'

'The hard-faced, ice-cold, feisty girl I know is going through a bit of a life-change. She just needs to learn to embrace it.' He stood up, walking over to the window, shoving his hands in his pockets as he turned round to face her again. 'There *is* room for everything, Amber. You *can* have it all.'

She wasn't sure that she could.

The afternoon stretched out in front of him like some never-ending movie he was bored of watching. Training was finished, a quick lunchtime drink with Gary and a few of the lads was over, and now he was back home. Bored. It was the Red Star Christmas party that night, so his evening was sorted, but getting through the afternoon was something else.

Amber was at work, he had no intention of calling his mam or dad because he wasn't in the mood for any kind of lecture, so he was just going to have to find a way of amusing himself.

He was about to reach over and fire up the laptop when his mobile rang and he answered it immediately, not checking the caller ID first. Big mistake.

'Are you at home?'

'Where else would I be, Max?'

'Oh, I don't know, Ryan. You've been spotted in so many places lately, you could be almost anywhere.'

'Yeah, you're funny.'

'Oh, I'm frigging hilarious, Ryan. Which is exactly what you're fucking career is going to be if you don't pull yourself together.'

'Jesus, Max, I'm not a kid…'

'Then stop acting like one. Grow up, look at what you have, and then think about what your life would be like if you lost it all. Because carry on the way you are and that's exactly what's going to happen.'

Ryan sat down, running a hand through his hair. 'I can control it, Max. It isn't like before, I swear; I know what I'm doing.'

'Famous last words, Ryan.'

'Max…?' But he'd already hung up, leaving Ryan staring at the phone. 'What the…?' Now he was pissed off. Now his afternoon had become even more frustrating. He needed something to take the edge off, something to see him through to party time – and he knew exactly what would take the edge off, but he was feeling lazy today. They could come to him for a change, even though it was a slightly risky thing to do. Somebody could see them, and it would only take one paparazzi photograph and an over-zealous reporter to start rumours that would spread like wildfire. But Ryan didn't care, not today. He was in a rebellious mood. Or maybe it was just the boredom. Either way he needed something to do.

Reaching for his phone again, he tapped in a password that took him to a secret list of contacts. Not that he thought Amber was the type to go checking his phone, but there was nothing wrong in being ultra careful. In his position. Pressing *call*, he spoke quickly to the voice on the other end of the line, making sure they knew exactly what to do before quickly scrolling down the list to find the second number he wanted. Once the edge was well and truly taken off he'd still need something to do, and with Amber at work, *she* wasn't going to be able to give him what he needed. He was going to have to look elsewhere for that. And he knew exactly where he could find it.

'Here you go,' Freddie Sullivan smiled as he handed Amber a steaming hot mug of tea.

'Thanks, Dad,' Amber sighed, cupping her gloved hands round the mug as she stood on the touchline, watching her dad's team prepare for their evening match with an afternoon training session. 'I didn't much fancy going home. I'm not used to it, not at this time of the day.' Freddie looked at his daughter, frowning slightly. 'Kevin's right though, pet. You *do* need a break. I can't remember the last time you had a proper holiday. Why don't you take yourself away somewhere, eh? You could go and visit your nan over in Marbella; she'd love to see you…'

'You know how it is, Dad. Ryan can't take a proper holiday until the season's over…' She looked at her father, taking a small sip of hot tea. 'You meant go without Ryan, didn't you?'

Freddie Sullivan looked down at the ground for a second, scuffing his football boot along the muddy grass, his hands buried deep in the pockets of his tracksuit bottoms.

'Maybe you should… maybe you should back off from him

for a little while, Amber.'

She continued to look at her dad, not breaking the stare. 'Why?'

'Because he isn't good for you, kiddo. He's… he's always had this reputation, this image that follows him around and I was never really sure how much of that was true, until I met him. Until he joined Red Star. He isn't good for you, Amber.'

She turned away, taking another sip of tea as she watched her dad's players take practice penalties at the far end of the pitch. 'I think I can look after myself, Dad.'

'Oh, I've got no doubt about that, Amber. But you shouldn't have to look after him, too.'

She threw her head back and sighed heavily. 'Will everyone stop blaming Ryan for the way I'm feeling right now? Please?'

'Something else on your mind, then?' Freddie asked, kicking a stray ball back onto the pitch.

'No,' Amber replied, probably a touch too defensively. 'No. Nothing else is on my mind. Well, apart from the fact I've been forced out of the office for a few weeks.'

'You should enjoy the time off, pet.'

'Yeah, you should.'

'What are *you* doing here?' Amber asked as Ronnie joined them on the touchline, taking the mug from Amber's hands and taking a drink of tea.

'I popped in to see you at work, but Kevin said you were here. He said he'd ordered you to take a few weeks off, and I have to agree with him. You haven't…'

'Had a proper holiday in ages, I know. I get it.'

'Anyway, I thought you'd be making the most of your free afternoon getting yourself a manicure or a new hairdo for the Red Star Christmas party tonight, seeing as Jim Allen seems to have ripped up his "no partners" policy for this year.' He looked straight at Amber. 'Any idea why he might have done that?'

She quickly looked away, his stare making her feel slightly uncomfortable, for some reason. 'How the hell should *I* know?'

'It is a bit strange, that,' Freddie mused, stroking his stubbled chin. 'Normally Jim's a stickler for protocol, and with every club he's managed, when it comes to the Christmas party, he's always been quite firm about no partners being allowed.'

'Why? Because he takes them all out for an evening of depraved debauchery that he wouldn't like the wives and girlfriends to know about?' Amber said, slightly more sarcastically than she'd intended.

'Well, your boyfriend might be able to advise him on the best places to go, if that was the case.'

'Ronnie…' Freddie said, a warning tone to his voice.

'Yeah, Dad's already covered the "let's batter Ryan" side of the conversation, so don't *you* start.'

Ronnie looked at Freddie, who just shrugged. 'I'd better get back out there before this lot start slacking off.' He quickly kissed Amber on the cheek. 'See you later, kiddo.'

'Yeah. See you, Dad. Thanks for the tea.'

Ronnie stood beside her, pulling the collar of his jacket up around his neck to shield it from the biting north east chill. 'So, what's your dad been saying, then?'

'That I should back away from my relationship with Ryan and go and spend some time with Nan in Marbella. On my own.'

'That's not such a bad idea.'

She looked at him, taking her mug of tea back. 'Oh, really?'

'Yeah. Christ, if *I* had that much time off I'd be over there like a shot. Sunshine and sangria over there in southern Spain, or snow and Christmas adverts being shoved down me throat in England? It's a no-brainer.'

'It won't work, Ronnie. I'm not going anywhere. And anyway, you don't even *like* sangria.'

'That's not the point, missy.'

'Whatever.'

'You're beginning to sound like him, now.'

'So, I take it you agree with my dad, then? You think that I should back away from Ryan, too?'

Ronnie shrugged. 'I'm not telling you what to do, Amber. All I'll say is, be careful. And remember, your dad doesn't even know the half of it as far as Ryan's concerned, because, if he did…'

'He doesn't. And he doesn't *need* to know.'

'And then there's Jim…'

'Can you shut up, please?'

'Well, like I said – just, be careful.'

She frowned, looking at him over the rim of her mug as she drained the last of the tea from it. 'What's *that* supposed to mean?'

'I think you know what I mean, Amber.'

She held his gaze, nodding slowly. 'Yeah.' It just remained to be seen whether she heeded those words of warning or not. 'I'd better go home. I've got to find an outfit for this party tonight, and I don't think jeans and a t-shirt are gonna cut it, somehow.'

'You'll look great whatever you wear,' Ronnie said, shoving his hands in his jacket pockets as he stared straight ahead.

'Yeah, well, I've still got a lot of work to do, haven't I? And it's not like I've got anything else to be getting on with, so I might as well go home and pamper myself.'

Ronnie turned to look at her again. 'Amber… If there was anything you wanted to talk about, you'd come to me, wouldn't you?'

She smiled at him, slipping her arm through his and squeezing it tight, quickly kissing his cheek. 'Yeah. You know I would.'

'So, you and Jim Allen…'

She let go of him, putting the now-empty mug down on the ground before she started walking back towards the car park. 'Like I said, Ronnie, I'd better go home and start getting ready.'

'So there's nothing going on between you two, then? Only, when you told me what had happened at Tynebridge a few weeks ago, in his office…'

'Yeah, well, maybe I shouldn't have told you anything at all.'

'No, Amber, hang on…' He gently grabbed her arm, swinging her round to look at him. 'I'm sorry. I don't mean to pry, it's just

283

that… Kevin said he was really worried about you. And whatever's going on, well, I don't think it's *all* to do with Ryan. Is it?'

Amber just looked at him for a few seconds before pulling her arm from his grip. 'I let things get on top of me, Ronnie. Okay? But I guess I've got the time to deal with it all now, haven't I?'

She resumed the walk to her car, but Ronnie wasn't giving up. 'Amber, come on, kiddo. What's that supposed to mean, huh?'

She turned round as she reached her car, leaning back against it. 'It means, I can concentrate on making sure Ryan doesn't throw his career away. Nothing more, nothing less.' Would he believe her? She hoped so. It was partly the truth, anyway. 'And not a word to Jim about Ryan, do you hear me?' She turned to open the driver's door before facing Ronnie one last time. 'So far nothing he's done has affected his football, and I intend to make sure it stays that way.'

Ryan lay back on the bed and smiled as he stared at the ceiling. That had certainly been one way to while away an afternoon, and all for less than a day's wages. He felt exhilarated, fired-up, ready to go all over again.

He turned his head to check the time on the clock by the bed. Amber should be home soon. He'd timed this perfectly, made sure everything had run like clockwork, and he'd managed to get the kicks he'd so badly needed without Amber having to know a thing. Jesus, he was good!

The sound of the door banging shut downstairs told him she was home and he smiled again, reaching down to gently touch himself. Hard and ready to greet his gorgeous girlfriend with a welcome home she probably wasn't expecting, but one he was sure she was going to love.

'Ryan! Are you up there?' Amber's voice drifted up the stairs and Ryan sat up, tying the towel he had wrapped round his waist a little tighter.

'Yeah. I'm in the bedroom!' he shouted back, unable to keep the smile off his face as he heard her run upstairs.

'Oh, good. You've already had your shower,' Amber said, throwing her bag onto the chair by the door, loosening her belt and slipping off her watch.

'Nice to see you, too,' Ryan mumbled, watching as she moved around the bedroom like she was on some kind of mission.

She swung round to look at him. 'Huh?'

'You. What happened to "*Hello, Ryan, hope you had a good day*"?'

'Well, I hope you *did* have a good day, because I've had a crap one.'

He stood up, walking over to her, slipping his arms around her from behind, kissing her neck. 'Oh yeah? What's happened? Tough day at the office?'

'You don't know the half of it,' she sighed, leaning back against him, wanting to feel angry with him because it was partly *his* fault she was in this mess, but she couldn't be angry with him. What good would *that* do? They might as well enjoy the Christmas party and work out where they went from here tomorrow. After all, she had plenty of time now, didn't she?'

'Do you want to talk about it?' Ryan asked, really hoping she'd say no. He was in the mood for sex, not conversation.

'Not really,' Amber replied, stepping out of his arms and slipping off her top. 'Suffice to say, Kevin's ordered me to take some time off from News North East. At least until after Christmas.'

'Really?' Ryan frowned, wondering if that meant she was going to be around the house more often. If she was, then maybe The Goldman was going to have a lot more of his custom. 'Why?'

She turned to look at him. 'Because my work has turned to shit lately, Ryan.' She threw her head back and sighed, pushing a hand through her hair. 'Look, it doesn't matter. I could do with some time off, and I was thinking of taking a fortnight over Christmas anyway. It's all good.'

'Is it?' Ryan was slightly confused now. He'd always thought Amber was the epitome of professionalism – the archetypal workaholic. Was it *his* fault she'd let her work slip?

'Hey, come on,' she smiled, slipping her arms around his waist, kissing his slightly open, unsuspecting mouth quickly. 'It's not *your* fault. Not entirely, anyway. But I guess what you *are* guilty of is being on my mind so much I lose all concentration.' *Just not always in a good way*, she thought.

He smiled, too, sliding his hand down her jeans, making her gasp out loud as his cold fingers touched her warm skin. 'Well, maybe having some extra time together isn't such a bad thing, huh?'

'Maybe not,' she whispered, pulling his towel away and taking a small step back to look at him, all toned and hard – very, very hard. 'It doesn't take long to get *you* in the mood, does it?' she smirked, reaching out to touch him, the feel of him in her hand making her stomach give one of those familiar flips. And despite the doubts she had constantly in the back of her mind about their relationship, and just why she was with him – because sometimes her reasoning was slightly blurred and there were times when she was never sure whether she was with him because she wanted to be, or because she felt a certain duty to help him – she didn't want to think about it right now. She wanted to have a good night; she wanted them *both* to have a good night. Everything else could wait. She had the country's most talented footballer right here in front of her, naked and sexy and hers. Right now he was hers, so she put any thoughts about the things he might have done or the women he might have been with to the back of her mind, and let her heart take over. Tonight was a night to let go and forget.

And Ryan couldn't have agreed more.

Chapter Sixteen

The Newcastle Red Star Christmas party was being held in one of the most exclusive hotels the region had to offer, although, much to Ryan's relief, it wasn't The Goldman.

With the use of its largest function room, and overnight accommodation booked for everyone so that nobody had to leave the party early, it was all set to be a night filled with celebrations and festivities that had cost something in the region of a small fortune. But, at a time when more than a few top-flight clubs had cut back on the Christmas party budget, Red Star had thrown money at theirs to celebrate the successful first half of a season that now saw them settled nicely in the top half of the league table, with a real chance of winning the title.

Giant Christmas trees dominated the entrance to the hotel, towering over everybody with their myriad of twinkling fairy lights, whilst inside waiters and waitresses stood with trays of champagne or orange juice to greet everybody as they walked into a lobby that was decorated like a winter wonderland, topped off with the biggest fire Amber had ever seen in the bar area. It crackled and roared as red and orange flames leapt up the chimney, sending out a glow and a warmth that you could feel the second you walked inside. It was almost magical, and for a second she was transported back to the wonderful Christmases she'd had as a child, followed by that familiar pang of regret that she'd never managed to pass those magical Christmases on to a child of her own. Maybe it could still happen, if she found the right man. Or maybe it never would. She was prepared for both eventualities.

'You okay?' Ryan asked, squeezing her hand as they walked through the lobby towards the party.

'I'm fine,' she smiled, leaning in to kiss him quickly. He looked incredible, she couldn't deny that. Tall and handsome, she could only describe him as drop-dead gorgeous in a dark suit and shirt, that beard of his only making him look even sexier. If that was possible. 'Christmas always makes me miss my mum that little bit more, that's all.'

Ryan squeezed her waist, pulling her against him for a longer, slower kiss and Amber found herself falling against him, his arms holding her tight. Why couldn't it always be like this? Because when it was like this, when he was holding her tight, it felt like a proper relationship. It felt safe, and real. But it was so far from that, and Amber wasn't stupid enough to think otherwise.

'Jesus, get a room you two, will you?' Gary smirked, sauntering past with his arm around Debbie's shoulder. She smiled at Amber, mouthing, '*Everything alright?*'

Amber nodded, smiling back, still holding onto Ryan.

'You look incredible tonight,' Ryan said quietly, gently stroking her fringe from her eyes. And he meant it. She looked sexy and beautiful in a black and silver baby-doll style dress and stiletto-heeled black ankle boots, her dark red hair loose around her shoulders in a barrage of big barrel curls, her make-up light but with the most stunning, smoky eyes he'd ever seen. She was one hell of a woman, and to look at her you wouldn't think she was eleven years older than he was. He was lucky to have her. He just had to concentrate more on making sure he didn't lose her, because he needed her. He really needed her. More than he ever let her know. More than he ever admitted to himself.

'You don't look so bad yourself, handsome,' Amber smiled,

kissing him again, once more letting his arms keep her close as their mouths moved together. It was at times like this that she remembered why she'd fallen for him in the first place. Maybe Debbie was right – underneath all the bravado and the footballer's ego there could quite possibly be the man of her dreams. Or maybe she'd just drank that first glass of champagne far too fast and let it go to her head, because she was starting to sound like something out of a romance novel. There was no such thing as a man of anyone's dreams, and she should know that better than anyone.

As he slid his hand into hers, Amber leaned in against him as they made their way into the large and possibly slightly over-decorated function room that was hosting the Red Star Christmas party. Waiters circulated through the mass of guests holding trays of canapés and glasses of everything from yet more champagne to what looked like mulled wine. An array of tables at the far end of the room surrounded a huge Christmas tree, all of them crammed with plates of food for a buffet that Amber suspected would contain a lot more than just a few sausage rolls and chicken legs. But it was the huge dance floor – presided over by a DJ she vaguely recognised as being a little bit famous – that seemed to be the main attraction. A few of the wives and girlfriends were already showing off their suspiciously well-rehearsed moves as they held their glasses of champagne aloft and sang along to a popular girl-band track that was pounding out of concealed speakers. Amber watched them, wondering if she'd ever be able to let herself go like that, because there was a little bit of her that really wished she could. But it had just never been her. She was so used to holding back, keeping a big part of herself locked away, reluctant to let anyone get too close.

'Another drink?' Ryan asked, squeezing her waist again.

She looked up at him, nodding.

'What do you fancy?'

'Surprise me,' she smiled, closing her eyes as he kissed her quickly, his mouth soft and warm against hers. *Jesus, Ryan, why can't things just be normal between us?* She watched him as he walked over to the main bar, smiling and chatting to people as he passed. He truly was a beautiful man, an incredible talent, but he was still so messed up. And until he admitted that to himself, Amber wasn't entirely sure what kind of future lay ahead for them.

'You look happy.'

Amber turned around to see Jim standing beside her, handsome and sexy – far too sexy – in a dark suit and white shirt, exuding the kind of charm that made him so popular.

'Yeah, well, looks can be deceiving.'

'Do I sense trouble in paradise?' Jim asked, his eyes scanning the room as he spoke.

'Me and Ryan are fine, if that's what you're referring to.'

'*Are* you?' This time he looked right at her, his eyes boring into hers.

'I'm having a few problems at work, that's all,' Amber replied, ignoring his question.

'Anything I can help you with?' Jim went on, resuming his scanning of the room.

'Not really. You're half the reason the problems exist.'

He looked at her again. 'I never meant to cause you any trouble, Amber.'

'It doesn't matter what you meant, Jim. The damage has been done. You're here, and I just haven't been able to deal with it the way I thought I could.' She hadn't been able to deal with it, full stop.

He said nothing for a few seconds, just continued to look at her, his eyes never moving from hers. 'You look beautiful,' he whispered, leaning over so his mouth was close to her ear, so close she could feel his breath warm on her face, which in turn caused her stomach to flip over so fast her breath caught in her throat and she had to turn away from him, so unsettling was his presence. So confusing. 'We can escape all of this,' he went on, pulling back slightly. 'If you want to.'

She looked at him again before quickly turning round to see

where Ryan was. He was talking to a couple of girls at the bar – a young, slim, dark-haired girl and a stunning redhead. Amber didn't recognise them as being any Red Star players' partners, and the way Ryan was looking at them, the way he had his arm around the younger girl's waist, his hand resting on her hip; the way she was staring up at him as he laughed at something the redhead was saying to him, it almost made her feel sick. Were they promising him something she just couldn't give him? So much for the perfect evening she'd imagined they could have. Why couldn't she have been strong enough to carry out her own threat of walking away the second something like this happened? Why couldn't she do that? Because, despite the tough image she'd like to think she'd created for herself, she was actually incredibly weak.

'They don't change, Amber.'

She swung back round to look at Jim. 'Well, you'd know all about that, wouldn't you?'

He looked down at the ground, laughing slightly. 'Yeah. I guess I asked for that one.'

Amber couldn't stop herself from looking over at the bar again. Ryan was still deep in some kind of conversation with the girls, almost as if he'd forgotten she existed. This was crazy! She was letting history repeat itself all over again – what the hell was she doing?

'I need a drink,' she mumbled, because it was blatantly obvious that Ryan wasn't going to get her one in a hurry, despite that being the whole reason he'd gone to the bar in the first place.

'Amber, listen,' Jim said, turning to face her, stopping her from walking away from him. 'Look, you know rooms are booked for everyone here tonight and…'

She looked at him, right into those green eyes of his, and she felt her stomach flip over again. A flip that seemed to go on and on, it wouldn't stop. Even though she wanted it to. She needed it to. 'Your point is?' she asked, her voice barely a whisper.

'We can get out of here, have a quiet drink upstairs. We can talk.'

'About what, Jim? About the fact I'm in the middle of something I can't even begin to explain with you whilst also being involved in a ridiculous relationship with one of your players? A player I care about…'

'But it doesn't look as though he cares all that much about you, honey.'

She looked over her shoulder, over at Ryan who'd now been joined by Gary at the bar, both of them still talking to the same two girls.

'Room 325,' Jim whispered, leaning in close to her again. 'Ten minutes.'

Amber watched him walk away, knowing she was an idiot for even contemplating following him, but where Jim Allen was concerned she was always going to be weak. Besides, Ryan had just knocked her good mood severely off-kilter now.

Taking a glass of something white and sparkling from a smiling waiter, she took a long sip and walked over to one of the huge floor-to-ceiling windows that lined an entire wall of the room, looking outside at the almost picture-perfect view of Christmas trees and fairy lights, all twinkling bright and colourful, lighting up the cold night with their magical glow. She'd always loved Christmas, she just had a feeling that this one wasn't going to be quite as uncomplicated as the ones she was used to. She had a lot of decisions to make, that was one thing she was certain of. A lot of decisions to make, and a lot of thinking to do. Should she make it a New Year and a new start? She'd never been the kind of person to make New Year's resolutions, but maybe this year it was time to change all that. Maybe.

'Why the fuck has he let partners come this year?' Gary groaned, watching as the redhead and her friend sashayed off across the room to see how many other Red Star players they could attract the attention of. 'If Debbie wasn't here I'd have been straight in for that redhead. She was up for it, I'm telling you.'

Ryan leaned back against the bar, downing a large mouthful of beer and sighing contentedly. 'You're gonna let it stop you, huh? Gary Blandford ignoring the calling?'

'I've told you, mate. Not when Debbie's around.'

'Doesn't look like she's that bothered,' Ryan grinned, indicating Gary's fiancée as she flirted quite openly with a tall, incredibly handsome-in-an-obvious-kind-of-way waiter who was quite happily reciprocating.

'Bitch!' Gary exclaimed, then smirked, sticking his hands in his pockets and leaning back, too, his body language changing immediately. 'That's my girl!'

Ryan shook his head, laughing. 'You're unbelievable.'

'Hark at Mr. Double Standards here. I didn't see *you* taking a step back from practically touching Ms. Brunette up, despite the fact your girlfriend's in the same room.'

'Shit! Amber…' Ryan said, suddenly realising he was supposed to be getting her a drink. What the hell had he been playing at? He guessed the effects of that afternoon's fun and games were still somewhat present, meaning that his thinking was still slightly clouded, his judgement a little off the mark. Obviously.

'You could find yourself in deep trouble now, mate,' Gary smirked as Ryan threw his head back and sighed. 'Look, quit fretting. She probably didn't even see you, she'll have been off somewhere with Debbie. The two of them are getting pretty friendly, by all accounts, which might not be a bad thing, actually. If those two become close it means they won't be spying on us quite so often.'

'Amber doesn't spy on me, Gary,' Ryan said, feeling slightly uncomfortable now. And he couldn't see Amber anywhere. Shit! Had she seen him and left? Jesus, what the hell was wrong with him today?

'Whatever, mate. I'm off to see if I can find that redhead, try and sort out something for later. If you get my drift.' He gave Ryan a knowing wink before winding his way through the crowd in search of his own idea of paradise.

Ryan threw his head back again, sighing heavily. The night had started off so well, but thanks to his brain taking five minutes off, he'd probably messed it all up now. And there was him telling Max he could control it this time around. It wasn't going to be the way it was before. Famous last words, Max had told him. Famous last words indeed.

Amber could feel her heart beating hard and fast as she stepped out of the lift, checking the room numbers as she walked along the quiet corridor, the noise of the party filtering up from below, muffled but just loud enough to make out the music playing. Every single part of her was screaming at her to turn around and not do this, this was exactly the way things had been all those years ago and yet still she came back for more. She couldn't stop herself. She'd tried, hadn't she? She'd tried, but it was like some kind of sick, invisible force pulling her towards him every time he was near. When she didn't have him around, when she didn't know he was there, it was easy – easier – to pretend nothing had ever happened between the two of them. But when he was this close, it was impossible. So, no. She couldn't turn back and walk away. He was a distraction she needed, and why not use *him* the way *he'd* used *her*? Didn't she deserve some kind of payback?

Yeah, you keep telling yourself that's what you're doing, Amber thought, her heart quickening even more as she finally reached Room 325. Lifting her hand up slowly, she balled it into a fist and made to knock on the door, but something stopped her. She paused for a second, closing her eyes, resting her forehead against the coolness of the wood as she tried to get her head together. But it was hard when it was all over the place and had been for months now. A few more seconds wasn't going to suddenly make her think any straighter, and as the image of Ryan and those girls filled her mind once more, she opened her eyes and stepped back slightly, tapping lightly on the door.

'Come in,' Jim's voice said from behind, and she carefully pushed it open, noticing the **'Do Not Disturb'** sign hanging from the handle, which only served to make her stomach take another almighty dip. She knew what was going to happen once she closed that door behind her, but seeing that innocuous sign swinging from the handle made it all the more real.

Turning the lock until it clicked, she looked up as she walked into the room. Jim was standing by the window, looking out into a darkness that was punctuated only by the twinkling fairy lights that seemed to adorn every bush and tree in the hotel's vast grounds. He was holding a glass of brandy in one hand, his other in the pocket of his suit trousers. His jacket was slung over a chair by the bathroom door.

'I've always loved this time of year,' he said, without turning round. 'Everyone always seems so happy.' He finally turned to face her, taking a small sip of brandy. He looked relaxed, which was more than Amber felt. 'Don't you think?'

Amber said nothing, just put her bag down on the dressing table and walked further into the room, rubbing her hands up and down her arms.

'Are you cold?' Jim asked, putting his brandy glass down on the windowsill behind him. 'I can turn the heating up…'

Amber shook her head. 'I'm not cold, Jim. Just, nervous.'

'Nervous?' he laughed. 'Of what? Of *me*?'

'Of what we're doing.'

'We're not doing anything, are we?'

She looked at him, wishing he wouldn't play these games. She had enough of that with Ryan.

He held out his hand and for a few seconds she just looked at it, not quite sure what to do. But before any sensible part of her brain could take over, she reached out and let him wrap his hand around hers, pulling her closer.

'We are now,' she whispered, playing with the open collar of his white shirt.

'What are you doing with him, Amber?'

She looked up into his eyes, a million memories flooding her head, tussling for space, crowding her thoughts – the memory of that first time she'd seen him as a twenty-seven-year-old player whom her dad had taken under his wing; the memory of the first time he'd kissed her, the first time he'd touched her. They were all still there, still as fresh as the day they were made. She'd never be able to shake them. Ever. She just had to accept that. He was so far under her skin that he could never be erased, that was just the way it was. And probably would be, forever.

'I don't know anymore,' she whispered, finally voicing a thought that had been going round and round in her head for weeks now. She didn't know. She didn't. 'But, if I'm going to hazard any kind of guess, I'd say it was to forget you. I'm with Ryan because I need to forget *you*. And I thought that being with him would help me do that.'

'And has it?'

She looked down at her fingers as they continued to fiddle with his shirt collar, shaking her head as her eyes met his. 'What do *you* think?'

'Then leave him.'

'It's not that simple.'

'Isn't it?'

She pulled away, walking over to the bed, turning her back to him. 'Things are complicated, Jim.'

'Complicated how, Amber?'

She inhaled deep, knowing she couldn't tell Jim too much for fear of him taking things out on Ryan by pulling him from the team, exposing his vulnerability; she risked letting the world know Ryan's problems, when that was the worst thing that could possibly happen. For everyone's sake.

'Ryan needs me.'

'That's bullshit, Amber. And you know it. Ryan doesn't need anybody, and we've been through this, honey. We've been through this, and you know as well as I do that he isn't going to change overnight. He's young, he's one of the most talented, most famous players this game has seen in a long while and he is going to milk that for all it's worth, believe me. I've seen it so many times before.' He paused for a few seconds as Amber turned around to face him again. 'I mean, I've been there. Haven't I?'

Amber said nothing. Yeah, he'd been there, and she'd been there with him. And now she was living it all over again with yet another handsome footballer who thought he could do anything with anyone and assume he could get away with it, no matter who got hurt in the process.

'Leave him, Amber. Walk away. He isn't going to change.'

'Because nobody will give him a chance,' Amber whispered, guilt flooding through her, which was quickly extinguished when those images of him at the bar reappeared once more, practically sealing the deal on what was going to happen in this room very soon.

Jim walked over to her, gently pushing her hair back off her shoulders, stroking her cheek with the palm of his hand as his eyes stared deep into hers. 'He doesn't deserve you.'

'And you do?' she asked.

He smiled, a smile that still had – and always would have – the ability to turn her world upside down. 'I love you, Amber.'

She wasn't sure how much importance she should put on those words anymore, after all, Ryan had told her he loved her, too, yet look at the way he was acting. If he loved her, then surely he wouldn't do the things he did? So why should she believe Jim any more than she did Ryan? She'd been right to avoid any kind of serious relationships over the years. They just complicated matters and intruded on life in a way Amber didn't welcome.

'I've always loved you,' Jim went on, his mouth moving closer to hers.

Amber felt her stomach dip and dive at a ridiculous speed and, despite every better judgement she could possibly have, she closed her eyes and let his lips touch hers, lightly at first before the kiss got harder, deeper, faster, until she had no choice left but to respond. She pressed her body against his, her arms sliding up around his neck, his hands pushing her closer as they rested in the small of her back. This was it. Those floodgates had been opened once more and the torrent was too quick to stem its flow, emotions too deep to ignore. Jim Allen was like some kind of cult she'd been sucked into, she couldn't escape him. She couldn't. She was too weak, too linked to him in some inexplicable way that she couldn't disentangle herself from this web he'd spun round her.

His fingers slowly moved up her back, carefully untying the halter-neck of her dress, standing back slightly as it fell to the floor, leaving her exposed in just her most expensive black and purple underwear. But she didn't care, she felt good – she felt sexy and turned-on and everything she'd always felt whenever Jim touched her. It was almost as if a kiss from him carried some kind of magic potion that cast its spell over her, turning her from rational to rampant in seconds.

She kicked her dress away, unfastening her bra as she walked round the bed, throwing it aside and turning round to face him, smiling as his eyes automatically lowered to look at her breasts.

Lying down on the bed, she stretched out, raising her arms above her head, arching her back, pulling one leg up and letting out a gentle moan that served its purpose. Within seconds he was naked, lying over her, his fingers exploring, causing her body to break out in tiny goose bumps wherever they touched. She didn't care about the shit going on in her life now. She didn't care that Ryan was a messed-up soccer star who didn't know how to control himself; she didn't care. She didn't care that her job was on the line, that her once-professional image was in question all because she'd let two men into her life that she should never have gone near. None of it mattered right now. All that mattered was that her childhood fantasy was back where he belonged, loving her the way she'd always dreamed he'd love her, touching her in places that made her crazy, that sent her head and her heart into a tailspin.

She moaned quietly as his mouth covered one of her breasts,

his tongue flicking, touching, his fingers moving down until they slid underneath the thin material of her panties. He pulled them down slowly, sitting up so he could watch her body finally become naked, and it was all Amber could do not to pull him down and make him take her there and then, so desperate was her need for him. Her breath was so fast, so shallow, she thought she might pass out, her whole body aching for him in that all-too-familiar way, an ache that was eased only slightly by his hand sliding between her legs, touching a warm wetness that he'd created. She threw her head back, stretching out even more as his mouth kissed the base of her neck, her fingers clasped together, every confusing emotion clashing against each other inside her head until all she wanted to do was feel him inside her so she could forget them all for a few beautiful minutes. But he was in no hurry, and Amber groaned loudly as he brought her to the brink of what would have been a spectacular climax with his expert fingers, pulling them away before she could enjoy their work. It was like a pain she couldn't turn off, couldn't escape from, and she wanted him back there, back to bring her that release she so desperately wanted. So desperately needed.

Opening her legs wider, he lay between them, his body resting against hers as his lips brushed over her shoulder, the side of her neck, until his mouth finally met hers in a kiss so beautiful she felt tears well up behind her eyes. This was how she'd always remembered him. This was the way Jim Allen had always lived inside her head, the way he was making love to her now. This was how she'd spent so many days, and far too many nights, wanting to be with him all the time but knowing it could never be that way. Could it *be* that way now? Or was she just confused by all the raw emotion flying around?

All she knew was that, when she finally felt their bodies become one, the wonderful feeling of calm he always seemed to bring her washed over her like a warm, comforting blanket. His hands were on her hips, keeping their bodies connected as they moved together in that perfect rhythm, their mouths touching in a series of quick, frantic kisses in between breaks to breathe. He was pushing hard, taking her over in the most explosive way, and there was nothing Amber could do to prevent her feelings for this man invading everything again – her life, her work, her relationships; he was there, constantly, and it didn't matter whether she wanted him there or not, he was always present. But right now she welcomed it, she needed it; like a drug she'd been denied for so long, but now she could grab that fix.

With one final push it was over, her body filling up with a white-hot pain that only intensified every confused and irrational feeling she'd been experiencing over the last few months. Yet, in a strange way, at the same time it also seemed to make everything that little bit clearer.

Keeping her eyes closed as Jim rolled over onto his back, she felt a sense of inevitability hit her. And maybe she'd been fighting it for all these months, ever since Jim had arrived back in the North East, she didn't know. She just felt that there was no way she could possibly move forward unless she admitted her true feelings. To everybody.

'Jim…' she began, turning to face him.

'Everything okay?' he asked, taking her hand, his fingers wrapping around hers, holding them tight.

Amber nodded, looking down at their joined hands. 'This isn't going to go away, is it?'

He shook his head, kissing her gently. 'No. It isn't.'

'So what do we do?'

'You know what I *want* you to do, Amber. I want you to leave Ryan and I want you to be with me. I want us to forget the past, forget what happened all those years ago, because this time things will be so, so different. No hiding, no secrets, no lies…'

'But there *will* be lies, won't there? Because I don't want anyone – especially not my dad – knowing what went on before. I know I was sixteen when it started, I know we did nothing wrong in reality, but… I just don't think it's a good idea to rake it all up, do you?'

He shook his head again. 'No, honey. I don't.'

She said nothing for a few seconds, staring at their hands, watching as his thumb stroked her knuckles, listening to his breathing. 'I don't know if I can leave him, Jim. I don't know if I can walk away from him, I really don't…'

He sat up, looking straight at her and she sat up, too, pulling the sheet up over her nakedness, feeling slightly exposed now. 'Has he got some kind of hold over you, Amber? Only, the way you talk about him, the fact you're so reluctant to walk away, it's all a little weird.'

'It's not weird, Jim.' She got up off the bed, retrieving her clothes and quickly dressing herself. 'But dumping him, just like that. For his *manager*? How is that going to look, huh?'

Jim got up, too, not bothering to cover his nakedness, and Amber couldn't help but stare at him – he might be forty-eight years old now but he still had a body that most men half his age would kill for. His playing days were over, but he hadn't let himself go. Far from it. 'You want to take things slow?'

'Jesus,' Amber sighed, running a hand through her messed-up curls. 'I don't know how I want to take things at all. I'm just so confused…'

He pulled her into his arms and she put up no fight, letting him hold her, loving the feel of his body against hers, closing her eyes as his mouth covered hers in another beautiful, slow kiss. 'However you want to play this, Amber, I won't push it. I promise. If you want to keep this just between us for the time being, then that's what we'll do. After all, we've got the rest of our lives together now, haven't we?'

She looked up into his eyes again, every ounce of resolve she might have had left disappearing within seconds. He'd won. The fight was over, she knew that. She had to be with Jim. She had to be. But how she told Ryan that, she had no idea.

301

Ryan needed to find her. The thought that she might have seen him behaving like a complete idiot felt like a thump to the stomach, a sobering-up the like of which he'd never experienced before. Despite the escape from reality he'd enjoyed that afternoon, something was telling him that maybe it was time to slow all that down now, before he burned himself out. Before he lost Amber for good. He'd treated her like crap over the past few months and it made him sick to think of what he'd done behind her back; how he'd thrown her trust back in her face when all she'd wanted to do was help him.

Leaving the party behind, he walked through the hotel lobby, bumping into Gary who was making his way back towards the function room, looking like the cat who'd got the proverbial cream.

'I take it you found Ms. Redhead, then?' Ryan asked dryly.

'Mate, that is one red-hot redhead! And it might be cold outside, but she's just managed to warm me up like you wouldn't believe. Man, I am buzzing!'

Ryan just looked at him. 'Your fiancée is in that room, you do realise that, don't you?'

Gary shrugged, sticking his hands in his pockets and grinning as the redhead sauntered past, throwing him a smile that screamed a thousand words. 'What the eye doesn't see… something you'd know all about, eh, Ryan?'

'Have you seen Amber?' he asked, ignoring Gary's comment.

'Amber? Hang on, yeah. I *did* see her a while ago, actually, on me way out to find Karli.'

'Karli?' Ryan frowned.

'Yeah. Ms. Redhead.'

'Okay. So you saw Amber. Where was she going? Did you see?'

'She was going upstairs.'

'Upstairs?' Ryan asked, frowning again. 'Why?'

'How should *I* know, mate. I didn't speak to her, I just saw her get into the lift. Maybe she was going to your room or something.'

'Oh, yeah,' Ryan said, breathing a sigh of relief. 'Of course.

Right, okay. I'll go see if I can find her, then.'

'You do that. I suppose *I'd* better get back in there and see how much the missus hasn't missed me. Catch you later, mate.'

But Ryan had already gone. The sooner he found Amber and got this night back on track the better.

'I made Ryan so many promises,' Amber whispered, leaning back against the wall opposite the lift, pulling Jim closer by his jacket collar, but only because the corridor was quiet. She was ready to push him away should anyone else appear. But the noise still drifting up from the party downstairs told them nobody seemed in any hurry to turn in for the night just yet. 'And knowing I'm going to have to break those promises…' She looked at him. 'I know exactly how he's going to feel, because I've been there.'

Jim looked away briefly before turning back to face her, placing his hand palm-down on the wall beside her head, leaning in to kiss her slightly open mouth. 'He'll get over it, Amber. Kids like Ryan, they always do.'

'Are you speaking from experience there, huh? Did you get over *me* that quickly, then?'

'Amber, honey, come on…'

She smiled, stroking his face with her fingertips, kissing him ever so lightly. 'Alright, I'm sorry, but… you're just gonna have to give me some time, Jim. Okay? You hurt me. You made it difficult for me to ever trust anyone again, so you have to realise that I can't just push what happened under the carpet as though it never happened at all. Even if that's how we're gonna have to act when we eventually go public. For now, though, it's just you and me.' She kissed him again, a little longer, a little harder. 'Until I work out what I'm going to say to Ryan, nobody else can know anything.'

But neither of them had heard the lift doors open or seen the figure step out. Neither of them had heard a thing.

'I'd say it's a little late for that, wouldn't you?'

Chapter Seventeen

'Does someone want to tell me what the fuck is going on?' Ryan asked, not quite believing what he was seeing in front of him – Amber and Jim Allen? He knew they were friends, but *this*? 'Have you two…? Have you been…?' He shook his head. 'No, this isn't right. I can see it on your face, Amber. You've slept with him. Just now. I can tell. You've just fucked him…'

'Jesus, Ryan, please,' Amber said, pushing Jim away and running over to him, trying to take his hand, but he pulled it back. She stared at him. 'Hang on a minute. Are you honestly gonna stand there and lecture *me* on cheating when *you* have been shagging Christ knows *what* behind my back because, whatever you've told me, I know it's still going on. I know…'

'He's my *manager,* Amber. He's my fucking boss!'

'Okay… okay, please, keep your voice down…'

'You might want to listen to her, Ryan,' Jim said, folding his arms as he looked at his star striker. 'She's giving you good advice.'

'What the fuck…?' Ryan made to go for Jim, but Jim stood his ground as Amber threw an arm between them, grabbing Ryan by the waist to pull him back.

'That's not a good idea, Ryan. Come on. Come on, we'll go somewhere quiet. We'll talk about this.'

He looked at her, still not able to take it all in. How long had this been going on? All the time he and Amber had been together? Or was it just some stupid, drunken mistake? The kind of thing that happened at Christmas parties. He'd like to believe the latter, but he knew how close Jim was to Amber – he'd just thought it was friendship, that was all. How wrong could he be?

'I can't do this,' Ryan said, shaking his head again, waves of confusion mixed with anger washing over him. 'I can't fucking do this. I've got to get out of here…'

'No, Ryan! Ryan, please…'

'Leave him, Amber.'

'No, I *won't* leave him, Jim. What if he says something? What if this all comes out now?' She knew that was a really selfish way of looking at things, but she couldn't help panicking. This was all so complicated, so hard to explain.

'Then we deal with it.'

'Jesus, I love the way you can be so calm about everything. You make it sound so bloody easy. Have you got any idea how he's feeling right now? Huh? How much this could hurt him?'

'It's you and me now, Amber.' Jim walked over to her, tilting up her chin so her eyes met his. 'It's you and me now.'

She shook her head, pulling away from him. 'Not yet, Jim. Not until I'm sure he's alright.'

And before Jim could stop her, she was running downstairs, hoping she could catch Ryan before he did anything stupid. Because only she knew what he was capable of right now, and that thought alone made her nervous.

Out of breath and with her heart feeling as though it was beating out of her chest, Amber finally made it down to the hotel lobby in time to see Ryan walking back into the party. She practically ran to catch up with him, finding him at the bar downing a large whisky.

'What do you want?' He wasn't really in the mood to talk to her. Not after what he'd just seen.

'I want to talk to you,' she replied. 'Please, Ryan. I can explain…'

He laughed. He couldn't help it. Was she *really* going to wheel

305

out the old *'I can explain'* cliché? 'Yeah. That's what they all say, isn't it?'

She was starting to get a touch aggravated now. How dare he stand there and act like the wounded victim? After everything *he'd* done? 'Listen, Ryan,' she began, trying to keep her voice quiet, because the last thing she wanted was a scene. 'I don't know where you get off acting all holier than thou, I mean, Jesus, you were practically fucking those two girls at the bar right in front of me…'

'Just how close a family friend *is* he, Amber? Has "Uncle" Jim always been this attentive to his best friend's daughter? Exactly how much does daddy know, huh?'

Amber glared at him. 'My dad knows nothing, Ryan. And if you care anything about me then you won't say a word. Please. There's a lot more to this than you know…'

He threw his head back and laughed again. 'Jesus Christ… But, do you know what? Things are suddenly a lot clearer now, like why Jim dropped me from that match a few weeks ago. Was it going on then, Amber? Did he get jealous of you and me and decide to exert his authority in the only way he knew how? Is that the way it was?'

'Look, Ryan – we're in one hell of a messed-up relationship, you and me. It's been like that from the start, and I don't think even *you* can argue with me on that score.'

'I love you, Amber. I fucking told you that, and I should have realised when you didn't say it back…'

'You never loved me, Ryan. How could you love me when you did what you did?'

'I love you,' Ryan repeated, looking right into her eyes. 'Yes, I've been an idiot, and if you must know, I was on my way upstairs to find you and tell you exactly how I feel and how much of an idiot I've been. How much I regret what I've done because my actions could have meant I lost you. And I didn't want to face that. Suddenly that scared me, y'know? But it seems like you didn't really give a fuck about me.'

'You are so wrong, Ryan. You are so, so wrong…'

'You never had any intention of sticking by me, did you? Not when you were sleeping with my fucking manager.'

Amber leaned back against the bar, closing her eyes for a second as she tried to take in just what was happening here. 'We need to talk, Ryan,' she said quietly, looking at him, but he was staring straight ahead. 'And here really isn't the place, is it?'

He turned to face her. Shit! He was never going to get his head around the fact she'd been sleeping with Jim Allen. But some sick part of him really wanted to know just what was going on between those two, even if he wasn't going to like everything he heard. 'Let's go upstairs. Come on. We can talk in peace up there.'

She didn't know whether to breathe a sigh of relief that he seemed to have suddenly calmed down, or whether to feel nervous because he could be so unpredictable. Either way, she was just glad they were getting out of there to somewhere more private. At least he seemed sober and sensible enough to realise that causing a scene wasn't the best move – for anyone.

Closing the door of their room behind him, Ryan watched as she walked over to the window, throwing her bag onto the floor by the bed. 'You said there was a lot more to this… what did you mean by that?'

She turned around, folding her arms against her as she leaned back against the windowsill. 'This isn't just… it isn't just a recent thing, me and Jim.'

Ryan walked further into the room, his hands in his pockets, looking at her through narrowed eyes. 'How d'you mean, not a recent thing? How long's it been going on? Before me and you?'

Amber turned away for a second, unsure as to what good telling him this would do, but he deserved to know the truth. She owed him that much.

'It started when I… when he was a player, for Red Star.'

Ryan frowned, keeping his eyes on her all the time, even though she was looking at the floor. 'That was… how *old* were you back

307

then? He was about *my* age when he joined Red Star, wasn't he?'

Amber nodded, still staring at her boots, her arms still folded across her chest. 'I was sixteen, Ryan…'

'Sixteen? Jesus Christ, Amber…'

'Let me finish, Ryan. Please.' She finally looked up, her eyes locking onto his, swallowing hard before she spoke again. 'I had this – this massive crush on him…'

'And he took advantage of that, did he?'

'Please. Just, let me finish. It went on for a couple of years, but nobody else knew. Nobody. Not my dad, not my mum, nobody. It was all this huge, exciting secret. Until he hurt me. Until he became involved with somebody else and just threw me aside like some used toy. So I left the North East, tried to forget him by throwing myself into university life and it worked, y'know? For a while. Until I moved back home to find him still around. Only, this time he was single again.'

'You went back to him?' Ryan asked, finding it really hard to believe that someone like Amber could be so weak. She just hadn't struck him as that kind of woman.

Amber nodded. 'For more years of secret meetings, lies… and then he did it again, didn't he? He hurt me – again. By this time his playing days were over, of course, and I didn't see why *I* should be the one to leave my home town… but I couldn't move on if he was around. I was so in love with him, so fucking in love, it wouldn't go away, even after everything he'd done. But I knew I couldn't get on with my life if he stayed in the North East, so he promised me… he promised me he'd stay away. He promised me…' She turned and looked out of the window, watching as a giggling couple ran across the large, fairy-lit patio area down below, throwing themselves behind one of the giant Christmas trees before indulging in the kind of kissing and groping that seemed rife at Christmas parties.

'And then he turns up as Red Star's new manager,' Ryan said, his voice monotone. 'After all those years… and you're still in love with him now, I take it?'

Amber nodded again, hugging herself as she continued to stare out of the window. 'I'm so sorry, Ryan.' She turned round, tears she didn't really deserve to cry beginning to fall slowly down her face. 'I should never have got so close to you, but I thought… I thought… You didn't deserve any of this.'

He walked over to her, pulling her arms away from her body, his hand slipping into hers. 'You thought that by being with me you could forget him. Is that it?'

She looked up into his dark blue eyes. He really was one of the most beautiful men she'd ever seen, and somewhere deep inside she felt so much for him, she really did. She just couldn't explain those feelings, couldn't understand exactly why she was with him; she couldn't work out whether she was with him for all the right reasons, or all the wrong ones, and that wasn't fair on him. 'I do care about you, Ryan. Please believe me when I say that, because it's true. But… but sometimes it feels as though I'm more like your mother than your girlfriend. All the worrying about what you're doing, where you're going…'

'It drove you back to him,' Ryan said, an almost resigned tone to his voice.

'Jesus, I don't know, Ryan. I don't know if that's the case, I really don't. Jim, he's… he's just always *been* there, y'know? There's never been any other man who can make me feel the way *he* does.'

'Even after the way he treated you in the past?'

'He's promised me that won't happen again.'

Ryan threw his head back and laughed a loud, cynical laugh. 'For Christ's sake, Amber. Have you heard yourself? What the hell's happened to that hard-faced ice-queen I fell in love with, huh? You're gonna let him do this to you all over again? Is that it? You're gonna throw it all away because Jim Allen has decided to walk back into your life?'

She pulled her hand free and walked over to the bed, sitting down on the edge of it. 'I can't forget him, Ryan. I can't spend my life with him here and me pretending I don't feel the way I do, that isn't fair on me. And it certainly isn't fair on you.'

He sat down next to her, leaning forward and clasping his hands between his open legs. 'I'll change, Amber. All the partying, all the crap that goes with this life, I'll bin it, forget it. I'll do that, I promise. Max was right…'

She looked at him, smiling a weak smile. 'I have to be with him, Ryan.'

'Why? When there's every chance he's going to hurt you again?'

'You don't know him like I do.'

'That's such a clichéd thing to say, Amber. Jesus, babe, you're such a strong woman, why are you acting like some lovesick teenager?'

Because that's what she was always going to be where Jim Allen was concerned – that sixteen-year-old, love-struck girl. She turned away from Ryan again, getting up and walking back over to the window. 'I've got to do this, Ryan. That's all I know. If I want my life to get back to any kind of normality, then I need to listen to my heart and I need to be with him.' She turned round to face him as he walked over to her. 'It's all I know, Ryan. *He's* all I know.'

'It doesn't have to be that way, Amber,' Ryan said quietly, reaching out to gently touch her cheek. 'You and me, we can make this work, if you'll let me.'

She shook her head, trying hard not to cry again. 'No,' she whispered. 'I've tried, and I can't – *you* can't. Deep down inside I don't think it's what you really want, Ryan. Not yet. But, promise me…' He turned his head away, but she put her hand to his face, making him look at her again. 'Promise me you'll pull yourself together and concentrate on your career. Please, Ryan. You don't need a babysitter, you don't need that, and Max is underestimating you if that's what he really believes. You are an intelligent man, a talented man, and I don't want you to throw that away, do you hear me? Promise me, Ryan.'

Ryan said nothing. He couldn't. Because only now did he realise how much she meant to him. Only now, when she was about to walk away from him, did he realise how much he really needed her. Only now did he feel something he'd never felt before – a sense of impending loss that almost took his breath away, and already he could feel a pain in his chest that hurt like hell. She was leaving him. For his manager. And she didn't think she was what he wanted? She was so bloody wrong.

'If I'd tried harder… if I'd tried to stop, if I'd made the effort…'

She stroked his cheek, smiling as she looked into those beautiful deep-blue eyes. Her handsome, beautiful boy. 'Jim was never going to go away, Ryan. I could never ignore him. I've been fighting it since the day he came back here, so… I don't know. But I doubt it.'

In a reflex action he couldn't stop, he lowered his mouth down onto hers, kissing her like he'd never kissed anyone before, because it was probably the last time he was ever going to feel her this close. And that pain only got worse as she responded, her mouth moving on his like this was just some bad dream and they were fine, really. They were okay, and she wasn't going anywhere. But she was. And he was just going to have to accept it. Somehow.

Chapter Eighteen

She was beginning to feel like a gypsy as she hauled boxes of her belongings back into her old house, thankful that she'd only ever rented it out and not sold it. It would be good to get settled back in her own home before Christmas. She loved this house. Back in her own territory, she felt as though she could finally get some kind of control back over her life because, for a time, she'd lost that.

Sighing heavily as the phone rang, she dumped the box she was carrying down on the hall floor before running into the kitchen to answer it, tucking the receiver between her chin and shoulder as she filled the kettle. 'Yeah?'

'Amber, it's Max.'

Amber let out a silent sigh, leaning back against the counter. 'What do you want, Max?'

'Have you seen Ryan lately?'

'No. I haven't. Why would I? We're not together anymore.'

'Yeah. So I heard.'

'And what's *that* tone of voice for?' Amber was slightly agitated now. Why was he calling her? She had a million and one things to be getting on with; she didn't have time for this.

'He needed you, Amber. *I* needed you.'

'Hang on a minute, that's not fair. You're making it sound like you wanted me to stick with Ryan to be nothing more than some glorified babysitter who could keep an eye on him for you.'

'But you *did* stick with him. For a while, didn't you? What changed your mind? I would've thought a woman like you could've pulled him back into line in no time, yet all he did was go further down a path he should never have taken. Again.'

'Okay, listen to me before you say anything else I could consider vaguely insulting. I stayed with Ryan because, at the time, I thought we had something. Do you understand? I cared about him, and yes, I wanted to help him. But as the relationship grew, it became evident that I couldn't stay with him just to get him through a bad time...'

'A *bad* time? Have you got *any* idea what that kid went through in London? He was washed-up, Amber. Or he would've been, if I hadn't managed to pull him back from the brink and get him the help he needed.'

'So, what's this, then? You can't be arsed to help him a second time?'

'I'm not his father.'

'Then maybe you should get in touch with his dad and let his parents deal with him.'

'It nearly killed them, Amber. Seeing their son go through what he went through, almost losing it all...'

Amber threw her head back, sighing silently again. 'I'm not his social worker, Max. And I can't let you pile guilt on me that I shouldn't be feeling. That isn't fair.'

'He needs you, Amber.'

'I can't help that, Max.'

She hung up before the conversation could go any further, but it was too late. The guilt had already set in.

'Where do you want this one?' Ronnie asked, coming into the kitchen with yet another box.

'Just stick it over there,' Amber replied, indicating the battered old sofa she loved so much.

'Okay. What's up?' Ronnie put the box down on the floor at

his feet and walked over to her.

'What am I doing, Ronnie?'

'Well,' Ronnie began, folding his arms as he leaned back against the counter beside her, '… I'd say you're moving house. Again.'

She looked at him out the corner of her eye. 'You know what I mean.'

Ronnie sighed, reaching back to flick on the kettle. 'Amber, sweetheart, I'm only going to irritate you if I start telling you what I think.'

'Irritate me. Come on.'

'I don't think you should be with either of them. But, if you really think things with Jim are going to be different…'

'I can't guarantee that, can I?' Amber sighed. 'I just know that I can't be without him right now.' She shrugged, pushing a hand through her hair. 'Maybe I just need to get him out of my system once and for all, who knows? But I feel so guilty about Ryan.'

'Why are you feeling guilty? Come on, Amber, he was never your problem.'

'Jesus, Ronnie, he was more than just a "problem". I feel like I've let him down.'

Ronnie pulled her into his arms, hugging her tight. 'Hey, listen to me, alright? Ryan is a mixed-up but extremely talented young man who just needs someone to give him a kick up the arse and tell him to grow up.'

''Cause it's that simple, right?'

Ronnie hugged her again, kissing the top of her head. 'He's either going to see sense or self-implode, either way, it's not your fight, Amber.'

'I care about him, Ronnie. That was never in doubt. He just frustrated the hell out of me.'

'Well, he's not the first footballer to act like this, and he won't be the last. You know that, kiddo.'

She pulled away, taking two mugs out of the cupboard and throwing teabags into them, covering them with boiling water

314

from the kettle. 'Doesn't mean I have to stop caring, does it?'

'No,' Ronnie sighed. 'But maybe you need to start getting your life back to normal now, sweetheart. When are you back at work?'

'I'm popping into the office between Christmas and New Year. I want to get sorted before the transfer window opens again in January.' She checked her watch.

'Somewhere you've got to be?' Ronnie asked, getting the milk from the fridge.

'I said I'd meet Jim.'

'Have you told your dad about you and Jim yet?'

She stirred her tea slowly, looking out of the French doors onto her small but beautifully organised garden. Everything in her life had been organised, once-upon-a-time. Everything compartmentalised, because that's the way she'd liked things. And now look at her. Everything was all over the place and she was still trying to get her head around it all.

'No. Not yet. We're going to wait, at least until after Christmas.' She turned back to look at Ronnie. 'And before you ask, no, we're not going to tell him anything about the past. As far as he's concerned – as far as everybody else is concerned – this is a recent thing.'

'You're gonna lie to him?'

'It's not lying, Ronnie. It's just not telling him something he doesn't need to know. It's different.'

Ronnie arched an eyebrow. 'Really?'

'Really,' Amber said, handing him his tea. 'Now, finish this and get out of here. Didn't you say you were meeting Anna later at the MetroCentre?'

'God help me,' Ronnie sighed, smiling. 'Christmas shopping is her idea of heaven, and my idea of hell.'

Amber couldn't help smiling, too. 'It's a necessary evil.'

Ronnie looked at her again. 'Are you happy, Amber? Only, you don't seem to have been *really* happy for a while. And I worry about you.'

'Well, don't. I'm fine, okay? I'm fine. Things have been a bit weird lately, and they're probably going to be a bit weird for a little while longer, but they'll settle down. Eventually.' She smiled at her best friend again. 'Ronnie, I… I love Jim. I always have. And I don't really expect anyone else to understand why, because I don't even know myself, all I *do* know is that I've got to do this. I've just got to.'

But that still didn't stop her from caring about Ryan. And all she could do was hope that he'd listened to what she'd said and was trying to finally put his demons behind him. She wished that for him with all of her heart.

The official club Christmas party might have been a washout, as far as Ryan was concerned, anyway, but the lads still had their own 'team night out' to look forward to, which was sure to be a hell of a lot more fun. No partners were invited, for starters. Not that that bothered Ryan anymore. He was back to being young, free and extremely single and he had every intention of using that to his advantage in any way he could later on when they hit some of the hottest, trendiest bars and clubs the city had to offer.

In the months leading up to Christmas, the Red Star squad devised a system to raise money for this annual night out – a team tradition, Ryan had been told, although he'd been a part of much the same kind of thing at other clubs, too – by setting up a 'fine' box. Players could be 'fined' for anything from a yellow card on a match day to a story appearing about you in the press, but if it happened to you then you were required to stick a donation in the collection tin and all the proceeds would go towards a 'bender of a night out', as Gary put it. And that sounded good to Ryan. Especially as he'd had to stump up quite a bit of cash in 'fines' himself, lately.

'I hear you and the rest of the squad are heading off into town later tonight,' Jim said, approaching Ryan in the now-empty dressing room as he packed his kit away, ready to leave the training

316

ground for the day.

Ryan looked at the man who'd taken Amber away from him, because that's the way Ryan saw things. It was *that* black and white.

He said nothing to Jim, just turned his attention back to zipping up his kitbag, slinging it up onto his shoulder as he made to leave.

Jim put an arm out in front of him, blocking his exit. 'I was talking to you, Ryan. I'd appreciate it if you didn't blank me.'

Ryan glared at his manager, feeling nothing but an anger he couldn't extinguish. It was getting harder and harder for him to face this man every day, knowing how Amber felt about him. Knowing he was responsible for her not being in his life anymore. It was hard, and Ryan knew he needed to get out of there before the rational part of his brain relented and let his real feelings loose. 'And I'd appreciate it if *you* didn't interfere in my personal relationships.'

'I didn't interfere, Ryan. Amber and me – it's something you could never understand. The connection we have, nobody can get past that. Least of all you.'

Ryan was so close to punching this guy, but Jim was too quick for him, grabbing his wrist before he had a chance to do something really stupid. 'I wouldn't recommend you do that, Ryan. Now, I've let the fact that you've been acting like a grade-A asshole over the past few days go, but you need to know that if this carries on, then we'll just have to find another way to make things work round here. Won't we?'

Ryan narrowed his eyes as he looked at Jim. 'What the hell's *that* supposed to mean?'

Jim said nothing for a few seconds, finally letting go of Ryan's wrist, taking a couple of steps back. 'Well, if it looks as though we can't work together as things are, we'll have to explore some other options.' He turned to leave the dressing room, but swung back round as he reached the door, looking at Ryan again. 'And if I were you, I'd behave myself tonight. Let's not give ourselves any extra ammunition. Okay?'

Ryan watched him leave, waiting until he'd been gone a good few seconds before turning and punching the wall hard, not feeling the sharp pain that shot through his knuckles as he leaned back against it, closing his eyes. Veiled threats aside, Ryan couldn't really give a fuck about his career anymore. It meant nothing to him. The game he'd once loved now just felt like an empty, vacuous pastime that was there only to intersperse the nights of partying, the days of making his own kind of fun, all of which took his mind off the things he really wanted. The person he really needed.

'You still here?' Gary asked, walking back into the dressing room. 'Jesus Christ, Ryan. What the fuck have you done to your hand?'

Ryan held his hand out in front of him, looking at the raw, blood-speckled skin across his knuckles, but still feeling no pain. He couldn't tell anyone about Amber and Jim. Not because he wanted to protect Jim, far from it. But he cared about Amber, and despite everything that had happened, he didn't want to hurt her. So he'd keep his mouth shut, even though it was killing him.

'We still on for tonight?' Ryan asked, picking up his kitbag again and sticking his injured hand in his jacket pocket.

'Too frigging right we are!' Gary replied, grabbing the jacket he'd left behind. 'It's gonna be one hell of a wild night.'

'Good,' Ryan said, more determined than ever to forget all the shit that was going on in his life right now. 'Because I'm just in the fucking mood.'

'If you want to tell your dad before Christmas…' Jim began as they walked along the sea front, the freezing cold December air more biting than bracing.

'I don't,' Amber said, wanting so much to snuggle in against him to shield her from the cold, or just to slide her hand into his like a proper couple. That's all she wanted to be – one half of a proper couple. She'd never had that with Ryan – she'd never had that at all, if she was honest. Thirty-seven years old and she'd never had a proper relationship. Her time with Ronnie didn't really count because they hadn't been together long enough for it to be considered a proper relationship – she'd been far too concerned about letting herself get too involved, as she had been for all those years since Jim Allen had first walked into her life. It might be nice to actually know what it felt like, for once. But not yet. Everyone knew she and Jim were friends, so to see them talking a walk together wouldn't be unusual. But to see them holding hands or snuggling in would only cause the gossip grapevine to go into overdrive, and Amber couldn't risk that. So they'd bide their time and take it slow. That was the way it had to be. For now. 'Let's get Christmas out of the way first, okay?'

They stopped to look out over the grey, choppy North Sea, the wind whipping up white-tipped waves that crashed loudly up onto the sand at King Edward's Bay.

'I'm really surprised you never wanted to go back to the States,' Amber said, finding it difficult to ignore the spark of electricity that shot through her as his arm quickly brushed against hers. 'Did you never think about it? After your playing days were over?'

Jim leaned over the railings, looking down at the small, sandy cove below that was almost deserted, bar a couple of dog walkers. But then, the weather was hardly conducive to a day out at the beach. 'It was never an option, moving back there permanently. I went over for visits every now and again, but my heart was here, Amber.' He looked at her, right into her eyes, and that urge to reach out and kiss him was so hard to resist. So hard that Amber had to turn away from him, focus on the clashing waves and the dogs barking at them then scampering away as they crashed loudly onto the sand. 'This is my home now. I have a great career, a good life… but having *you* by my side is going to make everything complete. Do you hear me, Amber? You're that missing piece of my own personal jigsaw puzzle; the part I need to finally make everything come together.'

She looked down at her glove-covered hands as they gripped the railings in front of her. 'I'm scared of peoples' reactions, Jim.

When they find out about us.' She looked at him again, taking in every line on his handsome face, that urge to kiss his mouth still one she was fighting with everything she had. 'It could end up in such a mess, couldn't it?'

He reached out to take her hand, but she shook her head, causing him to pull it back, shoving it in his pocket. 'This is crazy, Amber. All I want to do is hold your hand, act like any other normal couple...'

'But we're not any other normal couple, are we?'

'We *can* be, baby. Look, why don't we just bite the bullet, tell your dad, forget all this waiting. There's no need for us to put ourselves through that. We've made our decision. So let's get it all out in the open now and start living our lives, honey. Don't you want that?'

She started walking again, burying her own hands in the pockets of her warm and cosy winter coat as the sky began darkening above them, signalling the impending end of another day. Another confusing, head-wrecking day. 'Of course I want it, Jim. It's all I've wanted since I was sixteen years old.'

He gently touched her arm, making her stand still and look at him. 'Then let's go for a drink, sit down and talk about this. Okay?'

She smiled. He was right. What was the point in waiting? And maybe it would make Christmas that little bit less stressful if everyone finally knew the truth – or most of it, anyway. 'Yeah. Okay. Why not?'

Ryan downed another Jagerbomb, slamming the glass down on the table as Gary shouted over at the barman to line up another round. He didn't know how many he'd had, and he didn't care. Just as long as they were doing the job he wanted them to do, he'd keep on drinking them.

Another night, another bar with thudding music, free drinks and too many women to choose from. Ryan was throwing himself into it with everything he had, knocking back the alcohol like there was no tomorrow and, as far as he was concerned, he couldn't care less if there wasn't. All he wanted to do was numb the pain and forget what he could have had. Forget that Amber was fucking his boss; Jim Allen was the one who got to touch her now. Jim Allen was the one who got to sleep beside her, kiss her mouth, lie between those incredible legs of hers and put himself inside her. He couldn't stop thinking about it, couldn't stop torturing himself with images of the two of them together and the only way he could see to drown them out, to push them away, was to drink himself into some kind of oblivion before taking part in another mindless round of pointless fucks with women who had no idea how much pain he was in, because, when he closed his eyes it wasn't them he was fucking – it was Amber. If he tried to pretend it was her, then that pain lessened for just a few short minutes, and if the pretending didn't work, then he took it out on whomever happened to be underneath him, taking them so hard he made them cry out loud, but it was the only way he knew how to make himself feel any better. Even if it was verging on incredibly selfish. The girls didn't seem to mind. No one complained. Most of them took it as a sign to push back just as hard, digging their manicured nails into his back, screaming out loud like pain-wracked banshees as they shoved their skinny hips up against his. But even the white-hot release the sex gave him wasn't enough to make him pretend he could live with what had happened. He'd been stupid. He'd been an idiot. He'd been one selfish prick, but hey, she'd been no angel, either. He might have been sleeping around behind her back, but no woman he'd touched had meant a thing to him. They were all nothing but a release, an escape, a chance he hadn't been strong enough to pass up because these girls gave it to him on a plate. Amber, however, had been fucking a man she'd been in love with for over twenty years. She had feelings for Jim, she had a past with the man, and that changed everything. Jesus, he needed another alcohol kick, and fast.

'Hey, hey, take it easy, mate,' Gary said, watching as Ryan picked up two shots in quick succession, throwing them both down his throat at breakneck speed.

'Why, Gary? *Why* should I take it easy? I'm having the time of my frigging life here, so don't be a fucking killjoy and join that queue of people trying to tell me how to behave, okay? I'm sick of it.'

'Just, slow down, alright? We've still got training in the morning...'

'Fuck training. In fact, fuck it all, I'm done.' He picked up another shot, smiling as a beautiful blonde girl sat down next to him. Leaning over towards her, he began kissing her long and hard, breaking away only to throw the shot down his neck. The pain was slowly numbing, his brain was beginning to say goodbye to all those things he didn't want to think about; he was finally starting to feel calmer. As he'd worked out over the past few days, it took time. It took a few drinks, a couple of pretty girls; a line or two when no one was looking, and then he was ready to carry on. Without all that, he wasn't sure he could be bothered anymore.

'Move in with me,' Jim said, coming up behind Amber as she made them both a coffee back at his modest detached home in the little coastal village of Tynemouth.

She smiled, leaning back against him as his arms wrapped around her, his lips gently kissing her neck. She closed her eyes and gave in to his touch, enjoying the shivers running up and down her spine, the somersaults her stomach was turning. She could get used to this, but that was part of the problem. She'd gotten used to it before and then she'd been hurt. And she'd let that happen twice. But this time he wanted to go public, he wanted people to know about the two of them and that meant things were very different than before. This time he didn't want the secrets, the lies – this time he wanted the world to know. And this time it was *her* who was holding back from making it public knowledge.

She turned round to face him, running her hands up and down his arms as she looked into those green eyes of his. 'I think it's a bit soon for all of that, don't you?'

'Not really,' Jim replied, stroking her fringe from her eyes. 'It's been twenty-one years, Amber. It's taken us twenty-one years to get to this point so, no, I don't think it's too soon. I think we've waited long enough.'

She looked down for a second. If she was completely honest with herself, she was still trying to get her head around the speed at which all of this was happening. Just a few short months ago Jim Allen had been nothing but an aching memory at the back of her mind that she'd managed to control. Just a few short months ago Ryan Fisher had been nothing but a name, someone she knew about purely because of what he did, who he was. He'd meant nothing to her; he'd been just another footballer. He was so far from that now. And that guilt she felt at leaving him the way she had, it still stung deep. But she couldn't put her life on hold in the hope that he wasn't going to wreck *his*. She couldn't do it, even if she couldn't completely put him out of her mind.

'Amber, baby, he's going to be fine.'

She looked up at Jim, aware that she must've drifted off briefly. 'I... I wasn't...'

'He's all grown up; an adult. Even if he doesn't always act like one. He doesn't need his hand holding. *He* doesn't need you. He needs attention and adulation and everything else players like him thrive on. He doesn't need *you*. But I do.'

She smiled, reaching up to gently stroke his face. She wasn't sure she believed all of that, but maybe he was right. Maybe she had to stop worrying about something and someone she had no control over and start trying to live her life the way she wanted to live it. After twenty-one years of waiting.

'I love you, Amber Sullivan,' Jim whispered, his mouth resting on hers as he spoke, and with every word he breathed Amber could feel her heart start to beat faster, louder. She felt her knees weaken and her body ache for him; she felt everything she'd kept locked away, hidden inside, for all those years. Because, finally, he could be hers. All those dreams, all those fantasies and fairy tales she'd spent her life thinking about, they could come true now, couldn't they? So why couldn't she say she loved him, too? When it was so obvious she did.

'Maybe it isn't too soon after all, then,' she smiled, stroking his cheek with her thumb as his mouth lowered down onto hers again in a kiss so beautiful it hurt. 'We'll tell my dad soon, okay? Before Christmas.'

'That doesn't leave us long, honey. Look, he might think it all a bit weird to begin with, and who can blame him? It's a lot to get his head around, his old friend and his daughter, but…'

'He can't find out about our past, Jim.'

'Nobody said anything about the past, Amber…'

She was distracted by her phone ringing, but Jim grabbed her arm, stopping her from going over to answer it. 'Leave it. If it's important they'll leave a message.'

'Jim…'

'Leave it, Amber. Please.'

She shook her head, pulling free from his grip. She hated leaving phones unanswered – maybe that was all part of the control issues she had, but it wasn't something she could do, something she could forget about.

Picking up her phone, she looked at the caller ID. It was a number she didn't recognise, and not one from her own list of contacts.

'Who is it?' Jim asked, leaning back against the countertop and folding his arms. He obviously hadn't missed the frown on Amber's face.

'I don't know.'

'Then leave it. It's probably just a wrong number.'

She shook her head again, putting the phone to her ear. 'Amber Sullivan.'

'Amber? Jesus, thank Christ you answered.'

Amber frowned again, not recognising the voice on the other

end of the line, but whoever it was, they sounded more than a touch panic-stricken.

'Who is it?' Jim asked again, but Amber turned away, panic of her own suddenly setting in. Had something happened to her dad?

'Who *is* this?' she said, trying to keep her voice steady.

'Oh, erm, sorry. It's Gary. Gary Blandford. Ryan's teammate...'

'Gary? What... what's happened?'

'Shit, Amber, you've got to get over here quick, because I haven't got a clue...'

'What's happened, Gary? What's going on?'

'It's Ryan. And I really think you need to get over here fast because me and Debbie, we're out of our depth, Amber. We're out of our fucking depth.'

Chapter Nineteen

Amber raced up the drive of the house she'd only just moved out of, her heart beating out of her chest as the front door swung open and Debbie stood there, arms folded, her face pale and tired, despite the fake tan and the make-up.

'What's happened?' Amber asked, slamming the door shut behind her, her head spinning with feelings she couldn't even begin to describe. She'd hung up from Gary, told Jim nothing other than there was something she needed to do, and left his place without a word of explanation. What *could* she have said? When she had no idea what was going on herself. But she'd spent most of the twenty-five minute drive to Ryan's thinking so many things and hoping none of them were true.

'He's through there,' Debbie said, indicating the living room door with her head.

Amber said nothing, just pushed past Debbie into the living room, a hand flying straight to her mouth the second she saw him lying there. 'Jesus Christ, Ryan...'

'He's okay,' Gary sighed, leaning back against the wall, pushing a hand through his hair. 'He's alright. Now.'

Amber looked at him. 'What do you mean, he's alright *now*? What the hell is going on here?'

'We were out, at some bar in town, and he was... he was

knocking them back like they were tap water…'

'And you didn't think to stop him?'

'I fucking tried, alright? But he was having none of it, he was on a mission. He'd pressed that self-destruct button and nobody was gonna get in his way. Believe me.'

She turned back to Ryan, her heart breaking as she looked at him. He was a mess. His dark hair was all dishevelled, but this time not in a good way, and those beautiful eyes of his looked tired, dead almost, as he stared into space. Did he even know she was there? 'What happened?' Amber asked, crouching down beside the sofa Ryan was lying on.

'He was past drunk,' Gary went on. 'I mean, he was fucking legless, I've never seen anyone in the kind of state he was in, so… so me and a couple of the lads, we took him outside, tried to get him to sober up a bit, but it wasn't happening. He threw up a couple of times, but he just kept saying he wanted to jack it all in, he wanted to drink 'til it all went away. I didn't know what the hell he was talking about. He was just rambling on and on like that and…'

'Gary called me at home, asked me to come and get them,' Debbie took over, sitting down on the arm of a nearby chair. 'I don't think any taxi driver would've taken Ryan anyway, not in that state.'

'Is this just drink?' Amber asked, not taking her eyes off Ryan. 'Has he taken anything else?'

'I think he might have done a line or two of coke in the toilets,' Gary said, sliding down the wall until he was sitting on the floor.

'Oh, Jesus,' Amber sighed, throwing her head back. 'I could fucking kill you, Ryan Fisher… What?' She hadn't missed the look that had just passed between Gary and Debbie. 'Is there something you're not telling me?'

'When we… when we got him back home, we…' Gary looked over at Debbie, who gave him the nod to continue, '… we left him – for five minutes, that's all, I swear – we left him in the bedroom while we went to stick the kettle on and… and when we came back he… he was…'

'He was, what?' Amber's voice was quiet and calm, even though she had a feeling she already knew what they were going to tell her. She just didn't want to believe it.

'He was holding this… this bottle of paracetemol… I mean, he was sitting up, cool as anything, y'know? Despite being as wasted as he was. But he had this in his hand…'

'Was it empty?' Amber asked, her hand absentmindedly slipping into Ryan's. She hadn't even been aware she was doing it.

Gary shook his head. 'He was going on about having nothing left, he was finished. He just kept saying that, and he was turning this bottle over and over in his hand, so I asked him what he'd done and all he kept saying was it was over. It was over. That's when I rang you. We didn't know what the fuck to do; he was frigging scaring the shit out of me. I've never seen anyone in that state before, and I've been on some hellish benders in my time, believe me.'

'We made him sick,' Debbie said, her voice almost impassive. 'We had to. We didn't know if he'd taken anything or not, he wasn't in any fit state to tell us, so… so it was the only thing we could do…'

'Did no one think to call a bloody doctor?' Amber exclaimed. 'Get him to the hospital?'

'What? And have it all over the frigging news by the morning? That'd go down well.'

'Would you rather he'd fucking died?'

'I didn't take anything,' Ryan groaned, pulling himself up into a sitting position, putting his head in his hands. 'Okay? So stop bitching. I didn't take any of the frigging tablets.'

'You stupid, fucking idiot!' Amber shouted, standing up and pacing the floor. 'You stupid, selfish idiot!'

'Oh, that's rich, coming from you,' Ryan retaliated, looking up at Amber, suddenly sobering up. Sort of. Enough to know what was going on, anyway. Although his head was thumping, like someone was banging three sets of drums inside it. 'Calling *me* selfish after what *you've* done.'

Amber threw him a warning look, willing him not to say anything else. He got the message. Despite the state he was in.

'Shit!' he sighed, throwing himself back against the sofa cushions. 'What a fucking night!'

'You're telling me,' Gary said, pulling himself up from the floor. 'You were off on one, mate. Like you wouldn't fucking believe…'

Debbie looked at Amber, mouthing '*Are you alright?*' at her. Amber nodded, smiling her thanks at a new friend she was so glad to have. Without her and Gary, God knows what would have happened to Ryan.

'What the hell was it all about, mate?' Gary asked, throwing himself down in the chair Debbie was perched on the arm of. 'I mean, something must've…'

Debbie threw him a look, indicating Amber and Ryan. 'What do you *think* it was all about, Gary?' she hissed. 'Jesus, do you really not think before opening that mouth of yours?'

Gary looked at his fiancée with a genuinely confused expression on his face. 'What? Oh, come on. Ryan Fisher getting fucking suicidal over a woman? No…'

Debbie threw him another look, shaking her head and mouthing '*Sorry*' at Amber. Amber just gave her a weak smile back. She was suddenly so tired she couldn't muster anything more.

'Are you fucking kidding me?' Gary went on. 'He got himself in this state because him and Amber…?'

Debbie stood up, pulling Gary up with her. 'Come on. Before you say something you might regret.' She looked at Amber. 'Are you gonna be alright, chick? I'll just take this one home then come back and babysit Ryan, let you get off. But if you don't want to stay, I can always stick Gary in a taxi…'

Amber looked at Ryan, his eyes locking with hers. Decision made. 'It's okay. I'll stay with him. You two get off home, and… thank you. Both of you. I don't know what would have happened if you hadn't been around.'

Debbie came over to her, hugging her tight. 'It's what friends are for, chick. And anyway, this stupid bastard of mine should have been keeping an eye on him. They're nothing but big kids, the lot of them.'

'I'm not his frigging bodyguard, Debs.'

Debbie gave Amber one last hug, kissed her on the cheek and proceeded to drag Gary out of the room and out of the house.

Ryan waited until the front door had slammed shut before speaking. 'I bet you never thought you'd see this place again so soon.'

'Don't make fucking jokes out of this, Ryan. Because the last thing this is is funny.'

He sat forward again, clasping his hands together, his eyes looking up at her. 'I'm sorry.'

'Why did you do it?'

'I *didn't* do it, though. Did I?'

'You threatened it. And… and you've been on some kind of bender tonight, to get yourself in the state you're in now. Coke, Ryan… Jesus Christ, you *do* know they send people to clubs to do random on-the-spot drugs tests, don't you? You do know that could happen at any time, and you *do* know what it could do to your career if you're found with anything suspicious in your system? You *are* intelligent enough to work that out, aren't you?'

'You left me, for Jim Allen, Amber. You left me for my boss.'

'And you need to grow up and get over it, Ryan. Because I can't be here to hold your hand anymore.'

His eyes locked onto hers again, staring right at her. 'That's the thing, though, Amber. I fucking need you to be.'

She looked back at him, not breaking the stare, and when she saw the tears streaming down his face, she couldn't help but feel tears of her own start to fall down her cheeks, that tiredness she'd felt creeping in a few minutes ago now sweeping over her in an unexpected rush of emotion.

'I need you, Amber. I need you like you wouldn't fucking believe and it hurts every fucking day to wake up and know that I pushed you away, that I made you leave…'

'You didn't make me leave, Ryan. I've told you that.'

'I can't do this alone, Amber. I'm not strong enough, I'm weak. I'm weak, babe. I'm so fucking weak…'

He bowed his head as his body started wracking with loud, uncontrollable sobs and Amber felt her heart break all over again. She'd never seen anyone so broken, so defeated, and this was messing with her head, big time.

Sitting down next to him, she reached out to take his hand, squeezing it tight as he cried, pulling him against her, holding him close. What was she supposed to do? She couldn't leave him in this state, and she didn't want to. She didn't want him to go any further down that road he'd already travelled too far along, so she had no choice. Not really. He needed her. Jim was wrong. Ryan needed her.

'You stupid, stupid idiot,' she whispered as he lifted his head up and looked at her, his eyes red with tiredness and tears. He looked like the young man he was, and not the big lad he professed to be. 'You bloody, stupid idiot.'

'I can't do it without you, Amber. I thought I could, y'know? But I… sometimes I felt like Max had just set you up as this babysitter, someone to keep an eye on me and at times I resented that, even though I loved you. It all just did my head in, so bad. I mean, I'd managed alright all those years on my own in London…'

'You didn't, though, did you?' Amber said, gently stroking the tears from his tired face.

He shook his head. 'No. I don't suppose I did. I messed up then, and I've messed up now.'

'No, baby, you didn't mess up then – but you almost did. And if you don't stop what you're doing it's going to happen all over again, which is why you have to stop resenting Max, because you have no idea how much he cares about you. Yes, I know he's your

331

agent and a lot of them don't always have the best reputation, but *he* cares about you. And so do I.'

'You do?' His eyes widened, a hopeful look taking over from the tiredness.

'Jesus, Ryan, of course I do.' She ran her fingers gently over his bearded chin, her eyes following their every move. 'I didn't know what to think when Gary called me. A hundred and one things were going round in my head and every single one of them scared me, but…' She looked away for a second, her head spinning with the turmoil of emotions going on inside her.

'Amber…'

She looked at him, her heart breaking into a million pieces as his fingers wrapped tightly around hers, every fibre of her being telling her to think hard about what she was going to do next. But her mind was already made up. 'You *ever* scare the hell out of me like that again, Ryan Fisher…'

'Stay with me tonight, Amber. Please.'

She smiled, running her thumb lightly over his mouth. 'I'm going to have to now, aren't I? You're not safe to be left on your own.'

He smiled, too, and despite the state he was in, it lit up his handsome face, giving Amber so many reasons to never leave his side again. Even though there were just as many telling her not to go back. And she didn't really know what she was going to do past whatever happened here tonight. 'I love you, Amber Sullivan.'

She shook her head, stroking his dark hair. 'You need to get some sleep, Ryan.'

He looked into her eyes again, which set off another round of confusing emotions battling against each other inside her head, and what happened next she couldn't stop. She couldn't. Maybe it was the ridiculous amount of unexpected stress the night had brought, or the fact that coming face-to-face with his demons had scared her more than she'd thought it would, she didn't know. All she knew was that the feelings she still had for this man were real and they were still there. Despite everything.

She closed her eyes and felt his lips brush ever so gently over hers, igniting the tiniest of sparks inside her belly, her heart jumping as his mouth covered hers again, this time in a longer, slower kiss. And it took just seconds for the night to take its toll, for all the raw emotion and unexpected, still-repressed feelings to rise to the surface. It took just seconds for everything else to be forgotten as nothing but being close to him mattered. She should call Jim, but she knew she wouldn't. She didn't want to, because she didn't want to break away from Ryan, from what was happening here. She didn't want to let him go. He'd seemed to have found a strength from somewhere that meant he was stripping the clothes from her body so fast she was breathless, wanting only to feel his skin against hers again, his fingers touching her in all those special places. It didn't matter what he'd done tonight, who he'd been with, who he'd kissed, who he'd slept with; it didn't matter. Not right now. She was caught up in a moment that she hadn't wanted to happen, at first, but it was happening now, and she wanted nothing to get in the way of them finishing this journey. A journey back to them.

She let him push her back onto the sofa as he pulled the last of her clothes away, the cold air hitting her nakedness like a short, sharp shock, making her inhale deep, exhaling only when the warmth of his skin touched hers. Arching her back as his hands ran down over her waist, her hips and thighs, his mouth lowering down to kiss hers again, those confusing emotions showed no signs of subsiding as he pushed her up against him.

'Ryan…' she groaned, throwing her arms up above her head as his mouth moved down to her breasts, but all she wanted was to feel him inside her, taking her over once again, making her realise what she'd walked away from. She needed that so badly it was a physical pain, so deep and so real she felt it slice across her like the sharpest of knives.

'Open your eyes,' he whispered, his mouth gently resting on hers as he spoke. 'I want to look at what I've thrown away, I want to see the way you look at me when I make love to you… I need to see that, Amber.'

She opened her eyes, staring deep into his as he slowly pushed inside her, only the smallest and quietist of moans escaping as a beautiful feeling of peace and clarity suddenly took over from the madness and the surreal events this night had thrown up. One minute she was making plans for that life with Jim that she'd always thought she'd wanted, and the next she was back in the arms of her handsome footballer. And there was nowhere else she *should* be. She should never have left him, never have let him go through everything alone. The guilt she'd been feeling ever since the day she'd walked out on him should have told her that.

Wrapping her legs around him, she felt him push deeper, their eyes still locked together, everything else fading out of focus, ceasing to matter because, at that second, they were the only two people that existed. All she could feel was his body connected to hers in the most intimate and beautiful of ways as a warm and comforting feeling of numbness washed over her. And when that ride finally reached its finale, when that familiar, burning pain took over, filling her up, making her scream out his name as he held her as close as he possibly could, barely a millimetre between their bodies, she felt everything come spilling back in an avalanche of doubt – every ounce of confusion, every reason why this was the worst thing she could have done. It all came hurtling back, taking over her head like a crowd of uninvited gate-crashers, when all she wanted to do was lie there and hold him, kiss him, make everything better. She wanted to make everything better.

'Stay with me,' Ryan whispered. 'Please. Stay with me.'

She wasn't going anywhere.

'He's okay, Max. I promise. As far as I'm aware, we shouldn't be worried about anything appearing in the press. I know Gary won't say anything.'

'You can be sure of that, can you?'

334

'None of them were exactly saints last night, Max. All I know is Ryan's okay, although he's in no fit state to go anywhere near training today.'

'Can *you* sort that out? Try and smooth things over with the club?'

'Yeah,' Amber sighed, looking out of the French windows in the huge kitchen of the house she'd shared with Ryan for such a short time. The one that had never really felt like home.

'Only, I know you're close to Jim Allen. Just make up some excuse, tell them he's got some kind of contagious bug or something.'

Amber closed her eyes at the mention of Jim's name. If only Max knew exactly *how* close she was to Jim Allen. And what the repercussions of that might have on this situation now. 'They might want him to be checked over by the club doctor.'

'We can't risk that, Amber. If he's got any traces left in his blood...'

'I know,' she sighed again, resting her forehead against the cold glass, closing her eyes as the events of last night filled her head. Again. Because they were all she'd been able to think about for the past few hours as she'd lain in bed, holding Ryan close, remembering how it could be. And knowing how it really was. 'I know. I'll think of something. He should be fine tomorrow.'

'Are you staying with him?'

'I'll try to be around, yeah.'

'Amber... are you...?'

'I don't know, Max, okay? I don't know. I just want to get through today first.'

'Alright. Look, thanks. I know he's not really your problem...'

'No, Max. He's very much my problem.'

'He doesn't deserve you. I'll call you later, see how things are going.'

She ended the call and turned around, leaning back against the French windows, her eyes still closed. She was going to have to call Jim at some point today. He'd tried ringing her countless times over the past few hours but she'd ignored every call. What was she supposed to say? That everything they'd talked about last night was nothing but a sham? That she'd meant none of it? That it was all irrelevant anyway because she couldn't go through with it anymore?

Taking a deep breath, she put the phone down on the countertop and made her way back upstairs. Ryan was up and out of bed, and she couldn't ignore the small stab of disappointment she felt at his absence. She'd half hoped he'd still be in bed, ready to repeat the closeness they'd felt last night. She really felt like just snuggling up under the covers and shutting the world out for a few more hours. Reality wasn't high on her list of places to visit today.

Pulling on a pair of denim shorts underneath the Newcastle Red Star football strip she was wearing, she walked over to the bedroom window, looking out over the stunning view of fields and forests, the city looming far in the distance.

'You haven't made a run for it yet, then.'

She turned around to see him standing there, already dressed in jeans and a black t-shirt, his dark hair still all messed-up, his face still tired.

'Where've you been?' she asked, walking over to him, lightly running her fingers over his bearded jawline.

'I just went out for a walk. I needed the fresh air. My head's kinda hurting this morning.'

She smiled, pulling her hands away from his face and folding her arms across her chest, because she wasn't altogether sure what she should be doing with them.

'So,' Ryan went on, shoving his hands in his pockets, his eyes staring down at his black army boots. 'Last night…'

'I need to call the club. You're in no state to go to training today.'

'Amber,' he said, grabbing her arm before she could walk away. 'We need to talk, don't you think?'

She looked up at him, her heart aching as his dark blue eyes met hers. At times he looked like a lost little boy and that only confused her all the more. Who *was* the real Ryan Fisher? She didn't know, and she wasn't altogether sure that he did, either.

'I think we need to make sure things are smoothed over with the club first, Ryan. Before anyone starts asking questions.'

He reached out to grab her arm again, pulling her against him, kissing her so softly and so gently that she had no choice but to hold onto him and let it all happen. The feel of his lips on hers, the roughness of his beard on her skin, it was all just a huge reminder of a man she couldn't get her head around – but he was a man she loved. She loved him. In a way she couldn't really explain, and she certainly didn't love him the way she loved Jim, it felt nothing like that. But it still felt like love. And she had no intention of leaving him while he still needed her. If that's what he really, truly wanted.

'When I asked you to stay with me last night I meant it, Amber. I was off my head, I know I was, and I shouldn't have put people through that…'

She put her fingers to his lips, shaking her head. 'I know you regret it now. I know you do. Or, at least, I hope you do.'

'I do. I promise you, I do…'

'Okay. Okay, I believe you.'

'And when I said I needed you, I meant that, too. I want to kick this shit, Amber. I want to start enjoying my life rather than throwing it down the fucking drain, but I don't think I can do it on my own.'

'You don't have to,' she said, even though she felt as though she was acting on some kind of auto-pilot, the events of last night still too fresh in her mind for her to push aside easily. 'I'm going to be here, okay?'

He nodded, taking her hand and holding it tight, so tight she was afraid he might never let it go.

She smiled again, reaching up to stroke his cheek with the palm of her hand, kissing him gently, reluctant to pull away. But a sharp rapping on the front door was something neither of them could ignore.

'Who the hell's that?' Amber sighed, pulling her hand free of Ryan's.

'Leave it. They'll go away.'

Another round of rapping made Amber think that was highly unlikely. Whoever it was, they seemed extremely keen to be heard.

'You stay here. I'll go see who it is,' she said. 'I won't be long.'

She ran downstairs, flinging open one of the huge black double doors at the front of the house, her heart stopping in her chest as she saw the figure standing on the doorstep.

'Yeah. I was right. I thought I'd find you here.'

'Jim...'

He pushed past her, going straight into the kitchen, throwing a copy of a popular national tabloid newspaper down on the countertop. Amber took one look at it and threw her head back, sighing.

'I can only assume, because of the fact you ran out of my house last night without one word of explanation, and the fact you're here, in his house, that you knew about this? Am I right? Was that call last night to do with this freaking idiot?'

Amber nodded, her stomach flipping in a wholly unpleasant way now. 'He needed me, Jim.'

'Jesus Christ... He doesn't need *you*, Amber. What he needs is pulling into fucking line. He needs to quit this crap and concentrate on his fucking career.'

'I think he's aware of that now, Jim.'

'Is he? Is he really? You think so, do you?' Amber watched as Jim pushed a hand through his hair, pacing the dark-wood floor. 'He's got to get his act together, Amber. And fast.' He leaned back against the countertop, sticking his hands in his trouser pockets. 'Is he awake?'

Amber nodded. She was finding it really hard to look at Jim, knowing what she might have to tell him.

'I'll have a word with him, then we'll get out of here. You've done your bit. The rest is up to him.'

'Jim…'

He turned to look at her, his expression questioning.

'I… I can't leave him.'

Jim said nothing for a second. 'Can't, or won't?'

She looked out of the French windows again, the dark December sky matching her mood. 'Both,' she whispered.

Jim leaned back again, pushing a hand through his grey-flecked hair. 'You're going back to him?'

'I have to, Jim.'

'No, Amber. You don't.' He looked her up and down, taking in the denim shorts and the Red Star strip she was wearing. 'Did you fuck him?'

Amber folded her arms, looking down at the floor. 'He wasn't in any fit state for anything other than sleep,' she lied, looking up at him. 'So I'm not even going to answer that.'

His eyes locked onto hers. 'I don't believe this. We… we were about to start a life together, Amber, and, what? This jackass gets wasted and suddenly you're right back by his side? Why? Huh? You wanna tell me why?'

'It's not that simple, Jim…'

'Isn't it? What? Can't he throw up without you there beside him? Does he need you to hold his hand every step of the fucking way?'

'Yes. I do.'

They both looked over to where Ryan was standing in the doorway, his hands shoved deep in the pockets of his battered jeans.

'I need her to hold my hand. I need her, full stop.'

Jim just glared at him, but Ryan stood his ground.

'What I did last night, it was stupid. But it's nothing footballers of my ilk haven't done before. Getting drunk, making prats of ourselves, it's what we do, isn't it?'

'I'd prefer it if you didn't do it while you're a player at *my* club,' Jim said slowly, still staring at Ryan. 'I've got better things to do than deal with silly little boys who play games.'

Amber looked at Ryan, begging him not to tell Jim everything. He didn't need to know, nobody did. Nobody needed to know how low Ryan had got last night, how close he'd come to doing something really stupid. And the last thing Jim needed to know about was the drugs. Ryan wasn't an addict by any stretch of the imagination, but occasional recreational use was enough to see his career ended in an instant.

Ryan gave her a small smile, and a slight nod, which Amber took as a sign that he knew what he was doing. But she still felt sick. Still felt as though this could all come crashing down around them at any second and she really didn't know what she would do if it did.

'I'm sorry,' Ryan said, looking directly at Jim. 'No, I mean it. I'm really sorry, boss.'

'Sorry for being an idiot last night? Or sorry for involving Amber in your stupid games?'

Ryan's eyes never left Jim's as he spoke. 'Both.'

Jim turned away, laughing a loud and cynical laugh. 'Jesus. This is fucking crazy!' He turned back to face Ryan again. 'I should have your name ready to go on that fucking list when the transfer window opens up in January. I should make sure you leave here, get as far away from her as possible…'

'Jim…' Amber began.

He looked at her. A look which only served to make Amber feel more guilt, a guilt that hit her like some out-of-control speeding truck, so hard was the force of its impact.

'But *I* don't play games,' Jim said, his voice steady. Calm. He looked at Ryan. 'You get that fucking head of yours together, son, and get your ass down to that training ground, now…'

'Jim, please. He's in no state…'

Jim threw Amber a look that, this time, only served to make the guilt hit harder. 'I've got journalists – national *and* local – outside Tynebridge *and* the training ground, all of them wanting to know why *he* was in the state he was in last night, and right now the press office are trying to fire-fight, trying to explain that he's nothing but another overpaid idiot who thinks this world owes him a fucking living.' He looked at Ryan. 'So you get over to that training ground and you let our own doctors check you over. Who knows what shit you threw down your neck…' He looked at Amber again, '… and up your fucking nose. Don't hide shit like this from me again, Amber.'

'Hey, quit taking this out on *her*…' Ryan began, but Jim stopped him, throwing him a look that told him to keep quiet. There was only one person calling the shots in that room, and both Amber and Ryan knew it was neither of them.

'I'd rather we dealt with this at club level,' Jim said, his voice still steady, but obviously taking no crap. 'While we still can. I'll expect you there within the hour, Ryan. You can resume training with the rest of the squad next week.'

'Next week?' Ryan asked, frowning slightly.

'Oh, you can forget this weekend's match, Fisher. You can put that right out of your mind. I'm fining you for behaviour that could bring Red Star into disrepute and you're banned from this weekend's game. You don't even make the bench, kiddo. It might give you time to think about what you've done.' He looked at Amber, and she felt her stomach turn over so many times she felt physically sick. 'What you've *both* done. I'll see myself out.'

Amber closed her eyes as she leaned back against the counter, pushing both hands through her dishevelled, dark red hair, sighing heavily.

'It's gonna be alright, babe,' Ryan said, walking over to her, gently pushing the hair from her eyes.

She looked up at him. 'Is it? Pissing *him* off wasn't the wisest of things to do, was it? And I think we've *both* managed that.'

'He'll get over it.' Ryan leaned back against the counter beside her.

'Is that right? How do you work that out, then?'

He slipped his hand into hers, squeezing it tight, smiling slightly.

'Jim Allen is the ultimate professional, Amber. You know that better than anyone. And he's had to deal with bigger shit than this in his time as a manager.'

'What? One of his players sleeping with his ex-girlfriend?'

'You know what I mean.'

Amber looked down at their joined hands. 'What a mess,' she sighed.

Ryan moved so he was standing in front of her, his hands on her hips, pulling her loosely against him. 'If you really want to go to him…'

'Jesus, Ryan, I don't want to go to him, okay?' Didn't she?

'Well, you did before…'

'Things are different now.'

'What? Now that I've told you I'm weak and can't quite manage to dig myself out of the shit I've buried myself in unless I've got you to help me?'

'Do you know what? If you're going to start playing the big kid again, I'm out of here.'

'No, Amber, hang on,' Ryan said, pulling her back into his arms before she could walk away. 'I'm sorry. I'm just a bit… last night freaked me out, okay? I can't remember all that much about it, but I remember what I almost did, and that freaks me out. Big time.'

'That's understandable,' she whispered, resting her hands on his tattooed forearms, playing with the numerous leather bands he had tied around his wrists. 'But I really need you to grow up and start making this work, Ryan. Before it's too late.'

He smiled, a smile which sent her head spinning, despite the tiredness she still felt. 'You want me to grow up, huh? Was I not grown-up enough for you last night?'

She couldn't help smiling back, despite the guilt and the confusion and the pain she was feeling. For so many different reasons. 'You remember *that*, then?'

'How can I forget how good you feel?' he whispered, his mouth so close to hers now, his breath warm on her face. 'How soft and wet and beautiful…'

'Ryan…' she groaned, but before she could stop him his mouth had covered hers in another kiss that she knew was only going to lead to one inevitable destination. So all she could do was close her eyes, kick back and enjoy the ride.

Chapter Twenty

Amber sat at her desk, not sure whether she was glad to be back at work or not. It felt strange, after having spent so much time away from News North East, to be back in the thick of it, all eyes in the Sports Desk now on the January transfer window as a month of players moving backwards and forwards, joining new clubs or returning to their old ones, began. Usually Amber loved this time of year, but Christmas hadn't exactly been the kind she'd wanted. Ryan's time at Red Star wasn't an easy one right now. His relationship with Jim Allen was, understandably, strained, although nobody else knew about the Red Star manager's relationship with Amber, so only Ryan could really understand the dynamics that were now taking place. Jim hadn't resorted to any kind of under-hand or unprofessional tactics to get back at Ryan, but that didn't mean he wasn't keeping a very close eye on him.

Ryan had also been away a lot over the Christmas week. Red Star's Boxing Day match had been a home game but Jim had still kept to the usual routine of holing the squad up in a hotel the night before the match so, come Christmas Day afternoon, Ryan had left Amber alone to join his teammates. And as for New Year, the club's New Year's Day fixture had been away in the North West, so Amber had spent New Year's Eve with her dad – a quiet time, and one she'd used to reflect on just what the future might hold for her and Ryan. Because she'd missed him more than she'd cared to admit when he'd been away. At a time when she'd needed to be with him, he hadn't been there as much as she'd wanted him to be, but there wasn't anything she could do about that. She couldn't be with him twenty-four-hours a day, even if sometimes she wanted to be.

'Good to have you back,' Kevin smiled, perching himself in his usual position on the edge of Amber's desk.

Amber looked at him. 'It's good to *be* back. I think.'

'Get used to the time off, did you? Although, you didn't exactly take it easy, like I instructed you to.'

Amber sat back in her chair, crossing her legs. 'Things have been a bit – complicated, yeah. But I think we're getting everything back on an even keel.' She wished she felt as confident as she sounded.

'An even keel, huh?' Kevin repeated, arching a questioning eyebrow. 'So, you and the Red Star wonder boy… things settling down again now, are they?'

'If you mean, has he gone on any more benders, no. If he isn't with the squad, then he's with me. We're fine. So, yeah. Things are settling down, thanks.'

'What's he gonna do now you're back at work, then?'

'What do you mean, what's he gonna do?'

Kevin shrugged. 'Well, once training's over and he's got all that free time to kill…'

Amber stared at her producer. 'I trust him, okay? I think he's learnt his lesson now.' More than any of them would ever know.

Kevin shrugged again. 'Okay, well, I hope it works out for you both. I suppose he's got *you* to keep him in line now, so we shouldn't be seeing that talent going to waste. Red Star need him on top form if they have any chance of winning the league title this season.' He slid down from her desk, shoving his hands in his pockets. 'Oh, and Ronnie called for you earlier. He's on his way up to the North East. He's one of the pundits for Red Star's televised match on Saturday evening.'

Amber sighed, closing her eyes for a second. Ronnie. She hadn't seen him since before Christmas because he and Anna had spent the festive season over in Gran Canaria. But that didn't mean to say that he didn't know everything that was going on. And anyway, if he hadn't before, he'd know now, after talking to Kevin.

Her phone ringing pulled her back to reality and she looked at the caller ID, a smile instantly spreading across her face as she saw who was calling her.

'Hey, handsome,' she said, leaning back in her chair, looking out of the window at the traffic streaming past the News North East building. 'You not at training?'

'Sneaked off for a few minutes. No one'll notice. There's a story about Rob in the papers today – he's managed to get himself photographed with a married soap star, so the headlines are his, for a change.'

Amber smiled, absentmindedly turning her pen round and round between her fingers as she spoke. 'Is it good to have a day off, then?'

He laughed – that gorgeous, sexy, low laugh that made her stomach flip over and over, turning her into a giggling, teenage fan-girl. 'Yeah. You could say that. Things alright with you? And the press, I mean.'

Amber looked out of the window again, straining her eyes to see if she could see Red Star's training ground from where she was. She could see Tynebridge, but she'd never actually tried to see if the training ground was visible from her office window. 'Ryan, baby, I *am* the press. Nothing bothers me anymore.' Since her return to Ryan's side, media interest in their relationship had grown all over again, but Amber had learnt to deal with it. She'd had to learn fast, but she could handle just about anything they threw at her now, even if it was still a part of the package she could do without.

'That photo they had of you in the Herald the other week…'

'What photo?' Amber asked, her search for Red Star's training ground now over. She couldn't really see it from where she was, even though it wasn't all that far away from Tynebridge, which was clearly visible from her window, looming large on the horizon with its ominous, imposing, edge-of-city-centre presence.

'The one of you looking hot as hell in nothing but a bed sheet and a smile, because that was no holiday snap, babe, I'm telling you.'

She smiled to herself, remembering the photograph he was talking about. It had been printed alongside a story concerning her relationship with Ryan, and even though they'd had her down as a bit of a cougar, making a reference to the eleven-year age gap between them, Amber had just been flattered they'd used a picture that made her look good. Yes, even *she* let vanity get the better of her sometimes. 'That was from last year's News North East charity calendar. I was July.'

'Were you now? How come *I* never knew about this?'

'Because we didn't meet until August. Anyway, I'm sure you didn't call me in the middle of the morning to talk about calendar shoots.'

'Why not? Have you seen this year's Red Star calendar? There's something rather sexy in April you might be interested in.'

'Oh yeah? Would that have anything to do with a particularly hot, tattooed footballer showing us his considerable talent?'

'You've seen it, then.'

'Tracy's got one hanging up in the communal kitchen. Tell Gary he's cheering up January no end.'

'Yeah. I'll be sure to pass the message on. Listen, beautiful, do you fancy going out tonight? One of the lads is having a private birthday do in the nightclub at Tynebridge and...'

'Is that wise, Ryan? I mean, things have been going so well...'

'Amber, baby, I'm not suddenly going to set foot inside a club and fall off the wagon, am I? If that was going to happen then I had more than enough opportunities when I was away over Christmas. But I was a good boy, wasn't I?'

She couldn't help smiling. 'Yeah. I suppose you were. You were only bad when I wanted you to be.'

He laughed that low, sexy laugh again and it was all Amber could do not to grab her coat and head off to the training ground, find him, and give him some training techniques of her own. 'Why don't we *both* misbehave a little bit tonight, huh? I mean, you'll be there to keep an eye on me, won't you?'

'Ryan, please, I'm not your mother. I don't need to "keep an eye" on you. I trust you.'

'Yeah,' he said quietly. 'I know you do. So, you up for this, then? Come on, babe. Let me be a stereotypical footballer for a night, huh?'

'Yeah, okay,' she laughed, crossing her legs and resting her chin in her hand. 'Just don't expect me to be a stereotypical WAG. I'll see you later, handsome.'

'Talking dirty in the middle of a work day, are we?'

She swung her chair round and smiled as Ronnie pulled a chair over and sat down at her desk. 'Happy New Year to you, too. Kevin said you were on your way. I didn't expect you to be here quite so soon, though.'

'Traffic's quiet. And anyway, I was only coming from Hexham. I came up from London yesterday.'

'You look good. I take it the holiday was a success?'

'Yeah. I suppose so.'

Amber frowned slightly. 'What do you mean?'

'Oh, I dunno, Amber,' Ronnie sighed, pushing a hand through his hair. 'Anyway, what about you?'

She looked at him. 'Are you sure you're alright?'

'You're back with Ryan, then?' he asked, ignoring her question.

'I think you already know the answer to that one.'

'Why?'

'Because I love him.'

'As simple as that.'

'Yep. As simple as that.'

'I thought you loved Jim.'

348

She looked at him again. 'I will *always* love Jim, Ronnie. In some misguided, pointless kind of way. But I need to be with Ryan.'

'Do you?'

'Look, what is this? It's my first day back at work, okay, and I really don't need you turning up here with your interrogation techniques and a lecture.'

'So, your dad narrowly avoided learning about your relationship with his close friend. That was handy.'

She continued to stare at him. 'It could never really work, me and Jim. Too many memories. Too much history to get past. With Ryan it's… it's a new start. It's a brand new start.'

'And you think he's capable of that, do you? Of leaving all that shit behind and settling down?'

'Look, Ronnie, do you want to tell me what's bothering you? Because you're beginning to give me a headache I could really do without.'

'Nothing's wrong, okay?'

Amber arched an eyebrow. She didn't believe *that* for a second. 'Come on. We're going to the pub across the road.'

'Drinking? On your first day back?'

'It's lunchtime, Ronnie. And they serve soft drinks over there, too, y'know. Get up, come on. You're not leaving my sight until you tell me what's on your mind. Then maybe you can stop taking your bad mood out on me.'

Ryan jumped to reach the ball, heading it into the back of the net with more ease than any striker should be allowed to have. Jesus, he loved this game. Now Amber was back in his life that renewed energy she'd given him was back with a vengeance, despite the strained relationship he now had with Jim Allen. But, hey, in the fight for Amber's affections, guess who'd won? Jim would just have to deal with it.

'You coming tonight?' Gary asked, kicking the ball back to Ryan, squinting slightly as the winter sun shone low in the bright

January sky.

'Yeah. I called Amber. She's coming, too.'

'She's still on babysitting duty, then?'

'Fuck off, Gary. You more than anyone should know how much I need her right now. She trusts me, and I want her to see that I'm trying, okay?'

Gary shrugged, running along the touchline as Ryan kicked the ball out to him. 'What's with you and the boss, anyway? One minute everything's fine with you two and the next you could cut the atmosphere with a knife.'

'He's just pissed off at what happened, that's all.'

'Still?' Gary stopped running, bending over slightly, his hands on his hips as he tried to get his breath back. 'All that shit happened before Christmas. And, yeah, I mean, everyone expected him to be pissed off at us for a while, but that was weeks ago. You'd have thought he'd have calmed down by now. He's fine with me, so what've *you* done?'

'Leave it, Gary, will you? How should *I* know what's bugging Jim Allen.'

Gary stood up straight, a smirk spreading over his face. 'Hang on... no, it couldn't... Amber and Jim Allen...? I know he's a friend of her dad's, but... were they having some sort of relationship? Y'know, I always thought there was something strange about the way he was around her, the way he looked at her, I mean, we *all* look at her like that because she's pretty hot, y'know, for an older woman, but...' He looked at Ryan's expression. 'Jesus Christ, I'm right, aren't I? Jim Allen was fucking Amber! Then you go and get all messed-up, she comes running, and leaves him to come back to you! I *knew* there was more to it. I *knew* it.'

'Will you keep your fucking voice down, Gary?' Ryan hissed, coming over to him, shoving the ball at him so hard it almost winded the defender. 'Nobody knows about that, alright? Nobody knows, and that's the way it's gonna stay, because I do *not* want her hurt, do you hear me?'

350

Gary threw the ball down and held up his hands in mock-surrender. 'Hey, okay. Chill out. Her secret's safe with me.'

'Yeah. I wish I could believe that,' Ryan said, bending down to pick up the ball before throwing it back at another teammate. 'Seriously, Gary. I mean it. I don't want anything to mess up what I've got with Amber. I managed that all by myself once and I'm trying really hard not to repeat that mistake. So, any outside interference could really fuck things up.'

Gary folded his arms, looking straight at his best friend. 'You're serious about her, aren't you?'

Ryan nodded, pushing a hand through his dark hair. 'I love her, Gary. I frigging love her so much it scares me. And knowing the history she and Jim Allen have…'

'History?' Gary gasped, his face brightening at the prospect of more unexpected gossip. 'You mean, it wasn't something that just happened?'

'Jesus…' Ryan sighed, throwing his head back. 'Look, Gary, it's complicated, okay? Just keep your mouth shut, because you tell *any*one about Amber and Jim and I will fucking kill you…'

'Not literally,' Gary smirked, watching as Rob was sent flying in the wrong direction by a glorious shot from Joey Gardner, Ryan's striking partner.

'Try me,' Ryan said, fixing Gary with what he hoped was a warning look. 'Ruin this for me, Gary, and I will never forgive you. You may not feel much like settling down, but I do, okay? After tonight, Ryan Fisher's partying days are over.'

'I've left Anna,' Ronnie said, looking down into his pint.

Amber was speechless for a few seconds, trying to take in what her best friend had just told her. She'd thought everything was going so well, that Anna and Ronnie were made for each other. This was the last thing she'd expected to hear.

'Ronnie, I… Shit! What… why? What happened? I thought everything was good, that you two were getting on so well…'

351

'We were, Amber. Anna is such a great girl; she's a fantastic, funny, beautiful woman and, yeah, the holiday was good, but...'

'But what?' Amber asked, reaching out to take his hand as his eyes looked up into hers.

'It just wasn't going to work, Amber.'

Her eyes locked onto his, staring deep into his soul. He was her best friend, her very best friend, and he deserved to be happy. She'd thought Anna could have brought him that happiness, but it didn't look like that was the case anymore.

'Why?' Amber whispered, still holding his hand, her thumb gently stroking his knuckles. 'What went wrong?'

'Nothing, really,' Ronnie shrugged, breaking the stare, looking down at their joined hands for a second before pulling his hand away. 'Nothing went wrong. It was me, not her.'

'Christ, I hope you didn't tell *her* that. It's probably one of the worst things you can say when breaking up with someone, even if it's true.'

Ronnie looked at her again, downing a long mouthful of lager. 'Are you happy, Amber? This time? With Ryan, I mean. Given his reputation, his behaviour – his track record with women.'

'He's changed.'

'Well, forgive me for being cynical here, but you spun me that line before and look what happened.'

'What is wrong with you, Ronnie? Just because *your* relationship has broken down don't come here and rain on *my* parade, okay? What happened with you and Anna, it isn't my fault.'

Ronnie downed the last of his lager before standing up, his eyes fixed firmly on Amber's. 'Isn't it?'

Chapter Twenty-One

'I really hate this side of things,' Amber said, walking out of the en-suite bathroom, running her fingers through her damp hair. 'You said it was just going to be a birthday party for one of your teammates. I didn't realise that meant a full-blown, Z-List celebrity, footballer-filled event with press and paparazzi lurking all over the place.'

Ryan looked at her, arching an eyebrow, a slight smirk on his face. 'Y'know, for an intelligent woman you can be extremely naive.'

She poked her tongue out at him. 'You should let me know the full details before you make me commit to this kind of thing. I hate being photographed, and I've never liked being the centre of attention. I guess I should have thought about that, shouldn't I? Before I got involved with you.' She smiled as he walked over to her, half-naked and handsome, sexy and dangerous. Everything she should be avoiding but, at the same time, everything she couldn't leave alone.

'I always thought you were a bit of a local celebrity yourself round here. Y'know, this beautiful sports reporter with a father who once played for one of the region's biggest clubs.'

'It's not the same thing at all, Ryan,' Amber said, still smiling, running her fingers lightly up and down his naked chest. 'There's a big difference between being a face people see on local TV now and again and being the girlfriend of a famous footballer. And not just *any* famous footballer, but Ryan Fisher. You are a bit of a publicity magnet, mister.'

'Yeah, and not always for the right reasons,' Ryan sighed, pulling her closer against him, quickly kissing her forehead. 'I want things to change, Amber. I want to forget all of that crap and start thinking about getting my life in order. Coming so close to losing you, it… I've never been in love before, y'know? Never felt the things *you* make me feel, and it scares the hell out of me.'

She reached up and put a hand to his face, her fingers stroking his bearded jawline, her eyes looking deep into his. In just a few short weeks he'd changed so much and her only worry was that it was happening too quick, that he was doing it all because he felt he had to. Because he wanted to prove something to her. 'You don't have to do everything at a million miles an hour, Ryan. Just take it easy, let things happen by themselves.'

He trailed his fingers slowly up and down her spine, and even through the thick cotton towel she was wearing she could feel those familiar sparks of electricity sending her stomach into spasms of somersaults. 'I *want* things to happen, Amber. I want to forget the past and concentrate on the future – *our* future. Don't you want that, too?'

She smiled again, continuing to stroke his cheek, feeling so many things, so many emotions all jostling for space in her already over-crowded head that she felt quite dizzy. Had everything she'd felt for Jim actually been about Ryan? When she'd thought that being with Ryan was nothing but a way of avoiding her true feelings for Jim, had it not really been the other way around? She wished she had a definitive answer to that question, but she couldn't really say for sure. 'Yeah, of course that's what I want…'

He shut her up with a kiss, his mouth moving slowly against hers until she had no choice left but to give in to him, let his strong arms hold her close, his body hard, his breathing desperate as he pulled the towel away from her body. 'And *I* want *you*,' he

354

whispered. 'A million fucking ways, I want you.'

She felt her stomach flip over and over, an excitement only he was able to generate building up inside her – which was where she wanted him, and soon. Inside her. Deep, deep inside her.

'I want to take you places you've never been before.' His mouth was close to her ear, his breath warm on her face, his fingers playing with her, touching her, pulling away before they had a chance to do what she so badly wanted them to finish. 'Places only *we'll* ever go, away from the world and all the fucking shit it throws up. Away from everything, until it's just you and me.' He moved his head so his mouth was resting on hers, their bodies so close, so very close the heat was almost unbearable. Amber was burning up so fast, just the sight of him was enough to turn her legs to jelly and make her heart beat so loud she was sure he could hear it.

She put her hand on his chest, feeling his heart beating just as hard as hers was, signalling the start of a game that was going to be played out before either of them went anywhere. Unplanned, spontaneous sex. Something she'd never been all that used to, but with Ryan it was fast becoming the norm.

'Just me and you,' she whispered, closing her eyes as he pushed her back onto the bed, her body aching to welcome him, the pain of wanting him hurting so much she wasn't sure how much longer she could wait. But Ryan seemed in no hurry to end the game, no rush to take it to those final stages.

'I just want to look at you,' he whispered, letting his fingers slide slowly down over her breasts, making her gasp out loud as they continued their journey down over her waist, her hips, their eyes locked together all the time, neither of them breaking the stare. Not until the urge became too much, so overwhelming it was impossible to hold back any longer and she almost forced him inside her, raising her hips up so hard against his, desperate to finally feel him where she wanted him to be.

Closing her eyes, her stomach dipped as the combined feeling of his mouth kissing her slow and deep and his body entering hers took over, rendering anything else unimportant. When he was with her like this, when there was nothing else to distract him, nobody else there to tempt him away from her, this was a heaven she'd never even realised could exist. She'd never wanted to fall for a footballer; it had never been an option for her, after everything that had happened with Jim, but you couldn't help who you fell in love with, could you? As the old adage said. Because sometimes all those clichés were true.

She kept her eyes closed as his hands ran up from her hips, over her stomach, touching her breasts so lightly it forced another tiny gasp from her, a gasp which fast turned into a moan as his hands continued moving up her body until his fingers entwined with hers above her head as he thrust deeper into her. She could feel him there, feel him moving, feel him about to explode and when it happened it rocked them both, their bodies moving together to give each other an endgame they both wanted, both needed. He came first, filling Amber with a beautiful calm as white-hot pins and needles flooded through her, every jerk of his body, every move he made inside her giving her a release she didn't want to end because it felt so peaceful. So utterly perfect. And as he slowly withdrew, touching her gently with his hand, his eyes staring into hers as he helped her reach her own goal, Amber had never felt happier. She'd never felt so beautiful, so special, so absolutely sure of what she was doing as she did right at that second, with this man by her side.

'Jesus, Ryan...' she breathed, throwing her head back as the last of those post-sex shivers left her body. 'Now I know why I love you.'

He rolled over onto his side, resting up on one elbow as he looked at her, reaching out to stroke strands of hair from her eyes. 'That's the first time you've actually said those words,' he whispered as she turned to face him. 'The first time you've even alluded to loving me.'

He was right. She never *had* actually said the words, even though she'd been sure that she loved him for a while now. Ever since that night, really. The night he'd nearly thrown it all away. She'd just never been able to say it. 'That's because I do,' she said quietly, running her fingers lightly over his lips. 'I love you.' She couldn't stop her hand from flying to her mouth as she said those words, the shock and surprise that they'd actually come from *her* making her eyes fill with stupid tears, nervous laughter suddenly taking over. 'Oh, my God. Ryan. I love you. Yeah, I... I love you.'

She watched as his face broke into a smile, the way his eyes crinkled up at the corners sending those butterflies dancing round her stomach again. This was it! She'd actually said those words and meant them, or, at least, it felt as though she did. Maybe they never *had* been meant for Jim, even though she knew, in her heart of hearts, that Jim Allen would never go away. Ever.

But she'd fallen in love with Ryan, despite herself, despite everything. She'd fallen in love with him. Could she now finally let go of the past and start living?

Red Star's Tynebridge Stadium wasn't just a football ground. In this day and age of big money football, billionaire owners and exaggerated excess, very few grounds in the top flight of football were. So, as well as function rooms, executive boxes and hospitality suites on offer to those that wanted them, Tynebridge also had its very own nightclub and entertainment complex built adjacent to the stunning, purpose-built, recently-erected new stadium. It was used frequently by local celebrities for events and shows, had its own club nights open to the public at weekends, and it was the venue of choice for most of the region's top-flight footballers when they needed somewhere to host a private party – as was the case tonight – or as private as it could be when celebrities galore, as well as some of the biggest names in football, were expected to turn up, and press and paparazzi would doubtless be lying in wait, ready to snap anyone that could sell a photo.

Amber clung onto Ryan's hand as they got out of the taxi, the freezing January air making her shiver in the short, black, one-shoulder dress she was wearing.

'You cold?' he asked, sliding his arm around her shoulders, pulling her into him.

'Freezing,' she smiled, slipping her arm round his waist as they walked towards the entrance of the club, photographers seemingly jumping out of nowhere to grab that snap of Ryan Fisher and the latest woman in his life.

'Tell you what.' He smiled, too, his mouth close to her ear as they continued walking past the posse of paparazzi and their clicking cameras, the flashes almost blinding them. 'We'll get inside, grab a drink, then find somewhere quiet to warm ourselves back up.'

She couldn't help smiling back, turning her head to receive a much-welcomed – especially from the waiting photographers – kiss from her handsome footballer. That was the money shot, right there, and she didn't care who saw it. Not anymore. She was in love with this mixed-up, crazy man. She was in love. End of story. 'Like you haven't had enough,' she said, staring into his eyes for a second before they escaped inside the club.

'Hey, I'm Ryan Fisher. Nothing is *ever* enough for me, beautiful.'

'Shut up,' she laughed, pushing him gently before pulling him back against her, stopping to kiss him longer and slower, falling against him like a rag doll as his mouth touched hers, her fingers playing with the hair at the back of his neck. 'Oh, God, Ryan. You've got me going crazy here. I used to be so sensible, so grown up. Now all I want to do is drag you home and have lots of dirty sex.'

'Suits me,' he grinned, grabbing her hand and making to go, but she pulled him back, still laughing.

'Oh no, mister. *You* wanted to come here, so we're staying. For a little while, at least.'

'Am I still on a promise for the dirty sex, then?'

'If you're a good boy.'

'How good?'

'Very good,' she whispered, kissing the spot just below his ear which made him groan out loud, especially as she teamed that kiss with a sly feel, her hand quickly touching him down below, so quickly it almost didn't happen, but quick enough for him to know it *had* happened. And even *she* was surprised that just that slightest of touches had caused a reaction. 'For Christ's sake, Ryan, it doesn't take much, does it?'

He pulled her against him, kissing her again, both of them unable to stop laughing. 'You are so fucking good for me, Amber. You know that, don't you?'

She smiled at him, touching his rough cheek gently, loving him more each time she looked at him. How could he go from being a man she couldn't bear to be around to being someone so precious to her she was frightened to let him out of her sight? 'I think that, maybe, we need each other. Don't you?'

He smiled back, those gorgeous, deep blue eyes of his crinkling up again, making Amber just want to squeeze him hard and love him forever. Jesus, life could throw some curveballs when it wanted to.

'How come every time we bump into you two coming into a party you're practically fucking each other before the night's even started?' Gary grinned, sauntering past, with Debbie lagging slightly behind, rummaging around in her tiny clutch bag for something.

'Your way with words is so eloquent, Gary, mate,' Ryan smirked, sliding his arm around Amber's shoulders as they all walked into the club together.

'I say it as I see it,' Gary shrugged. 'Jesus, Debbie, sweetheart, what the hell are you looking for in there? You can hardly fit a frigging lipstick in it as it is. It's not as if there's any room to lose anything.'

'I'm looking for my perfume, if you must know.' Debbie finally looked up from her handbag search and smiled at Amber. 'Hey, chick. You look stunning!'

'Doesn't she just?' Ryan smiled, leaning over to plant a kiss on Amber's bare shoulder before kissing her mouth again.

'Isn't he gorgeous?' Amber breathed, not really wanting to break the stare she and Ryan were sharing.

'Fucking hell,' Gary said, folding his arms as he watched Amber and Ryan continue to smooch like a pair of teenagers on a first date. 'What the hell have you done with Ryan Fisher? Shit! Have the aliens finally abducted him and replaced him with robot Ryan?'

'Piss off,' Ryan laughed, keeping Amber close, his arm tight around her waist. 'This is what being in love is like, mate. You should try it sometime.'

'Hmm. He's never been a fan,' Debbie smiled, slipping her arm through Amber's, dragging her – rather reluctantly – away from Ryan's side. 'Come on, missy. Let those two get the drinks in while we have a girly catch-up.'

'Hey, Amber, you're not gonna go telling her what you two get up to in the bedroom, are you? Only, I'm not sure I can keep up with anything stud-of-the-year here can manage.'

'Fucking reel it in, Gary, will you?' Ryan sighed, pushing him towards the bar. 'Leave them to it, come on. I could murder a pint.'

Amber watched Ryan walk away, but not before he threw her a wink and a smile over his shoulder, which made her smile back, her stomach flipping over at a ridiculous rate. She literally felt her knees give way, so she was glad Debbie was still holding onto her.

'Girl, you've got it bad!' Debbie said, shaking her head as they walked over to a free table. 'Things really have changed since that night, huh?'

'So much so I feel like I haven't had time to draw breath since Christmas. He's trying so hard, Debbie. He really is. *Too* hard, sometimes.'

'Is that a bad thing? Amber, chick, that boy is in love with you. It's so obvious.'

'And I love him, too. Although tonight was the first time I've actually told him that. The first time I've been able to say the words and really feel that I mean them.'

Debbie sat back, crossing her legs. 'Whoa! No wonder you're

all over each other like a rash, then.'

Amber couldn't help smiling, looking over at the bar as Gary and Ryan laughed hysterically at something Rob was telling them. He looked so handsome when he laughed. His whole face lit up, those gorgeous dark eyes of his so expressive. Her young, beautiful footballer. Jesus! She really had to get a grip; she was fast turning into something from a clichéd romance novel. 'This is all so new to me, Debbie. These feelings, being so close to someone, trusting them… *learning* to trust them…' She stopped talking as she noticed the figure that had just walked into the club, her stomach dipping instantly. She watched as he began scanning the entire room – she could tell he was doing that, even though his eyes were covered by those familiar aviator shades.

'Amber? You alright, chick?' Debbie asked, gently touching her arm.

'Oh, sorry, yes,' Amber said, quickly turning to face Debbie, the smile that had briefly disappeared now back on her face. 'I'm fine. It's just been a long day, that's all. It was my first day back at News North East today, and I guess putting in a full day after all that time off was a lot more tiring than I thought it would be.'

'Oh. I see. Did everything go okay?'

'Fine. Straight back into the swing of things, what with the transfer window now open until the end of the month. It's all hands on deck trying to keep track of any local players moving on, new arrivals joining our clubs, you know how it is.'

'Gary's a bit worried about his contract, actually,' Debbie said, fiddling with the hem of her electric-blue dress. 'Jim Allen hasn't arranged any renewal talks, despite being in constant contact with Gary's agent.'

Amber felt her stomach sink again at the mention of Jim's name. 'They won't let Gary go, Debs. He's integral to the squad at the minute, they'd be crazy not to renegotiate.'

'Yeah,' Debbie sighed, pushing a hand through her blonde hair. 'That's what I've been telling him, too. I guess we just have to sit tight and see what happens.'

Amber took another look around the room, a slight feeling of anxiety now taking over from the excitement she'd been feeling before. 'Erm, I've… I'm just popping to the loo,' she said, throwing Debbie a smile before leaving the table, pushing her way through the crowd on her way out to the ladies'. She didn't really need to go, but what she *did* need was a bit of space, away from the mass of people inside the club. She felt a little claustrophobic all of a sudden.

'When you decide to end something, honey, you sure as hell make sure you have nothing more to do with it, don't you?'

She swung round, not in the least bit surprised that he'd followed her. She'd half expected it. 'What are you doing here? Since when did *you* start hanging out with the lads?'

'I didn't hurt you this time, Amber. This time I did nothing wrong. This time it was *you* who did the hurting, *you* who left *me*. Do you have any idea what that did to me?'

She couldn't help a small, cynical laugh from escaping as she looked at him. 'Sorry? You're seriously asking *me* that question? After everything that happened between us? You want to know if *I* have any idea how it feels, how much it hurts when someone walks away from you? Jesus…' She looked away, shaking her head.

'Okay. Alright, maybe that was… I asked for that.'

'Yeah. You did.' She looked at him, the aviator shades now stuck in the top pocket of his jacket, his eyes staring straight into hers. 'Look, Jim, I'm sorry, okay? The way things happened… none of it was planned. At the time I really thought that me and Ryan were over. I thought that was it, the relationship was finished. I couldn't take it anymore. But I was wrong.'

'It still hurt, baby. We were so close to that future we'd always wanted…'

'A future *I'd* always wanted, Jim. You deciding you want it after five minutes of being back in my life doesn't really count.'

'What changed?'

She stared into his eyes again. 'I guess I grew up. I stopped being that sixteen-year-old kid with a painful infatuation.'

'I loved that sixteen-year-old kid,' Jim whispered, reaching out to touch her cheek, but she quickly grabbed his wrist, pushing his hand away.

'She's not here anymore,' Amber said, letting go of his wrist as quickly as she'd grabbed it.

'You'll be telling me you're crazy in love with him next.'

'I am.'

It was Jim's turn to give a cynical laugh. 'Yeah. Sure. Come on, Amber. He's eleven years younger than you, he's nothing but a…'

'You might want to leave it there, Jim. Okay? I don't care about the age difference, I don't care about what he used to be or that he could sometimes be incredibly stupid. I don't care about any of that because he's finally growing up, and yes, I love him. I…'

'Like you used to love me?'

Amber stared at him again, their eyes locked together in a stare that neither of them seemed in any hurry to break. 'I think you already know the answer to that, Jim.'

'Everything okay here?'

Amber turned round quickly at the sound of that familiar Geordie accent, her heart jumping in her chest at the sight of him, tall and beautiful in the jeans, white t-shirt and black jacket he was wearing, his dark hair all messed-up and sexy. She ignored the concerned look in his eyes. There was nothing for him to be concerned about. 'Everything's fine,' she replied, holding out her hand, which he took without hesitation. 'Jim was just saying hello.'

Ryan's eyes met Jim's, both of them exchanging a stare that spoke volumes. 'Bit unusual to see you here, boss,' Ryan said, his voice slow and steady. Amber squeezed his hand as Jim's eyes moved to look at her.

'Well, I've never been in here before,' Jim replied. 'So I just thought I'd pop in, see what the place was like.'

'I'm sure Rob would like you to stop for a drink,' Ryan went on, his eyes still fixed firmly on his manager. 'If you haven't got any other plans, that is.'

Jim turned his attention back to Ryan. 'What other plans *would* I have? Now that you've taken the only thing I ever wanted away from me.'

Ryan stepped forward, his face almost right up against Jim's, but Amber quickly pulled him back, clinging even tighter onto his hand. 'She would never have been happy with you,' Ryan hissed. 'After what you did. How could she fucking trust you, huh?'

'And you think *you're* the one to renew her faith in footballers? Ryan Fisher, coke-sniffing, womanising prick…'

Ryan went for Jim again, and this time Amber had to really hold onto him to stop him from doing something verging on the stupid, grabbing onto his jacket and yanking him back, grabbing his hand.

Jim laughed – a small, low laugh – as he looked briefly down at the ground before once more meeting Ryan's eyes. 'You need to remember, kiddo, that I hold your fucking career in my hands. You need to remember just how much I know about you. And you need to know that I can bring you down before you've got time to draw breath, so you mess with me, son, and we'll see just who'll come out the winner. You might want to think about that.'

Amber stared at Jim as he walked away, her heart beating so fast she had to cling onto Ryan even tighter.

'Fucking bastard!' Ryan spat, pushing a hand through his hair, letting go of Amber as he started to pace the floor. 'Jesus, Amber, what are you doing talking to him?'

'Ryan, come on. I never wanted it to be like this, I never wanted the two of you at each other's throats, that was…'

'How can it be any other way? Huh?' He looked at her and she felt her stomach lurch even harder. 'Now that I know about you and him, know the history, know the way you felt about him… How do I know for certain you don't still feel that way? How do I know?'

'Hey, come on. Come on.' She grabbed his hand, taking it in hers and squeezing it gently, touching his cheek with the palm of her other hand, lightly stroking his soft skin, kissing his slightly open mouth in what she hoped was a bid to calm him down.

'I'm so fucking insecure, Amber.'

She looked into his eyes, a sudden need to just hold him overwhelming her. 'You shouldn't be.'

'You loved him for over twenty years. Twenty fucking years. How the hell can I compete with that, huh? How?'

She stroked his cheek again, his eyes filling with tears and it was all she could do to stop ones of her own from falling. 'Nobody's competing with anyone, baby. Alright? Jim Allen is my past – and that's where he should have stayed, but I wasn't prepared for him turning up like this. I just wasn't prepared. I let old feelings I'd repressed for so long take over and I shouldn't have done that, but maybe I needed to get them out of my system before... before I realised I can't go back to him.'

'But... do you... do you *want* to? Honestly, Amber. If someone could wave some kind of magic wand to give you the future you really wanted, would you go back to him?'

She shook her head, hoping he hadn't noticed the slight hesitation. 'No. The future I want is with *you*, Ryan. It's with *you*.'

He smiled, quickly wiping a stray tear away with the back of his hand. 'Shit, Amber. This is so fucking hard...'

'It doesn't have to be,' she whispered, standing on tiptoe to kiss his damp cheek, her lips finally resting on his, his beard tickling her skin, a feeling she'd grown to love. Because it meant it was *him* kissing her. It was *his* mouth moving against hers, there was no chance for her to imagine it was anyone else. 'It really can be very, very easy. Loving someone.'

He smiled again, pulling her against him, his mouth lowering down onto hers in another long, slow kiss, his fingers running up and down her back. 'You still up for that dirty sex later, then?'

'Yes,' she laughed, glad to see the old Ryan back. 'Now, come on. I could really do with a drink before I force you onto that dance floor to see what you're really made of.'

Ryan watched from the bar as Amber and Debbie stayed on the dance floor for yet another song, Amber's curves sexy and shown off to perfection in the dress she was wearing. Although Ryan still preferred her naked, lying underneath him, legs open, inviting him in to heaven. Jesus! One second, that's all it took for the beginnings of an almighty hard-on to start making an appearance. He was beginning to wish they hadn't come now. The idea of a party had been a good one at eleven-thirty that morning, but now all he wanted to do was go home, have lots of sex, and try not to think about having to leave Amber again tomorrow. With Saturday's match only two days away, it meant Friday night was due to be another evening holed up with the lads in the hotel, but if Jim Allen thought that was going to take his mind off anything other than football, he was wrong. Amber was all Ryan could think about now. She was all he *wanted* to think about. And nothing he could do, nothing *anyone* could do, could stop her from being the number one thing on his mind.

'So, it's serious, then?' Gary asked, handing Ryan another shot.

'Yeah,' Ryan sighed, knocking the shot back in one. 'It certainly looks that way.'

Gary followed Ryan's gaze as it fell back on Amber. She was dancing sexily to a dance track Ryan loved but couldn't remember the name of, her arms up above her head as she moved her hips in time to the thumping beat, throwing her head back and laughing as Debbie shouted something in her ear.

'She's probably telling her I've got a dick the size of a cocktail sausage, or something just as derogatory,' Gary said, leaning back against the bar and folding his arms.

Ryan looked at him, smirking slightly. 'Yeah, well, that's not a complete lie, is it, mate?'

'Says Mr. Hung-Like-A-Donkey.'

Ryan shrugged, turning his attention back to Amber. 'I've had no complaints. And I know I make that beautiful woman I get to sleep with every night scream out loud when I'm in there.'

Gary pulled a face, turning round to order another set of shots. 'I needed to hear that, didn't I?'

'And I want to be in there, right now. She is making me as horny as hell tonight.'

Gary downed another Jagerbomb. 'Well, I can't deny I'm still pissed off that *I* never had a chance to sample the delights of Ms. Amber Sullivan. She wouldn't go near any of us before *you* turned up, so what've *you* got that's so frigging different?'

Ryan grinned, sticking his hands in the pockets of his jeans. 'No idea, mate. But, whatever it is, she fucking loves it!'

'You fucking love yourself, you mean.' He looked at Ryan, his expression changing slightly. 'And what about her and the boss?'

'What about them?' Ryan asked sharply. 'It's over, Gary. And I'd really appreciate it if you didn't keep bringing it up, alright? It's over. And you've got to try and forget all about that because…'

'Okay, okay. I get it. I'll keep me mouth shut, don't worry.'

Ryan just looked at him, but said nothing.

'Want another drink?'

'Nah,' Ryan sighed. 'I'm trying to cut back, aren't I? Trying to slow down.'

'Whatever. I'm off to see if Rob's ever gonna stick his hand in his frigging pocket tonight. Just because it's his birthday, doesn't mean to say he can avoid getting a round in.'

Ryan watched Gary walk away, shaking his head as he turned back around to watch Amber. Jesus, she could move! He closed his eyes for a second, imagining her writhing around a metal pole wearing nothing but killer heels, until his dream was interrupted by someone sidling up beside him, an arm linking through his making him open his eyes.

'Hello, Ryan. Looking gorgeous, as usual.'

'Geena, Jesus, I didn't know you were coming tonight.'

'Well, I was hoping I *would* be. Later. If you're up for it. And if you make it as good as last time I'll have no need for the gym tomorrow, not after Ryan Fisher's given me a personal workout.'

Ryan looked at the young, blonde girl in front of him, knowing he'd met her before, but he couldn't quite remember where. He was surprised he'd even remembered her name, and he'd quite obviously slept with her, but he really wanted her to let go of him and leave. Right now. He felt nothing as he looked at her, except this fear that Amber would see her clinging onto him like a demented limpet and jump to every wrong conclusion there could be. This, what was happening here, this was his past. And he was trying very hard to leave all that behind.

'Look, Geena, can you... can you let go of me? Please?'

She looked at him, pouting like a child who'd had her favourite toy taken away. 'Ryan! What is *wrong* with you? Don't you want to play out tonight? I've even brought a friend with me, and she's *dying* to meet you.'

Ryan looked over at the dance floor again but, thankfully, Amber was still engrossed in the dancing, sharing another joke with Debbie. 'Things have changed, Geena.'

'What? You mean, you don't want to have sex with me anymore?'

He looked at her. What had he ever seen in this empty-headed, vacuous girl? Apart from a night of whatever he wanted, whichever way he wanted it, because he was sure she'd given him anything he'd asked for. At some point in the past. 'I'm with someone now,' Ryan said slowly, just in case she had trouble understanding what he was telling her.

'So?' she replied, examining her nails, the pout still present.

'So, Jesus... so, no, I *don't* want to have sex with you.'

She looked at him, resting a hand on his shoulder as she moved her mouth close to his ear. 'Not even if my friend joins in, too? Come on. Don't say you're not turned-on by the thought of me and my gorgeous girlfriend, both of us naked, both of us willing to give you absolutely anything you want. Absolutely *anything*, Ryan.'

He gently pushed her away, trying not to let the idea of her and whoever this friend of hers happened to be get under his skin. He'd probably indulged in the odd threesome in his time, he couldn't really remember. A lot of those nights had been nothing but a blur, but the idea of one now wasn't one he wanted to dwell on. Not at the risk of losing Amber. 'Go find someone else's head to fuck with,' he said, turning away from her, aware only of a huffy sigh coming from her direction before she finally got the message and walked away. 'Christ!' he sighed, leaning back against the bar, closing his eyes for a second, rubbing the bridge of his nose with his thumb and forefinger.

'Christ, what?' Amber asked, slipping her arms around his waist, quickly kissing his mouth.

He looked at her, smiling, a feeling of relief sweeping over him. 'Do you wanna get out of here?'

She smiled back, letting her hand slide up the back of his t-shirt as his mouth lowered onto hers for a slow, deep kiss. 'Yeah. I wanna get out of here.'

'Good,' he whispered, his mouth still resting on hers. 'Because I'm really not in the party mood anymore.'

She reached up to gently stroke his face, his chin rough beneath her fingers. 'What about our own private party, huh? You still in the mood for that?'

'Would that be the one with lots of dirty sex followed by very little sleep?'

'Yeah,' she breathed, letting his mouth close in on hers again, her stomach turning over and over in a zillion tiny somersaults. 'That's the one.'

He could feel himself reacting to her, the feel of her body pressed close against his, her fingers gently stroking the base of his spine, her breath warm on his skin. He was hard and ready, desperate to get back home and make love to her. If they made it that far.

'You ever fucked in the back of a taxi?' he smirked, running his fingers over her bare shoulders, down her neck, trailing lightly across her cleavage.

'No,' she laughed, throwing her head back as his lips brushed the base of her neck.

'Wanna give it a try?'

Chapter Twenty-Two

'Do you want to tell me what you meant the other day?' Amber asked, stopping Ronnie on his way into Tynebridge. She leaned back against the wall outside the main entrance where she'd been grabbing a bit of air before the match kicked off, keeping her eyes on Ronnie as she spoke.

He stared back at her. 'What I meant?'

'Oh, don't pretend you can't remember what you said, Ronnie, come on. You said that what happened with you and Anna, it was *my* fault…'

'I didn't *say* that.'

'You alluded to it.'

'I didn't mean it.'

'Didn't you?' Amber asked, following him as he walked into the main entrance, striding purposefully across the marble floor of the huge reception area which was now full of footballers, pundits, and a number of local celebrities who'd turned up to watch the game, not to mention members of the Red Star board. And Jim Allen. And it was his presence which caused Amber to momentarily lose track of what she was actually in the middle of saying.

'Didn't I, what?'

'Come on, Ronnie, I don't have time for this… When *I* said what happened with you and Anna – when I said it wasn't my fault

371

you looked at me and *you* said "*wasn't it?*" What am I *supposed* to think, huh? When someone says that? And then decides they're not going to answer my calls when I try to get hold of them. What's going on?'

'Nothing.'

She couldn't help laughing. 'Jesus, that's usually *my* line. Have we had some kind of role reversal go on when I wasn't looking?'

Ronnie stopped walking and turned to face her. 'Nothing's going on, Amber. Alright?'

'Actually, no. It's *not* alright. You can't go blaming somebody for something then refuse to tell them why.'

He threw his head back and sighed, pushing a hand through his hair. 'I'm sorry.' He looked at her. 'I'm sorry. I didn't mean to say what I did; it was just emotions taking over, that's all. It meant nothing. Okay?'

She narrowed her eyes slightly as she looked at him, not entirely convinced. His body language was a little strange, too. Like he was trying to hide something. 'Yeah. Okay.'

He leaned forward to plant a kiss on her cheek. 'I've got to get to work. I'll see you later.'

She watched as he walked over to the two ex-footballers who'd be joining him on the pundit panel during the televised match that afternoon, his expression changing, his body language automatically becoming more relaxed. So, there was nothing going on? Yeah, right. She believed *that*.

'Good to see you here, Amber.'

She turned to see Jim standing beside her, handsome as ever in his trademark match-day dark suit and white shirt, aviator shades tucked firmly in the top pocket of his jacket.

'You *knew* I'd be here. I'm working.'

He looked away for a second, smiling at the Chairman and two of the owners of Newcastle Red Star as they walked through the main entrance on their way to what Amber assumed would be one of the better-equipped hospitality boxes. There was always an element of corporate entertaining going on at big home games. And *this* was a big home game, for Ryan, anyway, because Red Star were playing his old London club that afternoon. And Amber knew how much it meant to Ryan to play the game of his life out there. To prove to himself, more than anyone, that he'd made the right decision to move back up north.

'It's just good to see you, that's all,' Jim went on, his eyes looking right into hers. And as much as she wanted to say something back, to tell him that she wished she could say the same but it wouldn't be true, no words would come out. She just stared at him, wishing he'd never come back here. Wishing he'd kept that promise to stay away, to respect what she needed him to do because him being around was only complicating everything. Even now. Even though she knew she wanted to be with Ryan; even though she knew she *loved* Ryan, Jim was still here, still a big part of her life. And there wasn't really anything she could do to change that.

'I've got to go,' Amber whispered, finally breaking the stare, hating the way she felt flustered. She'd never been flustered before *he'd* walked back into her life.

'Your dad's invited me round to his for lunch tomorrow,' Jim carried on, making Amber look up sharply. 'I gather you and Ryan will be there, too. I guess he wants us all to have a big family dinner, huh?'

Amber took a silent deep breath. 'You're not family, though. Are you?'

'As good as, honey.'

She continued to stare at him. 'Are you going to make this difficult for me and Ryan? Because that really isn't fair, Jim.'

'I love you, Amber. Yet you're with him. *That's* not fair.'

She wanted to say something, to make him understand that things could never be the way he wanted them to be but he'd walked off before she'd had a chance to even open her mouth. Great. Lunch tomorrow was going to be fun, and she really didn't need the stress of having Jim there. It was a difficult enough job trying to get her father onside as far as Ryan was concerned, without the added pressure of Jim. It was a situation fraught with tension, with three out of four people knowing a secret the other really couldn't find out about. Just one tiny thing had the potential to light a touchpaper that could really make things difficult, and Amber didn't want to think about the consequences that could arise from that. Maybe she was worrying unnecessarily, or maybe she really did have cause for concern. Who knew? She'd just have to wait and see, wouldn't she?

'Did Jim tell you he's joining us for lunch tomorrow?' Freddie Sullivan smiled as he arrived at his daughter's side. 'I saw you talking to him just then.'

She looked at her father, trying to return the smile he was giving her. 'Erm, yeah. Yeah, he did.'

'Are you two getting on alright?' Freddie frowned, shoving his hands in his pockets.

'Why… why wouldn't we be?' Amber asked, quickly checking her phone, noticing a new text from Ryan had arrived.

'I dunno, pet,' Freddie shrugged. 'He says he hasn't seen an awful lot of you since he came back up here, that's all. He feels like you're almost avoiding him.'

Jim Allen had seen more of her than most people, so he was lying there, but she couldn't really tell her dad that, could she? Sliding her phone back into her pocket, she looked at her father again. 'Why would he see a lot of me anyway, Dad? And I'm not avoiding him, why the hell would I avoid him?'

Freddie shrugged again. 'I have no idea, Amber. You tell me.'

'I'm not avoiding him. I'm just busy, that's all. And I'm sure he's got much better things to do than talk to me. We were never that close anyway, were we? Not really. He's more your friend than mine.'

Freddie fell into step beside Amber as she pushed open the double doors that led out of the main atrium and down to the Press and Players' Lounges. 'You were only young back then, I suppose. You had your own life… Listen, sweetheart, you don't *mind* me inviting him tomorrow, do you? Only, he *is* one of my oldest friends, and for some strange reason he's still without a girlfriend since he arrived back up north, which surprises me, considering what a handsome bastard he is. Had the women falling at his feet when he was a player here...'

Amber looked at her dad, not really in the mood to discuss Jim Allen's playboy past – a past that involved *her* far more than it should have done. 'Look, I've got to go and... y'know, catch up with some people in the Press Lounge, make sure I'm all ready for the match.'

'Of course. You go ahead, sweetheart. I'll pop into the Players' Lounge for a bit. There're bound to be some old faces in there I haven't seen in a while.' He kissed her quickly on the cheek. 'I'll see you after the game?'

She nodded, smiling what she hoped was a convincing smile. 'Yeah.'

She watched him walk into the Players' Lounge, and she was just about to push open the door to the Press Lounge directly opposite when someone grabbed her arm and pulled her round the corner.

'What the...? Ryan! What the hell are you doing? You're supposed to be in the dressing room, they're gonna kill you...'

He shut her up with a kiss and she just melted against him, leaning back against the wall as his hands rested on her hips, his mouth soft yet strong as it moved against hers. She hadn't seen him since yesterday morning, hadn't spoken to him for all those hours and this was something she'd missed. The kisses. She missed them when he wasn't around.

'You have got to get back to the dressing room, Ryan.'

He looked at her, those dark eyes of his staring deep into hers. 'Jesus. You're beautiful.'

'Shut up,' she laughed. 'Mind you, you *do* look incredibly sexy in that football kit. It's verging on a major turn-on, mister.'

He grinned, sliding a hand down the front of her jeans, kissing the side of her neck, making her groan out loud.

'Come on, Ryan, this isn't fair. You've got to get back…'

He grabbed her hand again, dragging her into an empty side room, locking the door from the inside.

'Ryan… what are you doing? If they…'

'If they, what? If they find me having sex before a big match they're gonna drop me?'

'They might,' she pointed out, already wanting him in her and sod the consequences. Despite the fact it was the last thing that should be happening. 'If they catch us.'

He grinned again, pulling her closer, unzipping her jeans as he kissed her slowly, his tongue touching the roof of her mouth, running along the back of her teeth, sending her whole body into spasms of unexpected pleasure. The danger of being caught, the fact they really shouldn't be doing this, it only made everything ten times more exciting.

'No one's gonna catch us, babe,' he said, sliding her jeans down, his fingers pulling at her panties. 'Relax.'

How could she do anything else when he was about to send her on a flying visit to heaven? Even the sound of voices outside in the corridor, the constant noise of footsteps walking backwards and forwards, was both a distraction and a turn-on. But the biggest turn-on was the fact he was going to make love to her wearing his full football kit. Jesus, she'd actually dreamt about this, and now it was happening.

'Ryan…'

His mouth covered hers, silencing her with another deep kiss as he pushed his way into her, hard and fast, the kisses matching the intensity as they fucked each other to within an inch of their lives in record-quick time. It took just a few beautiful minutes for him to reach his own goal, and a second or two more for Amber to reach hers. Then it was over. Done.

'You are in so much trouble if they find out,' Amber breathed, sliding an arm round the back of his neck, running her fingers along his rough, bearded jawline, her eyes watching their every move as she tried to catch her breath.

'They won't find out,' he smirked, pulling her jeans back up for her, his mouth so close to hers as he spoke. 'And I'm certainly not gonna tell them.'

'You'd better have enough energy left for this match.' She started playing with the hair at the nape of his neck, staring into his eyes, wishing they could stay there, just the two of them. Wishing they could shut the rest of the world out. This falling in love lark was hard work, having to fight those needy feelings that wouldn't seem to lie low, having to let him go when she really didn't want to. 'I love you, Ryan Fisher.'

'Hey, I love you, too, beautiful. I love you, too.'

She closed her eyes as he kissed her again, sliding her hand up under his football strip, touching his warm skin, which was a mistake, because the second she did that she felt that familiar stomach flip and a desperate need to have him again, but this time she pulled back. Stopped herself from getting him into any more trouble.

'You're not doing this just to piss Jim off, are you?' Amber asked, zipping her jeans back up.

'Now, why would I do that, huh?' Ryan grinned, running a hand through his hair.

She couldn't help smiling, pulling him back for one last kiss, pushing herself against him even though she'd promised herself she'd behave, let him get out of there before somebody found them. 'You *know* why.'

He grinned, slipping a hand up under her top and grabbing a quick feel before pulling away, opening the door and backing out of it, mouthing something incredibly rude at her as he finally left her alone.

Amber smiled a smile she felt as though she'd been waiting to smile for over a decade now. Ryan Fisher had well and truly got to her. And for that, she really was quite grateful.

Nobody had any idea of Ryan's forbidden warm-up routine. Nobody had any idea what he'd done just half an hour before kick-off, because he'd played the game of his life that afternoon. His energy levels had been up there, the adrenalin rush he'd got from fucking Amber in that side room had kicked in big time, leaving him raring to get out there and show his old teammates that he'd lost none of the talent he'd shown when he'd played with them. He'd been on the kind of form most clubs and their managers could only dream of, scoring two goals within ten minutes of each other in the first twenty-five minutes of the game, sending the Red Star supporters into a frenzy, raising expectations that their star striker was on a roll. And he was.

With another two goals in the second half – one in the dying minutes of the game – Ryan Fisher had bagged himself a hat-trick plus one, and another 'Man of the Match' award. He was fucking flying! By the time the final whistle came he was higher than any drug had ever made him, punching the air and yelling his delight at the home fans, sharing their excitement. Jesus! Life couldn't get any frigging better for him right now. He was playing like he'd never played before, he felt the fittest he'd been in ages, and he was in love. Shit! Who'd have thought? Ryan Fisher – in love.

'You did good out there,' Jim said, patting Ryan on the shoulder as he walked towards the tunnel, the sound of the crowd still deafening, drowning out the voice over the tannoy issuing instructions to the away fans to stay put. 'Well done.'

Ryan looked at his manager. Yeah, he looked as though he really meant that. Professional to the end, that was Jim Allen. Despite that one lapse near the beginning of the season – and Ryan totally understood why that had happened now – he hadn't done a thing to hamper Ryan's career at Red Star. Even if he *had* threatened to. 'Thanks, boss.'

Jim put a hand on his arm, stopping him from walking away. 'But pull another stunt like the one you did before this game, son, and I'll drop you faster than you can blink. You got that?'

Ryan stared at him, narrowing his eyes. 'What the hell are you talking about?'

'I can forgive *her* because, for some reason, she's acting like a lovesick puppy that can't bear to leave your side, but I know Amber, and she'll grow out of that. You, on the other hand, should know better. There are rules, Ryan. There are rules, and you either play by them or we find a way to make sure you have no other choice.'

'What the…'

'You get your kicks *after* the match, Fisher. Do you hear me?'

Ryan shook his arm free and continued walking towards the tunnel, a smile slowly spreading across his face. So, Jim Allen *had* known about the secret sex in the side room. Ryan had a feeling it wouldn't have escaped his notice; he let nothing get past him, and Ryan knew that. Did he honestly think he didn't know how closely Jim was watching him? Of course he bloody knew!

As he walked down the tunnel, crowds of people flocked around him, throwing questions at him, none of which he could make out through the cacophony of voices surrounding him. He had the post-match interviews to do, and then he had every intention of going out to celebrate – but not without Amber. Ryan was one half of a couple now, and he liked the feeling that gave him. He liked the security, the safeness. He liked the fact she was always there. Everything he'd steered clear of before, he now craved. How life could turn around in an instant.

As he pushed through the double doors at the start of the tunnel that led back into the ground, he was guided to the tiny corner of the corridor where the post-match interviews took place, craning his neck to see if he could spot Amber. He had no idea if she was doing the interviews for News North East; he hadn't even thought to ask her when he'd seen her earlier. He'd had other things on his mind. But, as he caught sight of her across the corridor, leaning back against the wall, her arms folded, he couldn't help but smile, a smile that only got wider as she mouthed *Well done, baby*. All that mattered was that she was proud of him. All that mattered was that she trusted him, that she loved him. If he had that, he knew he could cope with anything.

'*Wait 'til last,*' he mouthed back, wanting to get everyone else out of the way before he spoke to her. He wanted her to be the last person he saw before he went back into the dressing room. He needed that to happen.

She nodded that she'd got the message and Ryan continued on with the various post-match interviews they had lined up, all of them short and basically asking him much the same thing, but all the time he was just waiting for Amber to take her turn. Which she eventually did. Last in line, just as he'd wanted her to be.

He waited until she'd asked him the usual stuff, and he talked about the game, the four goals he'd scored, how it felt to be playing such a big part in helping his boyhood team have a chance of winning that league title. But, as soon as she'd thanked him for talking to News North East, he stopped her from walking away by gently taking her hand, asking if the cameras could stay rolling for a second. He pushed a hand through his dark hair and looked at her. The nerves were kicking in now, but he'd wanted to do this from the second he'd woken up that morning. He'd opened his eyes in that hotel room, in a bed on his own, and he'd known – he'd just known – that he had to do this.

'Listen, I… Before everyone goes I've got something I need to do. And it involves this woman here in front of me.'

Amber looked at him, a slightly confused expression on her face, which turned into something a little more anxious as he held her hand tighter, pulling her into shot. 'Ryan…'

He smiled at her, leaning over to give her the briefest of kisses, his nerves suddenly dissipating the second his lips touched hers. He felt on top of the world right now, and this would only make that feeling stronger, make it complete. He was way out of his comfort zone, but living on the edge was what he did best. And this was way out there. Nobody would be expecting this, not from him.

'I love you, Amber Sullivan. I love you, babe, and… and I want to ask you something…' His eyes never left hers, his fingers gently stroking a stray strand of red hair away from her face. Shit! He was really going to do this! And he'd never felt so frigging excited. 'I want to…' He leaned forward and kissed her again, his fingers wrapping themselves tightly around hers. 'Will you marry me?'

'You're supposed to report the sports news, not *be* the sports news,' Kevin sighed, quaffing a large mouthful of champagne in the Players' Lounge. 'Congratulations, though. Despite the fact our satellite friends got the bigger coup because their broadcast went out live, that should still guarantee us a few more viewers when our segment goes out in the late bulletin in an hour or so. Everyone loves a local fairy tale with a happy ending.'

Amber leaned back against the bar, sipping her own champagne. 'It's hardly a fairy tale, Kevin. And it hasn't even begun yet, never mind have a happy ending.'

'It'll be a frigging fairy tale when we do our own story on the pair of you, and your "romance".'

She looked at her producer. 'Huh? Sorry, did you just say you're going to do a story about me and Ryan?'

'Of course we're going to do a bloody story. We work on a local news programme, Amber. And, right now, *you're* the frigging news. Our very own Sports Editor has just got engaged to one of the most famous, most high-profile, most talented players in the country, a player who just happens to be both a local lad *and* playing for one of the region's biggest clubs – it's fucking manna from heaven!'

'I'm still getting my head around it all,' Amber sighed, watching Ryan across the other side of the room as he talked to Gary and Rob. He looked relaxed, happy. He looked like a different man to the one she'd first encountered here less than six months ago. Six months, that was such a short time in reality. Six months in which Christ knows what had happened, and she'd just agreed to marry him. Six months ago she'd been determined never to go near another footballer again, and she'd meant it. But then Ryan Fisher had walked into her life, and now, after everything she'd ever promised herself, she was about to spend the rest of her life with him. Jesus, just stopping to think about it for a second actually made her feel quite sick.

'Right, well, I'm off to start planning this story then,' Kevin said, downing the last of his champagne and slamming the empty glass on the bar. 'I'll see you in my office first thing Monday morning. Talk your fiancé round, okay?' He threw her a wink and a grin and walked out of the Players' Lounge. Amber turned to face the bar, picking up a bottle of champagne that was sitting on the end of it, pouring out the last of what was left inside, filling her glass back up again.

'I'd like to say congratulations, but I'd be telling you something I can't ever really mean.'

She turned to look at Jim as he leaned forward on the bar, his suit jacket now off and his shirtsleeves rolled up to the elbows. 'Then I'd rather you said nothing at all.'

He looked down at his clasped hands. 'It's killing me, Amber. I mean, it was hurting before, before he asked you to marry him, but...' He looked up at her, his eyes almost pleading, and Amber couldn't help but feel her stomach lurch slightly. 'What are you doing, Amber? You don't belong with him, you don't... Is this not just something you're doing to try and deflect from what you really feel for *me*?'

'You flatter yourself, Jim. And this really isn't the time or the place to be having this conversation, so, if you don't mind...'

He grabbed her wrist as she made to go, swinging her back round to look at him. '*We* belong together, Amber. *Me* and *you*. He isn't right for you, he'll let you down, he'll hurt you...'

'Then he's really no different to you, Jim. Is he?'

She walked off without looking back at him, knowing that wasn't the end of it, but she couldn't deal with him right now. She just wanted to be with Ryan. But it seemed the world and

382

its mother was conspiring to stop her from getting to him, even though he was only across the other side of somewhere that was smaller than the average living room.

'Engaged?' Ronnie asked, looking at Amber with wide eyes.

She stared back at him with eyes just as wide. 'Oh, *now* you want to talk to me.'

'You're seriously going to marry him?' Ronnie went on, ignoring her slight dig.

'I'm thinking about it, yes. You got a problem with that?'

'Amber… just a few months ago you were telling me this wasn't anything serious, and now he's proposing to you live on TV! What's *that* all about?'

'I love him, Ronnie. Okay? And, yes, this has come as much of a surprise to me as it has to you, because getting married isn't anything anyone expected Ryan Fisher to do, but, do you know what? I quite like surprises.'

'You never used to,' Ronnie said, an almost defeated tone to his voice. 'Shit, Amber. I hate the way things are changing.'

'It happens,' Amber smiled, taking his hand and squeezing it. 'And anyway, nobody's doing anything yet. He may have asked me to marry him, but any wedding is a long way off, believe me.'

'Glad to hear it,' Freddie Sullivan said as he joined them, a pint of lager in one hand, the other stuffed in his pocket. 'All I can say is, he'd better look after my girl or I'll have something to say to him.'

Amber sighed, throwing her head back. 'I need this, don't I?' She looked at her dad. 'You do realise I'm thirty-seven years old, don't you? And that I *can* look after myself.'

'Oh, yeah, I realise that, pet. I just hope you know what you're getting into with Ryan, that's all. Compared to you, he's still a bairn.'

She looked at him again. 'Thanks, Dad. Now I feel really old. Look, lunch tomorrow, is it going to be a problem? Would you rather me and Ryan didn't come?'

'Don't be bloody stupid!' Freddie admonished, taking a long sip of lager. 'I'm just acting like any dad would act when they find out their only daughter is getting hitched to football's worst kind of bad boy.'

'Yeah, that statement makes me feel really excited about bringing him over to yours.'

'He's gonna be part of the family, Amber. And if you say he's changed then I'm more than willing to give him the benefit of the doubt.'

Amber said nothing, she just let go of Ronnie's hand and finally made her way over to Ryan.

'Hey, gorgeous,' he smiled, sliding an arm around her waist and pulling her in against him. 'Everything okay?'

'Apart from the flack you're getting left, right and centre from my close friends and family, you mean?'

'I take it they're ecstatic about the engagement, then?'

'Over the frigging moon,' she smirked, closing her eyes as his mouth touched hers, an instant feeling of calm washing over her. 'They'll get used to the idea. I'm still getting used to it myself, if I'm honest.'

He kissed her again and she let herself fall against him, a sudden tiredness now joining that calm feeling. 'It feels so right,' he whispered, stroking her cheek with his thumb. 'I love you so much, Amber. I need you, babe, and I just want you to be there, in my life. Always.'

'I never had you down as the romantic type,' she smiled, letting her fingers slide slowly up under his shirt.

'Yeah, well, I'm full of surprises, me.'

'Do you wanna skip all this shit now? Go back home? Do some celebrating of our own?'

He grinned, sliding his hands down over her backside, pushing her harder against him. 'If that celebrating includes sex then I'm all over it, beautiful.'

'And in a little while, I'd quite like you all over *me*.'

'Jesus, Amber…' he groaned, running his hands up her back, underneath her top, '… you're killing me here.'

'Come on,' she whispered, her mouth touching his as she spoke. 'Let's get out of here. The only party I'm in the mood for right now is a private one.'

Chapter Twenty-Three

Ryan opened his eyes and turned his head to see if she was awake. She wasn't. He could hear her breathing, her eyes tight shut as she slept. Rolling onto his side, he pulled the duvet down slightly, exposing her breasts, watching as they rose and fell, feeling himself grow hard as he continued to stare at them. Sliding his hand underneath the covers, he gently pushed her legs apart, touching her down there, his thumb carefully stroking her, moving in a measured, circular motion, his hardness growing by the second as she became wetter, his fingers slipping and sliding against her. But he didn't move his hand away, even when she slowly opened her eyes and turned to look at him.

'I don't believe I ordered a wake-up call,' she whispered, her eyes meeting his as he continued to touch her. But she had no intention of stopping him; instead she stretched out, opening her legs wider.

Ryan was so hard now it was almost painful, but he was loving the feel of her against his hand, all warm and soaking wet, soft and smooth, but he wasn't going to be able to keep it up for much longer, not if he wanted to come inside her, which he did.

'Oh, God…' she moaned, her hands gripping the headboard as his fingers continued to stroke her, the rhythmic, circular motions speeding up slightly until he could take no more. Pulling the covers away from her naked body, he rolled onto his back, pulling her over on top of him, and within seconds she'd carefully lowered herself down onto him, leaning back to allow him to go deep. 'This is the *best* way to wake up.'

'You're telling me,' he groaned, jerking his hips up as she pushed down, making him shout out loud, fighting with her screams as early morning, red-hot sex took them both to that now-familiar place that neither of them wanted to leave. But the urgency meant that this was a super-quick visit to heaven.

'Do you think it'll always be like this?' Amber breathed, rolling over onto her back.

He turned his head and smiled at her. 'Probably not.'

'Oh, way to go, Ryan,' she laughed, playfully punching his arm. 'Are you saying that once we're married sex will cease to be exciting?'

He turned onto his side, propping himself up on his elbow. 'We're always going to have exciting sex, babe. I'll make sure of it.'

She smiled, too, gently stroking his cheek with her fingertips. 'Yeah, well, you'd better, mister. I've waited a long time to have sex like this and I'm not ready to give that up just yet.'

'So, you're only marrying me for the sex, then?'

'No,' she laughed. 'There're other reasons, too. I mean, you make a fantastic bacon sandwich…'

He started tickling her, making her scream and squirm as he grabbed her round the waist. Jesus, he was happy. He was so fucking happy, almost afraid it was just some kind of dream and that any second now he'd wake up and find that she was still with Jim Allen, that he really had lost her.

'What's wrong?' Amber asked as Ryan suddenly let go of her, sitting up and pushing a hand through his dark, dishevelled hair.

'I can't stop thinking about you and him, Amber. You and the boss.'

Amber pulled herself up into a sitting position, hugging her knees to her chest. 'It's over, Ryan.'

He looked at her. 'Is it?'

She rested her chin on her knees, nodding. 'Yes. It is.'

He looked away, focusing on the chink of light filtering through the curtains. 'It might be for you, but is it for him?'

She knelt up, reaching out for his hand, taking it in hers and squeezing it tight. 'I know this is a really difficult situation, Ryan. I know it is. It's far from ideal and…'

He turned to look at her. He'd never really stopped to just look at her, not in the early days. When he'd first met her all he'd really seen was this incredibly beautiful woman who'd provided some kind of challenge that he wanted to overcome, just to prove that he could succeed where others had failed. Lust had won over, and love hadn't even come into it. Not at first. But it was love he felt now, that overwhelming emotion that he'd never really experienced before; a fear of losing someone, constant anxiety that they were, one day, going to walk away from you, and it both unsettled and excited him. But the fact he'd never stopped to look at her, really look at her before – he couldn't believe he'd never done that because she truly was beautiful. Even now, when she'd been awake for just minutes, her face devoid of make-up, her hair all messed-up and sexy, she was beautiful. She may be eleven years older than him but that was something he didn't even think about anymore. It never *had* been an issue; and the fact that she was so different to the made-up, over-glamorous, almost desperate wannabe WAGs only made her all the more beautiful to him. 'As long as you don't love him anymore, that's all I need to hear, Amber. I just need to know that you don't love him anymore.'

She reached out to touch his cheek, leaning forward to gently kiss his slightly open mouth and Ryan felt his stomach leap around like it was on some kind of springboard. It had taken him twenty-six years to experience these feelings and now they were here he was in no hurry to send them packing. Not now he had the chance to keep them forever. 'I love *you*, Ryan Fisher. God help me, I love *you*.'

'Ryan,' Freddie Sullivan smiled – a slightly forced smile, Amber thought – as they walked into the hall of her father's house. 'Good to see you, son.'

Amber watched as Ryan shook her father's hand, giving him the bottle of Tesco's finest sparkling wine they'd grabbed on the way over.

'It's… it's good of you to invite me, Mr…'

'Freddie, please. Come on, Ryan. You're going to be family soon; we might as well start as we mean to go on.'

Amber didn't know whether to feel relieved that her father was at least trying to accept Ryan as her future husband, or nervous that he was just putting it all on and some time after lunch he was going to drag him into the kitchen for a private word about looking after her or having *him* to answer to. She felt like a teenager bringing her first boyfriend home.

Ryan smiled at Freddie, and Amber couldn't help noticing his shoulders sag slightly with relief. She threw him a reassuring smile and squeezed his hand before kissing her father quickly on the cheek. 'Something smells fantastic, Dad. What's for lunch?'

'Roast lamb with a rosemary and thyme gravy, roast parsnips and potatoes and a selection of four fresh vegetables.'

'Whoa! That sounds amazing!' Ryan laughed, then he looked at Amber. 'Have you inherited any of your dad's culinary skills?'

'Ryan, sweetheart, if you're marrying me for my cooking then you might as well call this engagement off right now.'

'Oh, there's a lot more to Amber than just her cooking skills,' Jim smiled, appearing in the doorway of the living room, looking casual and relaxed in jeans and a dark-grey shirt as he leaned against the doorpost.

Amber looked at him sharply, sending him a message with her eyes that told him to lay off the smart remarks. He just threw her a small smile back and took a sip from the wineglass he was holding.

'Anyway,' Amber said, quickly changing the subject, '… I could do with a glass of something white and sparkling.' She turned to

Ryan. 'Do you want to go and open that bottle we brought in with us, baby? Dad'll show you where we keep the glasses, won't you, Dad?'

'Yeah. Yeah, of course I will.'

Ryan looked at Amber with an expression verging on panic.

'He won't bite,' Amber smiled, kissing him quickly and letting go of his hand. 'And just refuse to comment if he starts asking any tricky questions. Go on,' she winked at him, making him laugh. 'And make that a large glass. It's Sunday, I want to relax.'

Ryan threw Jim a quick look before following Freddie into the kitchen.

'I hope that remark wasn't a sign that you're going to make this difficult,' Amber said to Jim as she walked into the living room.

Jim laid a hand on her hip as she pushed past him, causing her to swing round and stare at him. 'The engagement's still on, then?'

She looked down at his hand resting on her hip, waiting until he removed it before her eyes met his again. 'This isn't happening, Jim.'

'He's just a boy, Amber. A kid.'

'I love him…'

'Jesus Christ,' Jim sighed, throwing his head back. 'You're deluded if you think he's actually going to go through with this wedding. He'll get bored, fed up of having just the one woman to play with. Kids like that need variety, honey. They need choice, they want to play games with lots of friends, and you'll see that, one day. Or you could walk away now and save yourself the pain.'

She shook her head. 'What? And come back to you?'

'You were already with me not so long ago, baby. You were already there, talking about a future together, a life that we'd always dreamed of…'

'No, I'll stop you there, Jim. We've been over this before and I'm tired of saying it now – that life was a life only *I'd* dreamed of. Not you. You were too busy playing those games you talk about with all those "friends" of yours.'

He followed her into the room, closing the door behind them.

'How many times do I have to say I'm sorry, huh?'

She swung round to face him, knowing for sure that this had been a bad idea now. 'You've got nothing to be sorry for, Jim. It wasn't *your* fault I was naive enough to fall for you more times than I should have done. I should have learnt my lesson while I was still a teenager. But I didn't, did I? And that's *my* fault, not yours.'

He walked over to her, putting his drink down before resting his hand on her cheek, looking deep into her eyes. 'This will *never* go away, Amber. Not for me. I was an idiot, okay, I'll admit that. I knew you'd always be there and I took advantage of that, but don't think I didn't ever care about you, because I did. And when I finally grew up, when all that crap was out of my system and all I wanted to do was find the right girl and settle down… The right girl had always been there, Amber. Right there, beside me, and I just couldn't see it. Not back then. But I see it now. Ryan, he… he hasn't got it out of his system yet, honey. Jesus, I hate to say it, but he reminds me of me, which is why I *know* he isn't right for you. Not yet. He hasn't had that time to grow up, to realise what he actually has, and he *will* hurt you, Amber. He will, I can almost guarantee that…'

'You know nothing,' she whispered, wishing her heart wasn't beating at what felt like a million beats a second, wishing her head wasn't spinning and her stomach wasn't turning those somersaults it shouldn't be turning for him. It shouldn't be doing that. Not for Jim. 'You don't know Ryan like I do.'

'You don't know him at all,' Jim said, moving his mouth closer to hers, so close his breath was warm on her cheek, making her head spin more and her heart beat even faster until, in an action Amber just couldn't seem to stop, it was as if her whole body had frozen, rendering any movement impossible, his lips brushed against hers. It was a quick, gentle kiss at first, so brief it was hard to realise it had actually happened, until his mouth lowered back down onto hers in a deeper kiss, a longer kiss, a kiss that Amber couldn't break away from, she couldn't do it. It felt as though he'd cast some kind of spell over her and it would only break when *he* allowed it to. Or was that just some convenient excuse she was telling herself to account for the fact she'd wanted this to happen?

'No,' Amber spluttered, finally pulling away, backing off from Jim, shaking her head. 'No. This is *not* going to happen,' she hissed, wiping her mouth with the back of her hand. 'Me and you, it's over. It's done, finished. You're part of a life I just can't go back to and you need to realise that, you need to understand… You have to give me the space I need to move on because this – this isn't fair. On either of us. Jesus, Jim, you could have any woman you want…'

'I only want you.'

'Well, you can't have her.'

Amber swung round to see Ryan standing in the doorway and her heart practically stopped dead, her breath catching in her throat. 'Ryan…'

He walked over to Jim, waiting until he was right up in his face before speaking. 'I'll give you that one, okay? I'll give you that because you're quite obviously one hell of a persuasive bloke and I don't expect her to forget about you just like that. I'm not that naive. But you touch her again, and believe me, I won't be quite so calm about it.'

Amber looked up at the ceiling, trying to blink back tears that were threatening to fall, which was the last thing she needed. How the hell did she explain *that* to her father?

'I think you forget who holds the ace cards in all of this,' Jim said, a tone verging on the menacing in his voice.

Ryan let out a small, cynical laugh. 'You really want to play that kind of game, boss? You really want to put your own – not to mention the club's – reputation on the line by threatening me with blackmail?'

'I'm not blackmailing anyone, son.'

'It sounds pretty close to blackmail from where *I'm* standing.'

'You're punching way above your weight here, Fisher.'

'You reckon?'

'I *know*.'

'So, you're quite prepared for the possibility of Amber getting hurt, then? If you decide to carry out whatever threat you're making? And what *do* you intend to do, huh? Exactly how do you intend to use those ace cards of yours?'

'I could end your career like that. In an instant.'

'Then go ahead. I'm calling your bluff – boss.'

'Ryan…' Amber pleaded, desperate for this to end before her dad came back into the room.

'You can't have her,' Ryan said, stepping away from Jim, his hand sliding into Amber's, pulling her close to him. 'You can't fucking have her. And I guess you're just going to have to deal with that in whatever way you can.'

'Are you still mad at me for facing up to him?' Ryan asked, closing the car door, the sound of it slamming echoing around the underground car park.

'I'm not mad at you, no,' Amber replied, falling into step beside him as they headed for the doors that led from the car park into the main body of the MetroCentre, a large, out-of-town shopping and leisure complex on the outskirts of Newcastle. 'What you said to him… maybe it needed to be said. I just panicked that my dad might have overheard something, that's all.'

Ryan slipped his hand into hers, squeezing it tight. 'He didn't overhear anything, babe. He was out the back, chatting to one of the neighbours, that's the only reason I did what I did. I wouldn't have done it otherwise. Not there, anyway.'

Amber said nothing. She was just glad lunch was over. It had been a strained affair at best, although, thankfully, her father hadn't seemed to notice the slight tension between Jim and Ryan. But she hadn't been willing to stick around for any longer than they had to, making up some excuse about meeting Gary and Debbie for a drink, just so they could escape. And somehow they'd ended up here, at the MetroCentre, which was fine with her. She felt like a bit of retail therapy, maybe some dinner later. She didn't really want to go home just yet.

'You *are* still mad, aren't you?' Ryan asked, standing still and pulling her into his arms, kissing her quickly.

'Ryan, baby, I'm not mad, okay? I'm just… I'm just sorry I let him get to me. I didn't mean to…'

He shut her up with a kiss, just a quick one but enough to make her stop talking. 'It's okay. Jesus, Amber, you said yourself this isn't an ideal situation. And maybe we all just have to find a way to deal with it in the best way we can.'

They started walking again, Ryan's arm sliding around her shoulders as she snuggled in against him. 'What he said to you, though…'

'He won't carry any of that out, babe. They were just empty threats.'

'You think? You know that for sure, do you?'

'No, but he'd be stupid to try, wouldn't he? I mean, everyone knows I can be an arsehole at times, so him spreading shit about me isn't really gonna surprise anyone. Which means that the biggest threat he has is one that exposes what you and him had together, and that doesn't really affect me, does it? It hurts *you*, and I don't think he's willing to do that.'

'I hope you're right.' She stopped walking again, turning to face him. 'You could ask for a transfer. I mean, the window's open now, isn't it? For a few more days. Even if it's just on loan somewhere, away from here… it would give us some time…'

'Amber, baby, come on. That's not gonna work, is it?'

'Why not?'

'Well, for starters, the amount of money Red Star paid for me, no way are they gonna loan me out to another club when they're well on the way to being a real title contender. Jesus, I've only been there five minutes! No, it doesn't matter how pissed off Jim Allen is with me, he won't jeopardise the club. He's way too professional

394

to do that. The stick he got when he dropped me for that one game was enough, but if he tells the board he wants to loan me out… Can you imagine the questions he'd have to answer? And you *know* all of that, Amber. You've been around this game for too long, you know how it works. And what about *your* job, huh? You'd be willing to give that up just to avoid Jim Allen?'

It wasn't something she'd have been willing to do just a few short months ago. But the way things had panned out since then, if it meant she and Ryan could get some peace, away from Jim's – hopefully – empty threats, if they could just have some time together to work things out, well, she'd be willing to give up anything. 'Maybe we *need* to get away, Ryan.'

'And it's impossible at the minute, kiddo. It just can't happen right now, come on, you know that.' He tilted up her chin, making her look right at him. 'We've got to face this head-on, okay? He'll get the message, eventually. And, yes, maybe it's gonna be a little uncomfortable for a while, and maybe he'll do his best to get the odd dig in, but he'll get the message, Amber. I'll make sure of that.'

'I never wanted it to be like this,' she whispered, looking down at Ryan's hand in hers. 'But him coming back here, it's messed everything up.'

'Only if you let it.'

She looked up at him, smiling. 'Yeah. I suppose you're right.'

He rubbed his thumb over the third finger of her left hand, kissing her quickly, not caring if people were watching or not. 'Y'know, we're engaged, yet that finger is still looking a bit naked to me.'

Amber looked down, too, cocking her head to one side. 'I hadn't even thought about it.'

'Yeah, well, you see, that's where you differ from the girls I used to be familiar with. If I'd asked any of *them* to marry me, there's no way they'd have said yes until there was some obscenely-sized diamond on that finger.'

'Are you saying I'm cheap?' Amber smirked, sliding a hand

round the back of his neck.

'No, I'm not saying that. What I'm saying is, I think we need to find something to go on that finger, don't you?'

'I don't care about rings or fancy weddings or any of that, Ryan. I care about *you*. Nothing else matters. I don't need a piece of jewellery to tell me you're mine.'

'Not even a nice little solitaire? Maybe in a platinum band?'

She couldn't help smiling. 'Well, maybe a *little* diamond wouldn't look so bad.'

'That's my girl,' he laughed, quickly kissing the tip of her nose before his lips touched hers in a longer kiss. 'And after we find the perfect ring we can celebrate with a coffee and a doughnut, what do you say?'

'I'd say whoever said romance was dead didn't know what they were talking about.'

Chapter Twenty-Four

'So, which magazine are you going to sell your wedding photos to?' Debbie asked, crossing her legs as she and Amber shared a bottle of wine over lunch in a city-centre pub.

'Magazine?' Amber frowned, sitting back against the cushions of the comfortable navy-blue sofa they'd commandeered in a cosy corner of the pub.

'You'll have them falling over themselves to bag the exclusive,' Debbie went on. 'Me and Gary have just signed a deal with this one.' She held up a copy of a well-known, celebrity-filled magazine renowned for its coverage of weddings/parties/christenings, etc. of the rich and famous.

Amber shuddered as she looked at the magazine. 'Debbie, can I tell you something?'

Debbie put the magazine down and looked at Amber. 'Of course you can, chick.'

'I don't really know what I'm doing.'

It was Debbie's turn to frown. 'What do you mean?'

'All this talk of weddings and engagement parties and magazine deals – it's freaking me out. Big time. I mean, Ryan asking me to marry him in the first place was a big enough shock, but now it seems like I've been thrown into this whirlwind of publicity and I have no idea how to handle it.'

Debbie threw Amber a friendly smile. 'It's all been a bit full-on, hasn't it?'

'Just a bit, yeah,' Amber sighed. 'It doesn't feel like five minutes since last August when I walked into that Press Lounge to interview him and couldn't stand him on sight. And now I'm marrying him. It's crazy!'

'A lot's happened in those few months, chick.'

More than Debbie realised, Amber thought. She had no idea about Jim or the fact that he and Ryan were never really going to get along, even in a professional capacity. But even without all of that, things were still crazy.

'I feel like I haven't really had time to get my head around it all. I can't even escape it at work. Kevin wants to run a story on News North East about mine and Ryan's romance. He's even talking about doing some kind of feature on the run-up to the wedding, filming us as the date draws closer – a date, I hasten to add, that hasn't even been set yet and… I just want to take a minute to sit back and think about things, y'know?'

'Of course you do, chick. Look, what does Ryan think about all of this?'

'He wants to get married sooner rather than later. He'd like to set a date for some time soon after the season ends, but that's less than four months away, Debbie. And less than a year after we met. It just seems way too soon.'

'Do you love him?'

'Of course I love him. I love him like crazy, God help me.'

'Then, does it matter how soon you get married?'

Amber took a long sip of wine, wishing the alcohol would kick in and make her feel a little more relaxed about the whole thing. This whole situation was so alien to her. Marriage was something she'd never really thought about before. Ever. Except, maybe, for a brief period of time when she'd been with Jim. An infatuated teenager living her very own daydream. But, as an adult, it had never been high on her list of agendas, never been something she'd wanted to do. She'd loved her independence way too much. Until she'd met Ryan. He'd invaded her life and changed everything. There was no going back now, even if she'd wanted that. But marriage?

'I suppose not,' Amber said quietly. She looked at Debbie, picking up the magazine again. 'But I'm not selling my wedding photos to anyone. I'm not like you, Debbie. I hate being the centre of attention, even if my choice of fiancé seems to argue against that theory.'

'They pay for all sorts of things in return for exclusive photos, you know,' Debbie smiled. 'It's just a pity Gary and I aren't tying the knot until after you guys, then you could have seen what was involved. It might even be fun.'

'You don't think Ryan will want to go for this, do you?' Amber asked, with more than a hint of panic in her voice.

Debbie shrugged. 'I don't know. He does love a bit of media attention, but then, that was the old Ryan, wasn't it?'

'Do you really think he's changed, Debs?'

'Oh God, yes! No doubt about it. Gary's forever moaning that Ryan's no fun anymore because he never wants to go out as much as he used to. And he's finding it hard to find another partner-in-crime now that a lot of the Red Star players are finally starting to settle down.'

'Don't you want Gary to change, too, though? Surely if Ryan can do it then Gary can?'

Debbie sat back, taking a long drink before fixing Amber with a resigned look. 'Honey, he isn't ever gonna change, and I know that. He's going to be one of life's perpetual little boys, but I love him.' She shrugged again. 'I can't help myself. But at least I know how to deal with him. And let's face it, I'm no angel, either. We're two of a kind. Made to be together, because nobody else would put up with us.'

Amber looked at the delicate platinum diamond solitaire ring that now graced the third finger of her left hand. 'Things just feel too good to be true right now.' She looked back up at Debbie. 'And you know what they say – if something's too good to be true…'

'Just enjoy it!' Debbie smiled, picking up the bottle of wine and checking to see how much was left inside. 'No second-guessing, no questioning everything a hundred times over in your head. Enjoy it.' She stood up, tucking the empty bottle under her arm. 'I'll go get us another, then we can start planning this wedding of yours, alright?'

'You've got to let me and the lads take you out to celebrate,' Gary said, bending over to catch his breath as he took a quick break from training.

'We're having a proper engagement party soon, Gaz. We can celebrate then.'

'Jesus, Ryan. I know you've grown up and all that, but I'm talking about a night away from the missus. Just you, me, and a few of the lads, hitting the clubs, rocking up at the casino – it'll be a blast.'

'Can't we do all of that on the Stag Night?'

'Sod staying in Newcastle for the Stag Night. I was thinking Las Vegas.'

'Vegas? Gary, mate, is that not a bit over the top?'

Gary stood up straight, his hands on his hips, a confused look on his face. 'You *are* kidding, aren't you? I thought you went to Las Vegas for Danny Tate's thirtieth? And from what I read in the papers, it was one hell of a ride.'

Ryan couldn't deny it had been a trip to remember. Casinos waiting to be played day and night, women on tap; they'd had anything they'd wanted whenever they'd wanted it. They'd partied with the famous, slept with more girls than he cared to remember, and spent more cash than any group of people should be allowed to get through in three days. But the memories… Man, they were good! So good Ryan couldn't keep the smile off his face. 'Yeah. That was one trip I'll never forget.'

'So? Vegas for the Stag Weekend, then?'

Ryan still couldn't wipe the smile off his face. 'Why the hell

400

not, huh? I mean, Amber's bound to want to organise something with the girls, isn't she?'

'If Debbie's got anything to do with it, yeah,' Gary said, looking over at Colin on the touchline who was tapping his watch and throwing him and Ryan a look that said *Get back out on that pitch.* 'I've heard whisperings of Ibiza or Majorca. Do you think Amber would go for that?'

Ryan shrugged. 'Mate, I have no idea. But tell Debbie not to go too heavy-handed with it all, okay? Amber doesn't really go in for all that celebrity shit. It's way out of her comfort zone.'

'Well, she might have to start getting used to it. With you as her husband – Jesus Christ, Ryan. *You*? A husband? Shit, that's so not right.'

Ryan couldn't help laughing, because it was true. Or, it *had* been. Just a couple of months ago he wouldn't have even considered a steady girlfriend, never mind a prospective wife. But Amber had changed all that. She'd changed *him*. And he loved her for it. He loved her for saving him. 'It's who I am now, Gaz. So get used to it. You're gonna have to find a new playmate to go out with now.'

'Piss off, Ryan. You'll still be there, I guarantee it. There are only so many nights in a man can take, believe me. I've been there. So, anyway, this night out to celebrate your engagement. You up for it?'

Ryan stopped a ball shooting past him by standing on it, kicking it straight back to another player in the centre of the pitch. 'If it'll stop you frigging nagging, then yes, I'm up for it.'

'Get in! I knew you wouldn't be able to say no.'

'I can say no, Gaz. You just don't give me any bloody choice.' Ryan noticed Jim Allen standing on the touchline, dressed – unusually for him – in tracksuit bottoms, sweatshirt and football boots. He never took training, as a rule. That was very much Colin's territory. 'What's *he* doing taking training?'

Gary followed Ryan's gaze. 'Beats me. Maybe he's got something planned.'

'Well, I doubt he's dressed like that for the good of his health.'

Gary looked at Ryan. 'Shouldn't you just let that go now, mate. It's over between him and Amber. You said that yourself.'

'Is it?' Ryan mumbled, watching Jim Allen as he began kicking a ball around the pitch, showing quite clearly that age hadn't dulled his talent.

Gary frowned. 'Huh? What's *that* supposed to mean?'

Ryan looked over at Jim again, who was now standing with his arms folded, staring at Ryan. 'Nothing. It doesn't mean anything.'

'Whatever you say,' Gary shrugged. 'I suppose we'd better get moving, then. Hey, tell you what, how about a drink and a game of pool after this? We can talk about the night out.'

'Yeah,' Ryan sighed. 'Whatever.'

'Let's have a girls' night out to celebrate,' Debbie smiled, flicking through a rail of dresses in a small, high-end designer boutique that Amber had never been in before. This wasn't her style. She was more used to Next or New Look, maybe the designers section in Debenhams, at a push. That's where she was comfortable. Just looking at the price tags on some of these dresses made her feel quite faint.

'It's a bit early to be talking about a Hen Night, isn't it?' Amber asked, wishing they could hurry up and leave.

'I'm not talking about the Hen Night, silly,' Debbie laughed, picking out a tiny black dress with a silver halter-neck, holding it against her as she looked in the mirror. 'What do you think of this one?' she asked, swinging round to face Amber.

Amber thought it would barely cover her modesty, but Debbie had the kind of figure that – well, if Amber had a figure like that then *she'd* probably flaunt it, too. 'It's nice.'

'Nice?' Debbie said, arching an eyebrow. 'This is a £500 dress, Amber, it's more than *nice*.'

'*How* much?' Amber gasped, almost choking on that information.

'Listen, chick, now you're with Ryan you're gonna have to get used to shopping in places like this. You can't be going into Primark

402

when the paparazzi are following you.'

'The paparazzi aren't going to be following *me*, Debbie. Ryan, maybe, but not me.'

Debbie arched that eyebrow again. 'You have a lot to learn, missy.' She put the dress back and pulled out a slightly longer lime green one with spaghetti straps and an asymmetrical hemline. 'Anyway, about this night out.'

'What night out?' Amber asked, still wishing Debbie would hurry up and buy something so they could get out of there. She was gasping for a coffee.

'The night out to celebrate your engagement. And yes, I know you're having a proper engagement party soon, but this is different. I'm talking about a night out with the girls, away from the men. Dinner somewhere expensive, plenty of cocktails, the VIP section of a club… I might even organise a couple of strippers, what do you say?'

'Debbie…'

'Okay, you're too close to saying no there and I'm not going to let you do that. You're having this night out, so just leave all the organising to me and I guarantee you'll have a night to remember.'

'Really?' Amber asked, slightly nervous now.

'Really,' Debbie smiled, returning the lime green dress to the rail before pulling out a bright red one. 'It'll be fun! I promise.'

'Okay. I believe you,' Amber sighed. 'I suppose that means Gary'll be organising some kind of night out for Ryan, then?'

Debbie looked at her, reaching out to squeeze her hand. 'Listen, chick, I will make him swear on his life that he will *not* do anything stupid. Alright? It'll be fine.'

'It's not necessarily Gary I'm worried about, Debs. What if Ryan…?'

'He won't, Amber. He just won't. He's changed, I know he has. And you know it, too.'

'Yeah,' Amber smiled, relaxing slightly. Debbie seemed taken with the red dress, so that probably meant they could leave this

403

place soon. Half an hour in there and she was ready for another bottle of wine. But she'd make do with that coffee she was still gasping for. 'Yeah, you're right. And I can't hold him prisoner forever, can I? I've got to show him I can trust him.'

'Right. I'm having this one,' Debbie smiled, laying the red dress over her arm as they walked towards the cash desk. 'Are you sure you don't want to look for something to wear for this night out?'

'What? You've bought that dress for our night out?'

'Of course I have, chick. I don't want to be papped wearing something I've been seen in before, do I?'

'Jesus, Debbie, you're not wrong when you say I've got a lot to learn. I was just gonna throw on a dress I bought from Fenwicks for last year's News North East Christmas party.'

Debbie drew a sharp intake of breath, placing a hand on her chest in mock-shock. 'Amber, darling, you really do need my help.' She laid the dress she'd chosen down on the cash desk and smiled at the assistant behind it. 'I'll have that one, but if you can just hang on a few minutes, my friend here has yet to make her choice.' She took Amber by the hand, dragging her back towards the rail of dresses. 'Come on, Ms. Sullivan. I'm going to treat you to a dress that will turn people's heads.' She winked at her, and Amber couldn't help smiling. 'Especially Ryan's.'

'Engaged? I leave the country for five frigging minutes and you get fucking engaged?'

'I thought you'd be pleased, Max. This means I'm settling down, doesn't it?'

'Does it?' Max asked, leaning back against his black BMW that was parked next to Ryan's car in the Red Star training ground car park. 'Just like that? Is that how it works now, huh? I heard about your meltdown, Ryan. I read the papers, I've spoken to Jim Allen…'

Ryan couldn't stop the derisory snort from escaping, which Max didn't miss. 'Something wrong? Because, let me tell you this, kiddo, if you'd had any other manager in charge of this club I doubt the punishment you'd experienced would have been quite so lenient. So maybe you should be thanking Jim Allen rather than deriding him.'

Ryan said nothing. He wasn't in the mood to talk about Jim Allen. 'But out of all that shit, Max, I found Amber again, didn't I?'

'You should never have lost her in the first place. But I suppose we got there eventually. Maybe she can keep you in line this time. Turn you into a well-behaved boy, huh?' Max grinned.

'Piss off,' Ryan laughed. 'You coming on this night out Gary's got organised for me, then?'

'No, I can't. I've got meetings all this week and all of them involve ridiculously early mornings. But I trust you're going to be on your best behaviour?'

Ryan held his hands up, smiling at his agent. 'Scout's honour.'

'Hmmm,' Max said, folding his arms. 'I believe you. I think. But I've heard rumours of a planned visit to the casino, so I really hope you're ready to switch that willpower on, kiddo. And leave the women alone, alright? You know the old saying, why have hamburger when you've got steak at home.'

'Yeah, thanks for that,' Ryan mumbled, pressing his key fob to open the driver's door of his Jaguar. 'I think I know what I've got to do, I don't need babysitting anymore.'

'It's not what you *have* to do that's the problem, Ryan,' Max said, opening his own car door. 'It's what you *haven't* got to do that concerns me.'

Chapter Twenty-Five

Amber held the light green dress up against her as she looked in the full-length mirror. It was way shorter than she'd usually wear, but after a spray tan and a makeover in town that afternoon – courtesy of Debbie – she felt confident enough to show her legs. Even if it *was* still the middle of January. But, hey, that's what Northerners did, wasn't it? Go out in all weathers in completely unsuitable clothing.

Smiling to herself, she cocked her head to one side and shook her hair out, staring at the image looking back at her. She looked different, and it wasn't just because of the spray tan. She looked happier, more relaxed. Less uptight? Probably.

She lay the dress down on the bed and looked at herself again. Did she really want to go out tonight? No. What she *really* wanted to do was stay in, with Ryan, and do something normal like watch TV and eat pizza; the kind of things she was used to doing. She didn't want to go traipsing round the bars of Newcastle in the freezing cold, worrying about what Ryan was getting up to. Oh, it wasn't that she didn't trust him – or was it? *Did* she trust him?

She pulled the towel she was wearing away from her body and looked herself up and down. She wasn't perfect – far from it. But her figure wasn't bad, either. She had a little bit of post-Christmas weight still to shift and although Ryan had never once told her she was anything but beautiful, she still wondered if he'd prefer her to be slimmer, more toned; younger. The thought of Ryan made her smile, despite what she'd just been thinking about. He'd certainly had no complaints about her body lately, in fact, he couldn't get enough of her, so shouldn't that tell her everything she needed to know? She was just being paranoid, knowing he was going to be out there, no doubt surrounded by adoring women and the usual crowd of wannabe WAGs. But maybe she could give him something to think about before he hit the town on his own night out? Something to make him realise that he only really needed her.

She smiled again, grabbing her robe and wrapping it around herself, running her fingers through her hair. Yeah. She could make sure Ryan Fisher strayed nowhere tonight. And she knew exactly how to make that happen.

Ryan closed the door behind him and threw his bag down on the hall floor, pushing a hand through his slightly dishevelled dark hair. He was ready for this night out, although part of him still wished Amber was coming with him. Strange that he should now prefer a night out with her by his side rather than these separate nights they had planned, but he was already beginning to realise that life could throw up the weirdest of circumstances when you least expected it.

He just about had time to grab a quick shower and a change of clothes before he needed to head off and meet Gary and the lads in town and, despite the fact he'd much rather be taking his new fiancée with him, he was determined to have a good time. And Ryan Fisher was an expert in having a good time. Everybody knew that.

'Amber?' he shouted, walking through into the kitchen, taking his jacket off and flinging it down on a nearby chair, smiling as he saw her leaning against the island in the centre of the kitchen, flicking through a magazine. 'Hey, you're still here,' he smiled, relieved to see her. He'd missed her, and he hadn't really wanted to go anywhere without checking in with her first.

'I'm not meeting the girls for a while, yet,' Amber smiled back, closing the magazine, deliberately letting the robe she was wearing fall open. She was wearing nothing but a pair of killer heels, the rest of her completely naked, and Ryan could feel himself reacting within seconds. Jesus, this was the kind of welcome home he was well up for. 'I wanted to make sure I said goodbye first,' she said quietly, her eyes locked on his as he came closer.

Ryan reached out and gently touched her hip with his fingertips, letting them run lightly over her warm skin, his eyes staring deep into hers, his heart beating ten-to-the-dozen. 'Good,' he whispered. 'That's – that's good. Because I'd have hated you to run out on me without doing that.'

Amber smiled again, her whole body tensing up as his fingers travelled slowly up and over her waist, along her stomach, until they reached her breasts. She closed her eyes as he touched them, his thumb slowly flicking over her nipples, taking just seconds to turn them hard, and she bit down on her lip, throwing her head back as he covered one of her breasts with his mouth.

The taste of her was making him crazy. He was so turned on it was ridiculous. He was so hard and ready for her that it physically hurt and, without pulling his mouth away from her breast, he quickly unzipped himself but made no move to push inside her. Not yet. He wanted to take it as slow as he possibly could, make the most of her before he had to leave her yet again – something he disliked doing more and more as each day passed.

'Jesus, Ryan…' Amber groaned, gripping the edge of the island as he slid a hand between her legs, touching her, stroking her, his stomach flipping somersaults at the sheer anticipation of coming inside her.

'You are making me so fucking crazy,' he said, his mouth now touching hers as he spoke, their eyes locked together.

'I want you so bad, Ryan Fisher,' Amber breathed, her entire body tingling as it waited for the inevitable to happen. 'So, so bad.'

Ryan slid a hand round the back of her neck as he kissed her hard, his other hand still firmly between her legs, his body pushing against hers, both their breathing now heavy and fast. But he wasn't going to last much longer – he knew that. He could already feel that familiar crescendo starting its climb from deep within him, and in one swift movement he lifted her up onto the counter, pushing her legs wide apart, inviting him to finally make his presence felt.

They both kept their eyes open, staring at each other with an almost wild intensity as he pushed inside her, her body accepting his as though it was the most natural thing in the world, her legs wrapping around him, keeping him right where he wanted to be. He didn't think he'd ever get tired of the way she made him feel, the way everything was starting to revolve around her and this new life they were going to have together. He felt like a kid waiting for Christmas, waking up every morning knowing she was there, right beside him, beautiful and real and his. She was his. And she wasn't some glamour model or pop princess or reality TV star who just wanted to be seen with somebody famous to further their own career – she was a real woman, and he loved her. He loved her so fucking much. And he needed her more.

Leaning right back, both hands flat on the counter behind her, Amber finally closed her eyes, giving in to every touch of his fingers on her naked skin, his mouth covering first one breast then the other as he continued to push deeper into her, every thrust eliciting small cries of both pain and pleasure and she wished with every inch of her that this feeling would never end. Because he was a part of her now, hard though that might be to believe, given their somewhat sketchy beginning. He was a part of her, and she didn't want to have to think about what could happen if she lost him. Amber Sullivan had finally submitted to those sometimes hard and painful feelings associated with love for only the second time in her life, and she could only hope that, this time, the story didn't end the same way it had done before.

'I'm so close, baby,' Ryan whispered, his mouth touching hers, his hands now on her knees, keeping her legs apart as he gave that one, final thrust, that deciding push that sent that beautiful chain of events spiralling into motion. 'So close…'

She closed her eyes as she felt him come, felt him fill her up with that incredible warmth that once again sent her head spinning and her heart beating so fast she felt as though it could jump right out of her chest, but it was just a precursor to her own crashing climax. 'Oh, Jesus,' she breathed, clinging onto him as that wave of white-hot heat soared through her, shaking her body to its core. She'd never experienced sex like it – not even with Jim – and now she knew it could feel this way she didn't want to let those feelings go.

'I could stay inside you forever,' Ryan whispered, his hand on her cheek as he rested his forehead against hers, their breathing still heavy, their bodies still joined together in that most intimate of ways. 'You are the best fucking thing that's ever happened to me, Amber Sullivan.'

Amber smiled, running her fingers lightly over his rough chin. 'Yeah, well, you better believe it, handsome.'

'I love you so much; you know that, don't you?'

Amber nodded, quickly kissing him before returning for a slower, deeper kiss, wanting to taste him again, to feel how soft his lips were against hers, to keep that taste of him with her all night. 'I know, baby. I know. And I love you, too. I love you like you wouldn't believe. I feel like some teenager who's just bagged the best-looking bloke in school.'

He laughed, that deep, sexy laugh of his, looking down at her naked body as he finally withdrew, leaving a place he didn't really want to vacate just yet. He was happy when he was inside her. Nothing else mattered when he was there, nothing except the two of them. The rest of the world could just fuck off, he didn't need them, he didn't need any of it when he was with her, when he was this close to her. Is that what love really felt like? This overwhelming feeling of needing someone so much it actually hurt? A feeling that could creep up on you and take over before you'd even realised it was happening. 'We start talking about dates tomorrow, for this wedding of ours, you got that, gorgeous?'

She smiled again, taking a couple of seconds to just look at him, this young, handsome man in front of her. This famous footballer, this mixed-up kid who'd walked into her life and turned it on its head in a way she could never have anticipated. 'Yeah. Okay.'

He took a couple of steps back, quickly pulling himself together. Amber slid down from the counter and wrapped her robe back around her naked body, running her fingers through her hair.

'Amber?'

She looked up at him as he stood there, his hands in his pockets, his face carrying a slightly worried expression. 'Yeah?'

'I really will behave tonight. I promise.'

She couldn't help but smile as she walked over to him, slipping her arms around his waist and kissing him quickly, but still long enough to bank another taste of him that she could keep and pull out later when she needed to remember what this felt like. 'Baby, I'm your fiancée, not your mother.'

'I just want you to know you can trust me, that's all.'

'I know, Ryan. And I do, okay? I trust you.' She reached up to gently stroke his cheek, standing up on tiptoe to kiss him again, a longer, slower kiss, his hand resting in the small of her back, pushing her against him. 'I trust you.'

Chapter Twenty-Six

'Jesus! I swear they come out of fucking nowhere!' Gary said, leaning back against the bar as a group of glamorous young women descended on him and the rest of the Red Star players, all bright-white smiles and fake tan. 'But, hey, what can you do?' he grinned, sliding his arm around a very pretty brunette with pillar-box-red lipstick and over-made-up eyes.

Ryan watched as Gary did what Gary did best – ignored the fact he was engaged and only months away from being a married man himself to indulge in this age-old, off-pitch game that so many footballers enjoyed. A game Ryan had played himself so many times, it was just that now he was starting to feel a bit bored with it all. Because now he had Amber.

'Hey, handsome.'

Ryan turned to see an undeniably beautiful girl standing beside him, smiling the kind of smile he'd seen on the faces of these girls so frequently over the years. A smile that told him she'd be quite willing to do anything he wanted her to, he just had to say the word.

'Are you gonna buy me a drink, then?' she asked, edging closer to him, laying a French-manicured hand on his arm, her false eyelashes fluttering in what was most probably an involuntary action.

Ryan stared at her for a second. In the past he wouldn't have hesitated to do exactly as she'd asked, knowing what would be waiting for him at the end of the night. But things were different now. Things had changed. *He* was different. 'You do realise this is actually my Stag Night, don't you?' he said, wishing she'd remove her hand from his arm. The way she was touching him was making him feel slightly uncomfortable.

'So?' she pouted, moving her other hand down to his thigh. 'I can't see your fiancée anywhere, can you? And what the eye doesn't see…'

'Jesus Christ,' Ryan sighed, pushing her hand away. But she still made no attempt to move from his side, leaning back against the bar beside him.

'Jenna said you were usually up for anything,' she huffed, folding her arms like some petulant child who'd just had her favourite toy taken away from her.

Ryan stared at her in disbelief. 'Who the fuck is Jenna?'

She nudged her head in the direction of the brunette who was all over Gary, giggling like a schoolgirl at something he was whispering in her ear. 'She said you two had spent a pretty full-on night in The Goldman a few months back. Said you were a right kinky sod, too. The things you two did together…'

Ryan tried to tune her out as he looked at Jenna again, squinting slightly. Shit! Yeah, he remembered her now. She'd been one hell of a twisted bitch, he couldn't deny that.

He turned back to the pretty blonde beside him. 'What's your name?'

Her face brightened up immediately, her smile widening. 'Emmie. Short for Emily, but I don't like Emily. It doesn't really suit me…'

Ryan held up his hands to stop her from talking, closing his eyes for a second in the hope that, when he opened them, she'd be gone and he'd be left in peace. 'Look, Emmie – this is my Stag Night, sweetheart, okay? I'm getting married, I'm in love, and I know people are finding that quite heard to believe, given my past, but it's true. It's happened, so, whatever your mate Jenna has told you about me, that's all in the past. You got that?'

Her expression changed again, returning to that of the petulant child. 'You're not married yet, y'know.' She turned to face him, smiling a slow, sexy smile as she began fiddling with the collar of his jacket. 'You're still allowed a little bit of fun, surely?'

He pulled her hand off him, pushing her away slightly. 'No can do, sweetheart. You'd better go find yourself someone else, because I ain't playing anymore.'

'Spoilsport,' she huffed, picking her bag up off the bar. 'I really fancied you, too.'

And a couple of months ago he'd have fancied her back, but things were different now. He watched her flounce off in the direction of the rest of the lads, pushing a hand through his hair and breathing a sigh of relief.

'What are you *doing*?' Gary asked, almost running over to him.

Ryan looked at him, frowning slightly. 'Huh? What're you talking about?'

'Emmie. What are you doing shoving her away like that?'

'Look, first of all I didn't shove anyone, okay? And secondly, I'm not up for all that shit anymore, alright?'

'It's your Stag Night, Ryan.'

'Yeah, I'm aware of that, thanks.'

'Listen, mate, you're not gonna be like this all night, are you?'

'Like what?'

'Boring.'

'Boring?' Ryan laughed, pushing a hand through his hair again. 'I'm being boring, am I?'

'Just a bit, yeah. I was hoping me, you, Jenna and Emmie could have made a night of it later. They're both willing…'

'Yeah, I bet they are.'

'Oh, come on, Ryan. She hasn't got that ball and chain attached to your frigging ankle just yet, y'know. Cut yourself a bit of slack, chill out. Enjoy yourself. Come on. I'll get you a drink. What you having?'

Ryan looked at his best friend, a smile finally finding its way onto his incredibly handsome face. 'A large whisky. And… look, just… just don't try to push me onto women I have no intention of fucking later, okay?'

'The night is still young, mate,' Gary winked.

'Gary…'

'Okay, okay. I'll leave it. I promise. Come on; let's get you that drink and see if you can't loosen up a bit. This new you is fucking freaking me out.'

Amber watched as Debbie opened another bottle of champagne, whooping with delight as the cork exploded into the air sending a cascade of liquid streaming from the top of the bottle. This was all for her, this celebration. It was the first of many planned Hen Nights, apparently, as Debbie had told her before they'd all piled into the back of the bright-pink stretch hummer she'd hired to ferry them around town all night. None of this was Amber's style – all the brashness and the overt glamour. Oh, everyone was really nice, it was just that it wasn't really her thing. She wasn't used to hanging out in big groups; she wasn't even used to having a friend around all the time, if she was honest. Ronnie had always been her best friend, but he'd also always been at arm's length, almost, for a lot of the time, given his line of work. This being part of a large group of women was all a bit alien to her. But Debbie was doing her best to make Amber feel comfortable, even if the only place she really wanted to be was back home, cuddled up to Ryan.

'You okay, chick?' Debbie smiled, sitting down next to Amber, handing her a fresh glass of champagne.

'I'm fine,' Amber smiled back, taking a sip of the sparkling liquid.

'Just missing your man, huh?'

She looked at Debbie, sighing. Then she laughed – she couldn't help it. 'Jesus, how lame am I? It's just been so long, Debbie. So long since I've felt this way, y'know? And it's hard to get used to.'

Debbie squeezed her hand, sitting back against the huge, over-sized cushions that decorated the sofa they were sitting on in one of Newcastle's trendiest bars. 'Exactly *how* long ago has it been since you've felt this way, chick?'

'A long time,' Amber sighed again, throwing herself back against the cushions, too, taking another sip of champagne. 'Too bloody long.'

Debbie looked at her out the corner of her eye. 'Is there a reason for that?'

Amber stared straight ahead, trying to push any thoughts of Jim – no matter how tiny or how vague they might be – to the back of her mind, where they belonged. 'Let's just say things didn't exactly run smoothly in a previous relationship. He was… we… it was complicated. We shouldn't really have been together and… I fell in love. I thought he had, too, but I was wrong. It didn't end well. He hurt me and… I guess I put barriers up to prevent me from going there again. Until Ryan walked into my life.'

'He must have been someone really special…' Debbie sat up slightly, crossing her legs, fixing Amber with an intrigued look, '… to make you feel that way.'

'He was,' Amber said, staring down into her glass. 'I loved him so much and…' She shrugged. 'And he threw that back in my face.'

'Was he famous?'

Amber looked up sharply. What could have made her want to ask that?

'I'm only asking because, well, you've been around footballers and sportsmen all your life and I just thought… I assumed…'

'I was young and stupid, Debbie. Not to mention incredibly naive.' She knew she'd already said too much and it was time to steer the subject back round to the present – leave the past well alone. 'But that's all behind me now. I've got Ryan, haven't I? And we've got a future together. That's all that matters.'

'He really loves you, Amber. You're very lucky.'

Amber looked down into her glass again, unable to prevent

the smile from spreading across her face as she remembered the way they'd said goodbye to each other just a few hours ago. She could still feel him inside her, if she closed her eyes and thought about him, all handsome and hard. The taste of him on her lips, the touch of his fingers on her skin. She just wished he was here now, because she missed him like crazy. And she didn't like these needy feelings that seemed to be taking over, but she couldn't stop them. She loved him, it was as simple as that. She loved him. And she hadn't loved anyone as much as this since – since Jim.

'You alright?' Debbie asked, gently touching Amber's arm. 'You drifted off there for a second, chick.'

'I'm fine,' Amber smiled, draining the last of her champagne and standing up, shaking out her hair so it fell in a barrage of beautifully-styled barrel curls over her bare shoulders. 'I'm just nipping outside for some fresh air and a quick cigarette.' Suddenly she really needed one. So much for her New Year's resolution to give up. Again. 'Can you get me a refill?'

'Sure. More champagne?'

Amber nodded before pushing her way through the crowd towards the door that led outside, quite glad of the brief time away from the lovely but slightly overwhelming group of women she found herself out with.

'Amber?'

She swung round at the sound of his voice. That unmistakeable American accent. 'What... what the hell are *you* doing here?' Had he just followed her out of the bar? Because surely he hadn't just coincidently been passing as she'd walked outside?

'I'm allowed to come out for a drink now and again. There's no law against it, is there?'

He smiled at her, and she hated the way he still had the ability to make her heart leap about, even after all these years, and all the hurt he'd caused.

'It's just... just strange to see you somewhere like this, that's all.' She leaned back against the wall, rubbing her hands up and down her arms, although it was more of a nervous action than a way of keeping herself warm.

'I come to places like this quite often, honey. I gather it's *you* who's spent most of her life working rather than having fun.'

She looked down at her far-too-expensive new shoes. They were beautiful, but a few months ago she would never have dreamt of spending so much money on shoes, yet this new world she seemed to be involuntarily entering was making her do things she'd never done before. And that lack of control was something that bothered her. 'Did you know I'd be here tonight?' she asked, still looking at her shoes.

'I overheard Gary talking this afternoon. He mentioned you might be coming here at some point this evening.'

'You need to be careful.' She slowly looked up at him, all handsome and sexy and out-of-bounds. Very definitely out-of-bounds. 'That could almost be construed as stalking.'

Jim smiled, that wide and beautiful smile that could make her knees go weak and her stomach flip over a thousand times. But tonight she was managing to keep that in check. Just. Tonight the only man she had on her mind was Ryan. 'Call it – coincidence,' Jim said, moving closer to her, but Amber took a step back, keeping that distance between them. 'Are you having a good time?'

She narrowed her eyes as she looked at him, folding her arms in a slightly defensive manner. 'It's okay. I'd rather be at home, though. Like you said, I'm not one for nights out. But then, when we were together I didn't really have much choice, did I?'

Jim laughed, running a hand along the back of his neck before locking eyes with her again. 'We had a hell of a lot more fun staying in.' He reached out and gently touched her cheek with the palm of his hand. 'Don't you think?'

She quickly pushed his hand away, but she wasn't quick enough to stop him from moving in for a kiss, his mouth touching hers before she'd even had a chance to register what he was doing. But once it did, she lifted up a knee and kicked him hard enough to get the message across – she was off-limits. He had no right to do that to her. She wasn't his plaything, not anymore. 'No, Jim. That's enough, okay? It's over, finished. We're history, and you have to stop this, it isn't fair. It really isn't fair.'

'Because you're still in love with me?' he asked, trying to catch his breath, his eyes meeting hers once more, and she couldn't look away, even though she wanted to. She really wanted to.

'No,' she whispered. 'Because I love Ryan.'

Jim let out a cynical laugh, rubbing a hand along the back of his neck again as he broke the stare for a second. 'You love him.' He turned back to face her. 'No, you see, you *think* you love him, Amber. You *think* you do…'

'I do.' Her voice was quiet but steady. She wasn't going to let him unnerve her, not like he'd done before. She was older now, she could deal with this. 'And when I say those two words to him at our wedding, I'll mean them, like I've never meant anything before.'

'You're deluded,' Jim said, moving closer to her again, and this time she didn't step back. She stayed put. 'I'm *free*, Amber. I'm free, and I have been for years, because the only woman I ever really wanted was you, don't you see that? I only ever wanted *you*.'

'Then you had a really funny way of showing that.'

He reached out and took her hand, which was met with Amber pulling it away immediately, but her strength was no match for his and he grabbed it again, wrapping his fingers around hers so tight she had no choice but to let him keep hold of her. 'Things were complicated back then, Amber. You know that, Jesus, come on… If we'd gone public… But, now – now there's nothing stopping us. And we were nearly there, honey, weren't we? You and me, we were almost there.' He loosened his grip on her slightly, but she didn't pull her hand away. 'He isn't right for you, Amber. Marrying him is a mistake, and I think, deep down, you know that.'

'How can you possibly know what is or isn't right for me, Jim? How can you know that?'

'Because I've loved you for so long, baby. As simple as that. I've

419

loved you for so long.'

'I need to move on,' Amber whispered, finally pulling her hand away from his, pushing it through her dark red curls as she made to turn away from him. It was time to go. The champagne she'd been drinking had gone to her head slightly and she'd already behaved in a way she was going to regret in the morning, so staying any longer really wasn't a good idea. 'Goodbye, Jim.'

She'd just started to walk away when she felt his hand on her hip, swinging her back round to face him again, his arm sliding around her waist, pulling her against him so quickly she almost lost her breath. And then he kissed her – a kiss so gentle, so familiar that all she could do was fall against him. Suddenly she felt something she could only describe as akin to defeat. She was so tired, so confused, and being in the arms of this older man who'd been a part of her life for over twenty years, it felt safe. For those few, brief seconds she was right where she'd always wanted to be. With the man of her dreams.

But reality, as usual, was never far away. And as it hit Amber with a shock that could only be likened to someone throwing an ice-cold bucket of water over her, she finally pulled away from him, not looking at him as she spoke. 'Just go, Jim. Please.'

'Amber...'

'Please, Jim.' This time she did look at him, almost pleading with him to do as she said. To just let her go. Like she was trying to do with him. 'Just go.'

She watched him turn and walk back into the bar, her heart beating so fast it actually hurt. Leaning back against the wall and closing her eyes, she breathed in deep and exhaled slowly, trying to stop her heart from hammering hard against her ribs.

'You, and Jim Allen?'

Amber's eyes opened and her head spun round to see who that voice belonged to, and this time her heart almost stopped dead as she saw Debbie standing there, her arms folded, a curious look on her face.

420

'Debbie, I… How long have you…?' She felt her shoulders sag. And uttering those words '*It wasn't what it looked like…*' would be pointless. Actually, she couldn't even begin to think *what* it had looked like to someone who had absolutely no idea of the past history between her and Jim Allen.

Amber leaned back against the wall as Debbie walked over to her, closing her eyes as though hoping that, when she opened them, she'd be back home in front of News At Ten instead of here, in this nightmare situation.

Debbie leaned back against the wall beside her. 'Locking lips with your fiancé's boss, huh? Didn't see *that* one coming, I have to say.'

Amber turned her head to look at her friend, but said nothing. She didn't actually know what she *could* say.

'Are you having some sort of illicit affair?' Debbie asked.

'It's complicated.'

'Is that a yes?'

'We're not having an affair, no.' Amber took another deep breath. She didn't really want to have to explain everything, but she couldn't see another way of making Debbie understand what she'd just witnessed.

'Well, forgive me for stating the obvious here, chick, but it looked as though you two kind of know each other pretty well to me.'

'He's my dad's best friend, Debs. You know he is. He's known our family for over twenty years, so of course we know each other pretty well.'

'So your dad is aware that his best friend kisses you that way, then?'

She obviously wasn't going to let this one go. Amber threw her head back again. 'We're not having an affair, alright? Not anymore, anyway.'

Debbie grabbed Amber's hand, pulling her back towards the bar. 'Come on. I've got us another bottle of champagne and I think that's just as well, don't you? Because we really need to talk.'

'I'm not sure this was such a good idea,' Ryan said as he kicked the front door shut behind him. 'I mean, bringing them back here...'

'Relax, Ryan. Come on. Amber isn't going to be home for hours, yet. If Debbie's got anything to do with it, you'll be lucky to see her before dawn. Chill out, mate. This is much more discreet than taking them back to The Goldman.'

'Since when was discretion something *you* were bothered about?'

'I'm not doing it for me, you dickhead. I'm doing it for you. Trying to keep you away from any prying eyes. You know as well as I do that there are always paparazzi sitting outside The Goldman just waiting to snap somebody doing something they shouldn't. And *I* should know.'

Ryan sat down on the stairs, pushing both hands through his hair. 'I am so frigging wasted, Gary. Maybe I should just go straight to bed.'

'That's exactly what *I* was thinking,' Emmie smiled, emerging from the kitchen carrying a bottle of wine and two glasses.

Ryan looked up at the pretty, young girl in front of him, all bright eyes and beautiful smile, her expression full of hope and promise. Once upon a time he wouldn't have even thought twice about taking her straight upstairs and making all her dreams come true. But tonight he'd thought more than twice – he'd thought numerous times. And still he couldn't say with complete honesty that he didn't want to take her to bed. Maybe that was because he was drunk, or because the more he'd hung around Gary tonight, listening to him talk about his own second thoughts regarding marriage, the more that could have clouded his own thoughts. His own opinions. Tonight he'd been thrown straight back into the kind of life he'd lived and loved not all that long ago – the life that had gotten him into all kinds of trouble; the life a part of him still missed. But it could still all just be because he was drunk. In the morning he'd probably feel very different about everything, so, until then, couldn't he just enjoy these last few hours of being the Ryan Fisher he'd used to be? He didn't want to be that man forever, but one last ride – he could have that, couldn't he?

'I'm a bit tired, actually…' Ryan began, before stopping himself from saying anything more, anything that could actually deter her from doing whatever it was she'd come here to do. Because he kind of wanted to find out what that was. And yet, at the same time, he didn't. Shit! He really *was* wasted.

He felt around in the pocket of his jacket, finding the small plastic pouch of white powder Emmie had slipped in there earlier. So far he'd been sensible enough not to use it, but his resistance was wearing thinner by the second.

'Well, that would be such a shame, if you really *were* tired, because…' Emmie sat down next to him, slowly running her fingers through his dark hair, pouting away like some hard-at-work glamour model, '… me and Jenna, we had something planned that I guaran*tee* you'd want to stay awake for.'

He narrowed his eyes slightly, trying to fight the tiredness that was still there. He was just trying to ignore it now. But then, he *did* have something to hand that could take that tiredness away in an instant. If he was stupid enough to go down that route. 'Like what?' he asked, aware of Jenna sliding past them, making her way upstairs.

Emmie looked up at her friend, both of them exchanging knowing smiles. And then Ryan twigged exactly what was going on. Although he was more than certain he'd indulged in at least a couple of threesomes before, he just couldn't recall them all that clearly. And he couldn't lie and say he didn't want to go there again, and remember the experience this time. Of course he wanted to go there again, who wouldn't? When the opportunity was being handed to you on a plate.

'Gary says your bedroom is up here,' Jenna smiled at him, licking her lips in anticipation as her long legs continued to make their way upstairs. 'Second on the left?'

Ryan gave himself a couple of seconds to take in just what was happening, then he smiled back at her, letting his hand wander slowly along Emmie's thigh as her lips began kissing his neck. 'Yeah. That's the one.'

'Right. Well, I'll see you both up there. Soon.'

He watched her saunter up the last few steps before turning to look at Gary, who just arched an eyebrow and grinned at him. 'I think you're in there, mate. Twice.'

Ryan stood up, pulling Emmie up with him, pushing her back against the wall and kissing her hard, his hands sliding up and under her short dress. If he was going to do this, he might as well do it properly, after all, he had a reputation to keep up, didn't he? He wasn't married yet. And after tonight he was going to put all this behind him, once and for all. That was a promise he was making right now and, okay, so this wasn't the first time he'd made himself that promise, but this was truly, honestly, the last time he ever did something like this. It was nothing but one last taste of that life he had to leave behind, that was all. Just one last taste. And right now, it tasted good.

'Jesus, Amber... All that time and nobody knows *anything* about you and Jim Allen?'

'We've both done a top-class job of making sure our secret stayed just that. A secret. I mean, Ronnie knows, but he's my best friend. And he only found out recently. He wouldn't ever say anything to anyone.'

'What about Ryan? Does *he* know you and Jim used to... Does he know about your past history?'

Amber took a long sip of champagne. Not that she felt much like celebrating anymore. 'Yeah. He knows.' She looked at Debbie. 'Remember when Ryan and I split up last year? After the Christmas party?'

Debbie nodded, leaning forward to refill her glass.

'Ryan caught Jim and I, together. At the party. He heard us talking, saw us kissing... We owed it to him to tell him the truth.'

'Did you...?' Debbie's expression was slightly confused as she quite obviously started trying to piece together everything that had happened over that short period of time. 'You went back to Jim?'

'That's why Ryan reacted the way he did, why his behaviour changed,' Amber said quietly, staring down into her glass. 'I guess he found it difficult to handle the fact I was sleeping with his boss.'

'But... nobody else knew?'

Amber shook her head, swallowing another mouthful of sparkling liquid. 'No. We... we wanted to keep it a secret until we'd had a chance to tell my dad first, about our relationship, although we were never going to tell him about the past. He doesn't need to know what happened back then.' She fixed Debbie with a look that told her she meant what she was about to say. 'Nobody does.'

Debbie sat back, crossing her legs. 'So, Ryan was the only one who...' Suddenly, the proverbial penny seemed to drop and she sat up again, her expression changing instantly. 'That night – the night Ryan got completely wasted in town, the night he tried to... When Gary called you...'

'I was at Jim's. That's why it took me longer to get there.'

'That's why he was in such a state,' Debbie gasped, looking right at Amber. 'Isn't it? He couldn't hack you and Jim being together.'

Amber shrugged. 'I don't know, Debbie.'

'Oh, come on, Amber. I've never seen anyone in such a state before, and believe me, when you've lived with Gary as long as I have, you'd think I'd be used to seeing shit like that. But that night, Ryan, he... he was a broken man, chick. I thought he'd just got himself into that state because he couldn't hack the fact you'd left him, but, leaving him for his boss... Jesus! He must really love you...'

Amber tried to tune her out; she didn't want to hear any more. All the time she'd assumed everything was slowly starting to fall into place, when really it was still nothing but a huge mess. And tonight hadn't helped.

'So, out there. With you and Jim,' Debbie went on, sitting back and relaxing into the comfortable cushions of the sofa again. 'What was all that about?'

'I don't know,' Amber sighed, staring out ahead of her, mindlessly watching the crowds down by the bar below them, everybody mingling, laughing, having a good time. Was that what Ryan was doing now? Having a good time? 'He won't give up, Debs. Jim, he… he keeps telling me Ryan isn't good for me, that he can never love me like *he* can, but how can I believe anything he ever tells me when he lied so many times before? When he hurt me the way he did?' She looked at Debbie, wishing she hadn't had to tell her any of this, because the more people who knew about her and Jim Allen, the more chance there was of their past history being revealed.

'I won't tell a soul,' Debbie said quietly, taking Amber's hand and squeezing it gently, almost as if she'd read her mind. 'Not even Gary. I promise.'

'Thank you,' Amber smiled. 'And – and please don't think that I have any intention of letting what happened out there go any further, because it's over, between Jim and me. It's past history.'

'It can't be easy, though. For any of you. All working so closely with each other.'

Amber looked down at her hand as Debbie continued to hold onto it. 'We've just all got to accept that things change, haven't we? Whether we like it or not.'

'Jesus – fucking – Christ!' Ryan groaned as Emmie's mouth closed in on him, taking him on a ride to heaven that seemed like it was never going to end, and he wasn't in any kind of hurry for it to be over. His head was spinning, his body didn't even feel like it belonged to him anymore, but he didn't care. Why would he? When he had one pretty, naked woman between his legs and another with her quite obviously fake breasts pushed up against

426

his face? He hadn't done this kind of shit since leaving London and he'd almost forgotten how much of a rush it could be. He felt on fire! Like he could take on the world. Ryan Fisher was back on top form, doing what he did best, and there wasn't anything that could make him regret what was happening now, because this was who he was – he was King of the fucking world! Women loved him, men wanted to be him, and he couldn't help that, could he? He couldn't help being fucking amazing!

He opened his eyes as he felt Emmie move back up the bed, sliding along his naked body with the ease of someone who'd done this many times before, and maybe she had, maybe she hadn't. Maybe she was just extremely good at turning men on, he had no idea. All he knew was that she was now lying beside him, leaning over him to kiss Jenna, her hand reaching down to hold him, stroke him, take him on another crazy ride. And all he had to do was lie back, hold on, and let them do all the work.

Seeing Jim had taken the edge off her night, to some extent. Things felt so out of her control all of a sudden and all Amber really wanted to do was find Ronnie and escape somewhere quiet to try and work out what it was she really wanted to do with the rest of her life. Just a few short hours ago, when Ryan had made love to her, she'd thought that was it, all sorted. She'd fallen in love, and despite all her previous reservations about falling for a footballer, she'd thought she'd known that marrying Ryan and spending the rest of her life with him was all she wanted to do. But if seeing Jim on a night that was supposed to celebrate her impending wedding – if that had opened up this box of doubts, then surely she needed to think about this just a little bit more?

Despite the late hour, she quickly tapped Ronnie's number into her phone, leaning back against the slightly uncomfortable seat as the taxi travelled through the quiet Newcastle streets. She stared out of the window as they crossed the River Tyne, looking down at the Arena, smiling as she remembered all the gigs her and Ronnie had gone to there over the years – some of which she'd had to drag him to, rather unwillingly. But they'd always had such great times. Why did she suddenly feel as though everything was changing? Like she was never going to experience times like those again.

'Hey, kiddo.' Ronnie's voice seemed unusually chirpy as he answered her call, despite it being so late. 'You okay?'

'Erm… I didn't wake you, did I?' She was aware of another voice in the background – was she interrupting something? Oh God, sometimes she forgot he actually had a life of his own. She really had to try and stop being so selfish, calling him every time she needed a shoulder to cry on, but he was the only one who really understood her. The only one she felt she could really turn to, and over the past few weeks their relationship had felt as though it was shifting somewhere she didn't really want it to go, and she was scared. Scared of losing him. She was really scared.

'No. No, you didn't wake me, sweetheart. Is everything alright? Because you only usually ring me at this hour when you've got something on your mind. Do you want to talk?'

She could definitely hear someone else in the background and her heart sank. She knew he was back in the North East, back home for a little while, and she'd hoped she could have diverted the taxi in the direction of his Northumberland home. She'd hoped she could have spent the rest of the night sitting up with her best friend, watching rubbish TV, eating Chinese food and talking, because that's what she really felt like doing right now. It was *all* she felt like doing. But it sounded like he already had company.

'It can wait,' she said, not wanting to take him away from what-ever he was doing – and whoever he was with. Ronnie deserved a life, too. He wasn't responsible for trying to make her feel better about mistakes she might have made or decisions she couldn't make. She was just being stupid, anyway. All these doubts she was suddenly having about Ryan and marriage and her life changing in a way she could never have predicted this time last year, they were all normal, weren't they? They were nothing unusual. And surely she'd have more to worry about if she *wasn't* feeling anxious?

'You sure?' Ronnie asked, not hiding the fact someone else was there with him now as he whispered something Amber couldn't make out to whoever was there. 'We can meet up tomorrow, if you like?'

'It's fine, really. I guess it's just late and I've had a bit too much to drink.'

'Oh, shit, Amber…' Ronnie said, realisation suddenly flooding his voice. 'It was your Hen Night, wasn't it?'

'One of them, yeah,' Amber sighed, closing her eyes and rubbing the bridge of her nose.

'Second thoughts?' Ronnie asked, with more than a hint of expectation in his tone.

'No,' Amber replied, probably a touch more defensively than she'd meant it to sound. But weren't people just waiting for her and Ryan to mess up? Isn't that what they wanted? To all be proved right? 'No. Not really.'

'Not really?'

And she just knew he was arching an eyebrow when he asked that. She knew he was.

'It's been a funny old night, that's all. There's just a lot to get my head around. Still.'

Ronnie said nothing for a second, and she was sure she could hear him telling the person there with him to be quiet for a second.

'Are you sure I'm not disturbing you, Ronnie? I can hear you've got someone there with you. New girlfriend?'

'Erm… yeah. Sort of… Look, are you sure everything's alright?'

'It's fine,' Amber replied. Why had he suddenly started to sound more than a touch shifty? Like he had something to hide.

'Okay. Good. I'll call you tomorrow, alright?'

'Yeah. Okay. Goodnight, Ronnie.'

''Night, kiddo.'

Amber threw her phone back into her bag and looked out of the taxi window again as it made its way towards Gateshead, and

429

home. Tonight had been a test, that's how she was going to look at it. A test to see just how strong her love for Ryan really was. Her handsome footballer; the way he smiled, the way he knew just where to touch her to make her scream out loud – the way he could kiss her and make her feel as though she'd never have to worry about anything ever again. She loved him. Yeah, she loved him. Sure, he'd managed to barge his way into her once-well-ordered life with all the subtly of a force-10 hurricane, changing everything around her so fast it was as though her head had been spinning constantly since the day she'd met him. But maybe he was just what she needed. And all she had to do now was be brave enough to see if she was right, to take that leap of faith.

As the taxi pulled up outside their house, she was surprised to see lights on. Okay, it was late, but she still hadn't expected Ryan to be home. Not yet. Maybe *his* night hadn't panned out quite the way he'd wanted it to, either.

'Keep the change,' she smiled at the taxi driver, handing him more money than the requested fare. But that ride home had given her a little more clarity than she'd thought she'd get tonight, so she was grateful for the time it had afforded her to think. Jim Allen wasn't going to ruin the rest of her life. She wasn't going to let him, not this time. He'd taken enough years away from her. She'd wasted enough time thinking about him, wanting him, missing him. It was time to try and move on.

Almost running up the long, block-paved pathway to the front door, she felt a frisson of nervous excitement as she tried to fit the key in the lock with hands that were shaking, only to find that the door was slightly ajar. That nervous excitement was quickly replaced with something verging on edginess as she pushed the door open and walked warily into the hallway. *Oh, Jesus, please don't let it be burglars,* she thought, her heart starting to beat hard with a mixture of fear and nausea, which immediately turned to relief when she spotted Ryan's jacket thrown on the stairs.

She pushed the door shut behind her and flicked the latch,

locking it. He was home. Good. She was glad. After everything that had gone on she just wanted to cuddle up in bed with him and think about nothing but that brand new future that lay ahead.

Taking her own coat off and throwing it over the banister, she started to make her way upstairs, but within seconds her breath had caught in her throat and her stomach had tightened, bringing with it the return of the nausea and the nerves. Those shoes – two beautiful, glamorous, high-heeled shoes lay discarded on the landing, next to them a short, chiffon dress just covering the shirt Ryan had been wearing when he'd left the house earlier that evening.

And the giggles. They were coming from their bedroom. Giggles and moans and somebody cheering… What the hell…?

She stood outside the bedroom she shared with her footballer fiancé and rested her forehead against the door as a sickening realisation swept over her, cancelling out everything she'd ever felt over the past six months – everything. Before she'd even set foot inside the room, she felt numb, empty. She felt stupid. But she knew that was nothing compared to what she was going to feel when she finally opened that door…

Chapter Twenty-Seven

She slammed the door in his face. Childish, maybe, but what else was she supposed to do? He could say sorry until those proverbial cows came home but she'd never forgive him. Not this time.

She swung round at the sound of a key in the lock and as he tried to push his way in she fought back, desperately trying to stop him from getting inside before she realised just how pathetic this really was. She was starting to sink to his level now.

'Will you just listen to me? Please?' Ryan pleaded, leaning back against the now-closed front door, his breathing heavy and laboured. She could put up one hell of a fight, that was for sure. She'd almost won, there.

'I really can't do this, Ryan. Not right now,' she said, looking right at him, her eyes expressionless, cold. They reminded him of how she'd seemed when he'd first met her just six months ago – that wall had come right back up and it was nobody's fault but his.

'Amber…'

'I need you to go.' Her voice was barely a whisper. 'Because I'm really not in the mood to stand here and listen to any more lies.'

'Amber…'

He started to walk towards her, but she backed away from him, her arms folded against her, keeping that barrier between them. 'Please, Ryan, just go, will you? It's over. Us, the engagement, any

432

plans we may have had for a future together, it's over.'

'Look, I'm not going to stand here and say let me explain, because I can't. Well, I can, but… it would be a waste of time, wouldn't it?'

She continued to stare at him, but she said nothing. There was nothing *to* say. Like she'd said, it was over.

'I just want you to know that I love you, with all of my fucking heart, Amber, I love you, and… and what I did last night, it was – Shit!' He pushed a hand through his hair and turned away for a second, because her staring at him the way she was doing, it was tearing him apart.

'I trusted you,' she whispered, quite pleased with herself for keeping the tears at bay, but then, she'd probably cried them all last night, after she'd kicked him out, along with Gary and whoever the two slappers were that had been fucking her fiancé. 'You make me sick.'

'Shit!' He really couldn't see a way out of this. He felt like a cornered rat, banged to rights with nowhere to go but to face the music. The saddest song he was ever likely to hear.

'I knew when I opened that bedroom door that I was going to find you in bed with another woman,' Amber went on, her fingers gripping the thin material of the t-shirt she was wearing. 'But I can't even begin to tell you how I felt when I faced what was *really* going on in there. Finding you with *one* woman would have been bad enough, Ryan, but to see what I saw… to see what they were doing to you, what *you* were doing to *them*… Have you any idea how that made me feel? Huh? Have you?'

'Baby…'

He reached out to take her hand, but she pulled it away, backing off further, towards the kitchen. 'You can't possibly know,' she whispered, shaking her head. 'You can't. I came home, after a night of wondering whether I was doing the right thing in being with you in the first place, but… but I loved you, y'know? I loved you, so of course I knew I was doing the right thing, I mean, we all have those doubts, don't we? We all go through those topsy-turvy emotions, it's only natural. What isn't natural is making love to me, telling me we're going to start planning our wedding as soon as possible, and then bringing two…' She stopped talking, turning away from him, pushing a hand through her hair. 'What isn't natural is then, just hours later, sleeping with two women, in our bed – *our* bed, Ryan – while your teammate films it. Jesus, how sick is that?'

In the cold light of day, after the effects of too much booze and Christ knows what else had worn off, he couldn't help but agree with her. It *was* sick. It was wrong, and once again he'd let his ridiculous need for a life that wasn't even real take over, and destroy everything.

'I love you, Amber…'

'I don't care,' she said quietly, looking at him once more with eyes that were still trying to show no emotion, and they were just about managing it. 'I really don't care anymore, Ryan. I can't, because every time I do, something happens, don't you see? Every time I become involved…' She walked away from him, into the kitchen, folding her arms tight against her chest again. 'But not anymore.'

'Look, I know what you saw was…'

She swung round, fixing him with a stare that told him in no uncertain terms that she was in no mood to forgive. And she wasn't. As far as final straws went that one had been the perfect example. She'd already given him far more chances than he'd deserved. 'I really would like you to leave now, Ryan.'

He was about to try again, with another round of pointless explaining, but a loud banging on the front door stopped him from getting even one word out.

'What the…?'

Amber pushed past him as if he wasn't even there, going straight out into the hall and flinging the door open, not really having any idea what or who she expected to find outside. She was just irritated by the manner in which they'd made their presence known.

'Ronnie…?'

'You'd better let me in,' he said, an expression on his face that Amber couldn't really read. 'The shit is about to hit the fan, big time.'

'Huh? Ronnie? What's happened?' She followed him into the kitchen, where Ryan was now leaning back against the centre island, his arms folded. 'Are you still here?' she asked, not caring that she probably sounded a touch petulant now. She just wanted him out of her sight.

Ronnie looked slightly confused for a second, unaware of the goings-on of last night and the sudden shift in Ryan and Amber's relationship. But the tension in the room was quite obviously palpable. 'It's probably best he stays, for a while, anyway,' Ronnie said, pushing the confusion to the back of his mind, eyeing Ryan suspiciously as he threw a copy of a popular tabloid newspaper onto the counter. 'He might have some explaining to do.'

Amber was more confused than ever now as she walked over to the counter, picking up the newspaper Ronnie had just thrown down. And the second she looked at it, her heart almost stopped dead, her breath catching in her throat as she read the headline: *RED STAR BOSS AND HIS PLAYER'S FIANCÉE IN SECRET RELATIONSHIP PAST – Newcastle Red Star manager Jim Allen and News North East sports reporter Amber Sullivan – daughter of former Red Star player Freddie Sullivan and fiancée of bad-boy footballer Ryan Fisher – had a secret relationship that began when Amber was just sixteen years old and Jim was a player at the club, alongside Amber's father…*'

'How…? I don't…' Amber looked at Ronnie, hardly daring to believe what she was seeing written down in front of her. It had to be a joke, surely. Didn't it? Because this couldn't be happening. Not like this.

'Somebody's obviously blabbed to the press,' Ronnie said, taking the paper from Amber and placing it back down on the counter.

'So, who else knows?'

'I… I told Debbie. Last night…'

'Jesus, Amber, why?' Ronnie sighed. 'I thought you of all people would have been the one to stay discreet.'

'I had no choice,' Amber went on, leaning back against the counter. 'She saw Jim and me… She caught him kissing me, last night.'

'What the fuck?' Ryan gasped. 'What the hell were you doing with him last night, for fuck's sake? It was your frigging Hen Night?'

'Oh, and you fucking two slags in *our* bed on your Stag Night was acceptable behaviour, was it?'

'What the hell's been going on here?' Ronnie asked. But at least he now knew why there was an atmosphere in the room that could only be cut with a very sharp knife.

'Nothing,' Amber replied, shifting her gaze from Ryan and looking down at the floor.

'Nothing,' Ronnie repeated. 'Okay, so, something's obviously kicked off between you two but, thankfully, that's not making the headlines right now, is it? This is.' He looked at Amber. 'Do you think it was Debbie who went to the press?'

'No. I don't think it was her. She promised me she wouldn't tell anyone, not even Gary…' She stopped talking and looked over at Ryan, who was now shifting from foot-to-foot, staring out of the French windows opposite. 'Ryan… you didn't…?'

'He guessed, a while back,' he said quietly. 'I couldn't deny it, could I?'

'You could have fucking tried.' Amber pushed both hands through her hair as panic started to set in. What if her dad had seen this? How was she supposed to explain it all to him when she still had this shit with Ryan to sort out?

'Do you think it was him?' Ronnie asked, almost absentmindedly putting a hand on Amber's waist, stroking it gently, trying to keep her calm. 'Gary? Was it him who blabbed to the press?'

'I don't know,' Ryan sighed, dropping down to his haunches,

hanging his head. 'He promised he wouldn't say anything...'

'Yeah, well, we all know what promises from the likes of you can mean.' Ronnie took a quick look at Amber as she chewed nervously on a nail, staring out of the window in front of her. 'Could he have said something to anyone last night?' Ronnie went on. 'You were all quite obviously drunk, and we all know that can make mouths looser than usual.'

Ryan sighed again, standing up and throwing his head back. 'Last night, it was a fucking blur, man. I can't remember what I was saying half the time, or who I was saying it *to*, things were just so... I don't know. I don't know whether he said anything or not, but... I don't know.'

'You idiot,' Amber hissed, turning to face him. 'You bloody idiot!'

'Jesus, come on! I said I can't remember what happened last night, and anyway, how can you be so fucking sure it wasn't your new best friend who blabbed, huh?'

'Because she actually wants me to be happy, Ryan.'

Ryan's phone ringing stopped the argument from going any further and he answered the call immediately, his expression changing as whoever it was on the other end of the line spoke.

'What is it?' Amber asked, because it was obvious something was wrong.

'Shit!' Ryan said, throwing his phone down onto the counter behind him.

'Care to divulge what that was all about?' Ronnie asked, folding his arms and arching his eyebrows.

'Gary says he thinks we might have mentioned something to either Emmie or Jenna – the girls we were...' He stopped talking for a second, well aware that Amber would be able to put two and two together and work out just who Emmie and Jenna were. 'He can't remember what, exactly, but he remembers all of us talking about the boss, and... and apparently I said something about Amber and him having some kind of relationship when she was a teenager... It was probably one of them who...' Ryan sighed,

437

pushing a hand through his hair. 'I'm sorry, okay? Last night – shit! I can't even remember half of it, I really can't…'

'Well, that makes it alright then, doesn't it?' Amber said, her tone carrying more than a hint of sarcasm. She felt sick. Her stomach was turning to the point where she felt physically ill. Those two women – women who'd quite happily fucked her fiancé without a second thought to anyone else – they knew about her past? They knew about her and Jim? And they'd used it as a vehicle to make money to fund their pathetic, sordid little lifestyles.

She turned and ran out of the kitchen, only making it to the downstairs loo just in time to throw up a breakfast she hadn't even eaten.

'Amber?' Ronnie's voice filtered through the gap in the door, barely audible above the sound of the phone ringing.

'I'm okay,' she said, sitting back against the wall, wiping her mouth with a fistful of toilet paper.

'Yeah. You sound it.'

The phone's continuous ringing only served to make her more on edge, wondering who it was going to be on the other end – her father wanting to know why she'd lied to him all these years, more press wanting to hear her side of the story. She didn't know if she could cope with any of it today. It just didn't feel real, and if she was going to handle any of it with the dignity required to get through this then it needed to feel real.

'Whoever it is will leave a message,' Ronnie said, his voice kind, his presence now very necessary. If ever there was a day when she needed her best friend, this was it.

The doorbell ringing made her jump and she leaned forward, pulling her knees up to her chest, resting her forehead against them, just wanting to shut it all out for a few more minutes.

Ronnie was quiet for a second, then she heard him come back to the door, pushing it open and joining her inside, crouching down to her level. 'It's the press. And I'm afraid it's gonna be like this for a while, kiddo. They're already starting to gather outside and although it's probably the last thing you feel like doing, somebody's gonna have to tell them something at some point.'

'Jesus… Kevin's gonna go ballistic.'

'You reckon?' Ronnie almost couldn't keep the smirk off his face. 'It was probably him at the door; you know how he loves to be first when it comes to a local scandal.'

'It's not funny,' Amber said, trying not to smirk herself. 'Ronnie!'

'I know, I'm sorry. But, maybe talking to News North East is the way to go, don't you think? After all, they're your employers, so surely they've got the right to feature your side of the story before anyone else? Because you can't pretend this is just going to go away. It won't. Not for a while yet, anyway.'

'Shit! I can't believe this is happening. I'm just some local sports reporter who's really not that interesting. How the hell did I end up here?'

'I think you know the answer to that question already,' Ronnie replied, pulling her up to her feet.

'Speaking of questions,' Amber said, attempting to change the subject for a second, even though she knew it wouldn't last long, '… who's this new lady in your life, then? When I rang you last night…'

'You really want to talk about that now?'

'Yeah! Why not? I'm curious, nosy, call it what you like. So, *are* you seeing someone new?'

'Sort of,' Ronnie mumbled, looking down at the ground.

'Sort of,' Amber repeated. 'What's that supposed to mean? Ronnie…?'

'This isn't really the time to be discussing my love life, is it?'

'I think it's the perfect time,' Amber said, sitting down on the stairs and pulling her knees up to her chest again. 'Anything to distract me from everything else that's happening.'

'Yeah. Because burying your head in the sand is always the best option.'

'I'm not…' She looked at her best friend, who just threw her a look back as he sat down next to her. 'Okay,' she sighed. 'I am. But you can't blame me. I don't know what I'm supposed to do, Ronnie. What am I supposed to do?'

Ronnie was stopped from answering that impossible question by Ryan wandering into the hall, his hands shoved deep in his pockets, his face a picture of confusion.

'Are you still here?' Amber said, turning away from him. She couldn't bear to look at him, she just didn't really know why. Because what he'd done had made her sick to her stomach? Or because she still loved him and couldn't bear the thought of saying goodbye? For the briefest of seconds she almost felt sorry for him – he couldn't help the fact he seemed to like pressing the self-destruct button. But then she remembered the humiliation she'd felt just a few hours earlier when she'd seen two women all over him, witnessed him enjoying every sick second of the things they were doing to him. That managed to wipe away any remaining pity she might be feeling.

'Amber, I'm sorry,' Ryan said quietly. It seemed such an inadequate word, given the circumstances, but what else could he say? From the way things were panning out it seemed as though all of this *was* his fault. He should never have said anything to anyone, but then, maybe the thought of Amber and Jim being in such close proximity to each other all the time, maybe it was something that had constantly been at the back of his mind, even if he hadn't always been aware of it.

'You're sorry,' Ronnie repeated slowly, staring at this very famous but very mixed-up young man. 'Have you any idea what you've just done? Huh? Have you?'

'Hey, listen, before you start throwing accusations around, it wasn't actually *me* who spoke to the press, okay? It was…' He stopped talking, but Ronnie continued to stare at him, arching an eyebrow.

'You shouldn't have said anything, to anybody, Ryan. End of story.'

Ryan leaned back against the hall wall, closing his eyes for a second. He wished he could turn the clock back, to the point where he and Amber were making love in the kitchen, just a few hours ago, only this time he would make sure neither of them left the house. They'd have that night in that they'd both really wanted, and none of this would have happened. He'd never wished for anything more in his entire life.

'I think you two need to talk,' Ronnie said, pulling himself up off the stairs.

'Do we?' Amber asked in surprise. 'About what, exactly? The weather? Last night's TV…?'

Ronnie looked at her. 'Grow up, Amber.' He turned to Ryan. 'Both of you, sort it out. Like adults. I'll be in the kitchen fending off phone calls.'

'He's right,' Ryan said, looking at Amber. 'Maybe we *do* need to talk.'

'Now, you see, I disagree. I think we've done all the talking we need to do, Ryan. There's not much else we can say. And if you really think that we can salvage anything from this situation then you're even more deluded than I thought you were.'

'So, that's it, then? You're gonna give up without any kind of a fight?'

She stood up, staring at him for a few seconds before laughing, a quick, cynic-laced laugh. Then, without saying anything more, she walked calmly upstairs, into the bedroom she didn't think she'd ever be able to sleep in again, not without remembering the twisted scene she'd witnessed in there just a few hours ago.

She immediately started throwing the remainder of Ryan's things into a suitcase she'd already pulled out of the loft earlier that morning, determined to rid herself of any trace of him as soon as possible. Ronnie was wrong – they didn't need to talk. She wanted Ryan out of her life, so she didn't have to think about what had happened anymore. Besides, there were more important things to worry about now, weren't there? Thanks to him.

A tap on the door didn't distract her in the slightest. 'I've told you, I'm not interested. There's nothing left to talk about.'

'Well, I think there is, honey.'

She stopped what she was doing when she heard his voice. That soft, American accent that had captured her heart over twenty-one years ago and still refused to let go. She should have realised he was going to turn up, at some point. She certainly didn't feel surprised at his appearance. In fact, if anything, she almost felt relieved. Even though he'd doubtless caused the press and media outside much excitement on his arrival.

'Can I come in, Amber? Please?'

She walked over to the window, her head spinning with the confusion and anger and hurt that were all fighting to make themselves the dominant emotion within her, which was proving to be a tough job. They were all equally deserving of that title as far as she was concerned. 'Yeah. Okay,' she sighed, staring out at the view of Newcastle City Centre away in the distance. The city she loved. A city she didn't ever really want to leave, but if this mess she suddenly found herself in got any bigger she might have no other choice. Running away again might be the only option left open to her.

'Ronnie's explained what he thinks has happened,' Jim said, quietly closing the door behind him and walking towards her. She turned around to face him, leaning back against the windowsill. 'I guess this was always going to happen at some point, huh?'

Amber looked down at the ground, taking a deep breath as the doorbell rang downstairs. 'That'll no doubt be my dad.'

'We'll talk to him together, Amber. We've got nothing to be ashamed of…'

She looked up at him – this handsome man who'd taken over her life, because she'd let him. 'Haven't we? So, why all the sneaking about then, Jim? Why all the secrecy and the hiding and…'

'Amber!' Freddie Sullivan's voice boomed up the stairs and all of a sudden Amber felt sixteen again as all the guilt she'd felt back then flooded through her once more.

'Shit!' She threw her head back and closed her eyes, sighing heavily. 'We should have seen this coming. How could we have been so stupid?'

'We didn't know it would end up like this. How could we know that?'

She looked at Jim again. 'Talk about the past coming back to haunt us.' She could hear Ronnie downstairs trying to calm her father down, even though this wasn't his problem. This was her fault, and Jim's. Nobody else's. Yet here they were, hiding away from it all. Just like they'd always done.

'Maybe it's a good thing,' Jim said quietly, taking a step closer towards her.

'And how do you work that one out?' Amber asked, narrowing her eyes.

'Ronnie told me you and Ryan… He said the wedding's off. You and Ryan are finished.'

'He's got no right to tell you anything, considering he doesn't even know the full story himself. Today's events have kind of superseded all of that.' She looked at Jim again, his green eyes staring right into hers. 'Is Ryan still here?'

Jim shook his head. 'No, he's gone. I gather it was more than likely his indiscretion that caused all of this?'

'Probably,' Amber sighed, pushing both hands through her hair. 'It's just one big mess, though, isn't it? And we can't hide up here forever…'

'Listen, Amber, I can… I can put him on the transfer list, if that's what you want. The window is still very much open and… maybe it's for the best.'

Amber looked up sharply. 'For who, exactly? No, Jim, that's *not* what I want. And I'm not sure it's what the club will want, either. He's the best player Red Star have got, you paid millions for him just six months ago, why the hell would you want to sell him? That's letting our personal shit interfere with business and… and

443

we've got to deal with this like the adults we are.'

'I have the power to get him out of our lives, Amber, don't you see that?'

She looked at him, narrowing her eyes again, laughing slightly. 'Jim, you're a football manager, not the Godfather. And you don't really have the power at all, do you? You can't make that decision on your own.'

'They'd keep me over him, honey. I can guarantee that.'

She shook her head, her eyes still fixed firmly on his. 'No. No, we don't do anything that's only going to draw more attention to everything, that's ridiculous. All of this... it's nothing that can't be sorted. In time.' She wished she felt as confident about that as she sounded.

'What if I tell the board I think he's gone too far this time? That he crossed a line, that he... I know what happened last night, Amber. And before you start telling me I don't know the facts, I do, because Ryan told me himself. So I know he crossed that line. And if all of this hadn't have happened today I'd be hauling both him *and* Gary over the coals, believe me. The pair of them are still probably looking at a two-match ban, if I've got anything to do with it.'

'Is that wise? What did I just say? We don't need to bring any more attention to a situation we should be trying to diffuse.'

'So, you're happy to see him get away with it?'

'Jesus, Jim, come on. He isn't "getting away" with anything. He's just thrown our relationship down the toilet, he's ruined everything. So I really don't think he feels as though he's getting off scot-free, do you?'

Jim took another step towards Amber. 'Maybe... maybe this was the way things were always going to go.'

'I don't understand...'

'Fate. You and me. Everyone knows now, don't they? We can't hide it anymore, we can't lie and say it never happened, so...'

'So, what? Now the truth is out we might as well just get back

444

together, is that it?'

'Well, I wouldn't put it…'

'Jesus Christ, Jim…' Amber laughed, turning her head to look out of the window again. The neighbours were out in their back gardens now, shouting to each other over the fences, no doubt talking about the growing numbers of press gathered outside and the stories in the newspapers that had now made their street a port of call for the gossip-mongers. 'You make everything sound so easy.'

'Because it is. Or it can be.' He reached out to gently touch her arm and she swung back round to look at him, his eyes burning into hers as he spoke. 'No more secrets, Amber. No more hiding from the truth.'

'What that story doesn't tell the world, though, Jim, is how much you hurt me. All it focuses on is the fact we slept together when I was so young, not the fact that you hurt me so much, I… It doesn't tell the whole story, does it?'

'We can put all that behind us, baby, can't we? We can start again, don't you see?'

She pushed him aside and walked away from the window, going back to the job she'd been busy doing before – throwing Ryan's things into a suitcase. 'All I see is one huge mess that needs to be sorted out before I even begin to think about what's going to happen next. I mean, Jesus, this is actually as much *Ryan's* house as it is mine and yet I'm throwing *him* out! Maybe *I* should be the one to leave…'

'Do you love me, Amber?'

She stopped what she was doing and looked down at the t-shirt she was holding. Ryan's t-shirt.

'Amber? Look me in the eye and tell me you're not still in love with me?'

'That's not fair,' she whispered, throwing the t-shirt into the case and banging the lid shut. No. Ryan could be the one to leave. For now. Until she could move back into her own house, then he could do what the hell he liked with this place. He still had his city

445

centre apartment, so it wasn't like he was going to be homeless.

'Because I never stopped loving *you*.'

'Then you should have told me that a lot sooner, Jim.'

'You told me to stay away.'

'Because I thought you were leaving me for a whole new life! Jesus…' She leaned back against the wall, aware of more raised voices downstairs, of her father's rising above Ronnie's, and the guilt and the shame and the anger she still felt over everything suddenly overwhelmed her, bringing her close to tears. But she wasn't going to cry. Amber Sullivan didn't cry, she didn't do that. She was strong, she could deal with this. She could. She could deal with this. 'I didn't want you near me if I couldn't have you, Jim. I couldn't stand seeing you every day, with somebody else, and knowing I couldn't have you. But if I'd thought for one second that you felt the same way as me… if I'd known you'd really, honestly wanted me, too…'

'I should have gone with my heart, huh?'

She looked at him. 'I guess we messed up big time, didn't we?'

He smiled a small smile, walking over to her, and this time she let her heart skip a beat at the sight of him, let her stomach turn those familiar somersaults, felt her skin tingle at the prospect of him touching her. All those things she'd tried to batter down, tried to push aside and forget she'd ever felt at all.

'We should have come clean in the beginning, Amber, I know that now. But I got scared. I let my ego get in the way, I pretended you were nothing more than a fling, someone who'd always be there for me whenever I needed her, but all that did was hurt you. It wasn't fair, and I'm so sorry. I'm so, so sorry. You didn't deserve any of it.'

'We both made mistakes, Jim. I should have been wise enough not to let you back into my life a second time. I should have walked away, left you alone…'

'But I wouldn't have let you do that, because I *wanted* you to come back. I wanted you so much, Amber. I always did. I still do. But I was weak, scared of what people would say. Scared it would hurt my career. I was selfish. I was way, way too selfish.' He gently touched her cheek with the palm of his hand, his green eyes practically burning into hers. 'I love you, baby. I always have, and I always will. And there's not a thing you can do to stop that.'

This was so not the time for any of this to be happening, but she was vulnerable, weak. She was scared of what was going to happen and how the future was going to pan out, and what Jim was offering was a familiarity she needed right now. Because she wasn't sure she could face this all on her own. After all, they were in this together now, weren't they?

'Jim, I…' She closed her eyes as his mouth lowered down onto hers, and although she knew the timing couldn't have been worse, she let it happen because it felt safe. *He* felt safe. After all those years of knowing it was wrong, of knowing *he* was wrong, now he finally felt safe. Finally.

'*You* need to be thanking your lucky fucking stars,' Max said, pacing the floor of Ryan's riverside apartment. 'Because if it hadn't been for you and your reckless teammate blabbing to those women the pair of you saw fit to pick up last night, then *you* would have been the frigging headlines this morning, instead of featuring as nothing more than the shocked boyfriend who, apparently, knew nothing about his fiancée's secret past with his boss. But you *did* know, didn't you?'

Ryan nodded. 'Yeah, I knew. Anyway, none of it matters anymore, does it? Because she's not my fiancée now, is she?'

'Yes, and whose fault is *that*, Ryan?' Max asked, stopping when he reached the dining table Ryan was sitting at, leaning forward to look straight at his high-maintenance, high-profile client, his palms resting face down on the black glass. 'You, sitting here a single man again was going to happen regardless of all the other crap going down today. You saw to that yourself. What the fuck were you thinking?'

'I don't know,' Ryan sighed, sitting back and pushing a hand through his dishevelled hair.

'You don't know,' Max repeated, resuming his pacing, ignoring yet another call coming through on his mobile. It had been ringing almost continuously since the news of Amber and Jim Allen's past had broken, everyone wanting to know Ryan's reaction to his fiancée and his boss's secret affair. 'And I'll tell you another thing, kiddo, you also want to think yourself lucky those women you took home decided that Amber and Jim were more newsworthy than the fact they'd just slept with one of the country's top footballers on his fucking Stag Night…'

'You think I'm lucky, do you?' Ryan interrupted, feeling pissed off and angry now. Lucky was the last thing he considered himself to be.

'Yes, I think you're lucky,' Max said, his voice still carrying the agitated tone it had sported since he'd turned up on Ryan's door-step just a few minutes ago. 'You're lucky that everyone is focusing on your boss right now and not on what a fucking idiot *you've* been – again. That could have been your last chance, Ryan, you do realise that, don't you? Drink, women, drugs… how fucking stupid *are* you?'

'Jesus Christ, alright!' Ryan yelled, getting up and kicking the chair he'd been sitting on across the room. 'I get it. I've been an idiot; you don't have to keep going on about it.'

'Oh, but I think I do. Because you obviously don't listen to a fucking word I say! Or we wouldn't be *in* this mess now, would we? You had a great woman, a beautiful woman – a whole new future ahead of you, and your football was the best it's been in a long time, and what do *you* do? You go and piss it all up against a wall just because you can't let your old life go. A life that dragged you down and almost ruined everything you had, and you wanted to go there again? I'll never understand you, Ryan. I really thought we'd turned that corner, that you were finally settling down. I mean, that's why you came home, wasn't it? Why you left London and came back up north? To settle down? But you just couldn't leave it alone.'

Ryan sat down on his huge, oversized black leather sofa, putting his head in his hands. 'Quit with the lectures, will you, Max? I've had enough.'

'Really. You've had enough? Haven't we all, Ryan.'

'What's that supposed to mean?' Ryan asked, looking up at his agent.

Max leaned back against the dining table, folding his arms. 'It means, I'm not sure I can be bothered with the hassle you create anymore. Do you know where I'm supposed to be today? I'm supposed to be flying out to Barcelona to talk to a big-name player out there who's looking to move to England. He's talking to three of this country's biggest clubs right now – including Newcastle Red Star – and he wants *me* to represent him, but where am I? I'm here, aren't I? Sorting out another one of *your* fucking messes.'

'Shit! Max, I'm sorry…'

'Yeah, well, maybe sorry isn't good enough this time, kiddo.'

'Jesus…' Ryan sighed, throwing himself back against the cushions, closing his eyes. 'This is the worst yet.'

'No, it isn't. But it could have been. *You're* not a major priority at the minute. You got away with it because something bigger and far more interesting superseded *your* stupidity. Your career's safe, Ryan. This time. But your nine lives are running out fast, and you'd better get a grip before you really mess up.'

'Are you…?'

'I'm going nowhere, kiddo. I've been with you since you started out, since you were nineteen years old, do you really think I could walk away from you now? Despite all the shit you create, I'm not just your agent, I care about you, okay? God help me.'

Ryan felt a wave of relief wash over him. Max was like a second dad to him. He didn't know what he'd do if he wasn't around to help him out of all the trouble he seemed more than capable of getting himself into. He only knew that, if he hadn't been his agent, then Christ knows where he'd be now. Washed-up and finished before he was thirty, probably. 'I can't believe I've let this happen,' he said quietly, his voice almost a whisper. The past few hours were still a blur. His head still wasn't completely clear, and he had a bad feeling that, once the clarity that would definitely hit him some point soon arrived, he was going to feel a hundred times worse than he did now. And right now he felt as though his whole world was crumbling around him. 'I've really lost her this time, haven't I?'

Max looked at his biggest client – a young man he really did care about, someone whose talent was obvious to everyone in the world of football, but whose reputation went before him. And Ryan could have stopped that; he could have let his football do the talking, because he had more than enough talent to allow that to happen. People knew who he was because of the way he played the game. The skills he exhibited were there for all to see every time he set foot on a football pitch. People knew who he was because he was an incredible player. But they also knew who he was because of the way he lived his life *off* the pitch, and that was where the problems lay. He'd been sucked in by the lifestyle, by the money, the women. And whilst that was fine – he was a young man in a dream job, who *wouldn't* want to make the most of everything that came with that? – Ryan just had no idea when to press the stop button, when to step back and take a look at just what he was doing, and how it was affecting everything and everyone else around him.

'Why don't you go and stay with your mum and dad for a while?' Max sighed, walking over to Ryan and sitting down on the arm of the sofa.

Ryan looked up at him. 'Have you spoken to them?'

'They're worried, kiddo. And with every right.'

'I don't need to go running back to my parents, Max. I'm not a kid anymore.'

'Then you might want to start proving that, Ryan.'

Ryan put his head in his hands again, sighing heavily, before throwing his head back against the back of the sofa. 'Maybe I should think about leaving the North East altogether. I mean, coming back here, it didn't really solve anything, did it? All that's happened is that I've carried on exactly where I left off in London, so what was the point, huh?'

'Well, apart from the astronomic wage packet you earned by joining Red Star, not to mention the chance to play for the team you've supported all your life – a huge club with a worldwide reputation that has, quite frankly, turned you into a local hero – you had the chance to turn everything around, Ryan. You had that chance, and you blew it.'

Ryan stood up, sick of hearing Max's voice now. It was like having a broken record playing constantly in the background. He was well aware of the fact he'd blown it, he knew only too well what he'd thrown away, he didn't need somebody banging on about it on a regular basis, reminding him of the fact. 'All the more reason to make a new start somewhere else, then.' He looked out of the huge wall of windows that lined one entire side of his apartment, out at the view of a city he loved. Just being able to wake up every morning and see the Tyne Bridge, hear the noise of the city coming to life and feel the atmosphere this place exuded every time he walked around it, he loved that. He hadn't realised how much he'd missed it after all those years of living in London, until he'd come back home just those six short months ago. And Max was right. He'd had a chance to turn everything around, forget the past, leave those ridiculously hedonistic days behind him and concentrate on a footballing career that was setting him up for a pretty easy life in the future, if he played his cards right, and he could have done all of that with Amber by his side. Amber Sullivan. A woman he'd probably never really understand, but a woman he'd fallen in love with, from the second he'd set eyes on her.

'Well,' Max sighed, standing up and taking his phone out of his pocket as it rang again, immediately rejecting the call. 'I can't lie and say that there haven't been offers from other clubs for you, despite the fact you have a contract with Red Star. You're so much in demand that people are quite willing to pay an extortionate amount of money to get you out of that contract and into a new one…' Max looked at Ryan, wishing that things had been different. He was a good kid, deep down. He just had very little self-control, and that could well be his downfall if people didn't keep a very close eye on him. 'But, and despite the fact I'm probably kissing goodbye to a shed load of money here, too, I don't think you should be going anywhere.'

Ryan looked up at his agent. 'You think I should stay here, with all this shit going on?'

'Yes, because running away doesn't solve anything. Start showing people you're a grown-up, Ryan, and focus on what really matters right now – your football.'

He looked out of the window again, traffic streaming across the Tyne Bridge even though rush hour was long gone. But that's what Ryan loved about living in a city – it never really got quiet. 'It's all I've got now, isn't it?' he said, clarity slowly beginning to creep in, realisation hitting him hard. 'It's all I've got.'

Chapter Twenty-Eight

'How long does it take for people to move onto the next news story?' Amber asked, throwing her bag down onto her desk, slightly flustered from trying to battle her way into the News North East building through the crowd of press and photographers still gathered outside. They were probably the same ones who'd been hanging around her street when she'd left for work; they'd just followed her here.

'As long as it takes to get the conclusion they're after,' Kevin replied, handing her a mug of coffee.

She looked at her boss, frowning slightly as she took a sip of much-needed strong coffee. 'Huh?'

'You're giving nothing away, Amber.' Kevin leaned back against her desk, folding his arms. 'Okay, so, we gave them what they wanted to hear last week when you spoke to us, when you gave us that interview explaining what had gone on – and kudos to you for keeping your relationship with Jim Allen a secret all these years, by the way. That must've taken some effort.'

'Not really,' Amber mumbled, starting up her laptop. 'For a long time Jim Allen was in the past, where he should have stayed.'

'But then he signed on as Red Star's manager, didn't he? And the press would still like to think that's, in part, because of you. Makes a much better story, don't you think?'

She looked at Kevin, taking another slow sip of coffee. 'I'm not living in some romantic novel, Kevin. Jim used to play for Red Star; it's a club that's always been close to his heart. It makes sense that, when he was offered the job of manager, he would take it.'

'So, you're telling me he didn't give you a second thought when he accepted the job?'

'I've told you everything you need to know.' She opened up her emails, quickly scanning the list before frowning again, turning back to look at Kevin. 'And what do you mean, as long as it takes to get the conclusion they're after? *What* conclusion, exactly?'

'Well, everything's still up in the air, isn't it? Okay, so, your engagement to Ryan Fisher is off... That relationship's over, am I right?'

Amber nodded, feeling her stomach dip as Kevin spoke, but she ignored it, returning to her list of emails as Kevin carried on speaking.

'But as far as you and Jim Allen are concerned, everyone's kind of waiting to see what's going to happen there. Aren't they?'

'You including yourself in that?' Amber sniffed, not taking her eyes off her laptop screen.

'*Are* you and Jim Allen an item now?'

She waited a second before swinging round on her chair to look at Kevin, but she didn't answer his question.

'Is that it?' Kevin exclaimed as Amber swung back round to face her laptop. 'Is that all you're saying?'

'I didn't say anything,' Amber said, opening up the most urgent email in her inbox.

'Exactly! And this is why the press are still hanging around, kiddo. They're waiting for your next move.'

'You make me sound like something out of a David Attenborough documentary.' She looked at her boss again, smiling slightly at his exasperated expression. 'They'll get bored, eventually. Then they'll go away and look for the next newsworthy piece of gossip.'

'You reckon? Not today they won't, because you're off to

Tynebridge in a minute. There's a press conference to introduce one of the new signings Red Star have made during this January transfer window and we need somebody down there to cover it, so…'

'You're doing this deliberately, aren't you?'

'Doing what?'

'Sending me to Tynebridge when you know that puts me right in-between Ryan and Jim. It's like you almost *want* to throw me to the lions.'

'I'm asking you to do your job, Amber. That's all.'

'Yeah. Of course you are.'

'It all kicks off – pardon the pun – at ten o'clock, kiddo, so I'd get organised if I were you. See you later.'

Amber watched him leave, sighing as her phone rang from the depths of her oversized handbag. Reaching inside, she scrabbled around, trying to find the phone she'd casually thrown in there on her way out of the house, finally retrieving it from underneath a copy of the Newcastle Gazette.

'Amber Sullivan,' she said, answering the call without looking at the caller ID.

'I could have been anyone, including another journalist trying to prise more personal details out of you.'

'Ronnie,' Amber smiled, sitting back in her chair, happy to hear his voice. He was like a shot of calm amid the crazy, complicated mess that still lay all around her. 'You okay?'

'Should be *me* asking *you* that, really. And check your caller ID before you answer the phone next time, alright?'

'Yeah, alright. Sorry. I'm not used to this level of media attention, remember? Hang on… how did you know I *hadn't* checked the caller ID before I answered your call?'

'I know you, Amber, that's how I know. Anyway, how are things between you and your dad? Has he calmed down yet?'

Amber closed her eyes briefly, trying not to remember the confrontation she'd had with Freddie Sullivan after the news of

455

her and Jim's secret past had been revealed. To say he'd been disappointed would be an understatement. He'd been angry – obviously – not to mention upset, but most of all, betrayed. That's how he'd told her he'd felt when he'd first heard the news – he'd felt betrayed. And it was *his* reaction to it all that bothered Amber more than anybody else's.

'Well, yeah, he *has* calmed down a bit, I suppose. But to say his friendship with Jim is now severely strained is putting it mildly, really.' She opened her eyes and leaned forward on her elbows, resting her head in her hand. 'It was awful, Ronnie. When he said he felt betrayed, it broke my heart. Oh, he blames Jim for so much more than he blames me, but that's not the point. We *both* kept secrets from him, and we shouldn't have done that.'

'Finding out your best friend slept with your daughter when she was just sixteen years old is bound to have an effect on any father, Amber.'

'I don't want to go over it again, Ronnie. It's all still so bloody raw.'

'Are you sleeping alright?'

'Not really. There's a lot going on in my head, y'know? A lot to think about.'

'You're not thinking about taking Ryan back, are you? Only, I've seen the stories in the papers, how he wants you back and…'

'I'm not taking him back, Ronnie, don't worry.'

'Good girl.'

'Anyway,' she sighed, '… how's *your* love life going? Everything still going okay with your new girlfriend?'

There was a slight pause before Ronnie replied. A long enough pause to make Amber think something maybe wasn't quite as straightforward as it should be. 'I'm engaged, Amber.'

Now it was Amber's turn to stay silent. Did he just say he was engaged? When had *that* happened? 'Engaged…? I… When…? Aren't you… aren't you rushing into this slightly, Ronnie? I mean, this new relationship, this new woman, you've only known her

456

five minutes, haven't you?'

'Not really. Amber...'

'Not really?' Amber suddenly felt her stomach sink. 'Don't tell me... Not... You've taken Karen back, haven't you?'

'I didn't want to tell you just yet, Amber, but...'

'How long, Ronnie?' But Amber already had a sneaking suspicion she knew exactly how long it had been going on.

'I should have told you, but...'

'That's why it was never going to work between you and Anna, wasn't it?'

'I couldn't get her out of my head, Amber. You knew how much I loved her, what she meant to me, what our *marriage* meant to me...'

'She slept with another man behind your back, Ronnie.'

'And you'd know all about that, wouldn't you?'

Amber said nothing for a second. 'Okay. I probably asked for that.'

'Jesus... I'm sorry, kiddo...'

'That's why you were off with me, wasn't it? Just after you and Anna split up? Why you couldn't even look me in the eye...'

'Because I knew you'd react like this! And maybe now you'll know exactly how I feel about you and Ryan.'

'Yeah, but the big difference being, Ronnie, that I'm not taking Ryan back.'

She heard him sigh down the phone. 'I know what I'm doing, Amber. Really, I do. I can't let her go; I've got to give her a second chance. You gave Ryan a second chance, didn't you?'

'I gave him more than that,' Amber said quietly, fiddling with her pen. 'Are you *sure* about this, Ronnie?'

'You want me to be happy, don't you?'

'You know I do.'

'Well, Karen makes me happy.'

Amber sat back again, staring out of the window, shielding her eyes as the low winter sun made an appearance from behind a barrage of grey clouds, instantly brightening the day. It would've been nice if it could have done the same for her mood. 'Just – just be careful, alright?' Amber said, pushing a hand through her long, tousled hair.

'You're beginning to sound like me, now,' Ronnie replied, and she could tell he was smiling when he'd said that. She couldn't help smiling, too. 'So, do you think you and your dad are gonna be okay?'

'Yeah, of course we are,' Amber sighed, chewing on the end of her pen. 'It's just going to take a bit of time, isn't it? Not sure whether his relationship with Jim is ever going to be fixed, though…' She trailed off, checking her watch. 'Look, Ronnie, I've got to go. I've got to get to Tynebridge for a press conference in an hour.'

'January transfer window keeping you busy?'

'Whether I like it or not.'

'You okay with that?'

'It's my job, Ronnie. And if there's one thing I'm determined all of this won't do again is get in the way of my work. I can put my professional head on when need be, and you know that.'

'Yeah. Yeah, I do.'

She said nothing for a second, just stared out of the window again, her eyes following a double-decker bus as it pulled away from the stop across the road from the News North East building. 'I'm really happy for you, Ronnie.'

'Thanks, kiddo. That means a lot. You take care now, okay? And I'll see you soon.'

She hung up and threw her phone back into her bag. She'd see him soon. And that was going to have to do her, for now.

'You alright, mate?' Gary asked, sitting down next to Ryan on the touchline, both of them taking a quick break from training.

'What do *you* think?' Ryan replied, staring straight ahead of him.

Gary joined him in staring out at the rest of the squad kicking various balls around the muddy practice pitch. 'I'm really sorry,

Ryan. Me and my big mouth, huh?'

Ryan pushed a hand through his hair but kept his gaze fixed firmly on whatever was happening in front of him. 'It's not your fault, Gary. I should have kept my mouth shut, too. I should have done a lot of things, actually. Or maybe – maybe I *shouldn't* have done a lot of things… Jesus, I don't know…'

Gary reached out and quickly squeezed his friend's shoulder. 'Have you seen Amber? Since it all came out, about her and Jim?'

Ryan looked briefly at Gary before he turned away again. 'I've tried ringing her but she rejects my calls. And I've seen her around Tynebridge a couple of times but she just blanks me. All I want to do is make it better, y'know? I just don't know if I can. I only know I've got to try.'

'Is she… are her and Jim…?'

Ryan looked at Gary again. 'How would *I* know? I don't think so, I mean, even the boss has looked as though he's carrying the weight of the world on his shoulders. I gather the board have had a few words with him, because of everything that's gone on. Don't think he's going anywhere, though.'

'Yeah, well, they read the riot act to all of us, didn't they?'

Ryan didn't reply. His mind was starting to wander now. His concentration was wavering, even though he'd been warned to keep his mind on the football and stay focused. He might be Red Star's biggest signing in recent months, and he might be their star striker, but if he put another foot out of line he had no doubt that the consequences wouldn't be pleasant. Not this time. But he was finding it so hard to stay focused when all he could think about was Amber. He had no idea whether she and Jim had got back together – why would he? He'd hardly be the first person they told, would he? But there'd been nothing in the papers about any rekindled relationship and all he could do was take heart from that and hope that, despite their secret now being out, they saw no need to take that as some kind of permission to become an item again. He knew Amber. And she didn't strike him as the kind of person who'd jump straight into a relationship just to get over a broken one. But then, had she ever really jumped *out* of her relationship with Jim Allen? Had she ever really loved *him* as much as she'd loved his boss?

'I'm going to Tynebridge,' Ryan said, pulling himself up off the ground.

'What? Why? Ryan…'

'There's a press conference this morning, isn't there? For that new player we've just signed from Denby United. Amber'll be there.'

'You don't know that…'

'She'll be there,' Ryan said, striding purposefully towards the car park.

'Ryan!' Gary tried to keep up with him, almost running to catch him up. 'You can't just walk out of a training session.'

Ryan turned around briefly, smirking at Gary as he retrieved his car keys from the pocket of his tracksuit bottoms. 'Oh yeah? Watch me.'

Professionalism personified. That's what Amber could be when she set her mind to it, and that's exactly what she was as she ran the gauntlet of yet more press and paparazzi that were gathered at Red Star's Tynebridge stadium. Because they weren't just there to welcome the club's newest signing.

She held her head high but said nothing as she pushed past them into the main entrance, ignoring the questions being shouted at her from all angles.

She kept herself composed, despite the odd comment from one or two of her male counterparts, as they all waited in the Press Lounge for the press conference to begin. On the whole, her colleagues had been nothing but supportive, but there were always going to be a couple who thought their inappropriate remarks were hilarious. They weren't. But, despite the fact she was focused and her mind was solely on the job in hand, the second Jim Allen followed his newest signing into the room, she felt her heart flip over and her breath catch fast in her throat. As he settled himself behind the long desk there in the Press Lounge, ready to take charge of this press conference, Amber had to look down at her notepad, fearing people would notice her staring. But that's what happened when Jim Allen walked into a room – people stared. They couldn't help it. *She* couldn't help it. He was this enigmatic, charismatic, handsome, charming man who could hold the attention of a roomful of people just by being there. He didn't have to say a word to make people notice him. And Amber knew that better than anyone.

She was aware of more than a few of her fellow journalists and reporters taking a quick glance over at her as Jim smiled at everyone in the room. Of course people were curious to see her reaction, to see *Jim's* reaction. But they didn't know the full story. None of them did. And if she met his eyes for too long then she couldn't be entirely sure of what would happen.

Taking a deep breath, she finally looked up, crossing her legs and sitting up straight, shaking out her dark red hair slightly so it fell over her shoulders in loose waves. This was bread and butter to her – she'd done this hundreds of times over the years. It was her job. It was where she felt at her most comfortable.

As the press conference got underway, Amber focused on what it was she'd come here to do. And, as her eyes at last met Jim's, a brief smile passing between them, she sat back and waited…

Ryan locked his car and threw his keys back into his tracksuit bottoms as he scanned the car park, looking for Amber's car. And it didn't take him long to find it. Her pale blue Fiat 500 was parked just a few cars down from his.

Almost running towards the main entrance, he managed to dodge the waiting photographers and press still hanging around outside by pulling his hood up, covering his face enough to make sure that, by the time they'd done a double take, he was safely inside.

His phone beeped the arrival of a text message and he pulled it out of his pocket, pushing his hood back off his head. It was from Gary, informing him that Colin was on the warpath. But Ryan didn't really care. All he cared about now was talking to Amber, trying to make her see sense. He needed her to know that he really did love her and that everything he'd done had been – well, it had been stupid. He couldn't really call it anything else.

'Hello, Ryan,' Barry – one of the security guards who manned the desk in the main reception – smiled at him. 'You here to see Mr. Allen?'

Ryan looked at Barry, frowning slightly. 'Erm, no. No, I'm… Is the press conference still going on?'

'Finished about five minutes ago. Everyone's outside for the official photographs now.'

'Right. Okay. Thanks, Barry.' Without missing a beat, he headed towards the doors that led outside, standing quietly at the back of the North Stand as everyone crowded round the new Red Star signing. He was standing down on the pitch below, holding an official club scarf, Jim Allen by his side. The sound of camera shutters echoed around the otherwise empty stadium as Ryan craned his neck to see if he could spot Amber. He finally located her, standing near the front of the crowd of reporters. She was smiling as she talked to her cameraman, a smile which made Ryan's heart ache. He'd never felt this way before, and they were still feelings that confused him and scared him, but this time he had to gain some kind of control, and instead of hiding behind a façade he'd created just to keep up some kind of image, some ridiculous persona, he had to show her that he was serious. That he could love her like she deserved to be loved. Like he *wanted* to love her. Like he should have loved her before.

She looked stunning in a flesh-coloured, knee-length dress that seemed to cling to that incredible body of hers, even though most of it was covered by the long, cream coat she was wearing to keep out the freezing cold January temperatures. Her long legs were accentuated by high-heeled, nude-coloured ankle boots, and her long, dark red hair hung down her back in a barrage of tousled waves. She seemed relaxed, happy, even. Did she miss him as much as he was missing her? Looking at her now it didn't seem as though she did. But then, she was good at hiding her feelings, when she wanted to. Maybe, deep down, she was hurting just as much as he was.

He watched as she spoke to the new Red Star player, both of them laughing at something she said, and Ryan felt his stomach dip. This young man, this new addition to the team, seemed just as taken with her as Ryan had been when *he'd* first met her. He knew what an overwhelming day this could be for someone as young as this new player, but it seemed as though Amber knew just how to make him feel comfortable.

He watched as Jim Allen said something to her and she turned away immediately. Ryan craned his neck again to see where she was going, but she'd just taken a few steps back, allowing other reporters some time with the new signing. Had that been a knock-back from Amber to the man who couldn't seem to leave her alone? It had been a moment in time that had lasted just seconds, but it hadn't escaped Ryan's notice how many of the photographers in the crowd had turned their lenses in the direction of his ex-fiancée and his boss.

Looking down at the ground for a second, Ryan took a deep breath. Would she want to speak to him? Or would she just blank him like she'd blanked him so many times before over the past few days? The way she'd looked at him, as though he was just another footballer she had to deal with, it had been something Ryan had found hard to cope with. After being so close to someone, having them suddenly treat you like you didn't exist caused a pain the like of which he'd never experienced before. Life could really deal you some shit when it wanted to, but none of it came with a manual; nobody told you the rules or gave you any idea how to handle the crap that was going to come your way.

But Ryan had just had the biggest – the final – wake-up call.

And Amber had to know that. She had to. Because one thing Ryan had finally worked out was that he was nothing without her. He loved her. And everything else could go to hell.

She pushed the door of his office open, peering inside. He was there, standing by the filing cabinet, his suit jacket now slung over a nearby chair. He was flicking through a pile of papers as he talked into his phone, laughing quietly at whatever was being said on the other end of the line. She leaned against the doorpost, watching him for a few seconds while he was still unaware she was there. She was conscious of the noise of a post-press-conference stadium in the background; the hum of voices, the sound of people catching up with each other. They certainly weren't alone, she knew that much.

Walking inside his office, she shut the door quietly behind her, taking off her coat and throwing it down on the nearby sofa. He was still talking into his phone, but she heard him say goodbye, end the call and throw his phone down onto his desk. He continued to flick through the papers he was holding, pushing the filing cabinet draw shut with his elbow without looking up.

She walked slowly over to him, saying nothing. And he seemed so engrossed in whatever he was reading that he still didn't appear to have any idea that she was there. Which was fine. She didn't want him to acknowledge her just yet. There was plenty of time.

Biting down on her lip, she reached out and gently touched his waist, standing on tiptoe to kiss the back of his neck, the smell of him overwhelming her.

The papers he was holding dropped to the floor as he turned around, smiling at her. 'Well hello, beautiful.'

She smiled back, letting her fingers trail lightly over his cheek, touching his mouth, her heart beginning to speed up as he moved closer, his breath warm on her skin.

'I thought I'd surprise you,' she whispered.

'I used to hate surprises.'

'You won't hate this one.'

'You can guarantee that?'

'I can guarantee it.'

He pushed a strand of hair from her eyes, his fingers lightly stroking her cheek as they did so. Amber felt a long, warm shiver run right through her as he touched her, causing her to gasp out loud. The anticipation was killing her. And even though she knew what he felt like, knew just what it was he could do to her, it still felt as though they were here for the very first time.

His green eyes bored deep into hers and she pushed all the doubt, all the fear, all the guilt; all the feelings she might still have for Ryan, they were all pushed aside as she closed her eyes, Jim's mouth finally touching hers. His hand slowly pushed its way up under her dress, touching her skin, making her shiver even more. Backing up against the wall, she gripped the back of the sofa as he slipped his fingers underneath the thin material of her panties, pulling at them gently, his mouth still resting on hers. She felt hot, as though her whole body was burning up, and for a second she forgot that the door had no lock on it, that people were still outside, still hanging about. But their voices began fading slowly into the background as he pushed her panties down until she felt them fall to the floor. She stepped out of them, kicking them aside, looking into his eyes as his hand pushed up her dress again, that familiar tingling between her thighs leaving her in no doubt that this was going exactly where she wanted it to go.

Her breathing was so heavy now, her chest rising and falling so fast it almost made her feel dizzy. For over twenty years this man had been inside her head, taking over her life, and no matter how hard she'd tried, no matter how much she wanted it to stop, it always came back to this. It always came back to him. Always. And she didn't think it would ever change. Maybe she didn't want it to. Maybe she never had. Maybe that's why she was here now, letting this happen.

His lips were touching her neck now, lightly kissing that space just beneath her ear, a place that sent her crazy, sent a beautiful, warm shiver shooting through her again, which was intensified tenfold by the touch of his fingers caressing her inner thigh, threatening to enter a warm wetness that *he'd* created. And she wanted to feel him touch her there, she really did, just, not yet. She was enjoying the anticipation way too much, enjoying just being with him, even though they were playing a dangerous game. Anyone could come in at any minute, but that was also one hell of a turn-on. And they weren't exactly a secret any more, were they? So what would it matter anyway?

She smiled at him, gently pushing him away, pulling her dress back down as she walked over to the sofa. Jim's eyes followed her. He knew the game as well as she did, knew where this was going to end up and as she looked at him, handsome and strong and still as sexy as the first time she'd seen him, she knew she couldn't hold out much longer. Her thighs were tingling to the point of pain now, aching so much for him, telling her it was where he needed to be – inside her. She wanted to feel him so deep inside her; so, so deep that that feeling would never go away, even when he wasn't there. She wanted to feel that, to feel *him*.

She sat down on the edge of the sofa, swinging her legs up and lying back, stretching out. Closing her eyes, she slowly opened her legs, knowing he was watching, knowing he was aching to come inside her just as much as she wanted him in there. And it took just seconds for him to lie over her, still dressed in his white shirt and black suit pants, but that was another turn-on for Amber – he could rock a suit like nobody else. He wasn't known as the sexiest manager in football for nothing, so it was fine, it was okay that he was taking nothing off. It was just fine.

Amber stretched out again, throwing her arms up above her head as he pushed her dress up high over her thighs, exposing everything from the waist down, the cool air that suddenly hit her sending another shiver coursing through her. His thumbs were making tiny circular movements along her inner thighs and she could hear his breathing becoming heavier now, too, feel the touch of his fingers growing stronger until they finally found their destination, plunging inside her with expert precision and Amber had to bite down hard on her lip to stop herself from crying out loud. It was a beautiful pain, a feeling she'd craved, something she'd wanted him to do for so long now, but it was just the beginning, the first act of a show that had yet to get started.

He pushed a little deeper and Amber arched her back, lifting her hips up, a quiet groan escaping from between her slightly parted lips. It felt good, it felt *really* good, but it still wasn't enough. She wanted to feel that wonderful part of him that would take her to heaven; she wanted him to really become a part of her, and as he slowly withdrew his fingers, which in turn elicited another gasp from Amber, she felt the anticipation heighten as she waited for the inevitable to happen.

She kept her eyes closed, breathing in deep and exhaling slowly as she felt him lower himself down, felt him slip inside her as though it were the most natural action in the world. And maybe, for them, it was. Maybe it always had been. And maybe they'd wasted far too much time, time they needed to make up for now.

She opened her legs wider to let him go deeper, moaning quietly as he pushed harder into her, his fingers entwining with hers, his lips brushing her neck. Her body was burning up, waves of red hot shivers washing over her as they moved together, every inch of her warm skin tingling. And she could feel that crashing climax growing already, building with each kiss, with every move he made. She could feel it in the tips of her toes, creeping slowly up her body like a beautiful blanket of pins and needles, his hand in the small of her back keeping her close to him. And she wanted to be this close to him for as long as she could. She wanted to keep him there, with her, and believe that everything they were doing was right, even though she wasn't entirely sure it was. But it was time to make that move now. They had to do something, turn things around somehow so that everyone could finally move forward. This – what was happening here – it was just sealing the deal. She'd told herself that, if she'd felt everything she'd wanted to feel, if she genuinely felt it all when Jim touched her, made love to her, then and only then could she be certain they were doing the right thing.

And then it came, that incredible, white-hot wave of pain and pleasure that swept every other feeling clean away, leaving only a beautiful, tingling sensation that covered every inch of her body. His lips kissed the base of her throat in tiny, feather-light touches as she felt him spill out inside her, wiping away that last seed of doubt, and she closed her legs around him, keeping them there for just a little bit longer as she felt him continue to flood her body.

'So, I guess this tells me everything I need to know.'

His voice caused the perfect bubble she and Jim had created around them to burst in an instant. The spell had been broken, the moment suddenly lost.

'Ryan…' Amber began, pulling her dress down over her thighs as Jim sat up, running both hands through his grey-flecked hair.

'You should knock before you enter this office, Fisher,' Jim said, standing up and tucking his shirt back in before calmly walking over to a tray of various bottled spirits on a sideboard at the other end of the room. Amber watched him as he poured himself a whisky. It was as though getting caught having sex was an everyday occurrence to him. He was acting as though this wasn't anything unusual.

Jim turned to look at Ryan. 'Shouldn't you be at the training ground?'

Ryan stared at his boss for a few seconds, before turning his attention back to Amber. 'I wanted to see Amber.'

'Well, you've seen her,' Jim said, taking a small sip of whisky, despite it only just being past lunchtime. 'Now, I suggest you get back to doing what you're supposed to be doing before Colin feels the need to contact me about your behaviour. Again.'

Ryan looked at Amber. 'I need to talk to her.'

'Ryan, I…' Amber didn't know what to say. All along she'd known anyone could have walked in on her and Jim, she just hadn't expected it to be Ryan. 'I thought we were past all of this. It's over.'

'Is it? Is it really?'

'You walked in on us having sex, Ryan,' Jim said, walking back over to Amber. 'What does that tell you?'

'That she's in desperate need of a rebound fuck?'

In one swift movement Amber stood up and slapped Ryan hard across the face, before she felt Jim's hand in hers, pulling her back. 'Like I said, it's over, Ryan,' Amber hissed.

Ryan's hand went straight to his cheek, the heat of where she'd slapped him burning his palm. And then he just turned around and left, without looking back, without saying another word. He guessed he'd seen more than he'd needed to see, and heard more than enough. Amber had made her choice. It was now up to him to decide whether he could live with that, or not.

Chapter Twenty-Nine

'So, what do we do now?' Amber asked, turning to face Jim. Her hand still stung from where she'd slapped Ryan, and although she didn't regret what she'd done, she couldn't help but feel it had been purely because he'd hit a nerve. But Jim wasn't a rebound fuck. Not this time. This time things were different.

'Nothing's changed, baby,' Jim whispered, tucking a strand of her dark red hair behind her ear. 'Just because he caught us...' He smiled slightly. 'Didn't you get some kind of kick out of that, huh?' His mouth moved closer to hers, his breath warm against her skin. 'I was still deep inside you when he walked in...'

She pushed herself up against him, her arms sliding around his neck as that familiar tingle spread across her thighs again, despite herself. Despite the situation. 'I know you were,' she said quietly, remembering how beautiful he'd felt. Remembering how it had made her feel. But the guilt was still there, gnawing away at her every day – the guilt of what she and Jim had done to her father, more than anything else. But now she had the added guilt of Ryan finding her with Jim. Even after everything he'd done, she still couldn't help but feel he hadn't deserved that.

'I've been talking to Jorge over in Malaga,' Jim went on, pushing her back against the door, his fingers creeping slowly up her dress again. 'And it's all systems go. If that's what we want.'

Amber felt her heart start to race again, her skin breaking out in brand new goose bumps as his lips brushed over her neck, the closeness of his body causing her own to burn up once more. 'Jim... Jesus, come on...' Despite the fact she would much rather have indulged in another round of sex, bury her head in that bubble again rather than face reality, she knew this wasn't a game anymore. They had to talk about this. They had to decide. They had choices to make, and none of them were going to be easy.

Pushing him away, she pulled herself together, picking her panties up off the floor and pulling them back on. The time for playing was over. Real life had to take priority now. Whether she liked it or not.

'I understand that this is all very – scary, Amber...'

'Scary?' Amber laughed. She couldn't help it. 'You love this job, Jim. This club, it means such a lot to you, and to be able to manage it, and manage it well...'

Jim walked back over to her, gently brushing her cheek with the back of his hand. 'What really matters to me, Amber, is you. Yes, I love this job, but I can do this job anywhere. With any club. And you know as well as I do that part of the reason I came back here, back to the North East, it was because of *you*. Because it was where *you* were. It gave me that legitimate opportunity I needed to try and make you see how much I love you, baby. So I don't care if I have to leave this place behind if it means I have you. That's all that matters to me.'

She looked up into his beautiful green eyes, and this time she truly believed what he was telling her. Although she doubted whether she would ever be able to wholly trust him again. All she knew was that she couldn't fight it any longer. He'd come back, and she had to face up to the fact that she was glad about that. Even if nobody else was.

'But what about you?' Jim asked, noticing the hesitation in her eyes. 'You have so much more to give up than I do. You've got your dad, your job...'

She stopped him from talking anymore by kissing him slowly, just to give her time to think. If Jim took this job in Spain – and the offer was very much on the table – then it would mean a whole new start for both of them. Is that what she really wanted? Or was it just a case of history repeating itself? Would she not just be running away from things like she had done before? But one thing was different this time. This time she wasn't running away from Jim and the things he'd done to her – she was running away *with* him. And wasn't that what she'd always wanted? Deep down? Her and Jim. Together. Forever.

'Let's do it,' she smiled, stroking his cheek with her thumb, allowing a small frisson of excitement to flit through her.

'You sure?' Jim asked, pulling her close, and for the first time in a very long time Amber felt confident that she was finally heading in a direction she wanted to go.

'I'm sure,' she replied, still smiling. 'I'm more than sure.'

Jim smiled, too – that beautiful, warm and charming smile that had captured her heart over two decades ago. A smile that made her heart leap around like some out-of-control jack-in-the-box; a smile that made her stomach turn almost never-ending somer-saults. A smile that made her feel sixteen all over again. And she wasn't prepared to let that feeling go. She didn't want to lose him a third time. 'Marry me, Amber.'

That came completely out of the blue and it caught her slightly off guard. She felt her heart start to race again, but her mouth had gone completely dry. She just knew that if she tried to say anything no words would come out.

At the age of sixteen, she'd dreamed of Jim Allen saying those words to her – marry me. As an infatuated teenager she'd done the stereotypical thing of changing her surname to his, of daydreaming about what it would be like to be his wife, even though she was sleeping with him. But now that he'd finally said those words, she didn't know what to do. It was as if far too many life-changing decisions were being thrown at her all at once and she suddenly felt slightly claustrophobic.

He pulled her closer and she rested her head against his chest, breathing in his smell, closing her eyes as he kissed the top of her head, just holding her. And it was the most peaceful, beautiful feeling – standing there in his arms. Arms that could protect her, even though that had never been anything she'd wanted or needed – to be protected. Until now. Did she have to be strong 24/7? Couldn't she have some downtime and allow herself to be looked after? Something she'd fought so hard to prevent in the past.

'Yes,' she whispered, but it was like the words had come out of her mouth on some kind of auto-pilot.

He tilted her chin up, kissing her gently. 'Yes, you'll marry me?'

She smiled, something akin to a wave of relief spreading right through her. It was almost as if she'd just realised she'd been waiting all her life for this moment to arrive and now that it had, well; she was just having a bit of trouble believing it was happening, that was all. 'Yes. I'll marry you.'

She closed her eyes as his mouth lowered down onto hers again, a kiss that really had finally sealed the deal. She'd started this journey over twenty years ago, and although it had been a tough ride, and people she loved beyond anything had got hurt when that was the last thing she'd wanted to happen, she couldn't help but feel the time was now right to take this chance.

'I love you, Amber. I just need you to believe that.'

'I believe it, Jim. Now,' she smiled, running her fingers gently over the stubble on his chin. 'I believe it now.'

'So what's wrong?' he asked, noticing the slight and sudden change in her mood, her eyes turning away from his for a second.

'I need to talk to Ryan…'

'Amber, come on. He's a big boy now, and he's just going to have to handle this like a grown-up.'

'You don't know him like I do, Jim. He's really not as tough as he'd like to think he is. He's quite vulnerable…'

'Bullshit! Amber…'

473

'I was right here, in this position, about to start making plans to marry *him* just over a week ago. Remember?'

'And he blew it. Big time.'

She looked at Jim. She couldn't really expect him to feel the same sympathy for Ryan that she still felt. Even though she wished she didn't. It would make life a lot easier.

'You don't owe him anything, Amber.'

She gave him one last, quick kiss, smiling as she walked backwards towards the door, grabbing her coat on the way. 'I just want to talk to him, Jim. That's all. Try and make things right.'

'You think you can do that?'

She shrugged. 'Maybe not. But I can at least try.'

She gave him one more smile before she left his office, closing the door behind her and making her way back out into the main atrium.

'Did you see where Ryan went?' she asked Barry behind reception.

He looked up and smiled at her. 'You look happy, if you don't mind me saying, Ms. Sullivan.'

'Yeah,' Amber smiled back. 'Yeah. I guess I *am* happy. Sorry, did you say you knew where Ryan had gone?'

'I think he went back outside, into the stadium.'

'Okay. Thanks, Barry.'

She turned around and made her way back through the double doors she'd just come through, heading down the corridor that took her to the exits that led out into the stadium itself.

The freezing cold air hit her as soon as she stepped outside, along with the eerie emptiness that a deserted stadium created, the buzz and excitement the new signing had created now long gone. Looking around, she found Ryan sitting halfway up the stand, his hood pulled up over his head, his hands clasped between his open knees. He was staring straight ahead, out across the empty stadium, and for another of those brief seconds Amber felt a wave of feelings for this young man wash over her – feelings she couldn't explain, but they were still there. She couldn't switch them off just like that, not after everything that had happened.

She made her way over to the row of seats he was sitting in, sliding down onto the seat next to him. 'I'm sorry, Ryan.'

He didn't look at her as he spoke. 'Sorry for what, Amber? Sorry for the fact we're not together anymore, or sorry that I had to witness Jim Allen fucking you?'

She sat back, closing her eyes for a second and breathing out slowly. 'I really am sorry.'

'He only really came back here for you, didn't he?' Ryan said, finally turning to face her, not taking his eyes off her now. 'That's the only reason he came to Red Star, wasn't it?'

Amber slowly shook her head. 'That's not fair, Ryan. He came here because this club is very close to his heart…'

'Whatever.' Ryan finally broke the gaze and turned back to stare out at the empty stadium in front of him.

'Ryan, I…'

'Did you ever love me, Amber?'

'I… Of course I did.'

He turned to look at her again. 'Really?'

'Jesus, what *is* this, Ryan? When did *I* suddenly become the bad guy? It wasn't *me* caught fucking two women in *our* bed.'

'No, but I caught you…' He looked away, down at the ground. 'I'm sorry. I guess me seeing you with Jim…' He looked at her, realisation now flooding his face. 'I really blew it, didn't I?'

She smiled slightly, wanting to reach out and take his hand but she was afraid of the signals that would send out. 'Our whole relationship was a complicated mess, Ryan.'

'Is that how it really felt to you? A mess?'

She looked away. No. That wasn't how it had felt. Not all the time, anyway. 'No,' she whispered. 'But maybe we were kidding ourselves, Ryan.' She turned back to face him again. 'What I felt for you, it was real. I loved you, and…'

'But you were never really *in* love with me, were you?'

475

She wanted to look away again – to hide the guilt she was feeling? Maybe. But he deserved the truth now. 'Jim, he… he's been such a huge part of me for so long and… I tried to pretend it was over, Ryan, I really did, because I didn't want to go back there and leave myself open to that kind of hurt all over again, and I thought that if I could just… I wanted to believe that he wasn't the only man I could love. I wanted to believe that so much…'

'And you thought *I* might be the man that could help you see things differently? Is that it?'

'When it's said out loud it makes me sound so selfish,' Amber said quietly, staring down at her clasped hands again.

'I think we were both selfish, in our own ways,' Ryan sighed, sitting back and pushing his hood back off his head. 'I liked the idea of having this beautiful woman by my side, someone who was always going to be there whenever I needed her, but at the same time I couldn't let that old life go. And it wasn't fair on you.'

'It wasn't fair on *us*, Ryan. We never really gave each other a chance, did we?'

'I thought we were getting there,' he said. She looked at him again, his handsome face clouding over with a sadness she'd never seen in him before. 'After the Christmas party, when you went back to Jim, I… I thought you were all I wanted. I thought that losing you was the worst thing that could happen to me and…'

'Your head was all over the place, Ryan.'

'I acted like an idiot. Like some spoiled kid who couldn't have what he wanted and all I could think about was… I thought that if I tried to get your attention, tried to make you see that I couldn't cope without you…'

'Ryan… what are you talking about?'

He shook his head. 'It doesn't matter.'

'No, it *does* matter. To me.'

'That night, when Gary and Debbie assumed I'd tried to… tried to harm myself… I wasn't quite as wasted as everyone thought I was, Amber. I was sober enough to know exactly what I was doing.'

'And what *were* you doing? Exactly?'

He turned away, staring straight out ahead again. 'Like I said before, I thought if I could do something drastic enough to make you come running back to me…'

She narrowed her eyes slightly as she continued to stare at him. 'Do you mean…? What you did…? That was all *deliberate*?'

'I was desperate, Amber. I couldn't get you out of my head, couldn't think straight without you and I just thought… I just wanted you to come back to me. And I didn't care how I had to do that.' He looked at her. 'He doesn't deserve you.'

She laughed, and she hadn't meant to do that out loud but she really hadn't been able to help it. 'Pretending to be so low that you wanted to kill yourself? That's sick, Ryan. How could you do that? I was so worried about you, so scared; do you have any idea…?'

He continued to stare at her, his dark eyes boring deep into hers. 'He doesn't deserve you, Amber.'

'I think he does,' she said quietly, still slightly shocked by what he'd just told her. 'I love him, Ryan. It's as simple as that. I think I've been in love with him for most of my life, and I can't just push that aside and pretend those feelings don't exist, because they do. They do.'

'So, you never were *in* love with me, then?'

'I didn't say that. Jesus, I don't know…' She turned away for a second, pushing a hand through her hair, sweeping it back off her face. 'I just don't know, Ryan.'

'If he'd never come back here… Amber, look at me, please.'

She slowly turned back to face him.

'If he hadn't come back to the North East, do you think we would have stood a chance?'

'That would have depended very much on you, Ryan.'

It was his turn to look away, his eyes focusing on one of the groundsmen who'd come out to inspect the damage that morning's activities might have inflicted on his perfect pitch. 'It really was a mess, wasn't it?'

Their eyes met again, but this conversation, it wasn't making anything any easier. For either of them.

'So, you and Jim…' Ryan began, his fingers fiddling with a red and blue friendship bracelet he had wrapped around his left wrist. 'When did you… Was it straight after you found me and…?'

She shook her head, stopping him from asking the question he was trying to ask. 'No. No, it wasn't *straight* after, but… Well, once I knew that you and me were over, I… It was like a bolt of – of realisation, I suppose, if that makes sense. It just hit me. I could either continue to fight what I felt for Jim, or I could just give in to what I've always known. That I need him.'

Ryan smiled at her – a wry smile. '*You* don't need anyone, surely.'

She smiled back, taking a quick look down at her still-clasped hands. 'Yeah, you see, I do. I really do. This independence lark, it's really not all it's cracked up to be. Those tough-girl barriers I used to put up, they were only there to help me deal with the fact that I couldn't have the one thing I really wanted – Jim Allen. And maybe I should have been more truthful to you and more honest with myself from the beginning, but then, I'm not sure either of us really knew what the truth was, did we?'

'No,' Ryan whispered. 'No, we didn't. So, how long have you…?'

'Officially? A couple of days. Nobody knows yet. We haven't made anything public, although the press seem quite happy to draw their own conclusions anyway, regardless of what the truth is.'

'And what *is* the truth?'

Her eyes focused on her left hand – a hand that only a week or so ago had worn Ryan's engagement ring, but now it was naked again, waiting for the man she considered to be the love of her life to put his own ring on there. And just thinking about that sent another frisson of excitement shooting through her, making her shiver ever-so-slightly. 'The truth is…' No. She wasn't going to tell him that she and Jim were getting married. She wasn't going to tell him they were seriously thinking of moving to Spain where they could finally make that fresh start they both wanted so badly. It was only fair that her father should be the first to know those little snippets of information, although she was dreading *that* particular conversation. 'The truth is, it was time to face the fact that I can't live without him, Ryan. I can't do it. I pretend to be this strong, independent woman but all I ever wanted was for him to walk back into my life and tell me that he loved me. I never stopped dreaming about that day.'

'And what if *I* can't live without *you*, Amber?'

'Oh, I think we both know that's not true, though, don't we? You're young, you've got this incredible career, you can have any woman you want... Your future's sorted, Ryan. You don't need me.'

'Neither does he.'

Amber said nothing for a second, just looked away briefly again, watching the groundsman on the pitch below crouch down to examine a damaged patch of grass, shaking his head as he ran his hand over it. 'I feel like I can breathe again for the first time in decades,' she said quietly, turning to face Ryan again. 'When he walked out of my life a second time, when I told him to stay away from me... it was as though I'd made a decision, right there and then, to close a part of my life off, the part that belonged to him because, despite everything he'd done to me, I knew I would never stop loving him. And I didn't, I couldn't. So, to have him back, to *really* have him back, it's like – it's like that door I closed almost twenty-one years ago has finally been re-opened. And I feel like I can breathe again.'

Every word she spoke tore into Ryan's heart like someone ripping a blunt dagger right through it. It was a jagged pain, a gut-wrenching, agonising realisation and it was something he never wanted to experience again, so deep were the feelings it created. So maybe he should take a leaf out of her book and close that door that left him open to this hurt and this pain that no one deserved to feel. Maybe he should just go back to the shallow and materialistic lifestyle he'd indulged in before. At least that way he wouldn't have to experience this.

'I really think we could have made a go of things, Amber,' Ryan said, his voice barely above a whisper. 'I was ready to… I would have changed for you. I would have changed anything, for you.'

Amber shook her head again, not enjoying the way she was feeling right now, but what else could she say to him? That she thought they could have made a go of things, too? Maybe, in the heat of all the talk of engagements and celebrity weddings and brand-new, purpose-built mansions she'd got caught up in the whole footballer lifestyle. She'd let herself get carried along on that wave of fantasy because these people didn't live in the real world. *She* did. And now that she was back in it, she could see that, as far as her and Ryan were concerned, they'd never really stood a chance.

'I still love you, Amber. I want you to know that.'

She said nothing. There wasn't anything she *could* say. If he really did still love her – and she wasn't altogether sure that he did – then it wouldn't be fair for her to make him think she still had any feelings left for him, even if she did.

'I care about you, Ryan.' This time she did reach out and take his hand, squeezing it gently before standing up and leaving him alone. Saying anything more wasn't going to benefit the situation. She'd said enough.

Ryan watched her leave, not taking his eyes off her until she was back inside, out of sight. When he'd asked her that question – what if he couldn't live without her? – he hadn't really meant it, at the time. He wasn't the kind of person who needed just one woman; he'd proved that point good and proper, hadn't he? But as he turned back to look out at the now-empty-again stadium, the eerie quiet echoing around his head like a sudden migraine that wanted to make itself known, he suddenly realised he'd never actually spoken a truer word. Ryan Fisher couldn't live without Amber Sullivan. That was the truth.

Chapter Thirty

Amber knocked quietly on the door of her dad's office, slowly pushing it open. She felt sick. The nerves had taken hold on the drive over to his club's training ground and they showed no signs of abating any time soon, but she had to do this. Before the press got hold of everything and took it into their own hands. The last thing she wanted was for him to find out anything else about her and Jim's relationship from a newspaper.

'How are you today?' Freddie Sullivan asked, not looking up from his computer as Amber walked into the office, closing the door behind her.

'I'm… fine. Are *you* okay?'

'Well,' He looked up from his laptop, his eyes fixed firmly on Amber, '… apart from the fact I've just found out my best friend started sleeping with my daughter just days after she turned sixteen, I'm fine. You here for a reason?'

Amber took a deep breath. This really *wasn't* going to be easy. 'Dad, I… I'm sorry. For everything that happened, but it wasn't entirely Jim's fault…'

'No. I know it wasn't,' Freddie said, slipping his glasses onto his nose and turning his attention back to his laptop. 'You were a very grown-up sixteen-year-old, Amber. Possibly a little naive, but I'm sure you knew exactly what you were doing. He was the adult. At the time.' He looked at Amber again. '*He* should have known better. You were still a child.'

She looked out of the window, at the grey sky and the naked trees that shook slightly in the cold wind. It was a dull and depressing day, yet she didn't see that. She felt as though every day was a beautiful day now, and that was because she finally got to wake up next to Jim, and stay there. Nobody had to run off or hide away or leave as soon as the sex was over. She could lie in his arms and make those plans she'd always wanted to make but had never had the chance to, until now. She just had to make her father realise that Jim made her happy. He was the only one who *could* make her happy. She knew that now.

'I thought we'd been through all of this, Dad…'

'Yes, we have. But do you have any idea how it feels for me to look at him now and think about what you two… What you and him… You were sixteen years old, Amber. You were still my baby girl, do you get that? You were my little girl, and *he* was having sex with you.'

She winced slightly at her dad's words, turning away from him as she spoke. 'We're getting married, Dad.' It was the best way to deal with this situation. Just come straight out with it. Skirting around the issue wasn't going to help matters. Her father was never going to be jumping through hoops at the news, so what was the point in trying to make it any easier or drag it out for any longer?

Freddie Sullivan looked up at Amber again, sliding his glasses down to the end of his nose as he did so. 'Married?'

'Me and Jim,' she sighed, leaning back against the window sill. 'We're getting married.'

'You… I didn't even know you and him… You're *together*?'

She nodded. 'I love him, Dad.'

Freddie started searching through his drawers for something. Whether he needed that 'something' or not, Amber couldn't quite work out. 'You don't love him. You just think you do. You were infatuated with him, that's all.' He found whatever he'd been looking for and slammed the drawer shut, looking straight at her. 'It's time to grow up, Amber. You're not sixteen anymore.'

'No, I'm an adult, Dad, and regardless of what you think, I know my own mind, okay? And I know that the only man I've ever loved is Jim…'

'I brought that man into my house,' Freddie interrupted, '… over twenty years ago, and what does he do? He takes my teenage daughter to bed, turns her head, and this is what happens! You're not marrying him, Amber. I won't allow it.'

'I'm sorry?' Amber laughed, folding her arms, unable to believe what she'd just heard. 'You won't *allow* it? I might be missing something here, but when did we become Amish?'

'Don't be flippant, Amber.'

'You can't tell me who I can and can't marry, Dad. And I didn't come here to ask your permission. I came here to tell you what was going on myself before Jim and I go public.'

'Go *public*?'

She nodded, not looking forward to telling him the next bit of news, either. 'We're flying out to Spain in a few days. Jim, he's… he's been offered the manager's job at Malaga Athletico…'

'Whoa, hold on there, rewind a bit.' Freddie got up from behind his desk and walked out in front, leaning back against it. 'Malaga Athletico? But he picked Red Star over them, didn't he?'

'Apparently so.'

Freddie stared at his daughter, waiting for her to finish the story.

'We need a fresh start, Dad. Away from here. Away from the past, from the prying eyes and the press intrusion and… and Ryan.'

Freddie looked down at the ground for a second, scuffing his trainers against the front of his battered old desk. 'Yeah, you sure can pick 'em, sweetheart.' He looked back up at her. 'Why couldn't you and Ronnie have worked something out, huh? You two made such a beautiful couple. Why couldn't you two have stayed together?'

'We were never really in love, Dad. Not with each other. I've never felt that way about Ronnie and he's never felt that way about me, and anyway, stop changing the subject.'

'So, you and Jim are getting married then nipping off to Spain to live happily ever after sipping sangria on the terrace of your millionaire's mansion, is that it?'

'Now who's being flippant? Y'know, I could've just gone ahead with all of this without telling you a thing, given the way you feel about Jim…'

'I'm surprised you didn't. Why change the habit of a lifetime?'

She looked away, over her shoulder, out of the window. 'I didn't ask for any of this, and I certainly didn't want it to turn out this way, but…'

'It did. And I think we all need to start dealing with it like grown-ups, don't you?'

Both Freddie and Amber looked over to where Jim stood in the office doorway, his hands in the pockets of his trademark dark suit, his eyes covered by the aviator shades he always wore. Even in the midst of this less-than-comfortable situation Amber thought he looked hot. He looked handsome and sexy and she couldn't stop the memory of the shower they'd shared that morning from flooding her head, a beautiful shiver crawling up her spine that was making her thighs tingle and her stomach jump about.

'I'd prefer it if you didn't tell me how to handle this situation,' Freddie said, his eyes following Jim as he walked over to Amber, sliding an arm around her waist and leaning in to whisper something in her ear, which did nothing to calm her somersaulting stomach, her thighs tingling even more the second he touched her.

'You okay, honey?' he asked, squeezing her waist, sending what felt like a million tiny electric shocks coursing right through her.

She nodded, but she wasn't okay. Not really. How could she be when her relationship with her dad – the man she loved more than anything in the world – was so strained? They'd always been so close, and now this threatened to tear them apart, and she hated that. But she couldn't – she *wouldn't* walk away from Jim, or let *him* walk away from *her,* not again.

'Both Amber's mother and I trusted you, Jim.'

'We've already been through this, Dad...'

'And we'll go over it again, Amber. My choice.' He looked straight at Jim. 'Her mother and I trusted you. Yet you reeled her in...'

'He didn't "reel" me in, Dad. Jesus...'

'You took my sixteen-year-old little girl and you... I carry that image around in my head all the time now, are you both aware of that? Hmm? This image of my best friend having sex with *my* little girl, and no matter how hard I try, I can't get rid of it.'

Jim squeezed Amber's waist again, looking down at the ground for a few seconds, letting Freddie's words sink in. 'I really am sorry. For the way things turned out.' He looked up at Freddie. 'We didn't exactly go about things the right way.'

'You shouldn't have touched her, Jim.'

'I wanted him to, Dad. You have to believe that. It was *me* who instigated sex, *me* who wanted to sleep with him. It was *me*. And yes, maybe I *was* infatuated with him, at first, I can't deny that. He was this handsome, sexy older man, this famous footballer, and he was best friends with my dad! What sixteen-year-old girl *wouldn't* be infatuated by that? I wanted him from the second I saw him...'

'I don't want to hear this, Amber...'

'From the second I saw him I wanted him. More than I'd ever wanted anything, and I don't care if nobody understands how that feels, because *I* know. And, yes, he hurt me. He hurt me like you wouldn't believe, but all the time I was away at university he was still there, in my head, like some movie playing on repeat that I couldn't switch off. So when I came back home, and he was there, and he was single again... He wanted me, too, and I *know* I should have been strong enough to walk away because if I had then there's a possibility that none of this would have happened, but...' She looked up into Jim's eyes, and it was as though a waterfall of emotions were cascading through her, overwhelming her, almost, '... but I'm glad I was weak. I'm glad.'

'Even when he walked out on you a second time?' Freddie asked, throwing a quick glance in Jim's direction.

'I need him, Dad. And I need *you* to understand that. We're together, and it doesn't matter whether you approve or not, that's the way it is. The way it's going to be. But I love you, so much, and I really don't want this to get in the way of our relationship. I don't want that, Dad.'

Amber felt hot tears sting the back of her eyes, looking at Jim in the hope that would stop them from falling, but all it did was make them escape faster.

Jim leaned forward, kissing her mouth, his thumb gently wiping the tears from her cheek.

'I can't pretend I'm happy about this,' Freddie sighed, watching his daughter in the arms of his best friend. A man he'd once trusted. A man who'd betrayed that trust. But a man who, quite obviously, loved Amber. And *she* loved *him*. So who was he to stand in the way of her happiness? 'But I guess I've got no choice. Have I?'

Jim looked over at Freddie, his arm still tight around Amber's waist. 'I've loved her for over twenty years, Freddie.'

'Well, you had a bloody funny way of showing it for most of them, Jim.'

'I know. I know I did, but… Look, maybe it's time to stop raking over the past and move forward. We can't change anything that happened back then, but we *can* make sure the future is a good one. And all I want to do is make Amber happy. That's all I've ever wanted. And now I've finally got the chance to do that.'

Freddie looked from one of them to the other, shaking his head, his arms still folded against him in a slightly disapproving manner. 'The pair of you should have had your heads banged together a long time ago,' he sighed. 'So, Amber tells me you're flying out to Spain to look into the manager's job at Malaga Athletico. You're taking my little girl away from me, then?'

'Nothing's set in stone,' Jim replied, silencing his phone as it rang from within the confines of his jacket pocket. 'I haven't even spoken to the Red Star board yet, and I don't intend to until I've checked things out over there. But I think Amber and I… I think we need a new start. Wherever that turns out to be.'

'There's a lot to talk about. A lot to sort out,' Amber smiled, directing her words to her father, but looking at Jim when she spoke. 'All I know is that, somehow, we'll work this out. And then I might finally get that happy-ever-after I always dreamed about.'

'Shit!' Ryan said, slamming the empty glass back down on the table, even though most of it had ended up down the front of his shirt rather than in his mouth. 'Get another round in, Gaz, come on! Speed it up a bit, mate. I'm dying of thirst over here!'

'You need to calm him down,' Debbie hissed at Gary as he got another round of drinks in at the casino bar. 'He's on a hiding to nothing over there. Have you seen the state of him?'

'What do you want me to do, Debs? Carry him home?'

'If that's what it takes.'

'Don't be so fucking stupid. What are you still doing here, anyway? I thought you were meeting the girls at ten-thirty?'

'I am. I'm just not sure I should leave you alone, I mean, we've been here before, haven't we?'

'Jesus, Debbie, I think I can handle a pissed Ryan Fisher. And this is tame compared to some of the states he's been in.'

'You think so? He's not safe to be left on his own, Gary.'

'He's not *on* his own, though, is he?' Gary said, indicating the group of girls who'd draped themselves over Ryan in the corner booth they were sitting in.

'That's not what I meant. Just make sure he doesn't do anything stupid, okay?'

'I'm his best mate, Debs, not his frigging babysitter.'

She stood up on tiptoe, quickly kissing his cheek. 'Get him home in one piece, that's all I'm asking you to do. The last thing he needs is Jim Allen on his back, given the circumstances.'

'Gary! You got those drinks yet, mate?' Ryan yelled over as a young, blonde girl climbed deftly onto his lap and proceeded to stick her tongue down his throat, silencing him immediately. Ryan responded without missing a beat, circling her waist with one arm while his free hand plunged underneath her tight-fitting top, finding her left breast straightaway and squeezing it to within an inch of its life. 'Jesus, you are one horny bitch,' he groaned, feeling his hard-on push against the denim of his ridiculously expensive jeans.

'I need a pee,' the girl moaned, reluctantly climbing off his knee.

'Can I watch?' Ryan grinned, making a move to get up and follow her, until Gary put a hand on his shoulder, pushing him back down.

'Sit down and shut up, you dick,' Gary said, handing him another shot of vodka. He was beginning to wonder if Debbie was right. Maybe home was the best place for Ryan to be. He was getting steadily more out of control as the night wore on.

'Who *you* calling a dick?' Ryan slurred.

'Jesus. You really need to slow it down, mate. You're gonna be so fucked up in the morning, and we've got training, remember? Plus, Colin said the boss was probably gonna be around, too…' He stopped talking, well aware that any mention of Jim Allen was like lighting the blue touchpaper at the minute. And now was no exception.

'Fuck Jim Allen,' Ryan said, knocking back the shot and slamming the empty glass down next to the others he'd already put away.

'Yeah, real grown-up that, Ryan.'

Ryan glared at his friend. He was bored of sitting here, talking crap with him and being pawed at by these nameless, but ultimately very pretty women. Although he'd probably come back to them later. No doubt The Goldman would be getting the pleasure of his company in a little while. Mind you, he could quite as easily take a few of them back home with him, couldn't he? Now that there was no girlfriend there to nag him. Fuck Amber, too. He didn't need her. He needed this – he needed fun. And he was having plenty of that right here.

'I should get you home,' Gary sighed, taking Ryan's arm.

'Fuck off!' Ryan protested, shaking Gary off and standing up. 'I don't need looking after, alright?'

'Yeah, well, I think you do,' Gary said, standing up, too.

'Fuck off, Gary!'

'Is that the sum total of your vocabulary tonight, Ryan? Because you're starting to sound like some pissed idiot who's spoiling for a fight. Is that what you want?'

'All I want is to be left alone,' Ryan hissed. 'Is that alright with you?'

'Do you know what? It's fine with me. I'm done here. You go ahead and press that self-destruct button, because that's where you're heading, Ryan. This – this isn't helping. Let me know when you've sorted your fucking head out, okay?'

Ryan watched Gary walk away, grabbing the chair behind him to steady himself as he felt his knees give way slightly. Shit! He needed another drink.

'Ryan! There you are! Hannah said she'd seen you in here tonight.'

Ryan turned round to see a tall, dark-haired woman standing there. She was wearing a very short, very tight black dress and heels that made her legs look unbelievably long. If he squinted, she looked a bit like Penelope Cruz – with a Geordie accent.

'Do you remember me?' she asked, sitting down and pulling him down next to her, her leg touching his, her hand on his shoulder. 'Hannah and I were at a party down in London a few months ago, for one of your ex-teammates' birthdays. There were a lot of us there, I know, but I thought you might remember me because I was the one who danced naked on the table in your VIP area.'

Ryan grinned. Even in his drunken state he'd find it hard to forget that night. One hell of a party then some of the best sex he'd ever experienced. And the blowjob he'd received from this woman sitting beside him wasn't one he'd forget in a hurry.

489

'Yeah. I remember you,' he smirked, sliding his hand up and under the hem of her dress, and it didn't have far to go before it found just what it was looking for. 'Do you do repeat performances?'

Chapter Thirty-One

'I take it that rule about no sex on a match day doesn't apply to the manager, then?' Amber smiled, stretching out in what had to be one of the most comfortable hotel beds she'd ever slept in.

Even though today was a home game for Newcastle Red Star, Jim still kept to his usual routine of making the squad stay in a local hotel the night before, just to keep an eye on them – and some, more than others, *needed* keeping an eye on. But he didn't want to spend a night away from Amber any more than she wanted to be away from him right now, so she'd come with him to the hotel. And they'd spent the night breaking one rule in particular he imposed upon his players, in every possible way they could.

Jim propped himself up on one elbow and smiled at her. 'I think that rule was blown out of the water last night, baby, don't you?'

She kissed him slowly, loving the taste of him, the way his lips moved against hers. Loving the way he talked to her, the sound of his voice, the way he said her name, that accent of his so different to anything you heard on the streets of her native North-East England. All those years in Britain and Europe and he'd never lost that accent, that soft American twang that she found so unbelievably sexy.

'I don't want to get you into any kind of trouble, Jim.'

'Hey, who's the boss around here, huh?' he said, that smile of his sending her stomach somersaulting. 'Anyway, everyone knows now, don't they? About you and me.'

Amber turned to face him, running her fingers lightly over his shoulder, down over his toned arm. 'I hate being the centre of attention. This whole media circus that's following us around right now…'

'Says the TV sports reporter.'

'That's different,' she smiled, sliding the covers down over his hip, exposing more of his pretty-much-perfect body, for a man in his late forties. 'I work on local television. The celebrity status tag doesn't really count, does it? And anyway, I've always tried to keep a low profile. Until now.'

He gently pushed a strand of hair away from her eyes, staring into them as he did so. It reminded Amber of the very first time they'd made love, over two decades ago. The way he'd looked at her then was the same way he was looking at her now. Back then she'd wanted him like she'd never wanted anyone or anything before. She wanted him more than that now.

'And it's only going to get worse when they find out we're getting married. Why do you have to be such a high-profile manager?' she groaned, rolling over onto her back.

'Well, if it makes you happier I could seek out a nice little third division club to take charge of. Hmm? Does that sound like a better option?'

She turned her head and smiled at him, sticking her tongue out. 'You're funny. And you know what I mean.' She stared up at the ceiling, flinging one arm up above her head. 'All my life I've tried to avoid relationships with footballers, and especially with the extremely famous ones, but it was all a complete waste of time, wasn't it?' She looked at him again. 'Because I was always destined to *be* with one. To be with *you*. Why did we waste so much time, Jim? All those years…'

He trailed his fingers across her stomach, pushing the covers down so he could see her body in all its beautiful nakedness. 'We can't turn the clock back, Amber. But we *can* move things forward.'

She closed her eyes as his fingers slid between her legs, giving her no choice but to open them. Not that she'd intended to put up any kind of a fight. 'That sounds like a plan to me,' she groaned, stretching out again as he touched her, played with her, like he'd done so many times before, but now it was different. Now she had him for keeps. No more secrets. Well, apart from their engagement, and their possible move to Spain.

She bit down on her lip as she felt him move between her legs, felt his mouth take over where his fingers had left off and she really had to curb the rising feelings inside her – she was so close to just shouting out loud. His tongue was warm and soft against her, darting in and out of places she'd only ever really wanted him to see, taking her to that wonderful heaven she'd only ever really wanted to visit with him. He was driving her crazy!

Gripping the pillows tight, she turned her head to one side, biting down harder on her lip, but she couldn't stop a moan of pure pleasure from escaping as he pushed her legs wider apart, going in harder, giving her no option now but to give in to what he was about to give her – the most incredible orgasm she'd ever experienced at eight o'clock in the morning. It hit her like a tidal wave, crashing over her in a huge spasm of ecstasy that flooded every inch of her, her skin tingling as though it was on fire. That beautiful pain, that all-consuming, breath-taking feeling of wanting to feel nothing but this man inside her. She should have fought for him twenty years ago. She should never have let him go. He may have walked away from her, but she could have stopped him. If she'd really wanted to. But back then things had been so much more complicated. Were they really any less so now?

She kept her eyes closed as she heard him get off the bed, go into the bathroom. Jim Allen – the man who'd made her fall in love with him. The man who'd taken over her life. The man she was finally going to marry.

She couldn't help smiling at the thought of becoming Mrs. Jim

Allen, the relentless round of stomach flips making her feel like that star-struck teenager all over again, that young and slightly naive girl who'd fallen for the American accent and the footballer's legs and a face so unbelievably handsome it was no wonder he'd been the pin-up of the football world for a long, long time. Even now, with his slightly greying hair and the faint lines around those mesmerising green eyes of his, he was still so incredibly handsome. He was still lusted after by many, and she had no doubt that he'd made the most of all of that in the time he'd spent out of her life, while she'd felt no desire to be in any kind of relationship during those years. Because of him? If she couldn't have *him* then nobody else would do? She'd always known that was the reason, deep down. It had only been in the past few weeks that she could finally admit it was true.

'My beautiful, northern-English angel,' Jim whispered, sliding back into bed beside her, his hand gently stroking the curve of her waist. 'I love you so much, Amber. And I'm never gonna get tired of telling you that. Ever.'

She smiled again, reaching out to touch his rough chin, hoping, even though it was a match day and Jim Allen always liked to look immaculate on a match day, that he wouldn't shave. She liked the roughness of his stubble, loved the way it had felt when he'd been down between her legs. 'I can't wait to start my life with you,' she whispered, her skin tingling once again as he pulled her close, skin touching skin, the warmth of his naked body giving her a kind of inner peace she'd never, ever felt before. Was *this* what it was really like to be in love?

'Then let's do this sooner rather than later, what do you think? Just you and me, away from everyone else. We get married, and we tell no one. That way nobody can stop us, nobody can tell us this isn't right; nobody can disapprove or make us feel guilty for what we're doing – for what we've done.'

'Get married…'

'Next week,' he whispered, his mouth almost touching hers as he

494

spoke. 'Somewhere quiet, somewhere that will respect our privacy until *we* see fit to let people know we're finally Mr. and Mrs. Allen.'

Just hearing him say those words – Mr. and Mrs. Allen – sent a shiver of seismic proportions down Amber's spine, a tingle of excited anticipation she'd never felt before. 'Would we… would we not be rushing into things, Jim?'

He smiled, and that was all it took to knock those fleeting doubts right off the radar. 'Rushing into things? Baby, this has been twenty-one years in the making, me and you. We should be planning a wedding anniversary well into double figures by now, not the ceremony itself.'

'Yeah,' she smiled back, sliding her fingers between his, his hand clutching hers tightly. 'You're right. But – what about my dad?'

'Maybe one day, when everyone's used to the idea that we're together and there's nothing anyone can do to change that, we can have the whole wedding blessing thing. Y'know, the church, big reception, Freddie walking you up the aisle – but nobody will be able to change the fact that me and you, we're married. We'll give them all a day to celebrate with us, but nobody will be able to change what we've already done.'

'More secrets,' she whispered, letting go of his hand, closing her eyes as he touched her cheek, running his fingers over it so lightly it sent another shiver right through her.

'Not for long, baby,' he said quietly, moving in to kiss her long and slow. 'Not for long.'

She was lost in him again, every emotion she'd ever felt for this man colliding inside her until she was nothing but one big, emotional wreck, too in love to disagree with anything he was saying, and knowing he was right, anyway. Okay, her father had reluctantly agreed to accept the fact that her and Jim were together now, but she knew all too well that he would still try and talk her out of marrying him. Somehow. This way he wouldn't get the chance. And yes, she'd be betraying him again and that wasn't something that made her feel entirely comfortable, but she would do anything now to keep Jim by her side. She would do anything to make sure she never lost him again.

'Next week?' she smiled, staring into those beautiful green eyes of his.

'Next week,' he grinned. 'You up for that, gorgeous?'

'Oh, you bet I am, handsome. You bet I am.'

Ryan pulled the earphones he was wearing off his head and threw them down on the table that separated him from Gary on the coach that was taking them on the short journey from the hotel they'd been staying in to Tynebridge for that afternoon's match against another of the league's biggest northern clubs.

'Hangover kicked in, has it?' Gary asked, not looking up from the magazine he was reading.

Ryan ignored him and stared out of the window instead, watching as the frosty landscape whipped past them, passing cars with Red Star scarves sticking out of their windows, quite obviously on their way to the match. Gary wasn't wrong, though. His head was pounding. It felt like someone was holding a rave in there. Jim Allen might think that sticking them all in a hotel made them immune to any of the excesses forbidden on the night before a match, but he was deluded if he believed they all behaved themselves. Until they actually started checking their bags, the temptation to smuggle in drink, laptops and anything else designed to distract them from the focus of their game was always going to be there. Some of the lads were always going to be one step ahead. And none more so than Ryan. He'd brought the lot in last night – drink, a line or two of coke, his iPad. And he'd proceeded to spend the night drinking, getting high and gambling away three weeks' worth of wages in an online casino. He'd had a blast! He'd forgotten the kick he got from money being no object, from being able to pick a number, stick £1,000 on one of two colours and not give a fuck whether it came up or not. That was the mood he was in right now – he couldn't give a fuck. About anything.

'You're gonna regret this one day,' Gary continued, still refusing to look up from his magazine.

'When I want your opinion, I'll ask for it,' Ryan muttered, smiling down at a pretty brunette in a car beside them as the coach stopped at traffic lights.

Gary finally threw the magazine down and leaned forward, resting his elbows on the table. 'Y'know, I used to think *I* was the bigger prick around here, until *you* started to piss about.'

Ryan turned his head slowly to look at his friend. 'I'm not "pissing about" as you put it. I'm living my life the way *I* want to fucking live it. You got that?'

'I'm finished trying to help you, Ryan. I'm fed up of it. You need to grow up and deal with the fact that, just because you're some big-shot footballer who can usually have anything he wants, there are some things even ridiculous amounts of money can't buy.'

'And what the fuck's *that* supposed to mean?' Ryan asked, narrowing his eyes slightly.

'Oh, I think you know what I mean,' Gary replied, picking his magazine back up and opening it up at a random page.

'Fuck!'

'You got something on your mind?' Jim Allen asked, stopping by Ryan's seat as he made his way along the narrow aisle of the coach.

Ryan stared out of the window again, not in the mood for small talk with his manager.

'You gonna answer me, Fisher?' Jim carried on, leaning back against the seat opposite, folding his arms. And still Ryan said nothing. 'Have it your way,' Jim sighed as the coach turned into Tynebridge, pulling up outside the main entrance. 'But I'll tell you one thing, son – you'd better make sure you've brought a cushion this afternoon.'

Ryan turned to look at him, frowning. 'Huh?'

'You're on the bench, Fisher. And the next time you turn up on a match day looking like crap and smelling of alcohol you can consider yourself suspended.'

'It's going okay, then? The reconciliation?' Amber asked Ronnie as they sat in the Players' Lounge, grabbing five minutes of peace before the match started. Ronnie was commentating on the game for a satellite sports channel and she was doing a piece for News North East, so they were both there working, but it was good to catch up again. A lot had happened since they'd last seen each other.

'Yeah,' Ronnie smiled, and Amber couldn't help but feel incredibly happy for him. She'd had her reservations when she'd heard he'd taken Karen back, but, given her own circumstances, who was she to tell someone who they could or couldn't love? Relationships were a complicated thing at the best of times. People had to make their own decisions. Their own mistakes. She just hoped that, for both her and Ronnie, those mistakes had already been made, never to happen again. 'Yeah, it's going great. Y'know, maybe splitting up was the best thing that could have happened.'

'Really? How do you work that one out?' Amber asked, looking around the room to see if she recognised anyone, smiling at Debbie as she walked in.

'Because it made us *both* realise how much we really love each other,' Ronnie replied.

'Well, that's good. Isn't it?' Amber went on, slightly distracted by a text from Kevin asking where she was, followed by another one from Jim telling her to meet him in his office.

'On a match day? Not half an hour before kick-off?' Ronnie smirked, arching an eyebrow as he read Jim's text over her shoulder. 'Now that *really* doesn't sound like the Premiership's most professional manager. Is he dropping his guard a little? And what are *you* gonna be dropping when you see him, eh?'

Amber looked at him. 'Ronnie! That's private.'

'Nothing of yours is private anymore, kiddo. You're living your life in the sporting spotlight now.'

'Yeah, thanks for reminding me. And anyway, he only said to meet him in his office. It didn't say come and indulge in a seedy, pre-match shag up against his office wall while he finalises the team sheets.'

'Yeah, but you want it to be that, don't you?' Ronnie grinned.

'Shut up!' she laughed, hitting him on the arm with her phone. 'Jesus, Ronnie, you sound like a twelve-year-old. Is this what being in love does to you?'

'Yeah. And what does it do to *you*?'

'Ah, now, you see, *that* would be telling,' she smiled, getting up and running her fingers through her loose, tousled hair. 'See you later.' She threw him a wink and another smile and left the Players' Lounge, hoping she wouldn't bump into Kevin on her way to Jim's office. Maybe she wasn't the only one letting her professionalism slip slightly, but she knew Kevin would be okay. She was giving him more newsworthy stories for the programme than he'd had in years, so he was her best friend at the minute. He was still going to freak when he realised she'd married Jim by the time Newcastle Red Star's away game next weekend at Wigan came round.

But it wasn't Kevin she had to be worried about bumping into. 'Jesus, Ryan, you look like shit,' she said, realising there was no way of avoiding him now, seeing as the dressing room was directly opposite the manager's office. And, to be honest, she was slightly shocked at the state of him. To say he looked rough was an understatement.

'Yeah. Thanks for that. You on your way to see *him*?' He indicated Jim's office door with his head, aware that he probably sounded like some wounded boyfriend who was still sulking over the fact he'd been dumped for someone else, but, to all intents and purposes, that's exactly what he was. And he didn't care, anyway.

'Are you not well?' She was curious as to why he looked so rough. He couldn't have been out drinking, not when they'd all been confined to barracks, so to speak. But then, this *was* Ryan Fisher they were talking about here. Unreliable, didn't-give-a-fuck Ryan Fisher. 'Were you drinking last night?' she asked, leaning back against the wall and folding her arms.

'Who are you? My mother?'

'What are you playing at, Ryan? Why are you doing this to yourself?'

'What do *you* care?'

'You sound like a petulant teenager now. Just because we're not sleeping together anymore doesn't mean I suddenly stop caring about you. Don't throw it all away just because you can't handle a situation that isn't going to change. You're bigger than that.'

'Something going on here?' Jim asked, opening his office door and leaning against the doorpost, his eyes fixed firmly on Ryan. 'You going somewhere, Fisher?'

Ryan just threw him a look before shuffling back inside the dressing room.

Amber watched him go, a feeling in the pit of her stomach she couldn't describe. He looked truly awful, but wasn't he bringing it all on himself? She hadn't asked him to do what he'd done, to sleep with two women in *their* bed, but, in reality, hadn't it only brought forward a situation that had always been on the cards anyway?

'He's dangerously close to facing disciplinary action,' Jim said, noticing the look in Amber's eyes as she watched Ryan head back into the dressing room.

Amber swung round to look at Jim. 'Disciplinary action? Why?'

'Drinking the night before a match, turning up late for training, bad attitude… Do you want me to go on? Amber, honey, he's his own worst enemy. The kid needs to learn how to grow up and channel that talent he was born with, before it's too late. He's one of this generation's greatest players, no doubt about that, but if he carries on the way he is…' Jim pushed a hand through his hair, sighing. 'Anyway, I don't want to talk about him. Come on, come inside.'

She looked over at the dressing room again, listening as laughter and the sound of Ryan's voice filtered out into the corridor. He'd be okay. She was sure of it. But maybe she should call Max, give him the lowdown on Ryan's behaviour. Just to be on the safe side.

'Amber? Honey?'

500

She turned her attention back to Jim, smiling as she followed him into his office. 'So, what did you want to see me for?' she asked, watching as he closed the door behind him, holding out his hand. She took it, and in one swift movement he'd swung her round and pushed her back against the closed door, kissing her hard. She responded immediately. How could she not? He wasn't giving her that much choice.

'I just want to see you,' he smiled, slowly unfastening another button on her shirt, running his fingers lightly over her cleavage, drawing a small and quiet moan from her slightly parted lips. 'You okay with that?'

She nodded, closing her eyes as he bent his head to gently kiss her now-heaving breasts. It wasn't even kick-off on a Saturday afternoon and already they'd had sex more times today than she cared to remember. It was like they were desperately trying to make up for all those years they hadn't been together, all those chances to be this close that had gone by the wayside. Making up for all the wasted opportunities they'd never taken.

She buried her fingers in his dark, slightly greying hair as he freed her breasts from the confines of her fuchsia-pink bra, his mouth covering first one, then the other. She could feel him hard against her thigh and in just seconds he'd made her desperate to feel him inside her all over again, despite the fact it had been just a matter of hours since they'd last made love. That had been a slow and languid affair, whereas this one was going to, quite obviously, be nothing more than a quick fuck up against the wall. So, yeah, Ronnie had been right. It *was* what she wanted. More than anything. Even though she was supposed to be at work. That just made it all the more exciting.

With expert fingers, Jim slowly unzipped her jeans, pushing them down far enough to give him the room he needed to push into her, so fast and hard it took Amber's breath away. And she couldn't help but shout out loud, quickly biting down on her lip to silence herself. It was quite possible people knew what they were doing, anyway, but why give them any proof?

It was over in minutes, a satisfying rush of muffled moans and banging hips. Anything but romantic, but this wasn't exactly the place for romance. He'd needed her, she'd needed him, job done.

Amber quickly pulled herself together, running her fingers through her hair and shaking it out, hoping she didn't look too much like someone who'd just indulged in a quick one up against a closed office door with the hottest manager in football. She watched him as he tucked his white shirt back into his suit pants, positioning his collar so it fell just so, slightly open, and always no tie. He never wore a tie, not on match days. White shirt, dark suit – that was his uniform. And it suited him. As a player he'd always been a bit of a fashion icon, always immaculately turned out, the one that men all over the world wanted to follow. And he was no different as a manager. He was still as sexy-as-hell and a man who was both fancied and admired in equal measures by both sexes – men wanted to be him, women wanted to do him.

He turned round and looked at her, smiling that smile, and it was all Amber could do to keep those butterflies in her tummy from escaping again. Twenty-one years later and still he did that to her. 'You make me feel like the sexiest woman alive,' she smiled, walking over to him and sliding her arms around his neck.

'Well, I think you *are* the sexiest woman alive,' Jim whispered, his mouth close to her ear, the smell of his expensive aftershave overwhelming her senses.

'You going to make me feel like this for the rest of my life?' she asked quietly, looking up into his eyes as what felt like a million different, clashing emotions crowded her head.

'I'm certainly going to try,' he smiled, pulling her against him. 'Next Thursday. 1p.m. North Shields. The register office down by the river. That's where I need you to be, if you want to be my wife.'

She couldn't stop the smile that was already on her face from growing wider. 'Thursday?'

'Thursday,' he smiled back, his fingers sliding slowly up and under her shirt.

'Five days away... I'm not sure I can wait that long, Mr. Allen.'

'And I know a honeymoon in Wigan doesn't exactly sound like the most romantic thing in the world, but... it's the away fixture the following Saturday, and I'd love to be travelling to that game knowing you're finally mine.'

Was this really happening? Was she really standing here, in the arms of the only man she'd ever truly loved, just days away from becoming his wife? She was just days away from Jim Allen becoming her husband. If she thought about it for too long it was possible she might stop breathing. She hadn't felt this way since – well, since that first time with Jim, when he'd taken her virginity, and made her fall in love with him in a way that epitomised 'forever'.

'Thursday it is then,' she whispered, her mouth touching his as she spoke, her heart pounding so fast it was beginning to make her feel breathless. 'I love you so much, Jim. Jesus, I love you so fucking much.'

'Hey, come on,' he smiled, gently brushing away tears that had started to fall from her eyes. Tears of relief, of happiness. Of guilt? Maybe. But the relief and the happiness overtook that last emotion – for now. 'I know we took one hell of a long route to get here, but we're there now. Aren't we?'

She nodded, looking up at the ceiling for a second as she breathed out slowly, getting rid of the tears before she faced the real world back outside. 'I just can't get my head around the fact I'm...' She looked at him, the smile reappearing. 'It's a bit overwhelming, that's all. Everything's happening so fast.'

He raised an eyebrow. 'Twenty-one years, Amber. That ain't fast, honey.'

'You know what I mean,' she smiled.

He gently rubbed the small of her back, kissing her mouth ever so lightly. 'I love you, too, baby. I've only ever loved *you*...'

Voices outside calling for Jim broke the spell they'd both been under and he let go of her, grabbing his suit jacket and pushing a hand through his hair.

'I guess I'd better go to work, huh?'

'Yeah,' Amber smiled, straightening the collar of his jacket and kissing him quickly one last time before they left the privacy of his office. 'Me too.'

'I'll see you on the other side, then,' he winked, finally opening that door, the sound of a packed stadium on match day taking over the small and quiet world they'd been locked inside for a few blissful minutes.

She nodded, watching him walk the short distance across the corridor into the dressing room. The man of her dreams. The love of her life. Jim Allen.

'Is he okay?' Amber asked Debbie as they sat in the Main Stand at Tynebridge, watching the game. Amber hadn't wanted to sit in the press seats – mainly because she knew she'd just be grilled the whole time by Kevin, trying to get snippets of information out of her. She'd wanted to sit with her friend. But even that wasn't proving to be hassle-free, with comments from the crowd being thrown at her every so often, which she ignored. Although the temptation to shout a smart reply back to the less polite ones was almost too much to resist. Were they really *that* interested in what it was like to sleep with Red Star's manager? 'Ryan, I mean. Only, I saw him before, and he looked terrible. So I can kind of understand why Jim's put him on the bench this afternoon.'

'You don't think it's out of spite this time, then?' Debbie asked, turning her attention away from the action on the pitch to look at Amber.

Amber shook her head. 'Not this time. No.' Amber looked down at the touchline where Jim was shouting something at Gary, pointing in a slightly agitated manner at a fellow player he *should* have passed the ball to, a mistake which had cost them a sitter of a goal. 'I hope all of this isn't affecting Gary.'

'Gary's fine,' Debbie snorted, pulling her hat down further over her ears to shield out the biting January cold. 'And Ryan will be, too. He just needs a bit longer than most to get his head around things. For an intelligent guy, he can be a real child at times.'

Amber looked at Debbie, a touch surprised by her tone. 'Is something going on? Debbie, if he's drifting back into bad habits…'

'He's fine,' Debbie sighed. Amber raised both eyebrows in question. 'Okay. Okay, he's gone a bit – off the rails lately…'

'Off the rails? How? Is he drinking, gambling…?'

'Being a first-rate prick? Yeah, that just about sums it up. But he's okay, Amber. Really.'

'Really?'

'Really,' Debbie smiled, and Amber relaxed. Surely he'd learnt from his mistakes by now. 'We're keeping an eye on him, don't worry. And it's not like he's short of company to keep him occupied.'

Amber didn't really want to know about that side of things. It was that which had sealed the fate of their relationship, after all – his inability to leave the wannabe WAGs alone.

'Anyway,' Debbie went on, her tone of voice now signalling her recognition of a need to change the subject. 'Forget the trashy wannabes…' It was almost as if she'd read Amber's mind, '… you're Queen WAG now, chick. You're with the man *every* woman who loves football – and even those that don't – wants to fuck senseless. Jesus, even *I've* fantasised about Jim Allen when there's only been me and my trusty vibrator around.'

Amber looked at Debbie, a smile creeping across her lips.

'Is he any good?' Debbie asked, grinning widely as she shoved her hands deeper into the pockets of her bright pink padded jacket.

'Yeah,' Amber laughed, feeling like she was sitting in the school cloakroom having one of those conversations you had when you'd just discovered boys. 'He's alright.'

'Alright?' Debbie arched an eyebrow. 'Jesus, Amber, don't give away *too* many details, will you?' Debbie sat forward, on a roll now. 'Come on. Tell me *some*thing, chick. Like… I mean, for a man of his age…'

'He's forty-eight, Debbie. That's all.'

'Yeah, I know, but… the first time you had sex with him he was, how old?'

'Twenty-seven.'

'Two decades ago. And, let's face it, most men's bodies would have changed a bit over that period of time. Was he fit back then?'

'God, yes! You've seen photos of him when he was a Red Star player – he was like a walking dream, Debs. Six feet tall, dark hair, green eyes, not to mention that low, soft, sexy American accent of his.'

Debbie raised an eyebrow again. 'Jeez, you've got it bad, girl! Still feel the same way about him now? Or is that probably one of the most stupid and obvious questions I could ask you?'

Amber smiled, looking down at the touchline again as Jim stood in front of the dugout next to Colin, watching the game, his hands in the pockets of his immaculately-cut suit as he exchanged words with his coach. 'It's different now,' she said quietly, part of her wanting to confide in Debbie about the wedding next week, but another part of her knowing it really was for the best to keep it quiet.

'Different?' Debbie asked, pulling her scarf up over her chin. 'How? Is it not all hot and heavy anymore, then?'

'Jesus, Debbie…' Amber laughed, craning her neck as Jim disappeared from view for a second, reappearing from the dugout with Ryan. 'If you must know, it's hotter and heavier, okay? And can we stop this conversation right now, please? I'm gonna have to talk to him on camera at the end of this game and it's gonna be bad enough having all eyes watching us without me thinking about him naked and sexy-as-hell…'

'*Now* you're talking, chick,' Debbie grinned. 'So, he's still as sexy now as he was back then?'

'Sexier,' Amber smiled, watching as Ryan waited for the

substitution to take place, shaking hands with the player whose place he was taking before running out onto the pitch to a barrage of cheers and applause. Amber felt her stomach dip. Why did he suddenly feel like a stranger when only a few weeks ago they'd been closer than any two people could be? It felt odd. Like their entire relationship had never really happened.

'You okay, babe?' Debbie asked, gently squeezing Amber's arm.

'Yeah,' Amber sighed, sitting back in the red plastic seat. 'I'm fine.' He'd lied to her. He'd made her think he'd gotten so low that the only way out was to harm himself, just so she would come back to him. That wasn't right. But that was the kind of man Ryan Fisher was – the kind of man who thought he could have anything or anyone he wanted, no matter what it took to get it. He had a lot more growing up to do. It would never have worked. Never.

'It's been a bit of a roller-coaster few months, huh?' Debbie smiled.

'You could say that,' Amber said, watching as Ryan threw himself straight into the game, taking the ball from an opposing player with so much ease he made it look as though it was the simplest thing in the world to do as he ran with it towards the opposition goal. He may have looked like crap, but he was playing like the pro he was.

'He really *will* be okay, Amber,' Debbie went on, once again almost reading her mind. 'You've got to concentrate on your own future now. You and Jim. You lucky cow!'

Amber looked at her and smiled. A big, almost smug smile. Her and Jim. How good did that sound?

'Why the fuck are you going into the Players' Lounge?' Gary groaned, pulling Ryan away from the door as they made their way out of Tynebridge, ready for a night on the town to celebrate yet another Red Star victory. They were hurtling towards the top of the league table now, and spirits in the club were high. But the only spirits Ryan was concerned with right now were the ones that came out of a bottle. 'You know she's gonna be in there.'

'And you think that's why I'm going in there, do you?'

'I don't *think* anything, mate. I *know*.'

'You know fuck all. Let go of my frigging arm, will you?'

'You go in there and all it's gonna do is kill your mood for tonight. You'll end up being a miserable sod, moping over your beer all night and shagging the first blonde that gives you the slightest hint of interest.'

'And that's a bad thing?'

'The moping into your beer all night bit is, yeah. If I wanted *that* for company I'd go out with Andy Pearson. His divorce has just come through and I've never seen such a miserable bastard in all me life. Present company excepted, of course.'

'Yeah, you're a funny bastard, Gary. I'm splitting me sides here. Look, if I could just talk to her… I saw her before the match and I was, well, less than polite, I suppose…'

'You charmer.'

'Fuck off. But playing out there this afternoon, even if it *was* only for twenty minutes, it's cleared my head, y'know? Made me realise none of this is her fault. It's *me* who needs to sort myself out, get a grip…'

'You can get a grip with anything you want later on, so let's shift it, okay? The sooner we get home, get changed and grab some cash, the sooner we can get out and start celebrating.'

'Don't you see, though, Gary? I don't *want* to "get a grip", as you so eloquently put it, with anything or anyone else. I want Amber.'

'Well, unless you've been dropped on your head and suffered a bout of amnesia, you might have noticed that she is completely loved up with our great leader. Did you not hear him fucking her just before kick-off? Up against the office door I reckoned, it had to be. Must have been slamming into her so hard, the noise they were making…'

'Jesus Christ, Gary. Shut the fuck up, alright? I don't want to hear it.'

'Well maybe it's the only way you're going to realise that you can't have her, mate. And I don't think you ever could. It was never gonna happen, you and her. Not with him on the scene. And knowing their past history… You're gonna have to get used to it, Ryan, or let it destroy you. Your choice.'

Ryan looked at Gary for a few seconds, still not fully taking in what he was saying. Jim Allen had hurt her, in the past. Twice. He'd hurt her. And so had he, he knew that. He wasn't stupid. But Jim – he'd affected the way she'd lived her life for over twenty years. She didn't need him. 'Yeah,' Ryan said, slowly pushing open the door of the Players' Lounge. 'It's my choice.'

'Whatever,' Gary sighed, hoisting his bag up onto his shoulder. 'I'll see you later.'

The Players' Lounge was busy with the usual post-match buzz, almost full to the rafters with people catching up with each other, players' wives and girlfriends chatting away, making plans for the next girls' night out. Everybody seemed oblivious to his entrance, which he was glad of, for once. It wasn't often that Ryan Fisher managed to stay inconspicuous, mainly because he usually loved to be the centre of attention. But this afternoon he was quite happy to blend into the shadows.

Looking around, he finally saw her, at the other end of the room, leaning back against the wall. Jim Allen was standing next to her, one arm resting on the wall beside her so he could lean in close. Too close. Although they weren't exactly doing anything they shouldn't. They were just talking. But the way she was looking at him, the way her eyes never left his; the way his hand would gently touch her arm as he spoke to her – it was enough to make Ryan feel sick. He'd had that, and he'd blown it, because he couldn't keep his dick in his pants. Yeah, the whole situation was worse than it should have been because the man who'd stepped into his shoes was his boss – or had Ryan really stepped into *Jim's* shoes? Maybe everyone was right. Maybe she always was going to go back to Jim at some point, but how did they really know that? How could anyone really know that for sure? They'd been so good together, him and Amber. He'd brought her out of her shell, torn down those icy barriers she'd built around herself, and when they'd made love, Jesus, she could do things to him that he'd never forget. The way she'd made him feel was something he wasn't sure he'd ever be able to recreate with anyone else, least of all the legions of beautiful but ultimately second-best women that wanted to be with him.

He continued to watch Jim and Amber talk, watched as Jim took a quick look around the room, obviously checking to see if anybody was taking any notice of them. And he must have assumed they weren't because he then turned back to Amber and kissed her, his lips brushing over hers so quickly it was almost a blink-and-you'd-miss-it kiss, but it was long enough to tear into Ryan's heart. Shit! Now he knew why he shied away from relationships. If this was what it felt like, then you could keep all that crap. Never again was he going to let himself get caught up in feelings that hurt this bad.

Turning his back on an image he knew he'd be playing over and over in his head all night, he walked back out of the room, unnoticed and not caring. Tonight was all about forgetting now. And Ryan knew just how he was going to go about making that happen.

'I just want to go home, strip you naked – very slowly, I might add – and spend the night making love to you,' Jim whispered, his mouth close to her ear as they stood at the back of the packed Players' Lounge, grabbing what minimal privacy there was in a room so full of people. 'I want to explore all those places I haven't seen in so long, get to know them all over again…'

'Jesus, Jim, pack it in will you?' Amber said, conscious of the fact they were anything but alone. She could feel the tingling between her legs starting to happen already and she had a meeting with Kevin to get through first before anybody touched anyone

510

anywhere.

'You have no idea how much it turned me on, talking to you in that post-match interview. You were so professional, so cool, and all the time I'm talking to you I'm remembering what we did just minutes before kick-off.'

'Oh, yeah, that's real professional, Mr. Allen.'

He threw her that smile, and she couldn't help laughing. 'Well, I suppose I'd better go and do what we managers have to do on days like this,' he sighed, his fingers brushing quickly over her backside as he brought his arm down from the wall where it had been resting. 'Are you coming to mine tonight? You know I want you to stay over. We've got a lot to talk about.'

She couldn't tear her eyes away from his; the electricity between them was almost visible, so intense she could actually feel it crackling. 'I'll need to go home first. Pick up a change of clothes.'

'You won't need clothes for what *I've* got in mind,' Jim smiled, giving her hand a subtle and quick squeeze, his mouth touching hers in another brief kiss before he left her and headed off into the crowd.

Amber watched him for a few seconds, enjoying the dancing somersaults her stomach was performing

'Considering I've seen less distracted fourteen-year-olds at a One Direction concert you've done good today, Ms. Sullivan.'

She turned to look at Kevin, who'd sidled up next to her, sipping a pint of lager. 'I do try to stay as professional as I can,' she half smiled. 'No matter what's going on in my private life.'

'Well, you've had your moments over the past few months, I'll give you that,' Kevin said, looking at her out the corner of his eye, a smile slowly spreading across his face.

'It's been a bit of a confusing time lately, Kevin. Cut me some slack.'

He took another drink of his lager, looking straight ahead as Jim Allen finally managed to escape the press and reporters in the Players' Lounge and make his exit. 'I need you on board, Amber.

You're the best Sports Editor I've ever worked with. I'm just glad you finally seem to have found what you're looking for.'

She said nothing for a few seconds.

'I still can't believe you managed to keep all that a secret for so long. You and Jim Allen...' Kevin went on, shaking his head.

Amber sighed, leaning back against the wall. She really didn't want to go through this all over again. She'd done it so many times already; she couldn't believe there wasn't anyone out there who still didn't know about her and Jim.

'I'm sorry for trying to push you,' Kevin went on. 'For a story, I mean.' He looked at her, and she could see his human side appearing again. It didn't come out to play all that often, but she knew him well enough to know it was making an appearance now. 'I can see it hasn't been the easiest of times.'

'It's been complicated,' Amber said, wishing she could close her eyes and make the rest of the world go away, leaving just her and Jim. Alone. For a little while, at least. She'd really like that. 'But, hopefully, things are working out fine now.'

'And what about Ryan?'

She looked at her boss, unsure as to whether he was being a friend or digging for more information. 'What about him?'

'Whoa, don't jump on the defensive, missy. I'm just asking. I'm not the editor of some frigging tabloid rag, y'know. I'm not suddenly gonna publish every little thing you tell me in the form of some seedy, sex-fuelled story. Although...'

She couldn't help laughing. 'I know I'm paranoid, but... I still care about Ryan. But it would never have worked, Kevin. Not really.'

'And you and the Christian Grey of football management, it's for keeps, is it?'

She felt her stomach dip at that comment, hoping desperately that her face didn't give too much away. Yeah, it was for keeps. And by the end of next week everyone would know that – including Ryan.

'It's for keeps,' she said quietly, not really wanting to talk about this. Not here. Not now.

'Good. That's good,' Kevin smiled. 'I mean it, Amber. I'm happy for you.'

'Yeah, well, I wish everyone was,' Amber sighed, suddenly wishing she hadn't said that out loud.

'Your dad?' Kevin asked, raising a questioning eyebrow.

'My dad,' Amber replied. 'He'll come round. Once he realises this is it, that Jim and I are together and that isn't going to change.'

'I guess he's still getting over that hurdle of imagining his sixteen-year-old daughter… Well, he's had more to come to terms with, Amber, that's all. Jim and your dad go back a long way. He just didn't realise *you* and Jim went back quite so far – in that kind of way. How did nobody see the signs…?'

Amber took that as her cue to escape, grabbing her bag and sliding it up onto her shoulder, standing up on tiptoe to quickly kiss Kevin's cheek. 'I'll see you in the office on Monday, bright and early. Oh, and it *is* still alright for me to have next Thursday and Friday off, isn't it?'

'Yeah, sure, of course it is. Amber?'

She swung back round and smiled at him, a smile he returned.

'It's good to see you happy again.'

She threw him one final smile and began pushing her way through the still-crowded Players' Lounge, trying to find Ronnie, and hoping he was alone. She found him, talking to one of his TV colleagues over by the bar.

'Hey, kiddo,' Ronnie grinned as she joined them. 'You finished for the day now?'

She nodded, smiling at the man Ronnie had been talking to, an ex-footballer called David Henderson who'd once had the reputation for being one of the cleanest-cut players in the English league, except that Ronnie had told her different. But she was used to the stories these men could spin sometimes. 'I thought Karen was with you,' she said, leaning back against the bar.

'She's gone to see her mum and dad. They've just moved to a

new place in Cleadon, so she's gone to see how they're settling in, and to tell them the news that we're back together.'

'Will they be happy about that?'

'It wasn't me who ended the marriage in the first place, was it?'

'Fair point. You got to be anywhere in a hurry?'

'No.' He looked at David. 'We're done here, aren't we?'

David nodded, directing a wide smile in Amber's direction. 'It's good to see you, Amber.'

'Yeah, you too, David. It's been a while. We'll have to have a proper catch-up some time soon.' She took Ronnie's hand. 'I need to speak to you.'

Ronnie put his drink down, gave David a puzzled shrug then followed Amber out of the Players' Lounge. He didn't have much choice, really, considering she was holding onto him.

She didn't say anything until they were safely outside, away from any crowds and any prying eyes. 'Something up?' Ronnie asked, a purely rhetorical question which carried more than a hint of sarcasm.

Amber looked at him, suddenly wondering if she should tell him what she was about to tell him, but she had to tell *some*body. If she held it in much longer she was going to burst, or that's what it felt like, anyway.

'Jim and I are getting married. On Thursday.'

Ronnie stayed silent, staring at her as though she'd just said something really stupid. 'You're getting married,' he repeated. 'On Thursday.'

Amber nodded, keeping her eyes on his all the time.

'*This* Thursday?'

She nodded again. 'And I shouldn't really be telling you this because we've told nobody, not even my Dad...'

'Oh, good one, Amber. That's just what Freddie needs, *you* acting like you're sixteen again.'

'Can you just be happy for me? Please? Because I'm so excited I could scream!'

Ronnie said nothing, just raised another eyebrow.

'And what's *that* for?'

'What's *what* for?'

'That,' she said, raising her own eyebrow to show him what she meant.

'You *sound* like a sixteen-year-old, Amber. How can you possibly be sure that Jim is the one for you when you've only been together five minutes? It wasn't that long ago you were planning your wedding to Ryan.'

'I've loved Jim for over twenty years, Ronnie. Can people please try and start realising that? I can't get him out of my head, can't stop thinking about him, can't stop wanting him. So, regardless of what anyone says, we're getting married next week and if you can't be happy for me then it really doesn't matter. *I'm* happy – and that's all that matters. Because I haven't been happy in a long time. Not really. I've pretended I am, tried to believe that I could live my life without him, but I can't. And him coming back here, walking back into my life, it's proved everything I ever thought. I need him to survive. I need him to breathe, Jesus, it's *that* bad! And I wanted to tell you all of this because you're my best friend, and I love you. So, think what you like, but please, don't tell anyone what I've just told you. Don't tell anyone about Jim and I getting married. Especially not my dad. That's all I ask, Ronnie.'

'Hey, hang on, Amber…' He reached out and grabbed her arm, stopping her from walking away. 'Hang on. Look, I can't lie, okay? To you it might sound ridiculous, given the circumstances and your past history, to say that I think you and Jim are rushing into things, but I really do think you are. Can't you just take a bit of time to think about things?'

'We've been thinking about it for over twenty years, Ronnie. How much more time do we need?'

Ronnie let go of her arm, leaning back against the wall, pushing a hand through his hair. 'And you're sure – really, really sure – that you love him? That this is what you want? *He's* what you want?'

'I'm sure.'

He looked at her, their eyes meeting, a look passing between them that they hadn't exchanged in years, and it hit Amber like a bolt from the blue, because it was a look she hadn't expected to see in his eyes. Not now. 'Then I hope he makes you happy,' Ronnie whispered, breaking the stare and looking down at the ground, shoving his hands in his pockets.

'He will,' Amber said, not taking her eyes off her best friend. 'Ronnie…?'

He looked up at her again, holding out his hand for her to take, pulling her closer to him. 'I love you, too, Amber. You're the closest thing I've got to a little sister and I… I just want you to be happy.'

'I *am* happy.'

'Really? Promise me?'

'Promise,' she smiled, squeezing his hand tight, and before either of them realised what was happening, he'd leaned forward, ever so quickly kissing her, his lips brushing over hers gently and softly.

'Jesus, Amber, I'm sorry…'

'It's okay,' she said, bringing her fingers slowly up to her mouth, touching her lips. 'It's fine.'

'No. It's not fine. Things are confusing enough without stuff like that adding to the mix. I shouldn't have done it. In one breath I'm calling you a sister and in the next I'm kissing you. I'm so sorry, Amber…'

'Ronnie, come on. This is *me* we're talking about. How many times has something like that happened between us?'

'Yeah, at a Christmas party after too much drink or on your birthday when I reckon it won't do any harm to try my luck.' He looked at her again, right into her eyes. 'Or when we feel the need to treat each other as friends with benefits.'

She looked away, out at the sea of people still streaming out of Tynebridge, hoping nobody had seen that short exchange between her and Ronnie. He'd got one thing right, though – neither of them needed any more complications, not when they both seemed to be finally sorting themselves out. 'Well, those days are over now,' she said quietly, her eyes meeting his again. 'Aren't they?'

He nodded, smiling a weak smile at her. 'Yeah. They are. Look, Amber, I won't breathe a word about you and Jim, I promise. But shouldn't you tell your dad…?'

She shook her head. 'No, Ronnie. No. He'll come round, in time. I know he will. But, right now, I don't want anything to spoil this for me and Jim.'

He gave her another, bigger smile, pulling himself away from the wall. 'Well, I'm gonna be here in the North East all week, so you know where I am. If you need me.'

She nodded, wanting so much to hug him but wondering if, given what had just happened, it would send out the wrong signals. And what signals *were* those, anyway? 'Yeah. I know.'

'Good. Well, I'd better get off. I promised Karen I wouldn't be too long.'

'Tell her I said hi,' Amber said, watching as he almost ran down the stone steps that led from the main entrance.

'Will do,' he shouted over his shoulder before hurrying off in the direction of the car park.

Amber hoisted her bag up further onto her shoulder and started making her own way towards the car park, trying to push what had just happened to the back of her mind, because it meant nothing. She was going to see Jim in a matter of hours and that was all that mattered – all she really wanted to think about. She was going to see Jim. And the anticipation of what would happen the second she got there sent a shiver right through her, bringing a smile to her face as she remembered the way he'd touched her just hours ago in his office; quick, rampant sex that had made her feel like the most beautiful, vibrant woman in the world, something she hadn't felt all that often over the past few years.

'Someone's happy.'

She swung round as that familiar Geordie accent cut through her daydream, her stomach sinking when she saw him, leaning

517

back against his car like the cocky kid he still was.

'Ryan. I thought you'd be long gone.'

'It's not like I've got to *be* anywhere, is it?'

'Isn't the casino open by now?'

'Whoa, low blow that one, Ms. Sullivan,' Ryan said, shaking his head.

Amber felt instantly guilty. She hadn't meant to say that, of course she hadn't. He'd caught her off guard that was all. Suddenly she wasn't sure how to handle him. 'I'm sorry. I shouldn't have said that.'

He just shrugged. 'And it's not like I've got anyone to rush home to, is it?'

'Now who's aiming the blows low?'

'Enjoy the pre-match entertainment from the boss, did you?'

Amber looked at him, narrowing her eyes. 'What are you talking about?'

'Gary heard you, and Christ knows who else. In the boss's office, up against the door – fucking each other senseless, by all accounts.'

'Jesus, Ryan, come on,' Amber sighed, fishing out her car keys from the bottom of her bag.

'Is he that good, Amber? Is he *that* good that all he has to do is click his fingers and you come running? Or should I have just stopped at "come"?'

'You're being childish now. And I'm not having this conversation.'

'You can trust him, can you?'

She looked up at him, frowning. 'I've told you – I'm not having this conversation.'

'How can you be sure he won't do exactly what he did before? Huh? How can you be sure?'

'Because this time we've gone public, Ryan. We've told the world, they all know. There are no more secrets, no more lies.' Although she couldn't help flinching inside at that statement, knowing of the secret they still had and the lies they'd still have to tell until it was all done and dusted. 'No more pretending we're nothing

518

to each other.'

'And that's enough for you, is it? That's a big enough guarantee?'

'Go home, Ryan.'

She turned to walk away from him, over to her own car, but he grabbed her by the shoulder and swung her back round to face him. 'I loved you, Amber. I *loved* you.'

She stared at him, into those beautiful deep blue eyes of his, and although he still had the ability to make her heart give a tiny flutter, it wasn't anywhere near what she felt for Jim. And that told her everything she needed to know. 'It wasn't enough, Ryan,' she said quietly, taking his hand and squeezing it quickly before letting it drop, walking away from him without looking back.

Chapter Thirty-Two

'Now there's a sight for sore eyes,' Ryan grinned, sliding his arm around the dark-haired woman who'd slipped into the booth beside him. 'Sent from heaven to sort me out, good and proper.'

She smiled, sliding her perfectly-manicured hand inside his shirt, stroking his chest as she kissed him. Jesus, he was horny tonight, despite that conversation with Amber earlier. Or maybe because of, he wasn't quite sure. She'd looked hot, even in that simple outfit of jeans and a black shirt, her dark red hair pulled loosely back from her face. She'd looked like the beautiful woman he'd fallen in love with, and just touching her again, it only made him realise what it was he'd lost. Or should that be, thrown away? So it had hurt, but it had also turned him on, in some weird and twisted kind of way. She had that effect on him.

'When I got your call, how could I refuse?' the dark-haired woman purred, her fingers now stroking his rough, bearded jawline, promising things that Ryan knew she'd deliver. And soon, he hoped. Because he needed to forget. He needed to have every opportunity to think wiped clean away, giving him no chance to imagine what Amber could be doing to his boss – what *he* could be doing to *her*. He didn't want to know, didn't want to have to think about it, but at the minute he had no choice – images were filling his head. Images of her naked as Jim touched every inch of her body, just as he'd once done. Images of his manager pushing inside her, something Ryan would give anything to experience again, to feel that beautiful, warm wetness engulf him, taking him to heaven and back in one glorious ride. Shit! This was ridiculous.

'I need something from you, right now,' Ryan said quietly, his mouth close to the dark-haired woman's ear, his hand riding up her short dress, touching her thigh, telling her exactly what it was that he needed – a quick fix to tide him over until the longer game could begin. 'Come on. Let's get out of here.'

He grabbed her hand and they almost ran to the nearest toilets, shutting themselves inside the first cubicle they came to, his hands pushing her dress up over her thighs before they'd even locked the cubicle door. With a steady hand and one quick action, Ryan's companion had pushed him back against the wall, unzipped his jeans, sank to her knees and took him in her mouth, giving him that release he'd so badly needed. He threw his head back, closing his eyes as she took him in deep, bringing him to a shattering climax within seconds. Christ! How ready had *he* been? He'd almost come before she'd even had a chance to touch him.

'You have no idea how much I needed that,' he breathed, opening his eyes as she stood up, watching as she pulled off a couple of sheets of toilet paper and wiped her mouth.

'I aim to please,' she smiled, running her hand over him again, which made him flinch slightly. Just seconds after sex meant he was still extra sensitive, but that wouldn't last long. He'd be ready to go again, soon, and this time he wanted the games to last longer. Much, much longer.

'Something on your mind?' Jim asked, coming up behind Amber as she stared out of the window, her arms folded. 'Only, it's pitch black out there, so I'm not entirely sure what you're looking at.'

She said nothing for a second, just continued to stare out into the darkness.

'You saw Ryan, didn't you?' Jim's voice was quiet, his hand

resting gently on her hip.

'Can't you help him, Jim?' She turned round to face him, her eyes almost pleading with him.

'I don't know what it is you want me to do, honey.' Jim pushed a hand through his hair. 'It's not like I can put tabs on him or anything like that. The club can only do so much – we can't trail him 24/7.' He put a hand to her face, gently stroking the soft skin of her cheek. 'And it isn't your problem anyway, baby. Not anymore.'

'Maybe I haven't been fair on him…'

'Are you saying you regret breaking up with him?'

'Oh God, no!' She looked up into his green eyes, her hand covering his as it rested on her cheek. 'Jim, no. That's not what I meant. I don't regret leaving him, I just… I just wish things could have been different. I wish I didn't constantly feel that he was going to do something stupid or slip back into his old ways.'

'You can't spend the rest of your life worrying about him, Amber. Look, I'll do my best to keep an eye on him when I can, alright? He's a talent that shouldn't be wasted, I can't argue with that. But he's also going to make his own mistakes, no matter what anyone else tells him. And we can't really stop him from doing that if he's hell-bent on going down that road.'

Amber threw her head back and sighed. He was right, of course he was right. Ryan may have a talent that singled him out from the pack, but he was also pig-headed, arrogant, and likely to press the self-destruct button at any given opportunity. In fact, sometimes she had a feeling he did it just to spite people, almost as if to show them he could do whatever he liked and fuck everyone else. And there was nothing she could do about that, bar staying with him, and that wasn't an option. She couldn't stay with him, not out of pity. It wasn't fair. On either of them.

'You need to relax,' Jim smiled, letting his hand wander down over her neck, slowly trailing along her collarbone, his eyes never leaving hers. 'You're all tense.'

He wasn't wrong. She'd felt the knot in her shoulders tightening as she'd driven the short journey to Jim's house at the coast, and despite the many beautiful kisses she'd received from this man here in front of her since her arrival, all they'd done was ease rather than erase the tension.

She closed her eyes and threw back her head as his fingers continued to trail along her collarbone, his lips brushing over her neck, leaving tiny, soft kisses in their wake. Any thoughts of Ryan were slowly fading now. She didn't think he'd be wasting time worrying about her, so why should she spend time worrying about him? Not when there were far better things to do.

Jim's fingers slowly unbuttoned her shirt, sliding underneath the thin material to touch her skin, the coolness of his hand shocking her slightly, causing her body to shiver with the sweet anticipation of just what might happen next. She really couldn't wait to marry this man, to have him by her side in a way she'd dreamed of for so long. Too much time denying her feelings, and too long away from him had only served to make what was happening now that little bit more exciting.

'Upstairs,' Jim said quietly, his mouth close to her ear.

She couldn't help groaning as his hand slipped into hers, pulling her out of the living room towards the staircase that led to the first floor. Couldn't they just have sex there? In the living room? She was more than ready; the dampness between her legs told her that. It wasn't like him to look for the conventional place to make love.

Jim said nothing, just continued to pull her upstairs, kicking open the bedroom door, which Amber found quite a turn-on. She could do masterful. It just made him even sexier in her eyes.

As soon as she was through the door, he kicked it shut, pushing her up against the wall, his mouth urgent yet gentle against hers, his hardness already digging into her thigh. 'I want to taste you,' he whispered, his fingers entwining with hers as he searched her face for permission to do what she knew was coming. And just the thought of it sent her heart racing even faster, if that was possible. She was just glad she was leaning back against the wall or she was convinced her knees would have given way.

He found the zip of her jeans and pulled it down, deliberately slow, his mouth almost resting on hers as he did so, his fingers making her gasp as they slipped underneath the denim to touch her. A quick touch, but enough to speed up her breathing, her breasts straining to escape the confines of her pale green bra, eager to feel his mouth covering them.

He took her hand again, pulling her towards the bed. She knew what was about to happen, and she didn't think she could wait much longer. The anticipation was killing her now, a pain in her thighs throbbing to the point where she knew she'd have to find some relief soon. Very soon. Before it all became too much.

Shrugging her shirt back off her shoulders, she unclipped her bra and threw it aside, lying down on the bed and stretching out as Jim slowly pulled her jeans down, standing up for a few agonising seconds as he freed himself of his own clothes. Amber watched every move he made as that near-perfect body of his was revealed. The tanned skin, muscles in all the right places – at forty-eight he had a body that had hardly changed since the days when they'd spent all their free time doing this. Had she changed much in that time? She closed her eyes again, pushing any other thoughts from her mind as Jim pulled her panties down, leaving her naked and exposed, but it was the most beautiful feeling. She felt free, liberated, almost. She felt beautiful, wanted, needed. She felt so many things she couldn't explain, things she only wanted to feel. And she wanted to feel *him*. All of him.

She gripped the edges of the pillows as he placed both hands on her knees, pushing her legs apart before sliding another pillow underneath her, raising her hips up slightly. Once again the antici-pation built until she literally felt like crying out for him, screaming at him to do what it was he was about to do, because she couldn't take the waiting any longer. It was torture.

But within seconds the torture was over and the ride had begun. Amber couldn't stop herself from crying out this time as his mouth finally found its destination, touching her in the most intimate of places in the most beautiful of ways. His tongue was searching, probing, looking for that special spot but seemingly in no hurry to find it.

'Oh, Jesus… Jim…' Amber groaned, bucking her hips slightly as he pulled away, teasing her, making her crazy as he took her so far then pulled back for a second or two before lowering his head again. Oh yes. *Now* the tension was easing. *Now* she could feel herself relaxing.

Gripping the pillows tighter, she bucked her hips again, crying out loud as his tongue entered her for the briefest of seconds, sending a huge shiver right up her spine, but he didn't stay there. He knew that was enough, that the ride would continue in a different way, but he'd left her aching for more, now. He'd left her whole body crying out for him, a delicious ache spreading through her like some kind of beautiful, erotic poison. She needed him, and she didn't have to wait long to feel him back where he belonged. Sliding back up her body, his skin warm and smooth against hers, it took just seconds before she felt him slip inside her. And the relief was immense, her whole body tingling with tiny, white-hot pins and needles as she accepted him fully, wrapping her legs around him to take him in deep.

His fingers entwined with hers above her head, pushing her hands back into the pillows as he pushed hard into her, kissing her neck, whispering things to her that were both beautiful and filthy, turning her on more and more with every thrust, until the inevitable endgame began it's slow and steady climb, her body exploding with a force brought on by his final, almost violent thrust, a wonderful spasm of burning hot tingles covering every inch of her skin, her stomach dipping and diving as her thighs gripped him tight, waiting until he was empty. The feeling of him there, within her, was a feeling she didn't want to let go of. Not now. Not ever. Not after everything they'd been through, all those years of only wanting this but at the same time making sure it didn't happen. What had she been playing at?

As his own shuddering climax came to its natural end, he lowered his head down onto her chest, their hands still joined together, as were their bodies. And she was glad. She didn't want him to withdraw just yet, not yet. A few more minutes of feeling him this close, that's all she wanted. A few more beautiful minutes.

'Relaxed?' he asked, smiling slightly as he slowly raised his head. She smiled back. 'Yeah. I think so.'

'You think so?' he asked, arching an eyebrow. 'Do I need to do more? Huh? You wanna wear me out before we even get to our wedding night?'

She closed her eyes as she felt him slowly leave her body, rolling over onto his side. 'Jim…'

'Two seconds, baby,' he said, sliding out of bed and disappearing into the en-suite bathroom.

She lay back, drawing her legs up, staring at the white ceiling above her, her fingers fiddling with the edges of the pillows. She felt as though someone had just given her the most incredible full-body massage. She felt so relaxed, sighing contentedly as she stretched out.

'Jesus, Amber, just watching you do that makes me want to go in all over again,' Jim groaned, lying down beside her, propping himself up on one elbow.

'Help yourself,' she smiled, arching her back, her breasts full and in his face. Bending his head, Amber moaned quietly as he accepted her invitation, his mouth covering one of her breasts. She buried her fingers in his hair, pulling at it gently as his hand wandered down her body, trailing along her stomach, down over her thighs, until he found what he was looking for. And before Amber had any time to think about what he might do next, he'd slipped two fingers inside her, making her cry out loud again, arching her back even more, pushing herself up at him, which only served to make him dive deeper.

'I love you so fucking much,' he whispered, finally lifting his head to look at her. 'You know that, don't you?'

She nodded, opening her legs wider as his fingers continued to probe around inside her, sending incredible waves of pleasure washing over her. 'I know… Jesus Christ, Jim… that feels so good…'

His mouth covered hers, his thumb gently stroking her, heightening the whole experience tenfold until she could hold on no longer. He'd done his job, easing another orgasm out of her in record-quick time with an expert hand, kissing her hard and fast as her whole body shook, still with him inside her.

'That feels fucking incredible,' he groaned, slowly sliding his fingers out, leaving her breathless. 'You've got one hell of a grip on you, kiddo.'

She turned her head to look at him, smiling. She couldn't do anything else. She had a feeling that smile would be there for days to come. Everything she'd felt today, all those incredible, mind-blowing feelings she'd experienced, she wanted to feel them forever, feel him there in whatever way he could be. *Every* way he could be. She wanted to do things with this man that she had *never* wanted to do before, it was crazy! She wasn't some sex-crazed teenager out to experience everything she could because it was all so new, she was a thirty-seven-year-old woman. Yet she felt like that sixteen-year-old teenager when she was with Jim. Maybe she always would, but hey, if it meant they could share evenings like this, then she wasn't going to complain. 'We're gonna be okay, Jim. Aren't we?' she asked, a sudden vulnerability taking over as the tingles and the shivers subsided, giving way to reality. Which she didn't know if she was quite ready for yet.

'We're gonna be just fine, baby,' he smiled, gently pushing a strand of dark red hair from her eyes. 'I promise.'

I promise. Two words that she needed to believe more than anything. Two words he'd said to her before with consequences that had broken her heart a million times over. Two words that she hoped he'd learnt the true meaning of now, because she couldn't lose him again. She just couldn't.

'Prostitutes?' Gary questioned, grabbing Ryan's arm as he passed the bar. 'Are you serious?'

'I prefer to call her an escort of the more choosy variety,' Ryan said, shaking Gary's hand from his elbow.

'You sure about that? I mean, she's with *you* tonight, isn't she?'

'You're a fucking funny sod, Gaz.'

Gary leaned forward on the bar, taking a long swig of beer. 'She's a prostitute, Ryan, and you know it. Half the lads in the league have had her when they've visited the North East, it's what she does. It's how she makes her money. And I know we've all done it, mate, but at least the rest of us have been a bit more discreet.' He looked at Ryan, who was refusing to meet his eyes. 'She put her prices up yet? What with the recession and everything…'

Ryan finally turned to look at his teammate. 'Can you shut the fuck up?'

'Hey, alright,' Gary laughed, holding up his hands in mock surrender. 'Don't throw your toys out the frigging pram.'

'Just fuck off, Gary.'

'You're being a right arsehole at the minute, has anyone told you that?'

Ryan looked at Gary again. 'Yeah. And I wonder why *that* is?'

'Don't blame me, mate. I wasn't the one who shagged two birds in the bed I shared with my fiancée.'

'You could have stopped me.'

Gary stared at him. 'Hang on… What? You're seriously blaming *me* now?'

'Yeah. Why the hell not? I mean, you knew how much I loved Amber, how much I wanted to be with her, and yet *still* you forced me to come out on that stupid Stag Night…'

'I didn't tie your arms behind your back and fucking force you, Ryan.'

'As good as.'

'No, you aren't gonna tie this one on me, mate. No way. You're big enough and ugly enough to make your own frigging decisions in the end, and if you *really* hadn't wanted to come out that night, then you know as well as I do that you would've stayed at home, regardless of what anyone else was telling you to do.'

Ryan turned away again. He was right, Gary was right, to some extent. He hadn't been forced into anything, but maybe he *had* been worn down to the point where agreeing to whatever Gary was asking had been the easier option, just to shut him up.

'You're weak, Ryan. And all this has done is prove that.'

Ryan looked at Gary, an anger building up out of nowhere, because he hadn't felt it before. All he'd felt before was this urge to spend the night fucking some faceless woman in endless bouts of meaningless sex so he could forget – forget what, exactly? The fact he'd messed up big time? Yeah, Gary *was* right. But that didn't mean he was blameless. 'You shouldn't have pushed me so hard,' Ryan said quietly, knocking back two vodka shots in quick succession.

'Jesus, Ryan, come on. Deep down you *wanted* to come out that night. You *wanted* to fuck those girls, so don't stand there and deny it. If you'd really loved Amber as much as you say you did, then you wouldn't have gone anywhere near them, let alone take them home.'

'You pushed me,' Ryan went on, his voice quietly dark. 'You pushed me so far…'

'This is bullshit! Go and get your head sorted, Ryan, okay? Because you're doing mine in.' Gary took one last swig of beer before slamming his empty glass down on the bar, looking Ryan straight in the eye. 'She's gone. You lost her. Your fault. Now fucking deal with it.'

Ryan watched him walk away, balling his fists, digging his fingernails so far into the palms of his hands it hurt, but he felt no pain. Not from that, anyway. All he felt was a dull, nagging ache inside every time he stopped to think for a second, every time there was an opportunity for thoughts to process and images to appear in his head.

'Everything okay?'

He looked up as the dark-haired woman reappeared by his side, sliding a hand onto his arm as she sidled up close to him. 'Everything's fine,' he lied. 'Or it will be.'

She looked at him, frowning slightly. He downed the last vodka shot and slipped his arm around her tiny waist, leaning in for a long kiss, sliding his hand up her dress as he pressed his mouth against hers, feeling her reciprocate, wincing as she bit his lip as the kiss grew more urgent. He could take the pain. Anything that blocked out everything else going on in his life was good, if it distracted him.

He pulled away but kept his hand on her thigh, feeling himself grow hard at the feel of her smooth, warm skin against his hand. One more quick release – a proper fuck this time – then he'd hit the casino. Ryan Fisher needed to escape. And nobody was going to stop him.

Chapter Thirty-Three

Amber looked out of the upstairs bedroom window, peering through the blinds as the For Sale sign was hammered into the front lawn. It was real now. She was finally selling her beautiful little home to move in with Jim, but for how long? If things worked out with Malaga Athletico then he'd be selling his Tynemouth home, too. They'd be making a new life for themselves over in Spain, away from all the prying eyes and the questions.

Questions. They'd have plenty of those to answer tomorrow, when Amber arrived with Jim at the team's hotel in Wigan as their manager's new wife. Probably not the best timing in the world, but love had a funny way of making people rather selfish at times. Anyway, they hadn't quite decided when to announce the news. They were playing it all by ear, which made everything more exciting, but also more nerve-wracking.

Letting the blinds fall back into place, she turned around, looking at the simple white dress that lay on the bed. She had to smile. White. Yeah, because she was *so* virginal. It wasn't anything spectacular, but it was pretty, and it clung to her curves in the most flattering of ways. Teamed with a pair of modestly expensive, white, stiletto-heeled ankle boots she'd bought on a recent shopping trip with Debbie – although she hadn't told Debbie just why she was buying them – it was the perfect wedding outfit, as far as Amber

531

was concerned. Just enough to say 'bride' without making it look too obvious. Understated, that was the word.

She walked over to the mirror, carefully touching her just-styled hair that fell around her shoulders in a tumble of tousled, newly-coloured dark red curls. It was the look she wanted – simple. And it suited her, with her full fringe and – that word again – understated make-up. Some mascara, a light dusting of bronzer around the cheek and collarbone, and a touch of nude lip gloss, that was all she needed. She felt good. This was her wedding day, and although it was taking a little bit of getting used to, given that she was alone and about to get married in secret, she still had that excited feeling kicking around her belly. Every time she thought about Jim it felt as though there were a suitcase full of impatient butterflies trying desperately to gain freedom and fly freely around her stomach.

Sitting down on the edge of the bed, she picked up the photograph on her bedside table, a photograph of Jim receiving his 'Manager of the Month' Award. He was smiling the widest smile, his handsome face so relaxed and happy. She trailed her fingers lightly over the photograph, that little frisson of excitement rushing through her again as she looked at him. She was inextricably connected to this man, and she always had been. She just wished she'd had the conviction to realise that sooner.

But today wasn't the day to dwell on the past; it was a day to think about the future. Whatever that may entail. All she knew was that she was finally marrying the man of her dreams, and whatever happened after that, they'd deal with it.

The phone ringing roused her from her brief daydream. She placed the photograph back down on the bedside table and reached out to grab the phone. 'Hello?'

'Amber, it's Dad. You couldn't come over to the ground this morning, could you? I know you're not working today, and you've probably got plans, but I could really do with your help on something.'

Amber felt her stomach dip, her mouth suddenly going dry. She hated lying to her father. After everything that had happened, she'd promised she wouldn't do that again, she'd promised she'd be honest with him, and yet here she was, lying to him again. 'Dad, I… I can't. Not today. I've really got to be somewhere.'

Freddie Sullivan said nothing for a few seconds, his silence making Amber nervous. Could he tell she was hiding something from him? Did he know she was lying to him again? Oh Jesus, what was she doing? This was ridiculous!

'You can't spare me five minutes?' Freddie asked. 'If you're passing the ground on your way…'

'Dad, I'm really sorry, but I'm off to the coast today…'

'The coast?'

She closed her eyes, gripping the receiver tight. Freddie knew Jim lived at the coast. But so what if she was going to spend her day off with the man she loved? There was nothing unusual about that. Maybe she should head him off at the pass. 'I'm meeting Jim for lunch,' she sighed, hoping that would be good enough to placate her father.

'Lunch? It's 10a.m., Amber. You've got plenty of time to skip by here for a few minutes before you head off, and anyway…' He paused for a second, and Amber felt her stomach dip again, '… surely Jim wouldn't mind if you were a little bit late? It's not like you need to be there bang on time, is it? Isn't he working today, anyway? I mean, Red Star have got that crucial match in Wigan on Saturday…'

'I've got a doctor's appointment first, Dad, okay?' More lies. Now she felt *really* bad. Making up a trip to the doctors just to throw people off the scent was so old-school, and not particularly original. But it was all she'd been able to come up with on the spur of the moment.

'A doctor's appointment? Is everything okay?' Her father's voice sounded worried and Amber felt the guilt build again. Shit! A doctor's appointment was probably the worst lie she could have come up with, in hindsight. Her mother had been extremely secretive about her own doctors' appointments in the beginning, telling nobody about the cancer until it had got to the point where people had needed to know, and her father hadn't dealt with that all that well. Yet here she was causing him more anxiety with stupid lies to cover up her own selfishness.

'Dad, listen, everything's fine, alright? Everything's fine. It's just… it's just a routine check-up, you know, blood pressure check, that kind of thing. It happens every so often, when I need a new batch of pills…'

'Pills?'

Amber sighed, closing her eyes again and wishing this wasn't happening. She was digging herself into a bigger hole by the second. 'Contraceptive pills. I'm on the Pill, Dad. And when you're on the Pill they do regular check-ups, just to make sure everything's okay.'

Freddie stayed silent again, and Amber just hoped it was the mention of contraception that had shut him up. That uncomfortable realisation that his daughter did, indeed, do things he'd probably rather she didn't. And Amber was doing those things with a man whom Freddie had once called his best friend. Until he'd found out the truth. Could this get any more complicated? 'Okay,' Freddie finally broke his silence. 'Well, I don't want you missing your doctor's appointment. No matter how routine. Amber…?'

'What?' she asked, checking her watch and realising that she should be getting ready by now.

'You *are* being careful, aren't you?'

She frowned as she trailed her fingers over the soft material of her wedding dress. 'Careful?'

'With Jim, I mean.'

She paused for a second, not entirely sure what he meant by that. 'Yeah. I'm being careful, Dad.'

'Good girl. I worry about you, Amber. That's all.'

'I'm fine. Really. I'm fine.'

'Well, you just make sure you stay that way. I'll speak to you soon, sweetheart.'

'Yeah. See you, Dad.' She hung up and placed the receiver back on its base, throwing herself on the bed. This day was going to be a hell of a lot harder than she'd imagined it would be. She'd been letting herself get carried away with the whole 'Romeo and Juliet' romance side of things, forgetting completely about the reality of the situation. So the sooner she and Jim signed that wedding certificate, the better. Because she just wanted the rest of their lives to begin.

Max tried calling Ryan's number again, but still it went straight to voicemail, which was enough to make Max concerned. Ryan's phone only ever went to voicemail when he was doing one of two things – sleeping with women he deemed good enough to warrant no interruption, or throwing his life away in the casino. And normally Max would be able to cope with that. He'd rather Ryan hadn't veered slightly off the rails again, but he'd taken his eye off the ball, hadn't he? Concentrated on clients other than this errant, young, millionaire footballer with the lack of common sense and the fading self-respect. And now he was getting word back from Newcastle Red Star that Ryan hadn't turned up for training for the past few days, and nobody seemed to be able to get hold of him. His mobile was switched off and he wasn't answering his home phone, and there was also no sign of him at either his city centre apartment or his Gateshead home, apparently. He certainly wasn't answering the door, anyway, so Max had been told.

Max knew what had been going on in Ryan's life lately. He knew that he and Amber were past history, that she was with Jim Allen now, and Max could only guess – given that he knew how fragile Ryan could be at times – how that was affecting his young client. And that bothered Max. More than he wanted to let on. He recognised the signs, the warning signals, because he'd seen them all before.

He picked up his phone again and punched in another number,

but they didn't seem to be answering, either. Throwing his phone back down onto the counter, he picked up the just-boiled kettle and poured steaming hot water into a mug, stirring the coffee vigorously as his mobile's shrill ringtone pierced the air once more. He looked at the caller ID. It was a Red Star number, but not Jim Allen's. Did the manager even know what the hell was going on with his star striker? Or was he too busy rubbing Ryan's nose in the fact he now had his girl? Max sighed. It was childish to even think that way, but he cared about Ryan, and part of him was just frustrated that the kid hadn't been able to grow up enough to hold onto Amber. To make a go of a settled, stable life with a woman he'd loved.

Taking a quick sip of coffee, Max picked up the phone and held it to his ear. 'Yep?' He listened as the voice on the other end of the line enquired, once again, as to whether he'd heard from Ryan yet. Max took another sip of coffee. He was going to have to get down there and do some damage limitation, a little bit of spinning. Then, when he'd managed to save Ryan's career, he was going all out to find out just what the hell really going on.

She looked okay. Actually, she looked better than okay. The dress fitted her perfectly, hugging every curve in all the right places, her dark red hair falling loosely over her bare shoulders. She was going to freeze, of course, it still being winter and the temperatures far from tropical, but she looked okay. For a woman who was about to get married in secret to the man she'd loved for over twenty years. The love of her life.

A knock at the door made her jump slightly, knocking her back to reality, and she ran quickly down the stairs, peering out of the living room window to see who it was before she opened the door. She couldn't risk it being her dad. She was hardly dressed appropriately for a doctor's appointment.

'Ronnie!' she gasped under her breath, before heading off into the hallway and throwing open the door. She hadn't expected to see him today.

'You're still going through with it, then?' he asked dryly.

'No. I just thought I'd nip to Asda for some milk, I'm running low.'

He just raised an eyebrow. 'You gonna let me in? I'm freezing me bollocks off out here.'

'So eloquent,' she smiled sarcastically, standing aside to let him through.

'You look incredible, by the way,' Ronnie said, ignoring her comment and kissing her quickly on the mouth as he walked past her into the hallway.

'Thanks,' she whispered, lifting her fingers up to her lips where his mouth had brushed fleetingly over them. 'What are you doing here, anyway?'

He turned round, looking her up and down again, letting out a low whistle as he folded his arms. 'You really *do* look incredible. You going somewhere?'

'Jesus, Ronnie, will you quit with the smart remarks? I'll ask you again – what are you doing here?'

'Do you really think I'd let my best friend go off and get married without at least wishing her luck?'

'I don't need luck, Ronnie,' Amber said, fiddling with the top of her dress.

'I think everybody needs a little bit of luck, Amber.'

She looked up at him, their eyes meeting, locking together, and for a few seconds they just stared at each other.

'*I* don't,' she said quietly, finally breaking the stare, and the silence.

'Well, I could murder a cup of tea,' Ronnie sighed, turning and walking towards the kitchen. 'What about you? Or are you on the stronger stuff?'

'Tea will be fine,' Amber said, following him as quickly as she could in the heels she was wearing.

'And this is all still top secret, classified stuff then, is it?' Ronnie asked, filling the kettle.

Amber ignored the flippancy of his question and leaned back against the counter, folding her arms. 'Yeah. Well, I hope so, anyway. Just had a bit of a close shave with my dad, though.'

'Oh yeah?'

'Long story,' Amber sighed, looking over at the clock on the wall. Not long now until she escaped all these questions and so-called concerned friends. For a little while, at least.

'So, you're still sure you want to go through with this?' Ronnie asked, leaning back against the counter beside her, folding his arms, too.

Amber nodded. 'Yeah. I'm sure.'

He turned his head to look at her. 'You know that Ryan has been missing from training, don't you?'

Amber turned sharply to face him. 'Missing?'

'He hasn't turned up for days now. Nobody's seen hide nor hair of him since he was spotted in town at the weekend. He's not answering his phone, nobody's seen him at home…'

'He's not my problem anymore, Ronnie,' Amber said, turning away from him to stare out of the French doors into her small but pretty garden. A garden that, soon, wouldn't be hers anymore.

'And you mean that, do you?'

She looked at Ronnie again. 'If you've come here with the sole intention of hoping a missing Ryan will tug at my heartstrings enough to make me want to call things off with Jim, you're sadly mistaken. That isn't going to happen. I'm sure Newcastle Red Star have got enough people trying to locate him without me joining in. He's his own worst enemy, Ronnie. I can't help him anymore.'

'So, you really don't care about him, then?'

'Jesus… I didn't say that… Yes, I still care about him, but not enough to jeopardise my relationship with Jim. You got that? For Christ's sake, what now?' She sighed heavily as her phone started ringing, picking it up and answering it without missing a beat. 'Hello? Amber Sullivan…'

'Amber, it's Max. Max Mandell. Ryan's agent?'

Amber felt her stomach suddenly tighten in a huge knot. 'Max... What can I do for you?' She looked over at Ronnie, who just shrugged.

'Ryan isn't there with you, is he?'

'Ryan? No. No, he isn't. I haven't seen him since the game last Saturday, at Tynebridge. Why?'

Max paused for a second before answering. 'Ryan's just, well... you can probably guess what he's "just" doing. Sorry to bother you, sweetheart. Have a good day.'

Amber placed the phone down on the counter and looked at Ronnie again. 'They'll find him,' she said, walking over to the cupboard and taking out a packet of ibuprofen. 'He'll be off sulking somewhere, I know him.'

'Yeah. You know him. Which is why I'm surprised you're not more worried.'

She half-filled a glass of water and took a drink, throwing her head back and swallowing two tablets in one mouthful. 'He does this to seek attention, Ronnie. That's all. He'll be fine.'

'You think so?'

She fixed him with a look before checking her watch again. 'Yeah. I think so. Now, I've really got to get going... I need to call a taxi...'

'I'll take you.'

She looked up at Ronnie, a slightly surprised expression on her face. 'You'll take me?'

'Yeah, I'll take you, so instead of standing there repeating everything I say, why don't you go and make sure you've got everything.'

'What about Karen? Won't she mind?'

'She's off on an all-day shopping expedition to the MetroCentre with her mum and sister, so I doubt I'll be seeing anything of her until later tonight. I've got nothing better to do.'

'Gee, thanks for that.'

'You know what I mean. Go on, go. Go make yourself look

even more beautiful.'

'Are you saying I don't look beautiful enough?' she smirked, giving his arm a playful punch as she walked past him.

He looked at her, taking her hand as she slid past, his expression changing. 'Amber… are you *really* sure this is what you want? Are you really sure that *Jim* is what you want?'

She stared at him for a few seconds, looking right into his eyes. 'You giving me any better offers?'

The doorbell ringing made them both jump apart, Amber shaking out her curls as if to wipe away that split second of something she couldn't explain and didn't want to dwell on. 'Can you go see who that is, Ronnie? Please? And if it's my dad…'

'Yeah, go on. If it's your dad, what?'

She pushed a hand through her hair, throwing her head back, staring at the ceiling as though that would offer up the answer to everything. 'Tell him I've sent you over here to pick up something I've forgotten, *I* don't know…'

'You're really on top of all this, aren't you? I have absolutely no idea how you managed to keep an affair with Jim going for so long without anyone finding out.'

'It wasn't an affair,' Amber muttered at Ronnie's back as he walked away into the hall. She could do with a drink. A small glass of Dutch courage, but she didn't know if she had anything even vaguely alcoholic in the house. She'd been at Jim's over the past few days, so shopping hadn't been high on her list of things to sort out. She was in the process of opening and then banging shut cupboard doors in her search for that elusive drink when Ronnie came back into the kitchen, followed by a particularly stressed-looking Debbie.

'Debbie…? Is everything okay?'

Debbie frowned as she looked at Amber, taking in her dress, freshly-styled hair, and the small bouquet of flowers that lay on the table in the corner. 'What's… what's going on, Amber?'

Amber looked over at Ronnie, who continued to do nothing

but raise his eyebrows, something that was fast becoming an annoying habit of his.

'I'm… Me and Jim, it's… it's our wedding day,' Amber sighed, finally admitting defeat. She couldn't really get out of this one now. It was obvious she wasn't dressed for a trip to the bank.

'Wedding?' Debbie gasped, her eyes widening. 'I had no idea…'

'Neither did anyone else,' Ronnie muttered, folding his arms as he leaned back against the wall.

Debbie swung round to look at him. 'But… *you* knew? Didn't you? Or else, why would you…?'

'Be here? Well, I'm here to see if she's thinking straight yet. And I've only known for a couple of days. Seemed her and Jim didn't want anyone else to know about their impending, super-fast nuptials.'

'Ronnie, please…' Amber looked at Debbie again. 'What's wrong, Debbie?'

'It's Ryan.'

'Oh, Jesus,' Amber sighed, leaning back against the cupboards, staring up at the ceiling again. 'If you've come to tell me he's gone AWOL, I already know.'

'He hasn't gone AWOL, Amber. I know where he is. Both me *and* Gary know where he is.'

Amber turned to face Debbie again. 'You know where he is? Then – why don't you try letting some people know? I've had his agent on the phone, and I'm sure the club are looking for him…'

'He's not in a good way, Amber. Believe me,' Debbie went on.

'I'll make some coffee,' Ronnie said, quickly squeezing Debbie's arm on his way past.

'We thought it best to let him have some time alone before we told the club anything, and Gary's been doing his best to cover for him, which is why everyone just thinks he's been on a massive bender and now needs a couple of days to get over it.'

'And that *isn't* the truth?' Amber asked, wishing she could go to sleep, wake up, and start this day all over again, without all the crap that had suddenly landed on her doorstep.

'Well, yeah, I suppose it is,' Debbie began, shoving her hands in the pockets of her Juicy Couture sweat top. 'He was out on Saturday night, but then nobody could get hold of him on Sunday... Gary did a bit of digging and it turns out he'd spent most of the night in the casino... I don't even want to tell you how much money he lost...'

Amber gave a derisory snort, causing Ronnie to turn round and look at her.

'Anyway...' Debbie went on, '... Gary, he... When we couldn't get hold of him on Sunday... When Gary had left him on Saturday night...'

'Debbie, what's going on?' Amber asked, impatience starting to take over now. This was probably nothing but another one of Ryan's games and she really didn't have the time to play those, not today.

Debbie looked at her. 'It's happened again, Amber.'

'*What's* happened again?'

Ronnie frowned as he took a sip of coffee. 'Yeah. *What's* happened again?'

Debbie didn't take her eyes off Amber. 'You *know* what, Amber. What happened the last time. Only...'

Amber shook her head, turning to look out of the window again. 'It's all a game to him, Debbie. And this'll be no different.'

'Is someone going to tell me what you're both talking about?' Ronnie asked, putting his coffee down and folding his arms.

Amber looked at him, but said nothing.

'I saw him, Amber...'

'It was a lie, Debbie. What happened last time, it was a lie.'

Now it was Debbie's turn to frown. 'A lie? I don't...'

'He told me. He actually admitted it to me, he told me, Debbie. He pretended that he wanted to kill himself – he pretended he was so low it was the only option he had left, and he did that for one reason only. He did it because he knew I would come running. That's what he told me. But it won't work a second time.'

542

'Ryan tried to *kill* himself?' Ronnie asked, staring at Amber.

'He *pretended* to, Ronnie. There's a difference.'

'What the hell is going on here?' He looked from Debbie to Amber, trying to elicit answers from at least one of them.

'He couldn't have...' Debbie said quietly, her frown growing deeper. 'He's... he's in such a bad way, Amber. It's not like last time, not really. It's worse. This time he doesn't want anyone near him, he's refusing to leave the house, he's not eating... All he's doing is drinking and, from what Gary and I can gather, now that we've finally managed to get into his house, gambling via some online casino on his laptop. He looks a mess, he doesn't want to talk to anyone...'

'It's a game,' Amber said, determined not to let Ryan ruin this day for her, because he was having a damn good go at trying. Although he couldn't possibly have known he was ruining her wedding day. 'All of it. It's a game. He's just decided to play it in a more elaborate way this time.'

'I can't... I can't believe he would do something like that,' Debbie said, gratefully accepting a hot mug of coffee from Ronnie. 'I can't believe Ryan would lie about harming himself like that. I mean, I know he can be selfish, and childish, but – vindictive? Calculated? Manipulative?'

'I'm sure he can be all of those, too. Now, if you don't mind, I need to go finish getting ready. I've got a wedding to go to.'

She almost ran past Ronnie and Debbie, desperate to escape back upstairs, alone. She needed at least a few minutes to get her head together because this day was fast turning into something she hadn't expected. All she'd wanted was to be with Jim, begin their life together. She didn't want to have to deal with this, not today, and call her selfish, but this *was* supposed to be her wedding day. Didn't she at least deserve one day to forget about everyone else and do what *she* wanted to do? With the man she wanted to be with.

Taking a deep breath, she looked in the mirror, examining her reflection. She needed a bit of concealer under the eyes, maybe another coat of lip gloss, but other than that she still looked okay. Despite everything.

'*Why are you doing this to me, Ryan?*' she whispered to herself. '*Today of all days.*' And then, almost as if it had happened in a reflex action she couldn't control, she picked up the phone and tapped in Ryan's number, although why she was doing that she had no idea, because from what everyone was saying, he wasn't talking to anyone. And it seemed they were right. There was no answer, so she hung up quickly, throwing the phone down onto the bed. He'd be okay. He wasn't stupid enough to do anything really silly, and anyway, Gary and Debbie were there now, weren't they? He'd be okay.

Taking another deep breath, she opened the door and made her way downstairs, aware of Debbie and Ronnie's voices deep in conversation in the kitchen.

'I really need to go now,' she said, standing in the doorway.

Ronnie turned around, that look passing between them again that she shook off immediately. She didn't have time for this, not today. 'I really think you need to listen to Debbie, sweetheart. Ryan, he… it sounds as though it might be for real this time.' He turned his attention back to Debbie. 'We should get him to a doctor, if it's as bad as it sounds.'

'He doesn't want that,' Debbie said, her voice almost a whisper. 'We shouldn't have even contacted Max…'

'You've told Max?' Amber asked.

'Just now. I made her call him,' Ronnie said. 'I think he needs to know, more than anybody. He'll be the one who needs to do all the fire-fighting, if what Debbie is telling me is true. And I have no reason to disbelieve her.'

'So, you think I was lying? When I told you he made it all up, that he hadn't really wanted to kill himself? I was lying when I told you it was nothing but a ploy to get me back…'

'No, I'm not saying you were lying, Amber,' Ronnie sighed, dragging a hand through his hair. 'But, whatever happened last time, maybe this time he's not playing games?'

Amber looked from Ronnie to Debbie, then back at Ronnie, her voice quiet as she spoke. 'What am I supposed to believe, Ronnie? When he told me himself. And then he goes and does it again. What am I supposed to believe?'

'Maybe if he sees you, Amber,' Debbie said. 'Maybe if you talk to him he'll start seeing sense, because, right now, he's lost it. He's really lost it. The way he's talking...'

'Has he asked to see me?' Amber whispered, walking over to the table and picking up the small bouquet of cream and white roses nestled in amongst a barrage of baby's breath.

'He keeps talking about you,' Debbie replied. 'When he feels like talking, that is, which isn't often. Most of the time he just sits there staring into space, or he's logged onto his laptop, throwing his money away.'

Amber said nothing for a few seconds, just stared at her bouquet. 'When you say it's happened again, Debbie... has he... he hasn't tried to do anything stupid, has he?'

Debbie shook her head. 'Not yet, but we're worried about him, Amber. He isn't thinking straight...'

'I don't think it's a good idea. For me to see him, I mean,' Amber said quietly, checking her watch one more time.

'Amber...'

'Ronnie, please. Me going round there is going to do what, exactly? Give him some kind of false hope? Make him think I'm coming back to him because he quite obviously can't cope without me? Because he can, Ronnie. He can cope without anyone, and he knows that. It's a game, and I'm not playing. Now, are you taking me to my wedding or not?'

Ronnie gave Debbie a resigned look before walking over to Amber, pulling her into his arms for a hug. 'Yeah, I'm taking you. Come on. Let's go.'

Max stood in the doorway, watching as Ryan sat on the edge of the sofa looking like he hadn't had a wash in days, a change of clothes – a hot meal. The floor and tables were scattered with empty lager cans and bottles of spirits, the curtains drawn, the only light coming from the laptop screen on the coffee table in front of him.

This was Max's worst nightmare. It was like stepping back in time, reliving a situation he thought they'd never have to go through again after what had happened in London. Except that, this time, it wasn't really Ryan's lifestyle that had kicked everything off a second time. Not entirely, anyway. What neither of them had realised was that Ryan would fall so hard for somebody, at a time when it was blatantly evident he wasn't ready for a relationship. He still had issues to sort out, issues he'd thought could be rectified by falling in love, but he'd put too much pressure on her. And whether she'd realised that or not, Amber had really been little more than a crutch for Ryan to lean on whenever he'd needed someone to pick up the pieces, someone he could fuck into the bargain. From the start it had been an unhealthy relationship, Max could see that now, and he felt slightly guilty because it had been him who'd tried to push them together, tried to make Ryan settle down when he quite obviously wasn't ready for that just yet. Maybe if he'd fallen for some twenty-something wannabe WAG then things may have worked out differently, but instead he'd fallen in love with a woman eleven years older than him, who was, as everyone knew by now, very much in love with another man. Max was almost certain now that they'd both been using each other as some sort of shield, a way of trying to forget the problems both of them had been unwilling to face up to. Until now.

'I've called Colin,' Max said as Gary joined him in the doorway. 'Told him the usual cover story, that he's been on a bender, decided to disappear off somewhere for a few days without telling anyone. I've been peddling that one out for years now. It should at least buy us a little bit of time, though. But if he comes out of this, he's going to have to face club disciplinary action, at the very least… unless…'

'Unless, what?' Gary asked, shoving his hands in his pockets.

Max sighed, leaning back against the doorpost. 'I get him back into rehab.'

Gary gave a sharp intake of breath. He'd spent the morning listening as Max had told him the full extent of Ryan's past problems, and it was tough to take in. Because he cared about his best mate. He loved the idiotic bastard. And this had been a bit of a wake-up call for him, too. 'Do you think he's gonna go for that?'

'He's not really giving us much choice, is he? If he doesn't snap out of this soon… He's out of control again, Gary. This time it could signal the end of his career, and I don't think he deserves that, do you? No matter how stupid he's been. He really doesn't deserve that.'

Amber sat in the back of Ronnie's car, staring out of the window as they drove through Whickham village, her stomach dipping as they passed the road that led to the house she and Ryan had used to share; the house she knew he was back living in now. Their old home. Their beautiful, sometimes happy home. Because they had been happy – once upon a time.

'Do you want me to drop you off?' Ronnie asked Debbie.

'Here will be fine,' Debbie said. 'I could do with the walk and the fresh air, believe me.' She turned to look at Amber, smiling kindly. 'I hope today goes well for you, chick. And I promise, I won't say a word. To anyone.'

Amber couldn't say anything. Her mouth had gone dry and she had a feeling that, if she opened it, nothing would come out anyway.

She watched as Debbie said something else to Ronnie that she couldn't quite make out, and then opened the passenger door. And that's when Amber finally found her voice, although the words that came out of it surprised even her. 'Debbie, wait! Wait.' Debbie climbed back into the car, closing the door, throwing Ronnie a confused look before twisting round in her seat to look

547

at Amber again.

'I'll come and talk to him. I'm not sure what good it'll do, and I don't even know if it's the right thing to do, but…' She looked straight at Ronnie. 'I still care about him. And I don't want to see him throw his life away, even if he *is* playing a game.'

'Are you sure?' Ronnie asked, starting the engine again. 'Do you want to call Jim? Tell him what's going on?'

She shook her head. 'I don't intend staying long,' she said quietly, settling back in her seat as Ronnie turned the car around and headed off in the direction of Ryan's house. And anyway, she had a feeling Jim already knew what was going on. He wasn't the kind of manager who let things like this pass him by.

It took just seconds to get there, and Amber felt a thousand memories flood back inside her head as they pulled up onto the long, winding drive that led up to the modest detached house. But she had to remember why she was there. She had to put an end to this, had to make sure Ryan understood what was happening. She'd moved on, now he had to do the same. For both their sakes.

She left her bouquet on the back seat and followed Debbie and Ronnie to the front door, running her hands up and down her arms as a cold breeze hit her, reminding her it was still winter. But that wasn't the only chill she was experiencing.

'You okay?' Ronnie mouthed.

She nodded, although her stomach was turning major somersaults by the time Gary opened the door.

'He's in there,' Gary said, standing aside to let them through, indicating the living room with his head.

Amber stood in the huge hallway, looking around at a place that had once been so familiar but now felt like a stranger's home, despite the pictures she'd hung and the plant she'd bought for the sideboard in the hallway still being there. As was a picture of her and Ryan together. Both of them smiling. Neither of them realising that they should never have been together.

'We've tried talking to him,' Max began. Amber looked at him.

He seemed worried. And surely, if Max looked worried, then something must be wrong. Really wrong. Max knew Ryan better than anyone, so if *he* was concerned...

'Have you spoken to his parents?' she asked, looking briefly over at the framed photograph of her and Ryan on the hall windowsill.

'Not yet,' Max sighed. 'They're used to not hearing from him for days on end – he can be a real selfish bastard in that respect. But if things go the way I think they...' He stopped mid-sentence and Amber looked at him again, narrowing her eyes.

'If things go *what* way?' she asked. 'I mean, shouldn't his parents...'

'It looks like another trip to rehab, Amber,' Max said softly. 'It doesn't look as though he's leaving us with much choice. And if it comes to that, then yes, I'll have to talk to his parents. But after what they went through before, I'm trying to spare them as much anxiety as I can.'

'What's with the outfit?' Gary asked, looking Amber up and down. She'd totally forgotten she was dressed for her wedding.

'Oh, Christ,' she said, looking frantically over at Ronnie. 'I should have gone home and changed, shouldn't I?'

Gary frowned. 'Why? What's going on?'

'Amber and Jim – they're getting married. Today,' Ronnie answered for her. 'And it's too late to go back and get changed, Amber. Besides, it's just one of a number of things he's going to have to face up to, whether he likes it or not.'

'I know, but...'

'It's something he needs to know,' Max said kindly, seeing how anxious Amber had become. 'It's for the best that he understands, once and for all, that you're not coming back. Then we can take it from there.'

'Married?' Gary asked, looking over at Debbie, who just shrugged. 'You kept that one quiet. Jesus, you've only been together five minutes.'

Amber rolled her eyes, turning away from everyone for a second, composing herself, because she felt as though she couldn't breathe. Her stomach was in knots, her chest tight, her head fuzzy and confused.

'Amber?' Gary persisted. 'You're really marrying the boss?'

She swung back round, a more determined look in her eyes now. 'Well, I'm not dressed like this to clean the windows, am I?' She pushed past them all, stopping dead in the doorway of the living room when she saw Ryan sitting there, on the edge of the sofa. He was dressed in a navy blue t-shirt, jeans and battered old black Converse baseball boots. His hair was all over the place, making him look as though he'd just got out of bed, although Amber suspected bed was a place he hadn't seen for a while. He looked as though he hadn't slept properly in days. The room was littered with empty cans and bottles of spirits, the curtains drawn with just one slim chink of light filtering through a tiny gap in the middle. She looked over at his laptop screen – it was open at the blackjack table of an online casino. 'Ryan…'

He looked up, his eyes meeting hers, and she watched as his face just crumpled, tears starting to pour down his cheeks. She ran inside, sitting down next to him, scooping him into her arms as though he were a toddler who needed comforting, holding him as he cried, rocking him gently as sobs wracked his body.

'It's okay, baby,' she whispered, stroking his hair. 'It's okay.' Her eyes caught Ronnie's as he peered inside, but she shook her head, signalling that she wanted them to leave her and Ryan alone for a while. He nodded, and indicated the kitchen. She smiled that she understood, then turned her attention back to Ryan. 'What are you doing, you bloody idiot?'

He pulled away slightly, wiping his eyes with the back of his hand, turning away from her for a second.

'Ryan… you need to talk to me. You need to talk to *some*one…'

He turned to look at her again, his eyes red and tired. He just looked defeated, really defeated this time, and it pulled at Amber's heart. But she had to be sure – sure that this wasn't just another one of his games, another attempt to try and win her back.

'This isn't another… what happened last time…'

He looked down at his clasped hands in his lap, his expression not changing at all. 'I'm sorry, Amber. For what I did to you.'

She reached out to take his hand, squeezing it gently. 'Hey, I was hardly an angel myself.'

He looked at her, his face serious. 'I can't do this anymore, babe. I'm done…' He trailed off, looking straight ahead at the large, imposing fireplace in front of him where yet more photos of him and Amber stood. She felt her stomach dip again as she listened to him, guilt sweeping over her because Debbie was right – this time he wasn't playing games. This time he was serious.

'Come on, Ryan. This isn't like you. What's happened to the Ryan Fisher I used to know?'

His eyes met hers again. 'He died, Amber.'

His words filled her with a dread she'd never felt before. She'd known he was a mixed-up, confused young man, but nothing like this. This felt like a situation she couldn't handle, and a part of her was scared. What was she supposed to say to him? How much did she tell him?

'The truth, Amber,' Ryan said quietly, still looking into her eyes. 'I just want to know the truth. You and Jim… you and… is it the real thing? You and him? Are you… are you in love with him?'

She looked down at their joined hands, tears beginning to prick the back of her eyes but she couldn't cry. It wasn't her place to cry, this wasn't the time. 'Yes,' she whispered, not looking at him. 'To both those questions.' She finally met his eyes again, realising Max was right. He had to know the truth before he could finally start to deal with it. Properly. 'I'm… today, we're… me and Jim, we're supposed to be getting married…'

'Oh Jesus,' he whispered, turning away from her. 'Jesus…'

'Ryan, I am so sorry, baby. So sorry things had to turn out this way, but…'

He turned back to face her, wiping his eyes again. 'Shit happens,' he smiled weakly, and Amber couldn't help but smile back.

'We should never have been together, Ryan. Not really,' she said quietly, still holding tightly onto his hand. 'Me and you, we had so much baggage we could have given the reclaim section at Heathrow Airport a run for its money.'

He smiled again, stroking her knuckles with his thumb. 'I thought it was what I wanted, y'know? What I needed. A solid relationship. Something to stop me from going off the rails.' He shrugged, letting out a small laugh. 'Seems I just wasn't ready for it, huh? I saw you as nothing but someone who could be there to pick up the pieces, someone who would put up with the idiot I sometimes turned into, and I felt such a smug, lucky bastard because you were so beautiful into the bargain, and you wanted me and.. and I should never have let that happen. But I couldn't help it. I loved the lifestyle, the adulation, the fame. The money. I loved the fact I could have any woman I wanted just by clicking my fingers, until I realised that the only woman I *really* wanted had been right there in front of me all the time, and I'd blown it. Big style.'

'Things were complicated, Ryan. When I knew Jim was back in the North East… the second I found out he'd taken the job at Newcastle Red Star… I should never have got involved in a relationship with you. Never. It really wasn't fair on you. It was selfish of me because, when I think back, I'd only really thrown myself into a relationship with you as a way of trying to convince myself that I didn't still have feelings for Jim. That I could love someone else the way I'd loved him…'

'But you can't, can you?' Ryan whispered, his eyes boring into hers with an intensity so strong Amber could feel it burning into her. He truly was an incredibly beautiful man with a wonderful soul and a kind heart, she'd seen that side of him. She knew it existed. He just seemed scared to let it out.

She shook her head sadly, squeezing his hand again. 'No. I can't.'

He finally turned away, staring down at the dark wooden floor.

'So, that's it, then? You and me, it's over.'

'You have one hell of a future ahead of you, Ryan. Do you understand how special you really are?'

'It's all pointless if you're not with me.'

'That's bollocks, Ryan, and you know it. You don't need me. You don't need anyone.'

'Don't I?' he asked, turning his head sharply to look at her. 'Maybe that's the whole problem, Amber. Maybe I *do* need someone... someone to... to...'

'To *what*, Ryan? To save you? To stop this from happening? This is something *you* have to deal with yourself, do you understand that? You are an extraordinary footballer – don't let the pressure of a lifestyle you *think* you have to lead turn you into something you're not. And then, one day, someone will come along who you'll fall in love with...'

'She's already here.'

'No,' Amber whispered, shaking her head again. 'She isn't.'

He let go of her hand and stood up, picking up a can from the coffee table, shaking it to see if it had any liquid left in it.

'And that's going to help, is it?' Amber asked, watching as he tried another can. And another.

He swung round to face her as she stood up, too. 'Yeah. It is. Blocking it all out, wishing it would all go away... it helps.'

She said nothing, just walked over to the window and drew the curtains slightly, letting in a ray of bright winter sunshine before turning to face him again. 'Nobody's going to pity you, Ryan, you do realise that, don't you? You're young, you're in a dream career, you earn more money in a week than most people earn in two years. You can have anything you want, whenever you want it, or that's how people perceive you and others like you, anyway. So you throwing your toys out of the pram because you can't have *one* thing you want... well, it isn't gonna cut it, mister. The sympathy won't be there.'

He narrowed his eyes as he stared at her. What was she trying to do? Some kind of reverse psychology? Shit! His head was too fried to even try and get a handle on this situation.

'You need help, Ryan.'

'Do I?' Did he? He didn't really know *what* he wanted, or needed, if he was honest. Except, maybe, to sit back down, put his feet up, and watch another few hours of daytime TV. That's all he really wanted to do.

She walked over to him and he felt his heart start to beat faster as she reached out to gently touch his rough cheek, running her fingers over his beard, her beautiful pale blue eyes meeting his. 'I care about you, Ryan. So much. And if you throw this all away because of... Jesus, Ryan, I'm not worth it. I'm so not worth it.'

'You are to me,' he said, his voice barely a whisper as he reached up to cover her hand with his own. 'But... shit...' He broke the stare for a second, before turning back to look at her. 'You're really gonna marry him?'

She nodded slowly, bringing his hand to her mouth, kissing it gently. He could feel his heart splinter into a thousand tiny pieces and it hurt, it physically hurt. But that was all he felt. Everything else, any other feelings, they were gone. He felt empty.

'I'm not sure I'm cut out for this, Amber. This lifestyle, this job...' He felt more stupid, unwanted tears start to prick the back of his eyes but he couldn't stop them. It was as if there was some invisible tap that he had no power over, no way of knowing when the tears would come. But they were coming now, hot and fast, streaming down his face like some powerful, emotional waterfall. And, suddenly, he realised he'd been here before, in this cold, dark, lonely place where he felt no hope, nothing except the need to lock himself away from the world and drink himself into some kind of oblivion.

'It just doesn't matter anymore,' he whispered, still staring into her eyes, still hoping beyond hope that something... that she might tell him what he wanted to hear. 'None of it matters anymore, Amber. I can't do it. I can't.'

She reached out to touch his face again, her thumb gently wiping the tears away. 'Oh, you can, Ryan Fisher. You bloody well can. Do you hear me? You *can*. You are *not* going to give up. You love football, you've earned your place as one of this country's – if not one of the world's – greatest ever players and there's plenty of fight left in you yet. So you will *not* give up. You'll fight this, and you'll get back out there and you'll kill it. You got that?'

He watched her as she spoke, watched a determination in her eyes that he wished *he* could feel. But he just felt empty.

'Please, Ryan.' She was almost pleading with him now, begging him to try and sort himself out. 'You've done this before, and you can do it again. But this time, do it properly. Okay? Are you listening to me?'

He found himself nodding, agreeing to something he wasn't altogether sure he could go through with, but maybe she was right. Maybe he *did* need to try and find that fight. Try and do *some*thing – he just didn't know what that something was just yet.

'I never really understood how hard it was for you,' Amber said, slowly pulling away from him. 'And I should have done. I should have been less selfish, less self-absorbed with my own problems…' She slipped her hand into his, looking down as she squeezed it tight. 'We should never have let it get this far.'

'It wasn't your fault…' he began, but she put a finger to his lips, silencing him.

'Promise me you'll talk to Max, alright? He's there for you, and he'll do anything he can to make this right, Ryan. Anything.'

But he couldn't do the one thing Ryan really wanted, could he? He couldn't stop Amber from marrying Jim Allen, from disappearing from his world and into his manager's. And that was probably the hardest thing he was going to have to learn to deal with.

'Promise me, Ryan.'

He briefly looked down at their joined hands before looking back up at her, at her beautifully made-up face and a dress that he should have guessed signalled an unusual situation – she never dressed like that for a normal day at the office. She was dressed for her wedding. To another man. His boss. Shit! He had one hell of a lot to get his head around. 'I promise,' he whispered, holding onto her for those final few seconds longer before she slowly slipped her hand out of his and walked over to the door. 'Amber?'

She swung round to look at him.

'Be happy.'

She smiled, a smile that sent Ryan's heart racing, but which also delivered a painful inevitability that he should have seen coming a long time ago.

And then she was gone. Out of his life and into Jim Allen's, leaving Ryan with the realisation that the journey he had ahead of him wasn't going to be an easy one, but it was one he was going to have to take. Starting today.

Chapter Thirty-Four

Ronnie pulled the car into a convenient space close to the register office and switched off the engine.

'You okay?' he asked, looking at Amber.

She was staring out of the window, clutching her bouquet as though something really bad would happen if she let go. She nodded but didn't look at him. She still couldn't get the image of Ryan out of her head, broken and defeated. But underneath all of that she'd seen a glimmer of the man she'd once known – and the man he could really be. He was strong, deep down. And she knew that Max would make sure he got the help he really needed, but it didn't stop her from feeling a dull ache for what might have been – if they'd both been different people, free of the baggage they'd both carried with them.

'He's over there.' Ronnie's voice broke into her thoughts and she finally turned to look at him.

'Hmm? Sorry?'

'Jim. He's over there.'

She followed his gaze. Jim was standing in the doorway of the register office, checking his watch and looking around. She wasn't actually all that late, just by a few minutes, but he was obviously anxious as to where she was. And with good reason, really.

'Are you still going ahead with this, then?' Ronnie asked.

She looked at him. 'Yeah. Of course I am. Why wouldn't I?'

'Well, considering where you've just been…'

'I was never going to go back to Ryan. That wasn't why I went there, and you know that.'

'Are you glad you did?'

Amber sighed. It still felt as though everything that was happening today was some kind of surreal event that she wasn't really taking part in. A little bit of her felt strangely detached from it all. 'I think so… I mean, seeing him like that, it wasn't… it wasn't nice, but… He's gonna be okay, Ronnie. Isn't he?'

Ronnie reached out and took her hand, squeezing it gently. 'He's gonna be just fine, kiddo. Max has got it all in hand.' He looked back over at Jim, who was now pacing backwards and forwards outside the register office, his hands in the pockets of his dark suit. 'Maybe you need to have a word with him, though. He might have got wind of what's happened by now. I know Max didn't want to make the extent of Ryan's problems public just yet, but I'm sure the club, and his manager, will have been made aware of what's going on. After all, he isn't going to be available to play for a while, is he?'

Amber glanced over at Jim again. 'He must have known Ryan hadn't turned up for training for the past few days. He's not the kind of manager that lets things like that pass him by. He's always on top of everything. Why didn't he tell me, Ronnie? If he knew something was wrong?'

'Well, to be fair, sweetheart, nobody knew anything *was* wrong until today. Not really. Up until now everyone just thought Ryan had gone AWOL on another of his famous benders. And maybe Jim didn't want to worry you by telling you that. In his own way he could probably just have been trying to protect you.'

'You reckon?'

'I think so, yeah.'

She couldn't help smiling. 'You finally coming round to this marriage, then?'

He looked at her, a slight smile on his face, too. 'Don't rush me, kiddo. I'll get there. And are you sure you really want me to be one of your witnesses? Won't Jim mind?'

'I'd rather have at least one person I know and care about be there for me, Ronnie. Jim won't mind. He'll be fine.'

Ronnie leaned over and gently kissed her cheek, giving her hand one last squeeze. 'We'd better make a move. Before he starts going into some kind of meltdown. I've never seen Jim Allen so wound up.'

She smiled again, opening the passenger door but stopping for a second before she got out of the car. 'Ronnie?'

'Yeah?'

'Thanks.'

'For what?'

'For being my friend.'

He smiled back. 'I love you, kiddo. It's what I do.'

She looked at him for a few seconds, their eyes locking together in a brief moment of intensity. 'I love you, too, Ronnie.'

'Yeah. I know… Amber…?'

She was still looking at him, waiting for him to say whatever it was he was going to say.

'No… sorry,' he said, shaking his head. 'It doesn't matter.'

'You sure?' she asked.

'Yeah,' he smiled, climbing out of the car. 'I'm sure. Look, I'll see you in there, okay?'

She nodded, watching as he walked towards the register office entrance, exchanging a brief word with Jim before he went inside.

Taking another deep breath, Amber shook out her curls, composed herself, and looked over to where Jim had now stopped pacing, because he was looking over at her. And the second her eyes met his she knew everything she was doing here was the right decision. She wanted to marry this man more than she'd ever wanted anything in her life. The fact her heart had started to beat faster and harder just at the sight of him told her that.

His face broke into a smile and she smiled back, clutching her bouquet tight against her as she walked over to him, her eyes never leaving his, and then he was right there, in front of her. Her teenage fantasy. Her first love. The only man she'd ever really wanted.

'You look beautiful,' he whispered, sliding an arm around her waist, pulling her close.

'You don't look so bad yourself, handsome.'

He laughed that low, deep, sexy laugh and Amber felt her stomach flip a thousand somersaults, her head beginning to spin as the events of the day began to completely overwhelm her. 'Just kiss me, Jim. Please.'

He didn't need to be asked twice, and Amber closed her eyes as his mouth touched hers, moving against it in slow, soft movements.

'I thought you'd stood me up,' he said quietly, still holding onto her, his mouth still close to hers.

'That was never going to happen.'

He gently pushed a strand of dark red hair from her eyes as the cold, brisk, north-east breeze whipped her loose curls around her face. 'But you've been to see Ryan. Haven't you? I'm guessing that's why Ronnie's here.'

She nodded, pulling away from him, walking over to the railings to the side of the register office, staring out at the view of the North Sea. 'Did you know?' She looked at him. 'About Ryan not turning up for training all week?'

Jim nodded, staring straight ahead, his hands back in his pockets. 'I was made aware of it, yes.'

'And… and do you know what's really happened? Do you know the state he's in right now?'

Jim nodded again, sighing heavily as he leaned forward, resting his elbows on the railings. 'I've spoken to both Colin and Max Mandell. So, yes. I know the full extent of what's going on now. It's a mess…'

'He just needs to get his head together, sort himself out. You *are* going to support him, aren't you, Jim? I mean, the club aren't just gonna wash their hands of him…'

Jim turned to look at her, taking her hand and pulling her close. 'The club will give him all the support he needs, Amber. Believe me. I'll need to have a meeting with the Chairman tomorrow before we head down to Wigan, but I can assure you, honey, we'll do everything we can to make sure he comes through this. You have my word on that.'

Once upon a time his word hadn't meant all that much, but she believed him, now. She believed him.

'I feel so guilty, Jim. Did I push him too far? Did I do something wrong?'

'Hey, listen, it wasn't your fault, okay?' He ran his thumb lightly over her cheek, leaning over to kiss her gently. 'He was damaged goods, Amber. Before you and he got together.'

'So was I,' she whispered, looking deep into his eyes.

He looked away for a second, down at the ground, his hand still resting lightly on her cheek. 'It's time to make things right,' Jim said quietly, his eyes meeting Amber's again. 'For both of you.'

'Do you know where he's going? Max said something about rehab and I…'

'Amber, honey, he'll be fine. Max is talking to the club as we speak and between them they'll make sure he has the best care possible. Money's no object, remember? And it's in the club's best interests to make sure that kid is back to full strength and back on that pitch as soon as possible. Fighting fit and ready to concentrate on his career because, if he does that, then he's gonna be one hell of a legend.'

She looked into his eyes again. 'I care about him, Jim. I can't stop doing that, I can't turn those feelings off…'

'I don't expect you to, baby. Look, underneath all that crap he's a sensible kid. He knows what he really should be doing, and I'm sure he'll come out of this a better man. Trust me.'

Trust me. Two little words that he'd used so flippantly in the past with little regard for their meaning. But it felt different this time. This time she felt as though he meant what he said. Because he loved her. He really loved her. And she really loved him. No more lies. No more hurt. No more pain.

'I never loved him the way I love you,' Amber said quietly, glad of his arms pulling her closer against him as the cold breeze grew stronger, sending a sharp chill right through her. She wasn't really dressed to be outdoors for long periods of time. 'I thought I *could*, y'know? I thought I could, and then forgetting you would be so much easier…'

'If I hadn't come back, do you think you and Ryan would have had a future together?' Jim asked, playing with the loose curls that hung around her bare shoulders.

'I don't know,' she replied, exhaling quickly as Jim's fingers brushed against her skin, sending a welcoming warm shiver right through her. 'I doubt it. But I don't know.'

'Are you glad I came back?'

She looked at him, her face breaking into another smile, her fingers fiddling with the collar of his dark shirt. 'Yeah. Of course I am. Now. But you better be good to me, Jim Allen. This time, you better be good to me because I can't go through…'

He shut her up with a kiss, a long, slow, deep kiss that seemed to wipe clean away any more thoughts of anything other than why she was here, with this man. Even the cold sea breeze was having trouble bothering her now, because all she could feel was his body against hers, his arms holding her tight.

'So, you still wanna marry me, then?' he asked, that warm, rich accent of his melting her heart, bringing back a million memories and the delicious promise of a million more to come.

She smiled. 'Well, let's see… Amber Allen… it *does* have quite a nice ring to it, don't you think?'

Chapter Thirty-Five

The warm May sunshine beat down on Amber's face as she looked up at the bright, blue cloudless sky. It was a glorious day, and one Newcastle Red Star had been waiting for for as long as the club, and their supporters, could remember. There was no doubting how much of a success the club had become over the past few seasons, but one trophy had always eluded them – the league title. That prestigious accolade that put you right at the very top of the tree as far as English football was concerned. For too long that title had evaded them, been within their grasp only to slip away at the final hurdle, but now – now they had just one more game to play, one last game to win and the title would be theirs. They needed the three points a win would give them, a draw wouldn't do. A draw would see them having to rely on other teams' results going their way and nobody wanted that, so they were going all out that afternoon to win.

Amber finished her cigarette and walked back inside Tynebridge, smiling as she looked down at the thin band of gold glinting on the third finger of her left hand. Mrs. Jim Allen. She was Mrs. Jim Allen, and for the past four months she'd been the happiest woman on earth. No argument. To finally be Jim's wife was her dream come true, although it hadn't come without its problems, once word had finally got out. Her father had only just come round to the idea, Kevin had sulked for almost a week after he found out, claiming she'd denied News North East their very own 'happy ending' news story, although Amber thought there'd been more than enough news knocking around at the time to fill a multitude of shows, what with Ryan's absence from the Red Star squad and the rumours of his visit to rehab. Which hadn't stayed rumours for long. It had all come out, eventually, meaning that Kevin had finally got off her back and forgiven her for leaving him in the dark as far as her love life was concerned.

'Do you fancy a drink before kick-off?' Debbie asked, catching Amber as she walked through the main reception area.

'I'm gonna go see Jim,' Amber smiled. 'Just to make sure he's okay.'

'Okay?' Debbie frowned. 'Why wouldn't he be okay?'

'He won't thank me for telling you this, but he is incredibly nervous about this afternoon. It's not that he doesn't think the guys can do it, they can. He has every faith in them, and after the way they've been playing lately the title should be well within their grasp. It's just that, he puts so much pressure on himself. So much pressure to succeed, and he's always wanted this for Red Star. This title, this accolade. So to be able to give it to them with *him* at the helm… He didn't sleep much last night, let's put it that way.'

Debbie slipped her arm through Amber's as they walked towards the Players' Lounge. 'I'm really glad you and Jim decided not to move to Spain,' she smiled, leaning in towards her friend. 'I mean, what would I have done without my closest girlfriend there at my wedding? You're my Maid of Honour, I need you there.'

'And I'm gonna be right by your side, kid.' She squeezed Debbie's arm. 'It wasn't the right time to make that move. If Jim had taken the Malaga Athletico job, it would have meant we were running away and although, at the time, it seemed like the perfect thing to do, it would've been a mistake. Everyone needed to face up to everything that had happened – both in the past, and the present. Besides, he loves this club far too much to sell them down the river. And look what he's done for them? He's got them right where they've always wanted to be. He's about to make them champions. No, we'll be sticking around for a while yet, don't you worry.'

'Good,' Debbie said, planting a quick kiss on Amber's cheek. 'I'll see you in a bit, then, up in the hospitality box. We can talk about my Hen Weekend to Lanzarote during half time.'

Amber threw her a smile and left her at the door of the Players' Lounge, continuing down the corridor to the dressing rooms, taking in the noise and the excitement of this incredibly important day in Newcastle Red Star's history. The atmosphere was heady, the air thick with expectation, the noise coming from the Home Team dressing room loud and excitable. So no wonder Jim was nervous. He had a lot riding on this. He'd promised the fans victory, and if he didn't deliver he wouldn't be the only one who was disappointed.

Tapping quietly on his office door, she gently pushed it open, peering inside. 'Okay to come in?' she asked, catching sight of him behind his desk.

His face broke into a smile as he stood up and walked round the front of his desk. 'Hey, baby.' He opened his arms and she stepped inside, hugging him tight. 'Oh, Jesus, you feel so good.'

'Everything okay?' Amber asked, pulling away slightly and looking up at him. His handsome face was a mask of worry, but she knew that the second he stepped outside of the office he'd show no outward signs of the anxiety he was currently feeling.

'Everything's fine, honey. I'm just... This is it, y'know? This is what this club has been waiting for, and it's so close we can almost touch it... The guys are gonna do us proud this afternoon, I know they are.'

She smiled, reaching up to gently stroke his rough chin with her fingertips. 'I'm so proud of you, Jim. You've worked so hard to get this club where it is now. You're a hero to those fans out there.'

'Which is why we need to bring that title home, here to Tynebridge.'

'Baby, even if it doesn't happen, you *know* you'll still be their hero.'

'Managers have lost their jobs over less, Amber.'

'The board have just extended your contract, Jim. Last night. Why would they do that if they had any intention of sacking you? You're not going anywhere, handsome. Except, maybe…' She smiled, taking his hand and sliding it underneath her shirt, placing it over one of her breasts, '… inside me?'

He smiled, too, running his thumb over her nipple until it became hard beneath his fingers. 'Jesus, you kill me, baby. You fucking kill me.'

'You don't *have* to,' she whispered, standing on tiptoe so her mouth barely touched his. 'I just thought you might need a little bit of stress relief, that's all. Something to calm you down before the game. But I can always go away…'

'Hey, little lady. You ain't going anywhere. Get back here.' He pulled her against him, kissing her long and slow. 'You taste so good,' he groaned, pulling her shirt out of her jeans and pushing it back off her shoulders. 'So, so good.'

'That's why you married me,' Amber smiled, unfastening his belt. 'Come on. We haven't got much time before they start looking for you.'

He turned her round and lifted her up onto his desk, pulling down her jeans and sliding her underwear off, throwing it aside. With one swift movement he'd spread her legs and pushed inside her, causing Amber to moan out loud before slapping a hand over her own mouth, realising that making too much noise would only draw unwanted attention they didn't need. They wanted to be left alone for just a few more minutes and, after all, she was doing this for the good of the club, wasn't she? A calm Jim Allen meant he'd go out there and make sure those lads played to the best of their ability before her handsome husband brought home the rewards this club deserved.

Placing her hands palm down on the desk behind her, Amber

arched her back, pushing against him as he thrust deeper into her, his face buried in her shoulder to muffle his own groans. He was once again filling her up with every inch of him, taking her over, making her crazy for those few, beautiful minutes he was inside of her. This man had been her dream, her fantasy for over twenty years and now he was a reality she never wanted to let go of. History was not going to repeat itself, not this time. Not ever. And she'd do her utmost to make sure of that.

'You look a bit flushed,' Ronnie said, looking at Amber out of the corner of his eye as she joined him in the hospitality box where a group of them were watching the game. Even though she'd much rather have been watching it down in the stands with the real fans. 'You alright?'

'Of course I'm alright. Where's Karen?'

'She's over there.' He indicated to the other side of the box, where Karen was deep in conversation with Debbie. 'Wedding talk.'

Amber smiled. 'You nervous? About going for it a second time?'

He shook his head, taking a long sip of lager. 'I'm actually quite excited about it. We've experienced the pitfalls, made the mistakes, so maybe this time we'll get it right.'

'I really hope so, Ronnie. You deserve to be happy.'

He looked at her, and for a couple of seconds neither of them said anything. 'I'm happy, kiddo,' he said quietly. 'I'm happy.'

She smiled again, looking over at her dad who was talking to another ex-Red Star player whom Ronnie worked with on a regular basis in his TV work. 'It's all coming together, isn't it? For everybody. You and Karen getting married next month, then Debbie and Gary in July…' She broke off mid-sentence as the stadium erupted behind her and she swung round to see the Red Star squad run out onto the pitch. Jim walked slowly out of the tunnel after them, looking relaxed and calm with his suit jacket off and his white shirt-sleeves rolled up, hands in his pockets, aviator shades covering his eyes as the sun continued to beat down on a taut and expectant Tynebridge. Even from a distance he could make her heart skip and her stomach somersault an infinite number of times.

'Honeymoon period still alive and kicking, then?' Ronnie asked, rubbing the small of her back in an almost absent-minded action.

She turned back to face him. 'Yeah. It is.' Just the word 'honeymoon' made her stomach flip over again as she thought about the belated one she and Jim had yet to take in a couple of weeks, when the present season came to an end and the summer break loomed large. Jim hadn't told her where they were going yet – it was a surprise. But wherever it was, she couldn't wait to get there, to finally have her man all to herself for a blissful few days. She knew they'd probably have paparazzi trying to capture their every move but she didn't care anymore. If these past few months had taught her anything it was that there are some things you just can't fight.

'It's all gonna be okay,' she said quietly, looking back outside as the squad warmed up on the pitch, Jim standing in front of the dugout, issuing orders, waving his arms about to gain players' attention. 'Finally. It's all gonna be okay.'

Ryan turned his head and kissed the captain's armband that took pride of place on his upper left arm as the crowd went wild. If Tynebridge had had a roof it would have lifted off by now with the sheer noise that reverberated around the stadium. Newcastle Red Star were Premier League Champions, top of the tree, the best of the best. They'd finished the season at the very top of their game, as had he. He couldn't deny the past few months had been shaky, to say the least, before descending into a darkness he didn't ever want to experience again. But he'd come through the other side a stronger, tougher man. More determined than ever to concentrate on his game and become the footballer he'd always dreamed of being, because until now, he'd only ever really been half that man.

His month-long stint in a rehab clinic in the West Country had been hard, because, in the beginning he hadn't really accepted that he needed the help they were offering him. But one day something

568

had just clicked, a voice inside his head telling him to get a grip or he was going to lose it all, and if Ryan Fisher was one thing it was a fighter. So he'd fought – the addictions, the depression, he'd fought it all. And he'd finally won, arriving back at Tynebridge a player to be reckoned with. He had a lot to thank the club for. They'd stood by him, supported him, gave him anything and everything he'd needed to get back on track and back out on that pitch. Especially Jim Allen. Was that because of Amber? Maybe. Did it matter? No. He was back, and *that* was all that really mattered.

He couldn't lie and say that it had been easy, coming back to a club where the main topic of conversation was his boss's secret wedding to his ex-fiancée, but he was able to deal with things in a way he hadn't been able to before. This time he didn't feel the need to forget by drinking himself into oblivion or picking up the first woman who threw herself at him for a meaningless fuck that he hoped would wipe away things he didn't want to think about, things he was too weak or too frightened to face up to. He wasn't saying he was a saint, far from it. He'd just grown up a bit, learnt to control his life in a more adult fashion.

And now he was experiencing the very thing playing this game was all about – that incredible buzz, that overwhelming feeling of achievement players got from knowing they'd just taken their club to the highest level. He could have lost this. He *could* have. But he hadn't. He was here, wearing the captain's armband, and that spoke volumes as to how this club felt about him. He owed them, big time. And next season he'd show them the kind of player he could *really* be.

'What a fucking day, man,' Gary said, running over to Ryan and jumping on his back, giving him the kind of manly, celebratory hug players gave each other in situations such as this. 'You played a blinder out there. Four frigging goals, Jesus, you were on fire!'

Ryan shrugged him off before grabbing him round the neck and pulling him in for another of those manly hugs. 'It's what I do, mate. Ryan Fisher, goal machine.'

'And so humble with it.'

Ryan grinned, letting go of Gary, looking over at the rest of his teammates as they ran around the pitch in a lap of honour, although it was about the tenth time round for most of them. Nobody really wanted a day like this to end. This was the kind of high that everybody loved, the kind of high that players craved; the only kind of high Ryan needed now.

He looked over at the dugout. Even Colin was grinning away, that was how good a day this was. Their coach rarely cracked a smile most days, so to see him looking positively gleeful was an experience. But he couldn't stop his stomach from taking a dip as he saw Amber run out of the tunnel, flinging herself at her new husband – his boss. He watched as Jim caught her in his arms, swinging her up and around, both of them laughing until he put her back down. He watched as Jim kissed her, a kiss that Ryan didn't really want to watch but he couldn't tear his eyes away from them. And it seemed he wasn't the only one to notice it as wolf-whistles and cheers emanated loudly from certain parts of the stadium. It was difficult to watch, because nobody had said forgetting her would be easy. Or was it forgetting what they could have had that was the difficult part? He wasn't sure. He just knew that she looked happy, and that made him happy, too. She never really had deserved someone like him. Not the way he had been, anyway.

'Looking forward to the party tonight, then?' Gary's voice broke into Ryan's thoughts and he turned to look at his friend.

'Yeah. Yeah, of course I am. We've got shitloads to celebrate, after all. It's gonna be a blinder of a night.'

'You got that right,' Gary grinned, following Ryan's gaze as he looked back over at Amber and Jim. 'You okay, mate?'

Ryan smiled, grabbing Gary again as they ran towards the tunnel, ready for the onslaught of post-match interviews that awaited them. And, boy, was he ready for them! He was on top of the world, and he wanted the world to know that.

And then he saw her. Ellen. The beautiful Ellen, the first girl he'd bedded on his arrival here in the North East. Little, timid, PR girl Ellen – until he'd got her into bed, that is, and then a wild side you wouldn't know existed to look at her had been unleashed. And he'd never called her back. Never tried to have another go and see just how far he could *really* push her. Jesus! She worked here, and yet he'd never made an attempt to go there again. Still, no time like the present. 'I'm fine, mate,' Ryan replied, his attention now focused solely on making sure Ellen noticed him. 'I'm just fine.'

Her eyes finally met his and she smiled at him. A smile that carried more than a simple *'hello, it's been a while'*, and Ryan got the message loud and clear. She bore no grudges. She seemed quite happy to rekindle whatever it was they'd enjoyed all those months ago when he'd arrived at Tynebridge the new boy with a hell of a lot to learn. Quiet little Ellen, in her smart skirt and blouse, her hair pulled back in a neat ponytail – she promised everything and more that Ryan had been missing lately.

He grinned at her, walking backwards down the tunnel so he could keep eye contact as long as possible, make sure she got a message back that she understood. Oh yes. This day was just getting better, leaving him with no doubt in his mind now – Ryan Fisher was back!

Acknowledgements

A huge thank you to Sunderland AFC who kindly allowed me to have a little look around their fantastic stadium – that really helped, and I'm forever grateful.

And to whoever 'The Secret Footballer' is, thank you, too. Reading your book, 'I Am The Secret Footballer', gave me an insight into the world of professional football we don't normally get to hear about making me realise that, sometimes, things aren't quite as far-fetched as we may think they are...

Printed by RR Donnelley at Glasgow, UK